Dark Angels Prey

Elizabeth Genovese

Published by Silver Sword Publishers, 2019

DARK ANGELS PREY

First edition. November 3, 2014

Copyright © 2014 Elizabeth Genovese

Written by Elizabeth Genovese

Used with permission and many thanks to the *Hal Leonard Corporation*:
One Less Bell To Answer
Lyric by Hal David
Music by Burt Bacharach
Copyright 1967 (Renewed) Casa David and New Hidden Valley Music
International Copyright Secured All Rights Reserved

All Bible quotes are from the Douay-Rheims Bible, a public domain work.

Emily Dickinson's poem, Complete Poems, 1924. *Part Three: Love,* a public domain work.

Cover art design by Jennifer Quinlan
Historical Editorial
http://historicaleditorial.blogspot.ca/

Frankie G's Miracle

A supernatural novella
FREE at elizabethgenovese.com
In all formats!

1. A Peek Through the Veil

Ocala Florida, 1970

"Lots of requests for this dreamy ballad, folks. In the Number Two slot this week, right behind George Harrison's *My Sweet Lord* and originally recorded by Keely Smith in '67—here it is boys and girls, The 5th Dimension's *One Less Bell to Answer!*"

Young Joe Ross cranked up the radio in his dad's cherry red Chrysler Newport. His mom was so into the song and always played it for the horses because the horses preferred The 5th Dimension to Three Dog Night. He told that to Mom who told that to Dad.

'Neither,' Dad said. 'It's Joe's creative harmonica arrangements they like.'

Today was August 25th, his tenth birthday, a bad birthday. Last year his mom died in a freak accident. But Mom was sure present an hour ago at the party because he smelled her vanilla-orange body lotion all over the patio. And when Dad flipped the burger off the barbeque onto the grass, Mom's laugh burst out of Aunt Pam's mouth— Mom's silly, snorty laugh.

Nobody heard, not even Dad. Then he opened Aunt Pam's present, a little white prayer book, and Mom sighed. Still, nobody heard. Gaping like a rhino, he waited for reactions, waited for Mom to laugh or sigh again. But nothing.

'Your mom had a prayer book exactly like that when she was a kid, Joe,' Aunt Pam said, so he closed his hands tightly around the prayer book and squeezed—*you here,*

Mom? The book got all toasty in his hands and he scrunched his eyes shut. *You are here, aren't you, Mom?* The Mom-feeling stayed with him, but less on the outside and more on the inside, sweeter than brown sugar candy.

Mesmerized by three bands of changing color around his father's head, Joe edged closer. How come he'd never seen the colors before? Lately he'd noticed all kinds of new stuff, like right now seeing the curved road sparkle in the blues, pinks and purples. He pressed in on his stomach. This had turned into one of those days when he woke knowing the day would be crummy. He could tell because his gut always snaked up on him.

"Stomach feels weird again, Dad," he said, but his dad was too busy speeding to hear. "Dad, slow down. This is nuts!"

"Brakes! Brakes are gone! Put your head down, Joe!"

Oh no, Dad. Oh no. When the car swerved coming off the bend, he shoved his head between his knees. For a second it was like twirling on a ride when all you hear is a sharp whirr and a hum, like the dead hum on his busted fire engine. Then the car crashed against something solid and ricocheted back, spinning out of control. His father hollered his name, and the song blared right up to the bang ... *And all I do is cry ... One less bell to answer ... Because a man told me goodbye ...*

The smell of sulfur woke him and when his memory returned, he screamed. The burned Chrysler looked a whole football field away. How did he get so far out of the car and away from his dad? Then he saw it ... right in the middle of the road ... Dad's sneaker. He got cold all over.

Dad?

He hunched up on the roadside, scared to find his dad and scared of not finding him. Black mushroom clouds filled the sky. He'd call his father and he'd answer. He would.

"Hey, Dad?"

A hand rested on his shoulder. Comforted by its warmth, he straightened his legs and turned around, seeing nothing but beamy shafts of light–white on whiter. Everything might be okay. Mom had been around today so Dad would be around, too. They still loved him a lot, and now they were loving him from a better place.

A tear trickled down his face, falling into the cupped hand on his chin. Mom and Dad wouldn't be able to wrestle around with him again. Oh how he ached to be held, now more than in his whole entire life. But he couldn't ask this of a stranger, this beautiful stranger who'd brought friends, blurry friends with smiles he felt in his heart—like Mom at the party today. He stole another glance at the sneaker and let the tears come. So what if crying made him embarrassed. So what.

"Stop now," the stranger said, holding him close. "Don't be afraid to look at me, Joe."

The man wore the shiniest beauty on his face and seemed both young and old. He wasn't so scared anymore and his gut had stopped flip-flopping.

"Okay."

The stranger stared into him. "I'll guide you through your pain, Joe. Listen carefully to me."

"Who are you?"

"A friend. A *for life* friend." The friend tapped the little white prayer book. "I wrote a puzzle message for you because I know you like puzzles. But I have a more important message now and then I'll take you to the hospital."

"Important?" The Chrysler seemed two football fields away and the smoke had cleared.

"Study in the spirit. Then keep the child safe, Joe."

"What child?" The football field was spinning.

"Remember, Joe, study in the spirit ... and keep the child safe..."

∞∞∞∞

He woke up four hours later in Saint Gabriel's Hospital with two doctors, two cops and a teary-eyed nurse at his bedside. He was okay. No broken bones. Nothing fractured. No glass splinters from the windshield anywhere on him. *Miraculous,* they said. They were keeping him a day or two more because he'd had a bad shock. They were all so sorry his father died in the accident. But he'd have people to help him, his uncle was flying in to be with him, he wouldn't grieve alone. He had to believe that one day, life would be good again. On and on they rambled while the nurse sniffled and held his hand. Blah-blah-blah.

"We're leaving him the prayer book from the scene." It was a cop who said this because he saw the buttons glimmer on his uniform. "It's dated today with an inscription. Today's the boy's birthday."

The nurse coughed and sniffled some more while he strained to open his eyes all the way. No luck.

"Can I have it now?" he asked, floating off into twinkle-lights.

He heard the song as he drifted. Maybe somebody in the hallway had a radio. Maybe the crash tune was still stuck in his head—*One Less Bell To Answer. One less egg to fry.* He just wanted Dad and Mom back, wanted Fast Forward to train for the Derby. Thinking about the prayer book and Fast Forward taking the track killed the awfulness, pushed out the horror and destroyed it. Then he remembered the hand–the light–the stranger's message written in the book.

Remember your ABC's, Joe.

∞∞∞

"You're an amazing kid, Toots. You'll make it fine." Craig gave the chain a yank on the overhead light, and poof, no more blinding gamma rays. Geez, Craig was the greatest guy. Craig Matheson went to Harvard, was old, at least a couple decades older and he was proud to call Craig Matheson his 'Harvard' bud 'cause Craig was so brilliant, yes for sure. He was even prouder that Craig liked hanging with him better than his over-the-hill Harvard buddies who spent every summer at Claxton Farms. Craig nicknamed him *Toots* because he played harmonica for the horses.

"... Hope so, Craig. Mom and Dad wouldn't want me to chicken."

No point in Craig seeing him bawl like a baby. Besides, his friend looked sad and sick. He propped himself up and Craig tucked the blanket around his shoulders. Soon as Craig touched him, he got all droopy and tired again, felt mixed up and muddled in his head like the time he had to take antibiotics for a whopper cold. What was up with Craig?

"How's your 'apothecary on time versus variance' coming?"

Craig smiled, sort of. "Auxiliary hypotheses on *Time Reversal Invariance*. Well, my uncle still believes I'm wasting my time. I've decided to forget it for now, Toots."

"No way!" Craig had this theory about how time curved around people, and this theory meant more to him than Christmas and birthdays. "If I forgot about owning my own horse farm someday, I'd croak for sure! Those Harvard guys'll love your take on *Invariance*. I absolutely know it!" Thinking about Craig made his hurt go away, and already he felt his friend brighten up, except for the tiredness. "Don't dump your dream, Craig! Promise? Your uncle'll come around."

Craig gave him a play punch on the shoulder. "Thanks, Toots. Speaking of uncles, when's your Uncle Gord coming?"

"He's here now. He went back to the house to look into stuff. He said we can stay at the farm for another couple weeks after the funeral ..." *Think about Craig. Think about Craig. Say a prayer for Craig. Hey, God, please make Craig's hypothecary happen.* "... then we have to leave for Boston. So are you gonna do it?"

"Do what, Toots?"

"Not give up."

"Okay, Joe. I'll not give up."

"Promise? To the wire?"

"To the wire. Promise."

Zillions of fluttering moonbeams woke him in the middle of the night, fluttering and floating around his bed like angel bubbles. One moonbeam stretched to the ceiling and took the shape of a shining creature. It had to be his *friend for life* from the accident. Maybe Dad was with him. Mom, too.

"Listen to me, Joe," Friend said. The other beams floated to the foot and sides of his hospital bed. Had Friend told him to listen or was it his own loud thoughts? The thoughts flooded him with words—

Study in the spirit and keep the child safe. Use your pain to focus on others. The thoughts came faster than Forward's morning sprints around the track. *More loss. More pain. Later, your teammates will find you. Be their captain. Be their team leader. Help them get back, Joe. Help them get back so thousands can move forward. Keep your friends close and your enemies closer, as your enemy is a master at sneaking up from behind.*

Hear my voice, Joe—Marianlake.
"Marion Lake?"
Marianlake, Joe.

∞∞∞

Medford Massachusetts was already cold the first week of September. Joe longed to stay near his beloved horses in Ocala but Aunt Pam was his Godmother, not a blood relative. Besides, she couldn't afford to take him, which left his dad's older brother, Uncle Gord, the only relative he'd ever met.

Three short weeks ago, Fast Forward got his first racing shoes and Dad finally got him standing square in the starting gate with his head up and ready to break. Last week, Dad gave him the evil eye because he left his tool box on the kitchen table. And just last night he was in the stable hugging Forward goodbye.

Now everything had changed. He tried hard to comfort himself with thoughts of the Friend, which worked okay except for a scary dark moment that always followed. If he fought it, it didn't last long. He kept the prayer book close.

Uncle Gord looked like his dad around the eyes. Apart from that he found it hard to believe they were brothers. Gordon Ross was so thin, so bony pale-faced-weak-thin. And he never stopped smoking. It stank. He would cough, clear his throat, and then light up again.

"You'll get to see the four seasons here, Joe," Uncle Gord said on the drive out of Logan International. "And your Thoroughbred horse farms are around. May not be on every corner, but we still breed 'em here. Winters are something to see. You'll get to try some winter sports. Hockey's big. Would you like that?"

He nodded to be polite. Riding and hanging out in paddocks was his favorite thing to do in the world. Fast Forward would be really missing him now and wondering why he deserted him. Eyes stinging with tears, he turned his head away.

Medford had a population of 59,000, Mystic River fifty feet from the house and Medford Gas and Electric Company located centrally in town. Uncle Gord and practically everybody else in town worked at Medford Gas. It wasn't as nice as having pastures everywhere and being an hour and a half away from the ocean. He was near the water here, except this water would soon freeze, you couldn't body surf in it, and there were no boats on it this time of year. No Marion Lake either because he asked two people at the airport when Uncle Gord went to the bathroom. The top of the giant spruce in front of the house swayed in the wind, looking like it would topple. He wasn't in too big a hurry to see wintertime.

Aunt Beata had an early dinner waiting. On the plane he learned she was a widow raising a young daughter when she met Gord. She was waitressing in a bar outside Mexico City and Gord was vacationing there at the time. Wilomena–Willie, was three. Within four months, Uncle Gord sent for Beata, Willie, and Rosa Canites, Beata's mother.

At thirty-eight, Beata was ten years younger than Gord and still beautiful when she dressed herself up. She spent the rest of the time in tracksuits and wore her hair in a ponytail. Gord, who never complained, liked her in tracksuits so much that he bought her a closet-and-a-half full of them. Beata didn't have a vain bone in her body and Gord liked that, too.

He was midway through a cherry Jell-O when Willie burst into the house, slammed the porch door behind her and shouted, "Are they back yet?" He stood to greet her, surprised how much older she looked when she was a whole year younger. For sure they'd be friends and she acted like she had the confidence of the smallest jockey on the biggest horse. Except she didn't because he felt her stomach butterflies and the worry in her mind.

Pretty Willie walked straight up to him and kissed his cheek. "I'm glad you'll be living with us," she said, all smiles. Then the smile quickly faded. "But I'm sorry about your Mom and Dad."

His heart quivered like the cherry Jell-O on the spoon. He liked Willie as much as he felt sorry for her without knowing why. He even liked the question mark cowlick on the back of her head. But poor Willie's gut had this growing speck of sadness inside a circle of light. It was foreboding. He knew that word. His mom once explained it and when she tried to explain the word 'premonition' he didn't get it. A piece of the darkness was back though, which made him think of that word.

After lunch, Willie took him to his attic bedroom and helped him unpack. The mattress was as thin as a harness bellyband and the window too small to let in much light. There was a yellowed, girly chest of drawers under the window, probably yellowed from Uncle Gord's cigarettes. Wet glass rings and burn scabs crusted the top of the night table by his bed. Willie said her stepdad came up here to drink Cokes and read his Sports Illustrated in private. Everything smelled vinegary and moist, like a soggy beach towel.

"Gord said he'd get ya new furniture. Boy furniture," Willie said, noticing his disappointment. "We'll paint and put up pictures. I picked out the *Star Trek* bedspread. Do you like it?"

He did like it. He and Mister Spock went way back and he told her so, told her the black Princess phone was cool. But who would he call? Crumpling himself up under the covers, he cried himself to sleep, the longest bout of tears since the accident. He was still sniffling at midnight when an odd shuffling sound in the hallway made him bolt upright in bed. A long shadow lingered at his threshold door. Relieved when the doorknob didn't turn and the shadow walked away, he closed his eyes. Even if sleep didn't come, he had to keep them closed because they stung. Probably from all his baby tears. The next afternoon, he met the 'shadow' when he wandered into the basement.

That's where sixty-year-old Rosa Canites lived–in the 'cella' as she called it. It was another world compared to the rest of the house, not as neat or as organized and none of the colors matched. He liked that. Upstairs was like everybody else's living room. Downstairs was carnival-gypsy in the mist, the scent of lilacs after a hard spring rain. It excited him.

He was imagining a world with his parents and Fast Forward in one of her six crystal balls when she snuck up on him. "I wonder if she can see The Friend in one of these," he said, holding it to the light.

"Some people wait to be invited," said a crotchety voice with a trace of a Spanish accent.

He nearly dropped the thing. It was rude to sneak up on people. But he wouldn't dare tell her that, given the situation. "I'm.m Joe. I live here now."

"I know who you are. What're you doing down here?"

He didn't need the arthritic finger stabbing at his chest and pushed her hand away.

"Don't mind her, Joe," Beata said, padding down the stairs with a couple of Dr. Pepper's. "Mama doesn't like company much. Don't scare him away from us yet, Mama," she winked, handing each of them a Dr. Pepper. "We want to keep him." Then Beata left them alone.

Rosa was sure tall for a woman as ancient as sixty. And she looked like a gypsy with her long colorful afghan and those big hoopy, gold earrings. Her wavy gray hair hung loose at her shoulders, parted to the side. Funny how Rosa Canites seemed like the youngest person in the house.

"You read all these books?" he asked, trying to get the scowl off her face.

The row of wrist bangles clanked as she gripped his chin, tugging his head slightly to the left. "Your right eye is off-kilter, did you know that?" She was squinting at him.

"Only when I'm thinking real hard," he said defiantly.

Rosa's face softened. "Bring your drink over here and sit down with me ... and we'll get to know each other. I got in late last night and heard you crying. I almost came in but decided it wasn't the best time for strangers to get acquainted. God made tears to be cried, you know. Your tears are important." He was trying to stop his chin from quivering when she winked at him, "You're a great lookin' kid, you know that. Gonna break a lotta hearts, eh."

"Except for my right eye that's off." No one in his whole life ever mentioned his eye before, 'cause it hardly ever happened and no one else ever noticed. That had to mean something good because he was getting a 'cool, warm breezes' vibe from her.

Rosa leaned in closer. "But that's a special eye. When you concentrate with that eye, you turn it into an invisible third eye. And that's the eye that sees what most other people can't. It can work almost the same way my crystal balls do over there. You were wondering something about seeing the friend in them when I caught you. Who's this *friend*?"

It surprised him that he ended up telling her the entire story. He didn't even tell anyone at the funeral, not his friends or even Aunt Pam. He cried again, but he didn't feel like a suck crying in front of Rosa. She made it seem that crying was the sensible thing to do. He also told her about his mother—that if he got to her two minutes sooner instead of three, she might still be alive. If he had've sprayed the horse down a second time because the mosquitoes were bad that spring, he wouldn't have had to run for help in the first place.

They talked straight into dinnertime that day. Rosa, who almost always took her meals alone, joined them at the table. They spoke of many things–the education she gave herself through her books, her travels, his hobbies and old school friends. He showed her his special prayer book and she held it for a long time. When he talked she stared deeply into his eyes. Through the years, discussions of God and His angels would absorb them for hours at a time. The first time he ever asked about ghosts, she told him there were no such things. There were only dark angels pretending to be ghosts.

Rosa helped him work through the pain of adolescence–fights at school, a mediocre grade here and there, changing hormones, acne breakouts and girls. He eventually made many friends but Rosa was it. Best of the best. Rosa knew him like nobody else and sometimes she'd quiz him.

"How am I feeling today?" she'd often ask.

"Cut down on the Dr. Pepper," he'd tell her. "I shouldn't have to pop Rolaids for your stomach ache."

She always understood when he didn't want to discuss stuff, always respected his privacy. He loved her more for it. Besides, he knew that she knew he'd cave sooner or later and tell her everything.

A week after his arrival in Medford, Rosa took him to a 'spiritualist' friend of hers. Uncle Gord called her a phony. Beata called her a fortune-teller. And Willie called her 'so cool.' Rosa loved catching glimpses of the next world and he always accompanied her, though it made him uncomfortable and he never figured out why. They went to psychic fairs. Sometimes Willie and Beata tagged along, but never Gord. He stuck pretty much to his cigarettes and his pals down at the Lions Club.

His 'third eye' as Rosa referred to it, had developed by the time he was thirteen. Although the family was Catholic, Joe distanced himself from church-going. Worshipping alone felt more comfortable. Gord was still the final decision-maker in the family and if Joe didn't want to go to church, Joe didn't have to go to church, much to Rosa's consternation. This was the only thing they seriously disagreed upon.

The *Eagles* were big in 1975 and Joe and Willie got to see them at the Boston Garden. Since they were fifteen and fourteen at the time, Gord insisted an older neighborhood kid chaperone them. The older, more 'responsible' kid was the one carrying a fifth of vodka and an ounce of grass. When *Don Henley* and *Glen Fry* raised their guitars to *One Of These Nights*, that's when Willie took her first drink. It was also the first time she kissed him.

Winter sports were never his thing, preferring Korean karate and tai chi. All forms of smoking repulsed him after seeing what it had done to Uncle Gord who, weighing in at one hundred and eight pounds was more cadaverous-looking than ever. The smokers cough had worsened and he appeared to be two spits away from the grave, although he told everyone he felt like a breath of spring. Beata told him his breath was nothin' like spring.

Rosa sank more of her pension money into the lottery over the years, insisting they were going to hit the big one. Fifty bucks a week went into the 'big one'. But by 1979, shortly after his nineteenth birthday, Rosa won five hundred thousand dollars in the Massachusetts State Lottery. She put half of it into trust for his and Willie's education and future. She divided the other half among Beata, herself and Gord. Gord didn't leave her behind when he married her daughter. She never forgot that. He wasn't the warmest man in the world, but he provided for both her family and Joe. Gordon Ross succumbed to lung cancer the day after Christmas that same year, remembering to include his nephew in his will. Willie got dead drunk at his wake.

The martial arts and tai chi paid off. Months away from his twentieth birthday, he was a brawny six-foot-one with an infectious fireside smile and little-boy-lost look that always had the girls asking 'can I help you?' Rosa convinced him to wear his dark brown locks short to show off the high cheekbones and melting pot eyes never keen on making contact. He still felt self-conscious over the eye that sometimes went slightly 'askew'. Rosa said the eye that *rarely* went askew kept him humble.

Shooting for a four-year Bachelor of Science with emphasis in Equine Studies, he met Norma Chilling on campus during his first year at Amherst U. He'd been saving it for the real thing, but Ms. Norma the hot-spirited meteor, made it difficult to remember he was saving it. He wasn't in love with Norma, but aside from her knowing how to rile his hormones, he found himself attracted to her 'darkness'. Typically, he wanted to help, masochist and idiot that he was.

Sadly, there was more to Norma than fire and fun and he was still paying the emotional price for knowing her. A woman determined to get what she wanted, Norma wanted Joe Ross. She also carried a 6.4 oz. 22 Magnum Pug Mini which she could have carried in her sock. But Norma being Norma, toted it in a bra holster, which he unfortunately discovered one freezing December night after a party. Attraction to one's darker side was a battle he'd fight throughout his life, a battle hard-won and a blessing for those he helped, with the tragic exception of Norma Chilling.

"Start coming to church with me again, Joe," Rosa said, after Norma's inquest. "Father Jim would really like to talk to you. He can help you spiritually."

"Joe's spiritual enough," Beata shouted from the kitchen. "Leave him be, Ma. He'll go when he's ready."

"Sorry, R," he said. "But I need more than a priest right now. An angelic posse is what I need."

Rosa knew she'd get him there one day because Beata was right. He was spiritual enough. Rosa eventually got off his back because he was more spiritual than all of them any day of the week and twice on Sundays. Besides, they had a more serious issue to grapple with. And the issue's name was Willie.

∞∞∞∞

She had grown into a beauty. Odd thing was, people who didn't know better mistook them for brother and sister. Willie was happy they were not brother and sister. Willie'd been happy about that since the day he moved in. Joe Ross was practically all she ever thought of. She had boyfriends galore who were crazy for her, but none of them made her crazy, not like Joe.

For years Willie watched him. They even double-dated. She watched him most when he didn't know anyone was around. She went to Mass every Sunday for one reason–to pray for Joe's love. It began to work. Something changed and the change stimulated her faith. Father James was always going on about the power of faith.

'Amen I say to you, that whosoever shall say to this mountain, be thou removed and be cast into the sea, and

*shall not stagger in his heart, but believe, that whatsoever he
saith shall be done; it shall be done unto him. Therefore I say
unto you, all things, whatsoever you ask when ye pray, believe
that you shall receive; and they shall come unto you'.*

Willie memorized that passage, recited it a dozen times
a day. She truly believed Joe would be hers one day. So she
told herself to be patient. God would pick their time.

This ambiguous belief was her sacred amulet, giving her
strength to look the other way when girls pursued Joe,
though it was hard to stay straight during the double dates,
hard to watch him with his arms around some drooling girl
in the front seat. She promised herself there would be no
more 'drive-in' dates. They were just too painful. But she
hung in there because Joe was beginning to notice her,
really notice her.

∞∞∞

It was late August, three days after Joe's twentieth
birthday when Rosa and Beata rented a cottage near the
Cape until Labor Day. It was the perfect time to help Joe
put that whole Norma nightmare behind him and get
some distance between him and Willie. The plan was for
Joe to stay home and emotionally convalesce while they
absconded with Willie. Rosa wanted Joe to find himself
again, hang out with his friends and clear his head. The
plan backfired when Joe decided to join them. They could
always cancel the cottage, but to what purpose?

Maybe if she explained that Beata needed alone time
with Willie and she was tagging along to referee and
cushion blows, he would understand. But she couldn't do
that to Joe. She loved him and he needed his family, too.
She'd just have to make like an eagle and watch from on
high.

"I know I wanted to separate them but Joe needs us,
too," Rosa said while Beata packed her Birdwatcher's

Handbook and binoculars. "Joe's at loose ends after this dreadful Norma Chilling business. I wish he'd take a break from his studies next semester, maybe grab a friend and take a little trip. And Willie's been tripping a little too much if you get my meaning."

"Willie has a lot on her mind, Ma." Beata rearranged the binoculars in the suitcase for the third time. "Her nerves are bad. And Gord's death was hard on her."

Prepared to take issue, Rosa thought a moment, "Willie was never that close to Gord."

"Leave it alone, Ma."

She gave her daughter a pat on the cheek. "Okay. But sometimes it's better to attack a problem head on, even if it means pain. I know people who've spent their lives waiting for things that never happened. But not to worry, *mi querida*. After a few weeks away and some sage advice from her mother and grandmother, Willie's problems will get ironed out. You'll see."

Rosa watched her daughter overstuff that sorry old suitcase. Beata didn't look too convinced. Fact was she wasn't too convinced herself.

∞∞∞∞

They had been trying to motor for the last hour, except her mother had to check the new alarm system, her grandmother was at the neighbor's with more plant-watering instructions, and she had to make sure she packed all his favorite music. She stuck her head out the attic window and yelled down to Joe who was leaning against the car spraying his arms with DEET.

"You left all the Zeppelin and Stones tapes on your dresser! Don't you wanna take those?"

"If you want, grab them!" he shouted back. "You're the music meister. I leave all the musical arrangements to you." Then he smiled up at her.

She returned the smile, certain he smiled the same way at Norma. God, Norma went nuts over him, but then Norma was nuts, period. She ran her hands along his pillow and under his covers. It wasn't the first time she'd done this lately and it bothered her. He was making her so hot and feeling this way was wrong. She hadn't read a book in ages—couldn't concentrate, and she went on that last date because the guy was real good-looking and maybe Joe would get jealous.

But no luck. Good thing the guy was an out-of-towner. She got so drunk that night and had sex with him when they went parking by the Mystic River. They weren't even in the car. She had staggered out to get some air, to enjoy the view, to fantasize. Then he walked over and took her, right there against the tree. Late that same night, Joe found her crying on the back porch swing. He didn't lecture or get judgmental. Nothing. He simply scooped her up, carried her to her room and tucked her in. When she felt herself drifting off, Joe was still there.

It was a lovely drive up the coast highway and the healthy swig of vodka she took at their last pit stop helped her relax. They couldn't tell with vodka, as long as she stayed sober and wore the shades. It was hard to relax around Joe without a boost. Sometimes she felt herself slowly dissolving into him, piece by piece. Thinking this worried her so much she had to recite the passage in her mind again. Vodka and that miraculous little Bible passage from Mark dulled her obsession with Joe.

They were ten miles from the cottage when Joe tuned into a mellow radio station, an odd thing for him to do since he was a music lover who hated playing music in the car. The car was his think tank, he'd always say. He'd play music anywhere and everywhere else, garage, house, stable, closet, but never in the car. He'd made an exception to this rule today because there were three people to consider and it was a long drive. Also, he wasn't quite himself yet. He hadn't been returning calls to friends and lately, after a day at Moonlight Stables where he worked as a part-time groom and farrier, he neglected to shower after spending an afternoon with the horses. This was *not* Joe Ross, Mr. Perfect Hygiene.

"I don't want to get sick of all our own stuff too soon," he said. "We have close to a month up here." When Joe checked the rear view to change lanes, she glanced back. Rosa was catnapping and Beata was staring out the window, lost in thought. Then Joe took her hand and caressed it. Willie closed her eyes. *Thank you, God.* And again ... *thank you, thank you, thank you.*

∞∞∞

Nestled at the end of a private pine-lined driveway, it was not the typical cottage. It was more like a five-bedroom mansion without the pool, which they didn't need because they had the Atlantic Ocean twenty feet away. The back of the house opened to sweeping water views overlooking Cape Cod Bay all the way to the lighthouse point on one side and Angelfish Cove on the other, and sat impressively on a three-quarter acre of beach landscape. Willie curled her toes in the sand then ran into the water, gesturing for him to follow. Rosa grabbed his arm.

"Willie has expectations, Joe, expectations she's had most of her life and doesn't think we've noticed. And you're vulnerable right now."

"I know how she feels about me, R." He cleared his throat, watching Willie body-surfing a wave. "But you want to know if I feel anything for her. That's your question, right?"

"There are no secrets in this family."

"You sure? What about Willie's secret?"

"That's the main reason we're here and don't change the subject."

"You know I love Willie. Next to you she's my best friend."

"A set-up for catastrophe if ever there was one—a young woman desperately in love with the vulnerable hell escapee she can't have."

Rosa clattered her bangles at him and he laughed. "Oh the drama."

"You never talked to me about Norma. I mean *really* talked."

Willie was still waiting in the water so he gave her the high-five. He crooked his arm in Rosa's and they walked. "I hate re-living it. I re-live it every damn night when I shut my eyes. You were at the hearing. I shot my girlfriend and got away with it."

"Oh come on now."

"I know, R. I know. I'm not ready to get into a heavy about Norma. But I will. Sometime. Okay, *amiga mio*?"

"I worry about you too, you know. I need to know what's going on inside you. You're not an open book like Willie."

"It's the accident." He guessed from Rosa's expression that she knew instantly what he meant. He hadn't spoken of it in years and why it was surfacing now, he hadn't a clue. "The directive that ghost or spirit or angel, whatever it was, gave me. Can't shake it. It's stuck in my head like a grownup foot in a kid's stirrup."

"The child?"

"Yeah. I'm supposed to save a child? Whose? And when? And 'study in the spirit'? What does that mean? Then there's that *lake* place. I checked it out before we came, you know. There's no *Marion Lake* around here.

Okay so here's the thing, growing up I never concerned myself with it. All I thought about was horses. Until recently, this stuff was an old hazy dream, then suddenly I'm all obsessed. And probably for selfish reasons."

"What do you mean, selfish?"

He batted away a cloud of no-see-ums and snatched the DEET from his windbreaker. "I've wanted one thing my whole life. Had one dream. That Thoroughbred horse farm. I want to raise 'em—foal to yearling."

"And why is this selfish?"

"What if this *child* I'm supposed to save prevents that from happening?" He felt the veins cord in his neck. "Forget the what-ifs, R ... I'm terrified that's exactly what will happen."

Rosa gave his forearm a good shake. "No. You know why? Because you have choices, Joe. We all have choices. Remember that."

He drew in a tight breath. Poor Rosa. Here he was laying this stuff on her when she had a bigger horse to corral, a feisty filly named Wilomena and a daughter worried sick about her. In recent weeks, Willie spent more hours in the day hiding behind dark sunglasses and had taxied home drunk four times in the last month. He had to forget himself for once and find a way to help her.

They strolled back to the house and no Willie and no Beata in sight. "So what do we do about Misters' *Popov* and *Smirnoff?*"

Rosa sighed heavily. "Beata's call."

"Has she talked to Willie yet?"

"She's broached it. But you know Willie, she gets defensive. And then there's that pride of hers." Rosa started to say something then hesitated.

"What, R? Tell me."

Rosa told him about the chat she had with Beata before they left. In coming here, Beata wanted very much to put the period at the end of Willie's sentence. Beata was sure he would tell Willie there was no way for them, that it wasn't meant to be, that soon he would be on his way back to Amherst U or to whatever the world had in store for him. And she had to do the same thing. Once he'd had 'the talk' with her, Rosa and Beata could help Willie deal with certain realities. Beata also had serious concerns about him, seeing he was still a man with a beautiful girl willing to stop her world and get off for him.

"I assured Beata you'd behave responsibly. You always have. Told her you'd never cross any lines. You have wisdom way beyond your years, Joe. I keep forgetting you're only twenty."

He smacked a mosquito on his neck. Damn things. "Pedestals. Stop putting me on pedestals, will you please?" Willie shuffled onto the deck, sipping a can of Coke that was probably spiked. He waved up at her and drew in a long breath. "Well, say a prayer I don't disappoint, R." He whipped off his windbreaker and T-shirt. "Rain," he said. A few steps into the water, he observed the darkening horizon then turned toward Rosa, said it again, "Rain."

∞∞∞∞

Willie went to bed early that first night. The rain was disappointing. Joe was disappointing. He and Beata had been playing backgammon for hours. It was time to be alone anyway. She needed a real drink and preferred to do that in the privacy of her room. Pretending to be asleep would be easy if someone came knocking on the door.

Why did everything have to be so *complexifying*, as Joe liked to say? She poured herself a double vodka. Such a dilemma. It was getting harder to hide. The more she drank, the more she ached for him. And the more she ached for him, the more she laughed in the face of caution. Another double vodka and she might abandon what little pride she had left. She might mosey into his room and crawl into his bed.

"No." She drew the initial J in the condensation on the glass. "He comes to *my* room. He comes to *my* bed!"

After drinking herself into oblivion and waking sicker than usual, she checked her stash. Half a twenty-sixer before bedtime. Thirteen shots in less than two hours. She'd have to cut down for sure because she'd wreck her skin and bloat. Good luck attracting Joe looking like one of the Gorgon sisters.

She found him on the deck repairing the leather strap on Beata's binocular case, trusty red toolbox by his side, DEET on the patio table. Gawd, he had that toolbox since the day he arrived, that and the old harmonica he played so badly. Like it was yesterday, she remembered him lugging the toolbox up the stairs to the attic bedroom. A decade ago.

"Hey," he said, focusing on the strap, "Found a place where we can ride. Garrow's stable on the other side of the Cove. We'll have to check it out."

She slipped on the shades, her lips parting slightly at the sight of him shirtless and sweaty. "Good," she said, hoping the hangover didn't show. "When do you want to go?"

"--Mama, we're going to have to go back into town for those traps," Beata said, zipping onto the deck, Rosa behind her. "Where there's water there's rats."

"Rats?" Joe said.

"You want to go this aft, Joe?"

"What rats?"

"Beata thinks she heard rats scuffling around in the laundry room," Rosa said.

"We could stop in Angelfish Cove after. Check that out, too."

"Why don't you take a spin into town and pick up those traps, Willie." Rosa said.

"You wanna come, Joe?"

"I better have a look down there, B. Show me where."

He didn't even notice her grab her mother's car keys or shout that she was on her way *NOW* for those traps. He just took off inside the house with her mother. No *wait for me, Willie*. No *hang on, we're going riding, remember?* Nothing, forget it. She'd get the traps all right and on the way home she'd replenish the stash. She felt like having a few and right now she couldn't care less about trying to hide it.

The three of them were on the deck when she returned, Joe on the chaise fracturing a tune on his harmonica and R & B buried to the nose in sun hats, trying to read. He glanced up at her sheepish-like, so probably her gramma mentioned her storming off. She felt small suddenly, like she was dissolving into nothingness. *I'm melting. Meh-el-ting.* She considered snatching her mother's bird book and hiding behind it.

"Wasn't rats," Joe said. "It was a baby Sharpwater."

"*Shear*water," her mother the birdologist corrected.

"Must've come in through the dryer shaft, we figure."

"Oh."

"Sooooo, I was thinking tonight we go check out that Corey's Cafe you noticed on the drive in. Have dinner. Take a walk around the town after. My treat." He smiled that movie star smile and her eyes moistened under the sunglasses.

"Sure. Oh and hey—Ma picked up some fabulous raspberry chocolate mousse tarts. We can have ours on the beach after dinner. And I picked up a lovely California

Cabernet Sauvignon to complement." Was she imagining it or did Joe and Gramma exchange looks?

"It's a date," Joe said. They exchanged subtle looks again and this time she did not imagine it.

∞∞∞

Back home in Medford, Joe's little white prayer book fell from his bookshelf to the floor.

∞∞∞

The clouds hung low over the quaint village of Angelfish Cove. He and Willie strolled the boardwalk enjoying the Cove's music—cawing gulls and waves lapping the shore. The air smelled of buttery lobster and sandalwood incense. On both sides of the boardwalk, sunburned noses on medium-fried bodies' wandered along without care and outdoor cafes and shops of every description dotted their way.

"*Déjà vu,*" he mumbled, glancing at Willie who wasn't too talkative but for once, wasn't all riled up inside. Maybe she felt the presence here too, the spiritual ambiance, like the town was a 'portal' to somewhere. Willie took his hand when they crossed the street to where *it* stood–very much a part and *apart* from all the other attractions.

The tiniest record shop he had ever seen, for which it was aptly named *The Tiniest Record Shop*.

45s strung across the weensy storefront twirled in the breeze and *Stay* by Frankie Valli & The Four Seasons doo-wopped from a small indoor speaker. Willie headed straight for the album rack and he tapped along to The Four Seasons, checking for a clerk and a cash register. But no clerk and in place of a register there was a tomato juice can with 'Honor System' scrawled in black magic marker.

"More than six people would be vinyl sandwiches in here," he said. "You've probably seen confessionals bigger than this. Not that you need to go to confession."

When she blushed, he felt a twinge of guilt for teasing her and let her alone to surf through albums. Thumbing through a few albums himself, he noticed a conspicuous absence of recordings after 1970. Same with the 45s, Willie told him. And where was the shopkeeper?

A feeling of weightlessness inched from his feet toward his head, lifting him upward. He actually checked his feet to make sure they were still on the floor. No use bolting with Willie because the presence in this room had purpose, something to impart. He wasn't going anywhere.

A low intermittent buzz thrummed from the intercom above the door. Willie was okay, still happily flipping through albums. Good. Back to the intercom. More buzzing and scratchy static. And now that song. Oh, that horribly wonderful song ...

... *One less bell to answer. One less egg to fry. One less man to pick up after. I should be happy ... but all I do is cry ... Listen, Joe ... prepare yourself. Go out to the street and meet the players.*

Lord, what was this? Obviously, Willie hadn't heard 'the voice' part of the song. He got himself to the doorway and breathed. And breathed again. At the end of the boardwalk, a lobster trapper hunched over his day's-end catch, gulls squealing above him. Shafts of light streamed through the slats in the crates, centering him into a Zen-like calm. With maybe fifteen minutes of sunlight left to the day, he stayed in the doorway gazing tranquilly onto Main Street until Willie finished with the stack of 45s. What wondrous thing was next on the program, boys and girls?

"I wanna grab this *Chicago* album but there's not enough in the honor can to make change," Willie said. "Where's the guy? Is there a guy?"

Joe checked his wallet. "I'd spot you but all I have are twenties. Let's just drift and do dinner. We'll come back for the album."

While they strolled he gawked at everybody on the street. Okay, so where were these *players* he was supposed to meet? Players at what? In spite of the excitement, he remained calm. Just breathing the air was like a couple of good hits off a hash pipe. Part of this emotional quietude was coming from Willie, who hadn't suggested they stop for a drink somewhere. Feeling her calm center made him happy, however brief because he had to have 'the talk' with her tonight. She needed to get her life back and he needed to help return it to her. And to do that he had to be straight with her. God help them both.

It was a happy busy little town, filled with tourists, townies and summer stay-overs. Youngsters on roller skates. Oldsters carrying the latest in compact cameras. A pack of nuns headed in their direction. He counted them. Seven. Why would he count them? They walked in pairs until the seventh who trailed the others by several feet. She seemed younger than the rest, much younger and disconnected from the group. He decided her habit was the difference. The skirt was shorter, falling to the knee. She approached, and for a few seconds when they were shoulder to shoulder, he heard the Voice again,

Meet Sister Elizabeth.

Right. Okay. Time to dump his thoughts into the ether of his splintered subconscious and ask the meaning of 'Save the child' and 'Marion Lake'. But no answer came. No song. No intercom on the street, though he had faith that the answer was forthcoming. The path to the child would find him. He didn't have to go searching for the path. Finally it was going to happen and there was no stress, no stress at all, just this karma buzz. The Universe set the timer—*tick tick tick tick tick* and his life's purpose had begun, whatever it was. *Tick tick tick*. No need to be frightened.

Not yet.

"Joe, let's go over and check out the artist," Willie said.

Never had he seen such concentration. Off in a world of her own, she painted away. Nose and chin splotched with blue and red, her long auburn hair hung loose and free. She hadn't looked up yet, but it was an easy guess she had brown soulful eyes. There was something mystical about her and her hands had a spiritual quality, which amused him because he never thought of a person's hands as spiritual. *Begging your pardon, ghost of Raphael.* He peeked over her shoulder at the scape of Angelfish Cove, so haunting he wished he lived here.

"It's almost animate," he said to her.

"That's the idea," she said, eyes as warm as roasting chestnuts.

While Willie and the artist chatted about the absent clerk in the tiny record shop, he stood mesmerized by brush strokes made with a hand that seemed preternaturally guided. He felt a gentle tug at his spirit ...

... Joe, meet Maggie. My sweet client.

He had to ask the artist her name and when she answered 'Sally', his mind raced and his thoughts froze. Was Sister Elizabeth not really Sister Elizabeth? Were these people impostors? He hadn't had a serious anxiety attack since Norma's last night on this earth, but he felt one coming on now. So much for karma buzzes and Zen-like calm. One moment absolutely everything was coming together and the next ... well ... a snake in his belly and a pall of darkness nipping at the heels.

The anxiety hit Willie too, faster than a speed horse on a dirt track, so he led her across the street to Corey's Cafe

Beanery. Should he tell Willie about these seesaw emotions and bizarre battle taking place inside his head? No, she had enough on her plate. Then the answer hit him.

The Voice had instructed him to go and meet the 'players'. Of course. The nun and the artist were playing a role for his benefit. One day he would meet a nun named Elizabeth and an artist with red hair by the name of Maggie.

They grabbed a corner booth in Corey's and Willie ordered a screwdriver before he could protest. Didn't matter anyway because she always carried a flask in her purse she didn't think he knew about. He rubbed the back of his neck, relieved the prickling sensation had subsided. Rosa likened these types of feelings to visitations from dark angels. He'd have to give this some serious thought. The anxiety had gone yet again and for the moment he was at peace. *Players, Joe. Players. Don't freak out next time.*

He smiled across the table at Willie and her cheeks reddened.

2. Angelfish Cove

Over dinner they watched the sunset. He spoke of déjà vu and the subconscious. Mostly, Willie listened and drank screwdrivers. No one in the place had thought to question their age. The legal drinking age all over New England was twenty-one. He was ageless at twenty. Willie was nineteen and looked a beautiful twenty-five. The booze had done that.

On the way to the john, Willie made a pit stop at the bar, probably to change her order to a double. In all fairness to Willie, maybe she was asking the bartender directions to the john. Yeah, right. *Lead in yer head, Joe.*

A tall, balding, fiftyish-looking man stopped and introduced himself. "Hi, there. John Corey. Proprietor here. Hope you and your lady are enjoying yourselves."

"Very much, thanks." Joe singled out a photo in a cluster of several on the wall. "That has got to be the biggest bottle of liquor I have ever seen. Is that you in the picture?"

John Corey squinted at it. "Oh that one. Sure is. Me and my liquor rep. That's a ten-foot inflatable promotional bottle. Had it outside that night and took it in for the picture shot. *Needham's Bourbon.* Can you imagine the slogans we dreamed up with a catchy name like that? The company had a promo party in here that day. Yah, a whale of a slam-bang party it was, too. Yup. Went on into the wee hours."

"The guy sitting at the bar in the background doesn't look too happy."

"No he doesn't, does he. Didn't know him. Nobody seemed to. Remember him ambling in shortly before they took the *Needham's* picture with one of our locals. But then he disappeared and left the young man alone. Rep must've fed him one too many *Needham's* 'cause he kept mumbling something about a lost remote control. Remember I saw him toss it in the garbage. Just fling the thing. I had the bartender cut him off after that. Funny how I remember a stranger after so many years and little else about that night. I sure had my fair share a *Needham's* that night too, I don't mind admitting."

He uncrossed his legs and leaned forward. Why was this so intriguing? "How long ago was it?"

"Memory's saying late spring or early summer of '67. I remember 'cause that was the year I started slashing all my sevens with that little bar, 'cause the bank said my seven looked like a one. Been slashing them ever since."

Willie returned with their server who set down two drinks. John Corey glanced at the drinks, then smiled suspiciously at him, a smile that implied he'd look the other way if this was their last drink. They exchanged a silent understanding and John Corey bid them a good evening.

Willie's face was flushed—and expectant. Yep. She expected big things from tonight and before the night was over he'd have to find a way to break her heart without breaking her heart. He'd have to tell her they could never be an item and then with one more twist of the knife, 'Willie, you're turning into a drunk.' He was eight when he got pinned under a foal. No comparison to the weight he felt now.

How was he going to do this? Maybe he should put this off until they were home—in the morning. *No. It's tonight,*

Joe. Don't be such a coward. But he'd have her walk off the vodka first.

"Joe?"

"Come on, Willie." He reached for his wallet. "Let's get your *Chicago* album and then go have those chocolate tart things on the beach."

The tiny record shop with the absent clerk was closed so they returned to Corey's. The music from the jazz combo on the patio had bewitched them from down the street. Would've been nice to sit on the patio and kick back but he couldn't risk Willie ordering another screwdriver, so they listened from the sidewalk. The group's singer focused her eyes on him when she introduced their next number, an antique jazzy ballad called *The Look of Love*. At least it was antique to him.

"Know something?" He flagged his finger at Willie during the song's intro. "I was five or six when that song came out. I remember because my parents loved it. Don't they play anything contemporary in this town?"

"I don't ever wanna leave here," Willie said dreamily.

The soloist hadn't made it through the first verse when a small crowd gathered on the patio and street. Her voice was lilting and honey-like, a voice that made the senses shine, made lovers melt into each other. Beads of sweat broke out on his forehead and upper lip as the lyrics and melody captured him. What was the scoop with this town and old music? Did a person have to go backward to move forward? Odd thought.

The singer had a small chubby frame and an angelic voice, as though food and song were the only passions she'd ever known. He pictured himself guiding her when she was older. But something bad would happen to her on the road to the Future. He felt another bout of weirdness coming on and leaned further into the song's hypnotic

melody. What was this? Were the lyrics changing? Did the
singer just say his name...?

She'll need you, Joe. Her name is Dina.

During the song's outro, he dropped a five-dollar-bill
into the base player's guitar case and mouthed *beautiful* to
Dina. His heart was still knocking against his ribs when
they headed across the street to Pages Bookstore. He
couldn't resist turning back for one more look and found
her watching him.

"Thank-you," she mouthed back.

He nodded. 'Dina'. Hmm, what a voice. How many
more *players* were there?

"I feel all mellow inside," Willie said, entering Pages.

"Me too, and I feel like buying us something. Brilliant
idea here—how 'bout a book?"

"Or one of those." She pointed to the sun caps on the
wall behind the cash counter. "The green beanie one is the
same shade as my outfit."

Pages carried a variety of sun-hats in more colors than
the silks at Churchill Downs, all bearing the same logo,
angel wings with the word 'CAP' beside it. "Put that one
aside, please," he said to the clerk. "I'll pick it up on the
way out."

Like everyplace else in Angelfish Cove, the bookstore's
soothing mystical atmosphere mesmerized him. On the
upper level wall where the wide wrought iron staircase
ended, he caught sight of a painting that resembled the one
Maggie was working on. Maybe it was the incense again or
the chimes or the breezy ocean music, but he felt beckoned
by an invisible hand and loved it. Like Willie felt at
Corey's, he never wanted to leave, and the only noise was
clanking feet on the staircase and the occasional throat-
clearing. Coughing and throat-clearing reminded him of

Uncle Gord. Good old Uncle Gord and his nicotine cologne.

Willie's emerald green shorts and blouse blended right in with the carpeting, which happened to be the same shade of green. He admired the beamed ceiling and mahogany shelves. On the top deck in the far corner, customers cozied up reading by an enormous stone fireplace. This was like visiting friends in the country. Willie excused herself and went off to find the ladies room.

A stocky young man in a beige T-shirt sat alone at the reading desk, head propped in his hands. Didn't he just see this guy in the photo at Corey's Café with the same booze flush on his face? The young man's solitude touched him and there was no one around to care or even acknowledge his presence. Poor kid. Approaching him from the side, he made out two words across the back of his T-shirt, one of which looked like *Bogel* or *Rogel*.

"Excuse me? You all right?"

The young man didn't hear him. Before he could repeat the question something startled him. The boy seemed to vibrate, then fade. Either he was witnessing the smallest of earthquake tremors or having a dizzy spell. The boy's head jerked upward. Perhaps he sensed his presence, though it was obvious he didn't see him because he was looking *through* him. Was he blind? There was no cane around. The poor kid, clearly bummed out, folded his arms on the table and rested his head on them.

Maybe he should find the owner. Then again, he should probably mind his own business. Something cut into his ankle. A tiny glass shard had wedged itself above the bone. As he knelt to pick out the glass and tissue off the blood with spit, he noticed pieces of broken glass everywhere. And the store had darkened. He checked to see if the boy was okay but he had vanished. *What the hell?*

"Can I get you a Band-Aid for that?" asked a silvery soft voice.

He stood and wobbled back at the sight of those butternut brown, fawn-like eyes. She had strawberry blonde hair and looked around thirty-five. His heart fluttered. "No, the bleeding's stopped, thanks. But you might want to get someone to clean up all this broken gla..." When he pointed to the floor, there was nothing there.

"You sure you're all right?"

He shook his head slightly. "Yeah. Thanks. Probably too much sun today."

"I see. Well, enjoy."

"You work here then?" He wanted her to stay.

"Yes," she said, smiling, though not in the same way women usually smiled at him. "I'm the owner. Have a good evening."

"Um ... angelfish?"

"Pardon?" she asked with that same polite, glorious smile.

"The name of the town. I'm a tourist, though I live not too far ..." *For cryin' out loud, Joe, get to the point.* "Well, I didn't think the angelfish was indigenous to this area."

"The Atlantic spadefish is *Chaetodipterus Faber*. It's also called a moonfish as well as angelfish. Enjoy your evening."

He stood there gaping like a hungry basset, watching her walk away. What happened to the broken glass? Why didn't he get her name? He could always come back tomorrow.

Her name is Carol Ann. There are four yet to meet, but only one more this evening. You will not hear my voice again until 1996. This is the last time I am permitted to tell you this, Joe ... Remember to study in the spirit ... and keep the child safe. Goodbye.

Goodbye? They'd barely said hello.

He hoped to catch the owner at the cash when he bought Willie the cap, but no luck. The last thing he saw in Pages was the painting. His thoughts scattered and again he felt weightless, mesmerized. He moved closer. What was it? He didn't have to be an art connoisseur to know this was no masterpiece. Yet it was more—mystical, filled with light.

Dead center, a little blonde girl in daisy dungarees knelt in the grass with her magnifying glass, reflecting a trinity of sunlit rays shooting toward the heavens. How could a simple town setting with a hovering angel-shaped cloud make him want to hole up and lose himself in the thing? Willie had to drag him away from a captivating profile of another kneeling child. Dressed in a long white nightshirt with a striped towel over his shoulders, this boy was knees to the ground in the shade of a gnarly-looking tree. He had a hoop toy propped against the tree, which he appeared to be fixing.

"This segment doesn't jive," he told Willie. "The long nightshirt. The decrepit hoop. Even the tree."

"Whaddya mean, it doesn't jive?"

"It's like the angelfish," he said, frowning. "It doesn't belong here."

∞∞∞

When he saw the sign *You are now leaving Angelfish Cove,* he wanted to turn the car around and hump it back there. But to what purpose? The angel, if that's what it was, had ditched him for another gig. Only he could get deserted by an angel until 1996. He'd be thirty-six in '96. Bummer.

His sense of calm vanished with the Voice. It certainly knew a lot of women. Four women and more women. Women seemed to be his lot in life. A nun, an artist, a singer and a very attractive bookstore owner. Was he destined to have this child with one of them? Was that the idea? He'd choose the bookstore owner.

Twelve miles out of town they discovered a rock enclosure close to the waters' edge. While Willie grabbed a cushion that converted into a blanket, he uncorked the wine and poured a thimbleful of cabernet into their glasses. This annoyed Willie, who snatched the bottle from a hunk of shale and topped up her glass. Although Willie had sobered from the screwdriver's at Corey's, she seemed somewhat unstrung, no doubt developing a hangover. She sat close to him on the blanket, legs crossed, one hand stroking the wine glass like it was the fur on old Bentley the cat.

"You okay?" she asked.

"No, Willie," he said, staring at the mousse tart like it was a lab experiment. "Not really."

"Uh-oh." She swallowed hard. "We're here tonight because Gramma asked you to talk to me I'll bet."

"No. My idea, honest." He slapped a mosquito away from his leg. No doubt the little vampires packed suitcases and followed him.

Willie lifted the DEET from his jacket and handed it to him. "Then what, Joe?"

He wanted so much to tell her he loved her, but couldn't chance her misinterpreting. "It's just that ... well don't you think it's time we talked? I mean really *really* talked, Willie?"

"I suppose so," she said, shuffling her feet on the blanket.

There was no easy place to start. "I'm worried about you. Two things I want to say so please don't storm off into the Atlantic on me, okay?"

She sat up and crossed her legs. "K."

"Let me talk for a minute so I can get this out?"

"Go ahead, Joe."

He sucked in his breath. "First thing, I'm concerned about your drinking, Willie." He waited for a response and, surprisingly, there wasn't one. She simply sat there looking at him rather stoically, waiting. "So ... well ... you've come home in a cab several times over the last couple of months. And you don't seem to have any career plans. Um ... so, I'd like you to quit or at least cut it down significantly. She hadn't hit him with the bottle yet and he knew enough not to even broach the 'under age' thing. It was his turn to wait.

Considering this, Willie began nodding. Big nods. "I know, Joe." She said it like a whisper in a baby's ear.

"What, that's it? *I know, Joe*? A bit more, please."

"I'm worried about me, too. Ma and I have talked and when we get home I'm seeing my GP. Promise. I have cut down, but it's hard and I *am* scared, Joe. I think a lot about the drinking, then get scared and go get a bottle, bring it home or over to a friend's. This is when I used to actually have friends. Guess I've pushed them away."

"Why?" he asked, pleased how well this talk was going.

"I don't know. Guess I'd rather hang out with you. You sure you wanna talk? Then let's. Okay so you said there were two things."

Oh God. He knew how proud she was. "I ... think you have feelings for me."

Willie sighed heavily. Angrily. "Yeah, ya think? I've been sending you signals since I was thirteen."

"Where do you see us going, Willie?"

"Where do I ... I want you to love me! That's where I see us going, Joe. And I know you love me."

"Of course I love you. Just not in that way."

"Oh come on, I've seen you looking. And you didn't exactly push me away at the Eagles concert."

"I'm a guy, Willie. We look. And you took me by surprise at the Eagles concert. You're beautiful, and I do love you. And I want you in my life and to be a part of my life for as long as I live. But we cannot be together in that way. Ever."

"*Ever.* Wow. You really are sure of your feelings, aren't you. Well, Joe, I can't accept it. I can't accept it because I know better. You and I will be. Maybe not tomorrow, but we will be."

She was shaking her head in denial, so how was he supposed to get through to her? "I am not sexually attracted to you, Willie. Not in the slightest. You can't be hoping for something that's never going to happen. And when we get back to Medford, I'm going to look for my own place. Not because of you, but because it's time."

That last part was a lie. Their sharing the house would continue to complicate her life and he couldn't let her misread every smile, every nuance.

"Oh, so now you're moving out? And what happens to us?"

"Willie, there is no *us*."

"I mean our friendship. What happens to our friendship?"

"You'll always be my friend. My dearest friend. Will you still want me for your friend?"

"That and much more. You go ahead and move out for now, Joe. But you'll see—"

"Willie, no."

"I don't want to talk about it anymore tonight. Let's just take a swim and then go home. We'll talk more tomorrow."

"You okay?"

She kicked off those ridiculously-high platform sandals and stripped down to her bathing suit. She had that phony stoic expression again. "I'm fine. Now come on, I know you're wearing trunks under there."

Willie ran on ahead of him. She was hurting big time because he felt the stab in her gut and the pounding in her ears. And when he caught up to her in the water, she skipped around in a little shallow wave and fell against him. She put her arms around his neck.

"Joe," she said, trembling.

He pushed her gently away but she hung on tight and kissed him.

"Don't, Willie." His heart ached for her. It was like looking into a void, darkness without end. *Oh Willie* ... worse than Norma's darkness. "Willie, come on. You're right, we'll talk again tomorrow."

She collected herself somewhat, but those water droplets on her face hadn't come from the ocean, that much he knew. Crushed and humiliated, she spun around and started swimming to shore.

"Willie!"

"I'm all right!" she called back. "Let's just go!"

Before he reached the shore he thought he heard her calling, thought he heard laughter. But she hadn't because she was furiously gathering their gear. Now he was hearing things. If the Voice was back, certainly it would make itself heard and understood. This had to be nothing—like the laughter. Had to be the waves, the sounds of the night, some couple partying further down the beach. Then he heard it again, a distinct male voice calling him. He got out of the water and started slowly back.

He saw Willie warming herself in the blanket. Everything seemed fine except for whoever was calling. He yelled up to her, "Willie, who's there!" No answer. He got closer. She was alone, finishing off the wine. "Willie?"

Two feet away from their picnic spot, he saw a child vision as real as his fear. He buried his hands in his armpits and watched, shivering.

It was a boy child, bare from the waist up, squatting in the sand. He was fair and remarkably beautiful. He appeared weak and he'd been crying. He wanted to dry his tears, comfort him, but some dark thing would not allow him to move from this spot. The child reached for him with bruised and bleeding arms.

"You were supposed to help me, Joe," he lamented. "You have to help me." Droplets of blood pooled in the sand as he watched, unable to speak or move. "Please, Joe, help me."

The vision faded with the child's plea. He looked at Willie who hadn't seen a thing because she was searching for something in the cooler. Willie heard nothing, saw nothing. He slumped to the ground, the memory of the boy's face and bruises haunting him, a memory unlikely to fade with time.

Compelled to share this with Willie, he hoped she'd put their last exchange aside and listen. So he told her about the vision and afterwards he told her what had been happening all day, omitting certain feelings for the bookstore owner. But having polished off the rest of the wine, Willie was too drunk to process it.

"ESP," she said, eyes swelling. "I believe in it. *See.* You're special and me too because I'm with you. Some things're meant to be, Joe. No escaping."

He repeated the words absentmindedly, "No escaping."

It was past two when he walked Willie to her room with assurances that nothing would ever hurt their friendship. Into the wee hours he tossed and scratched at the mosquito bite behind his left knee, thinking about the fog he was in all day yesterday—the names, the voice, the young man in Pages, the child on the beach.

Who and where was this child? Why was he bleeding? How was he supposed to help him? Whose child was this? He looked to be the same age as himself when the accident happened. Ten or so. That was the first time he ever heard of this kid, about keeping him safe.

He got up ridiculously early and walked along the shore for a good two hours before returning to the beach house. It was wicked hot for September, hotter than Rosa's *chilaquiles* and they were practically sleeping on the ocean. He forced his thoughts back to Willie. Even Willie would be up by now. She always dragged herself out of bed at a decent hour no matter how messed up she got the night before.

He approached the beach house with the urge to flee, to grab his gear and hitch a ride to the bus station. If there was a bus station around here. Too bad he couldn't fast forward two weeks, then all this would be behind them. Willie would be angry but adjusting. She would have seen her doctor and he'd be apartment hunting. How exactly was he supposed to reassure Willie again this morning when she hadn't believed his reassurances last night? How in God's name could they keep her away from the bottle now?

Halfway up the deck stairs, he heard Rosa's bracelets clanking.

"Joe! What went on with you and Willie last night?"

"I ... you're gonna have to talk to Willie, R. She might not like me discussing last night with you."

"Well that's convenient. She's upstairs with Beata, beside herself. And Beata can't calm her down. "Now I want you to tell me what—"

He zipped past her on the stairs. "I'll go talk to her."

"No! Joe, she doesn't want to see you!"

My fault, my fault, he scolded himself, taking the stairs in twos. Could he have been any stupider having 'the' discussion with Willie last night when she was drinking? Why oh why didn't he wait?

Catching part of the conversation between mother and daughter, he stopped outside her room. It sounded too personal so he backed away, but froze when he heard Willie's hysterical voice,

"No! I prayed for him too long. I prayed for our love. God will make it happen, I know He will. He will, Ma!"

Willie's conviction frightened him. He could tell her one hundred and one ways that it was hopeless but he'd be wasting his time. Replaying the scene in the water, he remembered that fixated, hollow look in Willie's eyes. And with his head equally obsessed by the child-vision, there were no ideas forthcoming as to how to help Willie. How did things get so screwed up? He heard Beata now, trying to soothe,

"No, *mi amor*. He won't make it happen. You presumed He would and presumption is a sin. For whatever reason, you and Joe aren't right for each other and God knows that."

"No! '*Therefore I say unto you, all things, whatsoever you ask when ye pray, believe that you shall receive and they shall come unto you.*' You *know* that passage, Ma. I have faith in that passage. I believe that He'll give me what I want!"

"If it's His will, baby. That's what you should add at the end of all your prayers. 'Your will, Lord, not mine'. God knows it's not your fault. And He *has* answered your prayer. But you have to accept it, Willie. God's answer is no."

His stomach lurched at the sound of Willie's tormented voice. About one thing he'd been right—they could no longer live together as a family. This much was obvious. He'd wait until Willie was secure in their friendship before leaving. He couldn't go away with her thinking she'd lost that, too. Willie was family. With that thought, he stole down the stairs and joined Rosa in the living room, where they sat restlessly waiting for Beata.

"It was clear she was going into shock," Beata said an hour later. "I gave her a sleeping pill and she's out already. How much did she have to drink last night, Joe? She was pretty hung-over this morning."

"She had a fair bit with dinner but then she walked it off. Later on in the evening she drank the wine. I was too cowardly to say anything at first because I didn't want her getting defensive when I talked to her later. She said she'd planned to see her GP when we got home."

"She told me the rest of it, Joe."

"God."

"You did good by telling her the truth. Wish you had've talked to her sooner but at least it's done."

"I'm so sorry, B."

"No no. This couldn't have been easy for you, either. Norma and all."

Beata didn't have much else to say that afternoon. Every hour or so, she'd walk upstairs and stand outside Willie's room, listening for stirring sounds. Then she'd come down, plug in the tea kettle again and try to keep herself occupied. He suggested that given Willie's embarrassment, it might be better if he hopped a bus back to Medford. R & B's lack of response was their way of saying it was his decision. So he started packing and checking bus schedules for the morning. But he hated to leave Willie this way. Also, he felt drawn toward unfinished business in Angelfish Cove.

By five o'clock, Willie's frantic calls for her mother had them in a panic. "Get a doctor over here," Beata told him. "Hurry."

Beata found her on the floor in his room. Disoriented and drunk again, she had taken a wrong turn after using the bathroom. She looked at her mother through bloodshot eyes, shivering, "Ma, I'm so sick and scared." Her nightgown was vomit-stained, her panic escalating. "Ma, keep Joe away. Don't let him come up and see me like this. Please, Ma!"

"No, baby, I won't. Don't worry. Let's get you back to your own room."

Rosa, already in Willie's room changing the sheets, showed Beata the empty vodka bottle. Willie admitted stashing it behind her night table.

"Gramma," Willie pleaded, "please don't let Joe come up here."

"Joe will stay downstairs, *querida*. Now get into bed. Your mother and I are going to get the alcohol out of you. And a doctor's on the way."

"Doctor? I'm not going anywhere. Don't make me go anywhere! Ma?"

"You're staying right here, Willie. The doctor's coming because we think you've had an allergic reaction. I gave you a sleeping pill earlier and you put the liquor on top of that when you woke up."

"I'm going to be sick again."

∞∞∞∞

She was the typical young physician–overworked, tired, stressed and holding it beautifully together. After she had Willie throw up the rest of the alcohol, she pumped a high-potency B complex into her. Lots of water, lots of rest, absolutely no liquor! She wrote out a prescription for Ativan and asked the family to gather in the living room.

"Has your daughter had a recent fall, Mrs. Canites?"

"Ross. My daughter uses Canites, though. Not to my knowledge. But I found her in Joe's room on the floor. She may have fallen there."

"I'm most concerned with the splotching on Willie's back, Mrs. Ross. The splotching is indicative of liver damage. Are you aware that your daughter's drinking problem is chronic?"

"I suspected. That's one of the reasons we came down here. To decide what to do. But I didn't know ... are you telling me Willie is an alcoholic?"

"Based on one examination in your home, you're better prepared to tell me. Do you think your daughter is an alcoholic?"

Following a brief silence, Rosa spoke first. "I'm her grandmother and I say she is. Yes."

More silence.

"How is her emotional state? Anything she can use as an excuse for drinking?"

"Yeah, Doctor Lee. I'm the excuse," he said, talking more to Beata. "She has feelings for me I can't return and last night I told her. It's my fault she's up there in that condition."

"Well, I won't ask for personal details since I'm not your family physician. But she has suffered a recent shock. And the drinking is not so recent. She has a mild case of alcohol poisoning. Mrs. Ross, I would like to drop by again tomorrow and speak to Willie if I may."

The doctor was careful not to chastise. Willie was a grown-up, clever enough to seek out ingenious ways of getting liquor. She encouraged immediate action. Willie needed to get into a recovery program as fast as her family could get her there. A few more days in Angelfish Cove to absorb the shocks and mentally prepare wouldn't hurt. No more than a few days, though, she warned, adding that their family physician be contacted now so he could get things going from Medford.

∞∞∞

It wasn't the sopping pajama collar and pillow that woke her at 2 a.m. It was the pain from a tear-soaked right ear, most likely infected from all the splashing inside it. She tried to reach for a tissue to dry her ear and couldn't move, nor could she reach the water glass on her night table. She tried calling her mother but couldn't speak. Most of all, she wanted Joe. For the moment. She was familiar with all forms of sedation and when it wore off, she would want a drink more.

Her mother came in to check on her throughout the night, sometimes whispering words of love and encouragement, sometimes to sit and watch. Rather than feel comforted by her mother's presence, she agonized over the pain she was causing. Pain. Embarrassment. Humiliation before God. Her tired mind had played nasty tricks on her for so long. She'd manipulated a Bible passage toward her own end. Not for one single moment did she consider that God might have had something more important in mind for Joe.

Willie felt old in the worst possible way. What wisdom had she acquired from this nightmare, from all this pain? She dabbed at her eyes. The scent of his Calvin Klein was still in last night's outfit, casually thrown on the cedar chest at the foot of the bed. It occurred to her that it was already the night before that he pushed her off him in the water. So long ago. Practically yesterday. So far away—far away down the hall. It was 6:35 a.m. and she wanted to scream.

"Joe," she whispered, half hoping he would hear.

They hadn't found the three vodka twenty-sixers she'd stashed around the room. Sanity. Now she'd sleep more soundly than with that stuff the doctor gave her. She'd knock herself out and when she woke up, her mother would be up too, and together they'd put the broken pieces back together.

"Joe."

She was most impressed with the twenty-sixer hidden in plain view. The Cepacol bottle on her dresser did not contain Cepacol. She swallowed the un-green liquid. No one noticed it wasn't green. They did find two mickeys stashed in a boot here and a hat there, but nothing to seriously affect the inventory. She made a promise to herself—she would drink enough for calm and no more.

"Ohh, Joe."

Could it be possible that with the passing of time, Joe would come back to her? Sure, why not? They had ten years of solid memories. Straight from the beginning, they were friends. He was scared and confused because of what happened with that loony-tune, Norma. That's what was scaring him. Of course. He was only twenty. Best to let him go for awhile. He'd be back. See, the vodka was clearing her mind already.

Joe always slept with his door open a crack, so why not sneak down the hall and look in at him? She took two hard swallows from the Cepacol bottle and tiptoed to his room. Her heart pounded standing outside his door. He always slept so soundly. Enticed by the musky orange of his cologne, she stepped inside. The watch she gave him last

Christmas ticked on his bed stand in rhythm with the breaking surf. She didn't dare go closer.

No matter what season of the year, he always slept in BVD's. He had such a beautiful body and she wanted him more than her soul. If he asked her to marry him, she would never take another drink. True, they couldn't be together for some time. She would have to be patient. And he would date, that's for sure.

Girls were always chasing him. What if one of them got pregnant and seduced him into marriage? What if he actually fell in love with one of them? There'd be a wedding and he'd be bringing her home for holidays. She'd hear them making love at night. Feeling the contents of her stomach rising, she ran back to her room. Throwing up would give her a migraine. Okay—get calm, get calm. God, why wasn't she sleepy? It was the frightening thoughts she had in his room. Shoulda not gone in there.

She took in more vodka. How come it wasn't working so good? Her nerves pinged and her throat felt funny. Maybe if she got under the covers and tried to relax. She brought the covers up to her ears, but her legs wouldn't stop shaking and it was getting harder to swallow.

It had to all be in her mind because she could still breathe fine. As long as she could breathe fine she would not call her mother and embarrass herself further. It was just after 7 a.m. Soaking in a hot relaxing bath would help. No one would question it. If any of them heard, they'd feel better knowing she was up and getting on with her day.

She took her purse and the Cepacol bottle into the bathroom. She added bath crystals to the steamy water and sat on the edge of the tub. The steam made her feel dizzy. Removing a wallet-sized picture of Joe from her purse, she leaned over and set it by the faucet, reminding herself not to leave it in here after her bath. Now that would be embarrassing.

When the room started to blur, she took extra caution stepping into the tub. The worst possible scenario was to have a nervous breakdown, not to kill herself. The water was calming. She leaned back and stared at his picture, taken at that wild psychic fair they all went to last fall. Gord didn't want to go and Joe tagged along in protest. He took a stab at convincing Gramma that evil spirits liked to share stuff they knew, too, usually through people who charged big bucks for it.

Joe was standing in front of this bizarre-looking fortune-telling booth when she snapped the shot that day. Gramma was over at the next booth telling the guy that half the people in there were fakes. Ma was further down the aisle considering a crystal ball to buy Gramma for Christmas. It was a good day. Up to a point—

An elderly Asian lady approached her. Because of her poor English, she asked her daughter to translate. 'My mother says there are many bad spirits around you. You are in spiritual danger and she wants you to pray, to tell God you are sorry.' She'd asked the daughter if her mother was clairvoyant and the daughter answered, 'My mother is a visionary and she knows. Visionaries do not charge and their messages are meant for the good of all concerned. This means your family is also in spiritual danger. We come to these events to speak to people and remind them that God does not want them here. They are to seek their answers only from Him.' The woman's words haunted her for days.

The words haunted her again now and with the vodka buzz eluding her, she took another swig. There wasn't all that much left in the bottle anyway, so best finish it and get some Z's. Of course she knew she was in danger. The lady didn't have to tell her that. And yes she was sorry. But what about *her* future? What about her future without Joe? More tears came. Why didn't God want her to have him? What was wrong that she felt so sick?

Her throat hurt and she needed to throw up.

It was a struggle getting out of the tub. Maybe she could roll herself out by hauling one leg at a time over the side. Oh Lord, this was like that common nightmare when you're frozen in your body. Nothing—nothing but dead weight.

Summoning all her strength, she tried to move again and couldn't. She would have to call her mother for help now because she had to throw up. But her throat closed over the words and her heartbeat thrashed in her sore ear. She had no choice but to puke into the water and pound on the tub. Oh please—someone *had* to hear.

She bent over and expelled a trickle of gooey liquid. Her throat clenched. The rest of it wasn't coming out. Stuck! Her head jerked forward, slammed against the faucet and back again.

"Ma ... Mama!"

No breath! God, please! She stuck her finger down her throat to force an opening and gagged. She tried pounding again. No strength to hit. Pinkish watery blood leaked from her ear and nose, streaming down her shoulder and chest. Sleep would come now. If she could get back to bed, sleep would come. Now they wouldn't have to put the pieces back together. *Goodbye Humpty Dumpty*. Soon there would be no more pain. *God, I'm so sorry. Let me make it up to You. Let me—*

Willie looked at Joe's picture, smiled and slowly ... dropped forward into the water.

∞∞∞

Father James was waiting at the house when they got home the next afternoon, along with neighbors, several friends of the family and old friends of Gord's from the Lion's Club and Medford Gas. Rosa called a few relatives in Mexico City, due within the hour. Two attendants from DiNardo's Funeral Home had just returned from Angelfish Cove with Willie's body.

Beata, in and out of denial and heavily sedated, occasionally lapsed into fits of self-blame. She kept saying that she should have realized sooner how sick her beautiful daughter was. Then more of Willie's Ativan kicked in and she'd pace the kitchen, softly calling for Willie. Her lucid outbursts were in Spanish. When she cried, Rosa held her. When she was angry, she'd glare at Joe.

He'd never recover from the horror of finding her, facedown in red water, neck swollen, cowlick dried into a bloodied clump. His fingerprint bruises on her upper arms had yellowed. A reminder that he'd pushed her away in the water. *Don't, Willie.*

God Jesus God, it was two nights ago!

The bathroom reeked of musty copper. The worn photo she'd set shrine-like on the tub blinked at him like some slime-covered headlight on a backwoods road. He'd staggered up on numbed legs and locked the door, bending an ear to make damn certain he was alone with her. He wanted to be with her, talk to her, beg her forgiveness. So he rutted himself on the floor, left arm slung over the edge of the tub, fingers stroking the blood-crusted cowlick she waged hair wars with since they were kids.

He would later tell the police he had no idea how long he was alone with her. All he remembered was screaming her name. He screamed and then he cried. Whatever the higher purpose of Willie's death, if there was a higher purpose, he would never forgive himself. He knew God would, but he took no comfort in that.

∞∞∞∞

As with any death involving one so young, the loss was torture for them. Beata still could not go upstairs to her own room. It was beside Willie's. She hadn't gone upstairs at all since their return and slept down-cellar in Rosa's apartment. Rosa slept upstairs in Beata's room. That first night after finding the prayer book on the floor, he took it into Willie's room where he'd slept every night since.

Willie had so many friends, mostly old friends. In recent years, her obsession with him kept her from making new ones. Still, loving friends all exchanging memories filled the house. Father James had another priest tagging along with him these last few days, a Father Richard Vaux from Three Rivers, Quebec.

"It's actually pronounced *Twa Reevyare,*" Father James said, using a bad French accent.

He remembered Father James mentioning this priest from time to time and assumed they'd be close in age since they were so tight. It surprised him that Father Vaux was several years older, and a Dominican. Father James was a Jesuit. He didn't understand why, but he found Father Vaux curious. Obviously the Dominican felt the same way because he'd been watching him, intensely. With Father James off helping in the kitchen, he took the opportunity to strike up a conversation with this strange monastic French-Canadian.

"So I understand you live in a monastery?"

"*Oui,*" and then the priest laughed easily. "I mean *yes.* I promised myself I would speak English throughout my visit. I live in a Dominican monastery called *Marianlake.* It's very beautiful there."

His heartbeat pulsed and the hair stood up on his arms. "Marion Lake? A Dominican monastery, you said?"

"Yes. Marianlake doubles as both a house of retreat and a college where young men go to study for the priesthood. Don't tell me you're a candidate, Joe, I wouldn't believe it."

Laughing at the prospect felt good. So did hearing the words *Marion Lake*. "No. But I do feel like I should know more. Spiritually, I mean. I don't think I know nearly enough ... and lately ..." Maybe he should shut-up. There was no way to put it all into words, especially to a stranger.

Father Vaux grew serious. "You and Wilomena were very close?"

"Yes." He stared at his hands. Seconds ago he was excited about Marion Lake, and now, after hearing her name, he wanted to dash upstairs and yank the covers over his head. "I haven't heard anyone call her Wilomena in so long. We all called her Willie. And we weren't as close as she wanted to be, Father." What was he saying? Was he nuts?

"Don't blame yourself for complex things we humans could never understand. I think your Willie's suffering and death is providential, Joe."

"Excuse me, but you can't know that, Father." He felt instantly apologetic for the accusatory tone. But how could this priest know anything about Willie or the meaning of her death? "I'm sorry. It's a comforting thought anyway. It could even explain some of the weirdness, like the voice I've been hearing. I haven't told Father James any of this and frankly I'm amazed I'm babbling about it now. You know, when I was ten ... forget I said anything, Father. I'm feeling ... not right."

Father Vaux smiled sympathetically. "Don't feel ill at ease for saying these things to a stranger. This happens sometimes and it's a good thing when it does and I do recognize a spiritual struggle when I see one. One who lives the monastic life soon becomes familiar with spirits in all their disguises, both good and evil. Evil is always trying to destroy what is good. And Joe, I don't believe your spiritual struggle exists within."

He wanted to know everything about this man. Did he sense something? Did he see something? "If my struggle isn't internal, then where is it? What is it?"

Father Vaux patted his arm. "I don't mean to leave you hanging, Joe, but we have much to discuss. Come see me at the rectory tomorrow afternoon. It is my intention to bring you back to Marianlake in a few days. Someone there needs you."

It was like he swallowed a bee colony. "At Marion Lake? Who, Father?"

"There's a child who lives in Trois-Rivierés. A child who's been waiting a long time to meet you."

3. Marianlake

September, 1981

It was five minutes past noon and he'd already walked by Saint Jane Frances Parish three times. Didn't somebody important say procrastination was good for the soul? No, probably not, but didn't he wish. He really wanted to go to the cemetery first thing this morning, but overheard Beata tell Rosa that she was on her way there. She needed to spend time alone with her daughter.

'I still can't go upstairs, Mama,' she had said.

Procrastinating some more, he stepped inside the church before buzzing the rectory. It had been so long since he attended Mass, even though he'd assisted Father James on numerous occasions. Willie went every Sunday. She never went with R & B, always preferring to go on her own. She and God had this very private relationship. He knelt in the last pew and bowed his head. Less than a week ago they had explored Angelfish Cove. Willie was still here a week ago.

"Oh God, why? And who is this child?"

"You'll receive your answers soon, Joe." Father Vaux said from the other end of the pew. "Patience, remember."

Dressed in beige Levi's, a burgundy and white striped polo shirt and Reeboks, the priest looked younger than his fifty-plus years. Must've had something to do with 'the life'. "Patience isn't exactly a virtue of mine, Father."

"Nor mine," and he smiled. "Come on into the rectory where we won't be disturbed."

He declined Father Vaux's offer to lunch with him. Food was not going down too well these days and he wasn't exactly in a sociable mood. He was only here for information and to tell Father Vaux it was time to visit Aunt Pam in Ocala, maybe check out a few stables there. He felt uncomfortable going to Marion Lake. Sure he was anxious to hear about the boy, but he wasn't ready to throw his life into a brown paper bag and shake.

"Please, Father. You said the boy in Trois-Rivierés has been waiting a long time to meet me?"

"How do you know the child is a boy, Joe?" He reached for a chocolate truffle, admitting earlier that he was a chocoholic. "I said there was a *child* in Trois-Rivierés."

"Oh I know he's a boy. I think I've seen him. And years ago someone told me––"

"––to keep him safe. Father James told me of your parents' accidents. I'm so sorry. He also spoke of your Angel."

"Father, who is he?"

"His name is Alain. He is ten and beautiful. And quite special. He lives with his parents in Trois-Rivierés, a half-mile down the road from Marianlake. His father, Claude, is our veterinarian. We have a small dairy farm and a few horses. Alain is their only child and they adore him."

"What does he have to do with me, though?"

Father Vaux closed the box of truffles. "We made the first connection four years ago. Alain was six. Father Jim was visiting me at that time and one evening the Duprielles invited us for dinner. That's his name—Alain Duprielle. They heard me speak of Jim so often and they wanted to meet him. They've been friends of mine for many years. It was an evening to discuss friendship.

"Jim spoke fondly of the Canites family, how he loved Rosa but strongly disapproved of her occult practice. The crystal balls and psychics. The tarot cards. But you already know all this. I hadn't realized how close he was to your family until he took out the picture from his wallet. Alain, who was sitting on his knee, grabbed at it and became excited. 'Look Mommy,' he spoke solely in French at that time. Translated, he said, 'It's Joe. He's coming here, he's coming here. *Mon ami,* Joe! My friend, Joe.'"

Father Vaux sat quietly, waiting for a response.

Okay, so he was more intrigued, but he still wasn't taking off to Marion Lake. "Father James never mentioned him to me," was the lame thing he said.

Father Vaux's features softened. "Later that evening in private, he told me your story. I thought it best to wait for the second act. Jim and I realized there would be more to come. Better to let God say how and when, Joe. So, we waited."

"And was there more?"

"Alain began having an invisible playmate. He told his mother, Tracy, that his friend was the boy in the picture and that his friend's name was Joe Ross. The only name the boy ever heard was Canites. This was a year after Jim's visit. Alain was seven. As soon as I heard, I called Jim and inquired about you. When he told me your surname, I knew of course that there was a connection. Father Jim took it up with your Uncle Gordon who dismissed it at once. He didn't want you involved in any way with Alain. He said he'd had it 'up to here' with psychics and crystal balls and the like. Jim had to respect his wishes."

"So that was three years ago. Then what, Father? My Uncle's been dead almost ten months."

"For a long time nothing happened, at least nothing that Alain was sharing with his parents. And lately he's been having bad dreams. He's been quieter. Sometimes he appears frightened. There have been unexplained bruises on him and just last week he awakened in tears. He had been calling out for you, Joe, saying that you were supposed to come and help him. But the most frightening detail of all, I think, is that his mother found bloodstains on his sheets. But there wasn't a cut on him anywhere."

"You think somebody's messing with him?" he asked, psyching himself to tell the priest what he saw on the beach.

"Yes. I believe some*one* or some*thing* is trying to harm Alain and I don't know why. And he seems to be isolating himself more and more which is making it extremely difficult for us to get to the root of his trouble."

It mystified him how this information affected him so strongly. It wasn't like he knew the boy or anything. But the thought of some animal touching Alain, even thinking of him in any way immoral, filled him with rage. Two visions had obsessed him the past week—Alain bleeding on the beach, if it was Alain, and finding Willie in that tub. *Willie.*

He decided to wait to tell Father Vaux about that night in Angelfish Cove until he knew him better. It looked like Aunt Pam and Ocala would have to wait, too, because somebody was messing with the kid. He couldn't allow that, sap that he was.

"How soon can we leave for Marion Lake, Father?"

∞∞∞

Money would never be a concern. He had enough money from his share of Uncle Gord's inheritance and Rosa's lottery winnings. If he didn't want to work, he didn't have to work. There'd be no dead-end jobs or crappy employers. It was a nice thought to pursue except he wanted very much to work. He wanted that BS in

Equine Studies, wanted that horse farm in Ocala. He told Rosa the day they arrived in the Cape that it might not happen for him and it was a not-so-nice-thought he couldn't shake.

Overthinking—this was his problem. Was there a formula for effective thought-stopping? Maybe he'd find it in a peaceful place like Marion Lake Monastery on consecrated ground. He could study in the spirit as instructed, whatever that meant. And finally, he could take care of the child, though he wasn't sure what that meant, either.

Rosa was having a hard time dealing with the idea of his leaving.

"You're not telling me everything," she said, arms crossed in the kitchen chair. "You're going all the way up to Canada. The French part. You don't even speak French. And we don't know this Father Vaux. He's a good friend of Father James is all I know. What aren't you telling me?"

"You're right. I am keeping you in the dark about a few details and when I know more, you'll be the first person I tell. Think of it as a mission I'm going on." He was such a schmuck for leaving them this way, full of grief, frustration, questions. Yet living with guilt was fast becoming a way of life for him. "Rosa, we both knew I'd be leaving, even before Willie ..."

Rosa swung open the refrigerator and popped a cap on a Budweiser. "Never did need a glass," she said. "Comes in a glass. Never believed in drugs to calm my nerves, either. One or two beers–best thing. Wish Willie could've stopped at one or two." Then her mind trailed off somewhere.

"I thought we agreed you'd stick around another couple weeks," Beata said, standing in the kitchen doorway. She had dilated pupils and her hair needed a wash. "Didn't we?"

"It's already been two weeks, B."

"What time's your plane?"

"Takes off at four-thirty this afternoon." Quickly, he told the where, the with whom and omitted the why. "I don't know how long I'll be gone. I'll probably be home for Christmas."

Beata's smile threatened, "You're under twenty-one, Joe. So legally, I'm still your guardian. What? You think because you're not blood, I don't care?"

She looked exactly like Willie, standing tall, suppressing tears.

"B, I have to go."

"Everybody's leaving," she said. "How can you go when I'm still so angry with Willie, with myself. With you, too. How dare you leave me so angry, Joe? She turned her head away to hide the tears.

He put his hands on her shoulders, lightly kissed her cheek.

"Willie loved you so much." Her eyes were glassy from tears and Ativan. "I knew it even before you did. You could never be sister and brother. She took one look at you when she was nine and fell desperately in love. Imagine that? Nine. I thought it was sweet then. Thought she'd grow out of it. But she never did. Then the drinking. I prayed she'd grow out of that, too. Her father drank, you know. Oh, God! Why didn't we help her, Joe? Why didn't we help her?"

"I'm so sorry, B," his voice cracked. He had been asking himself the same question. "It's my fault."

"No!" Beata said. "We're all to blame. Even Willie. I blame Willie, too. Don't hold out on the people you love,

Joe. Willie kept too much to herself. If she had've told us more, maybe she would still be here."

"I say we go back to Mexico City for awhile," Rosa said, clapping her hands together, the gesture that meant a decision was final. "We continue our grieving in the place of our roots. Joe needs to get away, and so do we. By the time we get back, Beata, you'll be able to go upstairs. I think we'll stay with my brother, Blas. Joe, I'll write down his address and phone number for you. So you call and tell us what you're not telling us as soon as possible. *Comprende?*"

When it was time to leave for the airport, Father Jim honked the horn in the driveway. He was upstairs in Willie's room getting the one thing of Willie's he'd take with him. The cap. The cap he bought for her in Pages that night. His eyes blurred at the sight of the *CAP* initials. Fatigue. Grief. Guilt. Through all of it, the initials seemed weirdly significant.

They said their goodbyes, pretending it would be for a month or two. By Christmas, he'd be swapping stories with them in French. Rosa tried to get him to pinkie swear he'd be home for Christmas but something in his gut said they'd never be together again, not as a threesome. He hauled out his red toolbox and Fathers' James and Vaux helped him with the rest of his gear.

"I love you R & B," he said, hanging his head out the car window. Then he watched them until Father James' old station wagon clanked them out of view.

They took the long route leaving Medford, by way of the Mystic River. He needed to stop at the cemetery and say goodbye to Willie. As he knelt at her grave, a faint kiss grazed his cheek.

'*Don't worry. We'll fix it up,*' she had said that first day.

"I'm sorry the answer was no, Willie," he whispered, clenching the earth in his hands. "Please forgive me."

The early October wind swished its way through the treetops—northbound.

∞∞∞∞

He had read about Canada in National Geographic. After living in New England for the past ten years, he could handle a winter anywhere on any continent. Still, it was worlds apart different. They didn't have a bunch of small towns all linked together here. More like small cities spaced wastelands apart. There was no ocean in sight and no trace scent of fish in the air, but they did have the most stunning lakes and sunsets. Majestic purples bled into bright pink streaks with arcs of orange and blue. Small wonder this country was renowned for its sunsets. He could spend the rest of the month looking up. Where was Alain? Would he meet him tonight?

As they approached the outskirts of the monastery property, Father Vaux bore down an extra ten mph on the gas pedal. "I want you to see Marianlake before the sun sets, Joe. A wonder of tranquil beauty. On the outside. And I expect sleeping well without the burble of your Mystic River will take a little time."

"What do you mean *on the outside*?"

"Tomorrow, Joe. We'll have all day tomorrow during the guided tour I'm going to give you. Tonight is for relaxation. You'll meet Father Andre, eat, and rest your mind."

"Will I meet Alain tomorrow?"

"Yes. Tomorrow you will meet Alain."

Glancing uneasily at Father Richard, he tapped on his lips. "Uh, Father?"

"Mm?"

"You understand, right, that I'm only missing one semester? Then I have to get back to Amherst."

"Not a problem, Joe."

"Because I, well, I'll be missing my horses. Got to get the dream started, Father."

"Understood."

The twelve-foot wrought iron gates were cemented together by boulder-size hunks of flag and cobblestone. A brass greeting plaque, welded into the right gate, read,

Welcome to Marianlake Dominican Monastery. Erected 1847. Marianlake remains open to the public until 6 PM all year round.

It was a glorious time of year to see it. Rows of spruce, Scotch pine, maple and willows lined both sides of the winding road onto the grounds. With the exception of the evergreens, the fall colors were panoramic. Through the trees were picnic benches on open green fields to the left, large enough to squeeze in an eighteen-hole golf course. To the right, a herd of Canadienne cows grazed and lazed happily and he laughed when Father Vaux told him they were holy cows.

The property was vast, close to three hundred acres and the surrounding community consisted mainly of cattle and poultry farmers, though the downtown core did have an ancient recreation centre. They adored their hockey here, and the downtown core, by the way, was the size of a wink and a blink.

The main road led to a spectacular sight. He had been on estates before, but never one for the religious.

Prominently placed at the center of the monastery buildings was a twenty-foot statue of Mary. On the ground and of the same scale, a golden Rosary surrounded Her. Each ball, rather one *bead* in each decat weighed forty pounds. There was a praying bench directly in front of Her with two concrete semi-circular benches at the sides.

A long two-storey L-shaped seminary stood to the right of the statue, which housed six classrooms, a dining hall or *refectory* as they referred to it here, and a library and recreation area. The upper section of the L contained a combination gymnasium/basketball court. The dormitory building, adjacent to the seminary, had twenty-five cells on each floor. Currently, ten seminarians and four visiting monks from somewhere in Europe occupied fourteen of fifty cells. The monks, Father Vaux told him, seemed to be quite comfortable here because they were supposed to leave a month ago. The six priests in permanent residence lived in the rectory attached to the rear of the church.

The church, with its sanctuary recently modernized in pale pink marble and railed altar, somehow managed to retain its vintage quality. All the stained glass windows depicted New Testament scenes and the private alcoves with kneeling benches in each corner revered statues of saints whose images seemed supernaturally real. The old paintings, ceiling and walls had been well tended, all chips and cracks recently filled in. Most of the hundred or more votive candles looked lit. It was obvious that Saint Mary's housed a huge congregation. Mass every morning at nine o'clock. Four Masses on Sunday. Here, monastic life was lived among the people. The Dominicans were a community order.

Behind the church to the west was a partial view of a hill with the fourteen Stations of the Cross. A tiny chapel rested at the very top. From his point of view he could not see the cemetery behind it. As Father Vaux said, the grand tour would be tomorrow. It was beginning to get dark.

The monastery was directly in front of the lake and on the other side of 'Marianlake' were three large winterized cabins well-spaced apart. The lake itself wasn't that big. He guessed he could row across at warp speed in five minutes. There was also a road to the other side, so he could take his pick—row or ride. After they parked the car at the rectory door, he heard the hypnotic warble of a loon family half-hidden by bulrushes. For an entire minute he felt peace in his heart.

Father Andre Georges rushed out to greet them. He looked to be several years older than Father Vaux, though he seemed pretty spry for a man of his age. Must be the air up here. Did Alain live close by? Father Andre shook his hand.

"Glad you're here, son. Glad you're here. Come on, leave all that in the car. We're holding supper. Well, Richard, good thing we tuned up your rowing machine. Several ounces of chocolate applied directly to the midsection, I see."

"I better not hear that you put my eight a.m. regulars to sleep." After clapping each other on the back, he asked about his dog, "Any sign of Compo?"

"We haven't seen him, Richard." Father Andre sounded hopeful. "But he's around somewhere. Last night we heard his bark echo across the lake. We'll find him."

Following his transfer from Paris, his beloved City of Light, Father Andre had been the senior pastor at Marianlake for nine years.

"Do you usually speak in French?" he asked Father Andre at dinner.

"Heavens no," he said. "We can barely understand each other. I'm Parisian, Father Richard is Quebecois. We gave up a long time ago. Richard? Why are you so quiet?"

"Thinking about Compo," he said. "I thought Joe and I might have a look for him after dinner since we're setting him up in the middle cabin across the lake anyway."

"Tonight? Forget it, Father. I'm not going to allow you two to go groping around in the dark on the other side of the lake. A quarter-moon doesn't shed much light. You could fall, break something, and return full of holes and dents. I'm sorry, Richard, tonight we need to discuss matters of importance with Joe. He can spend the night here in the rectory."

"Matters concerning Alain?" he asked, rubbing his restless legs under the table.

"Yes." Father Andre set his fork down on the plate. "I have a full calendar tomorrow, Joe. I had hoped to spend the day with Father Richard and yourself and learned moments ago that I'm needed elsewhere. There are certain things I've asked Father Richard to withhold until your arrival, things I want you to know before you meet Alain."

A dog howled in the distance and he jumped, his restlessness taking a sharp turn into fear, the kind with the dark shadows. In his mind's eye, he saw Willie in that tub, saw himself struggling with Norma until the gun went off. He saw his mother in the barn, alive and vibrant one minute—dead the next.

He was far away from home in a place with men he hardly knew and his family was on their way to Mexico City. For ten years, he'd received supernatural warnings from either an angel or a demon to take care of some strange kid who needed him. When the dog howled again, he felt a dark angel type of presence.

At Father Andre's suggestion they moved to the living room. Midway, he stopped and furiously scratched at the mosquito bites still plaguing him behind his knee. He thought he got bitten once that night, but the bloodsucker bit him several times in the same spot and he was still healing. He got the bites before Willie passed him the DEET, seconds before he broke her heart. *Willie was still alive when he got these bites.*

He scratched and scratched, wanting to get to his room but didn't know where it was. This was so bloody embarrassing. He needed help. Nothing or no one around him was familiar. He couldn't catch his breath and his chest heaved.

Father Richard led him to the couch and sat beside him. "It's okay, Joe. Let the anxiety come. You've had all these feelings before and you know they go away. I don't want you to shrink away from them. I want you to ride through them now, you know, like a wave."

"Oh, God," he said, noticing their expressions had become obscured. "I feel like I'm being swallowed. So much has happened to me, you don't know. What am I doing here, Father? I don't know what I'm doing here, how I got here. Nothing."

"You already know a big part of the answer, Joe. The child. Place your focus on him and the situation will remedy itself. You're not alone, please believe me. It's perfectly acceptable for grown men to cry. Release."

"I don't feel so grown right now," he said as the tears streamed down his face. Father Andre asked how long it had been since he had a full night's sleep. "I think two or three weeks." He couldn't seem to stop sobbing. Suddenly it felt kind of good.

Both priests agreed that a sleeping tablet was in order. "You've been suffering through sleep deprivation, Joe,"

Father Andre said. "That accounts for the extreme lows and in the midst of this deprivation, you've made a major decision in coming here, leaving home immediately after your loss. Don't come down on yourself too hard. So we'll leave the talk for tonight and pick up first thing in the morning instead. Yes? Right now, with your permission, Father Richard and I are going to knock your lights out for a good twelve hours."

He managed a smile over his waning sobs. "I doubt I'll sleep."

Both priests laughed quietly. "You'll sleep," Father Richard said.

He awakened with senses completely recharged and all it took was a solid twelve and a half hours in the Land of Z's. That and Father Andre's coma-inducing tablets. He could take them all on now, even the dark angels. They'd been lurking last night when he had his little ill-timed anxiety attack. He was on the verge of learning more about Alain when his emotions fouled the race at the starting gate. But it wasn't just him. Some *thing* had been watching him since he arrived—watching from inside himself. If ever there was a time to control his thoughts ... He picked up the note slipped under his door.

Shower. Coffee ready in the kitchen. Then clear those cobwebs with a walk around the lake to the center cabin. Fr. Andre and I are waiting with breakfast.

—Fr. Richard.

The morning mist shadowed the ground like white angora. A flock of geese pecked and dined on blades of grass under a massive willow at the water's edge. Someone was reading in a drifting rowboat and an easy breeze knocked a fresh batch of autumn leaves in his path. A lone cyclist in a green pith helmet, number 72, whirred by him. No dark angels this morning. Not a one.

Short stilts and huge boulders supported the cabin's rise over the water. It had two floors and a verandah that hung over the lake on the lower level, surrounded by pine and maple on three sides. The pathway cut through the trees in back and the front verandah held a spectacular view of Marianlake, the monastery and the church. The cemetery was far to the west and a couple of horses grazed to his left. Now if the cabin had indoor plumbing, it would be absolute heaven. Father Richard heard him crunching his way along the leafy pathway.

"Good morning," he said, coffee mug in hand. "Don't tell anybody we gave you drugs your first night here, okay."

"I won't tell if you won't tell what an assh ... what an idiot I made of myself last night, Father."

"Nonsense. Come have some of Father Andre's scrambled eggs and premium-leaded coffee."

The inside was cabin nirvana—river rock wall and fireplace with two stacks of wood and kindling on the side. Colorful throw-rug and overstuffed couch. Bedroom, bathroom and shower upstairs, to his delight. Anyone would pay big bucks to vacation here. The harvest table in the kitchen was long enough to seat The Walton's and the place smelled of coffee and maple bacon.

They kept the conversation light over breakfast. Father Andre had canceled his morning appointments. Because of him. Because he was basketcakes last night. Andre couldn't carry on with his day without informing him of Alain.

"Let's sit on the verandah," Father Andre said. "It's almost ten now and the Duprielles are dropping Alain off at noon."

For a few seconds, his heart stopped.

"That gives us a good hour to talk before I have to leave. Father Richard will stay here with you, Joe. If you like. I know everything that happened on your tenth birthday, or rather as much as you've disclosed through your family and pastor. Now it's time you heard my story, which was clearly designed to begin with yours. I do not believe in coincidence. Hmm?"

He wanted to agree but never gave it much thought. Father Andre continued.

"In August of 1970, I was living and teaching in Paris. During this time I attended the ceremony for a friend who'd become cardinal. I ran into many old friends there, one was Father Vittorio Gianni with whom I studied and was ordained with in 1954. And like me, he loved to teach.

"At the gathering he introduced me to an American protégé, young Paul Crouse, ordained only two months. We became quite the trio, seeing the sights, exchanging political viewpoints, arguing and laughing. Vittorio and I were in our late forties and admittedly, my classes had become dull because I had become dull. My life was stagnating and my faith wavering.

"Two nights before my return to Paris, on August 24th 1970, the three of us went out for dinner and wine. When we retired late evening, we weren't inebriated but we were certainly feeling no pain as you young people say. Sleep came easy to us that night. And in that sleep, Vittorio, Paul and I shared the same dream. The same dream exactly.

"We were sitting in the garden, on the grounds of Saint Peter's when a beautiful youthful man with a glowing fair complexion approached us. He radiated warmth and light and we knew in our core that this man was a Messenger. No one but us saw him. It was a bright sunny morning with many people strolling the grounds.

"'A child is born this day,'" the Messenger said to us, "'a child chosen by God, who, many years from now will aid in the conversion of souls for millions. He dwells in the Canadian province of Quebec, a place called Trois-

Rivierés. The name of his house is Duprielle and the child is called Alain.'

"The Messenger went on to say that 'shortly after his tenth birthday, a small group of evil men will pursue him. Since the beginning of time, the devil's lot has been to seek out that which is good and attempt to destroy it. In His mercy, God is sending the child protection here on earth. I will make myself known to him also on this day. You will know him as he shares the same birth date as the boy and his name is Joseph.'

"As guardian, Joseph will face many tests, but his reward will be a hundredfold. It will all begin in the year 1981. Document my words and store them in the safest of three places. Read them often. For after a while, this dream will seem imaginary to you. Pray daily to retain your belief in this message. Your duties from now on will become clear when you awaken. Always study in the Spirit ... and keep the child safe.'"

"That's exactly what he said to me! Wow. Me? Me! My name from the lips of an angel." Finally, answers. "That was my *Angel*. He was around all of us when Alain was born on *my* birthday. But I don't understand, Father. You were told Alain would aid in the conversion of souls for millions. That's a considerable number. Is he going to be pope?"

The two priests exchanged glances then Father Richard excused himself for a moment.

"The Messenger didn't say, Joe," Father Andre said. "Alain is Catholic so that is a possibility."

"Wait a minute. Father?" He gripped the sides of the chair. "Please tell me ... Alain isn't? Okay here it is, Alain isn't ... I mean, they talk about the Second Coming and everything. He isn't ..."

This seemed to amuse Father Andre. "No, Joe. He isn't Christ reborn."

"Then who is he, Father Andre? Have you told me everything?"

The elderly priest leaned forward in his chair. "Have you told *us* everything, Joe?"

"No," he said, lowering his chin. "I haven't. I think I'm going to know Alain as soon as I lay eyes on him. Two days before Willie died we were on the beach this one night. We were in the water and she ran ahead to our blanket near the shoreline. I heard a voice calling me. It wasn't Willie's voice. I shot out of the water and when I got near the blanket, I saw a child. He told me I was supposed to help him. His arms were bloodied. And then he disappeared and Willie hadn't seen a thing. She was upset with me and had other things on her mind. Alain is blond, isn't he? Light blue eyes, almost gray?"

"Yes," Father Richard said.

"Father Andre, with all due respect, I think there's more."

"Perhaps there is and if there is, it will be revealed in time. Right now, Joe, you have to train."

"Train?"

"We humans exist in three modules. Spiritual. Emotional. And physical. If we concentrate on one and neglect the other two, we live empty lives. If we tend two of three, we plod along relatively content, but always feeling as though we're missing something. But if we tend all three, the last being the spiritual and most important, we're happy and blessed, even in the midst of our sufferings.

"Nurturing these three components takes work. When you were ten and your angel told you to study in the Spirit, he was telling you to start training. You built up your body and evolved emotionally, but you neglected the most important part. Well now you have much catching up to do. To take care of Alain in the manner God wants, you're going to have to go into training, Joe. You're going to have to strengthen yourself."

"How do I do that?"

"You start by reading. I will give you a list. These books will strengthen your faith and prepare you for spiritual battle."

"And if I don't get prepared?"

"More of what happened last night and on the beach," Father Richard said. "And in larger doses."

"You'll be fine, Joe," Father Andre said. He stood up slowly and rubbed his thighs. "I have an appointment now so I'll leave you with Father Richard and see you later this afternoon. Make yourself at home here."

They hadn't discussed expenses but Father Andre told him not to fret. "You take care of any long distance calls and we'll take care of the rest. Have fun with Alain. His English is almost perfect, thanks to his mother."

"So now I know everything about Alain?"

"Yes," the priest said. "Try not to worry.

Yeah right, don't worry. Sure, he knew everything. Andre flushed three shades of pink when he said that.

"He always leaves me with a lot to digest," he said to Father Richard, who seemed to be studying him. "You, too, for that matter."

"And the day's just started."

"Something wrong, Father?"

Father Richard scooted his chair in a little closer, patted his knee. "You're rested, yes? Feel like talking?"

"About?"

"About Willie. And Norma Chilling. About your mother."

He stuffed his hands into his pockets. "Seems the women who love me end up dead."

"It seems that way, Joe. Rosa and Beata love you and they're still here."

"True. But I'm still reeling from Willie. It's like she's right here walking the grounds with me. That day in Angelfish Cove with Willie—I haven't told you everything. And I'd rather no one else knows. Not yet. Not about my mother or Norma, either."

"Understood."

"Remember when you said in the rectory that you were waiting for act two?"

"Yes."

"Same here. I had quite the ethereal experience in Angelfish Cove the other week, that last day with Willie. And last night when your dog barked, I went a little wonky. Second lap around the track coming up, Father."

Father Richard hardly breathed as he reiterated the events in Angelfish Cove prior to the vision of Alain on the beach—the record shop, the Voice, the artist, the singer, the foxy bookstore owner, finishing with the broken glass episode and the 'evaporating' boy in the funny T-shirt at Pages.

"*Cher Seigneur, de le protéger,*" Father Richard said, explaining that he asked God to protect him. "Surely, you're right. You're meant to be here. We must let it all play out without resistance. Any similarities in the deaths of your mother or Norma?"

"No. Mom died in a freak accident with a horse, which I'll save for another day. And Norma was a sophomore at UMass Amherst who hung out with my freshmen class. Don't know why she picked us but she did."

Father Richard smiled.

"A buddy of mine dating her roommate said Norma had a mild form of schizophrenia, but had it under control. Mild schizophrenia. Now there's an oxymoron if ever I heard one. Strange, Father. When I learned that, I asked Norma out."

"You thought she had it under control at the time, so why strange?"

"When I was a kid, the year my mom died, I made friends with an older kid from Harvard who summered at the farm with his pals. Craig Matheson was terrifically brilliant but sickly, and we had a lot in common since we both lost parents. He lived in Cambridge with a wealthy uncle and after Dad died, I moved to Boston to live with my not-so-wealthy uncle.

"I remember Craig had been modifying some complex theory, a name I never got straight, even then, but he was excited about it and his uncle would have none of it. I guess he didn't want his nephew wasting Harvard bucks on some hackneyed theory. So he gave up, you know. So here the kid is with a busted dream and crap health. Sometime later I learned Craig had Type 1 Diabetes, but I knew he was sick before because I felt it off him at the hospital. I wanted him well as any friend would so I prayed for him during his visit. Nothing elaborate. But that's when I noticed my own pain diminishing. As long as I could concentrate on somebody else, I didn't hurt."

"But you still felt pain."

"Sure. But it wasn't *my* pain. And when Craig cheered up instantly and resumed the dream, I made a game of it. He stood up to his uncle, too, who eventually came around and supported him, even helped him with his theory when he got really sick. Craig died a few years after I moved to Boston. We wrote right up to the end and I know he died happy because the empathy stayed with me through his letters. I played that prayer game for years. And it was because of Craig. Selfish, really."

"Why selfish?"

"Because I used the game to end my pain. Like I said, I didn't hurt when I prayed for others. Anyway, Norma brought it all back. When she got dark, I got *empathy* dark, just like when I was a kid. And I've been having these intermittent moods since. I asked Norma out to see if the game would still work."

"And did it?"

He clasped his hands behind his head and looked up. "Oh sure it worked. She got happier and *crazier* at the same time. We went to a Christmas frat party the night she died. Willie met us there with her girlfriend. Norma was acting crazy jealous over Willie that night, saying there was something going on with Willie and me, all kinds of crazy accusations like that. I shouldn't keep using the word crazy, but anyway I had to get Norma out of there. And outside in the car ... well, that's when it all went down. I asked her if she had stopped the *Haldol*—"

"This was the medication she was on?"

"Uh-huh, an anti-psychotic. She told me it was keeping her down and she wouldn't take it anymore. So we argue and she pulls a 22 Magnum Pug from her *bra holster* and points it at my chin. Think I wet my pants, Father. She said, 'the girls won't be drooling over this face much longer'. I disarmed her, we struggled, the gun fired and Norma died two hours later in Cooley Dickinson."

"And the police thought it was deliberate?"

"Ah they did and they didn't. They gave me a hard time at first but cleared me at the hearing. It was tough on Willie, though. Willie said if she never went that night, Norma would still be alive. Now Willie's gone, too."

He appreciated Father Richard sparing him a mountain of useless platitudes. The priest listened, obviously sympathized, and that was it. When Father Richard brought the conversation round to Marianlake activities, he had difficulty focusing on what he was saying—something about a busload of high school girls.

With Alain due any minute, his thoughts reverted to concerns for the boy's safety. What if he blew that, too, like he did with Norma and Willie? The kid was ten. What do you say to a ten-year-old kid? So, Alain, I understand you're going to grow up to be this great spiritual leader. How may I be of assistance? Oh by the way, did you know that five minutes after my father was killed in a car accident on *our* birthday, an angel showed up and told me about you? So, do you think your parents'll trust me to keep you from getting dead?

Then it hit, the stomach knot, tense and tight as a bygone rival. Fortunately there was no fever. No feeling of the dark angel. No anxiety attack. Not to worry, folks, just a mild case of stomach cancer. A dog's howl startled him and Father Richard out of their chairs. Shades of last night.

"It's Compo." Father Richard reached for his jacket. "He sounds bad. I've never heard him bark like that. He's close, maybe two hundred yards. I'm going to get him."

The stomach cancer was worsening but with a little radiation he'd be fine. "I'm going with you, Father." Alain flashed through his mind again. "Sounds like he's barking at something."

Past the end of the pathway, after veering right about one hundred feet, he stumbled into Claude Duprielle who was yelling Alain's name. His wife Tracy was right behind him with a firm hold on her husband's jacket. Everybody started running in the same direction.

"Alain!" Mr. Duprielle shouted. "Alain had been walking ahead and must've broke into a run when he heard the dog. That dog sounds mad, Richard!"

With the barking yards away, they stumbled into a small clearing of leaves and pinecones. His stomach knot had expanded into something the size of a rubber raft as the young voice came at him, a young voice not calling for his father, but for *him*.

"Joe ... Joe ..."

There was no mistaking the blue and white streak at the other side of the clearing through a small opening in the bushes as the boy's jacket. He crept forward and the dog whined.

"He knows I'm here," Father Richard whispered. "He's got my scent."

"Move along with your friend, Richard," Mr. Duprielle said. "Let him catch more of your scent. Then call him."

Suddenly, a large muscular black Lab bolted from the bushes and charged his master. Inches away from him, the animal fell first forward and then rolled onto its side, as though restrained by a leash. Joe stepped off to his left, slowly making his way to the other side of the bush. It was obvious the dog could go no farther, that it was tethered. But there was plenty of slack in the rope. If spooked, it could get itself up and go back to the boy.

Father Richard called softly to it as it sat on its haunches, staring at him. It seemed half-crazed and bewildered. As soon as the priest diverted his eyes to check on his progress, the animal lunged at him, nearly strangling itself with the sudden movement. It then took three steps backward, its head rocking in a weird side to side motion and ran back in Alain's direction.

Within seconds, a large circle formed around Alain. Mrs. Duprielle cried out when she saw the animal baring its teeth at her son's throat. Alain, who had hunched down on the ground, his small body practically hidden under leaves and bramble, looked up at the people standing in front of him. When their eyes met, the boy stopped searching.

As much as he wanted to bask in the moment, he had to think. This was definitely not the time to get hypnotized by this kid's eyes. *Come on, Joe, think.* Dear God, it was really him. What a beautiful boy. Who is he, really? *Save the child.*

He waited. Father Richard's voice seemed to anesthetize the dog, though he was the definitive witness to familiarity breeding contempt, as if the animal was saying to its master, *I think I know you and if I do, how could you have done this to me?* Father Richard continued calling 'Compo' until finally it stopped snarling at Alain and timidly, with its ears perked up, crawled a foot closer to the priest. Just a little closer and he could snatch the boy out of its reach. Father Richard backed up a few paces. The dog crawled forward. One more foot, come on, one more ... he found himself counting the number of strides it would take to get in and out of there with the boy ... seven ...

"Alain!"

He rushed in and grabbed Alain's arm, slinging him over his shoulder in two perfectly executed tai chi moves. When the dog charged back in a rage, he made that last leap out of there with Baryshnikov precision. He and Alain fell to the ground with the dog inches away, nearly garroted by the rope. He was mindful of one thing—a smaller heart beating faster than his own.

"Are you all right?" he asked the child. In all his life, he never saw eyes fill up with love so fast, eyes with a freshly removed Band-Aid outline over the right brow and a double set of blond lashes. The cut over the brow might scar. Someone was definitely messing with him. In Medford, Father Richard had mentioned unexplained bruises. What exactly was happening to this kid?

"Joe," Alain said. "Ohh Joe. I knew you'd come."
The Duprielles and Father Richard came running over.
Tracy, all five feet of her, had obviously passed her looks onto her son. Claude towered over her at six-two. He looked to be in his mid-thirties with coloring similar to his own. Claude gave his wife's tummy a gentle pat as she dabbed away tears of relief with her coat-sleeve. Watching this gave him such a weird feeling, a feeling fast becoming routine. They couldn't seem to thank him enough and everyone laughed when Father Richard introduced them. Then the priest looked sadly at his beloved pet. The dog sat there with a low growl settled in its throat and rage ready to bust loose again.

"Claude? What do you think happened to him?"

"I don't know, Richard. He's not rabid. It's like he's been driven crazy somehow. I'll get a shot into him and take him back. We'll find out, my friend."

Father Richard's complexion suddenly paled with the reality of what might've been. "Who would do this?" he asked no one in particular.

The Duprielles happily let Alain spend some time alone with the young man who may have just saved his life, and so he and Alain walked back hand in hand. He felt the rhythm of Alain's pulse keeping time with his own. It finally hit him and it sure took its sweet time sinking in that he was chosen to perform this task. He had been especially favored, therefore important and valued. He smiled and gently squeezed the boy's hand. Now, which question to start with?

"So you knew I'd come?" Good a place as any to start.

"*Oui*," Alain said, revealing a remarkable display of confidence. "You told me that, Joe."

"I did? When?"

Alain jumped on a twig, enjoying the snap and crackle sound. "A long time now. I saw your face sometimes when I closed my eyes. Then you would talk. You wouldn't talk so often, though."

"What did I say?"

Alain stopped in his tracks and puffed out his cheeks, releasing the air in one burp. "Don't you remember, Joe?" he asked, somewhat frustrated.

Unfortunately, he couldn't. He had read about saints who bilocated. But he was certainly no saint. "No, Alain. I don't remember." Was Alain the saint?

"That's okay," he said. "I guess it's not important."

He laughed. The boy's immediate acceptance of the situation amused him. "What do you think our next adventure's going to be? Cowboys and Indians? Vampires?"

Alain giggled. "No. Lots of one color."

"Lots of one color? I don't get it."

"Then come on, Joe," he said, yanking his hand. "I'll show you. It's so amazing."

Twenty minutes later they came upon a clearing that stretched way beyond the scope of his vision. It was an explosion of orange in all directions. Acres of pumpkins. The only endless thing he had ever seen before was sky and ocean, blue against blue. But this—he could walk through this and not be swallowed up by it. Never before had he seen nature dressed solely in orange. Halloween. Witches. Broomsticks. Candies and costumes. Screams followed by laughter. He was standing in what had to be the best moment of the season.

They talked little on the way to wherever they were going and that was okay. He needed to recharge his batteries and forget the lurking dark angels. It was a beautiful, Oz-like, autumn afternoon. He turned his face to the sky.

"Will you come trick or treating with me, Joe?" Alain asked.

"You bet. No way would I miss Halloween with my new friend."

It was time happily spent in the field that day seeking out their two premium pumpkins, and they had an ocean of orange spheres from which to choose. Using his pocketknife, Joe cut a ten-pounder for Alain and a twenty-pounder for himself. Then they started back for Joe's cabin, laughing, carrying the pumpkins on their heads. So passed their first journey together. Over the next nineteen years, the memory of this day would strengthen their faith and preserve their sanity.

4. Players in the Dark

Although Trois-Rivière's division for Disease Control and Prevention had dropped cubes of anti-rabies vaccine into wooded areas, targeting the disease in foxes, Claude performed the test anyway. Marianlake was the typical small town, so within hours everyone would know about Compo going berserk. Alain and Compo were pals, and everyone acquainted with the dog loved him. Hopefully this would stay true.

Claude ran his hand affectionately over the dog's head, inadvertently turning his ear inside out. Something fine pricked the fleshy part of his palm. Swinging over his magnifier, he examined the ear closely.

"So sorry, Compo."

After Claude removed the sewing needle that had been halved and strategically concealed inside the dog's left ear, he checked his right ear.

"Our poor Compo," he said aloud in French, extracting the needle. "It's all over and life will be good again, yes?" He patted the dog.

He placed the needles in a small bottle and joined Father Richard in the empty waiting room. After seeing the needles, Father Richard Vaux thanked God for Alain's life. Any other dog would have ripped him apart. It was all beginning as Father Andre had said. It had to be those four European monks who mysteriously surfaced three weeks ago. They knew who Alain was. They must have seen the Document. If this was true—they knew more than himself and the Duprielle's. Like Joe, Richard felt something was amiss. Still, with all his heart he trusted Andre. If he was intentionally omitting something from his story, he had valid reasons. Perhaps it was Andre's way of protecting them.

The Duprielles didn't seem too concerned about solving the Compo mystery. Most likely they felt relief that their son was unharmed. And they did have bigger fish to fry, believing that Alain would grow up to be a great religious leader as told to them by Father Andre and foretold to him by an Angel of God. So naturally, Richard kept his suspicions to himself. But now there was Joe, who at twenty was still so very young. Had the great responsibility of what he was up against sunk in, the responsibility and the danger?

Eventually, Joe would have to get Alain away from Marianlake. How long would it take to prepare him for this journey? And how could Claude and Tracy let go? They'd be handing their son over to a post-adolescent stranger. Six of those brandy-filled chocolates he had stashed in his desk would do nicely right now.

"Return to the planet, Richard," Claude said. "I need your input."

"Okay. First thing we do is get Joe prepared. We've talked for years about this, Claude. Do you think you and Tracy can leave him? That time is near, maybe before the first snowfall."

"What choice do we have? I wanted to go along, see him safely tucked away somewhere. Now with the baby due in April, I can't leave Tracy. And you have a full class load. Joe's so young, Richard."

"In years, Claude. Remember, he was chosen. Besides, the third party should be a woman, I think."

"A woman. What woman? Tracy's the only woman who knows. You're not talking about his step-grandmother, are you? She's what, sixty-odd?"

Father Richard smiled shrewdly. Recently, an idea had come to mind, a persistent idea. "No. This particular woman is around Tracy's age. My concern is getting her out of the habit."

∞∞∞

"Blast!" cursed Sister Elizabeth Whyte after slamming down the phone. Then she checked the phone to see if she broke it. Plan B should've been ready in case she had to shift gears and she had two weeks left to wrap things up. It wasn't a mistake bringing the girls to Quebec. Certainly they needed all the spiritual boosting they could get. And maybe there was a genius in the bunch. No maybes. She was certain there was a genius in the bunch and she praised God for it.

In any event, all these beautiful, temporarily liberated teenage ladies were her responsibility. Sister Elizabeth decided to think positive. They would not get lost in the Canadian woods. They would not disturb the environment. And they definitely would not be eloping with any seminarians. There was only one problem to take care of and she wouldn't worry about that, either.

How was she going to break it to the girls? They came here to complete their projects and see the William Blake exhibition in Quebec City. Now the exhibit was put up exactly two weeks because the art gallery insured the safe passage of the work for the wrong dates. She failed to understand the paper rigmarole involved. Why couldn't they ink out the old dates and stick in the new ones? Everybody always had to complicate things these days. Oh the hell with it. Quebec City was huge, with lots to occupy them. She'd have to cut out the swearing, even if it was only *candy*-swearing.

"You'll never guess, Father," she said to Father Richard Vaux, noticing he shut his office door behind him. He never closed his door. Then she proceeded to condense the bad news into four sentences—in French. She liked to practice. But it was not very good French. Actually it was pretty awful French, but it amused Father Vaux.

"The art gallery did what?" he repeated, tittering. "They're setting fire to the Blake exhibit in two weeks? Run that by me again in your charming Brooklyn accent, Sister."

Father was right. It did translate better in English. Maybe she should save the French for the girls. "So what do you think, Father?" she asked, toying with the idea of dropping the subject altogether. He seemed so distracted.

"We'll come up with something for them, something cultural of course." He stopped the teasing and grew serious. "If you could get your superiors' endorsement, would you consider a hiatus from New York City, art and history?"

Sister Elizabeth squinted at him out of one eye. "How long a hiatus?"

"Oh I don't know. A year or twelve."

"Cut to the chase please, Father. My head's achy and I'm out of aspirin."

"You may need something stronger than aspirin by the time I'm through with you, Sister."

They dined in his office where they remained until midnight. Sister Elizabeth's mind filled with joy and wonder, allowing not one fraction of negativity to intrude on her thoughts. To be in the same room with the child was a blessing. But this—to live in the presence of a child who would one day grow to inspire millions ... she, along with this young man, would tend the soil, then sit back and watch while God grew the flower. Yes she was waxing a bit poetic. And yes she was a part of this now. Nothing could go wrong. Surely her superiors in New York City would sanction this mission, although they might not be too crazy about the deception. But there was no way to travel with them as a nun. No way to explain it. The habit had to go.

Life in its irony was returning something once violently taken from her. Father Andre, who had joined them shortly after dinner, had asked if she was up to changing her entire life. Yes, she told him. She was only thirty-five, still young enough to adapt. And it was finally payback time. She bartered away responsibility once, many years ago. It wasn't going to happen twice. But they didn't need to hear more about something they probably already knew. Certainly they would have checked her out. These people had to be thorough with both her spiritual and personal credentials.

"May I see the Document?" she asked Father Andre.

After hesitating, his reply was negative. "Not at this time, Sister Elizabeth." He offered no explanation and she found this curious.

"Be a lot of loose ends to tie up," she said. "I'll have to come up with something to tell the girls. And my family. Blast. What am I going to tell my family?"

Father Andre suggested she tell them she's been given the opportunity to travel, by accepting a single tutoring post for the Order. So simple.

Sister Elizabeth collapsed in the window rocker when she returned to her room. The light was on in the middle cabin across the lake and Joe's poor, restless shadow paced behind the drawn blind. No doubt all involved were restless tonight. Many lives were about to change. She rocked by the window in reflection and meditation until it was time to shut down her mind. When she finally fell asleep at 4 a.m., Joe's light was still on.

∞∞∞

With two tables left in the library on a Sunday morning, Joe wondered if most of these people were the after-Mass crowd or maybe more seminarians arrived last night. No matter. Thanks to the tai chi he could concentrate around chaos. They sure were a curious lot, these Dominicans, none of them concerned that he was Protestant. And so far no place was off limits. He had to wonder though, why the Catholics were letting a Protestant into their clubhouse. Actually he hadn't a clue about Protestantism, either, since his parents never practiced. He was more familiar with Catholicism since R & B and Willie were Catholic. Faith was faith and so far they showed no interest in converting him. He had faith. He was a believer. Good enough.

He rolled his eyes at Father Richard's reading list, *Passion and Death of Jesus Christ*, *The Evolution Hoax Exposed*, *The Incorruptibles, Saint Michael and the Angels* and last on the list, because Father Richard had them numbered, *Evidence of Satan in the Modern World* and all having the *impramatur*. Heavy stuff. He sighed loud enough to attract the attention of a young lady seated at the table across from him. Hearing her giggle made him look up and return the smile. She seemed familiar.

Being deliberately comical, he cocked his head to see the massive book in front of her. The thing had to be a twelve-pounder, easy. Still giggling, she held it up so he could catch a glimpse of the title. *Anatomy for the Artist*. A sketch of a naked male lay sprawled and facedown on the cover. He rubbed his right index finger over his left. Not appearing the least bit shy, the girl laughed, walked over and joined him.

"An art project," she said and he noticed the sweet chubbiness of her face and body. "But you, that's a mountain you got there. You must be a seminarian."

The thought of that picture gave him a good laugh. "Nope. Just suggested reading by a mentor. Hi. Joe Ross."

She thrust out her hand to shake his, which he found touching. "Hi. Dina Amodeo. I'm up here with my class for a couple weeks."

He felt a tingling sensation in his throat when he went to speak and an ache in his heart for Angelfish Cove. "But you're not really into art," he said to her.

She rounded her big brown eyes at him. "How did you know that? I can barely draw a straight line with a ruler."

"Oh, the sound of your voice and laugh. You've got the sound."

"What sound?" Dina asked, totally absorbed.

"That *singer* sound."

"Amazing." She shook her head from side to side. "I love to sing. Singing makes me the happiest. It's like, oh I don't know, I feel like I'm floating along in an air balloon. And when I land, I'm in this different place all wildly colorful. It excites me."

"Like the Land of Oz, right? Been there recently myself."

She nodded. "Mm-hmm. When I put myself in that balloon and take off, my voice always sounds better."

"Are you studying voice?"

"No." She seemed depressed suddenly. He didn't mean to do that. "I'd love to and I want to, but my parents think it's weird. I'm from New York City. Everybody sings in New York City. Everybody's got a band. Everybody's got talent."

"What about your talent?" he asked. "How much talent have you got?"

"Enough. Enough to make it if I apply myself."

"So apply yourself."

"It's not so easy."

"You want me to dump a bunch of clichés on you?"

"No, thanks. I've heard 'em. So tell me, since you're not here studying to be a priest, what brings you here, Joe?"

He should have better prepared for this question. Fortunately, one of the monks interrupted them. This one appeared younger than the rest, in his early thirties maybe.

"Excuse me," he said, pointing to a study quartet in the corner, "but my friends asked if you would keep it down. Exam tomorrow."

"Sorry," he said, detecting a trace of an Italian accent. There was a stale odor of wine on his breath.

"Ugh," Dina said, watching him walk back toward his group, "that guy is so creepy. He's been hanging around me and my friends since we got here the other day, eyeing us, you know? We found out he and three others just showed up here a few weeks ago. They're monks or something. He's very strange."

He wondered what exam these visiting monks were writing tomorrow since they were only *visiting*. He glanced over to find the monk staring at them. "Let's get out of here," he said, thinking it might be wise to memorize the monk's face.

Dina left her books behind and helped him with his. As they climbed into the rowboat, she asked him again, "What are you doing here, Joe?"

He sighed. Truth time. Always good not to have to keep track of lies. He wouldn't tell her everything, of course. "My step-cousin died last month and it hit me pretty hard. In a way I feel responsible. I'm having a hard time dealing, so Father Vaux, who is a good friend of our pastor back home in Massachusetts, suggested I spend some time here, getting, shall we say, reacquainted with the spiritual side of myself. Starting with this stack of books." He smiled and she immediately blushed.

"I'm sorry about your step-cousin. Were you very close?"

Every time someone asked him this question the black shadows returned. The guilt. Pushing Willie away like that.

"I'm sorry," Dina said. "If her death hit you really hard, then of course you were close. That was a stupid question. I ask stupid questions sometimes. My best friends think I'm going to stay innocent forever. Sister Elizabeth says I should stop, take a deep breath and think before I speak."

Sister Elizabeth. Another player in the game. "Sister Elizabeth?" Was all of Angelfish Cove lurking around here somewhere, lying in ambush? "Is she your teacher?"

"Yep. Art and history. I'm not so hot in either. So I flipped a coin and it was art. Now I have two weeks to learn how to draw. I need theme and color. Well, I know what color is. But theme, there you got me."

"It's a recurring idea in a work of art. Maybe Sister Elizabeth will help you. I'd like to meet her."

"Done, I'll introduce you." Dina bobbed her head once, as though accomplished. "Where we going with these books?"

"My cabin," he said, amazed she got in a boat with a stranger without asking sooner.

As they approached the middle of the lake, she began to hum. *In The Air Tonight. Phil Collins.* It had only been out a few months and already it was one of his favorites. "Sounds great," he told her, remembering the haunting voice of a much older Dina in Angelfish Cove. There was pain ahead for Dina. Some morbidly intrusive thing was going to steal away her innocence. He sensed it that night and the certainty of it now made him flinch in the boat. Could he prevent it? Maybe that's why he was here.

"Sing the words, Dina."

She sang and he stopped paddling. Her voice was that mesmerizing. One of the girls out sketching on the grounds put down her easel, shading her forehead for a clearer view. He could see the long flowing red hair. Another, dressed in a black habit, walked out to the deckchair at the end of the dock and sat down. Had to be her—Sister Elizabeth.

Eyes closed while she sang, Dina was already up in that air balloon on her way to Oz. She hadn't noticed the distraction she was causing on the other side of the lake. They had stopped what they were doing to listen and watch. Even the battlefield in his mind had cleared. Temporarily. He saw a fair-haired girl out there with incredibly long legs whisper something in the redhead's ear. His heart stepped up a beat. As Dina continued to sing, he continued to stare. And whoever she was, she stared back.

When Dina finished to echoing applause around the lake, he bowed to her.

"See? I'd start applying myself if I were you, Dina."

"What a cool cabin," Dina said, plopping down the books and sounding fourteen. "Sooo ro-man-tic." She knitted her brows and turned away from him.

"What's wrong, Dina? You're safe with me, believe me."

"I ... feel ... warm all of a sudden."

Uh-oh. He was uncomfortably familiar with 'warmness' in girls, though obviously, Dina wasn't familiar with it. How could she reach this age and not be? And why did this keep happening to him seeing as he was nothing special? The bites started itching again and his scalp prickled. But Dina was right about the heat.

"Joe, it's really hot in here. Don't you think it's really hot? I mean this is October."

He put his hand on her forehead and an even redder flush covered her face. "I hope you're not coming down with anything."

"Joe?" Father Andre stood at the door, Sister Elizabeth at his side. "Didn't you hear my knock?"

Instead of waiting for an answer, the elderly priest blinked his eyes and took to the couch.

"Isn't it nice in here, Sister?" Dina didn't wait for an answer, either. "I feel so warm all over. Actually I feel hot but it's kinda nice. Different from—"

"Dina," Sister Elizabeth cut her off, "the girls are waiting for you in the dining hall."

"See ya, Joe." She stopped in the doorway and gave him a cute little wave.

"See ya, Dina," he said, sniffing. Something smelled sickeningly sweet and musty in the cabin and Father Andre and Sister Elizabeth were looking strangely at each other and at him.

"Hello, Sister. Joe Ross." She looked younger and shorter than the Angelfish Cove *version* of her, but yes, this was Sister Elizabeth, a somewhat preoccupied Sister Elizabeth. What was this smell?

"Nice to meet you, Joe. You smell that? What is that?"

"Joe," Father Andre said, inhaling deeply, "seems we're not alone here. Do you smell anything unusual?"

"I do, Father. What do you mean we're not alone?"

"Sister? How do you feel?"

The nun answered with a raised eyebrow and a flushed face, then took her Rosary and wrapped it around her hand.

"We're not alone, you said?"

At once the odor disappeared and fresh air replenished the room, like someone had waved away the stench with a wand.

"It's gone," Father Andre said.

The three of them looked over at the doorway, and there *he* stood, Compo beside him, tail wagging. Alain stood silently, looking at him, affectionately patting the dog and smiling. The boy seemed half-present, a droplet of blood shining on his forehead. He lunged toward him but Father Andre held him back. It was then that he saw the boy was silently praying with his eyes fixed on him. Once again, he had never seen anything so incredibly beautiful as the glow on Alain's face.

As quickly as the odor had, the droplet of blood disappeared. Alain walked up to him as if nothing had happened and smiled.

"It's Halloween next week, Joe. We have to start our costumes today. *Oui*?"

He picked him up and hugged him. "Yeah, *oui*," he said.

∞∞∞

Sister Elizabeth watched Joe and the boy at play in the water. It wouldn't be easy for them. Separate or together they were quite the sight and wherever they went they'd draw attention. Alain looked like an angel and Joe, fantasy material for most women, seemed to act first before thinking things through. If not for Father Andre, Joe might have stopped a prayer in motion, which meant that that smell caused by that *Thing*, might still be lurking—which brought up another concern.

"He has a demon around him, doesn't he, Father?"

"Yes." Father Andre removed a prescription bottle from his pocket. "For a long time, I suspect."

"Lust?"

"Suspect so. But the entity is not provoking Joe, it's provoking the women around him."

"Why is Joe so favored?"

"Ah, the mystery question, Sister. He's done something to please God. And God isn't telling us what that is. Not yet."

"At least He's telling us about Alain—the whole miracle of Alain. And there's the Document you won't let me see."

"Joe doesn't realize he's favored because he doesn't know what it's like to be without miracles in his life," Andre said, ignoring the bait. "It's an old irritating cliché. We always take for granted that which we already possess, like the silver spoon at birth. He doesn't recognize the miracles because they present during his darkest nights of the soul."

"And there's Alain. Untouched and unaffected by darkness."

"He may be unaffected, Sister Elizabeth, but he's not untouched. Somebody tried to drive that dog crazy enough to attack the boy. Fatally. The police are conducting a discreet investigation and they have learned that he is the only one who takes that route to and from school every day. Someone familiar with his routine is watching him.

"A few weeks ago he was thrown from a horse he's been riding since he was five years old. We're dealing with evil in both forms, Sister. Mortal and diabolical. Joe has his work cut out for him. And so have you. Any second thoughts?"

She shook her head. Where Joe and Alain were going, she was going. "How long, Father?" This was a valid question.

"Perhaps a year. Joe turns twenty-one in August, as you know. Depends on how much he can handle alone, so when I said a year, I meant a year's stay for *you*."

"But I understand he's returning to his university courses in a semester or two."

"So he thinks," Andre said.

She had the feeling that certain details about Alain had been kept from Joe, and perhaps from her, and blast it all if that wasn't making her second-guess her decision. How long did they intend to keep Joe from the life he wanted? Something about Father Andre wasn't sitting well with her. Right from jump street she sensed he wasn't telling all he knew. Elizabeth did not care for secrets. She had a difficult enough time managing her own.

∞∞∞

Joe didn't understand his yo-yo moods—up, down, fear and darkness, serenity. With each visit, darkness revealed more of its face, then in marches Alain with his Angel of Light to save the day. Good thing, because his Angel of Light had taken a powder in Angelfish Cove. *Oh yoo-hoo. Remember me, I'm still here hanging.* Okay fine, he'd thank Alain's angel, whoever he was, for abating his fear.

"Alain?" he said, enjoying the sun's reflection in both water and mind. "What were you thinking before when you came into the cabin?"

Alain tossed a piece of driftwood into the water and cheered Compo on as he dove in after it. "Nothing. I see a face that I like to look at. Sometimes two faces."

"Whose faces? Are they people you know?"

Alain tightened his face. "Not sure. Sometimes I see a man. Then sometimes I see an older kid."

"Do you see them like you're seeing me now?"

"No. Different. I *see* them. Like TV in my head." Alain's expression saddened. "One time the older kid had tears on his face. It made me feel real bad for him."

"Why do you think the older kid was crying?"

Alain's scholarly expression almost cracked him up. "Because, Joe, things are just bad all over."

After another moment of watching Compo splash around in the water, Alain beat him to the next question. "Will you take me to Angelfish Cove someday, Joe?"

Chills moved up his spine. "Angelfish Cove? How do you know about that place?"

Alain circled his finger around his knee. Joe had come to notice that the boy spoke volumes with his body. "A person has to go backward to move forward," he said, still circling.

He simply didn't know what to say, so he gaped at him. If anyone could corner the market on emotional impact, it was this little boy. "Look at me for a second, Alain." Alain looked up at him with a trace of worry in his eyes. "When I was in Angelfish Cove, I wondered that very same thing—going backward to go forward. I was listening to a lady sing this old old song."

"Dina," Alain said. "I saw her come out of the cabin. And Sister Elizabeth was in Angelfish Cove, too, Joe."

Joe pulled the boy closer to him. "So were you, weren't you?"

"*Oui*. But I wasn't alone."

"Would you like to tell me about your visit there?"

Alain took the stick from Compo and tossed it out again. "Please don't be mad, Joe. I wasn't spying or following you, I promise."

"I know that, bud, I know. Tell me all about your adventure there, okay? 'Cause I sure had one."

Alain stretched out on his stomach, hands propped under his chin. "I was in my room and Mom was saying goodnight. Then I closed my eyes and saw the older kid's face. I didn't tell Mom. She put up my covers and said goodnight and I was still seeing him. He was on these really shiny white sheets and he glowed, Joe. It was great, like Star Trek."

Remembering back, he smiled.

"And then it was like I told you. TV in my head. He went away and I saw Angelfish Cove. I watched all the people until I saw you. And Willie. I saw the record store, the bookstore, the place where you ate. I saw Sister Elizabeth and Dina and even the other two. They're here, Joe."

Not exactly a surprise but he had to ask anyway. "Who's here?" He needed to know how much Alain saw that night.

"You know. The painter lady and the book store lady. I don't remember their names."

"It's okay. I sure do. Go on."

"And ... oh!" He pointed to Joe's cap. "I watched you buy that cap for Willie. Then later, things got scary. Mom and Dad don't believe me. Please believe me, Joe. They think I got them at school, but I didn't. I got them in my room—"

"Ssh. Slow down. Got what in your room, bud?"

Alain puffed out his cheeks again. "Bruises. Lots of bruises. I was black and blue and my arm got scratched and bleeding. I'm sorry–my English ..."

"Your English is great. How did you get black and blue in your room?"

"Something kept moving me around. It felt like a ride, only it was scary 'cause I couldn't see the thing that was taking me on this ride. It pushed me up against the wall into my Gordie Howe picture and that's how my arm got bleeding. Then I saw you, Joe. You were in the water and I think I called you. Or maybe it was the older kid who called you. I'm not sure."

"Well I'm sure I heard one of you calling me," he said, giddy and lightheaded, which was fast becoming a permanent state.

"Then you came out of the water. And when you saw us, the ride thing went away. It didn't bother us anymore. Then after I guess I fell asleep."

"Has the ride thing been back?"

"*Oui.* It was spinning around you when I got into the cabin, Joe. Didn't you see it?"

Numbly, he shook his head, legs pumping like pistons.

"Don't worry, Joe, it couldn't hurt you."

"I thought you said you couldn't see it?"

"I know." Suddenly Alain seemed pleased with himself. "But I saw it today. It looked like a big black shadow that went up to the ceiling. And it smelled bad. I guess I couldn't see it in my room 'cause the lights were out. But it was sunny in the cabin. Then I saw the man's face. Joe, whenever I see the man's face, I don't remember much after. But when I see the older kid's face, I see stuff. Like Angelfish Cove. Why don't I remember anything when I see the man's face?"

He wished to God he knew the answer. He was still back with the ride thing. "I don't know, Alain. Maybe Father Richard will know. Or Sister Elizabeth, maybe. Why don't we tell them everything you told me and then we'll ask them."

"Don't you want to tell Father Andre?"

"No matter. Father Andre has a lot of work to do after he finishes talking to Sister Elizabeth. Besides, I haven't really had a chance to talk to Sister Elizabeth yet myself. When you were telling me about Angelfish Cove and the beach, you kept saying *us.* Did you mean you and the older kid or you and the man?"

Alain tugged on an ear. "I'm not sure again. I only know I wasn't by myself."

Time got away from them. Alain had to join his father on 'animal rounds' and asked if he would bring Compo back to Father Richard. Sister Elizabeth and Father Andre were still chatting in his cabin as he rowed Compo across the lake. More and more, the elderly priest was not his cup of tea and it disturbed him. Or maybe it was sour grapes because Andre didn't trust him enough to tell him the whole story. He didn't need to be treated like a kid. He got the feeling that Andre was talking down to him half the time. And he didn't need secrets exacerbating his already disturbed state of mind. The last hour had been disturbing enough.

Three quarters of the way across, he stopped rowing and let the boat drift. Compo didn't look like he had any important appointments. It was so hard to believe this was the same dog that wanted Alain's throat for lunch the other day.

"You're really made of strong mettle, aren't you, boy," he said, with one eye on Compo and the other on the artist painting on the dock. She seemed so absorbed in her work. That had to be her. *Maggie.* When she looked up he tipped his cap and she nodded.

"I met one of your classmates earlier," he called out as the boat drifted in to dock. "Dina."

"Right, she told me," Maggie said, putting on her sunglasses and making the blue smudge on her nose even bigger. "Is that your cabin on the other side? The one in the middle?"

"Well it's not really mine," he said, climbing onto the dock. "I'm just keeping it company, courtesy of Father Vaux. Hi, Joe Ross."

"Margaret Page," she said, taking a step back as Compo charged by her toward the rectory. "Dina said your cabin was wonderful and I confess I snuck a peek at it through my binoculars. Would you mind if I sketched it from your dock?"

"Not at all. My dock is your dock. Margaret."

"Maggie," she laughed. "Margaret is better suited to an artist than Maggie."

"Yeah, but Maggie will work better for you in the '90s."

"The '90s! We're just into the '80s."

"Keep painting and you'll be a big hit in the '90s. As Maggie Page," he told her, remembering how much older she looked in Angelfish Cove. As a matter of fact, so did Dina and Sister Elizabeth. He gave himself a mental nudge. Uncanny resemblances aside, they were a cast in Angelfish Cove, actors playing a role, all for his benefit. There was one noticeably absent player left. "You keep to yourself a lot, don't you, Maggie?"

"What gave me away?" she asked, absorbed. "Dina said you were sort of psychic. True or false?"

"The psychic word makes me nervous. I do get vibes sometimes. I grew up around a grandmother who is into ESP, crystal balls and all that nasty stuff. No one can convince her that this is an occult practice, a veritable Christian no-no. Not that I'm a worthy example."

It amazed him how easily sharing this information trickled off his tongue. And it was clear that his disapproval of the occult arts was of no interest to her. Because she wanted to press about the ESP. Because she was a young woman unhappy with life in the present. Margaret Page wanted answers. Would she be rich? Would she be famous? She was adamant, insisted he had to be psychic. No one knew Dina could sing like that. So he told her she'd make it big one day, but that's all he told her.

He omitted her self-imposed isolation, all because of a door and what lay behind it. She would build a prison around herself. But his foresight was shadowed. A two-second glimpse at that door was all he got. And where the hell was this coming from? Oh God, what next? What, he was a visionary now? Getting vibes was one thing—but this? Maybe it was an intermittent thing. He could only hope and pray. *Shake it off, Joe, that's a good boy.*

"Who is that?" he asked, spotting the same monk he and Dina saw in the library.

"Oh not him again. He never seems to be far from the three of us." Maggie started packing up her paints and brushes. "Would you mind very much walking me back? That man makes me nervous."

"I heard he arrived with a few others." Maybe he should go over and confront the guy. But what would he say–hey Mac, stop looking at these pretty young girls or I'll punch your lights out? Or he could ask the guy if he'd been following the girls and of course he'd deny it. Best to just keep an eye on him.

"I only saw them once," Maggie said, casting a disapproving look in the monk's direction. "There are four of them. My sister complained to Father Richard about that one, though. I get the impression they're going to be asked to leave soon."

"Your sister?" For the first time he remembered the Angel's voice from the day of the accident. Respite. Glorious respite. But he was slipping off the saddle.

"Yes. My sister, Carol Ann. She would love your cap. The logo has her initials on it. And the angel wings—she got me into angels. I sometimes paint them."

CAP! Of course. The angel wings logo. Pages was the name of the store. Carol Ann Page. His head swam with questions. Questions for everybody.

"Joe? Is anything wrong?"

"Nothing's wrong."

If he sprouted wings he couldn't get off the grounds fast enough. He needed a lengthy alcohol-induced break. Better to meet the comely Carol Ann in a calmer frame of mind. And he didn't need his Angel telling him it would be a heavy. Nope, his Angel wouldn't be back until 1996. Yeah, a brief respite. He could slam down a few beers, turn his thoughts toward The Kentucky Derby and mastering those blow notes on *Long Train Runnin.* Maybe he could even practice being twenty again. For a few hours he could forget these last weeks and 1996.

After seeing Maggie to her door, he called for a cab. He had no idea what was in town and at this point he didn't really care. The cabby, whose English wasn't as bad as he pretended, dropped him off at the diviest looking bar he'd seen since he went slumming in Boston last year. A green neon sign flashed 'Patsy's', only the bulbs behind the *t* and *s* had blown, so it read, **Pa y's.**

"It's the Hilton, man. Thanks," he said, throwing a sawbuck in the driver's lap.

The inside was darker than he preferred and it smelled of stale draught beer. The place was also hopping for a late Sunday afternoon. He took a seat at the bar and ordered a Budweiser from Patsy, who happened to be the two hundred and fifty pound owner-bartender with a boxer's nose and a diamond pinkie ring blinding the patrons. Business must be good.

When Patsy picked up on his Boston accent they got to talking, mostly trivial bobble which felt darn terrific. Just a few hours—*I'm taking a few hours to mace my brain.* The affirmation worked. Once he'd polished off a bucket of suicide wings, he accepted an invitation to join a few of the regulars in a dart game.

He laughed when one fellow exposed his chest, pointing with pride to a pinprick of a scar near his heart, the result of a wayward dart. After he'd had a heart tattooed around it, his buddies nicknamed him Dart In The Heart. And Dart In The Heart had a girlfriend, a bleached blonde by the name of Candy Cane. No shit, the guys told him. This was really her name.

Lady luck was good to him. As it happened he won more than he lost and suddenly, beers with tequila chasers mysteriously appeared. They also disappeared just as mysteriously, along with three more hours on the clock. He was having himself a good time until his final trip to the men's room.

After that the evening fell into the crapper.

If he was completely whaled he still couldn't have missed the sign, scrawled with black magic marker in two-inch letters right over the urinal. He consoled himself with the thought that the name was common in Quebec. But he didn't stay consoled for long because forty minutes ago the wall was blank.

In capital lettering, the perv wrote Alain's name twice, one on top of the other. Nothing wrong with the top one. The second, however, was sobering. Someone had slashed a stroke through the first *A* in his name, replacing it with an *S*, making it read S L A I N. Imagination jacked, he got himself to a phone in a hurry. After dialing, the five or six rings before pick-up grated something fierce on his already sensitized nerves.

Come on. Come on. It's a school night, dammit.

"*Allô, oui?*" the young voice answered.

"Alain? Alain! How are you, bud?"

"Joe. Fine, Joe, except I really stink from being with the animals all day. Mom's makin' me take a bath."

"Good. Listen, I just called to say goodnight and I'll see you tomorrow. Is your mother still picking you up after school?"

"Yeah."

"Great. Okay then. G'night, bud."

Though he was a mess of gratitude and jumbled thoughts, his little escape was over. Reality was back. Hullo, Joe. Welcome home. After Dart In The Heart failed to talk him into another game, he figured the best thing to do was return to the cabin. He could fight off the gloom much better by the lake. The fridge had a few beers left in it, so maybe he could recapture the mood. Strangely, he was as anxious to get back as he had been to leave.

More and more, he'd come to trust his feelings, especially the disturbing ones. No doubt being around Alain was doing that, or Marianlake, or the little bit of spiritual reading he'd done so far.

There was a note taped to the fridge—in the same two-inch lettering, in black magic marker, undoubtedly written by the same creative psycho at Patsy's Bar.

Hi, Joe.

Please get your ass out of Trois Rivieres. The kid is dead soon anyway. You will be too if you stick around. Enjoy the rest of your evening.

5. Bed of Seeds

"So the police said they were going straight to Patsy's?" Father Richard asked him early morning in the rectory office. He sounded like a lunatic with the 911 operator last night.

"Yes. They wanted to compare it to the graffiti on the wall in the men's room—" The Tylenols hadn't helped. He would have done better to knock himself out with a blunt object and sleep the hangover away. It was reckless and stupid of him to get blasted. Alain was in his care now. "--and also ask around. Maybe somebody saw something."

"Seems you had quite the night," Sister Elizabeth said, louder than he needed to hear. "You think we'll eventually meet under cheerier circumstances?"

He smiled back at her and even that hurt. "As long as things like this really don't happen in threes, Sister. I'm sorry we didn't get the chance to talk yesterday. Disturbances."

"No apologies," she said, glancing at Father Richard, "been a little disturbed myself. Father, would you like to speak privately with Joe?"

"Won't be necessary. Make yourself comfortable, Joe. Any progress with that reading list?"

Imitating Alain's favorite gesture, he puffed the air out of his cheeks. "Not a whole bunch, Father."

All was silent in the rectory while Father Richard tapped his steepled fingers.

"Okay, Joe, here it is," he said. "The danger around Alain is escalating. And unless these people are caught, we all feel it's best Alain get as far away from Trois-Riviéres as possible, the sooner the better. When I say *we all,* I am of course including his parents and Father Andre. You've known all along that this was coming, Joe. Keep the child safe, remember?"

"I know, Father. But ... when?"

"As soon as things can be arranged—discreetly. Tracy is expecting another child this spring so Claude can't and won't leave her. The doctors cautioned against her having the baby. I won't get into that. Of course you're destined to accompany Alain. That, too, is obvious. But you're still only twenty years old, Joe. There will be too many questions asked by people on your travels. Bottom line is you'll need a chaperone. I know. Think of it more like an assistant." He raised a brow at Sister Elizabeth.

"I guess this is where I come in," she said.

"You're my chaperone?" He stood and opened his mouth, but no words came out. Women seemed to be his lot in life. He was going to be ambushed by women. But she was a nun. "But you're a nun."

"True," she said, kindly gesturing him back to his chair. "But I won't be traveling as a nun. I'm your new aunty. Fortunately, Alain and I have the same coloring. We can say you take after the other side of the family. We'll work out all those details later. And you'll need an accountant, a secretary, a tutor for Alain, a cook–although you can help with that."

"Oh, God," he said. "But you're a woman. And a nun. How can I be myself around you?"

"You'll make the adjustment," Father Richard deadpanned. "I have complete faith in you."

"Father, you said as soon as things can be arranged. How long?"

"Probably sometime around mid-November. Sister Elizabeth returns to New York City a week from today, November 2nd. She was going to spend this weekend in Quebec City, but plans went awry and most of the girls are behind in their work, anyway. So they all took a vote and opted out for the extra few days here to complete their projects."

"Does Alain know?" he asked. What a strange thing, this concept of time.

"His parents are telling him today. Father Andre flew to New York City last night in search of a place for you. That's the perfect town to get lost in and Sister Elizabeth was born there. By the way, the Vatican is footing the bill for this. We're blessed having Father Andre who knows people in high places. Normally they'd investigate at length, which they have done to some degree but Father's kept them informed from day one, so you needn't dip into your savings. You'll need that money when you're older, when this mission is a memory. By the way, your destination is top secret, Joe. I can't stress the importance enough. This means you can't tell your family. I'm sorry."

"You really believe Alain is in this much danger that he has to leave his home, everything?"

"Yes. Remember the document's contents? The Messenger said that 'shortly after his tenth birthday, his identity will be discovered by a small group of evil men.' I'm certain they're in Trois-Riviéres. Somewhere. We have to get Alain out of here."

"Have you seen the document, Father Richard?" he asked, hoping that didn't sound like he doubted its existence. He hated putting Father Richard on the spot, but geez, he would love to see the thing.

"No, Joe. I haven't. It's in Paris. Father Andre never did bring it to Marianlake when he came here in '71. That was wise, I think. Don't you?"

He didn't answer. And the normally talkative Sister Elizabeth had no comment.

With *The Passion* tucked under his arm, he left the rectory and crossed the courtyard toward the seminary. He had intended to sit and read in front of Mary's statue, but it was a bit too nippy for him. One week today was All Souls Day, November 2nd. He looked up at the statue. November 2nd would be a good day to get a Rosary said for Willie. Maybe Sister Elizabeth could say it, or was it Aunty Elizabeth now?

The wind stung his ears, especially irritating considering the shape his head was in. For Alain's sake, he hoped it would be warmer on Halloween. At least Alain had changed his mind, choosing to go as *Yoda* rather than *Luke Skywalker*. Originally it had been the other way around, until he convinced Alain that at six feet, he'd make a silly-looking Yoda. Once his giggles subsided, Alain saw the logic.

He entered the seminary, passing two classes in session as he headed toward the library. Father Richard was teaching one of them and Joe waved solemnly. His mood was low again. As a matter of fact, every time he got near this place it depressed him. It had nothing to do with pounding too many back last night, or the writing over the urinal at Patsy's or the note stuck to the fridge. It was this place, this old gloomy building. There was also that subtle sweet smell again, not quite as pungent as the cabin, yet something derivative. Rosa once told him that if alliteration came easily in a sentence, it meant demons were circling. Sickening sweet smell.

He lasted all of thirty minutes in the library since the smell was making him queasy. This wasn't a good day to concentrate on significant spiritual study. Too much on the brain. He'd stick to his original plan to return to the cabin, grab a warmer jacket and read outside. Fresh air was the best thing right now. Father Richard would be dismissing his last class for lunch any moment, so it was the perfect time to ask him the question slipping his mind since that first day.

"Hi, Father. Me again," he said, deeking his head inside the classroom door. "I got a question if you got a minute?"

"Sure, Joe, come on in. How are you? It's been ages."

A good man, Father Richard. He slid into the front desk beside the window, on which a student had etched,

Beware excess. Too much study impairs brain.

"Father, I keep remembering something odd you said about Marianlake the day I arrived. But we keep getting sidetracked. This place is full of distractions."

"Know what you mean. What was it I said that struck you as odd?"

He wanted to ask him if he noticed the smell. No, then they'd get sidetracked all over again. "You said that Marianlake was a wonder of tranquil beauty—on the outside. What did you mean by that?"

The priest seemed to carefully consider his words before speaking. "Just the word *monastery* seems synonymous with peace and tranquility, but this is not so. Decisions are made within these walls. Often they are the wrong decisions which bring heartbreak. You can see that by observing the number of empty cells in the dorm. Many who come don't belong here, Joe."

"Oh," he said, somewhat disappointed. "I interpreted your comment in an entirely different way."

"How was that?"

He hung his fingers on the neckline of his sweatshirt. "Probably seen too many movies. I took it to mean hauntings, spirits, that kind of thing."

"That's not unusual," Richard said casually, opening the window a crack. "Most monasteries have a great deal of spiritual power. Often there are entities of one kind or another disturbing them."

"Like the other day in the cabin?"

"Well, remember I wasn't there, though Andre and Elizabeth believe it was an entity."

The direct approach always worked best. "Father, have you had any reports of evil spirits here in the monastery?"

"Yes," he said, flatly. "Reported by those who are sensitive in nature, like yourself. Have you intuited anything else, Joe?"

He closed his eyes and whistled softly, rocking back and forth as though in a trance.

Father Richard laughed. "Guess you have. Tell me."

"Something's happening now, Father. Do you smell anything?"

"Yes. And I thought it was just me. Every year around this time, it comes and goes. I can't source the smell. One day last fall I went around sticking my nose in every potted plant in the monastery and rectory. Even the church. Nothing. Then Father Andre told me what happened in your cabin the other day. When he described the smell, I made the connection. But what we have here is a mere particle of matter in comparison, yes?"

He rounded his eyes. "Every year around this time, you said?"

"Makes sense, Joe, when you consider what's ahead. Let's go to the farthest point then move backward. A week today, next Monday, we have All Souls Day, when we pray for the holy souls in Purgatory. The day prior to that, on the Sunday, is All Saints Day, which is also known as Hallowmas, the Feast of All Saints. And hallow means to make holy, to consecrate. Now we step back one more day to the 31st - Halloween.

"Sadly, Halloween is the greatest hit and All Souls and All Saints Days are the flipside of the record. And happily, November 1st and 2nd repair most of the damage done on the 31st when demons are exceptionally destructive. It's a contest, Joe. During this period, they cleverly entrap souls by diversion to prevent them from praying for lost souls whose salvation lies in the hands of the saints and the human race. And who does the human race pray to at this time - they pray to God and all His saints."

"So you're not freaked by all the evil lurking in the shadows around here, Father?"

"Unnerved at times, certainly. But freaked? No. How could I be? If I was, I should seriously question my faith. Where there's good, there's always evil, remember? So weigh one against the other, bearing in mind that this is a monastery filled with those who practice the faith. To evil entities, we're the ultimate challenge, aren't we?"

"Guess so. But I don't need any more distractions, Father. I have to focus on Alain. That's my job, right? Got a dark angel with cabin fever after me and it was Alain who snuffed it out for us. How I don't know and couldn't process the information if I did know. But—"

"Think I know what you're getting at." Father Richard bookmarked a page and sat in the desk beside him. "Don't worry, Joe, we're right behind you. No matter where you or Alain go, we've got you covered. Even if all hell breaks loose and no pun intended. So what is it? You think some trouble is ahead?"

"I don't know, Father. I just have the urge to give my grandmother a call. We have this empathy thing going and she's always warned me to watch my spiritual back this time of year."

The lake looked a little too ripply so he chose to walk around it this time. Glancing ahead to the dock, he saw that Maggie took him up on his offer. But she wasn't alone. Curled up on the deckchair with her nose in a book, was the other one. The one with the mile-long legs. The snakes in his head slithered down to his belly. Had to be her. *Hmm. Carol Ann.* The last of the cast. That call to Mexico City could wait.

"Hi," he waved, approaching them on the dock. "Aren't you girls cold out here?"

"Used to working outside," Maggie said. This time she had a big splotch of orange on her chin. "Hi, Joe. This is my sister, Carol Ann. Carol Ann, this is Joe."

"Hi," they both said at the same time.

"Stereo," Maggie chuckled.

"I've been hearing all kinds of nice things about you," Carol Ann said, unfolding her legs and stretching them out. Thanks for walking my sister back yesterday."

"You're welcome." She had strawberry blonde hair. And these really light brown eyes with amber flecks. "It was my pleasure." He never used phrases like that. She had the tiniest little freckled nose.

"Dina's been running around singing your praises," Carol Ann said. "Literally."

Maggie chuckled again.

"That's quite the voice she has," he said. She was tapping her feet together. Uh-oh.

"True. But her voice won't help with the art project, though."

"Well, the voice out-ranks the project, I guess."

Carol Ann shifted in the deckchair, crossing her legs again. "It's not the voice she's going to be graded on next month."

"A course of action might be to arrange a course in effective study. Shall I start interviewing tutors?"

"Would anyone like a Dr. Pepper?" Maggie offered. "It's still cold."

"Sure, if you can convince her to put Juilliard aside for the moment."

"Is the problem me or too many Dr. Peppers?"

Carol Ann got off the deckchair and clenched a fist on her hip. "What right have you to give career advice to somebody you don't even know? Who do you think you are, Henry Higgins? You don't even look a second over twenty-five. Dina's been having major problems with this course. This project is her last chance for a pass. Now you come along and plunk her in the Land of Oz as she puts it. She's very impressionable."

"Last call for the Dr. Pepper," Maggie said.

"I can tell you're such a wonderful friend to Dina." What a beautiful pain she was. "So wonderful in fact that you've chosen to hang out here on the dock with your sister when you could be helping your friend with her art project, or at least, motivating her. You're right. I don't know her. But you do. So much for priorities."

Forgetting to say goodbye to Maggie, he walked off the dock, seething.

Well, she was certainly dazzled by his charm. Right. He had no time for girls now anyway. As to the question of priorities, he was overwhelmed with his own. He wouldn't think about her. He would try to forget that the first time he saw her she was maybe fifteen years older and he didn't want to stop talking to her, that Willie was there, that they were in Angelfish Cove, that magical place Alain wanted to see one day.

Too annoyed to return to the cabin for the warmer jacket, he zipped on down to the barn, which he'd wanted to check out since his arrival. What was it about this place? Peaceful, Father Richard said. Yeah well, he didn't like the sound of those fidgety hooves inside. It was a beautiful day, too early for the horses to be in, all two of them. Someone was with them.

"Hello," he called in. "Anybody home?"

"Just me," the familiar voice answered from behind the far stall.

"Dina? What're you doing over there?"

"Waiting for Misty and Jake to cooperate," she said, groaning theatrically. "I was considering them as models for my art project since they're always grazing behind the cemetery. But these guys have other things on their mind today."

"I don't get it."

"There's something wrong with them, Joe. I can't get them out and they're really nervous. Do you think we should call the vet?"

He reached out his hand in an effort to calm the older mare and she stomped the ground so hard, she got the other one going. Something was spooking these horses.

"Have they been out at all today?" he asked.

"No. And that's really strange, don't you think? They're obviously not themselves."

"Who is?"

"What?"

"Nothing. I think you should probably let them be for a while, Dina. They'll be ... did you hear that?" Before she could answer, he rushed out in back of the stable and returned a few seconds later. "Thought I heard sniffling or something. Sorry, hearing things. Leave the horses here and *I'll* go out to pasture."

"Uh huh. Okay then. Maybe you're right. I'll leave 'em alone and check on 'em later."

"You'd better get cracking on that project."

"How's your reading list coming along?" she asked, grinning like a third baseman after the tag.

"Touché," he said. "You go do your thing. I'll go do mine. And we'll compare progress reports tomorrow."

'Don't you know I have the power to save you or have you crucified!' Pilate had warned Him. Joe bookmarked the page and picked up the phone. He had to talk to them, especially Rosa, whose vibe could kick butt all the way from Mexico City.

He began with one of the handful of words he knew in Spanish, "*Si,*" he said to a deep voice two minutes later. "*Donde es,* Rosa Canites, *per favor?*"

It worked, whatever he said. He distinctly heard Rosa's bracelets clanking on the way to the phone. "Joe? Tell me it's you," Rosa said.

"Okay I'll tell ya," he chuckled, happy to hear her voice. "How are you? How's Beata? I miss you guys. Did you get my letter?"

"Yes I did. That's quite a little boy. Too bad Beata's out walking. She'd love to talk to you. Anyway this is long distance. You're still at the monastery in Canada, aren't you?"

"Yeah, at least until—"

"Joe, every morning and night when I pray for you, for the past week now, there's this odor. Not pleasant. That's a warning, Joe. Something evil. Listen to me. I want you to wear the Scapular I tucked in your shaving kit. I want you to wear it on Halloween. Really, you should be wearing it all the time. Do you hear?"

"I will," he said. There was no point in telling her that things weren't smelling too healthy at his end, either.

"And make sure Alain is wearing a Scapular, too."

He asked her to hang on to answer an enthusiastic knock at the door. Unable to locate his tongue when he saw Carol Ann standing there in those tight jeans and denim jacket, he simply gestured for her to enter. He returned to the phone, eyes glued to Carol Ann.

"Sorry, R, uh, a friend just stopped by. Don't worry. I'll call you Saturday afternoon."

"And Sunday morning. After Halloween. There's something malicious there, Joe. You can't really talk anymore now, can you?"

"No."

"We'll talk again during the week."

"Hug Beata for me. How is she really?" He watched as Carol Ann moved about the room looking at things, pretending to ignore him and his conversation.

"She taking pills, Joe."

He felt Rosa's sadness.

"But I don't wanna talk about that now," she said. "You go visit with your company. I love you. Be very very careful."

He told her he loved her too, and hung up. "My grandmother," he mentioned to Carol Ann, in case she was interested.

"This isn't easy for me," she said, drawing an extra breath. "But I'm here to apologize for what I said on the dock. You didn't deserve that."

He wondered how a girl eighteen or nineteen could look this elegant in blue jeans. "Forget it. It was nice of you to come and tell me."

"You know, we've only heard Dina hum and sing a little when she didn't think we were listening. But we never guessed ... I don't know how you managed it, and on the lake with everybody around her, listening."

"This place tends to hold the mirror to the soul. You get to see your needs up close."

Carol Ann shook her head, giving him a probing look. "How old are you, really? Forty? Sixty? Is this Shangri La?"

"Right now it is."

"You're really confident around women, aren't you?"

Yeah right, a regular Byron. "I am around girls."

"What's that mean?"

"It means I'm less confident around women."

"But you're comfortable with me because I'm just a girl, so I make you feel confident. Gee, it must be fun to play Father Superior."

He moved a few steps closer and she retreated. Interesting. She was a little afraid of him. For different reasons, he was a lot afraid of her. Oh God, she could be too serious a distraction. "Why are you so determined to twist everything I say? I have my faults, sure, but superiority is not in my character profile."

"So you're saying you're no different?"

"I didn't say not different, I said not superior. There were and are controlling factors in my life, so my childhood slipped away from me. Are we going somewhere with this?"

"I don't know anymore," Carol Ann said, skittish. "I'll take notes and bring it up at our next meeting. I have to go."

"Wait, Carol Ann." He placed his hand gently on her forearm and stopped her at the door. "Why do you want to stay mad at me?"

"Because," she began, turning her face away from his, looking deliciously vulnerable. "You make me feel like a woman in a little girl's head. And I don't like it much. Guess I don't like you much."

Before he could speak, she had halfway disappeared past the trees on the path. Such a hurry. Why did she bother to come here and apologize if she didn't like him so much? No. This conversation was not over. If he rowed across the lake he could beat her to the other side. Actually, forget the oars. To be certain, he'd crank on the motor. No contest, even against those gorgeous wings she had disguised as legs.

Two minutes later, feeling damp and foolish, he stood in the middle of the road with his arms folded, patiently waiting for her to catch up. If she wanted to get by him, she'd have to climb over him.

"I'm too mystified to let this go," he told her, wiping lake-spray from his face. "So I apologize. I don't know what I did to make you dislike me but I apologize anyway."

"Don't," she said, looking contrite. "I shouldn't have—"

"Please," he warned in fun, "let's not get into trouble again. There's a good chance I might end up in the water next time. Vespers are almost over now which means it's getting close to dinner. Also explains why it's so quiet around here. If you can get away for a couple hours, I mean if you'd like, I know where we can get the greatest wings. Only a ten-minute cab ride from the grounds."

"Sure, okay," she said, no hesitating. "On one condition."

"What's that?"

"I ask a lot of questions. You think you can hack it?"

"No wing-dinging me if you don't like my answers?"

"Deal. I'll go tell Sister Elizabeth."

"I'll call us a cab."

By the time they got to Patsy's, she knew about the loss of his parents, Willie's death, his course outline at Amherst

U, the name of the hotel he already had booked for the Kentucky Derby next May, tai chi and his favorite sandwich—roast beef and Swiss cheese on dark rye. And clams. He once shucked four plates in an hour. Of course, everything else, which was his reason for being here, had to remain top secret. He did mention the bond he had formed with Alain and that was all. He wanted to know everything he could about her, but she wasn't exactly giving him the opportunity to ask questions.

"Why do they call him *Dart in The Heart*?" Carol Ann asked, after Dart introduced himself and left.

He shrugged. "He got a dart in the heart one time when he was having a game."

"Silly question," she laughed. "What are Vespers?"

"Vespers is the name for the prayers priests say daily between four and six p.m."

"Have you ever thought of becoming a priest?"

"No," he said, grinning. What a great detective she'd make. Or reporter. Then, he knew otherwise.

"Out of curiosity, how does one get to be a priest?"

"Well, a guy goes to his parish priest who fills him in on the criterion. He needs a baptismal certificate, reference letters and most important, a university Bachelor's degree. Then he has to pass a medical exam. Once this is over, he meets with the seminary rector. If he's accepted as a candidate, he begins to study for the priesthood, which takes about seven years."

"Father Georges is the rector at Marianlake, isn't he?"

"Right. Father Andre Georges. And Father Vaux is the Dean of Studies. Both of them are real scholars. A string of letters after their names."

"We've all heard bits and pieces of their classes. What subjects do they teach?"

He accidentally brushed his leg against hers under the table and liked that she kept hers where it was. "They teach many subjects. Scripture, Christology, Sacraments, the Trinity. Minimum to maximum knowledge of psychology. Let me see, uh, Canon law, Bioethics. They also have to learn how to preach and run a parish. Administration. All that fun stuff. I learned a lot about them when I did odd jobs at our parish back in Medford."

"Excuse me. You said *bio epics*?"

"Bioethics," he said, smiling. What a curious little nose for news she had. "A study into the ethics of biological and medical research. Do you know what the word seminary means?"

She had been staring at him. After a few seconds, she shook her head. "Guess I'm more into history," she said, trying to hide her embarrassment.

His nerve endings tingled. *Oh no*. "It means bed of seeds."

They experienced some awkward silence after that, during which time Carol Ann sipped and re-sipped her Dr. Pepper. He rapped a set of knuckles on the table in a concentrated effort to make them sound inaudible. Their eyes kept missing each other's. Below the table, there was a whole other conversation taking place. He rubbed his foot against her ankle accidentally on purpose. When he stopped, she responded in kind.

"How is it you sound so much older than you are?" she asked, shyly casting her eyes downward when he looked at her. "I mean, in your interests, the way you see people, your vocabulary, everything?"

"I've spent a lot of time reading. Not so much fiction. More psychology and inspirational. And I love great music, except in the car." He patted his jacket pocket. "Never go anywhere without my harmonica. I can't think of a time in my life when music was not around me, not profoundly affecting me somehow. There was always music in the background while I was reading. We lived in a quiet house. Willie and I tossed records and books back and forth for years. In Angelfish Cove, we walked into this great bookstore ..."

"Don't stop. Tell me. Where's Angelfish Cove?"

"In Massachusetts, a few miles off the Cape. Getting hungry?"

She said she wasn't hungry yet and neither was he. He didn't want to eat. What he wanted was to tell her all about Angelfish Cove, but that was off limits, which meant 'CAP' was off limits. Was Carol Ann off limits, too? He didn't want her to be. He hadn't felt this comfortable talking on a date since Norma. Someone stuck a quarter in the jukebox and out popped a tune by Styx called *Babe*. So they danced on a floor that had room for maybe six people. It concerned him how much he wanted to know what she was thinking. He had about a week left in Trois-Rivierés and so did she. Frustrating. They were both going to New York and he couldn't even tell her that much.

Looking down at her face, he pulled her closer. The five adorable freckles on the bridge of her nose resembled a tiny snowflake. For the first time since he was old enough to have these feelings, he wasn't thinking about sex. He was thinking about making love.

"I'm glad you're not mad at me anymore," he said, happily conscious of the dreamy way she was looking at him.

Carol Ann's lower lip trembled. "I don't know what to say. Guess it's this song. Reminds me that we leave a week today."

"I'm good at writing," he said.

She put her face closer to his.

"I couldn't stop at one," he whispered. The song was over and soon this evening would be.

He introduced Carol Ann to Patsy when he set down their food.

"Did the cops get back in touch with you?" Patsy asked, no doubt assuming Carol Ann knew all about it.

"No not yet. So I don't know what they've learned. Did you see anyone in here last night you didn't know, Patsy, aside from me?"

"No. But we were pretty busy, Joe, and I was stuck behind the bar most of the night. If any strangers had a drink, I didn't see the cash, man. So I didn't see the stranger. I think the guy musta come in just to draw on my headroom wall. Hear you had another note waiting for you."

"So much for a discreet inquiry."

"Got a cousin on the force," Patsy said.

When Carol Ann asked what was happening, Patsy shot him an apologetic look and made himself scarce. Guessing she was preparing to ask the first question from her list of twenty, he told her as much as he could which wasn't much at all. The horse. The dog. The notes. That was about it.

"But why, though?" she asked, insatiably curious. "Everyone's asking *what* and *when*. They know *where* and of course *who*. So don't you find it odd that they don't have a list of possible *why's*?"

"I'm sure they're not telling as much as they know," he said, admiring her resolve.

Carol Ann leaned forward and twisted an invisible moustache. "This *eez mysteree* big," she said in a French accent. Lord, if she was any cuter he couldn't stand it. "What do *yeu* think this is all about?"

"Your guess is as good as mine, Inspector. I say Alain saw or heard something he wasn't supposed to and doesn't know the significance." Judging from the fake smile, she wasn't buying it. "Let's talk about something else. About you."

"Not much to talk about, really," she said, between fries. "I'm going to try to get into Smith next year if I can pass the boards, which I should be able to. I skipped into thirteen, which hopefully, will impress them. That's how Maggie and I came to be in the same grade. She's actually a year older. And that's about it. Shooting for a major in history."

"What are you going to do with it?"

"Shape young minds and teach, probably. Or maybe something in communications. Not sure yet. Joe? Does your heart belong to anyone?"

It amazed him how casually she asked the question. "No. Does yours?"

"No."

The pretense at sophisticated poise disappeared when she caught him staring. Done with the food, she fidgeted with her hands. It wasn't hard to tell where her heart was, from his side of the table. It seemed to hang in midair between them and it had a big question mark on it. If she was offering, he'd take it. He wanted to hold her and say sappy stuff.

Shortly after eleven, the cabbie dropped them off at the gatehouse, which also doubled as Marianlake's souvenir shop. It surprised Carol Ann to find the door unlocked.

"There are only two locked doors at Marianlake," he explained, "the gates after six. And the sacristy." He wrote a brief note, attached a five-dollar bill and left it beside the cash register. "Something I have to pick up for Alain. He probably has a pile of these already. But still, you never know."

"What's that?"

"This," he said, showing her the Scapular medal made of brown cloth, "is worn as a sign of love and devotion to the Mother of God. Remind me to get it blessed."

He turned off the light and saw Carol Ann leaning in the doorway waiting for him. The moonlight had accented her strawberry blonde hair with bands of soft pink. There was an aura around her. Sky blue at first, then red and more red. Blue for love. Red for passion. And she knew when not to speak. Finally, he had someone he could be happy with in the silences.

He walked over to her and rubbed his lips gently around hers, tasting vanilla with his tongue. Barely touching her, he caressed her face and neck with the back of his hand. He kissed her forehead, massaged her ears with his lips, and then he held her. And held her.

Carol Ann tightened her arms around his neck and kissed him feverishly, pressing herself hard against him. She flexed her fingers back and forth along the ripple of muscles on his shoulders, locking herself into his strength. Soon he would have to stop kissing her this way. God, why did he have to?

Why? Because you have to leave her soon, Joe. Haven't you messed up enough women?

Seeing the image of Willie in that tub again was like squeezing your eyes shut during the scariest scene in a horror movie, which never worked because you always ended up peeking through the hand covering your face. Gently, he pushed her away.

"What is it, Joe?"

"I ... we should be getting back. Sister Elizabeth will be after me with her ruler."

Blast. Now he went and hurt her. His stomach clenched as he guided her down the five slippery steps covered in wet leaves. The third step sloped in the middle and just his dumb luck that she slipped and he had to catch her.

Carol Ann grabbed onto him. "Joe, hold me. I'm afraid some horrible thing is going to snatch you away. This is ... I don't know how to feel this way. I don't know."

"Carol Ann," he whispered, kissing her. He loved saying her name. "Carol Ann. I think we're both feeling the same way." He took her hand. "That's why I'd better get you back. Don't you think so too, Inspector?"

She ran her thumb along his hand. "Are you being noble because I'm a good girl and you respect me or because we're on hallowed ground and it wouldn't feel right? Or, maybe it's neither and you've taken this secret vow of chastity. Yep, I bet that's it."

"Amazing," he teased, "How did you know? Seems I cannot keep secrets on this hallowed ground."

"Not with Carol Ann Page on the force," she laughed then squinted at something off in the distance. "Joe, the lights in the barn are on. They don't usually leave them on at night, do they?"

"No. I'll go have a look. We'll say goodnight here then."

"No we won't. Forget it. I'm going in there with you."

"Do you always intend to be this difficult? Is this what I'm in for?"

She kissed him playfully on the cheek. "Yes, but you'll get used to it pretty quick. I promise."

As they approached the barn, remembering how weird the horses had acted this afternoon, he called in for the second time today. No answer. He motioned for Carol Ann to stay near the door, then went in and nosed around. Obviously the horses' dispositions hadn't improved, and their coats looked about as tangled as their nerves. He wanted to get Carol Ann away from here given that the last person in here wanted the same thing and left in a hurry, forgetting the lights. The scent in the air changed suddenly. He switched off the lights and pulled Carol Ann into his arms. Holding her seemed to divert him from the creepy sensation of being watched.

"This is the second dark doorway we've stood in tonight," he said, thinking how every eerie occurrence today had come in pairs. This afternoon he heard what sounded like a sniffle. Now it was a cough.

"All right, that's it!" he shouted, turning the lights back on. Who's in here!"

"It's me, Joe."

Carol Ann walked over to a hidden nook beside the saddle bench and found a groggy Dina lying on the hay, covered up to her chin with a horse blanket. "Dina, what are you doing here?" she asked in a tone one would use on a five-year-old.

While Dina explained, he tried to source the familiar smell coming from nowhere and everywhere. Sickeningly sweet. The girls were still talking and hadn't noticed. Why was that? Something was different about it, something in the smell tainted by synthetics. Of human hands. Menthol and lemons. Rosa was right as usual. There was a malicious presence here at Marianlake. Immortal and mortal evil had joined forces. Dark angels preyed.

"What's wrong, Joe?" Carol Ann asked after Dina had gone inside the dormitory.

"Dina, she's like a little girl, isn't she?"

"Very much. One of the things we love about her. What is it?"

He felt sick, nauseous. The entity had followed him from the barn and she still could not smell it. Yet Dina had noticed the lemony menthol but not the other. Carol Ann noticed neither. Maybe it was nothing more than what Dina said. Acute sense of smell. All those years of sniffing out ingredients in the spaghetti sauce.

"I'll see you tomorrow," he said, tracing his finger along Carol Ann's lips. "Everything's fine, don't worry. You better go in."

He couldn't go back to the cabin. What did he think he was doing? He couldn't get involved now. He was taking off in a week and probably wouldn't see Carol Ann again for years. Memories stabbed at his core.

Because he had feelings for her, she might get hurt now.

No, that couldn't be because he considered that at Patsy's while they were playing footsies under the table. She was going to have a bookstore named 'Pages' in the '90s. Nothing was going to hurt Carol Ann. She would be absolutely perfect and that's all there was to it.

He returned to the barn and calmed the horses. He brushed them down, talked to them, and played a little harmonica for them. Every once in awhile, a vague lemony scent wafted under his nostrils. Fortunately it wasn't that revolting 'entity smell' that sickened him earlier. This was quite pleasant, probably lemon balm used to treat thyroid or depression. Sure, that was it. These horses were jumpy. A bit of lemon balm tossed in the water trough would fix 'em right up. Already they felt better and it couldn't be his harmonica playing. Alain's father must have come in today and lemon-balmed them.

On the walk back to his cabin the nauseating sweetness caught up with him again, thick and treacle sweet. The *thing* moaned with pleasure in his ear and he hunched at the side of the road and vomited. When it moaned again, he reached into his coat and squeezed Alain's Scapular. The *thing* stopped. Why was it following him? Who was it after? Life could change on a dime. So fast—on one thin dime. He had to grab Alain and get the hell out of here.

At the rear entrance of the monastery, the wind rustled a tiny piece of paper scented with menthol and lemon below Dina Amodeo's second-floor window.

∞∞∞

Five extremely busy days passed at Marianlake. With the exception of Dina, Sister Elizabeth's class completed their projects. Dina preferred to keep a close eye on the horses and so chose to complete her project in the barn. No amount of coaxing, bribery or promise of straight A's could lure her outdoors. After a lengthy examination, Claude Duprielle found nothing wrong with them. And no, he told Joe, he hadn't given them a lemon balm or any essential oils, though it wasn't a bad idea.

Father Andre returned from New York holding the key to Joe's future home in a modest section of Long Island. Each day's breakfast meeting continued through lunch as they drafted their assignments. Finally all arrangements had been made. They were leaving in one week. Carol Ann and company were leaving in two days, allowing Elizabeth ample time to escort the girls back and then return for Alain and Joe. Her girls had no idea she would not be around to grade their projects and her superiors thought it might be wiser if they said her goodbyes for her, *following* her departure. Reluctantly, she agreed.

Given the emotional aftermath of seeing Alain's things packed away in three suitcases, the Duprielles convinced themselves to sell the business, then secretly join Alain and share in this incipient drama as soon as the baby was old enough to travel. Father Richard stopped Father Andre from telling the couple this was a pipe dream. When they were ready, Providence would help them accept the reality of the situation.

Joe didn't get too far down that reading list. Instead he spent every available moment with Carol Ann. His heart ached to tell her the truth. Although she knew they had to say goodbye for a while, she had no idea how *long* a while, no idea that she would be unable to contact him. When Alain let it slip that soon they'd be going far away to have adventures, he made a near-perfect recovery. Still, Carol Ann was suspicious. The guilt hurt him more than the secrecy.

Their feelings for each other were obvious to everyone, particularly Sister Elizabeth who realized that this passion might one day lead to danger. And their decision to wait before making love was torture for them. They would become lovers when there was no rush to say goodbye. Over the Christmas holidays they could brainstorm for their future. This romantic notion belonged solely to Carol Ann.

Joe knew the fairy tale had a different ending. Three times he'd begun writing a letter to her, trying to explain why they would have no Christmas together. All three attempts ended up in the fireplace. That inner voice he'd grown to trust told him to finish the letter. There wasn't much time left. On this Halloween eve, Marianlake Dominican Monastery was rapt with secrets.

6. DaRk AnGeLs PrEy

There had been no TANGIBLE entity assaults since that night on the road. This allayed two percent of his jitters since the thing's shadow on all of Marianlake had seeped into his pores. The horses were still jumpy. The panoramic fall color disappeared overnight. Everyone seemed infested with dark thoughts. The lake had turned muddy and three in the loon family lay dead in the reeds with no apparent cause.

Rosa was still feeling the *malicious presence* in Mexico City. Alain, at home dressing for the big night, felt it too. Claude told him over the phone that his son was in some kind of 'kingdom come' and this was the best English translation he could offer.

"Is he wearing the Scapular?" he asked, recalling how spiritually significant this was to Rosa.

"Yes," Claude said. "Since you gave it to him last Tuesday. Twice it ended up in the bathtub with him. Tracy had to take the hairdryer to it."

Conversation was strained around the Duprielle dinner table. He felt sorry for Tracy and Claude. A nun and a young guy they barely knew were taking off with their firstborn in a week and Father Andre hadn't yet addressed all their concerns. The baby kicked and that lightened the mood—for a minute. Eventually they accepted the vibe, relinquished forced attempts at conversation and ate the rest of their meal in silence until Alain skipped into the room half-dressed in his burlap Yoda jumpsuit. Yoda's head and cane, prominently displayed on the living room sofa, was an ominous sight from all perspectives. Like eyes in a portrait, it followed them everywhere.

"Don't worry," Alain said. "The force will be with you tonight."

∞∞∞

The neighborhood was a *Star Wars* panorama. Jedi knights, Darth Vader's, Yoda's and R2-D2's demonstrated their Jedi moves at every corner. He had to wonder what the trend of the moment would be come 1996. Some of the actual characters standing around the bar in *Star Wars* came to mind.

"How come you didn't get me an edible *light-saber*?" he asked Alain, after he saw a kid snacking away on his.

Alain didn't hear the question. "Joe," he said, near to a whisper, "I won't let them hurt me if you won't let them make you change. Mostly they wanna make you change, Joe."

Even under the mask, he could still see those eyes. Who was this child going to grow up to be? "How are they going to change me, Alain?"

"I don't know. But they could. Promise me, Joe. Promise me you won't let them make you change."

"I promise." Then a gust of wind blew off his headband.

The wind intensified, whistling and blowing out pumpkin candles in its wake. The neighborhood looked like someone hung a closed sign over it. By eight o'clock, bits and pieces of costumes lined the streets. The kids were getting bigger, taller. Now it was grown-up Halloween. Cars screeched up and down Dalhousie Circle, the street on which he and Alain walked. With their bags almost full, they'd be in by nine, no problem.

A crowd had gathered in front of a house six doors down. Joe moved to cross the street, but the number and density of spectators on the other side had increased. One guy sat swilling a beer in a lawn chair near the curb. Though he couldn't see, it seemed obvious they weren't typical drunk and obnoxious revelers because they sounded frightened. When Alain told him he had sticky hairs on his arm, he tightened his grip on the boy's hand. Something was very wrong outside that house.

"What's happening?" he asked a teenager who was unsteady on his feet.

"A fight, man," he said, attempting to light a cigarette with nervous fingers. "Bad one."

"I wanna see," Alain said, freeing his hand from Joe's. And off he went zigzagging toward the front.

Given his size, it took him several minutes to sidestep the mob and catch up with Alain. Then he found him inches away from the action, nearly hypnotized from horror. He put his arms around him but Alain refused to move, *if* they could move. Moving in any direction would be impossible. The crowd had doubled and there wasn't a cop in sight.

Both fighters looked to be in their late teens, with one a head taller and more muscular. And he'd had training. His lip was swollen and bleeding and he had a black eye. At this stage of the fight he was holding back, yelling at his opponent to stay down. His reasons were obvious.

The eyes of his bloodied opponent were swollen shut. He was thin, rail thin. He was also proud. This was a matter of honor. His girlfriend stood on the curb, crying and screaming at him to stop. Tear-dried ribbons of black eyeliner mottled her face, making her look ravaged and grotesque. She kept grabbing at him, begging him to stay down, but he pushed her away. He continued to push away everyone who tried to help him.

"Make them stop!" the girlfriend pleaded to the crowd. "Somebody please make them stop! Call the police!"

The boy laid on his side, crying blood and coughing up teeth. His jaw was broken. He made moves to get up again.

"Stay down, man!" implored the larger boy, eyes filled with fear. "I mean it!"

"Please stay down," Alain yelled.

He held Alain closer, wishing he could get him the hell out of here, wishing he could break up the fight, but he wouldn't risk letting go of him. Besides, that boy over there would die first rather than accept help. He looked at the people around him. Could he trust one of them to hold on to Alain while he attempted to stop the fight? No, dammit! He couldn't chance letting go of Alain.

Ignoring pleas from the crowd, the boy managed to get on his feet. He weaved over to his opponent.

"Billy, no!" the girlfriend shouted. "No! No!"

He swung with all he had left, managing one clean blow to the chest. Blood spurted everywhere. The girlfriend screamed. Alain felt a thrust of weight inside his trick or treat bag. The big boy hit him again, gently, gently enough to shut him down. More people screamed.

Billy's legs buckled and he called the girlfriend's name. She ran to him but it was too late. The boy was dead. Killed by pride.

A police cruiser arrived on the scene.

Joe carried Alain for two blocks until he spotted a bus stop bench and set him down. He assumed Alain didn't know the boy died and figured he just had the wind knocked out of him. That was fine. He didn't need to know.

"How 'bout a treat before we go home?" Alain said, practically recovered. "Somebody gave us red licorice."

Alain's hand was all the way down in the bag when something made him cringe. Slowly, he withdrew his hand, pulling out a gray, white and red sweatshirt that had been slashed several times.

"Nohh. How did he get my shirt? It was in my closet, Joe. Ohh No."

He grabbed the shirt from Alain's hand, a New York Yankee shirt. Reggie Jackson, 1977. Yankee colors were gray and white pin-stripes. This one was red, saturated with blood. Still damp, it had a note attached. What was it with this twisted creep and notes?

Poor Reggie. Didn't even see it coming. Newsflash, Joe—the kid doesn't have a week.

Was he nuts remembering Reggie Jackson in that '77 World Series now? Jackson hit three homers in the sixth game to clinch the series against the Dodgers. The shirt, a Christmas present from his parents that year, was Alain's most prized possession. Who was this asshole!

Visibly shaken but toughing it out, Alain said, "It's okay, Joe. Jedi's control their fear."

∞∞∞∞

Maggie Page regretted her decision to stay in and sketch tonight. She loved the remoteness of this place. Until now. She was an artist, familiar with angles and distortion. But these angles and distortions were unmistakably deranged. There was nothing on which she could properly focus, no perspective she could scale. The ceiling seemed higher and the doors looked crooked. For the first time she was uncomfortable with windstorms and rattling windowpanes. She remembered a line from somewhere, *evil is not always quiet.*

The idea of spending the night alone hadn't bothered her earlier, before her classmates took off to a hockey game in town, before her room heater died.

"Hold your hand over this please, Brother," she asked, after snaring a seminarian in the hallway. "Why is it blowing cold air?"

"It's hot air," he said, pushing up his glasses. "Put your hand over the vent."

Maggie shrugged. "Huh. Okay, guess it's feeling better now. Thank you. Oh, have you seen Sister Elizabeth anywhere?"

"She left a little while ago with Father Vaux. They went over to the Duprielles for a visit. I have the number if–"

"No that's okay. Just wondered."

"Well, I'll be retiring now," he said. "We have to be up at 5 a.m. to say Matins. You shouldn't stay in your room alone. Why don't you join your friend, Dina, in the stable?"

"Maybe I will catch up with her. Thanks."

When the heat disappeared with the seminarian, she sighed and put on a heavier sweater. Good. No more cold air blowing out of the vent now. Actually, there was nothing blowing out. Getting back to her sketch would ease her jitters and worry about her sister. Carol Ann was at Joe's cabin right now, waiting for him to return from trick or treating with that little boy. This was the first time she ever saw her sister wait alone for a guy. And the way Carol Ann looked at him, well that was new, too.

After almost two weeks here, she had memorized the statue of Mary in the center courtyard and so continued to work, unaware that the room temperature had dropped a few more degrees, that her left hand was cold and her right hand was warm.

Her hand moved erratically over the page. Heavy leads of black replaced soft leads of gray. Smooth rounded strokes became jagged and broken. The temperature dropped several more degrees as the cold, moving upward from her hand, now covered her left side. The cold hand reached over and took the pencil from the warm hand.

In a dreamy alpha state, oblivious to the cold, she worked the sketch to completion. It wasn't until ten-thirty that things came back into focus. Clearly, she had fallen asleep. Her bottom was warm, almost hot. One singular nagging thought prompted her to look under the covers. Stunned by what she saw, the sketchpad fell to the floor. She'd wet the bed in her sleep. Never before in her life had she wet the bed. Not ever. How absolutely embarrassing.

'Well, Maggie, this is something you don't wanna share with the girls.'

She jumped out of her clothes as quick as she could and stripped the bed, then dumped the sheets in the hamper. What a relief that the mattress wasn't stained. Bless the guy who invented mattress covers. She picked up her sketchpad and noticed the blackened area of flooring underneath.

Maybe the floor was black all along and she hadn't noticed. The area looked like one of those Rorschach tests, resembling a vampire bat. Shuddering, she flung a throw-rug over it. Odd how she fell asleep like that while working. She leafed to the last page in the sketchpad and went numb at the sight of the drawing.

Hideous and grotesque! She stared at her hands. How could they have created such an aberration? It was a sketch of bat-like creatures with human faces. Seven in total. Four in back, three in front, all posing nicely for her. The second from the left in the back row smiled through crooked teeth and crimson eyes. With their wings extended, they appeared to challenge Heaven, and there was a red door in the background, slightly ajar.

She covered her mouth with icy, shaking hands. The creature in the front row frightened her most. He didn't seem evil like the others. His sad, tormented eyes radiated softness, discomforting warmth. What did she know of sadness like this? Or suffering? She hadn't lived long enough, experienced enough life to know. And she didn't want to know, not ever.

Did God have a direct line to stave off evil? Was there a spiritual knight in charge of automatic drawing? She'd better find out fast because people she loved needed to stay safe. The thought of doing something helped her regain a modicum of emotional strength. Who really drew this vile picture?

Maggie put her hands together and looked up.

"Dear Lord, what is in me that drew this picture? Send someone to help us please, Lord. So scared ... so scared."

She buried the sketchpad under a pile of school books and rushed out the door. Outside the dorm, she turned toward the barn, then changed her mind and headed for the seminary. No sense in rattling Dina. She'd wait in the library until there was life around here—and escape that room upstairs. Escape.

A sliver of Hell was in that room, in that picture ... with those *things*.

∞∞∞

Dina knew about fear. Two years ago she was in a car accident and sustained three cracked ribs. She experienced fear for the first time at age seven after seeing a young burn victim in church one Easter Sunday. Mass had not yet begun when in he walked with his folks.

The congregation smiled at his beautiful Easter suit. Not her. All she saw was the disfigurement, the severely scarred face. Terrified at the sight of him, her father had to carry her out. Through tears, she looked back for one last glance. He had been watching her. And he too was crying.

That poor little boy. To this day, she felt guilty for making him cry.

Shoulders tight, Dina flinched at every noise. Images of the horses dying flashed through her mind. Crazy, crazy thought. She'd stay with Misty until the class returned from the hockey game, in spite of that creepoid monk giving Jake a rub in the next stall. She had to nix the Halloween heebie-jeebies. That's right. *Stuff it, Dina. Stop being a baby*.

The monk smiled at her and she managed to relax her face and smile back. She was being mean, really she was. The monk guy seemed nice enough. Because he'd been hanging around her for the past few weeks didn't make him bad. Creepy, yes. Bad, no. He was probably lonely. His friends weren't around much and he needed the horses for company, something she understood. Maybe she should talk to him. Funny though, she could have sworn Father Andre asked him and his friends to leave. They must've come to some arrangement with Father Andre.

"What did you say your name was?" she asked him, not meaning to yank at the knot in Misty's mane.

"Steve," he said. His pupils were large and glassy.

"That doesn't sound very foreign to me. I mean, because of your accent. Where you from, Steve?"

He came around into her stall. He offered her a lemon drop.

"No, thank-you," she said, wrinkling her nose. He stunk of menthol and lemon. "Only use 'em when I get sick."

As she brushed Misty's bangs, she caught his reflection in the horse's eye. The stranger's hand moved toward the top button of his leather jacket. Slowly, he undid the other four buttons. The temperature must've dropped because she felt so cold suddenly. She brushed and she watched ...

through Misty's eye. She said some words to the man who called himself Steve, without having any recollection of what she'd said. Some silly, meaningless words.

The strokes down Misty's bangs became mechanical when she saw his skin reflected through the horse's eye. No shirt from the waist up. She didn't want to look below his waist. Something made her not look there. All she needed was to get the four words out and put them in a question. It was hard to talk or move. It was harder to look over there. His reflection was getting bigger. A head. Eyes. *Just four words, Dina. Ask them!*

"What are you doing?" She heard a little girl's voice come out of her mouth.

He was standing close behind her, so close she felt his lemony breath against her ear. He showed her his pocketknife, traced it around her lips, held it to her throat.

"Shush, Dina." She felt the draft on her legs. Her skin prickled. "Not one word. Close your eyes and keep them closed until I tell you to open them."

She would go to some faraway place in her mind and stay there for a while. Misty stomped as the stranger who called himself Steve bent her over and her face squished into Misty's belly. She'd go practice at Radio City Music Hall in New York ... ohh ... *go there, Dina, go there!*

"... Bend, Dina, bend," the choreographer ordered her. *And he forced her nose to her knees for the workout.*

"It hurts so much," she complained. "Ohh, it hurts."

"No pain, no gain," he said, grabbing her legs and snapping them apart like a wishbone at Thanksgiving dinner.

For a moment the pain was unbearable. But she had to go through this because she was a star and she had to stay on top. One of the dancers in the show dropped a small carton of milk on the stage.

"Ohh, man, what a mess," she said. "Somebody please clean this mess up."

She told the choreographer they had to break. Her thighs were stiff and sore and her bottom was killing her. A cast member offered her a lemon candy, but the smell made her nauseous.

"Ugh. Get it away. I hate those things."

Some guy was talking to her while he rushed off the stage. She couldn't quite grasp it all. Something like ... 'open your thighs.' No no. It was ... 'open your eyes, Dina. Open your eyes.' Then he turned left behind the stage curtain and disappeared.

Dina opened her eyes and found herself sitting on a mound of rough, scratchy hay, staring into Misty's middle. Her chest was cold and bare. She fastened her bra but had trouble buttoning her heavy Scottish cardigan, the small buttonholes too awkward for her stupid, sausage fingers.

She exhaled deeply and looked at her legs, breath hitching at the sight of her panties and jeans twisted below her knees. *No wonder this hay is so pinchy*. Her bruised thighs had swelled and there was dried sticky stuff all over them.

"I must've slipped in the spilt milk."

Dizzy and disoriented, it took her a long time to get dressed. She kept stopping, trying to remember the thing she forgot at Radio City Music Hall. Shortly after midnight, she left the barn and stumbled back on wet grass toward the dormitory, slipping and falling in a pile of leaves. It didn't hurt so bad as long as she remembered *no pain, no gain*. The moon was full and the wind howled around her. So cold. Where was everybody?

Dina rested her cheek on the side door, staring beyond Mary's statue to Radio City Music Hall. It looked like a big tomb with all the trees kneeling over it. What was it she forgot? She continued to wonder about that as she crawled up the stairs to her room on the second floor. Someone must've died at Radio City. Yeah ... and she didn't stick around for the funeral. How horrible of her. Who was it that died there? *Who?*

∞∞∞

Something was wrong. Carol Ann sensed it in his voice the moment she picked up the phone. He was still at Alain's talking to his folks. Sister Elizabeth and Father Richard were also there, so he was going to be late, probably after midnight, he said. What was going on with Alain? It wasn't that Joe didn't want to take her trick or treating with them. It was more like he couldn't take her with them. Lately, she'd come to notice how much she hated being away from Joe, even for an hour. She was leaving day after tomorrow. That didn't give them much time.

Joe sounded tired on the phone, but said he still wanted her to wait for him. All right, enough. Tonight she would tell him she loved him. They had made all these plans for Christmas, beyond Christmas, and they never exchanged those three words. Actually, she had done the planning. Joe mostly listened. Sometimes he looked sad. Whatever he was keeping from her was driving her mad. She had never worried about anything or anyone this much until Joe Ross showed up in her life from out of nowhere, changing her whole world in one short week. What a corny cliché. But love really did do crazy things to a person.

She sat by the fire with a quilt on her shoulders. Why couldn't she get warm? Not to worry. Soon, Joe would be here holding her in his arms, kissing her, telling her he wanted her. And she would giggle and remind him that they'd have to wait until Christmas.

None of these beautiful thoughts helped. Her spine tingled. Her throat was dry. Her arms and legs felt stiff. *My mind is sore.* She grabbed a floor cushion and edged close to the fire. The crackle sound amplified and the room temperature dropped. Was the fire ejecting cold? No, absolutely not.

Her eyes followed a thin stream of smoke to the large mirror by the front door. "Hazy daze," she whispered to herself, walking dreamlike to the mirror, counting the number of hooks around it. Eight hooks for coats and keys and umbrellas. What else? Joe's CAP cap dangled on one of them. Such an old mirror. So many specks and streaks in the glass. The harder she looked, the more she found. The specks mingled with the streaks and multiplied, like spots on a rash.

Barely cognizant of her dissolving image, she watched the spots form into letters, then into words, and finally into sentences. Dizzy and weightless, she strained to read the words in the mirror ...

Urgent Message for Carol Ann Page!
EOJ LLIW SSORC TAHT DLOHSERHT YNA TNEMOM NOOS. EH STNAW UOY WDOB DNA LUOS, LORAC NNA. EKAT MIH SIHT NROM GNIRUD EHT LLITS LLUF NOOM, DNA EHT NOISSAP SEVIL REVEROF NI EHT NAM.

Mesmerized in front of the mirror, she waited for a second message. Nothing. There'd been an obvious presence here. But it was gone now, thank-you very much. She'd read about supernatural manifestations in monasteries and the like and always promised herself that if ever she ran into a ghost, she'd handle it with grit. Her father had said it a hundred times when she and Maggie were growing up, 'You gotta get tough, girls. Handle life with grit.'

Now if only she could stop shaking.

Hearing Joe approaching on the pathway, she had to think fast. No. She would not tell him. He might think she was making it up in order to nail him body and soul, like the message said. That would hurt just too damn much. It would also damage their relationship. That was the real test. That thing wanted to break them up. Well, just try, tweety pie. When Joe opened the door and flashed that movie star smile, she flung herself into his arms, wanting him more than ever.

"Hey," he said, in between kisses, "were you spooked here all by yourself? Not to worry. Luke Skywalker to the rescue with his light-saber. Good thing I couldn't eat it after all."

She continued kissing him, deeper and longer. The last part of the message was closing in on her. She didn't write it down. Could she retain it? Suddenly it was exam time with fifteen minutes left to cram, only she couldn't find the crib notes. *Take him this morn, during the still full moon. And the passion lives forever in the man.*

"Joe, I don't want to leave in two days. Would you like it if, if I could find a way, that is, well if I didn't return with the class?" His hands fell to his sides and the pained expression in his eyes about did her in. "What, Joe? What is it?"

∞∞∞∞

It had been a horrible night. They instructed him to keep silent about his plan. In light of this evening's events, he had to take Alain and go in, what—hours?

"During morning rush-hour traffic," Father Richard had instructed. "That will be the best time to disappear into the crowd. Sister Elizabeth will have to join you in New York."

"What do I tell Carol Ann?" he'd asked, near panic.

"Sorry, Joe," Sister Elizabeth said, "I know Carol Ann very well. She won't let up until you tell her everything. She's like a dog with a bone. Tell her you have to get back to Medford on a family emergency. Then call her in a few weeks or leave her a letter explaining as much of the truth as you can. At least with a letter, she can't box you into a corner."

"How much of the truth can I tell her?"

For several seconds, no one uttered a word until Father Richard spoke. "Maybe you should stick with the family emergency for now. Only your grandmother can know you're taking care of Alain. And even she won't know your whereabouts."

"Oh God," was his brilliant rejoinder.

"Joe, please say something," Carol Ann asked, clinging to him. I'm getting worried."

He walked her over to the couch and sat her down. Then he looked into the eyes of the girl he loved and flat out lied. "Carol Ann, I have to leave even before you. I have to head back to Medford first thing in the morning."

"In the morning? Why, Joe?"

"My, uh, grandmother isn't well. Doctor's afraid of a stroke. My aunt wants me home tomorrow."

"I'm so sorry. For your grandmother. For you. For me. Will you call me as soon as you know how she is?"

He pulled her into his arms. This was the way it had to be. This was for Alain. Alain had to come first. "Let's hold each other till sun-up."

Carol Ann whispered in his ear, "we don't need to wait until Christmas. Wanting you this much is torture for me. Let's make love tonight."

"Carol Ann, you don't ... there are things I haven't been able to tell you."

"I know that. I love you, so I know. Something to do with Alain. I got vibes and I know keeping certain things from me isn't your decision. You'll tell me when you can. Only, when do you think that will be?"

"How I wish I could say."

She curled her fingers around his hand. "Do you love me?"

"Yes. But I'm not going to make love to you and then leave you. And what if something happens and I can't make it back for Christmas?"

Carol Ann bit the inside of her cheek. "Is your grandmother really sick?"

"My grandmother has been through hell."

"That's evasive, Joe. Clever and evasive."

She could drive him so crazy. God, how he wanted to pick her up and carry her upstairs. "Carol Ann Page on the force again?"

"Be straight with me, Joe."

He had to get tougher with her now. The last thing he wanted to do. "Don't grill me, Carol Ann. You said it— keeping certain things from you is not my decision. Come on, let's throw a blanket down in front of the fire. I need to hold you."

She gave him a pained stare then grabbed the blanket off the couch. He hated hurting her, and she seemed somewhat needy and unstrung, glancing over at the mirror a couple of times. What was he doing to her? What was he doing *with* her? He was absolutely nuts to get involved now. But he loved her and wanted her, and soon he'd have to say goodbye to her.

"We still have hours," he said, feeling her soften as they cuddled on the blanket. "But I don't want you to get in trouble with Sister Elizabeth."

"I'll leave just before sunrise," she said, running her hands along his shoulders, "before everybody gets up. We'll say our goodbyes then and I'll be back in my room before I'm missed."

"All the priests will be up," he snickered at her.

"You think a priest is going to squeal on me? I doubt it."

"It's been a whirlwind, I know, Carol Ann. A lot of stuff will come along and confuse you. Through it all, remember I love you. That's the only truth I can give you now. One more thing, Inspector, and promise not to question me on it?"

She agreed, reluctantly, but she agreed. "Okay. What?"

"*Angelfish Cove.*"

"What, Joe?"

"That's all I can say. Remember it—Angelfish Cove."

He kissed her deeply, and they continued to kiss and doze and talk and kiss some more until four-thirty in the morning. As he held her, he felt two sensations with perfect clarity—the warmth coursing through their bodies and the tender loving pain at the thought of parting. To add to the intensity of these emotions, he had the disturbing premonition that it would be years until they could be together again.

Before sunrise as they prepared to tear themselves away from each other, Carol Ann asked, "Joe? On a scale of one to ten, how much *can't* you tell me?"

He stroked the side of her face.

"That much, huh."

"Yes."

Suddenly her patience turned to frustration. "I don't know if I'm going to be able to handle not knowing where and how you are, not being able to get a hold of you. Help me out here, Joe."

"I'll call or write, probably both as soon as I can. I promise." Already he was feeling guilty. Again. Damn it, again.

"It's almost five," she said, swallowing hard. "I have to go. What time are you heading out?"

"In three hours. I'll walk you back now. I love you, Carol Ann, but I really need you to help me keep it together."

They walked back to the dorm in silence, arms around each other's waist, sniffling from the chill in the air. "How am I doing?" she asked when they reached the walkway. "Not even a chin quiver. Aren't you proud of me?"

He grabbed her and squeezed her so hard he felt the knots on her spine. "You have no idea how much I want to haul you back to the cabin and make love to you," he said, practically kissing her breathless.

"Take care of your grandmother," she told him. This time there were tears in her eyes. "I love you. Carry me with you wherever you go. Bye, Joe." And she ran off down the walkway.

He waited until she was safely inside the dormitory, then beat it back to the cabin to pack. Once he got there, he sat on the veranda and stared vacantly across the lake, eyes tearing, unsure of where he was going. When he snapped out of it, he had an hour left to pack and write Carol Ann that note, his beautiful Carol Ann who knew he wasn't going to his grandmother's. But there could be no letter of explanation. A simple love note with a cryptic message was all he dare leave behind. For Alain's sake, he could tell her nothing, not for a long time.

∞∞∞

Father Andre showed up at 8:00 and Father Richard arrived at 8:15 with Alain. The boy had already said private goodbyes to his parents. All agreed that it was wiser to depart from the cabin rather than Alain's busy street. Joe was secretly relieved. He had done the goodbye scene to death with the Duprielles last night. He didn't have the energy to go through it again this morning. Carol Ann's perfume was everywhere.

"Joe, I know emotions were running high last night. But I expect you'll take better care of yourself from now on. It's obvious you haven't slept." This was a polite reprimand from Father Andre. "You must study, Joe. There's a reason. Remember? Sister Elizabeth will help tutor you. No more distractions."

"There won't be, Father. Sorry. Didn't count on falling in love."

"Sometimes I forget how young you are. I'm sorry, too. You're hurting, I can see. But you'll be fine. Did you know that every time one person prays for another, an angel goes and sits on that person's shoulder? You have an army of angels accompanying you to New York, Joe."

They spoke more of plans, times, details and the little gray brick bungalow waiting for them in West Hempstead, Long Island. Everything he needed was in the manila envelope Father Andre handed him. Sister Elizabeth would join him in five days. It was all in the envelope, Father Andre repeated, advising him to memorize its contents.

Compo had rushed through the door ahead of Father Richard and Alain. Funny how animals sensed a person's comings and goings. The dog was all excited. Usually, at this time of the morning he was curled up in his favorite kitchen corner digesting breakfast. Alain, comfortably dressed in his Star Wars cap and black and red tracksuit, appeared drained. But as always he was handling it with heart and faith. He whisked over and gave him a playful jab in the arm.

"I'm all ready, Joe" he said. "I packed snacks for the car and the plane and everything. We're all set. You ready?"

"You bet. Let's get those adventures started."

"We'll be waiting outside, Joe," Father Richard said. "Take a minute if you like."

"Thanks, Father."

He watched the clouds hover over the monastery buildings. No more angry gray and black sky. All negative presences had departed. For now. The air was clean on this November 1st and the nip helped dispel the fatigue. What was waiting for them beyond those gates? Would dark angels follow? Nothing seemed to make any sense. Surely Alain would be safest right here on Marianlake property, right here in this cabin. From the first night he and Willie set foot in Angelfish Cove, he felt he was being tested. He had more than a heavenly directive to reckon with. Apart from proving himself to everyone in the Penthouse, he had to prove himself here on Ground Level. And so far, he'd spent most of his time staving off intruders in the Cellar.

A small hand slipped into his.

"Is our new house near a lake do you know, Joe?" Alain asked.

"You bet. Father Andre knows we're part mer-men." Alain's eyes looked like two rolling cameras. Film. Cut. Wrap. Marianlake was in the can and going with him.

He thought of the last thing Carol Ann had said and checked to make sure his note to her was secured under the sugar bowl. She would understand its cryptic message. The little symbol after his name might be a bit of a struggle for her, though. He considered removing it. No. She was his little inspector and she was good with puzzles. Soon as he got another copy for himself he'd send her the Flower Book. He needed it to code and translate messages to her and wasn't about to call home and ask for Beata's copy.

Carol Ann loved flowers, so yeah, she'd figure it out, especially since he'd already dropped hints.

"Pitter patter. Let's get atter," he said. That line always made Alain smile. And over the years he would say it often.

So they left Marianlake. Strange. As they passed through the gates, neither he nor Alain turned their heads for one final look back. It wasn't necessary. All memories would remain clear and intact until their return ... in 1996.

7. Scarred Wrists & Obscured Messages

New York City, November 1981

Carol Ann WAS ON HER THIRD FLIP through the Flower Book and the mailman only dropped it off an hour ago. Father Richard had passed on Joe's note to her the morning he left Marianlake, that annoying, cryptic jumble of words. She tightened her jaw. No more tears, please. How could he possibly know she could no longer read, that is, read *normally*? Could Joe have intuitively guessed that a book of flower meanings was more appropriate under these bizarre circumstances?

He'd pressed a forget-me-not inside the book. She just couldn't read the words 'forget-me-not,' not from left to right. Wherever did he get a forget-me-not in November? She stared at his name again--EOJ. This was how her mind perceived it. EOJ. For the past three weeks she had written his name on a hundred scraps of paper, praying that one more signature would fix things. Her palm stung from hammering her fist. First the self-blame for falling in love with no safety net. Then the tears. The tears always followed the emotional self-abuse.

His name was Joe Ross. Would she ever again see it as Joe Ross? Since the day after Halloween, she had seen it as 22OR EOJ. That thing, whatever it was, had given her this grisly visual.

"It doesn't look like the name of the guy I'm in love with," she sobbed to Maggie. "It looks like an address in Greece."

Dyslexia was the name given the condition, the cause of which involved neurological dysfunction. The specialist said it may have resulted from various causes and there are a number of subtypes of dyslexia that probably exist with different origins and symptoms. *Oh puh-leeze.*

"So what does all that tell us, Doctor?" her mother asked. "It sounds rather vague to me."

Cheers, Mom.

The doctor continued to speculate, refusing to take a stand and isolate the cause. "Some theories suggest that the two hemispheres of the brain develop in an unusual manner," was the twaddle he offered while spinning his pencil. She sat there thinking up more creative things he could do with it.

"You can tick specialists off that list until Marianlake reveals its secrets," she said to her parents and Maggie at dinner. "I told you what happened to me in that mirror. And there's Maggie's story. Next we have Dina. God only knows what happened to her. She's not talking. She's just getting weirder by the minute. Why do you both insist on taking me to doctors? This thing is not medical."

"Well what would you have us do, Carol Ann?" her father asked. "If you'll stay calm, we can brainstorm."

"My hand tremor has stopped," Maggie said in her quiet, matter-of-fact way. "Maybe I can get some work done now. Carol Ann's right, Dad. It's not medical. Torch the list." With that, she left the table and pussyfooted off.

She looked at her sister in amazement. "How does she stay so calm all the time? She's always so together. It drives me nuts."

"Maggie de-stresses by painting," her mother said. "Wish you'd find a distraction, Carol Ann. And as for this Joe of yours, I think you should try to forget him. I hate to say it, but sending you a book about flowers and their meanings is a little strange. He should've called by now, or written. And why didn't he leave you his grandmother's number? Medford, was it? Something's definitely amiss. Just put him right out of your mind, dear. Out of sight, out of mind. That's what I always say."

"Yeah well, I always say absence makes the heart grow fonder, Mom."

She couldn't lose face by telling her parents that she did have the Medford number, which she got by sneaking it from Father Richard's Rolodex the day they left Marianlake. When she called, the operator apologized— that line had been temporarily disconnected. Surprise, surprise. Somehow she knew he wouldn't be there. He lied and it hurt. It hurt bad. Couldn't he sense how much she needed him now? That evil sadistic thing had scrambled the guts out of her visual perception and he wasn't here to hold her, to tell her why this was happening.

"He loves me, Mom," she said near tears again, advertising the fact that she was not the mature eighteen-year-old she believed she was. "I know it. I do." And she wept openly, something she always hated to do in front of anyone, even family. In the past twenty-four hours, they had seen more of her tears than they had in her life. She was turning into a whiny, lovesick puppy and she hated it.

With the little flower book tucked neatly under her arm, she scratched on her sister's door and entered. The wall Maggie had primed white shortly after their return from Marianlake had thoroughly dried. She flipped through the book with one eye on her sister. Maggie barely acknowledged her as she furiously drew random notes and lines at the corners. The day they bought the white primer, Maggie expressed concern over the mural's outcome, said there was no ending in her head. There wasn't even a middle. And the beginning had a mind of its own. All she knew was that she had to paint a mural on her wall and she had to begin now.

"Will you read me his letter again, Mag?" she asked, now that Maggie seemed cognizant of her presence. "It's all ass-backwards and I can't stand looking at it this way. There's something he wants to get across to me in this letter or in this book, I know it. But as long as the dyslexia lasts, I can't figure it out."

Maggie clasped her hands under her chin, giving her one of those wide-eyed, brainstorm stares. "Is the library still open?"

"Yeah, it's open till eight. Why?"

"Been thinking. Why don't you take the letter and photocopy it? Then enlarge it. Then ... hold it up to the mirror. Should read normal for you. What do you think?"

"You're a genius!" She slipped the letter out of the Flower Book and held it in front of Maggie's vanity mirror. "I can read it fine. You're right. Once I enlarge it, more's the better. At least I can read *somewhat* until the dyslexia clears. Won't be a drag on any of you guys. Be nice if I could stop feeling sorry for myself for five minutes, wouldn't it?"

"We've all been through hell," Maggie said. "And we don't know why. Don't know what any of this is about. I think the answers lie with your vanishing Joe Ross. I know you. You're not going to sit around with your nose in that flower book much longer, are you?"

"No." She narrowed her eyes. "Joe was into something. And now Sister Elizabeth has suddenly resigned with one more term left to teach, to take some mysterious tutoring position. Betcha Alain is the student. I saw some strange things going on up at Marianlake, but I didn't pay much attention at the time. I got suspicious in a hurry a few days before we left, though."

She told Maggie of the morning breakfast meetings that lasted for hours each day. She told her what Patsy let slip about the vandal's sick message on the men's room wall. The boy himself nearly made a major slip and even Joe appeared overly frustrated at times with what appeared to be information he could not share with her.

"There were secrets there," she said. "Big secrets."

Maggie smiled. "Is Carol Ann Page on the force?"

"Oh you bet. Major."

"Where you going to start?"

"With Father Richard. I'll be giving him a little phone call."

"If he's involved in whatever this is, he won't tell you anything."

"It's what he doesn't tell me, Mag. What he doesn't tell me will point me in the right direction. I have this idea on how to get a message to Joe and if it works, that'll mean Father Richard is very definitely involved."

"Father Richard isn't going to fall for anything. He's too smart."

"I'm more in love than he is smart."

Within the hour, she was back with an enlarged photocopy of Joe's letter and a very determined mind. As she passed Maggie's room, she gave her door a playful scratch to let her know she was back in case she needed to talk. The door-scratch had been with them since they were kids. It was their way of expressing their availability to each other without interrupting studies or a masterpiece in the making. This time there was no response. Maggie sounded awfully busy in there.

She got comfortable in her favorite overstuffed chair and pulled the full-length mirror practically nose to glass. She attached Joe's enlarged goodbye note to a clipboard and faced it at the mirror. It felt so wonderful to read normally again. The dyslexia would pass. Affirming this to herself had kept her mentally and emotionally sound. So far. But if she didn't hear Joe's voice soon she might lose it. The large words hung frozen in the mirror. If only she knew what to look for.

Dear Carol Ann,

I can't stop thinking about last night. I love you. No matter what happens, always remember that.

There's this 'errand' I have to do and I don't know how long it will take and I wish to God I could share it with you. But sharing would mean breaking confidences and I can't do that. You don't know how much it hurts me to keep you in the dark.

Carol Ann, though I don't know when we can see each other again, I will be in touch with you ASAP. My means of communication will seem weird, but remember—there's a reason. Study the Flower Book and think about Angelfish Cove. Just think about it. And please have patience, baby. Thoughts of you are keeping me together.

Goodbye for a while.

I love you.

JOE ±

She stayed up until sunrise picking the letter apart with the growing fear of not seeing him again for a very long time. The letter was so obscure. An *errand*, he wrote. *Breaking confidences. Weird means of communication*, which definitely meant the phone was off limits. Joe would be communicating through the Flower Book. This was the only breakthrough she had. Twice he told her to think about Angelfish Cove. Why? As soon as she could get away, she would go there. Right after New Year's.

Joe knew all along that they would be apart for some time, reminding her yet again in the letter. *Goodbye for a while*, he said. Then there was the most mystifying obscurity. What was that thing after his name? An underlined cross, perhaps? A plus over a minus? Was he telling her that he was going off to another monastery of some kind?

She sat by her window, watching the snow fall until dawn, obsessing over the bowl of alphabet soup she'd been staring into for a month. What was that logo thing after Joe's name? Her eyes were dry and strained. As she crawled under the covers, the memory of changing batteries in her old portable radio flashed through her mind. Something about positive and negative. Two opposing forces. The connection was then lost in sleep.

∞∞∞∞

It would be some time before she figured out how close she had come to an answer this night before sleep claimed her. The future would bring her another sign, another symbol. And by 1996, she would see it everywhere.

∞∞∞∞

"Father Richard? How are you? It's Carol Ann Page. Joe's friend."

"Of course. Carol Ann. It's nice to hear your voice. How are you doing?"

"Well actually, that's why I'm calling, Father. Not so good. There's been some–I don't know how ... Father, I had a real screwy experience up there on Halloween night and so did my sister. And I suspect, Dina most of all."

"Tell me."

She told him everything, from the frightening message in the mirror to waking up dyslexic a few hours later. Of course she omitted how close she and Joe got, though Father Richard had to know since she started weeping when he gave her Joe's note.

Father Richard spoke slowly, too slowly, like he was carefully choosing his words.

"Carol Ann, there *was* a presence here that week. Joe experienced it more than once as well. I don't know how much he told you, but I'm certain, given his obvious feelings for you that he must have spoken of some spiritual matters of concern. It's difficult to get into it in depth over the phone. But you're more than welcome to come back up. The dyslexia will disappear the moment you return to a positive mindset."

"That won't happen, Father Richard, not until I talk to Joe. You see I haven't heard from him except for a book he sent me with a forget-me-not pressed inside. I'm afraid I'm not going to hear from him for awhile. I need to tell him about this. He needs to know about Maggie and Dina, too. Do you know how I can get a hold of him?"

"Well I know he's in Medford with his grandmother. She hasn't been well. And that number's unlisted, Carol Ann. He left so suddenly that morning that he neglected to leave the number with us. But he did say he would call as soon as the dust settled. And I trust that he will. The moment he does, I'll pass on your message."

"Thank-you, Father."

"I'd like to discuss the other matter more with you, Carol Ann. It's important. Dark presences linger in the mind when you're emotionally vulnerable. I want you to say your Rosary every day. Do you think you can come back up to Marianlake for a few days?"

"I'll try, Father. But I need to talk to Joe first. I promise I'll let you know. I'll keep you informed."

Elizabeth Genovese

"Don't wait too long. And don't worry about Joe. What he feels for you is real."

"I needed to hear that. I'll be in touch soon."

"Very good. Say the Rosary. Tell Dina and Maggie to say it, too. Bye, Carol Ann."

"Bye, Father Richard."

Carol Ann stroked the receiver. Up and down. Up and down. He lied. He lied! Unless one of those dark presences snuck into his head, erased his memory and torched his Rolodex, he was lying. Why? She liked Father Richard. She really did. She closed her eyes. *Please, Joe. Please hear me calling you. I need you.* Now it was a waiting game.

Four excruciatingly long days passed without word. If it wasn't for school winding down for the holidays, her time would have been spent clock watching and mail waiting. Anxious to share these feelings with Maggie, she scratched on her door several times but she was unavailable. Maggie was often unavailable these days. Come to think of it, she had skipped class five times since their return. This mural project was obsessing her because Maggie hardly left her room now.

Dina had suddenly become Miss Congeniality at school. Massive personality change. The once shy, very innocent girl had transformed or transmuted as Carol Ann kidded. Dina was practically a woman of the world now and had taken over the choir. Carol Ann didn't know what to make of her. Not yet. She was so strange. And yet she was finally beginning to open up with confidence. Certainly this was a good thing.

The plant and the other baffling item arrived four days after her chat with Father Richard. Tiffany's Florists. Tiffany's Florists was right here in Brooklyn, ten minutes from her home. When she phoned for info about the sender, no one knew a thing. She called three times, spoke with three different people, and received the same answer—a money order was couriered to the shop and the name on it was indecipherable.

He had sent a flowering lemon geranium and a small container of oats. *Oats.* This did not sit well with her parents who, since they thought he was strange before, believed he was one cheese short of a cracker now. Feeling the little man with the heavy hammer inside her heart, she looked up their meanings in the Flower Book. Why did it have to be this way? Even Maggie stopped work long enough to hear this.

"So what's it mean?" Maggie asked, splattered head to toe with rose-colored paint.

"The lemon geranium means 'unexpected meeting,'" she said, breathless. "We're going to see each other soon."

Maggie looked skeptical. "And the oats? I must know."

"'The witching soul of music.' I don't get it. Is he going to meet me somewhere with music playing in the background? A club maybe?"

"Your guess is as good as mine, Carol Ann. I hope it's soon, though. These little mysteries are getting on the folks' nerves, not to mention what it's doing to you."

The memory of his dark eyes searching hers as they cuddled in front of the fire made her want to open a window and scream out his name. "I love him, Maggie. And sharing it with you now is like bringing him back. You were there, not in the cabin with us, but you and Dina were there. Oh God, where is he, Maggie? What's he into? Who's he with? I'd be happy just hearing his voice."

"No you wouldn't," Maggie said. "Hearing his voice wouldn't be enough. It'll never be enough again. Don't forget to water the geranium."

∞∞∞∞

Dina listened to the sirens from her hospital bed. The busy, wintry Brooklyn streets had nothing on Marianlake with its morning loons and Joe's harmonica echoing across the lake at bedtime. She tried to think of more pleasant sounds but only the dark sounds came forward. A scream for attention in the next room. A hacking cough from across the hall. And an alleyway scuffle ending with the rattle of a garbage can lid clanking down the lane.

Somewhere in the midst of this depressing racket was a sound that did not belong—the stomp of a horse's hoof. That hypnosis doctor must've done something weird to her. She placed her palms over her ears and curled her legs into a fetal position. What her GP had said, it couldn't be true.

Maggie and Carol Ann slipped quietly into the room. After exchanging hugs and kisses, she had diddly to say. They were never a trio for small talk, especially under serious circumstances.

"I guess you've heard I can't remember any of it," she said, plumping a pillow. "Except for bits and pieces when they put me under hypnosis this morning. So any news at school yet about Sister Elizabeth?"

"No," Maggie said. "Still nothing. We would tell you right away. Oh well, at least Mrs. Mlynarsky doesn't grade as tough. She gave you a good mark for your project."

Carol Ann jumped up and held her head in her hands. "My God! Dina gets admitted for a rectal infection then finds out she's been raped. And you two are talking grades. Dina, talk to us."

"Marianlake," she said. Saying that word seemed to take all her strength. "In the barn. Some guy attacked me in the barn. I don't want to remember his face—that's as much as they figured out while I was under. They kinda put two and two together because they told me I kept droning on about Radio City Music Hall. Can you believe that?"

"Did it happen Halloween night?" Carol Ann asked. "And did it get really cold in the barn just before?"

Maggie frowned at her. "Carol Ann, go slow."

It was like somebody shut the blinds on Dina's eyes. She preferred to stay with her friends, thank you very much, but still had to close her eyes. But she didn't want to go to sleep.

Too bad. You're going to sleep NOW.

"We better come back tomorrow," Maggie said. "She's been through too much today."

The girls were halfway out the door when the blind rolled up with a snap. "Ay!" she hollered at them. "Where the hell you two think you're goin'? You just got here. We got important stuff to talk about, man. Real important stuff."

The girls stood there, dumbfounded.

"Get your butts back here. Now first of all, the fact of the matter is I was raped. Okay? Now I don't want anyone at school to find out. Hell, I don't even know the details. And you know what? I don't wanna know. It happened. It's over. Finito. They can't make me remember things I don't want to remember. Unfortunately, since I'm a minor, my parents still have all the say. So I'll play along with them. In the meantime, what I really want when I get outta here is to sing. Joe turned me on to my talent. Tell him to call me, Carol Ann. I got an actual gig over the Christmas holidays at my uncle's club. You remember the Club One Two? And I want Joe to be there. When you gonna be talkin' to him?"

"I don't know," Carol Ann said, grabbing onto Maggie's arm. "We haven't been in touch, not verbally."

"Whaddya mean, *not verbally*? What kinda shit is that?"

"He's out of town for awhile. I should hear from him soon."

She narrowed her eyes at Carol Ann.

"Joe has some very important things to take care of," Maggie said. "We're not quite sure what yet, but everything will be fine, don't worry. Give us your club date and we'll be there at table number one."

"Yeah." Carol Ann strained to smile. "And I'll pass it on to Joe. But we should talk about you, Dina. You've changed since we got back from Marianlake. We all have, but you the most. What happened to you is so—"

"Drop it Carol Ann." She yanked the plumped pillow from under her head and flopped back on the bed. "I can't deal now. Too wiped. Dealing with my parents over this whole thing was the worst, you don't know. They even got the cops involved back there in Three Rivers. I'm tired. Let me get outta here first and then we'll get into it. Anyway guys, please don't get your feelings hurt, but I am beat. I'll call tomorrow. I might even be out tomorrow or the day after."

Two policemen were waiting outside the room to take their statements. The girls' description of the four visiting monks matched those of Fathers' Andre and Richard. It was just 'unfortunate' for Dina that she was having memory problems. Even after talking with her doctor, it was clear they weren't buying the rape. They had seen one too many girls on trips away from their parents. It was also clear that the police would be of little help. Carol Ann cried herself to sleep for Dina that night. Maggie, near completion of her best work ever, painted into the morning hours.

∞∞∞∞

Dina stayed up half the night with a notepad, trying to decide which songs to perform for her first gig. She had absolutely no intention of telling a soul she remembered what happened in the barn on Halloween. Actually she had forgotten already. She had passed the memory on to sweet little Dina before that guy spilt the milk on stage at Radio City. And sweet little Dina didn't want to come out and play much no more.

Even in the wake of 'this tragedy,' her dream was very much alive. She had the music in her and she owed it to Joe goddam Ross. Since that magical day out on the lake when she heard her chops for the first time, she knew what she wanted. She liked this new energized Dina. The music was in her soul now, right where it belonged.

She shuffled down the hall toward the Coke machine in her fuzzy slippers, munching cheese doodles and humming between swallows. A guy who looked sort of familiar was at the desk talking to the nurse's aide, but she couldn't place where she had seen him. He had dirty blond hair and was a few years younger than her. He wasn't fat, but he was big, and tallish. And why the hell should she care? Nope. It wasn't registering. When the nurse pointed in her direction, the guy looked startled and bolted to the exit.

"Wait a minute!" the aide called after him.

She ran up to the nurse's station, leaving a trail of cheese doodles behind her. "Who was that guy?"

"He said he was a friend of yours from school," she said, apologetically. "And he wanted to know how you were doing. I can call security if you like. It'll have to be quick, though."

"No." This was weirdly exciting. "I think I do know him. Just can't place him. And he's no friend of mine from school, I can tell ya that. This is gonna drive me nuts. I wonder why he ran?"

"I wouldn't have given him any information," the aide said, sheepish, "except that, well, he knew what happened to you. I'm so sorry, Dina."

"Shit! Shit! Shit!" She'd die if this got out. "Well, he already knew, didn't he? Damn, how does he know? Soon as I remember where I've seen him, I'll get my dad to pay him a visit. But I gotta tell ya, I'm a little pissed off. None of you guys should be giving information to anyone who isn't family. I should report this, but since I'm leaving today, forget it."

"Thanks," the aide said, relieved.

"S'okay." She carried on down the hall to the Coke machine, humming.

Dina blew them all away at the audition the first week in December. Her Uncle Rocco and the rest of the staff said she was amazing. 'Why had his niece and the rest of the family been holding out on him?' he'd asked. He said she gave him goose bumps, especially after belting out *In The Air Tonight*.

"Hey Dina!" her uncle said on her way out that day. "What happened to the shy, giggly girl who helped me bus tables here last summer?" Actually, they all wondered. She was kind of wondering that herself.

Uncle Rocco gave her three nights to show her stuff— Thursday December 10th through Saturday the 12th. If all went well, she could earn herself college tuition, if she desired. She desired. But not college. She had no interest in college now and when she told the parents, they handled it well.

Considering 'the tragedy,' the parents weren't about to give her an argument, however she had to promise to see the shrink twice a month. That was the deal and she took it. Humpty Dumpty Dina would one day be together again. Soon she'd get to sing at the Club One Two. That's all she wanted, to sing like Joe said she could. And it would happen big time for her, she absolutely knew for absolutely certain. Because Joe said so.

She kept the two secret letters from everyone, including Maggie and Carol Ann—such sympathetic words from a friend who knew about the rape. The letters kept her from flipping out these past weeks in ways the shrinks, family and friends never could. She longed for another letter. Too bad she could never tell anyone, not even the girls. But she was asked to promise these letters be kept secret. She would keep the promise and the secret, somehow knowing that if she did, more letters would come. And come they did ... for the next ten years.

∞∞∞∞

Maggie painted her signature in red at the bottom right of the mural wall, then tuck-taped the sheet-cover at the upper corners. Since Carol Ann had arranged a little impromptu brunch this afternoon, she decided to formalize the affair. It was time to ditch the coveralls, which she'd been living in since their return from Marianlake. Today, she wanted to look like an angel from Christmas past. Everyone always said she was a throwback to an earlier age and these were not unkind words. She would love to go back in time.

She chose a full-length, emerald green velvet skirt with a striking century-old Victorian tape lace blouse. The simplicity of the 'to-the-knees' train that flowed in back was her favorite feature. Everything had to flow today and it would. It was a perfect day. Even the heavy snowfall was perfect. Fortunately, friends and family were not traveling from remote areas. Absolute perfection, though? Really, could there be such a thing when the person who inspired the work had mysteriously disappeared? Dina was having her club debut in five days. Hopefully, Joe would be there, if only to see Carol Ann.

Ready two hours early, she swished about the house in her long skirt, sipping on eggnog, enjoying the fire and decorations, remembering that gorgeous autumn day in the pumpkin field. She was setting up her easel and canvas when they seemed to appear out of nowhere trailing a red wagon filled with pumpkins.

'This is definitely finally it,' he had said. 'I think this little guy wants to decorate his entire street. He's just not telling me. Hi, Maggie.'

'Hi, Joe.'

'You're painting the field?'

'Yes.'

'See all the faces?'

She smiled, thinking he was teasing. 'Pumpkin faces? You kidding?'

'Not on the pumpkins,' he had said, slicing vertical lines in the air. 'Between them. There are faces everywhere.'

'And in the trees, too,' said that beautiful little boy.

'See ya later, Maggie.'

'Bye, Joe.'

She did see faces everywhere that day. Just like Joe said. Carol Ann nudged her back into the present.

"You look fantastic. Can't wait to see *it*."

"Thanks. Sorry I didn't give you your usual sneak peek."

Carol Ann helped herself to a sip of her eggnog. "You hardly leave the house anymore. Since we got back, you've run paint supply errands and been to see Dina in the hospital. That's pretty much it. They're calling you the 'drop-in' at school."

"We'll be done for good with school in a few months and my grades are fine. They're not as high as yours Miss Skip a Grade, but I'm not worried. There's been a pull to the house, to my work. I can't seem to leave it for long. It's practically all I think about, my work and our lives. Yours. Mine. And Dina's."

Carol Ann's eyes saddened. "And Joe's."

"Yes. And Joe's."

"Why no sneak preview for me this time?"

"I read somewhere that if the work is still in progress, you should save the energy for the work alone." She smiled mischievously at her sister. "But it's done now."

"Does that mean you'll bring me up and show me before the others?"

Maggie had taken to locking her bedroom door, a recent habit. Privacy, which was never important in the past, had now become a way of life. She took down the white sheet and watched her sister's eyes widen. Carol Ann gave out a little yelp and stood gaping until it was time to dress.

∞∞∞

With Carol Ann playing follow the leader, twenty guests squished themselves into Maggie's bedroom, including Dina who was right in the middle of things, plugging her upcoming debut in five days. The festive atmosphere included playful nudges, a few suggestive comments and developing attractions. As always, the usual percentage of men glared at one or the other of the beautiful Page sisters. One in particular was eyeing Carol Ann like she was the only grape on the vine.

Carol Ann asked for their attention.

"My sister showed me this painting a couple of hours ago and my heart is still pounding. Most of you know Maggie is an artist. But what most of you don't know is that Maggie is an ARTIST. Daddy, will you unstick the corners, please? Ladies and gentleman, I'm so proud to show you the work of my sister, Margaret Joanna Page!"

The golden hair fell to the shoulder, waving easily around the face. The wings stretched to the farthest corners of the wall, thirteen by seven feet. Both wings had a face. In the top tip of the right wing, a blond child looked upward in wonderment, a small black cross on his cheekbone. In startling contrast on the upper tip of the left wing, a black dash lined the cheekbone of a handsome, dark-haired young man. His pained, watery gaze looked beyond the guests, the room, and the time. Later, several guests asked Maggie what the boy and the young man were seeing.

The golden crown over the Angel's head seemed to subtly revolve and its sea-blue eyes stared directly into the soul from a radiant, ageless face. Some intuited personal messages filled with warmth and hope. Others received admonitory or scolding messages. Some felt touched by God. Most felt pressured by something dark and threatening.

Painted from the waist with crossed hands splayed on its bare torso, shafts of light streamed through long-fingered spaces.

"Is there something in or behind the shafts of light?" someone asked.

"Petitions are being received and set forth," the artist said.

What had touched her, they wondered. What was her muse? The wise noticed the absence of pride in the artist, detecting not one hint of vainglory, seeing only love and gratitude.

Though she'd never been demonstrative, she wanted to hug every person in the room. She'd have to send them all thank-you cards, maybe include a snapshot of the mural. But a heart full of gratitude wasn't enough. Friends meant well, but friends were not professional art critics. She needed to learn from an expert whether or not this painting could succeed in the art world on its own merit.

She was only nineteen-years-old and she didn't know anybody.

When her parents suggested the guests move downstairs and crack open the champagne, Carol Ann and Dina stayed behind.

"Maggie?" Dina asked, straight-faced, "do you think you could bring your wall to my opening?" Then she giggled, almost the way she used to. "Seriously Maggie, it's absolutely the most fantastic painting I've ever seen. Did you get the idea at Marianlake?"

"Sort of," she said, noticing how fascinated Carol Ann was with the faces in both wings. Anticipating her sister's next question, she said, "It's not a dash. And it's not a minus sign. While we're at it, that mark on Alain's cheekbone is not a cross."

Carol Ann's shoulders drooped. "That letter he wrote me, that odd looking thing after his name. It's been driving me crazy and you know what it means, Maggie?"

The sisters hinted that Dina excuse herself for a bit.

"Forget it," Dina said, boldly crossing her arms in front. "I'm part of this, too. I'm not moving."

"I painted those in yesterday. That's when I knew. It's a *can't see the track for the horses*, as Joe used to say." She walked up to the mural and touched Alain's cheekbone. "It's a 'positive' sign."

"So you're saying that that dash on Joe's cheek is really a negative sign? Is that it?"

She nodded and Dina looked lost.

Carol Ann rubbed her index finger up and down the side of her nose. "So what was Joe trying to give me, an algebra lesson? All right, I end up with a positive over a negative. What does that tell me? There are no numbers. So I can't divide the denominator by the numerator. And I have no way of knowing which is greater. So all I have are the signs–positive and negative. Two opposing signs. Two opposing forces. Maggie! It's so simple—"

"I didn't know what they were." Maggie needed her sister to understand. "I think that was for you to figure out somehow. I only knew what they were not."

"Over the phone, Father Richard told me there was a presence at Marianlake, that Joe experienced it more than once. And we all discovered the presence was negative. Father Richard insisted the three of us say the Rosary every day. He also said that 'dark presences linger in the mind when you're emotionally weakened.' He was referring to the dyslexia. If I take his spiritual prescription, he thinks the dyslexia'll disappear."

"I don't know if I get this," Dina said. "Somebody clue me in. Does this mean that Joe is bad because he's the negative guy? And the kid is good because he's so positive?"

"Not at all." Carol Ann sat down beside her on the edge of the bed. "I believe it means that there's a battle going on and the two of them are helping each other. It could be your classic good against evil thing, but what the story is, I have no idea. Joe drew that logo after his name because he wanted to remind me of Marianlake. And I don't mean our falling in love.

"I think he wanted me to go beyond that and really focus on what he once referred to as *dark angels*. On our first date, he bought Alain a Scapular medal to protect him. After Halloween I understood better. All three of us were in the presence of these dark angels. Maggie with the sketch. Me with the mirror poem and dyslexia. And Dina– you worst of all. We won't get into that."

Dina wiped the dribble under her nose with the back of her hand. "But I got my voice. And Maggie got that." She pointed to the Angel who now seemed a very real presence. "And Carol Ann, you got—I'm not sure what you got."

Carol Ann smiled. "I think I got Angelfish Cove."

"And what does that place have to give you?" Dina asked.

"I don't know yet. Another mystery from Joe. Dina, your uncle's been advertising your club date in the paper. If Joe's in New York, he'll be there, I know it. I have to see him. I can't go anywhere until I see Joe."

One of the neighbors let himself into the room. After apologizing for the interruption, he suggested steps Maggie must take now.

"I don't know if you remember, Maggie," he said, "but I've been producing the community news over at PERK since you girls were babies. And I've struck uranium finding a young artist of your caliber in my own neighborhood. Now I know we're only local, but it's a beginning. What say we get a film crew over here? By tonight, you and your masterpiece could be on the eleven o'clock news."

Before Maggie's humility could sabotage the offer, Carol Ann answered for her.

"That would be absolutely fantastic. She'd love it."

And so for Maggie Page ... it was beginning.

∞∞∞

Carol Ann sat front and center at the Club One Two for all four of Dina's performance nights and this was closing night. Maggie was there of course, along with Mr. And Mrs. Page, followed by the Amodeo clan, probably around a hundred of them—nieces, nephews, cousins, Godchildren, neighbors and their various others, all smiley-faced and numbed with pride.

Maggie and Dina were suddenly hotter than char. Somebody from one of the big Manhattan TV stations saw the spot that aired on PERK and broadcasted it on 'New Names In The News,' a popular affiliate show in New

York City. People were still calling the station, asking how they could get a photograph of Maggie Page's Angel. She was approached by three agents and today signed on with one of New York's finest. Heidi Rotterman never took on novice artists with an empty portfolio and no resume until she saw the Angel.

New Names in The News flashed three frames, enough footage for Heidi to jump on the phone to PERK. Within the hour she had Maggie's Brooklyn address and an appointment set. Forty-eight hours later she had Mr. Page's signature on a contract that all but guaranteed the unknown artist fame and fortune. The Pages were still celebrating. As for the artist, well she wasn't saying much, then she never did. But she had been quieter than usual. And today she did something else she considered important. She called a locksmith who replaced a month-old lock with an expensive upgrade on her bedroom door.

∞∞∞

Dina had no trouble keeping up with the attention. She was not only singing on that lake now, she was also rowing across it at warp speed. She had them on their feet by the end of the evening the first night. Last night, she had them on their feet after her first number. Tonight, who knows. The night was just beginning. She too, had been approached by several notables—managers, record distributors, voice coaches, agents, scouts. Uncle Rocco had friends with clout and when Uncle Rocco told people he had friends with clout, he always added, 'Certainly no pun intended.' For once, the cloutful friends were very pleased. The Amodeos and the Pages clinked champagne glasses. Wasn't it wonderful that both their daughters were on New Names In The News this same week.

An hour before the first set, Dina paced her dressing room, tip-toeing from one flower arrangement to the next, reading the cards, re-reading the latest letter from her secret friend, and feeling as emotionally high as a bundled up four-year-old watching the Santa Claus Parade. Against the shrink's advice, she continued to block out the rape, burying it someplace deep. When it tried to surface, she'd bury it deeper, which was getting easier to do. Too much bad stuff back there in the brain.

She liked the new Dina. She liked her a lot. What she didn't like was the extremely weird-looking plant someone had placed smack dab in the middle of her dressing table. The thing had no color and the leaves looked pleated with funny-looking, furry extensions sticking out the top. She removed the note from the small envelope and read it. After that, Dina couldn't get into the hall fast enough.

"Hey, Mac!" she yelled at a staff member walking by with an armload of tablecloths. "Where's the attic!"

She had to step around all the broken tables, lamps, chairs, and anything that needed fixing was up here collecting dust. Rocco must've realized the kitschy Italian posters weren't exactly compatible with his current décor—chic and cool in chrome and glass, with lots of torso parts hanging around. She wasn't sure she liked that look, either. He seemed to have this thing for hands and lips.

Her throat dried suddenly as she climbed the last few stairs to the attic. Had to be *his* cologne. Mesmerizing. Everything about him was mesmerizing. She had to stay cool, get some saliva back. No messing up the throat right now. Stage time was under an hour away. But he'd know that and he would get her back in shape. He was the one responsible for everything that was happening in their lives right now. More of his cologne wafted straight into her nostrils and she felt guilty for being aroused. He belonged to Carol Ann.

Several shafts of light beamed upwards through wooded slatted cracks in the floor and walls. She could hear murmurs from the capacity crowd below.

"Watch your step, Dina," he said, in that gorgeous deep voice. She saw the hand come out to assist her, followed by the arm, then all of him. He greeted her with a hug and his perfect smile made her feel all melty.

"Joe," she said, hoarsely. "Well where the hell have you been?"

He held her fingertips in each of his hands and that's when she noticed his wrists. How could she not have noticed before? On both wrists, she saw tiny healed-over scars. They weren't slash scars. More like a pattern or design. Swirls of some sort. Looked like curly-Q's raised slightly off the skin. She remembered everything else from Marianlake except for the barn because little Dina had taken the barn with her. Perhaps she had taken the memory of these strange marks on Joe's wrists as well.

"I've missed you," he said, letting go of her hands.

"Where you been, Joe? So much stuff has happened. You have no idea. And Carol Ann has been really crazy. I've got a million and one questions to ask you."

"Dina, I came to see you." His eyes were soft and sad. "It's you I want to talk about and we don't have much time. You have a show to do. I'm so proud of you."

She didn't know what to say or ask first. "Did you hear me sing?"

"Yes." He smiled at her again and tapped his heart. She found she could swallow now. "You're not going around in circles on a lake anymore, are you?" He took a step closer. "Your voice moves my soul. But it cost you, didn't it, Dina."

Knowing what he meant, she instinctively fought back the disturbing emotions attempting to surface. "I'm fine, Joe. You have no idea what's been happening."

When she started to tell him, he placed his hands on her shoulders. "Shh. I know everything that's been happening. You, Maggie and of course, Carol Ann. Originally, I planned to meet Carol Ann here. I sent her this message. Can't now, not after what I heard happened to you. I don't have much time and can't see you both. Dina, when I heard what happened to you on Halloween, it made me sick. I know the cops have dropped the investigation. But I came to tell you I'll find this guy. I promise. Right now, I need you to tell me about him, everything you can."

"I don't remember," she said stubbornly, really not wanting to remember.

"Remember for me now."

"No, Joe. Let it go. I have."

"You haven't let it go. Where's my little Dina? Let me talk to her."

"She's hurting like hell, Joe. Let her rest."

"Let me see her, just for a minute or two. I'll help her with the hurt."

"Like you helped your friend, Willie?" She didn't understand where that came from and it made her stomach turn, more so now that she had wounded him. She threw her arms around his waist. "I'm sorry, Joe. So sorry. So sorry."

"It's okay. I'm paying for Willie. I'll always pay for Willie."

"I have to go to the outpatient clinic at Brookside Memorial," she said, dreading her next appointment. "They do hypnosis on me. They're making some headway, but I can't get past Misty's face. Remember Misty in the barn?"

He nodded and swept a lock of hair away from his eye. She noticed his wrists again.

"I saw you inhaling the air when you came up here," he said. "Do you like my cologne?"

It was her turn to nod.

"You and I always had sensitive noses. Do you remember that smell in the barn those last few days?"

She began to feel uncomfortable, pulled out of herself like some huge hand reaching in and yanking out spirit, like the time she had that real bad flu and floated out of her body for a few seconds.

Joe took her hand and held it. "Close your eyes, Dina. Don't be scared. I'm going to take something out of my pocket and I want you to smell it. Not look at it. Smell it."

She heard the rustling of paper. Menthol and lemons. And the entire scene re-played itself in Misty's eye. The floor clouded below her as she described the man who called himself Steve. Odd name for a man with an accent. It was so wonderful to be able to talk to Joe about it, to tell him everything he needed to know without having to hear it herself. When she returned from a floaty, drifting place, he smiled and braced his hands on her shoulders.

"I have enough," he said. "I'll find him, Dina."

She noticed that his eyes looked past her, like he was looking a hundred years down the road. There was a tear in the corner. "Thanks for not making me remember. I remembered for awhile then made it go away. I made your little Dina go away, too. Even know where she went. What I don't know is where you've been. Where did *you* go, Joe?"

"I wish I had the time to tell you. But I have to get back."

"Get back where? Where the hell is back, Joe? Carol Ann is freaking."

"Will you be seeing Carol Ann on Christmas Eve?"

"Yeah."

"Don't tell her or Maggie you've seen me. Not tonight. You can tell them Christmas Eve when you tell Carol Ann to be by the phone at ten o'clock. If all goes well, I'll have made arrangements for us to meet. Tell her I'll be making it quick on the phone. Tell her to expect no conversation, Dina."

"Why can't I tell her tonight that I've seen you?"

"I know Carol Ann's hurting now. If she finds out I was here and didn't take the time to see her, not even for two minutes ... well, she wouldn't understand that, trust me. I've been watching her down there. She keeps looking around for me and I keep disappointing her, don't I?"

She watched him stare at Carol Ann through one of the slats in the floorboard. His dark brown eyes softened with love and she guilted up for finding him so attractive. For the first time she didn't like the new Dina so much.

Joe took out his harmonica and tooted it once. She smiled.

"Something could go wrong, Dina," he said. "If it does, I'll contact you to cancel the message to her. Please wait until Christmas Eve before telling her you've seen me. If you don't hear from me before, tell her early so she can keep the phone clear. I'm sorry to put you in this position."

"Joe, anything can happen with the phone. Shit. You know that."

"I'll try for ten minutes. I gotta go, Dina. You'll be all right. Sing *In The Air Tonight* just for me."

"Can't you tell me anything? Are you living here in New York?"

"Not far. But also not for long. Bye."

He kissed her on the cheek and made large strides away from her in the darkened attic.

"Wait a minute," she called after him, "what happened to your wrists? Joe, are you all right?"

His voice was already in the distance, telling her not to worry, that he was fine. Stupid, crummy word-*fine*. Everybody always lied when they said they were fine. And if they weren't lying, which was rare, they were leaving whole bunches of stuff out. She stood there like a big old lump until twenty minutes before show time, hoping the lingering scent of his cologne would float her away again, just float her away to her own private Land of Oz.

8. Road to Rome

Downtown Manhattan was a snow-covered dream world on Christmas Eve. Macy's and Gimbel's windows were decorated to their very festive nine's with bell-ringing, beard-adjusting Santa's ho-ho-ing on every other corner. Small groups of Salvation Army carolers managed to crack smiles on some of the most hardened of hearts as they walked along the busy streets. Alain jerked his head around in awe at this Currier & Ives-like scene.

"Don't we have tons of hours left, Joe?" he asked, watching him check his watch.

"Only a couple. Sister Elizabeth would like us back by nine."

"Elizabeth. Remember, we're not allowed to call her *Sister* anymore."

"Right." In some ways, Alain was a better secretary than Sister ... than Elizabeth. Was it coincidence that the cadaverous-looking guy across the street was also in Macy's an hour ago? He wasn't carrying any packages, either. "How 'bout a bite to eat? The sign on that deli over there says they have Santa Dogs."

"Pitter patter," Alain said.

They chose a table with a street view in the busy deli. The skinny guy was still out there, and real, not some foul-smelling spirit. He had to corner him, pretend to shake him up—unless Father Andre sent him. Well, he'd find out, but he needed a plan. While Alain gave a spiky-haired young waitress their order, he noticed two large stacks of bread in front of a double door.

"Is that the service entrance?" he asked her.

"Yeah," she said, arching her hip at him.

"Where's it lead?"

"Alley out back. Why? Those shopping bags are full of loot, right, and you need a quick getaway?"

"You guessed it," he chuckled, noticing her noticing his wrists. "So may we use it?"

She paused. He smiled. She smiled back. They could use it.

Alain, who was always full of questions, let this entire scenario pass. He found this curious. Lately he was finding more and more things about Alain that made him curious, like his expertise at time management. It amazed him how quickly the boy completed his homework assignments from Elizabeth. Last night he had five completed pages of history answers returned within the hour. But when he was nosing around him, it would take Alain the same amount of time to write one page.

"I'd rather go out the front, Joe," Alain said when he paid the bill. "Why do we have to go out the back?"

"Because I'm waiting for someone. Now when we get outside, I want you to stay by the door. You don't move from the door, okay bud? And you don't say anything."

He tried to read Alain's face and couldn't. Although he was unable to read minds, he could pick up on emotions, lies, bits and pieces of the future. He wondered if growing up with Rosa helped him tap some of those unused portions of the brain. Or was Marianlake the beginning, the real beginning? Alain's emotions and everything else about him were becoming increasingly difficult to read.

At Marianlake, Alain spoke volumes with the simplest expressions and gestures. He still used them, only now their meanings seemed to suggest something more. The answers he needed were undoubtedly with Alain and whatever the boy knew, he wasn't sharing.

The alleyways in Medford, Massachusetts were nothing like this. This was New York City and its alleyways were always buzzing, typically with accidents waiting to happen. The sleeping wino a few feet away could actually be a cop on a stakeout, unless he passed up his last liquid dinner to buy those snow-white shoelaces. And the long hair sticking out of the heavy woolen cap was conditioned to its very satiny ends. He could only hope that police business would not interfere with his own.

Light footsteps and the jingle of keys moved slowly toward him. He looked down at Alain and reminded him to stay by the door, promising him that he wouldn't be farther than a few feet away in any direction. The approaching man was definitely thin enough, but he seemed older. He checked on Alain again then casually stepped forward, friendly like.

"Got some kick-ass hash, man. Ya interested?" he asked, close enough to notice it wasn't the cadaverous guy after all.

This guy was older and seemed wired. Something was about to go down. He had to get Alain away from here real fast, only somebody was beating him to it. The young skinny guy who'd been tailing them suddenly had him by the hand, pulling him inside. Joe leapt for the door and yanked Alain back by the collar. He wasn't sure, but he could have sworn he heard Alain tell the guy in French to hurry and go. With one hand on Alain's collar, he managed to yank the guy back with his free arm, thrusting him against the brick wall. He couldn't have weighed any more than a hundred and ten pounds. His face seemed oddly calm. Then all hell broke loose in the alleyway.

As a small Salvation Army band sang *Hark The Herald Angels Sing* out front, the wino joined forces with seven others in back. Somebody yelled 'freeze'. So everybody froze right on cue. The guy he offered the hash to was cuffed and Mirandized. All this against the Sally Ann's peaceful carols, and he still had the guy pinned to the brick wall. This entire scene seemed so ludicrous, orchestrated somehow. But like Willie's death, that thought didn't make sense.

"I got questions," he whispered, taking a finger-pulse on the guy's throat. "Now we're gonna pretend like we're talking friendly for a minute until the cops disappear. Understand? Nod once for yes."

The guy obeyed, eyes as tranquil as Marianlake that first morning.

"Question number one," he said, pumped. "Why are you following us? And before I give you a chance to get verbally creative on me, I'll check the ID." He patted every pocket the guy had—jeans, ski jacket, lumberjack shirt. He even checked out his boots. Nothing. And Alain said nothing. He just stood quietly with his eyes glued to him, sucking on his lower lip. "Who are you?" he finally asked. The guy, more of a kid really, didn't seem scared or bothered in the slightest.

"Everything is happening exactly the way it's supposed to happen," he said. "But there's a long road ahead of you yet."

"Answers! I want answers!"

The boy looked at him like he was a long lost brother. "The man who attacked your friend–you'll find him in Florence. His name is Stephano. Other information awaits you in Rome. Take the child there."

"What! God, I'm so sick of these cryptic puzzle games." He tightened his grip around his neck. "I want your name."

"My name is Rafe."

"Rafe. Rafe what?"

Joe had no idea how *Rafe* did it, but suddenly he was holding his hands, palms up with his wrists exposed.

"Pay strict attention to these," Rafe cautioned, referring to the swirls of developing scars on his wrists. "Study for five years in Rome. Study in the Spirit, Joseph. And keep the child safe. There will be tests."

"Joe," Alain called to him. "This policeman here is looking at us."

"Merry Christmas," the officer said. "Sorry for the disturbance, but we had you covered. Best you keep the boy out of laneways, though. Night."

This exchange had taken less than ten seconds but when he returned to business, Rafe was gone. Sure. Why not vanish into thin air? After scanning all possible exits, he looked questioningly at Alain.

"Did you see where he went?"

Alain shrugged. "I was watching you."

He squatted to Alain's level and searched his eyes. "Let's get home. We'll finish the tree and then we're having a long talk. Okay?"

"Mm-hmm. Where's Rome, Joe?"

Sister Elizabeth was having eggnog with her nephew Ronny when they got back to their homey digs in West Hempstead, Long Island. It was a quaint little suburb, similar to Alain's home in Trois-Riviérés. Joe looked at the sand dollar hanging on the tree and remembered Ocala. Ocala seemed like another dimension now. Still, every time he thought of Florida, his stomach flipped over the way the car did that horrible day. Then there was the touch of the

Angel's hand. Was he around now because he sure could use him?

"Left you guys part of the tree," Ronny said, enthusiastically running the words together to sound like one. He was such a pleasant kid who spoke so fast that he forever sounded out of breath. The extra pounds on him accounted for that. During childhood, almost all of Ronny's imaginary playmates were angels and he insisted they hung out with him, everywhere and always. They even helped him with his homework. Ronny's candor regarding the angel visitations, coupled with the fact that he was overweight, made him the focus of many cruel jokes.

He used to get beat up a lot as a kid, he told him. Lots of blood. And he had one non-angel imaginary friend named 'Joe'. Joe decided the non-angel imaginary friend part had to be a call for male-bonding and attention. But he simply did not have the time for Ronny right now. Alain was his primary concern.

Ronny shrugged off the jokes easily and continued to develop his interest and high aptitude for languages, something that baffled his teachers and family. At seventeen, he already spoke three languages, was working on a fourth, and was practically devoid of ego. He admired that quality in the kid, believing humility was a gift he hadn't received, especially given the pride he took in his horse-smarts. As far as Ronny's family knew, there hadn't been an angel sighting in years. As far as they knew.

"Everything go okay today?" Elizabeth asked. "You get all your whatchamacallits?"

"We're going to Rome," Alain said, eager at the prospect of another adventure. "Eh, Joe?"

"What's this?" Elizabeth put down her eggnog mid-sip, but was instantly distracted when Ronny said he had to get home to his mom, that he was already in for it because he was so late.

"Tell ya in a bit," he said, casting a goodbye smile in Ronny's direction.

"Merry Christmas, everybody," the teenager said. "Bye, Aunt Liz. See you tomorrow."

Elizabeth always seemed saddened by Ronny's departures and lately, her goodbye hugs appeared clingier. At the door, Alain extended his Christmas wishes to Ronny in French. Ronny had said he enjoyed listening to Alain speak French since this was the fourth language he was working on. Ronny and Alain exchanged whispers before he left.

"Everybody's forever learning something from everybody around here," he said, running his hands through his hair. "Everybody's getting answers, Elizabeth. Except me, of course."

"Oh my. Somebody's got a reindeer in his knickers." She got up and fixed him an eggnog with cinnamon. "What's up? And what's this about Rome?"

Following his recap of the day's events, Elizabeth sat there scrunching up her face at him. "So you're going to take off to Rome on the basis of this information?" she asked, flatly.

"I don't get you. Every time something happens you turn your head away. This Rafe character knew about Dina and where to find her rapist. *Study in the Spirit, keep the child safe.* These scary things on my wrists. Just how would you explain all that?" He checked his watch. 9:30 PM. Sugar-plum fairies started dancing around in his stomach.

"Are you still planning to arrange a meeting with Carol Ann in Angelfish Cove next week?"

"Yes. I've got to see her."

"Do you plan to bring Alain with you?"

"Course not. It'll only be for a few days."

Elizabeth absent-mindedly bobbed the cinnamon stick up and down in her mug. "Not a good idea, Joe, if you don't mind my saying. How will you be able to keep him safe with you there and him here?"

Tired of being the polite yes-man in a plan he still knew nothing about, he decided to let the hammer fall. The hell with it. Alain was in his room wrapping gifts. No chance of him overhearing.

"Alain is always safe. Haven't you noticed?" he said with a slight edge in his voice. "Horses. Dog attacks. Intruders. Really, what's he need me for? We're supposed to be deep undercover here in New York. And what happens, we have cherubic, golden-haired nephews hanging around on a daily basis, a walking target while he runs girlfriend errands for me. He's checking on friends in the hospital with entire police squads loitering about. Oh yeah, and he takes impromptu walks with Alain around the neighborhood. Then there's you—who sees her sister a couple times a week and the Marianlake crowd have absolutely no objections to this. I, on the other hand, can't talk more than a minute on the phone. How come no one's designed me a bag yet? You know, something stylish to wear over my head."

He checked his watch again and continued, hoping he wouldn't sound this agitated when he talked to Carol Ann. Fifteen minutes left. "Look at the hassle Father Andre and I got into the other day when I wanted to see Dina at the club. He tells me I need to keep up with the lives of these three young ladies, as he calls them, and then he won't tell me why or let me see them.

"I got this hole in my gut, Elizabeth. This big gaping hole. I feel like I'm mutating. Look at my wrists. Every day the marks look different. And nobody, not even God will give me an answer. It hurts because it seems that all of you know more than I do. Even Alain. God help me, on this Christmas Eve, will I get even one answer? Elizabeth ... do you know who Alain is?"

∞∞∞

He was right. Everyone did know more than he did, including herself. This very frustrated young man did not deserve to be kept entirely in the dark. Still, her loyalty belonged to the higher forces. And poor Joe had a long way to go. She answered his question.

"No I don't," she lied.

Joe didn't believe her and she knew it. It was a silent stalemate.

"Call Carol Ann," she said. "Go to Angelfish Cove. We'll manage here."

He looked at her with a pained stare. "Am I going to make it there? Is something going to prevent me from seeing her?"

"We know Carol Ann will make it there, Joe. That's the important thing."

"Why did I see your clones in Angelfish Cove? *Meet the players*, I was told. There hasn't been a night since that I haven't asked myself–players in what? And then there you all were, waiting for me at Marianlake. But Alain ... Alain was in Angelfish Cove for real that night. Then Willie died. Willie ..."

"Make the call, Joe. Hearing her voice will help you. Make the call and then we'll start celebrating Christmas. You, me and Alain. Let Willie rest. Her death was for a reason. You were given a glimpse of Willie's destiny from day one, or at least the destiny she chose."

"I should not have had the talk with Willie that night, not after she'd been drinking."

She gave Joe's arm a squeeze and left him to make his call in private.

∞∞∞

Carol Ann picked up on the first ring.

"Hi," he said, picturing that little freckle cluster on her nose.

"Joe. Oh Joe," was all she managed.

"Carol Ann, please listen carefully. I can get away from January third to the sixth. Meet me in Angelfish Cove. I've made a reservation for you at the Twin Cedars Lodge, a mile north of the main drag. You won't miss it."

"Will you be there on the third?" she asked in a voice higher-pitched than usual.

"That's my goal, but stay put until the sixth, okay?"

"Where are you now?"

He didn't answer.

"Is Alain with you?"

Again he didn't answer.

"Can't talk anymore, Carol Ann. We'll save it for Angelfish Cove. And baby–I know about the dyslexia. Don't worry. You won't have it for long. Merry Christmas."

"Joe? Joe! You still love me?"

"Yes I still love you. You have no idea. I wish you did then all this wouldn't be so hard on you. I really have to get off the line now, Carol Ann. I'll see you soon."

He had no business falling for her, continuing with her. If he loved her, he should terminate this impossible relationship. Carol Ann didn't need to end up like Norma. Or Willie. Alain and Elizabeth found him by the phone with his head propped in his hands.

"Carol Ann okay?" Elizabeth asked.

He fluttered his lips at her. "Insecure, confused, frustrated. I'm such a gift to women." Alain was standing there in his Santa PJ's with the feet in them and he had to laugh. "I'm sorry, bud. It's your first Christmas away from your parents and Compo and Marianlake. And I'm being a stick-in-the-mud. Why are you so flushed and sweaty?"

"I always get warm on Christmas Eve," he said as though this were the most natural thing in the world. "Joe, let's put on Christmas carols and finish the tree now." He grabbed his and Elizabeth's hands and yanked them into the living room.

"Okay, shall we decorate from the bottom up or top down?" Elizabeth asked, tearing the plastic off a box of gold ornaments.

"Bottom up, of course, but lights first," Alain said.

It had always frustrated him that he could never get an empathic vibe from the boy, except tonight. Alain's legs and stomach were tingling and his ears burned. "Alain, come here." Alain scooted over and he ran his hand across his forehead. "You feel okay? You're awfully warm. Elizabeth, feel his forehead."

"I'm sure he's okay, Joe."

He raised a brow at her and plunked Alain on his lap. Something was definitely amiss here. "Bud?"

"Told you, Joe. I always get warm on Christmas Eve. Don't worry. Usually I stay by myself in my room for awhile. But not this year. This year I'm allowed to feel like this with you and Elizabeth. But more you."

Elizabeth was as calm as cool breezes at her end of the couch. "What do you mean you're *allowed*?"

"Jesus. He's inviting you to His birthday party. That's all. Please get all the sad parts off your face, Joe. *Gai Noël, oui*?"

"Are you telling me you know Jesus personally, is that what you're saying?"

"Mm-hmm. But so do you, Joe. I probably hear better, though."

"Hear what better?"

"Here." Alain took his hand and held his wrist on his forehead. "You keep your wrist there and I'll close my eyes." Alain re-arranged his position on his lap and closed his eyes. Within seconds, tiny beads of sweat broke out on both their foreheads.

He glanced over at Elizabeth again.

"Go with it, Joe," she said.

While Alain silently prayed, a burning sensation developed on his wrists. It was mild enough to tolerate and he'd experienced it before. But this time he felt an internal burn. He closed his eyes. Fear and worry over the future disappeared, seemed insignificant now, workable, answerable. He saw his life from a proper perspective, the way he had when he went up in an air balloon on his seventeenth birthday and looked down on the shrunken landscape.

As a powerful force smothered his darkest angels, the whisper of a voice from deep within spoke to him—

'A huge thumb', Humor said to his soul. 'I will always hold your enemies down for you'.

'Who is this child?' he asked in his mind. *'One question and one answer on this special night. Please.'*

The answer came, *'Not who is this child? Rather, who are you and how much will you sacrifice for this child? Go to Rome, Joseph. The child comes in answer to a prayer.'*

He hung on to this beautiful peace and once again recalled his first morning at Marianlake. The mist, the loons and the easy breeze had sucked the tension out of him. That walk around the lake to his cabin had been another slice of heaven revealed. If only he'd known at the time.

He didn't want to open his eyes, but it was hard to ignore Alain's playful knocking on his cheekbone. He winked one eye open and the boy giggled. "If you tell me what you heard, I'll tell you what I heard. And I'll throw in a couple of cookies."

Alain, who wasn't buying the bribe, gave him an impish look. "Everything I hear comes out in French, Joe. I don't know how to say it in English."

"Please tell me."

Alain glanced down at Joe's wrists.

"Look at your wrists," Elizabeth said, still in the land of cool breezes.

The skin was pinkish, but fast fading. All the swirls on both wrists had disappeared, replaced by three small letters raised two millimeters from the skin in dimensions of one half inch by one inch.

"S t C," he said dreamily. "Save the child."

Sister Elizabeth and Alain exchanged looks.

"I don't know how to describe this feeling," he told them, deciding to keep the interior message to himself for now.

"A feeling of perfect piety and consolation," Elizabeth offered. "These are gifts, Joe, meant to be temporary. After they've faded, you'll be intentionally left on your own to prove your sincerity or discover your insincerity. So beware of pride. Whatever good is in you belongs to God and things you can boast about that are placed in you are at His disposal."

"Do you think I'll have to wait until 1996 to piece all this together?"

"No. I think you'll learn more as you go. Obviously." She pointed to his wrists. "I think we'll all know as much as we're allowed to know in the given moment."

"Does all this scare you sometimes, bud?"

"I was scared on Halloween when my shirt got wrecked and bloody."

"Weren't you scared the day we met, when Compo was in that mean mood?"

Alain lifted his chin. "No. 'Cause I knew you were coming. And we already talked about this. Can we finish the tree and all the other stuff now?"

They finished the tree at a quarter of eleven, topping it off with the largest angel they could find in West Hempstead. It had golden hair, just like Maggie's angel. If only he could tell her how very proud he was of her. She was the one he hadn't yet been in touch with. Still centered and calm, he realized that God was taking care of things all along. Now he could feel and demonstrate this truth. Without having to look at his wrists for confirmation, the *StC* would comfort him when this feeling had gone. Elizabeth was right. Though this state was not permanent, it was the perfect time to decide their next move, while he was in the 'zone'.

"I can't go," he announced to Elizabeth, holding his finger down on the green ribbon she was tying on a gift. Alain was busy putting the crib together and flicking radio channels. He repeated, "I can't go."

"To Angelfish Cove?"

"Yes."

"Why can't you go?"

Thinking of Carol Ann as the proprietor in that amazing bookstore of hers, *sometime* in the future, he said, "I'd distract Carol Ann from something that has to happen. Something has to happen to her while she's there. And we three have to go to Rome."

"This might be your last chance to see her—for a long time, Joe."

The thought of not seeing Carol Ann saddened him to no end. "I know it. But she has to do her thing and I can't mess with that."

"You'd better call her right back then. Tell her there's been a change in plans."

He poured Elizabeth a hot apple cider and plunked a cinnamon stick in it. "I can't call her back, not until she gets to Angelfish Cove. She may not go if I call it off before."

"I know you're right, but I feel bad for her. You're going to say goodbye to her, aren't you."

This wasn't a question. Somehow she knew. And Alain, who stopped what he was doing to watch them, knew what *he* knew. The insights they shared on this sacred night had rendered them a kind of spiritual triumvirate. The room was full of Angels. The right kind of Angels.

"Yes," he said. "I have to let her go. For now. Maybe I knew it all along and just couldn't stand the thought. Couldn't accept it. Guess I'm getting a lot of special help tonight."

"Are we going to Rome 'cause Rafe said to?" Alain asked from across the room.

"Not because of him." He looked at him curiously. "I want to find a priest Father Andre mentioned. Something very special happened there a long time ago and I would like to talk to him more about it."

"You mean Father Vittorio Gianni?" Elizabeth asked, taking a quick breath.

"Yeah. Father Richard told me he's still working in the Vatican. Took me two weeks, but I finally got him on the phone this morning. He's agreed to meet with me as soon as we arrive. He seemed tight-lipped about Father Crouse's whereabouts, though."

The cinnamon stick Elizabeth was playing with tipped over the cider. Refusing his offer to clean it up, she said abruptly, "It's my mess. Now I guess I'll have to clean it up, won't I?"

Father Paul Crouse. She always got weird whenever his name popped up. Secrets. Everybody had secrets. He wondered what hers was. "Any time you need help cleaning up a mess, I'm here."

Elizabeth patted his cheek. "Thanks, Luke Skywalker. I'll remember that."

Staring passionately at the crib, Alain said, "I wish we were inside here ... visiting."

∞∞∞

When Joe called her in Angelfish Cove to say his temporary goodbye, as he referred to it, she cried and cursed him. Then she cried some more. He told her he would always love her. That would never change. He promised to keep an eye on her, Dina and Maggie. The most she got from him was that he was calling from a payphone near Times Square. In his typical cryptic fashion, Joe asked her to remain in Angelfish Cove then return as soon as she finished school, without telling her why. So she screamed at him again and hung up.

He must have been prepared with a bag of quarters because he called her back and told her he was sending her something. With every word he uttered that came closer to their end, her body got colder. Then Joe choked out his final 'temporary' goodbye and hung up. Denial was the easiest emotion to deal with and she immediately called Father Richard who advised her to let him go. She spent the night awake, obsessed and more deeply in love than ever. The following day, Willie's 'CAP' cap arrived at the lodge.

For a week she walked around Angelfish Cove in a fog, crying, phoning Father Richard two more times, hanging out around the big empty glass factory that had gone bust many years ago. Glass-blowing was a pretty big deal in New England and this old building was something of a white elephant, from what she heard around the lodge. Too bad because it certainly had atmosphere and was fixable.

One day she nearly froze to death standing by the ocean, staring up at the house Joe often spoke of—the place where Willie died. Obviously boarded up for the winter months, she continued to stare until something compelled her to enter. There was no resisting the temptation. She could be close to Joe again, like Willie was–only five months ago.

Carol Ann reached into her bag and swapped her fur hat for Willie's cap, which she took everywhere with her. *I'm not walking through a house. I'm walking through a dream.* After finding a couple of loose boards on one of the basement windows she climbed through and drifted slowly through the house, spending time in each room, particularly the kitchen. They would have shared their meals here, talked and laughed.

From Joe's description of the house it was easy locating his room upstairs at the end of the hall. She lay down on the bare mattress. Joe's room. Joe's bed. The house smelled coppery cold and musty. She stayed on his bed twenty minutes or so. She would NOT go into the bathroom, and actually managed to get two steps down on the stairs before turning around. She had to go into that bathroom as surely as she had to stay here in the Cove without Joe. And she had to get close to Willie.

Chugging in a breath at first sight of the tub, she caught a scent in her throat, a faint, lingering scent of orange floral. Willie's *On The Wind* cologne. Joe said she wore nothing but, that he always knew what to buy her—Christmas, birthdays, or to cheer her up, especially these last two years when she started drinking heavily. Was she imagining the orange scent intensifying? She shook out her hands and cleared her throat.

"Okay, what gives with the noses in the Marianlake crowd? ... Willie?"

Her answer came from the tub faucet where a large yellow tear hung ready to fall. She watched and waited. Willie had known Joe most of her life and loved him almost as long, probably cried an ocean of tears, probably died of a broken heart. And she had what—two weeks with him?

"Damn you, Joe! I can guess what Willie felt over there in that tub. Damn you, damn you! You're history, Joe Ross. Willie ... you find him for me and tell him he's history!"

Maybe it was the current of her breath flowing over to the tub that released the tear. She'd never know, but she huddled in the corner on the floor until dark. Before leaving, she affirmed the resolution—she would forget Joe Ross, just put him completely out of her mind.

"Thank-you, Willie."

Willie wasn't around to remind her that resolutions made in the wrong frame of mind were always mistakes, that one could easily misinterpret signs in the wrong frame of mind. Important signs.

On the drive back to the lodge, a road-sign that read, 'caution, bridge slippery when wet,' appeared to glow. There was no bridge in sight, but she didn't notice that when she backed her Pinto to the shoulder. She read the sign from left to right probably twenty times to be certain it was true. It was. Yet she saw only the obvious—the dyslexia was gone.

"Thanks again, Willie," she said, re-reading the sign on her way out of Angelfish Cove the following morning.

Again, the sign's true message escaped her.

Three years later in late spring of 1984, she would return to Angelfish Cove for good and thank Willie once more for inspiring her to lease the old glass factory. But her decision to cast Joe Ross from her mind was a terrible mistake.

∞∞∞

On January fifth, Joe Ross, Elizabeth Whyte and Alain Duprielle arrived at Leonardo Da Vinci Airport in Rome. Forty-five degrees Fahrenheit and it felt like a spring evening to them. Father Richard had booked them into a little *penzione* in Ottavia, outside Rome's center core which pleased him because it was only a ten-minute bus ride to Vatican City. And Father Gianni was now teaching at Vatican City at the Academy of Sciences. They had an appointment first thing in the morning. Hopefully, Father Gianni wouldn't give him the same run-around as Father Andre where the Document was concerned.

He also wondered if Father Gianni kept in touch with Father Paul Crouse, the third member of the Dream Team. Still no word on him. Something went on between Father Crouse and Elizabeth because the mention of his name made her jumpier than a colt with a dog around his hooves. When he finally queried her about it, she said they did know each other years ago, that he had counseled her through a problem and that was that. He couldn't get anything more out of her.

"They don't want you to see that document, Joe," she had said back in New York. "That's blatantly obvious. They wouldn't let me see it, either. How far do you think you're going to get with Father Gianni?"

Their 'Dream' Document. Everything recorded from the collective dream the three priests' shared, had to answer at least fifty of his questions. The Christmas Eve magic had worn off. Probably still back there in New York along with Carol Ann. The saddest thing of all was that during moments like these, his Marianlake memory of her seemed incomplete, like one of Maggie's pre-painting sketches.

He had to abandon her, had no choice there, but now longed to return to their past and hold her. He wanted to hear Dina sing again, the way she had on the lake that day. He wanted to see how Maggie was doing with her Angel. Angels were always the constant. With her paintbrush, Maggie had captured the one thing they all had in common. Angels. Why had the bad ones been eerily quiet? Where were all these bad guys, anyway?

Alain had fallen asleep in the cab when they arrived at the pensione. It was close to 11 PM and he and Elizabeth were walking zombies. Given the jet lag and the hour, they were unable to appreciate the century-old three-storey rooming house. The second and third floor balconies circled the house. One side faced Vatican City, offering a view of the top half of Saint Peter's Basilica. The opposite side was all Mediterranean Sea, deep blue and timeless. They had the timeless side.

"When Father Richard was making your arrangements," the proprietress said, "he told that you grew up always near water." Lena, an extremely elegant lady in her mid-sixties, smiled graciously as she spoke to them in warm, broken English. "This is to your satisfactory? Si?"

Elizabeth, who had the adjoining suite, answered her in perfect Italian and complimented her lovely home.

"Oh," Lena said, on her way out. "Always I'm forgetting to tell about letter. Yesterday a man, very thin, dropped it off for you, Mr. Ross. I leave on your night table. *Buonanotte*."

"Bwona notey," he said and Elizabeth grinned.

After tucking Alain in, he opened the letter, figuring it was a greeting and the usual instruction or two from Father Andre. These instructions typically included the location of the nearest church, library with reading list, and banking details. However, the letter was not from Father Andre. Suddenly he was wide awake, knocking on Elizabeth's door.

"Rafe," he said, nervously tapping the letter. "How do you suppose he found us? Who the hell is this guy anyway? Less than two weeks ago he shows up in an alley in New York City. Today he's in Rome ahead of us, telling us in a letter who raped Dina last October back in Quebec. Some guy. Some guy by the name of Stephano Tartura, or something. I'll find him in Florence, he says, working at a joint called the Giardino Cafe. Okay, so after I punch the guy's lights out, what do I do? Why couldn't he give me this information in the alley Christmas Eve? Who the hell is this Rafe guy!"

Elizabeth pointed him to a Florentine davenport while she went and turned off her bath water. "You'll probably be able to ask him yourself who he is. He's around, obviously, so it's logical that he'll choose a time to present himself. Try and get some sleep, Joe. Your appointment with Father Gianni is very early in the morning."

His gaze bounced around the room. "I'm so tired of whining about all these mysteries, Elizabeth. I've been given a directive that seems like empty words because I don't know the meaning behind the words ..."

"... Study in the Spirit. And keep the child safe," Father Gianni reiterated at 8:45 the following morning.

They had been strolling through the Old Gardens in Vatican City for fifteen minutes and he was too tired to appreciate its beauty, though the forty-degree nip in the air was curing the jet-lag. Why was it he never seemed to be at his best for extremely important meetings with extremely important members of the clergy? Pontifical clergy at that. He looked up at Father Gianni, way up, and wondered if he had ever considered a career with the NBA. Maybe the scouts didn't come out this far. In his late sixties, Father Gianni was the perfect senior *Lurch* with hands the size of watermelons and the voice to match.

"I'm a little grumpy and don't mean to sound disrespectful, Father," he said, stopping in his tracks to face the distinguished priest. "Please tell me why the Document is being kept from us, Sister Elizabeth and me? Confirm that there are parts of the dream that you all detailed in the Document that I'm not supposed to know."

"There are," he admitted in that *Lurchy* voice. He took Joe's hands and examined his wrists. A soft smile crept into his expression. "There are details of the purpose of your mission. Details of Alain Duprielle. You have received validation of good and evil. You already suspect that there are certain people in your life with whom you have a connection. You were introduced to their spirits in Angelfish Cove then met them in the flesh at Marianlake where you experienced evil. And that evil was a fragment, a mere particle of that which you will have to face in future."

Father Gianni rubbed his index and middle fingers along his right wrist and continued. "These impressions come straight from God, Joe. So you need not be afraid. But you must study in the Spirit with all your heart. You have made the commitment to this call, but you have not yet taken responsibility for it. And that is why you are floundering. You are accountable. You are in charge.

"Studying over the next few years will prepare you for 1996 and *studying* is your prime directive right now. So you will stay in Rome for five years. You will apprentice with me. For you, these will be uneventful years, so you will not have to spend this critical time gazing over your shoulder."

"So why New York, Father? Why didn't we come straight to Rome in the first place? And can you *pleeze* tell me something of what will happen in 1996?"

"Sister Elizabeth had to renew her passport. Also it was important that you stayed long enough in the States to learn of the sudden changes in your friends' lives. And as for the year in question, I am permitted only to inform you that if you study hard and keep your eyes on these." Again, Father Gianni took hold of his wrists, "God will give you special graces and some answers in the interim."

One thing he had to know, "Does Alain have some of these answers?"

"He does. But he has a directive as well. Even the child inside the adult soul understands that his knowledge must remain between himself and God. You will learn everything in the end."

"In 1996?"

Father Gianni smiled.

"That's fourteen years away."

"It will pass quickly. I promise you."

"But I have ..."

"What, Joe?"

"... Dreams. I have a life I dreamed of since I was five. Five years?" It was back—the heart palpitations, the irrational worry, the churning stomach. "I'll be in Italy five years? I have a girlfriend. *Had* a girlfriend in the States."

"I'm sorry, Joe. But try to keep in mind that dreams change."

"Not mine. What's to stop me from leaving Alain in the Vatican's care, just walk away and go home to Medford? He'd be fine here with all of you."

"He would. But you wouldn't."

"It's a muddy track on race day you're giving me, Father." He lowered his voice. "Who wrote the notes back in Trois-Rivierés? The dog, the bloody shirt on Halloween, all of it?"

Father Gianni's blank expression didn't exactly come across as convincing. "Now go to Florence and apprehend this Stephano Tartura. Do nothing more than turn him over to the authorities. Nothing more. Then return Monday morning at nine to begin your studies." Father Gianni's eyes softened. "Get on that bus and don't worry so much, Joe. Help is on the way. In two weeks, you will be seeing things quite differently. For now, focus on Dina."

He spent the first half of the four-hour bus ride twisting his brain into a pretzel, *negativizing* on why they kept dodging all his questions and the second half trying to tame his fueled emotions. How did Alexander tame Bucephalus so quickly he tried to remember as he stepped off the bus in Florence. It was near three in the afternoon, which meant he'd been grinding his teeth for fourteen hours straight.

He took in the lush greenery surrounded by mountains. Most of the homes and apartment buildings were made of yellowish cinder blocks with faded red roofing. The Arno River ran straight through the middle of the city with the Pitti Palace and Boboli Gardens below it. Michelangelo's *David* was only five blocks away at the *Galleria dell Accademia*. How Maggie would love to see it. So would he, for that matter. But he hadn't the time because he was here to catch the sick pervert who raped his friend. Why, after the miracles shown him these past months, did he still want to pound the living shit out of a human being? It was a privilege and a gift to personally apprehend this criminal for Dina, was it not? So why wasn't that enough to satisfy him?

He sat at a low-profile table in the Giardino Cafe, unconscious of his tightening fists and white knuckles. Dina's entire personality had split in half and here was this guy, recommending the house antipasto to big-tipping tourists. He spotted him. This Stephano creature was the monk impersonator at Marianlake who asked him to tone it down in the library, the one who gave Dina and Maggie the creeps. Cheap way for cons to travel. Five stars for the sting on Father Andre. Too bad the guy was going to *see* stars.

"Good afternoon, sir," Stephano said in a sickeningly phony voice. "Would you care for anything from the bar?"

Joe removed his sunglasses. "No thanks," he said, standing. "I could recommend something from the bar for you, though. Like a good lawyer."

When Tartura made serious moves to bolt, he grabbed him and pushed his face forward on the table, holding him there until blood oozed from both sides of his nose and down the tablecloth. Some lady screamed and half the cafe was already on their feet. He took a fistful of the guy's collar and shoved him against the wall. Seeing Tartura's blood-covered face barely satisfied him. What Tartura really needed was a slight modification of the reproductive organ, for which he was happy to assist.

He pounded him in the groin and Tartura doubled over. That was one. Now two.

"Sorry Dina and Misty have to miss Act Three," he said, folding his hand around the rapist's genitals.

"Please, please don't do this!" Tartura begged in fractured English. "That place was evil that night. I'm sick. I have trouble."

"Yeah well, you're gonna have more," he said, tightening his grip. Just as he was about to change Tartura into a soprano, he felt a hand squeeze his bicep.

"Let him go, Joe, the police are here. Let them take over." It was Rafe.

He released Tartura and the knots inside his brain and stomach subsided. "Well, if it isn't my travel agent. What other place would you recommend I beat people up in? Care to tell me who you are now?"

"The name's Raphael and we'll speak again another time. Don't misdirect that passion of yours, Joseph. Revenge is a bad companion."

When the police stepped in to begin questioning, Rafe disappeared. An hour later, the authorities charged Stephano Tartura with the brutal rape of Dina Amodeo and extradited him to the United States the following day. Joe sent his friend a wire.

I got him for you, Dina. Wake 'little' Dina and sing one for me.

—Joe

∞∞∞

In 1982, the U.S. received pictures transmitted by the Voyager 2 of the planet Saturn. Dina Amodeo toured nightclubs in New York State and polished her style. Photographs of Maggie Page's Angel became world-famous. Carol Ann Page began dating Brent Tennison, a man who looked alarmingly like Joe Ross. With Father Gianni's help, Joe Ross began to seriously study in the Spirit.

In 1983, Benedetto Bettino Craxi became the socialist prime minister of Italy. Young Alain Duprielle miraculously resuscitated a toddler from a hit-and-run. Elizabeth Whyte told Joe Ross her secret. Beata Canites died from sudden cardiac arrest in her Medford, Massachusetts home.

Rosa Canites swore she saw Willie by her casket.

In 1984, Indira Gandhi, India's prime minister was assassinated by Sikh extremists. Carol Ann Page married realtor Brent Tennison and set up residence in what used to be Angelfish Cove's old glass factory. Maggie Page had a celebrated art showing in Greenwich Village and left hyperventilating shortly after the opening. Dina Amodeo recorded her second album, *Lake Oz*, which topped charts worldwide within two years.

Five more years passed. It was 1991, the first year of awakening for all the players, the year angels of darkness and Light began calling them home. Alain Duprielle, who now bore the marks on his wrists, turned heads wherever he went. Joe Ross, like the impressions on his wrists, had greatly changed.

In the spring when the ground was soft and wet in Trois-Rivierés, Father Andre Georges hired a team of excavators to level the pumpkin field on Marianlake's back property. Father Gianni was on his way from Rome with Father Paul Crouse at his side. And Marianlake's newest resident, a man by the name of Walter Bayard, unfolded a blueprint on the floor of Joe's old cabin that would one day impact the lives of millions.

9. I Want Him Back

Angelfish Cove, 1991

Carol Ann shipped the divorce papers with the other deadwood memorabilia because they reminded her of *him*. Dina once introduced her to a friend with the same name as *him* and she never called the poor guy by name, couldn't bring herself to say it. She had to knock it off. This was a *him day* and she'd been suffering through these once a month for the past year. Why oh why were thoughts and memories of J ... *him* haunting her after all these years? She taped the box and added it to the pile, then did what she always did on *him days*—she got her sister on the phone.

"Well," Maggie said, "the shrink didn't work. The hypnosis didn't work. Maybe it's time we took a different tack."

Poor Maggie never tired of consoling her. Her poor sainted sister. Her poor wealthy, famous, beautiful, sainted sister. "What do you mean?"

"Now don't jump on me again. Let me finish. Okay?"

Crap. She knew what was coming. "Okay."

"Maybe it's time we looked for him?"

She would have none of that. "Oh no. Absolutely not. He could be married. He could have a pile of kids."

"He could be fat. He could be bald."

"Maggie, please. Let's change the subject."

"Think about it, okay?"

"Don't tell Dina I'm obsessing. She'd go track him down and drag him back here by the hair."

"Would that be so terrible?"

The thought gave her the shakes so she ignored the question. "Thank-you again for storing my stuff. I'll have so much room in the basement now for inventory. I'm sending you a pile more boxes, by the way."

"Welcome. How are the renovations coming?"

She held up the phone so Maggie could hear the banging, drilling, sawing, cursing. "Hope this building grows up to be a bookstore sometime before the millennium." She sighed heavily.

"What?" Maggie asked.

"Why didn't I go with my first instinct to open the bookstore seven years ago when I moved here? Instead I chicken and let Brent, who couldn't sell a dying man a prayer, talk me into setting up that dud of a realty company and we cram our bad marriage into the top floor."

"Poor Brent."

"Yeah. Poor Brent."

"I'm sorry, Carol Ann, I didn't mean to throw—"

"It's okay. He has a chance at a life now. In my absence."

"Stop that," Maggie said. "New store. New life for Brent. New life for Carol Ann Page. Right? To new beginnings. Let me hear you say it."

"To new beginnings."

They talked more about Maggie's work and then she returned to her packing. Wow. Maggie and Dina had such remarkable success, on professional levels. Personal—not so much. Once upon a time she'd accomplished something remarkable when she aced the entries for Smith College. Aced them. Then she had to go drop out after one year.

She once told *him* she wanted to shape young minds and teach. What happened to that major in history, that dream? Her family asked the same question.

She told them, "I decided I don't care to remember the past."

Of course the folks thought she was referring to Marianlake and everything that happened there. But it was never about that night of horrors or the dyslexia. It was about him. Everything in the past was always about him. Was it because he wouldn't make love to her, because they had only two weeks, that in light of his new adventures she'd be fairly forgettable? Was it because she fell in love with him too fast? Did that do something to the karma? Or maybe it was because she married a guy who looked so much like him.

She settled. This was probably the reason success was absent on all levels in her life—because she forced *him* out of her mind all those years ago. She should've known then that forcing anything in life never worked. Maggie had a point. It was time to consider looking for him. No and no! She had to stop her brain from circling this wagon every time she got a headache.

If she got out of the house, got some fresh air into her lungs, she'd feel better. She grabbed her old battery-operated radio that broadcasted one station in the Angelfish Cove area—COVE 1010, and reclined on the lounge out back. Oldies but goodies was all COVE 1010 ever played, and nothing but static on every other station. Where did the town get their transmitter—the Oracle City of Delphi, for crying out loud? There wasn't a blasted song played after 1970 and why nobody in town complained was a mystery of mysteries. They loved the oldies, that's why. But her curiosity got the better of her that first year in Angelfish Cove, so she paid a visit to the little station.

The DJ was nowhere around that day. She did meet a secretary who plunked tapes into the machine every hour or so, but the DJ was on vacation. Two weeks later she learned from a new secretary that this elusive DJ, whose name she couldn't remember now for the life of her, was running the station from Boston.

She tried writing the DJ in Boston a couple of times but he never acknowledged her letters. No big deal. Yet if she had managed to get some contemporary music on the station, maybe she'd think less often of *him*. He'd mentioned the music the first time he told her about Angelfish Cove. He too had wondered.

Even the little record shop on the main drag continued to sell ancient music. No doubt the DJ owned a piece of that place, too. Frustrated by the good old oldies, Dina always had a few choice words for the proprietor on every visit. The proprietor, when they were lucky enough to catch him in the almost-always-empty shop, didn't know who she was, had never heard of her. Two Grammys, two platinum albums, three successful world tours, some scandalous press and he had not seen nor heard of Dina Amodeo. So it continued that the Cove station and the almost-always-empty record shop with the always-open-door preferred to stay linked to the past. Go figure.

Given the noise, the memories, the worries, the debts, the divorce, anxiety seemed to be punching a hole in her gut. She turned off the radio and went inside. At least she had *Pages,* the name she'd chosen for the bookstore. The name might be unoriginal but it was her name and she was sticking with it. Besides, using the old maiden name was the one thing she felt positive about these days.

A large shipment of books was on the way up from Boston, due late afternoon. As her silent investors, she prayed she would not disappoint Maggie and Dina. Maggie reminded her to pay very special attention to the walls in Pages. Maggie liked the words 'very special.' She used them often, usually to refer to one of her paintings, but never in a conceited way. One of her 'very special' paintings was also due to arrive later today and she had promised Maggie she'd hang it in a place of prominence.

"This painting is alive," Maggie told her before they hung up. "I don't know how, but it has us in it." Somehow Maggie knew stuff. Always did.

Temples pounding, she grabbed her BoSox windbreaker and tacked a *Back by 3* note on the front door. While heading to Corey's for lunch, she realized she wasn't the only one spending too much time alone. Maggie didn't socialize and hardly ventured out of the house these days, if one could call it a house. A mansion is what it was. Of course, who was she to talk? Friends hadn't come easily to her in Angelfish Cove. Having a husband who was a failure in marriage and finance didn't exactly leave her feeling sociable. Pangs of guilt again. It wasn't Brent's fault. It was mostly hers.

For obvious reasons she never should have married Brent. She was destined to live in this town with someone else and the day she and Brent took up residence here was the most despairing day of her life. This was the typical small town where everyone knew everyone's business. She was special, though. Hah, right. She was special because she was the best friend of that famous singer, whats-er-name. And she was also the sister of that other really famous one–the mysterious and reclusive Angel Lady artist. The townsfolk were fascinated with Maggie. Since there was an angel somewhere in every one of her paintings and her own sister resided here, Maggie was an honorary townie, *in absentia.*

Her favorite place in town was the beach house a few miles south of the main drag. She never mentioned her faint connection to it with anyone, not even John Corey. The townies still spoke of the beautiful young girl who drank herself to death in the bathtub ten autumns ago and the handsome young man she loved but could not have.

Sure, Carol Ann Page was special ... because of who she knew, not for who she was. She slapped the menu down on the table in Corey's Cafe Beanery. The self-pity had to go. So did the headache. It didn't help that the noonday sun was blind-siding her on the right.

"Perhaps if we move the table over, out of the sun?" said an unfamiliar voice.

She squinted upward at the lovely raven-haired waitress bearing the nametag 'Iris'. She looked to be her own age, around thirtyish, with a face that resembled Ava Gardner in her prime and piano teeth that gleamed from across the room.

"Thanks," she said, grateful to the stranger for her consideration. "This is the last table for two in here and this sun is killing me."

Iris gripped the table to pull it forward and that's when she noticed her wrists. There was something familiar here but her brain could not make the connection. Déjà vu. Long ago. Something.

With an increased pulse came the compulsion to play detective. "You're new to Corey's?" She introduced herself, but Iris didn't give her a surname.

"Had to get out of Boston," Iris said, "and I couldn't get past this town. So I stopped in for lunch one day last week and here I am. You're *that* Page, the sister of the famous artist?"

Trying to stave off another wave of depression, she nodded.

Iris took her order and politely excused herself. From a few feet away, she said, "Bet you inspire your sister. I just bet."

Inspire Maggie? In that moment her headache disappeared.

Something about Iris compelled her to hang around and relax a bit, so for the first time in her life she ordered a drink in the afternoon. A screwdriver. When Iris went off shift at two, she asked if she would like to join her. Iris accepted and suggested they go for a 'walk 'n talk' in the spring sunshine.

"I used to drink screwdrivers," Iris said as they strolled along the creaky boardwalk. "A long time ago. I don't drink much anymore, maybe a little wine now and then."

"Me, too," she said, careful not to allow Iris to form any false impressions. What she could not figure out was why she cared. She never cared what strangers thought of her. She wanted to hear Iris's story, especially the story behind those peculiar marks on her wrists. "I hardly ever drink. I must be having a very nice afternoon, thank-you. That was nice what you said about me inspiring my sister."

It was clear Iris did not care to reveal her past, which intrigued her all the more. Carol Ann Page-Tennison-Page was on the force again and it felt good. She learned that Iris was of Latin descent and grew up in New Jersey. Coming from a neighboring state and having an uncle who hailed from Jersey, she knew the accent. And Iris didn't have it. The slight accent she did have sounded indigenous to the New England area. She did say she had come from Boston last week. Funny. One could end up an Oxford scholar and still never completely shake a Jersey accent.

They found themselves outside Pages greeting a courier who was standing in a pile of cigarette butts at the front door. In the time she had spent at Corey's, the books also arrived, along with Maggie's painting. One of the carpenters signed for the books, but the courier had orders to release the painting in the hands of Carol Ann Page.

The courier didn't seem the least bit ruffled over having to wait, so she sent him to Corey's for a meal on her before he headed back. Two of the workmen carried the painting upstairs and she invited Iris to follow. Iris seemed unusually protective of the painting, taking care that they watch the corners.

"If you want privacy," Iris said, "I can understand. Obviously this is from your sister."

Carol Ann shook her head. "Uh-uh. I love showing off Maggie's work. I'm so proud of her. I remember her first ..." Her voice suddenly trailed off. The depression had returned.

Then Iris said an odd thing. "Don't go past. Don't go future. Stay here because there's always something in the here your soul wants to tell you."

When Iris spoke of not going to the future, she spoke with her hands, holding them up which exposed her wrists. The identical marks on both wrists mesmerized her. The first mark was unmistakably the letter *S*. She had to ask. Even the unveiling of the painting could wait. She had to know.

"Please tell me ... um, those marks on your wrists?"

"Don't you want to see your sister's painting first?"

"For some strange reason I can't explain, I'm compelled to know about those marks. Obviously you didn't try to commit suicide. You never would've lasted long enough to carve out all that detail. Ohh. Please forgive the cold, clinical observation." *Real smooth, Carol Ann. So compassionate.*

"No apologies. You're welcome to take a closer look. It's okay. It's the least I can do for letting me share your first glimpse of that." She nodded at the painting.

Carol Ann gently ran a finger over Iris's left wrist. She couldn't believe herself. She had known this woman less than three hours and she was not a toucher. "The *S* is all I can make out. Where did the marks come from?"

"They appeared suddenly a few weeks ago. I just woke up with them one morning, but the impressions weren't as pronounced until I got here last week. These marks ... well, I believe they're spiritual, a sign. And I think you're the one who should find out what they mean, Carol Ann. There's a connection in this town, between these marks and you, an answer to start you on your way. You know how I knew for sure?"

Dizzy and excited, she shook her head and wondered whatever happened to that old Flower Book. Why on earth would she think of it now?

"--I knew for sure when I first saw you today. My wrists burned. It was awful. And then I felt your headache. It went away, didn't it?"

"Yes. The Iris is such a pretty flower. I used to have this book with ... never mind. Not important now."

"Don't let this throw you, Carol Ann. Please keep it together. I can't stay long in Angelfish Cove, but probably I'll be able to come back later."

"Where you off to?"

"A couple of friends to visit, some family matters to clear up. Remember, stay focused in the present. The past can drive us nuts if we let it."

"I need to ask you a million questions, Iris."

Iris's laugh filled the room with heart. "I'm sure you do, but I can't answer them for you. I can point you in the right direction. And I can share any insights I have with you before I leave. You going to unwrap the painting?"

Angel Reclining, Maggie called it. Reminiscent of the late '60s, it was a main drag scape of Angelfish Cove. The artist had captured its timelessness. The summer boardwalk. An elderly couple pointing at a lobster catch. A rear view of a man standing in front of the tiny record shop wearing a large, khaki T-shirt with two scrambled words printed on the back. Something 'gel' in the first word. And something 'tory' in the second.

Maggie remembered to paint in Corey's Cafe Beanery and old Len Marvick's Hardware Store on 98 Main Street right down to the candles, incense and large box of fireworks in Marvick's window. It amazed her how perfectly Maggie recalled the predominant lime green shade in the store's rainbowed '98'. She'd painted in a sign perched on top of the fireworks that read,

Draw for contest noon, July 4th.

With so much going on in the scape, she found it difficult to spot Maggie's signature angel. She grinned at the cute girl catching sunrays with her magnifying glass. What was she looking at, a bug, a worm? One ray solarized either a toy train car or streetcar because it was all silvery with a bunch of windows. In the distance was a partial view of a green barn with a golden horse weathervane on the cupola, a wayward baby duck in the bay, a beautiful boy with a towel draped over his shoulder, checking out a hoop toy. And the amazing *Pages Bookstore*.

She would not be humble about the store. Why downplay the magnificence of the new store in the name of being humble? Working from a bad photocopy of a sketch, Maggie managed to duplicate it in all its glorious pulchritude. As usual, Maggie's second-sightedness was uncanny. But hey, where had she stashed the angel?

"Do you see it?" she asked Iris.

"Yes. But I won't spoil your fun, Carol Ann. And I have to get going."

She gave Iris her business card. "Before you leave," she said, patting her arm, "I'll make you dinner. I think we have to talk more."

"Me, too. Before I go, we'll talk again for sure." Then Iris headed out, dodging buzz saws and sidestepping electrical cords.

Figuring she'd gain a better perspective from a distance, Carol Ann leaned against the wall and stared at the painting. Just as she was about to phone Maggie to ask where she put the angel, she spotted it. Prettier than melting butter on pancakes. She had the angel reclining as an unobtrusive billowing cloud that stretched right across the top third of the painting. Hair falling to the side, its head rested on its hand, supported by the elbow. And of course, it was reading one big sucker of a book. What a perfect gift for Pages opening.

The longer she stared, the more intently the angel seemed to read. What was the angel reading, for crying out loud? Jolted by the memory, her pulse accelerated.

'And he had all these squiggly scars on his wrists', Dina had said. *'Really weird-looking. I don't remember seeing those at Marianlake. Do you, Carol Ann?'*

'No', she'd said. It was so many years ago. *'There were never any scars on his wrists'.*

A gentle knock on the door snapped her from what would soon become an obsessive thought. Her stomach quivered. Whoever was out there in the hall had been knocking for some time because she heard it over buzz saws and chose to ignore it. Amazing how one memory could put the present entirely on hold. She opened the door.

"Mrs. Tennison?"

She found herself staring into the softest brown eyes she had ever seen. He looked seventyish and balding, with shimmering thick silver hair at the sides. He was around five feet five and a little round in the middle, but held himself like gentry.

"It's Ms. Page," she said, admiring his beautifully tailored suit. "I'm newly divorced. I wanted to use my maiden name again." She could have simply said 'Ms. Page' without offering any explanation. "Can I help you?"

"I was thinking perhaps we could be of help to each other." He smiled. "My name is Edmon Fendi, Ms. Page, and I come to you recommended by John Corey at the Beanery."

His teeth had a yellowish tinge and she detected a stale odor on his breath, but not enough to be offensive. He certainly knew how to dress. Then she noticed his hands ... so white and smooth. Not a wrinkle or a line. No age spots. At first she thought he was wearing surgical gloves. "What is it that you do exactly, Mr. Fendi?"

"May I come in?" he asked in a butler-like tone.

"Of course. So John Corey sent you? You don't look like a handy-man." She noticed his brown eyes soften more when he spotted Maggie's painting. His smile seemed familiar.

"I was employed by Menlo and Wright Publishing in Boston for twenty-seven years. I retired last year as Acquisitions Coordinator and I'm not handling retirement well. Been around books most of my life. Books and food. Cuisine is my avocation, you might say. And if you need somebody to hammer in a nail for you, Ms. Page, I'm your man. To be honest, though, never hammered a nail in straight yet. It may go in crooked, but it goes in crooked in the right place."

She smiled with uncertainty, feeling ambushed by the weight of responsibility. She needed to sit. *Ambush. He* was so fond of using that word. Thinking of him flooded her with waves of desire as tiny sparkles of eye-stinging light danced around Mr. Fendi's head.

Could Dina have been mistaken about the scars on his wrists? What about Iris's wrists? Her eyes caught hold of the *Vanity Fair* magazine on the coffee table. But her eyes were not seeing the words *Vanity Fair*. Her legs buckled. Before she passed out, she saw the words as *ytinaV riaF*.

She came to on the couch, tucked under her floral chintz cuddling blanket. A lemony herbal scent wafted into her nostrils. That Vanity Fair magazine brought it all back—Marianlake on Halloween night all those years ago. The message in the mirror. The dyslexia.

"Oh, God," she said, taking notice of John Corey and the kind eyes of Edmon Fendi. "It can't be happening again." That true grit inherited from her dad was nowhere to be found, not even in the most secret deepest part of her. Okay, so who stole the grit? Who swiped the courage?

"The doctor's on his way, Carol Ann," John said. "You're all worn out, that's what. Yuh, I'm sure. Ed's brewed you his fixer-upper herbal tea. Fix you up great."

She looked at Edmon, almost getting lost in his eyes. "Sure you wanna work for a manic-depressive?"

"Is that a self-diagnosis, Ms. Page?"

She managed a smile. "Tell me about yourself, Mr. Fendi."

The man answered in the abridged, which she appreciated considering she felt like crap on a plate. There was obviously more to him than a list of credits longer than the Academy Awards. Gesturing with those beautiful, elegant white hands, he spoke in a quiet resonant voice pleasing to the senses and she found his essence distracting. She needed distraction. *Thank you for that, Mr. Dapper. You're hired.*

Edmon Fendi's first official task as part-time assistant was to hang the *Angel Reclining* in the top foyer in front of the wrought iron staircase. Edmon had been with her two short weeks and with his help, opening day was happily moved back two weeks. More sample dyslexia had not returned but she ditched the Vanity Fair magazine, anyway. Looking at it made her cringe.

Days before the grand opening, the curious began pressing their noses to the glass. She had advertised straight down to Boston, but it was the reports circulating in several newspapers and telecasts that brought them in from all over the U.S. One tabloid reported that Dina Amodeo was flying in now that her lawyer had negotiated a settlement with the injured party. Another newspaper said it was hype for her upcoming American tour. Carol Ann knew better. The last thing Dina needed was more bad publicity.

Behind Dina's legion of admirers were Maggie's fans. Maggie Page was a notorious recluse renowned for missing her own showings, whose beauty, mystique, and genius had touched the world. In a rare interview, bashful Maggie confided to the press that she and her sister were close.

With the *Angel Reclining* a banner headline, Maggie's fans assumed she'd show for Page's opening. Acting as her sister's envoy, Carol Ann received the attention modestly. She loved Maggie and Dina with all her heart, but come on, everybody was here to ogle *them*. No one got this crazy over the opening of a regular bookstore owned by a regular person.

The crowd would be so darned disappointed. Dina's court date was no rumor and the rages had worsened. This time she almost killed someone. Last night on the phone, Dina said she was trying to finagle a way to postpone the concert dates. She was afraid of herself, she said.

And Maggie, well, she would try really hard this time, though it was torment living with this darkness in her head. The fear and agoraphobia were so bad that some days she couldn't leave her bedroom to venture into other parts of the house—her house, a hermit's castle surrounded by high walls and invisible motes, the perfect place for self-imposed exile.

Maggie wasn't the only one in the family with demons. Hers was a pervasive, bottomless-well emptiness, spreading like ignorance and lies. At least Maggie didn't pop lorazepam to get to sleep. But the store opening was tomorrow afternoon so she had good reason to pill-pop. No worries, though. After the opening she'd return to hot milk and happy thoughts. She felt so alone. No old friends. No family. Her parents were at Maggie's now and decided to extend their stay. They had canceled their Boston flight an hour ago.

"What do you mean you can't make it at this time?" she asked her mother. How much was Maggie leaving out of their recent conversations? Maybe it was time to investigate this 'darkness in the brain' further.

"Carol Ann, we're not worried about you. We know you're fine. But Maggie—"

"What isn't Maggie telling me? What's really happening there, Mom?"

"She's been overworking herself. And we can't get her out. Well, you know."

"Put her on the phone, Mom."

"Can't. She's sleeping. Finally. Call her in a few hours, Carol Ann. Honey, your Dad and I are so sorry. We wanted to be there very much but we can't leave your sister right now, not until she's completely rested. And the press is here straddling her property line with binoculars and cameras. I can see them as we speak. We'll come and see the store as soon as we possibly can, I promise. And we'll call you tomorrow. Is Dina coming?"

"No."

"Because of that big to-do in New York?"

"Yes. She has to hang around for a court appearance and if she's lucky she can get off with community service. It depends. It's all rather sticky."

"Why did she want to go and hit that guy? She's got the world by the tail."

"Apparently not, Mom. Everybody has their dark angels."

"Their what?"

"Their demons, Mom."

It seemed family solidarity was prevalent on sad occasions. For the first time she felt a hint of resentment towards Maggie, so she called Iris and invited her to dinner tonight. Edmon wanted to go over last-minute details then suggested she retire early but she wouldn't hear of it. She needed a shot of hope and maybe Iris could help give it to her. This 'darkness in the brain' was damned disturbing.

Iris showed up at seven carrying a plant covered in lavender crepe paper and a box from Hoffman's Bakery.

"Thank-you's are not necessary for the chocolate cheesecake," she said, carefully setting both items down on the kitchen table. "And the plant is not from me. I met the florist at the door. It's nice to see someone have Christmas all year round. First your painting and now this."

It was odd how Iris chose to cover both wrists with thick ivory bracelets. Looking at them calmed her. An hour ago she was a mess and now she was calm. How nice it would be if this mysterious, lovely lady would stick around Angelfish Cove a little longer.

"Hi then, in lieu of thanks," she said, wanting to give her a welcome hug, but then she didn't know her that well. "Edmon's picking us out a red wine. I made linguini with clam sauce. You're not allergic to clams, are you?"

"No. I was weaned on them. Who's Edmond?"

"Edmon. My new, nearly indispensable assistant, courtesy of John Corey."

"Did you plan to have an assistant?"

"No. He just appeared. The same day you did as a matter of fact. He's been a great help to me. To tell you the truth this should be such a happy time, but instead I've been tense and distracted, and overly self-involved. That's not usually me."

Iris seemed empathetic, suggesting she check out the plant. "Nature has a way of grounding people. Doesn't take much. A flower. Birdsong. The smell of air and earth this time of year."

Silent and reflective, she removed the crepe paper and found herself staring at the most peculiar-looking plant she'd ever seen. Wheat-gold in color, it had two predominant shapes consisting of six feathery protrusions and leaves in various sizes resembling 'ears'. The baby ears were kind of cute. There was no card.

"The tag says, *Auricula*," she read, puzzled. "What a weird-looking thing. I wonder who sent it?"

Iris smiled nostalgically. "Auricula. Years ago I had this little flower book. Do you know what auricula means?"

For the second time in days, she remembered her own little Flower Book and its gift-giver. Was it simple coincidence that Iris had one, too?

Iris pushed the plant across the table toward her. "In the language of flowers it means *painting*."

An electric jolt shot through her. "Painting? Oh how I wish I knew who sent this?"

"I'm guessing you hope it's from someone in particular?"

She leaned in close to the plant. "I don't dare hope it's from this particular someone. It was so many years ago. A boy I was deeply in love with sent me this strange plant, then disappeared. He sent my friend Dina one, too. Before that he sent me a book about flowers and their meanings. Like your book. And around that same time, I was told he had marks on his wrists. Like your marks. You didn't stumble into Angelfish Cove by accident, did you, Iris?"

Iris's eyes narrowed when Edmon appeared with their bottle of wine. Edmon's soulful eyes widened. Intrigued, she made the introductions, wondering why they took an instant dislike to one another. Then some people had bad hair-trigger chemistry for no reason.

Suddenly the most 'talkative' thing was the auricula. This was so silly ... or maybe it was that the auricula was *listening* the hardest. Even if the plant did have ears, this last thought was the silliest. She had to say something. They were all standing here, three pairs of eyes gaping at the thing.

"Did you pick us out a nice red, Edmon?"

"A vintage Amarone," he said, smiling softly at the guest, awaiting her approval.

Iris stared blankly at him, her eyes dark.

"Well goodnight, Ms. Carol Ann. Ms. Iris, it was a pleasure. I hope you'll be joining us for Pages opening tomorrow afternoon?"

"Wouldn't miss it, Edmon," Iris said, giving a nod her way.

As he left the room, she could have sworn she saw blue sparks shoot out the back of Edmon's heels. It lasted a split second, but she saw what she saw. Her nerves were more banged up than she thought. First the headache, then the frightening return of the dyslexia, followed by the fainting. Now this. Time for a physical. Time to find out who Iris was. What was happening to Dina? And Maggie wouldn't come out of the house. What the hell was going on?

"Iris?"

"You trust who you trust, Carol Ann. Go with your instincts."

"When I introduced you to Edmon ... I don't even know your last name."

"It's Valez. Tell me about the boy you loved."

"No. Tell me again about your wrists. I'm not in a daze this time, which means I'm no longer convinced you wandered into this town accidentally. Don't buy it, Iris."

Yielding to her curiosity, Iris removed the bracelets. "I was in Boston," she said, pouring their wine. "A month ago I dreamed I was in a bookstore. It was Pages. And I saw you—you and your strawberry blonde hair. It was a lot shorter than it is now. Then behind you I saw a dark-haired young man. And beside him was the most incredibly beautiful blond child I had ever seen. He had this angelic face that seemed to glow.

"Then I heard an unfamiliar voice in the dream. Though I like to think I wasn't dreaming but I'm not sure. The voice said *Save the child*. The next morning I woke up in a fever with these on my wrists, and an overwhelming urge to take a vacation. So I took a leave of absence from my waitress job, hopped into my car, and here I am. Then I saw you, the girl in my dream. Look at the letters on my wrists, Carol Ann. Does this touch any part of you?"

She let out a little gasp. The marks were more pronounced than a few days ago when she could only decipher the *S*. Now the impressions had morphed into three intelligible letters. "S t C," she said, touching them. "*Save the Child*. So much of this seems familiar, from some part of my past. The boy I loved years ago. There was a little blond boy around him back then. He'd received threats of some kind and the next thing I knew they'd disappeared. Even my favorite high school teacher disappeared. I always suspected she was involved. And involved in what I couldn't tell you. It was Halloween. Something horrible happened to all of us that night and continued to happen to all of us ever since..."

Was she rambling? Sure she was rambling. Was Iris making sense of all this? Barely touching her food, she chattered through dinner like a dizzy kid climbing off a ride. She couldn't stop herself. After all these years, she couldn't shut up about him. Joe. Her Joe. She felt the passion ignite again. Remembering his brown-sugar eyes, his voice, his touch, awakened her from this ten-year sleepwalk.

She'd decorated Page's patio and umbrella tables with white twinkle lights and used track lights to line the alleyway beside the store. The air smelled of seaside goldenrod and dogwood. She adored New England in late April with its crisp night air and shimmering stars. Cassiopeia was out tonight.

The wine made her a little giddy which felt wonderful. Such a fabulous prelude to tomorrow's opening and she hoped her guests were having as great a time—Iris, the auricula, and of course the Cassiopeia Constellation. She looked up, imagining the wife of Cepheus and the mother of Andromeda bowing down to toast her success and return her lost love. Poor Brent got such a bum rap because of her lost love.

"Poor Brent," she said, shoulders curled forward. "I married him because he resembled Joe. How could I not know that at the time? Even at the altar, it was Joe I was seeing."

"Don't beat yourself up over the past," Iris said. The nip in the air had blushed her nose and cheeks. "You have an opening tomorrow afternoon. There are things to come, things that will feel different when the wine wears off and Cassiopeia turns away from the light. Remember, auricula means *painting*. Something in your sister's painting, perhaps? What happened a decade ago at Marianlake. Joe's disappearance. The marks on his wrists, and mine. Dina and your sister.

"You have a mystery to solve, Carol Ann. Either that or a mystery will solve itself around you. I don't think it's a leap for me to say you're going to experience some serious conflict. Too bad I have to leave the day after tomorrow and don't know when I'll get back, but I will get back, I promise. You'll piece it all together, I know it. What do you think?"

"What do I think?" It might have been the wine talking but who cared. She winked at Iris. "Carol Ann Page is back on the force."

"What is it?" John Corey asked the next morning, referring to the auricula, now back on the kitchen table. He had been flicking one of its baby ears. Two mildewed boxes dated 1969 beckoned the hung-over deadwood that was herself to move in closer for an inspection.

"It's called an auricula and all I know is that it can take a lot of abuse. What's in the boxes, John?"

"Books. Walter Bayard left 'em when he moved out of Angelfish Cove back in '70."

"Walter Bayard? Why does that name sound familiar?"

"Of course it should sound familiar. He practically designed Angelfish Cove single-handed. Matter of fact, he was the only real in-town DJ we ever had. Used to love to play with electronic thingamajigs. He was always inventin things. Seems I remember him saying something about inventin the big one when he disappeared. Real stand-up religious guy Walter was."

"You never told me," she said, trying to hide the fact that she was a little ticked at John. It was this past year that they got better acquainted, but surely he must have remembered her when she moved here seven years back. "I tried like hell to locate Mr. Bayard when I first moved here, John, don't you remember? Nobody seemed to know who was running the Cove station at the time. I remember writing him a couple of letters in Boston, but he never answered me."

"I don't recall that," John said, squinting at the auricula. "Nope. No recall."

"How come he doesn't update the music? Is he still alive? Do you know who runs the station now?"

"Whoa, Carol Ann. Loosen up them reins, girl."

She had to smile. She was getting advice to slow down from Angelfish Cove's 'flying' restaurateur. John always looked like he was on roller skates at the Cafe. She poured him another coffee and put the guns back in her holster.

"Okay. Let's start with the books then. Why are you giving me Walter Bayard's old books?"

"Better you than me. It was Ed's idea, anyways. Never would of crossed my mind and they were dustier than an old saloon up there in the Cafe's attic. Ed was right. They should be on display. That would do old Walt proud. But don't sell any of 'em, Carol Ann. If somebody wants to buy one, guess I'll contact the family somehow. They're still in Boston. Think Walt's grandson's keeping the Cove station alive for us. Not sure. Nobody but you was ever interested. Yuh, we all like that early stuff. Don't you?"

She'd spent enough time going backwards, thanks. "I like it fine, John. But there's been some great stuff since. How does Edmon fit into this?"

"He reminded me a few days ago when we were talkin about your opening. Been steppin over them books up in that attic for years and never thought of doing anything with 'em. 'Bring 'em down from there', Ed said. Now you can dust off the important ones and put 'em in that fancy glass case you got downstairs." John touched the auricula again, smiling and staring thoughtfully at it. "Walt sure used to love to read from them books on the air some nights late. He used to read from a story he wrote about Angelfish Cove.

"I had him make me a copy. Bringin the books reminded me of it, so I brought it with me figurin you'd be interested in readin it. Years ago it was. I recall him sayin he wrote the whole thing entirely in I-talian. Or come to think of it, it mighta been Latin. But of course, mine's in English. The man spoke a few languages, you know, Carol Ann. He was real educated."

"And you brought it with you? Please read it to me, John. The vision's a little bleary this morning."

"As you like. But shouldn't you be gettin ready for your opening?"

"I have a couple hours yet. Hair's done. Makeup's on, except for the lips. Go ahead, John. Read it."

John Corey took out two pieces of paper from his shirt pocket and carefully unfolded each page. Carol Ann clasped her hands behind her neck and stared out the kitchen window into the spring sunshine. The window was opened enough for the curtains to gently rustle and every few minutes the scent of lilacs filled the room. Of course, this morning the scent was making her nauseous.

"It sure wasn't a day like this," John began. "It was winter, New England blue cold out there. I remember listenin to Walt's voice while I stared at my own window. It was around midnight and the window was prettied up with ice patterns. Men look at that stuff, too, Carol Ann. Anyways, as the story here goes ...

"One cold winter's mornin', somewhere back in the '60s, God was up in Heaven having Himself a look down here. He kept looking around, checking things out when He spotted one of his angels and called him back up for a minute.

"I want you to find me a place," God told the angel, "a place where a select group can study for a miraculous event in the '90s."

"A type of place in mind, Sir?"

"Serene and anachronistic," God said, "free from distraction. Choose a timeless place with four seasons where they can reflect and learn the meaning of faith and love. It is to be a place of preparation."

"Excuse me, Sir, but exactly what will they be preparing for?"

"To face their demons."
Confused, the angel asked why. "I don't understand. They face their demons every day."

"Not demons of this caliber," God said. "Humans require my help to conquer these demons."

"Why will the demons be in pursuit of them, Sir?"

"*Their mission's yield will elevate souls with a glance. To do this, they must be purified through love. Stand in my light as we cross into Terra Incognita.*" Then God ordered the angel to stay close.

As the angel stood in God's light, the sky streaked black and gray. The only color was the golden hue cast by God. The angel gasped, for it had never seen a place without color. There was no wind, nothing moved and the angel could neither smell nor taste.

Frightened, the angel said, "Sir, may we make this brief? I believe I've taken leave of my senses."

God said, "On Earth, you know to work beyond your senses. It would be wise to remember that here."

Then God returned the angel's senses and it heard footsteps, slow and soft. The ground warmed beneath its feet. The humid atmosphere filled with stench enough to unbalance a nation. It found itself looking into the eyes of an androgynous figure so profoundly beautiful that it forgot the light and absentmindedly stepped forward. In its brief encounter with darkness, before God pulled it back, the angel was mindful of a thing it had never known—an awareness of its own form.

Disregarding the angel, the demon stood dutifully silent, waiting for God to speak.

As God filtered his Light through the angel's essence, it saw the ugliness that eluded it a moment ago. An aura of red and blue flame surrounded the demon. Away from the Light, it saw only external beauty.

"Look hard into the demon's eyes," God warned the angel, "so you may communicate that it is not one of mine. At times this will be difficult, for often it is the artificial light that seems genuine. See that they ask for my help in all trials. There is one more task for you, but first we will leave this place."

Relieved, the angel memorized the demon's eyes and its aura. And as they left, it looked back to find the demon hovering and it realized that no matter where it went, the boundary separating lightness from dark would always be fine.

"And the final task, Sir?" the angel asked God when they had stopped at the place between Heaven and Earth.

"There is another location that I have chosen for them to complete their mission. You will know it. It is named after my Daughter. Plow the pumpkin field in the rear of the property in 1991 and see to it that your forces gather there in 1996. I will send Lucifer's conqueror, the Prince of Angels to assist you. Soon, many of you will go ahead to personally guard my young leaders. Remember, Raphael, this is their final look back. So organize and prepare them well. I do all this in answer to two selfless prayers spoken from the heart."

With those words, God returned to Heaven and Raphael returned to Earth and found the serene, timeless place God had asked for.

The story intensified Carol Ann's obsession. "Marianlake," she said. "That's the place. I know it. I'm going to see Joe again. I can't believe it. Oh dear God, this is so incredible! John, you've got to tell me what the mission was that Walter Bayard wrote about. If the *yield* elevates souls, it must mean a miracle of some kind! So, what is the yield?"

"He would never say, Carol Ann," John said, squinting at her. "The book he translated his story from was in one of those I-talian languages, remember."

"Do you know anything more about this book, anything at all?"

"I never saw it, dear."

Iris was right. She *was* involved in this mission, whatever it was. Again, more thoughts of Joe filled her with desire. She looked at the auricula and said dreamily, "He *did* send it."

John Corey sat back and watched her dig through both boxes, looking like a human drill breaking concrete. A few minutes later, coughing away dust, she told him they had come up bookless. There was nothing in them, at least nothing bearing any resemblance to a foreign language. Walter Bayard had to have taken this mystery book with him when he left Angelfish Cove.

Oh, but wouldn't it be great if he hadn't.

10. Angel Reclining

An hour prior to Pages opening, Carol Ann asked the press to set up by the fireplace upstairs. Originally part of her and Brent's apartment, she missed the stone fireplace once she included it in the store's layout. But it was okay that her apartment had shrunken considerably because Edmon knew where to get his hands on an attractive portable at a reasonable price. Edmon had been an angel.

"This place looks so gorgeous." Iris said. Edmon offered her a glass of Dom Perignon and she politely refused.

She noticed how Iris's eyes tracked Edmon around the room. "You don't like him?" she asked.

"Don't know him," Iris said. "At this stage of my life, I'm trying to get away from making judgments. *Sooo* ... that was quite the story you heard this morning. If you're right and Joe did send the auricula, that means there's something in your sister's painting he wants you to find. It has to be that book."

Carol Ann stepped back and stared curiously at the painting. "How would Joe know about the painting? The art world's heard, but no one's seen it before today."

Iris looked around to check for eavesdroppers. "That's not the issue, but finding that book is. I disagree, Carol Ann. I think that book is somewhere here in town."

"Why do you think that?"

"Because of the sequence of events. Way back, Joe wanted you to move here. Remember? So if everything is unfolding exactly the way it should, the book is here—

somewhere." Iris peeked out the window at the growing crowd. "Did you insure the painting?"

"Maggie insured it for me and she upgraded Pages security system." She hated feeling sorry for herself, but geez, her big day and no parents, no Maggie, no Dina, although Maggie had called earlier and sent three dozen yellow roses. "I must get myself out of this mood. Either I'm extremely high or incredibly low and it comes on so suddenly. My little one-minute bout with dyslexia scared me more than I thought. I feel like I'm becoming manic."

"Keep an eye on those mood swings. It's important you don't let your emotions control you."

A townie acquaintance rushed up, all excited. "Press are ready for you, sweetie. Go put Pages on the map."

"Thanks, Judy." Judy returned to the press corner, taking the staircase two steps at a time. Not bad for a sixtyish rotund woman. "Even Brent couldn't make it but that's fine. I don't know why I invited him, anyway. And all this media are here because of Maggie and Dina."

"Carol Ann, you gotta stop this. Focus on the wonderful things happening now. Think of Walter Bayard's story."

"I find myself thinking mostly about Joe," she reflected. "Every conversation, every look, every kiss ..."

"Obsessing over Joe wastes a lot of time. Don't you think?"

"Carol Ann!" Judy was waving her up to the top deck.

"Break a leg," Iris said. "We'll have a glass of bubbly when you're done."

Naturally, the press inquired about Dina's latest boner. She handled it. And naturally, the press inquired about Maggie's conspicuous absence. She handled that, too. The cameraman changed the color of the lens filter twice, insisting it needed darkening. There was much too much stress in her face. Another rock to toss into the worry bag—would she still be pretty by the time Joe re-entered her life?

"We're fine," the cameraman said. "That last take'll do."

The news crew shut down and headed for the champagne and cheese table. Forgetting compliments like the great interview she gave or Pages mystical atmosphere, she focused on the negative, like the multiple takes and a face full of stress.

"That's a long line out there, Ms. Carol Ann," Edmon said. "Shall we open to the public now?"

He looked splendid in his Armani suit. His shortness and stout middle didn't matter because it was always the soft eyes they noticed. "Open those doors, Edmon. Time to rock'n'roll."

Accompanied by John Corey, Iris strolled over and stood with her.

A three-piece jazz combo, courtesy of Dina, swung into *Harlem River Drive*, a heartening tune rich with soft fluted notes. Outside, the cops apologized to the people in the block-long line.

"Sorry, folks. Once the store's reached maximum capacity, two can enter for every two leaving."

This was the drill. The crowd up front didn't protest too much since gawking at the next two in line seemed preferable to the festivity inside.

One of the men was elderly and in a wheelchair, casually dressed in a spring sport-coat, expensive tracksuit and a Red Sox baseball cap. The soup-strainer mustache and nerdy glasses gave him an air of eccentricity. He wore unseasonable heavy gloves and spoke little, content to toy with his 35 mm Nikon, focusing, checking, shooting. Considering the gloves, he managed the camera nimbly much to the amusement of the couple in back.

The young man beside him was driving all the ladies to distraction. Tall, in his early twenties with thick blond hair falling to his shoulders, he too dressed casually in black jeans, black sweatshirt and an olive green leather jacket. He wore a large watch on one wrist and an athletic tensor band on the other. One girl, three people down, sighed every time he moved. He gazed tranquilly at the sights.

Inside, the champagne had improved Carol Ann's mood. "Well, John," she said, body swaying to the rhythm of the sax, "why don't we simply contact Walter Bayard's family? Geez, it's hot in here. You know, guys, I think I've drunk more in the past week than I have in my entire life. I have also been starting most of my sentences with *I*. I've always hated that."

Edmon refilled her glass and she bowed to him in gratitude.

"Can I chat with you a minute?" Iris asked. After isolating themselves in the psychology section, Iris asked if she was still sober enough to talk seriously.

"Half-sober," she said. "So talk to the right half."

"I'm leaving first thing in the morning."

"Listen, what is all this urgency, really? John adores you, so do all the regulars at the Cafe. What's up, Iris? I've had a couple of drinks so I'm practically inhibition-less."

"I have a mystery of my own to solve. This should really wait till I get back."

"Oh come on, I think you're holding out on me, Iris Valez, if that's your name. That brand on your wrists proves you're more connected to my past and present than I am. I certainly don't have any marks on my wrists. You know what endeared you to me? In many ways you remind me of the female equivalent of Joe. Joe was the most cryptic person I ever met. I love mystery and excitement. Always have. An addiction of mine. So tell me, if you want me to accept any more advice from you—what's your real story? And can I have the unabridged version, please?"

Iris tugged at an earlobe. "Okay. I admit I have been holding out on you. But only a wee bit." She pressed her thumb and index finger together. "You like mystery? Well good, because like everybody else, I have secrets, too. But I can't break confidences, sorry. I *can* promise I will tell you everything eventually. Carol Ann, I don't know how all this is gonna turn out."

"I'm not asking you to be a fortune-teller. But you have to tell me one thing."

"What?"

"Do you know Joe Ross?"

Iris sighed. "I know someone who *knew* Joe Ross. And that's it, girl. Afraid that's all I can tell you, except that I'm leaving tomorrow to check out someone else who's rumored to have the same marks on her wrists. I'll give you an update when I get back."

Iris offered her hand, which she refused. "When will that be? Any ideas?"

"You're really upset with me, aren't you?"

Carol Ann swept away fresh sawdust from the top shelf. "Not so much upset really. Just incredibly frustrated. You can't break a confidence. I respect that. That's where I entered the scene with Joe. Things were going on with him that he couldn't tell me. Now history's repeating itself in you. Knowing you know someone who knew him–how whacky do you think that makes me?

"We're connected to this thing, Iris. And you can't tell me what you know. And me? Suddenly I'm obsessed with the past. My sister and best friend are getting weirder by the minute but I'm not spending a whole lotta time thinking about them, am I? Never in all my life have I been so self-absorbed. You know, with all this going on I have to remember I'm running a new business here. I can't screw up. That's another thing—I seem to have misplaced my confidence. I'm losing little bits and pieces of myself. Man, listen to me. Just listen to me."

"Don't rag on yourself, Carol Ann. You know, the devil turns us into puppets when we live on our feelings. That's how he corrupts us. That happened to me once or twice. So don't you give in to self-abuse of any kind. Okay?"

"I would never do that." The second she emphasized the word *never*, a bolt of heat shot through her. "I always seem to attract you religious types."

"How convenient," Iris said, showing all four thousand teeth.

"That man over there in the wheelchair looking up at the *Angel Reclining*," she said, fixating on the ramp she suddenly remembered she forgot, "how's he supposed to get upstairs? Gawd." She went scurrying over. "My apologies. Pages *will* be wheelchair accessible. We're putting a ramp in next week. There's so many things on the blueprint that ... well, I opened a little ahead of schedule."

Pages was only wheelchair-accessible at the entrance. How could she forget a ramp to the top floor? How could the architect omit it from the schematic? Why didn't she simply admit the error and promise to correct it? She was such a doughhead, and a schmuck for lying.

"It's fine, Ms. Page," he said. "Andrew Gillis. I have my 35-millimeter here with a zoom lens I don't really need at this distance. But I'm glad to hear you're installing a ramp."

Something in his voice warmed her. For sure she'd install that ramp now. He caught her noticing the heavy gloves. "I didn't mean to stare. New England is still fairly chilly in the spring."

"A touch of arthritis," he said. Then Iris caught his eye and she introduced them.

She oughta knock off the champagne. Ha-ha, maybe it was the devil making her see things, like the hint of recognition between Iris and Mr. Gillis. Iris's mouth curled upward and Mr. Gillis looked down after their introduction. This was sort of the flip side of what happened between Iris and Edmon.

"Nice meeting you, Mr. Gillis," Iris said, then walked off into the thick of the party.

While mingling, she searched for Iris. What was wrong with peeping through the odd keyhole, anyway? Voyeurism to the lesser extent was a common human frailty. Iris was talking with two elderly gentlemen. The senior demographic was huge today with one towering above everyone. Edmon stood on the sidelines, peeping through the same keyhole.

"Who are they, Edmon?" she asked, noting his heavy breathing.

"Priests," he said icily, "minus their typical ornamental attire."

Apparently, priests put Edmon on the edge of disdain. This was the first time she had heard the cassock referred to as *ornamental attire*. "They must be here for Maggie's painting. Don't you think?"

She may as well have been talking to the clouds in the painting because Edmon, duplicating the look of disdain he had a moment ago, seemed preoccupied with the young man on the top deck. How could she have missed this blond Apollo?

"Who is that? Wow. Probably one of Dina's. Or maybe an actor."

As if he heard, the young Apollo turned and leaned on the brass railing. He acknowledged her with a smile, which she returned. Everybody looked up at this point. His eyes moved from hers to the man in the wheelchair, now chatting up Iris and the priests.

"John has the rest of the champagne chilling at the Cafe, ma'am." A flake of skin hung from Edmon's dry, chapped lips. "I'll run the car over and pick it up. Be back as soon as possible."

"That's fine, Edmon. Do you think you're ever going to get past this Ms. Carol Ann and ma'am business?"

"Old-fashioned coot, that's me," he said, and when he smiled, his lip cracked open and bled. He hurried off faster than she could say 'here's a tissue and I'll fetch the champagne because I need you at the cash register.' Judy had already voided five bills by her last count. Well, Edmon would have no trouble figuring out the cash tonight. He was a whiz with numbers, like everything else. What a Godsend.

"Hello."

Oh to be ten years younger. Up close the young Apollo looked more like an angel. "Hello. Carol Ann Page. I'm the owner."

"Hi. I'm Al. I know who you are. I overheard you introduce yourself to my uncle before. The man in the wheelchair?"

"Oh, of course. I suspect your uncle is really here because of the *Angel Reclining*. I saw him taking pictures." She found herself searching for things to say. He excited her so, not because of his beauty. It went far beyond sexual attraction, more towards the soul. Only thoughts of Joe could do it for her in that other department. She wished Maggie were here. She wished *Joe* were here.

"My uncle is a big fan of your sister."

"And my sister would love to do your portrait. You look like you could have wings and a halo." He had a familiar laugh. Déjà vu or something. *Settle down, Carol Ann. Quit obsessing about the past.*

"Tell your sister that I would be happy to sit for her. Any time."

The band segued to *In The Air Tonight* and the fragrance of pine drifted into her nostrils. Perhaps the memory of Dina's voice blending with the hoot of the loons and rustle of autumn leaves was getting to her. Oh, it had been so long. Too long. Al's uncle wheeled over and she took a deep, savoring breath. Maybe she should sit, or grab an oxygen mask.

"I'm afraid I'm a little dizzy. All this smoke, I think. I should've put up no smoking signs. But because we were having a party—"

"You have a nice little patio outside. Why don't we go out and sit," Mr. Gillis suggested. "You can tell me and my nephew about Angelfish Cove."

The spring air smacked of nostalgia. It seemed they instinctively knew not to speak while she sat back and relished the rest of the song. Al listened with his eyes closed and Andrew Gillis stared past the alley to Main Street. From this angle, his mustache looked crooked and fake, not so for the dark eyes hiding behind the coke-bottle glasses. She fought to resist asking another nervy question. Ah, what the hell. It had been a strange day.

"Would you mind removing your glasses for a minute, Mr. Gillis?"

"Excuse me?" he asked, posture stiffening in the chair.

"My uncle's glasses are tinted," Al said. "His eyes are sensitive to sun and most forms of artificial light."

She wanted to hide behind one of Maggie's paintings. "I'm sorry, Mr. Gillis. That was so rude. Don't know where it came from. I keep apologizing to you, don't I? I'm not usually this spacey. There I go again."

"No apologies." He reached out to touch her but pulled back. "I should be the one apologizing to you, Carol Ann."

"What on earth for?"

"I think we should head back to the Inn, Uncle Andrew," Al said. "You want to be there to get your call. It was great meeting you, Carol Ann. I wish you every success with Pages."

She walked them down the alley to the boardwalk. "I love books but I must tell you how much I admire your sister's work," Andrew said, shaking her hand goodbye. "That's quite a painting in there. Did you notice the book the angel's reading?"

"No, not really. Did you see something?"

"Yes. I'm intrigued by that low-profile *O* on the cover. We'll be around for a couple more days. If you happen to talk to your sister before we leave, I'd be interested to know what the O stands for."

"Funny," she said, intrigued. "I never noticed the book's cover. It took me long enough to notice the angel made of cloud. I will ask Maggie. For sure. It's the least I can do to change your impression of me. First the ramp. Then the glasses."

"I liked my first impression of you," he said, "my very first impression."

"We'd better pitter patter, Uncle Andrew."

"Goodbye, Carol Ann."

"Goodbye, Andrew."

She accompanied them to the end of the alley and watched a while as they made their way down the boardwalk. As Al pushed the chair toward the cove and the orange setting sun, the memory of Joe with Dina singing her heart out in that rowboat came to life again. It was the first time she ever saw him. Why oh why did Joe want her to move here and how long would it take to get the answer? She would phone Maggie right after the party and ask about that unobtrusive O. Imagine. The auricula knew all along. Too bad it wasn't sharing its secret message or lending its ears, so to speak. Too bad Andrew Gillis didn't take off those glasses.

As it happened, Maggie reached in and plucked the letter O out of her mental grab bag. There was no special significance attached to it, she had said, adding, "But you know of course, that most of this stuff doesn't come from *me*."

Carol Ann decided to give this news or absence of news to Andrew Gillis in person. Unfortunately, by mid-afternoon the next day, Andrew was nowhere in sight, so she spoke with Al instead, which was no hardship. While the Inn buzzed with strangers, so many strangers—so early in the season, she noticed Al yank his sleeves down to the knuckles as soon as he spotted her in the lobby.

"You're leaving?"

"Yeah," he sighed. "We have to get back to Boston. My Uncle will be sorry he missed you."

"Everybody's leaving. My friend, Iris, left first thing this morning as well. Andrew still in his room?"

"No. He's out sightseeing. I'm picking him up on the way. I hope we'll meet again, Carol Ann."

When Al said goodbye, he did an odd thing. He shook her hand and massaged her wrist with his thumb. It tingled. She'd spent her life taking time getting to know people. But that was before Iris came along. And now Al and his uncle. Was it mere self-gratification that made her want to be instantly important to them? She didn't want to let go of his hand.

Jerry, the Inn's one and only porter thrust a set of keys into Al's hand and grabbed two suitcases smothered in stickers—Rome, Paris, London, New York and Quebec.

Both bags had sticky, empty spaces beside the lock clasps. Obviously, something had been removed. Probably initials. No time for questions over one lousy cup of coffee because Al seemed anxious to be on his way.

"Take care," he said, climbing into the van, "of yourself and Pages. You'll be all right. Believe in God's will. That's what my uncle always says."

"How does one even recognize God's will? I'd do it if I knew it."

Al smiled tenderly. "That takes some living, I guess. But you'll come to discern it. The route is often strewn with tears. Don't ever stash the pain."

She would have felt more comfortable hearing this from Andrew Gillis. How could a kid eight to ten years her junior be packin' this much wisdom? But he was no ordinary kid, even though he spoke in clichés a lot.

"See ya, Al. I'll give you the discernment update when next we meet."

By the time she reached Pages and reviewed morning sales with Edmon, she decided to defer the quest for God's will until tomorrow. She had to ease some of this anxiety first. Edmon suggested she heat up a spot of brandy with herbal tea and unwind in a salts bath. He would look after the store for the remainder of the day. She'd get it together by tomorrow, for sure. Maybe somebody would call by then. Iris or Dina. Maggie. Somebody.

She was reading an article in *TV Guide* when Dina called from New York late in the afternoon.

"You're what?" Dina asked. She was on one of those awful speakerphones and her voice echoed unnaturally. "Pages first full business day and you're reading? Who's minding the store?"

To her shame, she blamed her lack of drive on nerves and no sleep. Dina the workhorse was not buying any of it.

When she was in her 'Rockstar' personality, she said exactly what was on her mind, not always stopping to consider feelings. Still, in this personality, Dina was at her best on-stage and had trained herself to deaden scary emotions.

"Listen, Carol Ann, this Edmon sounds like an effing jewel, but letting some other guy run the show is not your style. What are you doing sipping brandy in the afternoon? I thought I'd find you near cash register noises."

"I told you, Dina," she said, irritated by the yapping of puppies on the other end. "It's been a weird twenty-four hours. I feel so alone here. And nervous—"

"You feel what? Alone and nervous? Well welcome to my world. Hey maybe I should come out there for a few days before I go to Quebec. That's *if* I go to Quebec. Everything's fixed with that mess I got myself into. Out of court settlement. Man, decking that guy in the cojones cost me quantitybucks. Carol Ann? You still with me?"

She felt groggy from the brandy. "Quebec? What are you ... you doing a concert there?"

"No." Dina's voice lowered and she disengaged the phone speaker. "My therapist's been saying since last Christmas that I should get my butt out to Marianlake because of the nightmares. I told you. Some of that stuff has been backing up on me. But I told her no effing way I'm going back there. But the nightmares haven't stopped so I decided to prep myself for the place."

"I don't get it. What do you mean by *prep*?"

"I've sent someone out to Trois-Rivierés to keep me posted on Marianlake, take pictures, that sort of thing. If I have to go back there I'm getting psyched first. Remember that huge pumpkin field in the back, the one Maggie painted?"

"Of course."

"They plowed the whole thing under a few weeks ago and my guy's finding holes in the story he got. And nobody else in town seems suspicious. That field is as many miles long as it is wide and it's owned by the Vatican. So you know what I did? I called Father Vaux. After all these years he's still there. So is Father Andre. Anyway, Father Vaux sounded happier than a Vette in the fast lane when I told him it was me. We talked for an hour. He asked about you and Maggie. He *remembers*."

Jacked with adrenaline, she caught her breath. "Did you ask him about Joe?"

"Figured you'd get around to him first. Sure I asked him. He told me he hasn't heard from Joe Ross in years. You remember that little boy, Alain? Well I had George, he's my spy out there, look up the kid's family. I remembered meeting Claude, Alain's dad, when he came out to check on the horses that time. He was the town vet, remember?

"Anyway, the family upped and disappeared shortly after we left in '81. Not a trace of them anywhere. George is still working on it. Strange though, because I asked Father Vaux if they still had horses up there and he said they did. Then get this—he tells me not to worry, that they were getting the best in veterinary care. *Claude* was there taking good care of them. Of course I pretended not to notice the slip. So, my guess is he was probably lying about Joe, too."

"Probably," she said, staring absent-mindedly at her wrist. "That won't be the first time he's been caught in a lie. The thought of his knowing where Joe is makes me a little nuts. So what did he say about the pumpkin field?"

"Well now this just gets too weird. Listen to this– Trois-Rivierés had this big sports centre and last February it burns down. Father Vaux says it's such an old building, that in recent years it couldn't pass code and because it had the only hockey rink in the area, town officials looked the other way. So one night it goes up in flames because of faulty wiring. But George's been digging and the word is there wasn't one electrical thing wrong with that building. For a while, the rumor was arson. Anyway, that rumor got buried as soon as Marianlake donated a new town centre, which is being built on that field. That's what they're clearing it for."

"So Father Vaux says."

"Right."

"And you don't believe him."

"No way. They've broken ground and poured the concrete. George says the aerial view looks almost maze-like. Whatever they're building up there, George says, ain't no sports centre, that's for damn sure. And get this, they haven't hired or consulted any locals for its construction. They won't even let anyone on the property. Not in back. George went to Mass there last Sunday and afterwards he took a casual stroll in back and they got the whole thing cordoned off. A lot of Italians roaming around securing the area. He couldn't get near it."

"So does this George have any idea what they're really doing?"

"No. He said the aerial view looks like a huge X'd-out circle or crossed-out circle. Take your pick. And the X overlaps the circle. But then you drop down a couple thousand feet, he said, and it looks like a big sun with four lanes or extensions coming out of it. Those are the *X-extensions,* I guess."

"But then, why can't the circle part be the arena? Why would he say it couldn't be a sports centre?"

"Because the lanes or extension parts are dug deeper with the circle part raised. George thinks the extensions are going underground. In the country? Why? And get this, the spaces between each lane are dug even deeper. Very strange layout for a sports centre if you ask me."

She wiped the sweat from her upper lip. Joe could actually be up there somewhere. "That is really strange. What I'd like to know is what they're going to tell the townspeople. How long can they keep them away? The locals have to be wondering about their tax dollars."

"They'll have all that worked out in advance, I'm sure. When the time comes, they'll have a story ready. Funny, though. Some of the people George talked to on the quiet don't buy the idea that it could be something other than a sports centre."

"So you think Marianlake's up to no good?"

"Well don't you after everything I told you?"

"I don't know, Dina. I really don't know. Joe was seriously involved with something at Marianlake, something he couldn't tell me. You know that. And I don't believe Joe would involve himself in anything illegal. And that little boy, Alain. It had something to do with him. Then everybody disappears. Father Vaux's caught in another lie. And other strange things have been happening in my life."

She brought Dina up to date, ending with Al's advice. She told her about Iris and the marks on her wrists, similar to what Joe had. How Iris was going off to investigate more wrist sightings. The auricula and its message. Walter Bayard's story and his book. The dyslexic episode and her recurrent negative state of mind. She reminded Dina, for the one-hundredth time, how Joe had encouraged her to seek out and move to Angelfish Cove. Despite everything Iris had said, all she could think about was taking off to find him.

"Iris told me it's all connected. Something evil is stirring among us. But this conversation has snapped me back. I felt good around Iris and the two men I met yesterday, but as soon as they took off, I withdrew into this black cloud that's been shadowing me. So you, me and Maggie have got to keep it together.

"Together, and I know it sounds corny, but together we can fight this intruder. When I'm alone, this negative force frightens me. You don't know how much I wish I could leave Angelfish Cove to look for Joe. Though Iris said I should stay here, taking say ... two short weeks couldn't hurt. And your tour's postponed for a couple of months, so you're available. Dina, would you help me look for Joe?"

After a lengthy pause, Dina's voice returned girlish-like. "Hi. I'm still here. I may not be the rockstar you were talkin' to a minute ago, but it's sort of me."

She would never get used to this. Dina once told her to think of it as simply changing channels, except her head was the TV. "Ohh. Do you remember all of our conversation?"

"Yeah. It's even not as faint as it used to be. The Rockstar's listening in too. But she's relaxing. We're getting along better. Oh I hate this, Carol Ann. I can't sing as well when I'm me. I'm all messed up and scared."

"I'll stay with you on the phone, Dina, for as long as it takes."

"Talk about staying together," Dina giggled, pathetically.

Carol Ann blinked away the tears.

"Did you ask me to help you look for Joe?" Dina asked.
"Yes."

"I don't think that's such a good idea, Carol Ann. Besides, Joe knows where you are. I agree with you about the auricula. I think he sent it, too. And you have the store now. Wait for destiny. Don't get all hung up on Joe again. Try to forget him for now."

"Dina, the last time I decided to forget Joe Ross I married his double and moved here."

"But Maggie ... we'll need Maggie. It should be the three of us and I know Maggie is not ready to tackle anything like this. You know that."

"Maybe it's time I went to see my sister."

"Don't get mad at me, Carol Ann, but your motives are slightly selfish. It doesn't seem right to me."

"Okay, you're half-right, I'll admit. But I also want to see my sister. Will you meet me there?"

"What about Pages?"

"Edmon's had a hundred years of experience. It's for two or three weeks, Dina."

"Oh all right. But you have your work cut out for you with Maggie."

"We'll meet at Maggie's. The three of us will talk it out together. Man, it's been so long since I've seen her."

"Okay, so where do we go from Maggie's?"

"Medford to speak to his grandmother. Then on to Marianlake. If anyone can get us in there, you can. And your therapist did say you should go because of your nightmares."

"I know, but I don't wanna push something I'm not ready for. And what about you? I don't want you messed up again. Oh I don't know right now about Marianlake. Give me some time, Carol Ann. Let's get our buns to Maggie's first. I still don't feel right doing this."

"Dina, what happened to us happened a decade ago. Why after a long dormant period is Marianlake in our thoughts and lives again? And I'll wager something's going on at Maggie's end. In fact, I know it. She would've shown at the store opening. Don't you think we should look into this? Well I'm looking into it and I don't care how many dark forces I encounter along the way. It's time to rekindle that grit. You with me, Dina? Dina?"

There was another pause on the line, followed by a familiar voice humming scales in a perfect a cappella.

"I don't think going off in hot pursuit of an old boyfriend who might be dead or married or a priest has anything to do with grit. If ya ask me it sounds more like lunacy, something I'm real acquainted with. Sounds more like what happens when you mix fantasy with hormones. Ah, what the hell. See ya at Maggie's."

11. Ladies in Waiting

Medford, May 1991

When Iris saw Rosa cleaning windows on the top floor of the house, she turned her back to her. Funny, with all Rosa's bags of money, she managed the house without help and even with Willie and Beata gone, refused to downsize. She was probably hanging on to the house for Joe now that he was home from Italy for good. Unable to bear living in the house alone, Rosa spent most of her time in Mexico after losing her beloved girls.

While Joe was out for a run, she strolled the Mystic thinking of him scrunched in a wheelchair two sizes too small for him, wearing the dark shades and goofy mustache. She felt happy, happy to be part of this extraordinary mission, though there were many things she could not share with him. But Joe was accustomed to secret directives now, having learned that not all secrets are bad. This time it was Alain who told her she'd have to wait to reveal her identity, which was okay. She liked being a mystery to Joe.

This week's task was to quietly move him and Alain into the Angelfish Cove beach house, decidedly more of a pleasure than a task, except for the getting-them-into-town-quietly part. And oh what a task it would be since Carol Ann didn't go one day without driving by the beach house. And Joe had to have that beach house. No other home in Angelfish Cove would do.

Father Richard tried numerous times to dissuade him from the move but Joe was adamant. Joe was Joe and the beach house was going to be their corner of operations. No arguments. For all involved, the opening phase of the mission would be difficult, even those endowed with supernatural gifts.

She was glad Joe insisted on preparing them in the beach house. Like Carol Ann, she wanted to be near it too, for different reasons. Soon. Soon they would reunite as a team to battle an incoming force of corruption with no face and no rap sheet as she once heard him say at a strategy dinner in Rome. Manifestations of evil were clearly present.

That dinner was three years ago. The US frigate 'Stark' had been hit by an Iraqi missile in the Persian Gulf. A severe earthquake killed tens of thousands of people in Armenia. Joe predicted it would not be long before Iraq invaded Kuwait. He was right–it happened last year, beginning the Persian Gulf War.

Having faith in Joe's instincts, she agreed that the beach house was the best place to kick this thing off. In it, perhaps he could finally forgive himself for Willie, receive a little absolution—from Joe *to* Joe. For all his guidance and intense study these past years, he was still human. God had left him enough flaws to keep him close and humble, though he was always humble. Now he was home and his peaceful days of study in a Roman garden had ended.

'I don't mess with stress,' Joe told Father Gianni. A few days prior to their return to America, Alain went out and got him a sweatshirt with those same words printed on the back. When she saw Joe running in her direction, she quickened her step. She couldn't help herself. It was easy quickening her step towards him, difficult stepping away.

Catching him in her sights, she waved. "Well hello, Mr. Gillis. These Mystic River runs can't be good for your arthritis?"

Joe's laugh hadn't changed, one long note followed by two short. "Hey whaddya know, the only other person my age working this gig. Hope you can saddle a horse, lady, or it's Mr. Ross to you." Having returned from Europe with all the customary gestures, he kissed her on both cheeks. "I hoped we'd get a chance to talk at Page's opening, but I guess it would've been awkward. Besides, I was emotionally distracted. Somewhat."

She chuckled at that one. "Emotionally disabled. Somewhat."

"Observation noted, Iris." Then he grinned and pointed at her heels. He loved to kid her about her heels. "Um, speaking of disabled. Next time you might want to reconsider walking along this river in those *highalized* heels."

"Advice noted, Joe."

"Okay, pretty lady. What brings you to Medford? I thought we'd be meeting back in Angelfish Cove."

"I had a long power breakfast downtown with Alain. He didn't tell you?"

"Nope. Alain handles Marianlake business. And he gets to use his French. He's already mastered Medford. It's *Mez Bah* here, he found out. If you ask for a *Mars Bar*, you get change for a video game. Is Carol Ann all right?"

She loved that his voice retained its Boston flavor, that he still said things like *Medfid, gahbidge, cah* and her favorites *'propahly and howevah'*. "Well, that's why I'm here. I wanted to talk to you personally about Carol Ann and the girls. I realize we only know each other through Father Andre's covert meetings, but at Pages opening I sensed you wanted to share a bit. I understand Elizabeth won't be catching up with us for awhile."

"No. She's spending time with her son. But it's okay. I have Alain. He has this way of showing me how to collect all the crap in my head and dump it into one corner. To see it objectively, he says. Then I can start waste removal. What did you want to tell me about the girls?"

"They could be heading for a spot of trouble. I mean, more than usual."

"Times like this I wish I had Alain's technique, you know, destroying the fear thoughts. Actually, Alain doesn't have fear thoughts. Yeah, Carol Ann seemed rattled. Attached. Her attachments worry me. No need to tell me how Dina and Maggie are, either. But I wasn't prepared for Edmon."

"There's something else you should know. You may have to cut your visit short, Joe." She watched him tame the May breeze in his long dark hair with a rubber band. She would always love him. He didn't have to give anything back. She could, though—precisely why she asked for this assignment.

"More complications?"

"It's Carol Ann. Seems she has it in her head for the three of them to go searching for you and she figures a chat with your grandmother is the best place to begin. I talked her out of it, then Edmon talked her right back into it. He has the advantage being with her day and night. He's won this round."

"Has he won any other rounds?"

"Seems he's teaching her everything you ever wanted to know about self-gratification. He can handle Pages so she can relax in a hot tub. He'll hire someone to do the gardening so the sun doesn't wreck her pretty skin. He'll *run* Pages so she can sink deeper into her obsession for you.

She could hold us up, Joe. Now she's on your team. What do you want to do?"

He took a couple of deep breaths, tapped on a rock with his toe. "I see Carol Ann hasn't learned how to grip the hammer before she swings. So. We're on our way there and she *thinks* she's on her way here." Tapping some more on the stone, he said, "Not to worry. If I know Maggie, she'll talk them into returning to Angelfish Cove, which is exactly where I need them to be."

"Isn't it too soon? Besides, you'll want Maggie there as well."

"Right. So start praying, Iris. We need Maggie out of that asylum she lives in, and I have a hunch Maggie may be the first to get the marks. I gather she thinks the girls are going for an overdue visit with no secret agenda?"

"Yep. You sure it's wise to reunite the girls at this time? You're not settled in the Cove yet and it may be difficult keeping your presence from them. If they're separated, it would be easier for you to go to them when they need you, without the others knowing."

"We have to stop speculating at some point. Could be this is the way it's supposed to happen. The strength of one will be beneficial to the others. I'm worried about Carol Ann, though. If things don't go well for her, she could return to us psychologically and spiritually damaged."

"You going to take that chance? You may have to intervene."

"I can't intervene, you know that, Iris. Doesn't mean I'm not tempted, but Carol Ann isn't the only one I have to concern myself with here. We'll take care of her when the time comes. But I have to stay detached. Her feelings for me have nothing to do with the big picture. And the big picture is my priority."

"Pardon the reminder, but you're still human. You certain you can keep yourself detached? You loved her. And that love was filled with a promise or two she never got to collect. She's going to want a return on her investment, Joe."

"I'm not the same person I was with Carol Ann. Or Willie. Except that for everything I've learned, through faith, through the miracles, all of it ... I still see Willie in that tub every day of my life. That's why I want the beach house. I can reconcile my past with Willie there. Ironic. Willie was my dark angel when she was alive. And she still is."

She reached out her hand for his. "Willie's no dark angel, I can promise you that."

He flashed her that movie star smile. "Oh excuse me for taking pride in the fact that I've finally learned to let remarks like that slide. There was a time when I would have insisted you tell me how you know that. Now I let you brass pass. So you see, progress. Every once in awhile, Alain throws a test at me. Usually when I'm at my worst."

"Best time."

Joe laughed and agreed. "I guess I'd better tell Rosa a little more about Carol Ann and the girls. She's going to be taking a trip to the Cove at some point, without the crystal balls, I hope. Poor Rosa. No matter how much I tell her, she's going to know I'm leaving the flathead out of the toolbox. As for my Vatican credentials, she's having a tough time buying the job description. And Alain mystifies her. She said she could peel off ten of his layers and still not get a handle on him. She's incredible. Would you like to come in and meet her?"

"I uh, I'm afraid I'm a little pressed for time, Joe. I'm going to head back to the Cove now. A few more things to do at the beach house before you and Alain get there."

"Not even time for tea?"

"Sorry. Gotta rush. Tell me something though, if you wouldn't mind?"

"What's that?"

"How did you feel seeing Carol Ann again?" When he took his time answering she felt shame for wanting to read his mind, but she'd require permission for that. "You don't have to answer, Joe."

"No, it's okay. How did I feel?" Joe clasped his hands behind his neck and looked up at the sky. "Embarrassed wheeling around her store in that getup. Desire because I wanted to touch her. It was like falling off my own world and hitchhiking through hers. And don't get me *stahted* on the memories. Telling you it was tough detaching and returning to business, Iris, but it got done. Seems they managed to teach me a few things in Rome besides Italian. Carol Ann hasn't found the book yet, has she?"

"No. Edmon's convinced her that Walter Bayard would never have left it behind in the Cove. He's managed to wipe out everything I said—the book in Maggie's painting, even the point of your auricula. He's got her thinking that the auricula's real message is of a romantic nature. Oh well, we'll all be back there soon. So you're going to show yourself to them individually then?"

"I'll be there at the first sign of any wrist action."

"Hope that's soon. I find I'm a little impatient."

"I know, me too. But I can't help advance them to higher levels until they discover a little more on their own. You know of course that I also can't show up at Marianlake in '96 short a team member. If one person on the team hasn't received the marks, none of us go. How are the others doing?"

"Rafe doesn't tell me."

"Gee that's a surprise. Man, I wish they'd asked me to find that book instead of Carol Ann."

"You can't be doing Carol Ann's chores for her. She asked me straight out if I knew you, you know."

"What did you tell her?"

"I told her I knew someone who knows you."

"Very clever. That's still the truth."

"The truth by a hair. I was all prepared to lie, but I got lucky."

Joe smiled reflectively at a noisy bullfrog partially hidden by reeds. "I was at her wedding, Iris. I sat in the back in my disguise of the day and watched her walk down the aisle with this guy who looked so much like me I almost threw up. Made the trip in from Rome and everything. Had to fight everybody off. Had no understanding of why I needed to go.

"They all warned me it was a bad idea. Alain was the only one who left me alone. He also talked them into letting me go, and he was still a kid, isn't that amazing? He told them that when I got back from the wedding I'd be ready to learn about detachment for sure. He had that right. I felt like a baby cutting a tooth when I got back. I couldn't get the pain out of me fast enough. Couldn't understand why the pain was still there."

"But you've never been able to let Willie go."

"Told you, Iris ... Willie's my dark angel. She always has been."

Iris drove back along the Atlantic Coast to Angelfish Cove, speaking quietly to Rafe. He could hear, wherever he was. She was concerned for Joe and the girls. The girls hadn't exactly been walking in clover these past years and if they knew what lay ahead, they would quit now.

Rafe showed her droplets of blood on the midday sun. He let her smell the rising sulfur in the earth. Then Rafe showed her a final mind-numbing vision—a shocking underworld behind a door. A red door.

∞∞∞∞

Maggie whipped the sheet off the canvas and stepped back. This was one she should've burned. Instead she found herself taking her precious Number Six brush and tweaking the thing. Should she paint her front door red? Was that the message? Should she show this anomaly to Carol Ann and Dina? For two days now she'd been tweaking and pacing—the rooms, the staircases, the grounds, twiddling the Number Six like a drumstick through anxious fingers. She used the brush for filling in extra-fine spaces and shading areas between the wings and shoulders, below the nose and around the Kewpie-doll lips. Except she wasn't using it to paint angels these days.

Her mother kept her first Number Six, worn down to the nub after painting the angel mural in the old studio bedroom. She longed to see the mural again. Ten minutes. Five minutes. Though she'd hung a sixteen by twenty blow-up in her room, the folks had the real thing. She had seriously considered transporting the wall but the old home was more home than this complex ... this *Masada*.

"*It's not really about the wall,*" she prayed to the great Archangel, "*people need me and I'm letting them down.*"

She concentrated her prayers on her internal and physical walls. Getting her essence over it was one thing. Getting her body over it was something else. Walls and doors. One door in particular was too frightening to open, not yet, though at some point she would no longer have the option. But what about the return of Carol Ann's dyslexia? Could it be the door had already opened a crack?

She always faced her fears on canvas. Except today. Enough for today. She set down the brush and threw the sheet over the picture. As much as she ached to leave, how could she risk an entity trailing her to the home of a loved one? Drifting down the stairs with spiritual confidence, she headed toward the one place she felt *alone*—in the garden by the statue she'd commissioned of the Archangel Michael. She'd worried about it remaining anchored, given this discomforting May wind.

She brushed away a lock of hair whiplashing her cheek. It was too late to call off Carol Ann and Dina's visit. Not that Carol Ann would let her. She sat on the bench in front of the statue and gazed at it with reverence.

"Please protect the girls from the darkness in this house."

∞∞∞

Dina put aside a couple of extra bulky sweaters to pack. It wasn't exactly summer yet. Stupid idea, this trip. Why the hell did she have to agree to it? How come little Dina hadn't been humming so much lately? She liked it in there, that's why. She was usually happy inside, tucked away in her safe cozy corner. No smell of horse shit. No sound of leaden hooves pounding her in the head. No menthol and lemons. She hated for Maggie to see her like this. No wonder little Dina didn't want to come out and play no more.

"Well neither do the rest of us in here," she said to the bathroom mirror. "But don't you worry, Chubby Buns, I'll stay out and about. You've always been safe with me."

What's to keep you safe from me, Rockstar?

She scrambled back from the mirror. "No playin' around, Chubby Buns. Cut it out."

Little Dina called to her in a sleepy voice, *I didn't do nothin'. Tired. Let me finish my nap.*

"Anybody there with you, baby?" Rockstar Dina asked.

She listened to the silence in her head for several minutes. The little one must've fallen asleep. She'd been sleeping a lot lately.

"You're hearing things, girl. Finish packing your stuff, then go play with the pups. The puppy people'll cheer you up."

Taking the stairs in twos, she sprung up three floors onto the 24th floor roof of her Manhattan penthouse. Good thing she got it when she was still being a good girl. Before the rages. That snooty board of directors wouldn't let her lease the broom closet now, not after she kicked that hairbag in the testacola's.

"Too late all you old farts. I'm here for five more years."

They'll deal with it. She wiped puppy licks from her face. The board was used to this kinda bullshit. She wasn't the only wackadoo in the building.

The romp and roll with the puppies' mother helped shake the scary voice. That voice could've come from anywhere. The radio. Anywhere. She looked at Compo Rose and gave her a long hard kiss on the snout, leaving the usual amount of Rosy Rich lipstick. Compo Rose's favorite flavor.

"Did you know your namesake got his name from hanging around compost heaps? Admit it. You do, too. Maybe I'll send one of your kids to Father Richard. What do you think?"

Dina's secretary poked her head around the corner. "Scuse, Dina. Gerald says the plane's ready and will you be picking up more passengers en route? And Carol Ann called. She wants you to pack some lorazepam. She says her doctor won't give her any more until next month."

"Okay thanks, Becky. Tell Gerrybarry not likely." Dina referred to her pilot and co-pilot as Gerrybarry, which never failed to amuse Becky. "Call Carol Ann and tell her we'll pick her up around four, so we should get to Maggie's in time for dinner. And Beck?"

"Mm?"

"Did you have the radio on a little while ago?"

"No. Been downstairs in the office all morning. Shall I tell Gerald you'll be ready to take off in an hour then?"

"Sure, fine." It could've been the radio alarm in her bedroom. The thing never did work right. And since when did Carol Ann start taking lorazepam?

∞∞∞

Dina's private plane touched down in Suffolk County, Long Island at 5:45 PM. They had decided it best to arrive together since this might turn out to be something of an intervention. Maggie had not left her mansion in nearly two years.

"She's never been much for talking," Carol Ann reminded Dina as they stepped off the plane. "Even when we were teens, she'd shut herself up in her room whenever she was working on a project. As far back as that she isolated herself, but we never made anything of it. Maggie always preferred the solitude. I miss how close we used to be."

"And she still won't hear of therapy," Dina said. "Once was enough for her. But she talked me into sticking with mine. Go figure."

In the limo, hawk-eyed Dina pointed out that this was her fourth mug of water in one and a half hours. "Either you're turning into a camel or you got dry mouth. Or could be you're diabetic or hungover. I'd say it's dry mouth and that's from booze or drugs."

Carol Ann folded her arms across her chest. "Booze or drugs? I think you know me better than that."

"Oh yeah, sure. Sipping brandy in the afternoon. And what's with the lorazepam?"

"I use it to sleep, Dina. All this excitement, Pages, Joe— the thought of seeing him soon. Isn't it obvious?"

"How many milligrams did the doctor give ya?"

"Two."

"How many pills in the bottle?"

"Sixty. Will you be making your point soon?"

"My point is that you're taking more than you're tellin' me. If your doctor isn't giving you any more until next month, you've obviously gone through the sixty already. You want me to do the math for you?"

"No thanks."

"I got a couple more questions, Carol Ann."

"Save them."

"I'm not so sure about this Edmon—"

"I said save them, Dina."

They didn't exactly arrive at Maggie's in the best of humor. There were also a couple of reporters on the road snapping pictures while they waited for clearance at gate number one before taking a private road to a second security station at gate number two. At this station they waited for visual confirmation from the first station. When they got to the front door, they had to show themselves again.

Dina, who had run out of patience two stations ago, shouted into the intercom, "Effen ay, Maggie! Didn't you tell these guys we were coming? Who do you think you are, me!"

A phone rang on the inside and a moment later the doorman welcomed and escorted them into the living room which looked more like an undersized ballroom. White furniture. White walls. Italian and French Renaissance reproductions adorned the walls–Donatello, Fontainebleau, Michelangelo. Maggie's paintings were noticeably absent on this floor.

Maggie had always felt uncomfortable displaying her work amidst renowned artists, even reproductions. Her paintings occupied another part of the house, several rooms in fact. Outsiders often wondered whether the owner's dominant trait was egotism or humility.

"Wow, this is breathtaking," Carol Ann said, turning in a slow circle. "Do you know it takes five hundred and seventy gallons of paint to cover the exterior of the White House?"

"Really," Dina said, dryly.

"True. Maggie tell you she commissioned a sculpture of St. Michael, similar to the one at Capilla del Cerrito in Mexico? At eleven feet it's smaller, but still powerful-looking. Wonder where it is."

"Dracula always did have great taste," Dina said.

"I heard that," Maggie said, making a splendid entrance, complexion peachy white against an emerald green lounging suit. Thick locks of hair draped her shoulders like satiny, red ribbons and she seemed to float as she crossed the room to greet them.

Carol Ann wondered how her sister, the recluse, could look so good. What place did Maggie go to in her mind to get her looking so lovely and confident? It had always been hard to tell where Maggie's head was. Her reserve accounted for much of that—her reserve and the closed doors.

Dina ran over and gave her a mushy hug and kiss on the cheek. "Look at you. We yak on the phone all the time and I haven't seen you in almost two years." *She's a grown-up, isn't she, Rockstar. You think you'll make a good grown-up some day?*

Maggie smiled and studied Dina for a moment.

"Hey," Carol Ann said. "How's my brilliant sister?"

Following a long embrace, Maggie voiced her concern. "You're ten pounds underweight, Carol Ann. What's the scoop?"

Unable to get over how beautiful Maggie looked, it took her ten seconds to concoct a scenario involving Joe, visualizing how he might react to Maggie now. He hadn't seen her in years, and he always liked Maggie. With one look he could fall madly in love. But maybe he *had* seen her. She lived in this big place and never left it. What a love nest it would make, with everything in it so perfect, with Maggie so perfect. Yes, perhaps they had seen each other.

She blurted out the words, "Have you heard from Joe Ross? I have to know, Maggie. Have you been hearing from him all these years and not saying anything? Tell me." Carol Ann felt small and foolish. "I'm so sorry, Maggie. I guess it's obvious how I lost the weight. I've been obsessing over the past and haven't been sleeping well. We haven't really talked about Marianlake in a long time. I'm kind of a wreck."

"Carol Ann, slow down," Dina said.

"Come on." Maggie slipped her hands into the crook of their arms. "Let's have some supper and champagne. We'll get into things, Carol Ann. Dina, are you all right?"

Dina burst into a fit of nervous giggles. That question always made her giggle. "Sure," she said, tapping her temple, "we're all fine in here, by gum."

Maggie had an elegant dinner waiting in the solarium. Surrounding gardens and ponds covered in blooming water lilies shimmered through white and green floodlights. In front of a Romanesque gazebo stood the great Archangel, watching over them as they clinked champagne glasses.

During dessert, the wind kicked up, giving the illusion of plant-life struggling to get safely inside. Tulip petals and leaves slapped the solarium panes, twisting and pressing traces of color onto the glass. Two young poplars by the gazebo seemed near the breaking point. Maggie rushed to the intercom and ordered them secured. Empathy poured from her as if the young trees were children instead of poplars. It was the most visible display of emotion the girls had seen in years.

"All we're missing is the howling of wolves," Dina said, against a musical setting of *Für Elise*.

Carol Ann refilled her champagne glass. "This weather reminds me of that Halloween night at Marianlake. Remember how the wind howled?"

Dina rubbed the chill from her arms. "I remember."

You don't have the guts to remember the whole thing, Rockstar. And little Dina never could. She's gone, by the way.

"Enough!" Dina slammed her hand down on the table. "Enough, please! I've been hearing this voice inside my head since this morning. And it ain't exactly friendly. Oh, God. Oh, God. I'm so tired. I am so incredibly tired." Tears streamed down her face. "Carol Ann. I can't go to Marianlake. At least not now. I'm not in the right frame of mind now. But I promise you, when I get my paddle back in the rowboat, I will go. I'll go for you because ... because if I don't go for you, you'll hurt. I don't want to see you hurt anymore. And since I'm obviously taking lousy care of myself, maybe I can take better care of you two." For a second her hands grew hot and her mind filled with peace she hadn't experienced in ten years, peace too fleeting to mention.

"Tell us about this voice," Maggie asked, wiping away tears full of black mascara from Dina's face.

"For a couple of weeks now, little Dina has been tired, so tired all the time. She wasn't coming out as much, preferring to delegate memories, stress, and career to me. Me. Ms. Altered States. Can you believe it? But in spite of my tantrums, I get things done. And I'm great in performance.

"The last time little Dina really came out was on the phone a couple of weeks ago. She wanted to talk to Carol Ann. That night at Marianlake, I felt her die inside me. But at first I didn't know whose funeral it was. You know the rest. After the rape, my therapist resurrected her. Then the squabbling. Years of it until a month ago. I felt her leaving me, and I miss her.

"This morning she told me to let her sleep. A few moments ago when I freaked, the voice said I never had the guts to remember everything that happened up there and that little Dina was gone. Your little Dina. She's gone, guys. Whoever's taken her place, well, your guess is as good as mine." Dina hunched over in her chair, pulling at her fleshy knuckles. "Stubby, chubby hands. I hope Joe can hear me calling tonight. Wherever he is."

Carol Ann stared boldly into her sister's eyes. "You're the riddle in this trio, Maggie—our puzzle. You, our vestal virgin. We used to be so tight ... but now I don't know who you are anymore. Please tell me. Because if I have to drug you to get you out of this place, I will. I need you out in the world with me. Now."

"Why don't you tell me why you're really here?" Maggie asked in a soothing tone, leaning in.

"Because we need you, Maggie. We need you to help us find Joe Ross."

"We? Or you?"

"All right, me. Dina has some reservations, but she has agreed we should go."

Dina narrowed her eyes at Carol Ann.

"Joe Ross," Maggie said, holding her eyes shut for a moment. "He's an obsession, Carol Ann. Why do you want to find him now? After ten years, don't you think it would be healthier for your self-esteem if he were to find you? What if he's married?"

Hearing this relieved Carol Ann. Maggie *really* didn't know anything about him. "I have a feeling he's not. And I think he's still involved in the goings on at Marianlake that Dina spoke of. So he hasn't contacted you then?" She wouldn't ask again.

"No. Don't you think I would've told you?"

Carol Ann raised her voice a notch. "I don't know what to think about you anymore. You started locking doors right after we returned from Marianlake and you've been locking them ever since."

Maggie drifted over to the window facing the statue. Remembering a poem by Emily Dickenson, she quoted it in part, "... *what fortitude the soul contains that it can so endure—the accent of a coming foot—the opening of a door.*" Flinching at the windstorm, she turned to her sister. "You want to know about doors, Carol Ann? Follow me, you two. And I'll tell you all about doors."

Maggie's private studio and gallery were on the second floor, with the staircase covered in mural scenes on both sides. Going up on the left side toward her studio, clusters of various scenes of Cape Cod Bay and Angelfish Cove filled the area. Between each scene, angels stood and hovered in the air, posed in the direction of Maggie's studio. Their expressions radiated beauty and serenity. Most of the colors were soft and earthy in tones of green, blue, peach, autumn oranges and cloud whites. Filled with sunlight, the mural depicted daytime scenes.

Preoccupied with the opposite wall, Carol Ann polished off the last of the champagne in a couple of gulps. "A bit of a shudderfest on this side," she said, referring to the dark colors and angels with cautionary expressions. "And they're all looking the other way."

"It scares me," Dina said. "The whole thing's at night. They all look so ... annoyed."

"What's that at the very end?" Carol Ann asked, retracing her steps. "That red thing?"

"A door," Maggie said. "Quite a contrast from my work as the world knows it, don't you think?"

"No kidding," Dina said. "I think I'll get myself back in the sunshine."

"So much red," Carol Ann noted, fascinated. She stopped again at the red door. "What's with the door, Maggie?"

"You've never noticed that before?"

"Well how can we?" Dina said. "It's the first time we're seeing it."

"No it isn't." Concentrating on the door, Maggie's complexion paled as she stared at its threshold. "I've had a red door in everything I've done for the past ten years. I made them subliminal. The artist child in me played *Hide the Door*. My supporters played *Spot the Angel*. The Angel has brought me fame, been my inspiration. But the Door has given me awareness to the suffering, the tormented. Come on. Let's go into the studio."

A lovely, summery contrast to the staircase walls, Maggie's studio was a smaller, rounder version of the downstairs ballroom with a huge bay window as its focal point. Painted in soft butter yellow, she accented the room simply, using three pieces of white rattan furniture and floral cushions. Because of the curve in the wall, most of her paintings rested on easels. The work in this room was Maggie Page as the world knew her—beautiful, mystical, and a hint of romance without the whimsy. It was feet-on-the-ground but heads heavenward. 'Nothing lore-ish, purely spiritual.' wrote a famous art critic. A large cheesecloth-covered canvas stood conspicuously isolated at the far end of the room. Maggie guided them through every painting but that one. When the girls asked about it, Maggie rubbed the chill from her arms.

"Later," she said.

They had more champagne and chatted merrily, focusing on externals for Carol Ann, who enjoyed articles and magazines on the latest in skin care and figure-flattering wardrobes. Diets and exercise. Holistic herbs and vitamins.

"And lorazepam," Dina said.

Every ten minutes or so, Carol Ann worked Joe's name into the conversation. Her voice would deepen then and she'd sigh and roll her shoulders.

"God, he was so beautiful," she said dreamily. "He'd always listen so intently with those sweet brown eyes, interested in everything I said. Brent made me feel a little of what I felt with Joe. For five minutes. But Brent was a puddle after a rain and Joe was the Atlantic Ocean. Lately I haven't been able to stop thinking about him and it's beginning to interfere with my life—"

"Beginning?" Dina said.

"*And* I just opened the store and can't focus on it. Not a healthy start, girls. I've no interest in dating and I haven't practiced my faith in ages. Remember when I used to go to Mass every Sunday?

"A few months ago I started taking the lorazepam for sleep." She glanced at Dina. "Hardly ever drank and now I don't hesitate to pour one if I'm stressed or worried. Which is often. If Joe were here I'd be okay. Really, I would. Hey, it's only been a decade since I've seen him, right? I have to practice a little patience."

Dina spoke of the rages and broken love affairs. She spoke easily of her therapy and the progress she'd made, according to her psychiatrist. Dina was of a different opinion. She admitted some of her fears—never making love or having normal sex again. Actually she never did have normal sex. She was a virgin on that Marianlake trip and was now tormented by the fear that her illness might escalate to schizophrenia.

"And the voice I've been hearing all day, guys? Different. Nothing like little Dina's voice."

Speaking of voices, she could lose hers. And losing her voice was the biggest fear of all. Fame had been trouble-free so far, a dog day at the beach compared with the rest of her problems, though it was becoming difficult trying to separate the two. That started two years ago in Florida on a walk in a lemon grove owned by an important concert promoter.

"I didn't throw up or pass out like you'd think," Dina said, tightly clasping her hands till her fingertips turned pink. "Oh no. I got real creative and threw myself at him. I stripped naked from the waist down. I felt drugged and probably looked it, too, according to what he told me later. You'd think a guy who was a friend, a guy who's been doing business with me for years and knew something of my history, would do the decent thing, right? Well, he didn't. Instead he violated me every way imaginable until the pain got so bad I screamed at him to stop. So he stopped. Wasn't that sweet?

"Then like some alley cat after the mating ritual, I attacked him. Scratching. Punching. Hitting. You name it. And you know what? The bastard got turned on all over again—and went for me. Again! But I threw up. And not too soon. I guess my stomach contents dribbling down his chest was finally enough to turn him off. Believing I had the flu, he calls his *girlfriend* to take care of me. I threw up a lot that weekend—smelling that lemon grove right outside my window.

"Can't get near a horse or a paddock, neither. Remember how I loved horses? Almost as much as Joe, probably. I get the shakes when I'm near one now because I can still see that bastard's reflection in the horse's eye. So you see guys, even if Joe hacked off the prick's man-tonsils in Italy—it wouldn't have been enough."

12. Coming Home

"Butterscotch," Joe told her all those years ago. "That's you, Maggie—pure butterscotch posing as peppermint. So much sweetness inside."

She was painting in the pumpkin field that day when Joe and Alain walked by balancing pumpkins on their heads, and after dropping Alain off, Joe returned for a chat. That chat lasted an hour.

Once or twice a year, Carol Ann asked about her love life. 'Not a priority right now' she'd always answer. Mere mortal man wasn't good enough, Carol Ann kidded. 'You're in love with the angels'. Her sister wasn't far from the truth. Her sister had also grown impatient waiting to hear of that other matter, the one that kept her from Pages opening—her self-imposed exile.

"You can say it," Maggie said. With champagne blushes on their cheeks, the girls had curled themselves into the studio's wicker chairs. "Agoraphobia. Isn't that such a perfectly trendy name in the '90s? I want to see the Potala Palace in Tibet. I want to go to Florence and see the statue of David. I want to spend an entire afternoon in the Louvre as close as I can get to the Venus de Milo. Imagine. She's three hundred-plus years older than Christ. I want to see all the greatest art in the world. But I guess I have to get out of the house first, don't I?"

"You can start with us," Carol Ann said, using the opening to segue. "I want to go to Medford and talk to Joe's grandmother and I want you to come with us."

"Back to that are we," Maggie said. "If I leave with you, it won't be to hunt down Joe Ross. I want you to return to Angelfish Cove. It's time we all did. Together. And that's what Joe wanted you to do, remember? It's the reason you settled there. Why do you want to go off in search of the mountain, when clearly it's in your own backyard?"

"You suggested I look for him! What, I was hearing things?"

"No, of course not. I know I suggested it. I thought closure might help you stop obsessing. Joe never gave you closure. But now I believe you should see Joe when you're in a better, clearer frame of mind."

"He's never forgotten me, Maggie. Look at the auricula."

"Of course he hasn't forgotten you. But he was using the plant to direct your attention to my painting. And then there's all this book business you told me about. Joe's still on this mystery mission of his, Carol Ann. You may have to accept the fact that his mission has nothing romantically to do with you. There may be something big going on here—huge. Let me try to tell you both why I'm so terrified of leaving this house. And about the *door* that's been in my head since we left Marianlake. The red door.

"Now I don't know how or why, but I think part of Joe's mission is to tackle what's behind that door and we're involved, us and Sister Elizabeth, wherever she is."

"So how are we involved? What is this door thing?" Dina asked.

Carol Ann tottered to the window seat and tucked her knees to her chin.

"That painting over there ... makes my hand shake." Maggie glanced over at the solitary canvas then massaged her right hand. "Last week it didn't stop shaking for two days. I had to hold it steady with my left hand to work, and

I couldn't do any fine strokes at all. I'll get my sketchbooks."

The sketches were the antithesis of her paintings, suffused with dark, undulated strokes. Disturbing midnight blues mixed with gray mists heavily dotted her backgrounds. A trace of yellow that shone from under the red door, gradually increased with every sketch, and it was obvious that the 'night side' of Maggie's hallway mural had evolved from these sketches. She had assembled the sketchbook during the last half of the '80s.

By 1989, the door had opened considerably. The entity casting a yellow shadow had misted out the door, and sketches done from '90 to the present were the most disturbing of all. Against a black background, Maggie had drawn a smoky gray and white mist. Clearly, there was something sinister about the sketch. Carol Ann and Dina began to shift and squirm in their seats.

"Look closer," Maggie said. "Look closer at the mist. Don't look at the door."

Hundreds of eyes filled the mist. Hidden around the eyes were shapes that took the form of a tree, a mirror with reflective eyes, letters, a bed, a sword, a man, a paintbrush. And so it went.

"Why didn't we see all these things at first?" Carol Ann asked. "Every single stroke is a picture. Are all those things coming out of that room behind the door?"

Maggie nodded.

"So then what gives with this door?" Dina wiped the hollow between her breasts with a tissue and brought it up dampened into shreds.

Maggie got the covered painting and carried it back on the easel to the girls. "I painted this a few days after Pages opened, Carol Ann."

It was a duplicate of the *Angel Reclining*–with one exception. The Angel wasn't reading the book. It was stretching an arm toward Pages, not quite reaching it. Pages had a few alterations, too. Maggie painted the store's interior with more detail. The people, the bookshelves, the wrought iron staircase. She had doors everywhere. Every one of them painted red.

Squishing in beside Maggie on the loveseat, Carol Ann noticed another peculiarity. "The book on the Angel's lap. On mine, the O is showing. In this one you have the O and a D. So you painted this after I called and asked about Walter Bayard's book? You said then that you didn't know what the O stood for."

"Still don't." She searched her sister's face for that old inspector-ish curiosity, which was there to some degree, but only, she guessed, because of Joe.

"What's with all the red doors in Pages?" Carol Ann asked, eyes sparkling.

Speaking of it aloud terrified her even more than thinking about it. But her love for them raised her above the fear. Dear God, she needed them to understand. "As you both know, I haven't left this house in two years. Prior to that, there were those awful panic attacks every time I had to go out in public. I've read all the books on agoraphobia. True, I always enjoyed solitude, but never at the exclusion of friends, family or work. There is no pathology in my past that could explain this. I sought therapy once. I won't do it again.

"At Marianlake, Joe predicted I'd become a celebrated artist, but I believe there was something else he wasn't telling me. I could read it on his face. And also at that time, the sixth sense in my work was developing, enhanced by every conversation with Joe.

"The apprehension, the mounting fear or whatever you choose to call it evolved around one thing and that one thing was Marianlake. Like the tree of life, it has many branches. I began painting those branches, ending recently with Angelfish Cove. Joe doesn't want one of us there, Carol Ann. He wants all of us there.

"And somewhere in that town there's a red door. As God is my witness, I know *it* has to be found and I know that *book* has to be found. I also know that Hell is behind that door because I've seen it. Again, don't ask me how I know, but we all have to see what's behind it." She looked searchingly at her sister. "And that's where Joe comes in. It's some kind of a test and he's got to help us pass it."

"Why the ten years?" Dina asked, hand cupped over her mouth. "You talk of Hell. Well I think we've already paid dearly for everything we've got. Are you telling us now that we're in for more of it? How come?"

"I told you, Dina, I don't know. A test like I said. And I don't know what we're being tested for. One thing for certain and this is common sense—we're going to end up back where it all started. Dina, have you heard any more of the goings-on up at Marianlake?"

"No. Except that George thinks it's weird that the people in Trois-Rivierés are so blasé about the project. Nobody seems to care."

"Joe will know," Carol Ann said, anticipation glowing on her face. "Tell us about this Hell you've seen that's kept you locked up here."

Her heartbeat thrashed in her ears. "There's a refuse dump that never stops burning. It burns on a corner of a lake that also burns, and this lake is not a metaphor. It is real. Inside the lake are charred demons in animal form, with flames shooting from their eyes and mouths. They're not standing in the lake. They're buried in it. This lake has condemned souls in human forms, too, being tortured for the sins that sent them there. The egotistical are humiliated. The lazy continually prodded. The thirsty drunk drinking fire. They float up and down, lament, hate, and despair."

She stopped to catch her breath. "I can't swallow," she said, patting her throat. "When I get scared, I feel like I can't swallow." Dina rushed to her and Carol Ann rubbed her back. "I'm afraid if I leave this house, that door is going to find me. That horrible place is real. This is not the first time you're hearing about it the way I said. Many of the saints and mystics have had visions of it. I'm certainly no saint, but with my sister in the same town as this door, how can I stay here?

"There's a large screen in my mind that acts as a kind of projector. It plays when it wants, like your voice, Dina. And when it plays, I sketch. I chose this life for myself. It did not choose me. I chose it out of fear. If I let the fear win now, I sacrifice my sister and my best friend."

Making up her mind this very minute as she spoke diminished the fear. After covering the painting with the cheesecloth, she carried it back to the far corner of the room, returned and faced the girls. "What say I find that door before it finds me? Tomorrow, ladies, we leave for Angelfish Cove. Together."

Saying the words bolstered her, but she felt feverish with a burning sensation in her wrists.

Moments before dawn, Maggie Page received a visit from an old friend.

∞∞∞

The fever did not frighten her as much as her aching hands. She asked God to give her any cross He chose and then apologized for being such a selfish coward. If arthritis were to strike her hands, she didn't think she could cope.

The windows rattled from the wind and the rain came down in sheets the way it did in old horror movies. Nature had an angry tune in her head tonight. *Sheet music*, she joked to herself. She laid on her back in bed on sweaty sheets, hair a sopping tangled mess, massaging and squeezing her hands. How long had she been awake and lying here thrashing around? The skin on her wrists felt sensitive and mottled, like a developing rash.

"Okay, getting scared now."

A soothing voice reassured her, "Don't be frightened, Maggie. Everything is as it should be. This is a reward, not penance. Close your eyes."

A ball of swirling yellow light appeared on the screen in her mind, growing larger until she felt comforted by electric rays coursing through her body like a warm lullaby. The ball of light split into millions of atoms and fragments, leaving her adrift in tranquility. Perhaps the fever had killed her. If so, then hello death, pleased to meet ya.

Something or someone was in the room with her.

The silhouette on the wall moved closer until it overshadowed her bed. She remained peaceful, saturated in happiness. The right side of the bed dipped from weight and she heard breathing, a contented sigh. A slow hand stroked her hair.

"Who?" she asked in a little voice.

The hand continued to caress. "Man, you're gonna need a gallon of conditioner to straighten out this mess," he said.

She couldn't believe it. Was this happening? "Joe?" Then she heard that lovable, deep chuckle.

"Maggie. You know, you *can* move. If you would turn your gorgeous head to the right a tad and tilt that busy little chin up another tad, you'll be able to see me."

It was Joe, alright. Really and truly—Joe. The years had been generous to him. Shafts of daybreak beamed through the window, showing the caramel highlights in his dark shoulder length hair. Dark too, were the eyes she remembered so well after all these years, deep chestnut with glistening flecks of honey. He was almost as beautiful as the fairer *St. Michael* would look if he sprung to life. Suddenly she thought of her beautiful sister, Carol Ann. She touched her lips and swallowed a lump that was hard going down.

"What is it?" Joe asked, tenderly. "What's taken away that lovely smile?"

"Carol Ann. You're not going to leave without seeing her, are you?"

Joe smiled. "Of all the questions to pick at this moment, you choose that one. I can see how the love earned you those marks."

"Marks?"

He took her arm and gently placed it in a shaft of light. "These marks, Maggie."

"They're like yours," she said with uncharacteristic emotion. Joe laughed when she grabbed one of his wrists and compared them. "I've heard of these marks. Dina told us she saw them on you years ago. And Carol Ann met someone named Iris who has them. *S T C*. What do the letters mean, Joe?"

"Recently I've learned that that's not a *T*, Maggie."

"You've lost me."

"It's a cross. A symbol separating the S and C. And within days you're going to be hearing more about it. There's a couple of thousand people in the world who have it, with a couple thousand more who will develop it over the next five years. Dina and Carol Ann, too."

"You didn't answer me, Joe. Now I know the letters don't mean *Santa Claus*."

"For years I thought they meant *save the child*. But that's another story." Joe held onto her hand, "Santa Claus was pretty close. They mean ... *Second Christmas*."

She didn't quite get that. "You mean, like a Second *Coming*?"

"No, Maggie. I'm afraid some of the answers to your questions will have to wait a little longer. Right now I have other matters to go over with you, then I gotta get out of here. I won't be seeing Dina at this time. Or Carol Ann."

Her face slackened. "Carol Ann wants to see you so much."

"Me too. But I can't."

"Why not?"

Joe disregarded her question. "Maggie, listen to me. I'm on my way to Angelfish Cove. Do you remember that little boy from years ago? Alain Duprielle?"

She sat up and he covered her shoulders with the blanket. "Yes."

"Well, he's all grown up now and he's been with me since Marianlake. Alain and I are two of thousands involved in *Second Christmas*, on making it happen. We'll be preparing you, tutoring you over the next five years. Everyone with these marks is going to experience something so wondrous that I can't find a superlative to do it justice. But here's the catch—we earn it. We have to face certain dark realities, downsides, demons. Call it what you want."

"You mean like tests?"

"Exactly. We'll have help, but in the end, we get to choose–as always. These marks on all our wrists come straight from God. They too, were earned. I suspect you earned yours when you decided to face the thing you fear most in order to keep safe two people you love most. These marks are here to help us, to strengthen us, even to give us insight at times. What is the thing you fear most, Maggie?"

It was still difficult to picture, but that was okay. Joe was here. "The red door," she said.

"Yes." He leaned in closer. "It is real. It's in Angelfish Cove. And we're going through it, but not until Alain and I prepare you, all of you. More on that later. My brave Maggie, you're going to leave this house today. You can't tell the girls you've seen me. Come on now, don't pull that face. I'll contact you from Angelfish Cove in a day or two and we'll talk more.

"When the girls ask you about these marks, you can tell them about the fever and the beautiful feelings, but you have to leave me out of it. I wasn't here. You never saw me. So you don't know what the letters mean. I'm sorry, Maggie. It has to be this way for now."

"You're always in such a hurry. Always off somewhere. Tell me something, my vanishing friend. Who you working for?"

"Technically I'm working for the Vatican. Alain and I are research associates, employed by the Vatican Institute of International Development."

"Oh puh-leeze." Hearing Joe's laughter made her laugh, too. It had been a while.

"My grandmother has a tough time with that one as well," he said, alerted to a toilet flush. "Really, we'll get into all your questions later."

"Are you married?" She had to ask.

"No."

"So this thing, this mission is wonderfully special?"

"Yes, Maggie. Have you been very frightened all these years?"

"Since that Halloween night at Marianlake, I've been tortured by glimpses of this red door. As the years passed the door opened more. So I saw more. For every painting of beautiful Angel light, I've had to pay with sketches of the hell behind that door. Both sides of the record, plus and minus, but too much minus. You know?"

He nodded sympathetically.

"As the entities behind the door grew, I retreated. I was terrified they might follow me out, Joe, becoming like an airborne virus or something. What's going to happen today? Will they follow me out?"

"Maggie, look at Dina. They've been on our tail for ten years. But God's touched you this morning. You'll have the courage to leave here, don't worry."

"I know you don't have time to get into any more of this now, but can I ask you one more question?"

"You Page women never ask just one more question. Sure, go ahead. As long as it's not a *Second Christmas* question."

"How has it been following Carol Ann?"

Joe raised the collar on his leather jacket. "I suspect through a memory, a memory that's become an obsession. Any form of obsession is like worshipping a false god. Idol worship. And I'm the memory. I'm the idol. Serious consequences often follow."

"How do you know all this about us?"

"It's surprisingly easy to keep track of people. I've been blessed with some extra insight through everyone involved in this project. Also I have a great PI."

She giggled again. "You like my work?"

"You paint like an angel. And Dina sings like one."

"And my sister?"

"Heavenly legs."

"Joe, I'm serious. She hasn't really left the past in the past. I want to know what she's in for. How 'bout you? Have you left the past completely behind?"

"All of you began in my past."

"That's cleverly evasive."

"Don't you think Carol Ann deserves to hear those answers from me first? And as for the future, as I said, there are tests we have to pass, Maggie. Your red door. You've endured so much pain in your isolation, even more than Dina. No question you've earned a bit of respite now. I wish I could promise you'll have it. As soon as the marks develop, one becomes stronger, able to understand what the poverty of love entails. One learns not to fear suffering.

"Half the time we wouldn't know we were suffering if our fear wasn't constantly reminding us of it. I spent five years in Rome learning how to love and detach. I'm still learning. So now I'm taking another five years to pass on what I've learned to our little group. I hope the timeframe sunk in, girl. 'Cause that's how long we're all going to be together before this goes down."

"Ohh, Joe. Five years. How long before Carol Ann gets the marks?"

"No way to know. I was at Pages opening, you know, dressed in a silly getup. I was in a wheelchair and she laid some heavy guilt trip on herself because there were no ramps in the place. That's not like Carol Ann. What's up?"

"She ... hasn't been herself. Why the disguise, Joe? If you didn't want her to see you, what were you doing there?"

"Two reasons. First, to buy a little piece of real estate on the quiet. Second, to bond my insight with yours. I guess Carol Ann's already asked you about the book the angel's reading."

"Yes she has. I wish I could help you out, but I don't know where I get this stuff. What's the story behind this book?"

"Too long a story. I'll save it for the beach and a bowl of chowder." He ran his hand across her forehead. "Fever's gone. The euphoria will stay with you a day or two, long enough to get you out of here and moved into Angelfish Cove. There'll be no anxiety attacks once you pass through that gate. That much I can promise. It's stopped raining, Maggie, and the sun's all the way up. Pitter patter. Alain and I are driving from here to the Cove, so you'll probably get there before me. All my friends are fresh out of private jets these days. Besides, we can't have me spotted by anyone inside the house, can we?"

"How did you get by all my security?"

Joe smirked and raised his brows. "See you soon." Then he kissed her on the cheek and slipped quietly out of the room.

Maggie passed the next two hours staring at her wrists.

∞∞∞

The basement in Pages was Edmon's favorite place in all of Angelfish Cove. He loved coming down here to dream and scheme. It was the perfect place to try Joe Ross and his merry little band of angels. There were no windows. Accordingly, there could be no sun. The air was dank, to which he'd added a pinch of decay—enough to lazy up the mind and impede their mental dexterity.

He so enjoyed the challenge of renovating the room for her. A storage room was what little Ms. Page wanted. Well, she would have it, only it would store a little more of his inventory and a little less of hers.

Ah, such a remarkable door. He stood admiring the paint job—all three coats of blood red paint soulfully applied with every stroke of the brush. 'Course, these boring little chippies wouldn't want to get anywhere near his soul, assuming he had one. He kept the door locked at all times but could enter without a key, apart from *Mr. Halo*, Ross's creepy sidekick. He had to smile again. This room was the reason he returned to Angelfish Cove.

Joe Ross would be taking them on their little purification walks in this room. Oh the joy, the rapture, if they entered before J.R. waved the green flag. In that event, it would be a hell-walk. Tch, sorry all. *Ms. Cap* was on the brink of entry now since he'd already started messing with her. But Carol Ann was for killing time, for laughs. He mustn't get too distracted, seeing it was that big fish kid he wanted to hook and reel in. That's why he really returned to the Cove.

There was a disadvantage though—they had to *know* about the door. He had his rulebook and superiors, and damn it all, Joe Ross had his. Not long now before they'd know all about the door, know it was off limits. But he still had to go through the motions of telling Ms. CAP that he randomly chose the color red to do some touch-up painting, and she'd react as she always did, with that cute little indecisive nod. Ah well, Rome wasn't destroyed in a day.

He opened the door and sauntered through the room. There *it* was, resting unobtrusively on top of that grimy old file cabinet, driving him mad. Walter Bayard's book. He didn't feel like smiling so much now. In a big way that book, being part of the agreement and all, had more power over him than Rafe and the rest of them. Not fair. The door was off limits to them and the book was off limits to him.

Opprimo Diabolis. 'Overpowering the Devil'. If he so much as farted near it he would be, for lack of a better phrase, sent down. He had to get the kid to bring the book out, after which, it would be Ms. CAP's responsibility to return it to Joe Ross and his superiors. Good luck with that, folks. Once the book was out of here and in his rightful hands—goodbye, *Mission*. Hell's baby bells, he loved it down here!

∞∞∞

While Joe unpacked, Alain sat in the deck chair ocean-gazing. The ten years had passed quickly. Joe knew about the ruse with Compo and the horse, for which Claude felt terrible. But no harm had come to the animals. Joe also knew that Claude wrote those notes. He'd followed them that Halloween and dropped the bloodied shirt into his trick or treat bag. It really didn't take Joe long to put it together. He figured most of it out in Rome a couple of weeks after they extradited Dina's rapist. Joe understood it would take a life or death situation to tear him away from Carol Ann and his studies. The 'ruse' was the only way they could get him to Rome, which is where they needed him to be.

Father Richard Vaux had no idea they'd selected Claude Duprielle to manipulate the dog and write the threatening notes until the morning he and Joe left Marianlake. What Joe didn't know was that his bruises were fake and that Tracy Duprielle was a gifted makeup artist. To this day he still didn't know about the bruises.

To the same extent, given all the disguises and secrets, their present resembled their past. This was his sole complaint when he spoke with his CEO's. It wasn't fair to Joe, especially since he was the only one without secrets. 'Sorry, Remiel', they always said. 'Joe must wait it out.'

Iris was on her way up to the deck. She had been ten miles down the road when he heard the *Gloria Estefan* cassette blaring in her old VW. Iris loved those Latin rhythms. Latin rhythms and four-inch platform heels.

"Hello there," she said gaily behind clunky shoe noises. He'd have to remind her to wear sensible shoes around here, but then he understood her reasons for not wearing them. "Gorgeous night, isn't it?"

Alain motioned her to sit down and glared at her.

"What?"

"I was wondering," he said, gray eyes sparkling like icicles on snow. "How are you doing with all of this? Really?"

"Where's Joe?"

"He was unpacking. He's going through Maggie's personal file now."

"Oh, I'm all right, Alain. I have my moments, but they pass."

"Being around Carol Ann doesn't upset you too much?"

"It did in the beginning. The first day. But she's beautiful and kind, so I got over it real quick. H.G. Wells said that time changes space. Now here I stand on this deck, on this special night, one of many, I'm sure ... and at this very moment I feel that this space is still exactly the way I left it and that time hasn't changed it at all. I say this with all due respect to Mr. Wells."

"Funny you should bring up his name. Joe mentioned him just the other day. Wells had asked the questions, *can man control his destiny? Can he change the shape of things to come?* Joe told me he felt that Wells believed it possible. He said he did, too."

"I know you and Joe don't share the same opinion of Wells, but look now though–he's actually going to get the chance to see the result of how man can control his destiny. One man's destiny, one man's answered prayer, thousands of destinies affected. It boggles my mind, even with my new gifts."

"You mean your *spiritual bounty*," he teased. He had said it in French, a language he still enjoyed speaking every once in a while. Iris was fluent in all languages, another bountiful gift. Still he wondered why she had not yet learned to master her own emotions. Considering her tragic past, he hoped so see her enjoy a reprieve. Poor Iris. No sweet surrender yet.

Alain observed the subtle change in Iris's body language when Joe walked onto the deck nibbling a wedge of pizza.

"Hi, Iris," Joe said. "Welcome back. My grandmother called and wants to visit soon. But what I can't figure ... what's wrong, Iris?"

"Nothing. Just a chill. When does she want to come?"

"She's not sure. As soon as her friend's feeling better, she said."

"I don't know if her visit is such a good idea, *Uncle Andrew*," Alain said, grinning at Iris. "Our plates are pretty full with the girls, don't you think?"

"No argument. But what was I supposed to tell R– don't come? Don't get me stahted on that now. I'll get all sidetracked. My pizza'll get cold. And Carol Ann's working in the store tonight. What I can't figure out is why the town isn't buzzing about Maggie and Dina. Gee, I wonder if anybody we know had something to do with that. Any ideas? Dear *nephew*?" He squinted at Alain.

"Rafe dropped by earlier," Alain said, taking a lazy stretch on the deck chair. "He has this tranquil effect on people, what can I tell you." He faked a yawn and they laughed. "So I don't think they'll be getting any special treatment."

Joe leaned on the rail and looked at the shoreline. "For a moment I thought I saw Willie playing in the waves. I wonder if Willie minded my giving her CAP cap to Carol Ann. I'd wanted to connect her with Pages. Pages and

Willie. I'm clueless as to why I'd want to connect Carol Ann with Willie. Thinking back on it now, I don't know why I did that."

"I don't think Willie would've minded," Iris said. "She loved you. Who knows, Willie's spirit might have put the thought in your mind to stay connected to you."

"I'll always stay connected to Willie." Joe stared vacantly at the sky. "I don't know, Alain. Maybe it was a mistake buying this house. Every time I walk in that bathroom ..."

Alain got up and joined him. "When you decided on this house, you were in a different state of mind. You knew Willie wasn't dead, not in the spiritual sense. You felt her presence in positive ways. You wanted to reconcile the past in order to let it go. Do it, Joe. Do it so you can help Carol Ann reconcile her past with you. Of everyone in our group, I think Carol Ann will be the most difficult. We got that feeling at Pages opening."

"Yeah, and I don't mind admitting to both of you that it scares me. Even with these marks and everything I learned in Rome, I still have my defects, which will become problematic at some point. I don't know how you do it, Alain. Look at him, Iris. Women drool over him everywhere we go and he always manages to keep his hormones in his pocket. I mean, neither of us are priests. We took no vows of chastity. You're amazing."

"What if I promise to fall madly in love and get married in 1997? Will that make you happy?"

"It will if I get to choose for you." Joe grinned at Iris. "I know. Priorities. Right, Iris?"

Alain cleared his throat. Iris had been staring at Joe like he had a flock of seagulls flying around his head.

"Right." A flush crept across her cheeks. "The time is going to go by so quickly. Besides, in a way, you and Alain already have enough women in your life. You can't avoid Carol Ann for much longer, Joe."

"I know. I'm trying to figure out the best way to approach her without shocking her into a stroke. And I did want to spend a little private time with Maggie first. Then again, I don't want her getting mad at Maggie for keeping secrets. There are too many secrets floating around already." Joe arched his eyebrows at both of them.

∞∞∞

He didn't want to upset the peace he'd been enjoying for the last little while. One hour alone with Carol Ann could ruin everything. And the others couldn't know how insecure he felt ever since Maggie asked how he felt about her. When Maggie told him Carol Ann still loved him, an alarm went off inside, not only in his head, in every other part of his anatomy. This wasn't anything like a burglar or smoke alarm. This was one of those Californian brush fire–evacuate-the-entire-area alarms.

Alain waved him off the deck when Iris went below to talk with someone under the balcony. Okay—time to evacuate the area. He and Alain made fast tracks into the living room.

"Think fast, Joe. What do you want to do? It looks like they're on their way up, all three of them."

"Who?" His heart started hammering. "Oh hell."

Iris came running in ahead of them. "Sorry, Joe. Carol Ann spotted me on the balcony. She's out for a late picnic dinner on the beach. She's got Maggie and Dina with her and she's already wondering what I'm doing here. What could I do? I had to invite them up. Think fast, Joe."

Taking a hard left around the fireplace toward the stairs, he said, "Alain, you know what to do. Stall until I think of something. And in the meantime, if you think of something first, I'll be grateful." Hearing the slap of flip-flops behind voices, he bounded up the stairs.

Alain returned to the deck, giving Carol Ann a glimpse of the back of his head.

"Hi," Iris said. Carol Ann introduced her to Maggie and Dina.

"I'm a fan of both of you," Iris said. "Maggie, I was at Carol Ann's the day your painting arrived. She let me stay for the unveiling. It is so beautiful."

"Thank-you," Maggie said, graciously.

"This is a great place," Dina said, tilting her head toward the deck. "Is that your hubby sitting outside?"

"I wish," Alain called in. "Bring everybody out here, Iris."

Carol Ann's mouth flew open. "Al!" she shrieked, giving him a hug. "When did you get back? Is Andrew with you?"

"Late this afternoon," he said. He let out a big-time sigh and the girls exchanged looks. "Let me offer you a little Courvoisier, ladies. You're going to need it."

"Hopefully we won't," Maggie said.

"Am I missing something here?" Dina asked.

Carol Ann dry-washed her hands. "You can pour me a Courvoisier, Al. A double."

"I'll get it for you," Iris said. "Actually I'll get one for all of us. Actually I'll bring out the bottle."

When she left them, everyone got silent for an awkward moment until Dina spoke.

"You know, you sound familiar. Your voice. And I know voices."

"I know you do." Alain smiled warmly at her. "I remember the first time I heard you sing."

"Oh? You caught me in concert. That's nice."

"Well you only sang one song, and you were in a rowboat. I can still hear your voice echoing across that lake. I was ten at the time, but I remember."

Iris returned with the bottle and a tray of snifters.

"Wait a minute ..." Dina slapped a hand against the side of her mouth. "I know. Alain! You're the little boy Joe Ross hung out with at Marianlake!"

"Yes."

Maggie put her hand on Carol Ann's shoulder.

"Carol Ann," Alain said. "I'm sorry for the deception. There were reasons. But I don't think now's the time."

Carol Ann took a sip of cognac. Her hands shook so badly when she put the drink to her lips, Maggie had to assist her.

Iris turned her head away.

"Alain ..." Slightly unsteady on her feet, Carol Ann walked up to him, "do you still keep in touch with Joe Ross?"

Maggie glanced down at her wrists.

"Yes," Alain said. "He's my best friend."

"Then I can call him?" she asked in a strangled voice. "D-do you have his number handy?"

He didn't answer. It took Carol Ann seconds to notice that Alain wasn't looking at her, that none of them were looking at her. Carol Ann followed their eyes to the doorway, to where *he* stood. *Him*!

The love of her life.

Joe Ross—her obsession.

13. For the Love of Pain & Desire

"Joe," she said, eyes sparkling with tears. Carol Ann ran to him, clung to him. "Finally. Oh Joe, I can't believe this."

He wanted to kiss her breathless. Instead he rocked her in his arms and kissed the top of her head. Lord, he felt the knots on her spine. Had she lost more weight since Pages opening? What else had he missed looking through those dumb Coke-bottle glasses?

"Carol Ann. You sure took your sweet time finding me."

"Well, you know, things to do."

He searched their faces. They wanted answers and after waiting a decade, they deserved them. But this wasn't exactly the best time to update them. Maggie, who was better informed, sat patiently with hands folded on her lap. But Maggie was functioning on zero hours sleep and just left her home for the first time in two years.

Maggie blew him a kiss. "It's good to see you here, Joe."

Poor Maggie was still processing his dawn visit and her branded wrists. Dina looked like a lost little girl whose parents had forgotten to pick her up after school, her sweet mind no doubt reeling from surfacing teenage memories.

"Gotta get my hug in here." Dina squeezed in front of Carol Ann. "Ay! Show me the DEET and the harp."

They all laughed when he extracted both from his jacket and tooted the harmonica.

And Carol Ann. He owed her an explanation, a big one. How was he going to explain it all to her, make her understand? He felt the longing in her thin, trembling body when he held her. How did this happen to her? The hurt in her eyes stabbed at him when he escorted her to the deck chair beside Maggie. Back in her life five minutes and already he'd upset her.

"It's been ten years since we were all together," he said, accepting a snifter of Courvoisier from Iris. "Except we were drinking Dr. Pepper last time. You ladies are so beautiful. And successful. Not that I have the right to be, I'm extremely proud of you. In case you were wondering, I've kept tabs on your lives. I've never forgotten you. Not for a day." Oh, these wonderful, expectant faces. "Wow, where to begin. Think I'm stalled at the gate."

"Perhaps we should keep it light for awhile," Alain said. "Everybody's feeling emotional, I think. I'll put on some music. Something upbeat."

Carol Ann teetered over and slipped her hand into his. "How light are we supposed to keep it? How long do I have to wait before I can start asking you questions, Joe?"

"Give him a minute, Carol Ann," Maggie said. "He didn't expect us to show up here tonight. This is about more than the two of you."

"So you keep reminding me," she said sharply. "You seem the better informed, Maggie. Where did you get your information? Please share."

"Hey, guys," Dina said. "This is supposed to be a reunion. A happy time. We haven't had too many of those."

"I really feel like I'm intruding here," Iris said. "You all should have some time alone, so I'll say goodnight."

"You're not intruding, Iris." He let go of Carol Ann's hand, hating the way her face paled at his familiarity with Iris.

"So you two *do* know each other." She cast a foul glare at Iris. "Why did you lie to me?"

"Because you would've asked me too many questions that weren't my place to answer. Talk first to Alain and Joe. Then tomorrow I'll come by Pages and we'll talk."

The second Iris pulled out of the driveway, she turned to him, "Are you and Iris well acquainted?"

"Iris and I met a few years back in Rome." She'd already had too much to drink and it was still early. "Alain and I spent five years there studying. And the past four plus years, both of us have been traveling, working for the Vatican and that's where I met Iris, at a dinner meeting. We're friends, Carol Ann, that's all. I never married, in case you were wondering."

"I'll admit, I was naturally curious," she said, attempting to flirt.

"I can't get this laughing tune out of my head," Dina said, plunging her ears. She appeared anxious and breathless. "But maybe it isn't in my head because it's so loud. Laughing and twangy guitars. What is it? Can you hear it, Joe?"

"Alain?" he said. "This is where you come in, bud."

Alain trailed his deck chair over to Dina and positioned it such that their knees touched. "Is the tune intermittent?" he asked.

Dina nodded, gazing into his eyes.

"Do you think you can get your head to raise the volume?"

Dina became agitated again. "Why would I wanna do that?"

"Close your eyes and try to raise it and I'll show you," he told her.

Dina covered her ears.

Alain gently pulled her hands away from her ears. "Now try to lower the volume," he said, still holding on to her hands.

Smiling now, Dina stared at him in wonderment.

Alain returned the smile. "Getting bored with that same old tune, were ya?"

Dina managed a chuckle.

"Close your eyes again. You're familiar with recording studios, so you know where everything is. Find the volume control and power it off. Then sit quietly for a bit."

They all waited a short minute.

"Now hit the power button and turn it back on. Okay. What do you feel like listening to? Doesn't matter. Switch to another station. Nice music? Good. Turn it up a notch. Wait a few seconds. Then power off."

Dina squeezed Alain's hands and thanked him. "It worked. What did you do?"

"I swapped your juices–negative with positive," he said, laughing when she scrunched her face at him. "I'll get into details for you later. But right now we need to give a little time to Maggie." Alain turned to Carol Ann. "Guess you were surprised when you saw your sister's wrists this morning?"

Carol Ann took a long, drawn-in breath. "Yes. Now she looks like you, Joe, and Iris. Is this a special club? Can I join?"

"In a way it's a club," he said, wiping DEET off his palms. "And I was with Maggie when she joined. I asked her to keep my visit to herself until I could get the three of you together. So don't be mad at her. I didn't expect to see you all so soon and wanted to present the facts after we'd been back in each other's lives awhile, when we were calm. Now Alain has accomplished that with Dina, and Maggie got it through osmosis. But you're too wound up, Carol Ann." He said to the others, "If you guys don't mind, I'd like to take Carol Ann for a stroll on the beach."

Although Alain hesitated, the girls said that was fine.

∞∞∞

They walked silently along the beach for the first few minutes which was fine with her. He had been back in her life less than an hour and already she'd made a fool of herself. How silly her clingy greeting must've seemed to him. How girlish. She really knew nothing about him. Her chin trembled. He would have to see her after she'd had a few too many. A ways down the beach a man laughed shrilly, laughing at her it seemed. Suddenly it wasn't yesterday anymore, and ten years really *had* gone by.

"This is nice," she said, crossing her arms as they walked.

"Mm," he said, collecting his thoughts.

Well this was a hubbub of conversation. Maybe Maggie was right. Joe hadn't returned for romantic reasons. She felt disgusted with herself for being jealous when he hugged Dina and winked at Maggie. He looked like an angel, so it was clear he'd done extremely well without her. And she probably looked damaged to him, which must've said it all.

Joe's thoughts were no doubt with Willie seeing this was his first day back in the beach house. So probably this was a good time to ask how he was managing. But she didn't want to discuss the 'Willie' memories. She wanted to discuss the 'Carol Ann' memories. She crooked her arm into his. *Look at me, Joe. Look at me! Kiss me hello.*

He still wore black jeans, white T-shirts and probably still bought his boots at GH Bass. His long hair fell in sexy wisps over his eye and he smelled like crisp sheets and morning air. Those melting pot eyes seemed focused away from her. Oh God, she wanted them focused on her. She wanted his body too. Like his mind, it had grown stronger, more muscular. He and Alain apparently spent time working out and that Alain was pretty terrific-looking.

Obviously they were close, had been all these years during her absence. They had traveled together and shared this 'mission' thing. How *close* were they? Joe stopped and looked down at a piece of driftwood.

"I was at your wedding," he said, brushing the driftwood aside with his foot. "In back of the church."

She reached for his arm and tugged him closer. "You were there?"

"Yeah. Did he ever hurt you?"

She shook her head, tried to swallow. "It was the other way around. I hurt him. He had his weaknesses but he loved me. "You were really there?"

His eyes explored hers and she went weak in the knees. "Tell me."

"I didn't love him back but did a great job talking myself into believing I did. It's amazing how good we are at talking ourselves into things. Don't you think? I guess you noticed the resemblance?"

Joe's expression pained. "When the priest said *speak now*, you don't know how close I came to standing up. For some time I blamed myself for your marriage." He took a moment to collect his thoughts, which got her tugging on an earlobe. "When you look back, Carol Ann, what do you remember, I mean specifically?"

What the hell did he think she remembered? Art projects? "I remember the intensity of it all. What we felt and how fast we felt it."

Joe took her hands in his. "Don't you remember Halloween night—what happened to everyone?"

"Yes, Joe. Of course I do." That stupid man down the beach was still laughing. *Shut up already.* "I was one of the one's stuff happened to, remember? But we also said goodbye that night, and that memory tends to override the others a bit. You told me you loved me, said you always would. You told me to remember Angelfish Cove. So? Here we are—ten years later. But where are we really, Joe?"

He kissed the tops of her hands then let them go. "Right where we're supposed to be at this time."

"You're as cryptic as ever. No more. I want answers. I deserve that, don't you think? All I got from you was a goodbye phone call in a lodge three miles from here. That phone call was the last time we spoke. You said *I love you, Carol Ann. Always will*. Remember? Then the next day you send me Willie's cap. Which I wore inside the beach house after I broke in, by the way. Like that, you were gone, Joe." She snapped her fingers. "So I said goodbye forever to you right there in that bathroom. Probably from the very room Willie said her goodbyes."

"I'm so sorry." He grazed his fingertips along her arm, stirring every nerve ending in her body. "I was in love too, and confused. So much was happening to me. We just buried Willie. Then I meet Father Vaux at her wake and my life changed. You happened—and I fell, too. But I had priorities, Carol Ann, priorities that tore me up inside because they were so much bigger than us." Joe looked cautiously at her. "They still are."

She decided to let the tidal wave wash over her. "Then what *are* these priorities? What is it that is so much bigger than us?"

"I don't ... tonight isn't the right time."

"Please, Joe."

He didn't hesitate long. "You've heard of Walter Bayard, the man who pretty much built Angelfish Cove?"

"I have." She noted the glint of excitement in his eyes.

"It all started with his saying a prayer that God answered in a way even Walter could not imagine."

"What prayer?"

"To return love and hope to the world. To do that, we get to take something of the past and move it forward. And nothing gets disturbed or changed in the process. So hang on to your inspector's cap, Carol Ann, because we're all going back in time. For twenty-four hours."

It was her turn to stop and gape at him. What on earth had he been into?

"I know it's hard to fathom," he said, grinning like a boy. "But Walter Bayard created a time gauge he can install at subterranean depth in any location."

Oh, come on! "Don't get me wrong, I mean, it's incredible. Okay, so—you're telling me this has all been about time travel?"

Joe gave her one of his cryptic smile-frowns. "Not quite all. Alain and I are going to have a meeting with everybody later in the week. But this gift, Carol Ann, we have to earn it, spiritually train for it. Confront our demons for it."

"You're talking inner demons, right?"

"I'm talking demonic entities."

"Oh come on, Joe. I admit to weirdness that Halloween. But the mind—the brain is a powerful thing."

"How can you say that? Look at your sister and those sketches."

"My point exactly. The mind is a powerful thing."

Joe sighed, picked up a stone and tossed it into the water. "We'll table the debate for now. And the time travel? Your thoughts?"

The idea was a little too out there and she didn't want to hurt his feelings. "You're getting us all together for a meeting, you said?"

"Yes. You may walk away with a different mindset after that meeting."

Joe always liked that word, 'mindset'. "More open-minded, you mean?" He didn't answer. Instead he set his jaw and launched another stone. "Okay. What did you mean by *earn* and *spiritually train* for this thing?"

"Healthy love is where it's at, Carol Ann. To get it we internally cleanse. Then we ready ourselves for a fight. I know. Please allow me to be my usual cryptic self a while longer. Thing is, I need you, Dina and Maggie together. I didn't intend to talk mission tonight, but you always had a knack for prying information out of me. Why don't we talk about you? What you're feeling. Us here in the present. Your expectations."

"My expectations?" She couldn't believe this. He was speaking to her like a mayoral candidate wanting her vote. "Well let's see. I know I'm not a priority. But I do expect you to put your big picture aside for the moment and honestly tell me what feelings you have for me, *here in the present*. Because I still love you. You want to really go back to the past, Joe, for twenty-four hours? How 'bout going back five minutes? That's how far back the past seems to me. Internally cleanse, you say? I tried internally cleansing you from my system and guess what—no soap." She would not turn into a teary mess. She would not. "I've told you how I feel, Joe ... you?"

∞∞∞

Carol Ann hadn't once asked about his life, his dreams, if he ever got that horse farm in Ocala, did he still play the harmonica badly, or his mosquito phobia. Nothing. What she wanted from him after the ten-year absence was the fantasy reunion, her own self-gratification. And he was still on this mission so their situation hadn't really changed.

"I'll always love you. But ten years have passed. I've changed. You've changed. We're not in a position to pick up where we left off. I wish with all my heart we could."

It saddened him knowing his love was genuine and her love was nothing more than idealization, obsession. He could walk away. She couldn't. Dear God, would he have to stand around and watch another woman he loved break apart again? In a word—no. He'd have to distance himself from Carol Ann.

"You're looking to me for your happiness, Carol Ann, and no one is responsible for the happiness of another. You don't love me. I'm not even real. You made me up, attached a memory, face and body. All I am is a fantasy. And sadly ... fantasy is your drug."

"How the hell do you know so much! Have you been here? Speak for yourself, mister. You say you still love me? You don't know the first thing about love, Mr. Me and My Priorities. You gave, you took away and then you took off. And you're still taking off. Still love me, huh? I don't think so. We'll see who knows what about real love.

"You go ahead and express your love your way, Joe, as twisted as it is. And I'll express it mine. In the meantime, I'll stick around. I have to. I'm a key player on your team. Right? So I'll play the reluctant rookie for you. Must check out this *big* picture of yours, mustn't I? Drive the girls back for me, will you. I'm going home. See you at the team meeting, Coach."

That fiery little strawberry blonde would no doubt put them all in jeopardy. His eyes narrowed as he watched her storm off down the beach toward the man laughing in the night.

∞∞∞∞

In his eagerness he'd told her they were taking something of the past and moving it forward. That was a slip and to his relief she didn't ask what. *What* exactly, were they moving forward? In recent weeks he'd twice overheard the word *cargo*. Still, he couldn't tell her what he didn't know. He couldn't explain that there were secret directives still floating about out there, that he would know more about the mission when he was ready to know. He trusted Alain and that was good enough for him. But he wondered, though. Every day, he wondered.

Sleep wanted nothing to do with him, so he got out of bed and leafed through today's briefing material. The 'dream team' Fathers had couriered individual *how-to's* on fact presentation. One wanted to dump it on them and wait for the fallout. The other paraphrased the Good Book saying, 'don't give them too much solid food. Just give them a little milk'. Perhaps Dina and Carol Ann were not ready to comprehend all of it. But he was the boss, they wrote in their unique ways. He knew best. He could field their questions. Yeah, but what about his questions? Ah, some things never changed.

It was past 4 a.m. when he turned in, hopefully for the last time. Something caught his eye while lowering the blind. What was out there? He flicked the blind up again and saw a red Cougar parked three beach houses down. With only seven beach houses on this road, all having garages and long driveways, there was no need for guests to park on the road.

Carol Ann had a red Cougar.

For the first time in ages he didn't think. He reacted. What was she doing out there at four in the morning? Had she been drinking? *Blast!* He jumped into his jeans and stumbled through the darkened living and dining rooms. Soon as he unlatched the patio door, an exhale startled the hell out of him. Alain was in the dark, reclined on the Lazyboy. He had been watching her.

His gut fluttered while he waited for Alain to speak first.

"She's been sitting out there for over an hour now," Alain said, not shifting his gaze. "Sitting there in the damp sand, staring up here. There's still a touch of frosty air in this May neck of the woods, especially this time of the morning. It's a May day in the truest sense, isn't it?" Alain turned his head to him, eyes glistening in the moonlight. "Do you want to go out to her, Joe?"

"Can she see us?" was his overwhelmingly brilliant question.

"No. Not unless you turn on a light. If you turn on a light, she'll go away, won't she."

It wasn't a question. "I don't want to startle her ... embarrass her. Oh God, look at her. Tell me, man. Tell me what's going to happen to her."

"I can't do that, Joe. No, I mean I *really* can't. She has to choose her weapons."

"Choose her weapons? She doesn't even know where the arsenal is."

"But her soul knows, doesn't it? The little dove always knows."

"I want so much to go out to her, but I put us at risk if I do. She's too vulnerable, emotional, and to me–still beautiful. It's harder this time, Alain. I don't know why. I'm in possession of certain gifts and it's harder."

"Because you loved her. Do you still?"

He was too gutless to love her *still*. And he didn't have to answer. Any answer would sound lame, anyway. "Why is history repeating itself, can you tell me that?"

"History has been repeating itself since the hour following the beginning of time. Get her ready, Joe. Time will be up before we know it and she's deteriorating emotionally. I'll take care of Dina for you. And Edmon at his worst."

"Who is Edmon? Isn't it time I knew?"

Alain took a lengthy pause. "His name is an anagram."

Waves of heat rippled up the back of his knees. It was '81 all over again. "You going to make me get out the Scrabble tiles like in *Rosemary's Baby*?"

"Edmon Fendi," Alain said, expressionless. "It means *Demon Fiend*. He was the one playing that little tune in Dina's head last night. But that was just for kicks. I suspect he's after Carol Ann. He wants her for something or he's using her as a lure. I'm not sure for what yet. She heard laughter on the beach ... guess who?"

"And we can't disclose his identity?"

"No. If and when she or the others come upon the realization that Edmon is what he is, then we can confirm their suspicions. Learning how to recognize evil is between them and God. Our job, among other things, is to teach them how to listen. We also teach them awareness. Big load but they're big people. Take another look at Carol Ann out there. Judging from her body language, would you say she's aware?"

He slinked over to the window and inched open the curtain. "Carol Ann lives her life asleep. 'Often it's the artificial light that seems genuine.' Remember? Who has been shining their light on Carol Ann, I wonder?"

Alain considered the question then shifted his thoughts elsewhere.

∞∞∞

"I've taken certain liberties with your coffee, Ms. Carol Ann," Edmon said at 9 a.m.

Carol Ann removed the cash register cover. For a second she wasn't quite sure whether it was all a dream or a nightmare. Was Joe really back in her life? Yes. He was. Sort of. "Smells sweet," she said, staring longingly at the coffee. "Did you spike it?"

"I did."

"Good man. Is our part-timer complaining about the extra hours?"

"She seems to genuinely enjoy the work. I asked her to come in at ten, in case you wanted to help your sister and Ms. Amodeo settle in."

Carol Ann took a generous gulp of the coffee, heavily laced with Bailey's and Grand Marnier. "This is a very special day, Edmon. I've been waiting years for this day. James Dean is alive and well and back in Hollywood."

Edmon seemed bored by the allegory. "I put the promotional material for the book fair down in the storeroom," he said, revealing bottom teeth tinged with yellow. He had a habit of grazing his teeth along his lower lip. "Did some painting down there recently. When Judith gets in I'll take you down and you can show me what else needs doing."

"How 'bout doing me one more of these." She waved the empty mug at him.

Pages was hopping when Judith arrived at ten with Iris right behind her.

"Where can we go to speak privately?" Iris asked.

"Well I do have an apartment upstairs, Iris."

"Are Maggie and Dina out and about already?"

She slammed the cash drawer shut. "Dina checked into the Twin Cedars Lodge last night. She's got the whole top floor. Fancy that. And until she can get herself a cabin around here, Maggie's staying with her."

"I see."

When they got upstairs she was too jittery to sit still. Although the special coffee's helped, she found herself wanting something stronger. She felt like such a fool. What if Joe had seen her this morning, sitting on the beach looking like a pathetic, lost little puppy? A wet puppy. She wanted a lorazepam, but the bottle was in the kitchen and she and Iris were in the kitchen.

"You've been drinking a little," Iris said.

"No," she lied, eyeing the cupboard. "I have this annoying canker and it's tripping my tongue."

"I can smell it, Carol Ann."

"Oops. Alright, so you can smell it. Need new shock absorbers, Iris. Big bumps in the road, you know. Is it true? Are you and Joe only friends?"

"Yes. We're only friends, I swear."

This time the tears were tears of relief. Where did that spunky girl get to, the one that Joe knew at Marianlake? And however did Dina manage? There was enough hell in being just one person.

"I'm a little emotional." *Open the cupboard and pop the damn pill.* "Didn't sleep last night. Did you want to talk to me about anything in particular?"

"I wanted to tell you the meeting's at eight tonight. Alain and Joe have a lot on their plates today. The phone and a couple of other things have held them up. Joe offered to help Maggie find a cabin this afternoon. He thinks he knows of one a few miles outside of town. It'll be perfect for her painting."

"What's she doing for a car, or is Joe helping her with that, too?"

"Carol Ann, don't let bad thoughts control you. Maggie loves you so much. She would never allow herself to think of Joe in that way."

The relief was fleeting "But Joe might want to think of Maggie in that way. She's so beautiful and they've always had this special friendship."

Iris tapped her fingers on the counter. "He has a special bond with Dina, too. Are you going to be jealous of every woman he knows? Every person he knows?"

"Oh probably. In case you don't know this already, Joe says he loves me, but he obviously loves me like a sister. Because he doesn't want me. He told me I don't really love him. Can you believe that? So since he doesn't want me, it's likely he'll replace me. He attracts women like crumbs attract ants. But they have to get by me first. I'll get him back. I'll make him love me again."

"Carol Ann, you can't make someone love you. I know. Besides, Joe already loves you *unlike* a sister. Can't you wait? Can't you give this time?"

"Time! Tell me you're kidding. I would never, and I repeat, never interfere with Joe's work. I know how important it is to him. I have to prove to him that he can have us both. We don't have to wait another five years. I could lose him in five years."

She knew how Iris loathed hearing people say they'd 'never' do something. That word always made the devil dance. It was no use pursuing this conversation because she couldn't listen to Iris now anyway. Unless Iris was in secret-spilling mode.

"You're not going to lose him. Remember, eight tonight at the beach house. Eat something and try to take a nap this afternoon."

"Joe might drop by."

"He told me to tell you he'd see you tonight."

"Great. He can find time in his busy schedule to see my sister today, though."

"Stop with the negative thoughts already. You need yourself to show up at the meeting tonight in a better frame of mind. Sleep will help. So will you try to do that?"

"I still don't understand why you neglected to tell me you know Joe. Gawd, he was right there in front of me in that wheelchair and you didn't say a thing."

"I couldn't, Carol Ann. I'm so sorry. I had confidences—"

"Yeah yeah, I know. Confidences you couldn't break."

"Forgive me?"

Trying to play the hard-hearted woman, she stiffened against the counter. "Lucky for you I like mysteries."

Iris chuckled. "Well good, because there's more on the way."

"Please don't tell Joe what I said. Don't tell him the way I am this morning."

∞∞∞

Maggie loved the cabin. It reminded her of Joe's cabin up at Marianlake, only smaller. Nothing wrong with smaller. What mattered was solitude, which she had to have. Always. Hidden by evergreens at the southern tip of Angelfish Cove, the cabin had a private dock and was only four miles from the main drag. And the '89 Ford station wagon she bought from John Corey's friend was perfect for her needs. For the first time she felt peaceful inside, peaceful and undisturbed by thoughts of the red door or the dull, nagging headaches.

Remembering Dina's headaches, then Carol Ann's, she smiled. Her turn now. Did best friends share or what? But she couldn't share this, not if it meant drawing attention to herself or worrying them with what-ifs. Best to keep the headaches in dry dock and not mention them at all.

"I love it, Joe," she said again, playfully visualizing masterworks. "Thank-you."

"You're welcome." Joe laughed at Dina who was on her knees checking for phone jacks.

"Told ya, Maggie," she boasted. "No phone jack. You gotta do the phone thing right away. Don't you dare consider not putting a phone in here."

"I would never consider not doing that," Maggie said.

"You're right," Joe told Dina. "Better get that taken care of. Call them now and order one, Dina."

When Dina made moves to locate the nonexistent phone, they burst into laughter. Maggie's peace was somehow contagious. As though it was the most natural thing, they drifted into silence and went about their business. Maggie walked around with a notepad, looking in cupboards and making a list. Joe grabbed his trusty red toolbox, checked the fuses and hooked up the cable on the TV. And Dina did nothing except sip Coke and rock on the old porch swing overlooking the Cove. When she began singing the slow, haunting lyrics to *In The Air Tonight*, Joe and Maggie stopped what they were doing and listened ...

It was a day for Joe and his toolbox. At a quarter of eight he finished the wire connections from one phone to a triple-speaker setup on the dining room table. Alain added two leaves to the table and foraged for extra chairs. Dina, first to arrive, immediately regarded the speakers and her knowledge of them intensified her cat-like curiosity.

"Sorry," Alain said to her, "Gotta wait for the others. Has your mystery voice returned for a visit?"

Dina pulled her extra-large sweatshirt down over her hips and pushed up her sleeves. It was so matter-of-fact with them. So easy to talk about, like being overdrawn at the bank or bouncing back from an argument with a promoter. So she had a couple extra personalities kicking around in her head. No big deal.

"No," she said, temple-tapping again. "The Rockstar's in here takin' care of business and I'm out here with you. The mystery me is still in hiding, though. I wonder if I'm always going to be this way. Or if I'm gonna get worse. I get so angry sometimes, Alain. I fill up with this rage and then I forget where I am and who I am. I don't remember belting that guy in the b ...

For some reason, she couldn't say *balls* in Alain's presence. She didn't know why. He was grinning at her and she blushed. "Anyway, I let him have it and I don't remember doing it. Could I kill somebody? Maybe next time I will. Funny you know, when I got this gift, I also got this curse."

"That's usually the way it goes," Alain said. "A cross with a gift. And a gift with a cross."

"I don't get it."

"Could be the gift's the Cross, and the Cross is the gift."

Dina scrunched up her face. "Both sound the same to me."

Carol Ann arrived last, twenty minutes late. Joe tapped his watch and wished he hadn't once he saw that wounded look. Her eyes were swollen, either from sleep or tears and she appeared sedated, not quite with them in the present moment. This was one night she needed her cookies together. Joe took her off to the side.

"I need you focused," he said, clasping his hands on her forearms. "Remember that Carol Ann Page who loved being on the force?"

She answered yes and smiled dreamily at his hair. "Well, the *inspector* would be in her glory tonight, because tonight her questions are getting answered. Think of all those questions hanging around collecting dust for ten years, Carol Ann. Stay with me here."

"There's nothing in the world I want more."

He resisted the urge to groan theatrically. There had to be some way to get through to her. "I'm not going away. I am not going to disappear on you again. What's in store for us we can't know right now, but trust that whatever happens in the future, you will be happy. I promise you that, Carol Ann. Work with Alain and I on the bigger picture and I promise you will be happy. Work with us starting tonight. All you have to do is listen."

"Can't I ask questions?"

Now that was more like her and not the lovesick schoolgirl he saw on the beach this morning. He'd refrain from mentioning that. She'd been doing a good enough job humiliating herself these days. "Of course you can. Come on, let's get stahted."

He cleared his throat and motioned them to sit at the table. "We better get rolling here. Dina's jumping out of her skin."

"That better not be a play on words," Dina said, giggling.

He rubbed his palms together. "Let me begin by informing you that we are a group of ten. Four cannot be with us tonight, but they will be joining us on the speakerphone set-up you see in front of you. Three of the four you know—Fathers' Andre and Richard. And Sister Elizabeth. Shortly after we left you at Marianlake, Alain, Sister Elizabeth and I went to Rome, and that's where we met Father Vittorio Gianni. He was my spiritual instructor and friend during the five years I spent studying at the Vatican. He was at Page's opening, by the way, Carol Ann. You must've seen him, the giant?"

"Oh yes," she said, "I spoke briefly with him. I remember how charismatic he was."

"Father Gianni bears the same marks as the rest of us, with the exception of yourself and Dina. Eventually both of you will receive them as well, when it's your time. Maggie's time came the other morning. But I'll get back to these marks later. Right now it's my time to tell all of you why we're back in each other's lives after ten years. Truth is, we've never really been out of each other's lives, have we?

"I know that at certain points you've sensed me nearby, physically or in your thoughts. Same here. We established a connection at Marianlake. I don't think any of you will give me an argument there. But what if I were to tell you that we made the connection before Marianlake? What if I told you we connected right here in Angelfish Cove many years ago?

He took a second to search their faces. Was he going too fast? He'd find out soon enough. "You've all heard bits and pieces, bits you've collected and other cryptic pieces from me. These marks—" He held up his wrists, "Dina first saw them on me years ago in New York. My little foliage messages, the latest of which was the auricula sent to Carol Ann." Carol Ann narrowed her eyes. "Auricula means *painting* in flower speak, as you've discovered.

"Without going into too many details now, we knew that Maggie completed a painting with an angel reading a book, its title beginning with the letter O. The language in Maggie's paintings has been our map and compass for years. There you have Maggie's link to us, her painting, inspired by light and dark forces. Remember the positive and negative logo in her first painting back in Brooklyn?"

Alain came over and whispered in his ear, "*Begin with Walter.*"

"This is all very complicated," he said. "Let me get us back on track. In the late 1950s, a man by the name of Walter Bayard resided right here in Angelfish Cove. Originally from Boston and coming from old money, he relocated here with his wife in '58 when he was thirty, stayed twenty years then returned to Boston for personal reasons. He was an architect by trade but had an aptitude for electronics, loved to tinker with sound. Light and time travel fascinated him. The little radio station in town was one of Walter's favorite toys. His grandson runs it from Cambridge now and sticks with the oldies, per Walter's instruction. He wanted to keep the timelessness in Angelfish Cove. And he has."

He flipped open one of the file folders in front of him and passed copies of Walter Bayard's story to the girls. "I know you've all heard this story from Carol Ann, via John Corey. Please take a few moments to read it over to yourselves now. Take more than a few moments and read it twice. It's the reason we're all here."

As they read, he took the DEET from his jeans and sprayed a liberal amount into his palms. Blood-sucking mosquitoes. His mother was distracted to her death by these vampires. Rubbing the spray on his neck and arms he wandered out to the deck and watched the moon hovering over the ocean. A honking flock of geese glided toward the Cove. The peace he'd known these last few years was no doubt about to end, his training about to be tested.

For many years he'd assumed Alain was the *child* he had to keep safe, but there was always something in Father Andre's dream story that didn't ring true. Then there was the vision of Alain on this very beach that night with Willie. If it was Alain. Realistically it could've been any boy that age with Alain's coloring.

But Alain was a man now who most certainly did not require his protection. So who out there did? He was driving himself nuts again. Mulling over Alain's birth announcement in the 'dream team's dream' always made him crazy. The heck with it. This was not the time to get distracted with more questions. This was a time for soothing and answers. *Lord, I have five years to prepare them. Is it long enough? Am I equal to the task?* Alain had been standing silently beside him. As usual he always seemed to appear during his worst moments of self-doubt.

"I couldn't help overhear your promise of happiness to Carol Ann," he said, steepling his fingertips below his chin. "You sure about that?"

"Of course I'm sure. How can you ask me that? If she works with us, she'll be happy. But she has to work with us. I think I drove that point home."

"True. You did. But I notice that Carol Ann has selective hearing. When she equates the word happiness with you, her mind is conjuring a whole different scenario, and that scenario revolves around a box spring and mattress. I don't know. Maybe it was wrong of me to suggest you take care of her and I take care of Dina. We could swap. What do you think?"

"Not gonna happen, bud. She'll think I deserted her all over again. And I just finished telling her I wouldn't go away. Can you tell me the same thing?"

"You know I can't. What else is bothering you besides Carol Ann?"

He took a slight step back and pulled at the rail. "We're both older than our years. We've had to be. But you ... you're seventy in a twenty-year-old body. I've always respected your privacy, Alain, and the night I received these marks I was told you had your own directive. But Dina told me something today that won't go away."

"What was that?"

"She told me your family disappeared from Trois-Rivierés shortly after we did. She also said that Father Richard led her to believe that Claude was still there taking care of the horses. Every time I ask about them, either you or Father Richard has some handy answer about their working for us on this project up at Marianlake and that's all I can fish out of both of you. I remember you telling me their involvement was top secret, so I respected that, too. But now Dina tells me they're not in their house and haven't been since we left. So where are they? Can you tell me that much?"

"Yes," Alain said, unruffled as always. "They're living in your old cabin. Claude has a gambling problem, or had, so he sold the house years ago. And since they are deeply involved in this project, Father Richard suggested they live at Marianlake. Walter's in the cabin next door with Ronny Fergel. Remember Ronny? Elizabeth's son?"

He always thought it odd that Alain referred to his parents by their first names now. He never did growing up. Alain rarely spoke of his family at all. "Sure I remember Ronny, although at the time I thought he was Elizabeth's nephew. I heard he was working with Walter but I don't know in what capacity."

Alain smiled knowingly. "He's Walter's assistant, his right arm. He's also taught Walter to speak fluent Aramaic. Ronny was always a whiz with languages, remember? Even my brother, Simon, has picked up a little." Alain laughed when his jaw dropped.

"Wait a minute. Let's rewind the cassette here. *Fluent* Aramaic? Have Walter and Ronny been back?"

"Let's say the fluent part slipped out. And let's add that more can slip out when we're done here tonight."

"My God." It struck him that this miracle was actually going to happen. "They've actually been back! Oh man, I have to talk to them, see them."

"You're about to get your wish. Elizabeth has decided to visit the girls and Ronny's decided to join his mother. Then Walter, who's decided he needs to see Angelfish Cove again, is accompanying Ronny and Elizabeth. But I suspect he's coming mostly to talk to you."

Carol Ann walked onto the deck looking like she had the words *still waiting* tattooed on her forehead. "We're ready, Joe. Um, anytime soon?"

"Pitter patter," he said.

Pulse racing and mind reeling, he returned to the table and stood before the group.

14. Burnt Offerings & Auld Lang Syne

After what Alain just told him, handicapping a Thoroughbred would be easier than delivering the mission speech right now. Carol Ann already thought they were all nuts. *Walter and Ronny have been back! Focus, Joe. Jump in, boy.*

"You'll be interested to know that Walter Bayard is temporarily residing at Marianlake. He is overseeing experiments of a time machine he's created. That's right. H.G. Wells stuff. And this time machine has room for ten. Five years from now, it will transport 3,640 people back in groups of ten to the years 5 and 6 for twenty-four hours. The time machine will be operational for one year—from December of 1996 to December of 1997. Is everybody with me so far?"

The women barely moved and he continued.

"Beginning December thirtieth of '96, the first group will get into this time machine and spend twenty-four hours with the Holy Family. To worship. *Not* to change. It's Walter Bayard's dream to bring hope and love to the world by restoring and rejuvenating belief in God."

"Will it just be Christians going back?" Maggie asked.

"No, Maggie."

"Isn't this an ecumenical stew you're all brewing? You're going to have a lot of cooks in the kitchen here. So many denominations separated by doctrine."

"Many cultures walk in God's light. This goes beyond our understanding."

"But what about the Vatican?" Carol Ann cut in. "They're actually sanctioning a trip back to visit the Son of God with many people who don't even acknowledge Him as the Son of God?"

"All three thousand plus people going on this trip have been chosen," he said, trying his best to stay clear of denominational politics. "So it follows that they belong in God's tapestry."

"It's really what it's all about, isn't it?" Alain said, folding his arms on the table. "Understanding. When we fear our demons, we're empowering them. We have to understand each other, through awareness and love. And Joe and I have five years to teach you that. There are three hundred and sixty-four other group leaders going through the same thing. Joe is your group leader as I'm certain you've guessed and I'm his second-in-command. As opposing forces surround us, massing and arming, it's our job to bring you into the light—to enlighten you. You must learn how to fight them without fearing them."

"Are we going to be controlled in any way?" Dina asked in a childlike fashion that tugged at his heart.

"No," he answered. This was not happening the way he'd intended. Something was draining their energy, making the enormity of this mission sound more like mission impossible. For the first time it sounded implausible, even to him. For the first time it seemed too fantastic. Why were they not processing this gift, this wonder? Had evil forces crashed the party?

∞∞∞

"Maybe we should empower ourselves with an opening prayer," Iris said.

It was not really her place to suggest but Joe needed her. After all, he was the reason she was here. She really wasn't supposed to see Joe again until 1996, but obviously there were shifts in the plan when they called her to sub for Father Crouse. He was now going with another group, which worked out best for Sister Elizabeth. Life was always changing and flowing. Flowing and changing. A lesson she had learned too late.

"Since everyone's standing by at Marianlake, Joe, and the speakers are set, let's get the group on the phone. Let's have a party. A few people still haven't met and Elizabeth is excited about talking to her students again. What do you think?" She felt Carol Ann's covetous glare.

∞∞∞

"Why not," Joe said. At times there was a familiarity about Iris, but he could never keep that thought in his head long enough to investigate. Something always drove it out. "The only one in our group you haven't met is Father Vittorio Gianni. The Giant. As I said, he was at Carol Ann's opening. So there's the six of us, Fathers' Vittorio, Richard and Andre. And Sister Elizabeth Patrick Whyte."

"And Walter Bayard?" Carol Ann asked.

"He's going in the first group, but you'll be meeting him. You're all going to find out soon enough, that his assistant, Ronny Fergel, is a huge part of this. Ronny is Elizabeth Whyte's son."

A moment of awkward silence followed.

"Did he come before or after final vows?" Carol Ann asked.

"Those are private details better left for Elizabeth to share with you."

"Who's this Rafe I keep hearing whispers about?" Dina asked.

Brief silence again.

"He's whom we call Triple C," Alain said. "Chief Celestial Coordinator."

Before anyone could comment on Rafe, a familiar feminine voice from one of the speakerphones distracted them. "Hello, my ladies."

Dina's face beamed. "Sister Elizabeth? Is that you? I know that's you."

"Dina? My famous songbird. I know your voice, too. Anywhere. Carol Ann? You there?"

"I'm here Sister. It's been many Halloweens. How are you?"

There was a brief pause as they all stared at the speaker.

"I'm good, Carol Ann," Sister Elizabeth said. "Maggie Page, are you there?"

Enthusiasm was all over Maggie like a child approaching a playground. "When can I paint your face? I've missed it. When can I *see* your face?"

"Very soon, Maggie. I was so happy to hear that you're out and away, that you've received the stamp of this mission. And Dina ... I hurt for your hurt. I'm so sorry."

Dina's eyes watered. "I've known that for years, Sister. Thank-you."

"Thanks for the puppy, Dina." It was Father Richard Vaux. "I've called him *Pancake*. Warmest hello's everyone."

Everyone said a 'Hi, Father' in unison.

Next out of the speakers came a piercing, stabbing voice. The room temperature plummeted.

"How are Robin and his merry little band?" it asked, sounding amused.

"Who is this?" Joe asked. "Father Richard? Where's that voice coming from?"

"Seems to be emanating from your end, Joe. There's a familiar odor here ... but I can't source ... could be close to someone in your group."

Father Andre cut in fast. "Everyone, try not to be afraid. Courage, Dina. We're with you."

"That awful odor," Dina said, palms perspiring and a nerve rash fast developing on her cheek.

"Oh, I'm offended," it said, *"but on my budget, a pot pourri of menthol and lemons is the best I can manage. Dina always appreciated it, didn't you, Chubby Buns?"*

Nostrils flared, Dina sneered into the empty space in front of her.

"Aw, I can see you're upset. Please accept my humble offering."

After saturating the room with the scent of menthol and lemon, the demon groaned with pleasure when Dina leaned forward and retched in her sweatshirt. It was all happening again––the vibration of Misty's stomping hooves and the searing pain of the rape. Alain held her down while she shouted obscenities at her invisible rapist, flailing her arms and kicking, cutting her finger on the broken glass she had knocked over.

Sister Elizabeth called out to her in an attempt to pacify but Dina remained deafened to all voices but one. The harder Dina kicked and cursed, the more Elizabeth sobbed. And *the thing*, whatever it was, started whistling *Auld Lang Syne* over a staticky background. Carol Ann's body went rigid and her eyes bulged. Maggie closed her eyes and prayed. Joe phoned Marianlake and spoke one on one with Father Andre without averting his eyes from Dina. He assumed *the thing* was still listening in at this point because of the lingering odor.

Alain calmed her some, though that last outburst caused her to claw her quarter inch nails into his chest, creating four deep, open gashes. Nothing came out. There was no blood, except the blood on Dina's hand. Everyone waited—for one of the Marianlake voices on the phone, for *that thing*, for Joe's counsel, for the blood to come out of Alain's chest. They all watched in wonder. In seconds, the gashes disappeared before the blood dried on Dina's hand.

Giving them a reassuring look, Alain asked the entity, "I assumed no dark angels would be permitted on the premises tonight. Obviously I was wrong. How did you get in here?"

"Hitched a ride on the rockstar," it said. *"I've been her escort for days. And the days have been rich with all kinds of informative goodies. But that's unimportant. You can have your little songbird. I'm through with her for now, and in case you're wondering, Remiel, my disciples are not intimidated by you. Now let me speak to Iris and then I'm out of here."*

Alain spoke with authority, "You're not getting anywhere near Iris."

"Let me speak to Iris!" the thing barked. *"Let me speak to Iris or Dina's head winds up in a permanent cast."*

"It's okay, Alain." Iris said. Its voice seemed to be coming from everywhere. "What do you want from me?"

It spoke softer now. *"I want you bounced from this game. You're a wild card. Somebody's not playing fair, for heaven's sake. You tell your associate, Rafe, either he removes you from Ross's group or I will be forced to do a whole lot more than prepare tests for the enlightened. Somebody important is going to walk out of that Red Door with a mind so damaged that Walter Bayard will wish he'd said that prayer to MY superior. Are we clear on this?"*

"We're clear," Iris said. "Leave Dina alone and go."

"Don't worry, Iris. I won't give away all your little secrets. You have one week to square it with high command. I'm gone."

"Joe. Everyone. It's Father Andre. Everything is all right now. It's gone, I promise you. Alain, how's Dina?"

"She's drained, Father, but fine otherwise." Alain noticed they were all gaping at him and Iris. Joe, too. There was not a scratch to show that Dina's fingernails had been anywhere near his chest.

Elizabeth's voice cracked through the speaker, "Alain, why did it call you *Remiel*?"

"It's another of my given names," he answered. "I guess it prefers to call me that."

Joe considered the possibility that 'Remiel' was the *first* given.

"Why does it want you out of the group, Iris?" Carol Ann's brandy snifter trembled in her hand.

"I don't know," Iris said. "That's the truth. Maybe Rafe can tell me."

Joe smiled at her. Again the familiarity was warming, but as far away as a dead man's memories. Why did that *thing* want her out of the picture? Odd. He recalled his first day in Medford when Willie took him up to his attic room. Willie hoped he liked the Star Trek bedspread because she had picked it out for him. Weird time to remember that.

"How soon can you get a hold of Rafe?" he asked her, still trying to shake off the bedspread memory.

"Probably within the next couple of days."

"Iris," Father Andre said in a commanding voice. "Don't you be intimidated now. Rafe was the one who placed you in this group. He must have had his reasons."

"Thank-you, Father, but we have Dina to think about. That thing has been harassing and threatening her. And I'm not much help here. Should I head back to Marianlake and work with Walter and Ronny?"

Carol Ann's eyes brightened.

"No," Father Andre said. "Stay put. Wait and talk to Rafe. He'll ease your mind."

"Hey guys," Dina said. "I've been through hell for years. I'm practically used to it and besides, with all of you around me, I'm really not that scared anymore. So don't worry about me. We're a team now, really a team. And that thing's creepy voice is out of my head now, too. Oh man, it's like having a slice of the peace Maggie was talking about. Sister Elizabeth, are you still there?"

"Right here, dear, like I'm in the room with you. And I am in more ways than I can explain."

"I'm sorry about my cursing fit earlier. Will 'going back' fix the anger part of me, do you think?"

"Yes," Alain told her, admiring the beginnings of love on her large wrists. Only he could see them.

"Joe, tell us about the Red Door," Maggie asked. "I've been painting it for years. And it's terrified me for years. What is it?"

Joe took the moment to have a chuckle. Of course there was no order. Naturally there was no control. He learned how to surrender control in Rome. When this was all over he'd show Rome to Carol Ann—if they were meant to be.

"There is an old Tibetan ceremony for students of the Dalai Lama. The name of the ceremony is *The Room of a Thousand Demons*. Before the ceremony begins, the Dalai Lama tells them what they can expect, what this ritual entails. One at a time they enter a small room with the door shut. There is an exit at the opposite end of the room. Although the distance between both doors is insignificant, few make it out. And those that do, make it out enlightened.

"The room is filled with a thousand demons, all with the power to throw your worst fears at you. If you've got a hate-on for snakes, guess what you'll see. If it's heights, insects, or the devil himself, it goes down. If you have a fear of drowning, you could find yourself alone in polar waters, gasping for air. Get the idea?

"What the students are taught prior to entry is that these frightening images are not real, though they feel real with overwhelming clarity. And the fear paralyzes most. Too, the knowledge that the demon's images are false does not always successfully temper their fear, so the Dalai Lama urges them to keep their feet moving. If they keep their feet moving they will make it to the other side.

"So, the *Red Door* is our version of Tibet's *Room of a Thousand Demons*. There are 365 Red Doors at various locations around the world. One for each group. All of them ready last week. And *everybody* going back goes through that Red Door. I guess you can call it a kind of purification chamber. God will not allow any negatively impaired minds to return to the years 5 and 6. He wants us all to receive the Child's Light and in order to properly receive, we must have our reason since it's in our consciences and reasoning minds that God lives and communicates to us.

"Now comes the scary part. I said the Red Door is our *version* of 'The Room of a Thousand Demons.' In our case, the demons we encounter will definitely not be of the mind. You probably gathered as much from our little broadcast, earlier. But some of you have already seen them, haven't you? Some of you have certainly heard them before this evening. So trust that no one in *this* room will walk into *that* room unprepared. Though we will certainly cover this in depth later, there are those who insist our Red Door rooms are no different from the Tibetan room. Pray we can persuade them otherwise.

"Now ... it will take a year for everybody to return in groups of ten. But we have these wrist impressions, and having these will enhance your study and concentration.

Some of you will receive them late and have much catching up to do. Why that is I don't know. Perhaps those who receive the marks late have bigger lessons to learn and require less time to study, who knows. The bottom line is we will all be ready in '96.

"Over the next five years you will have your worldly affairs to manage of course. Life will go on. It might be toughest on Dina who has an upcoming tour and is a national celebrity with many obligations. If necessary one of us will accompany you, Dina. But we'll X that square when we come to it.

"So—the outside world. There are so many of us and our wrists have not escaped attention. There are people trying to emulate us. One young man nearly died trying. God's grace was with him. He wanted to be a copycat, not a suicide victim. These impressions come up above a main artery and that's what will intrigue the press the most. As you know, the *SC*, which is separated by a cross, stands for Second Christmas. For years I thought the cross was a small letter *t*, making it look like StC, until the small t evolved.

"Naturally you're not to discuss its meaning with outsiders. When you come across another of us, and some of you will, there's only one way you'll know they're genuine. Try to touch their wrist during a handshake. There will be heat and no doubt in your mind they are one of us. I suspect we have these marks in order to recognize each other. They must not make us prideful.

"As for the impersonators, there are a lot of makeup artists out there. You might see some on tabloid shows insisting SC stands for vile things like–Sadistic criminals. Satan's church. Satan's children. But the most popular will undoubtedly be Second Coming. Oh the irony of it all.

"Okay, here's the question. How do we explain it? What do we tell people? One of our very own is famous, unable to hide the marks indefinitely. It's a given that less is more, so we tell the world we fell asleep with a fever one night and woke up the next morning with the marks. We don't remember anything. We were asleep at the time. The truth, right?

"To keep them off our backs, some of us have agreed to be tested and probed by the medical profession. I can't wait to see what they come up with. And unfortunately there may be some of our own who fail their tests for whatever reason and end up saying the wrong things to the wrong people. Stay close to us, study with us, and let us teach you. This has nothing to do with control or manipulation. This is not a giant hoax or cult. One of the things we're attempting is to return your freedom, not take it from you. Stay close to God and you will know in the deepest part of you that this is genuine.

"As this gets big and it will, people will follow you. They'll want to touch you, tell you their problems. One of us in Germany suggested using makeup art to cover the marks but he was told that it wouldn't work and was asked not to do it. He went ahead and did it anyway and the cross burned through the makeup molding in ten minutes. But feel free to wear anything removable. Wristbands or whatever. I assume the molding denied their existence too much and that's why it didn't work. Again though, impostors always find a way to convince somebody, don't they?" He watched Carol Ann refill the brandy snifter. He figured he lost her somewhere around the end of the Red Door and the start of the outside world. Of course that little radio show starring The Dark Angel of Marianlake hadn't helped her nerves.

Swirling brandy in the snifter, Carol Ann asked him, "You said it'd take a year for all these groups to go back?"

"Correct." Maybe he was wrong and she was gaining tolerance for the stuff.

"Yeah well, the Christ Child wasn't in Bethlehem for a year after His birth. They had to make tracks outta there because of Herod, remember?"

Joe sighed. "Yes, that's true. An Angel appeared to Joseph in a dream and told him they had to escape to Egypt. And that's where they stayed until Herod died. So the chronology team working with Walter has determined that they remained in Egypt for at least two years."

"Don't tell me you're going to have thousands of us wandering all over Egypt?"

"No, Carol Ann," Elizabeth joined in from the speaker. "We'll all remain within a five-mile radius of the birth cave."

"I don't understand," Maggie said. "Will everyone be seeing Jesus in the same time, at the *same* moment—over twelve months?"

Joe knew the question would get asked and Maggie had asked it—the question he was not looking forward to answering. "The machine's chronology apparatus does not toggle back and forth. Once a date is set, time can only move forward. However, it can transmigrate through geographical locations as well as time, this way we don't leave Marianlake and end up back in Marianlake, Year 6. So the team can control the place, location, and forward time. They just haven't built in time reversal. If somebody got in there tonight and set the thing for yesterday's date, Walter's dream is over. It's not for me to question why he built it the way he did. I'm sure he had his reasons."

"You sure all the kinks are worked outta that thing?" Carol Ann asked.

"No problem," he said, hoping she'd pack in the brandy for the night. "There was no need to go backward in time when all Walter had to do is set the machine one or two minutes ahead for each group. There are one thousand, four hundred and forty minutes in a day. Ten thousand and eighty minutes in a week. Walter could set the gauge in half-minute increments if he wanted but there's no need." Dina and Carol Ann looked doubtful so he shot Alain a help-me look.

Alain stood and held out his arms as if to embrace them and Maggie and Dina smiled. Carol Ann poked her tongue in her cheek. "Joe's seen the machine. I've seen it. And it's been repeatedly tested. That said, Walter and Ronny have already been back and forth with their crew during the course of their experiments. However, as Joe told you, the time gauge can only go forward. So they've set the date *way back*, beginning with the Year 1 and have been moving continuously forward in time.

"History has conflicting reports as to the year of Christ's birth. Years 1, 3, or 6. We've confirmed Him in 6. Ronny, as some of you may know, is multi-lingual. He's taught Walter fluent Aramaic and you will learn the basics, at least enough to get you through twenty-four hours. One or two people might have to learn more. We'll see."

∞∞∞

Alain glanced at Maggie. She too would need a fluent handle on the language—she'd be staying a while. At least he could inform Joe of that soon, though he had to leave out the ending. Joe had to wait until after 1996 for that part. And there were many parts.

∞∞∞

"I don't know." Carol Ann was not about to apologize for having reasonable doubt. "There could be a screw-up. Some reason some*one* has to go back. And they won't be able to. Supposing somebody gets left behind? How can you go back and get 'em if you can't go back and get 'em? Nothing is fool-proof."

Part of Joe agreed with her. "Even if the last passenger was somehow left behind, all he would have to do is wait one minute into the future. And that's where the machine would return to pick him up. The machine will still have moved forward in time from its last point of entry. Don't worry, nothing will go wrong. Right, Alain?"

"The risks are minute," Alain answered with confidence. "Always remember who's at the helm here. Then you won't be afraid. God is actually allowing us to go back and visit His Son. That's a gift. I don't think He's going to ask you to give it back."

Carol Ann wouldn't let it go. "Yes but you said the risks are *minute*. And Joe said *nothing* will go wrong. Isn't there a slight discrepancy in these two statements?"

Somebody's throat cleared from one of the speakers.

"Okay," he said, trying to remain patient with her. "Alain and I are both optimistic people, but we're optimistic in different ways. We each believe the outcome is going to be just splendid. However, opinions differ on the 'getting to the outcome' part. There are never any guarantees, Carol Ann. That's true. But God is the exception. With God there are always guarantees."

For a few seconds everyone got lost in their thoughts.

"Joe," Maggie said, "we understood that this project is being explained up at Marianlake as construction for a sports centre."

"Right," Father Richard hollered through the speaker and they all grinned. "Father Gianni's on the site with Walter as we speak. He said he's sorry he can't be here for our lovely multi-directional conversation but he's showing the Centre to the town mayoral board. Can you all hear me all right?"

"Loud and clear, Father," he chuckled. "Better adjust the hearing aid."

"To answer your question, Maggie, and for the rest of you, it's being explained as a hockey rink. Later there'll be additions, probably a pool. But our concern is with the rink. Lots of big fans here, you know."

Carol Ann gave her head a shake and Maggie raised her brows.

"A hockey rink?" Dina bunched up her face. "And there's people in there now? What if they find the machine once they're in there? Some people have an eye for things that are different. What if they see something they're not supposed to?"

Carol Ann nodded enthusiastically.

"Everybody," Father Andre said, "a section of the hockey rink *is* the machine."

"And at the end of '97," Joe said, twisting the cap off an *Evian* water, "its sole function will be a hockey rink. At the end of our mission, when the last person returns, Walter's time machine will be permanently shut down. We get it at the end of '96. The townspeople get it at the end of '97. As a hockey rink. In the meantime, when outsiders come to look at the *rink,* that's all they'll see.

"The disk-like section that is the actual machine is barely visible since its components are attached beneath it. And there's so much construction happening, no one's going to ask. The control panel is hidden below the rink floor and inaccessible without a key. Before the rink opens to the public, the panel will be destroyed. Then of course the ice goes on top, the race is over, we're grazin' in the paddock."

"Kind of sad that it'll never be used again," Maggie said.

Nobody said anything.

"Isn't this disk-like machine with ten people sitting on it, appearing out of thin air, maybe going to attract a little attention in ancient Judea?" Carol Ann asked, her sarcasm getting on the nerves of some. "Or do you have a cloaking device like in *Star Trek*?"

"It will land in isolated areas previously selected," Alain said. "Meanwhile, back here, the exterior wall of the rink, along with the major portion of the rink's flooring will remain intact during our comings and goings. Any officials on tour, prior to the opening, will notice nothing missing.

"Now picture a circle within a circle. It's the inner circle and people on it that slowly constrict, fade, and de-materialize. Scouts go ahead and seek out isolated terrain, suitable for landing. These scouts are archaeological experts, by the way. They've acquired knowledge of ancient Palestine, Judean maps, artifacts, etc. They know enough not to land in a market place, let's put it that way. Then they have to locate the Family once they get there. And that could take time."

"I still have my concerns," Carol Ann said, widening her eyes, a facial habit she had recently acquired. "I'm sorry but this is really all too incredible to swallow. It's hard for me to fathom."

"I would love to hear about their excursions back," Maggie said. "You must know something, Alain."

"Sorry. Confidential."

"Is it ever," Elizabeth said. "My own son is involved and I can't pry a word out of him. I guess you all know of my son by now. Anyway, Ronny's not talking, which is unusual for Ronny."

Maggie had been staring curiously at Alain. "You seem to be more in touch with the brass somehow. Am I imagining things? That was a powerful demonstration of self-healing after Dina dug her nails into you. That I did not imagine. Neither did the rest of us."

Alain cranked the kinks out of his shoulders. "My being the coffee and donut man gives Joe more time to concentrate on you. I do the legwork and update him. So you could say that yes, I do spend more time with the brass. As for the self-healing ... that's probably better left for another day. Joe and I learned some amazing things in Rome."

"I think you're leaving the raisins out of the pudding," Carol Ann said. "Why did that *thing* single out you and Iris? I remember it said you didn't intimidate its disciples. Why would it say that?"

"I had certain spiritual gifts when I was a child and connected with Joe. He had gifts, too. Remember? I didn't intimidate that demon because I was first introduced to them in my childhood, growing up practically on Marianlake, practically raised by priests. I learned how to fight them, and how *not* to fear them as I said. Remember, you empower the demons you fear. I have no fear of them and they sense that. And fear is what they thrive on. Joe and I will knock that fear out of you. Naturally they want to sabotage this mission. Evil passionately desires hatred and chaos in the world, not love. Each of us in our own way will spread that Love around all over again after our return."

"So many people will think we're totally *pazzo*," Dina said. "Which I'm used to."

"History repeating itself," Joe said thoughtfully. "Concentrate on the positive things that will happen in the new millennium. We can help take some of the evil away."

"Are we talking about saving souls here?" Carol Ann asked.

"We're talking about the elevation of souls," Father Richard clarified, still shouting. "We're talking about love and the gift of faith."

Maggie had stretched out on the couch at this point. "Joe, where's *our* Red Door?"

Uh-oh. He looked to Alain to field this one.

"Finding the door was my job," Alain said, "and I have asked for extra protection for Carol Ann, since she lives closest to it. Take a deep breath, Carol Ann. It's in your basement. Believe me when I tell you, you had no worries about accidentally entering the room. Haven't you noticed that every time you went to go down the basement, something distracted you?"

Eyes round as stove burners, Carol Ann nodded.

"It's exactly what you imagine it to be," Alain continued, "a big red door. Stay away from it. All of you. Nothing to fear, Carol Ann. Just don't go down there. Don't discuss it with outsiders, who, by the way could wind up behind it for whatever reason. Delivery people. Who knows. It is a storage room after all. Not to worry. The room only affects those involved in this mission. Anyone else who inadvertently enters will be safe. They may have a bout with the blues for a day or two but other than that, they'll be fine. Besides, the door's not a priority since none of you will be in that room for a while."

He lifted his brows at Alain, who suggested they call it a night. Everyone was getting heavy-headed, so the group said their goodnights, which took another forty-five minutes. There were more questions that could not wait. More doubts to express. The evil parts were easy to believe, but as always the glorious parts were easily unbelievable.

He told the girls all their questions would get answered one on one throughout the week. Also, things sounded like they were getting busy at the Marianlake end. Father

Gianni had returned with several unidentified voices accompanying him. Oh to be at Marianlake now, knockin back Buds at Patsy's with Dart In The Heart and the rest of the boys. He was glad Patsy's Bar was still going strong. Father Richard admitted dropping by once or twice a month for darts and a kibitz with Patsy. He didn't understand this nostalgia. That *thing* had obviously left its mark.

∞∞∞

Wanting another turn with him alone because she felt gutsy, Carol Ann waited until everyone left. Brandy did well for gutsy, especially after hearing their spiel about that red door. In HER basement. What the hell, the room was all a mind thing, anyway. She had the Dalai Lama's word on it. Joe even said that some didn't believe the demons were real. She wouldn't tell him she agreed. Of the *mind,* folks—not real. Got that? Besides, Edmon did all the storeroom stuff, so she had no reason to go down there.

"Night," she waved to Dina, the last to leave and drifting so happily in her little Judean world in spite of that grisly *temporal lobe* episode earlier.

She wished she could buy it all. But it was still five years away. Joe, Alain and Iris were so big on living in present moments. Ironic. Well, here was a present moment coming up, which was not going to be a repeat of this morning's psychotic error in judgment. She found him in the kitchen, loading the dishwasher.

"It's been quite an evening," she said, passing him a sandwich tray.

"Yes," he said, head practically in the dishwasher. "Lots to digest. Lots of missing raisins."

"I came back here last night, you know." He looked so surprised. Why? Because she was out there or in here admitting she was out there? "I guess I was still in shock seeing you again. I was going to come to the door but it was so late and then I lost my nerve. I wanted to apologize for the things I said on the beach. Um, did you happen to notice me out there, reclining under the stars?"

"Mm hm. To be honest, Carol Ann, I didn't know what to do. Then I thought I might embarrass you if I went out."

She looked away, paced to the opposite end of the kitchen. "Joe, I'm a little out of control I think. Edgy nerves and ghosts from the past and limbo feelings. I'm filled with jealousy for everyone you look at, even Alain. Can't eat. Can't sleep. I didn't start thinking about you when you came back into my life. The thing is I never stopped thinking about you. You say it's not love, well, whatever it is, it's causing me a great deal of pain." She would not cry. "I believe it's love. And you haven't even ... you don't seem to want to ... oh crap. You must think I'm awful with everything that's going on and all I can think about is us."

"Carol Ann, don't do—"

"No please, Joe. Believe me I know what I'm doing to myself. You see I'm scared all the time now. I'm more scared when I walk away from you. I'm terrified when you walk away from me. And you want to know my biggest fear? Good thing we're not in that red door room now because my biggest fear is that I'm turning into Willie, that I'm putting you through that all over again. And the worst part is I know if you made love to me all night, I would still be scared in the morning. The fear would still be there, probably worse. I don't know what's going to happen to me, Joe. What's going to happen to me?"

She let the tears come and he rushed over and pulled her into his arms. The tighter he held her, the harder she cried.

"Oh God!" she sobbed, "this incredible thing is happening to all of us and I can't keep my mind off myself. I try. I try so hard. Sometimes I even hate you. Sometimes I want to hate you. God's not going to give me those marks, Joe. How am I supposed to earn them in this state of mind? I could spoil things for all of us. And right at this moment, I don't care. I don't care and that terrifies me, too."

Joe lifted her face to his and wiped her tears. He looked like he had more pain in his eyes than she had in her heart. "I ache to make your pain go away. The thought of you carrying it these past years ..." He took those marvelous hands off her. *Oh no, don't pull away, Joe.* "You know, even if I let you possess me, it wouldn't be enough for you right now. This mission would always come between us and I know you'd hate an intermittent relationship, which is oxymoronic as far as I'm concerned. It would kill what we have."

"Do you want me to wait for you? For us?"

"I can't ask you to wait five years. How can I?"

"You don't want us now. You can't ask me to wait. You were away a long time, Joe. Is there *someone*? Iris, maybe?"

"No, Carol Ann. There's no one. Not Iris, not anyone. I would tell you. Don't you know that I would tell you?"

"I don't know anything. You. Me. Not anything."

"You will. We have time. Told you, I'm not going anywhere. Let me drive you home. In the morning I'll pick you up and bring you back here for breakfast. How's that sound?"

They drove in silence along the cove and when he pulled up to Pages alleyway entrance he leaned over and kissed her cheek. "I'll always be here for you, Carol Ann. Until they drop me in the cold, cold ground."

"Promise?"

"Promise. Your waiting is my waiting, too. Remember that."

Through what had to be osmosis, she felt his strength and found a modicum of peace. "And that door in the basement can't harm me?"

"In a day or two you'll forget it's there."

She pretended to bite the inside of her cheek and he laughed. After he escorted her to the door, she gave him a little nod. "Okay, Joe, whatever you say. Just don't keep me too long at breakfast. I'm a working girl, you know." Then she walked into Pages with dignity, something she hadn't known for a long time.

∞∞∞

With a more secure Carol Ann safely inside, he drove around the corner and parked the car. No better time than the present to get centered, to rise above these volcanic emotions he shared with Carol Ann. It was tough being with her not knowing where her turbulent emotions ended and his began. All his life he could distinguish another's feelings from his own. Not so with Carol Ann. He still wanted her, but he couldn't tell her that.

'O that this too, too solid flesh would melt, Thaw and resolve itself into a dew!'

Right, but Hamlet didn't have to endure five years of longing. He took a few deep breaths, put the seat back and closed his eyes. He counted backward from twenty, picturing each number floating amidst a constellation of stars. Meditation was like looking down from the universal sky. He could gain his perspective when the world appeared smaller. And if ever the world needed to look smaller ...

From the alpha state he observed emergent images with perfect clarity, like headlights reflecting snow. These images seemed new, though mixed with old, if that made sense. Still in Angelfish Cove he seemed to be walking along Main Street in another time. He heard music from the late '60s. There was a party going on at Corey's Cafe Beanery and John had an inflatable ten-foot bourbon bottle out front. The image faded before he caught the name of the distillery.

Haunted by images and music in this strangely familiar scenario, he snapped himself out of it. This was the second similar feeling tonight. He couldn't figure out why he thought he was in the late '60s since Angelfish Cove never got out of the '60s. Well, not really. So it was like two sets of '60s. He started the ignition. Answers would come when he was ready to hear them. Yet he wanted to return to Corey's party more than he wanted to hightail it back to Carol Ann. Was something summoning him *from* there or *to* there? Joe shook it off and pulled away from the curb. His instincts were correct, though. There was an answer waiting for him there.

Alain's van wasn't in the driveway when he got back to the beach house. But he was too exhausted to worry.

15. The Red Door

Angelfish Cove, 1991

Alain held the palm of his hand against the door, praying for discernment and counsel, expressing his gratitude in advance. As a warrior, fear did not abide in him, though he empathized with the emotion in humans.

The basement smelled like urine and burnt popcorn, intensifying when he stepped into the darkened room, a sign the demon lied when it said he did not intimidate its disciples. It was time to execute tactical and intelligence maneuvers against Edmon's superior.

While he stood in the moonlit room waiting for the enemy to speak, he recognized the demons' attempt to mask their fear with defiance. Taking gratification in his keen perception unsettled him. The room certainly had its tricks. Two minutes here had already made him prideful.

The cautious shuffle of footsteps edged toward him.

"Welcome, Remiel," Edmon said. "What do you think of our room? It will do nicely, don't you think?"

Alain ignored him. He was here to speak with the demon at Marianlake that Halloween. "Speak," he said to the thing hidden in the shadows. "I'm here regarding Iris."

"There's one too many of her sort in Ross's group," it finally said. "Your people are not playing fair, Remiel. Alas, I'm beginning to repeat myself."

"This isn't a game," Alain said, stepping closer. He felt the thing recoil. "Since you goaded my presence by crashing our party tonight, I've come to tell you that Iris stays. That's the end of the matter."

"I don't think so. Too much history there. Too much loooove," it droned. "Replace her. You see Remiel, I am quite capable of humility. Iris is working through you. You think I can't see that? Since you can do no more than hint, you're using her to give solutions. C-h-e-a-t-i-n-g. Splendid isn't it, that we are permitted to create problems you are not permitted to correct? We do well guiding in pastels while you guide in abstract grays. So, Joe Ross solves this problem on his own. When he walks through that Red Door, he walks through without Iris. I'll repeat this for the last time—there's one too many of her sort in Ross's group."

"I don't do ultimatums," Alain said. "True, she's not one of us. Not yet. Still, nothing changes. Everything is happening as intended. Iris stays. If you don't feel ready to give us your best test when we walk in here, perhaps you should withdraw and make enhancements among your own. Why not select a more qualified disciple? Would that suit you?"

"Don't provoke me, ALAIN," it threatened. "I have such an easy target in Dina."

"I'm tending to Dina. That means she'll have no problem with you as long as I stay close to her."

The demon sighed theatrically. "Is this a display of pride?" Clearly pleased, it moved closer now that it had a crumb from which to feed.

Searching the demon's eyes, he empathized with its sorrow, sweet lovely sorrow amassed over centuries. *No.* He was too long in this room. Even for him. A step backward returned him to the light of his birthright. "I love Dina. She won't be hurt."

"Oh I can make her fall in love with you as well, Remiel. You know I can. But ... that play is already in performance elsewhere and getting rave reviews. Speaking of Carol Ann, she's sleeping softly tonight. Joe had tender words with her earlier that moved me so. But her strength will wane. Give it a week or two and then we will all enjoy watching her life spiral downward."

"Iris, Dina, Carol Ann. Aren't you forgetting Maggie?"

Phlegm rattled in its throat as the demon compounded the existing stench with sulfur dioxide.

"No verbal response for Maggie. Interesting. And Elizabeth?"

"Her existence *has* been taxing," it said.

Alain understood that answer too well. God turned Elizabeth's tragedy into a miracle. "The priests?"

"We have come to an understanding of each other, an acceptance," it admitted. A mist had settled in the room. "We had our time and they suffered greatly. Once they understood their suffering was a gift from me, I lost them. I lost them to awareness of the full armor of God. That armor is an abomination, Remiel."

Alain didn't buy the demon's emotional exposé. It seemed to be on a fishing expedition—with Iris as the bait. They desperately wanted Walter Bayard's book but could not touch it while it remained in this room. Since no copies existed they had to entice someone to remove it for them. He knew Carol Ann was the one chosen to discover the book and return it to Walter. So what was keeping Edmon from bringing her in here?

It was simple. She owned this bookstore. It made sense for her to walk in here, see it, pick it up, and take it from the room. She was certainly in enough emotional turmoil that he would have no trouble luring her through the Door without Joe's knowledge. And he would have no trouble taking it from her. What were they waiting for? Unless ... *whom* were they waiting for, if not Carol Ann? He decided to conduct a little fishing expedition of his own.

"You first joined Dina when she was preparing to visit Maggie? Is that right?"

The demon nodded, its apprehensive eyes narrowing into two fine shafts of yellow.

"At that time, Carol Ann and Dina had decided to talk Maggie into searching for Joe. They wanted to start in Medford." He continued speculating with more energy. "And Carol Ann had asked Dina to go to Marianlake to see what she could learn. What a perfect way to get yourself into Marianlake without detection. With Dina as the host, you could get a closer look at Walter Bayard's machine. Only two objects in your possession can serve you in the ruin of souls, Walter Bayard's book, inches away, and his machine. How am I doing?"

"You state the obvious," it said. "But I'll admit I was disappointed at Dina's change in plans. That's some protective wall your people have around Bayard and that fascinating machine of his. Protective, but not completely impenetrable."

"What's kept you from making Carol Ann fetch the book from here?"

The demon sharpened its tone, "This exchange has grown tiresome, Remiel. And it's a bad day to discuss strategy with foes. My apologies for being uncooperative. Now if there's nothing else, I really must be leaving. Truly, I find your presence in this room offensive."

"Remember who remains at the helm."

"Oh that's right. You have your CCC. But you must remember something too, Remiel. I'm the DA." Amused with its joke, it retreated into the shadows and vanished.

Alain picked up the book and held it reverently. "*Oppressis Diabolus*," he said, reading the title. "I'm guessing your Latin is probably perfect, Edmon?"

Edmon chose to answer with his thoughts.

'*Overpowering the Devil,*' Alain heard. '*Once that book is out of here, it will fall into our hands. And it will stay in our hands. Your people will never have the opportunity to practice what's inside.*'

"*Never*? Don't you know that word makes the devil dance, Edmon? See you around the campfire."

Alain turned into the alley beside Pages and sat on the terrace. Hard to believe he was here with Joe not two months ago. How unfortunate that he wore those dark coke-bottle glasses that day. Why did the same detail in the *Angel Reclining* keep eluding Joe? He had noticed everything else in the painting, so why miss this? He had seen it one hundred times and still he did not see.

Alain did not have the gift of foresight. With as many roads as there were choices, he could do little more than pray Joe would *keep the child safe*. He could also do no more than hint as the demon was quick to remind him. Poor Joe. If only he could jump in and take over for him. If only they had more than five years to prepare. Now he was sounding like Joe. No question he was too long in that room. Although he had an occasional brush with it, negativity did not abide in him. *Reality* did, however. Alain closed his eyes and called out softly for Rafe.

Something felt very wrong.

∞∞∞

By the first week of June, the fourth estate had made the 'mystery marks' known throughout several parts of the world. In prior months there had been all kinds of rumblings, a blurb in a paper here and there, but no attention-getters. Now everybody seemed to be talking about it. Talk and tabloid shows. Tabloid papers. Radio. The story seemed to have come out of the Louisiana bayou, of all places. Joe met Louisiana's group leader in Rome, the same night he met Iris. Most of the group leaders around the globe were present that night but Joe spent the evening talking to this fellow. His name was Tim Pink and Joe thought he was a hoot.

Joe phoned Tim to see how he and his group were holding up and Tim said they were hangin' in. One of his people had prematurely passed through their Red Door. This person saw no harm in spinning her version on three national talk shows. It was embellished of course, which is why she saw no harm in declaring that SC stood for Satanic Contra, that God specifically chose them to 'stamp out evil in the world'. And those stigmatized with SC had the power to stand up against the world's darkest forces.

After being probed and tested, the marks proved genuine, but the girl's psychological examination uncovered a pile of neuroses. Her appearance on national TV had generated worldwide curiosity. Suddenly there were T-shirts, posters, hats and key chains. Others like herself were spotted and followed. Many were harassed. If all the crazy stories were lies, what was the truth? Why weren't most of these people talking, why were they running and where were they running? The media had become frustrated and desperate for answers.

Tim Pink advised Joe to be cautious. The marks were no guarantee they'd be able to hold their own in that room. Without sufficient spiritual training, dancing with the demons was an invitation to disaster. When Joe asked Tim how the girl was faring, he said she had begun to see herself in a healthier light. Rafe had paid her a visit. But there'd been other outbreaks of this sort and Tim believed it was due to premature entry into that 'hellhole' of a room.

He also told Joe that rumors had surfaced about the Angelfish Cove chapter from both Marianlake and Roman headquarters.

"Of all of us, you guys are the only ones who personally associate with Wally Bayard," Tim said. "Aside from your obvious past links to Marianlake, there's more history there. It's no secret his assistant's related to one of your own, that another one of yours is a bad-tempered rockstar. And I also understand that Maggie Page is yours, too. You know she's been painting that Door for years, right Joe? And for the last little piece of resistance, I heard you guys have Bayard's book. Joe-Joe, is this true?"

Joe made non-committal noises from his throat.

"Be careful, man," Tim warned. "Be extra careful. You're under a cosmic microscope, man. I've had my troubles here but I don't think I'd trade places. What's your status?"

Joe gave his harmonica a squeeze. "We got the whole group coming in two weeks plus Walter and his assistant. Plus Alain's family. Even my grandmother wants to come and I haven't figured out how I'm going to talk her out of it yet. I'm strokin' along but Alain isn't his usual cheery self. Preoccupied, you know. This worries me."

"Do they all have the marks?"

"No. Two haven't received them yet. I know we have a few years left but I'd feel better if everybody had them now, you know what I mean? You're right. We're beast-bait here, Timmy."

"One more thing," Tim said. "Sorry for sounding like an alarmist, but you got like air masses comin' together there, man. I hear tell that Wally's assistant doesn't have them. Maybe you heard."

He hadn't heard. He seldom spoke with Elizabeth and when he did, she never mentioned it. Alain would've told him if he knew. Why would a sweetheart of a kid like Ronny Fergel, who saw angels everywhere but in his soup, not have received the sacred brand? Ronny wasn't in his group but he felt responsible for him. He was Elizabeth's son and he'd soon be camping on his turf. And this *kid,* all of four years his junior was Walter Bayard's right arm. He didn't need this now. He and Alain had enough on their plates.

Tim ended the conversation saying he'd keep Joe's group in his prayers. He thanked him, adding that a cloaking device wasn't such a bad idea. Tim didn't get it but that was okay. They could always use the prayers. To take his mind off things, he took a little drive over to the Pinetree Inn. Three out of five room reservations were in order, making the Fathers' all set. But reservations had mistakenly booked Walter Bayard and Ronny Fergel for the wrong date. For some unknown reason, they had them coming in August. And the Inn was booked solid for June and July. The desk clerk at the Inn contacted the Twin Cedars Lodge where Dina was staying and they didn't have so much as a broom closet to spare. "What next?" he said to Alain. "What next?"

∞∞∞

The third week in June, a wind-blown Sister Elizabeth Whyte railed the corner onto Angelfish Cove's main drag in a white 1984 Ford Mustang G.T. 350 convertible. A distinguished looking, white-haired man rode in front with her and a young, portly man in his late twenties lounged in back. They stopped at Corey's Cafe Beanery for lunch before heading to Joe's. Actually lunch could have waited. The distinguished man, a cross between Captain Nemo and Rod Serling, really wanted to say hello to his old friend, John Corey. The young man tapped a restless leg on the floor as he perused the menu.

While they waited for their order, Elizabeth called the Inn to check on the room. She wasn't sure which one in her party of three was going to be taking the room, but they wouldn't be checking in for a few hours yet. Last night Joe had asked her to come straight to the beach house. 'Don't worry about accommodations,' he'd said. 'Everything's worked out.' Elizabeth was anxious to get there. All three of them were. But first things first. Walter hadn't seen John Corey in eighteen years.

∞∞∞

The waitress didn't get the man's name, so John assumed he was meeting the brewery rep due to show up. He squinted ahead at the white-haired man sitting with the woman and the young fella. Definitely not the brewery rep. He offered Walter his hand, glanced quickly at his companions and then looked inquisitively at this man who looked more like a Supreme Court justice than a beer rep.

"Hi there. John Corey. I didn't catch what brewery you're from?"

The elegant *Captain Nemo* stood and shook his hand. "Truth is, I'm more of a spirit man," he said, grin deepening.

"Walt!" He gave Walter a hard embrace. "I knew I'd see you again before they put me in the cold New England ground. Just knew it. It was the white hair that threw me."

Walter embraced him in kind then introduced his party. Even though Elizabeth was out of habit, she wore her Carmelite Order pin and introduced herself as Sister Elizabeth Patrick. Walter introduced Ronny Fergel as his friend and assistant. John wrinkled his brow at Ronny. The lad looked familiar, then he shook a couple hundred hands a month, many of whom were stocky and blond. Ronny Fergel could look familiar to anyone.

"Look at you," Walter said, clasping his shoulder. "You have a few years on me and still no signs of geezerhood. What's your secret?"

"I tell ya," he said, deadpanning, "the single life and all the beans I can eat."

They spent an hour playing catch-up. Elizabeth sat quietly while Ronny wolfed down the New England clam chowder and two wedges of strawberry rhubarb pie. He and Walter joked about the old days, the radio station, fights over the Cafe's original blueprint. Walter designed all but two buildings on the Cove's main drag.

"It feels like I never left, Johnny," Walter said.

The two men had diametrically opposed backgrounds. One was grade-eight-middle-class and as blue-collar as one could get. The other was raised in Boston with the proverbial silver spoon, graduating from Yale with a B.Sc. in Architectural Engineering. One couldn't distinguish a moron from an oxymoron and the other spoke four languages. They had their differences, yet they had no differences.

John couldn't help noticing the marks on Walter's wrists, the marks he'd been hearing a great deal about on the news lately. He saw traces of the marks beneath Sister Elizabeth's cardigan and the lad didn't have any. He had to ask, not out of nosiness but because he genuinely hoped his old friend hadn't become one of them religious fanatics. Too many a them in the world. As far as John was concerned, most of them turned into Jim Joneses at some point.

"There's been a lot a talk, Walt," he said, carefully choosing his words. He tried not to look at Walter's wrists. "People out there saying crazy, far-fetched things about those SC marks. What do they mean, Walt? I'll believe what you tell me."

The two large creases on Walter Bayard's forehead deepened. "There was a fever," he answered. Ronny stopped eating and Elizabeth pulled her cardigan sleeves down to her knuckles. "I went to bed with a fever contained in my body like flame under an asbestos suit. But there was no fear, strangely enough. There is also no memory, Johnny. I woke up and I had these. We're investigating their meaning. We're talking to others with the marks. We're cross-referencing similarities, differences, things of that nature."

Right. He knew fancy talking malarkey when he heard it. He'd heard folks answer big questions using lots of words that answered nothing. Maybe he should skip the questions for now. Maybe save them for a private talk later between him and Walt.

They had been apart a lot a years. People changed. Could be Walt was one of them people. He patiently waited until his old friend finished talking some more of his twaddle which took a few minutes. The young lad still seemed familiar, more now than an hour ago. Ronny was like a big kid and he enjoyed his reaction to the 'Book Fair' sign that Edmon was stringing up across the street in front of Pages.

"Oh far out, Mother," the lad said, enthusiasm spilling out all over the place. "A book fair. Wild. We gotta go to that!"

∞∞∞∞

Ronny excused himself and said goodbye to John Corey. He told his mother and Walter he'd meet them in front of the bookstore when they were ready to leave. He simply *had* to go and check out this book fair thing. The man hanging up the sign over there seemed very friendly because he'd been giving him several welcoming smiles. He hurried up crossing the street when he saw the elderly man stepping down from the wobbly ladder.

Ronny held the ladder steady until the man's feet were on the ground. "Gotta be careful on these things," he said, extending his hand. "Hi there. Ronny Fergel."

"Hello. Edmon Fendi. I thank you for your assistance."

For a second Ronny forgot why he had come over. It passed quickly. "Um, a book fair, I see. What kind of books?"

"What kind do you fancy?"

"Theology. Technology. Languages. I speak several languages," he boasted. He never told people stuff like that. Never boasted. "I have an aptitude for languages. They come easily to me. I learned French from a friend living right here in town."

In French-Canadian, Edmon told him to return tomorrow. There would be books on any subject he desired. Switching to Parisian-French, Edmon assured him that he would find whatever he fancied, then complimented him on his grasp of both dialects.

Edmon asked if anything was wrong.

He shook his head and folded the ladder. He never allowed a dark thought to linger, so why was he thinking so hard about Compo dying in a frozen Marianlake two winters ago? He had been exercising him that afternoon. It was to be the last toss of the twig. Then the ice broke and Compo never made it back.

"Guess I'm a little wasted from the long drive," he said.

"*The Bagel Factory*," Edmon said, reading the back of his favorite T-shirt. "What is that, a bakery or supermarket where you work?"

Ronny giggled, childlike. "It's where I work but it's no bakery. *Bagel* is a combination of my employer's surname and mine. You might know him 'cause he used to live here years ago. Walter Bayard?"

Edmon ran his tongue along his lips. "I've certainly heard of him, but we've never really met. He left town shortly after I moved here. Your boss, is he?"

Ronny felt so drawn to this place. He wanted to go inside. And he could swear he heard Edmon repeat his question, although not in so many words, or not in any words at all. He wasn't sure. "Yes. My boss. He's an architectural engineer and I'm his assistant."

Come back tomorrow, Ronny. I'll take you on a tour.

"Can I come back tomorrow?" he asked. "Maybe you can give me a tour."

Edmon smiled. "Of course." *Don't mention our conversation to anyone, Ronny.*

Ronny stared back at him and waved goodbye. "Okay."

∞∞∞∞

Including Joe and Alain, there were fifteen in the beach house that night. And it was a party. A social. It was time to lighten up, to play a little and get reacquainted. For Carol Ann, Maggie and Dina, it was their first introduction to Father Vittorio Gianni. Although he attended Pages opening, Carol Ann's encounter with the tall priest had been somewhat covert. Joe affectionately referred to him as a 'high priest'. It became obvious that they shared a tight bond, having spent all those years together in Rome.

The girls were also happy to finally meet Walter Bayard, Ronny Fergel, and Alain's ten-year-old brother, Simon. Joe could not get over his resemblance to Alain at that age, telling everyone how remarkable it was. 'It's Alain ten years ago,' he kept saying. Yet no one seemed to agree with him and he couldn't understand that. Even Claude and Tracy said that Simon took after Claude, minus the blond hair. Joe was mystified. Until Tracy put the boy to bed, he could barely keep his eyes off Simon. Mid-evening he caught the tail end of a conversation on the patio between Alain and Iris, which baffled him all the more—

"I know exactly what he's thinking," Alain said.

"What are you going to do?"

Alain chuffed out a breath. "Guide. Let it happen the way it was meant."

What Iris said next struck him as very odd. "And soon my *real* work begins."

They went inside then and he laughed to himself. Ten years ago this would have been one more thing to drive him nuts. But he knew Alain and he trusted him no matter what. He could never forget that once a very long time ago he was told that Alain had a directive of his own, so he took the secretive side of Alain on faith. And love. But something was up. They were all here tonight, the entire group, plus Claude, Tracy and Simon. And of course, Ronny and Walter.

Walter wanted to speak privately with him later this evening, perhaps at the Pinetree Inn. Walter and Ronny decided to take Elizabeth's room and she would stay with Dina at the Lodge. For tonight, Father Richard offered to let Ronny bunk with him so they could have their privacy. Joe figured he was in for a long night and kept the coffee brewing. As the others sang, danced and drank, he got wired on caffeine. When Walter hinted it was time to drive him to the Inn, he knew he'd have no problem staying awake. He didn't want to miss one word of whatever this amazing man had to say.

Shortly after 11 PM he parked in back of the Pinetree Inn. They hadn't said a word in the car, though it was all of a two-minute drive. This was his first time alone with Walter. They'd met briefly on three prior occasions but he'd never had a one on one with the man. He always seemed to travel with an entourage, or had a group of some description hanging around him.

In Rome he learned the dangers involved in glorifying humans. Now he was a hair away from remembering to apply all he had learned. Walter Bayard was the one who hit this ball out of the park. His prayer, his conversation with God, his dream. Walter was responsible for a large part of his own destiny, and the destiny of nearly four thousand others around the globe. He built this town. He built that incredible machine. He was taking all of them to the Year 6. *Okay, Joe, no glorifying humans.*

It was a balmy 73°. Walter stood in the parking lot with his hands in his pockets enjoying the boardwalk view. He closed his eyes and concentrated. "Do you hear that?"

"I hear the water rippling in the Cove," Joe said.

Walter pointed to the poplar tree a few feet off the boardwalk. "See that poplar? So soothing. Years ago I used to sit under it on days and nights like this. I would close my eyes and listen. When the wind blows through a poplar, it sounds like the most delightful rainstorm. Torrential sound, actually. Let's sit under it now."

After they made themselves comfortable under the tree he closed his eyes, relaxed enough now to ask Walter the real reason for this visit. "You're not here just for our meet 'n greet, are you, Walter?"

"No, Joe, I'm not. I'm here to share some information with you and then I expect you'll have some questions for me."

"Is this information confidential?"

"Some, yes. Before we get into specifics, I need to talk to you about my machine." Walter reached into his pant pocket and removed a somewhat crumpled envelope. He passed it to him. "Inside you'll find all directions, locations of and combinations to my safe and desk at Marianlake. Notes. Diagrams. Sketches.

"There is also a third remote in the making. I'm nearly finished, Joe. Twenty hours more and I'm done. It doesn't hurt to have a spare, although I doubt we'll need it. If one is lost, we can still function with one. All we need are the log entries. Time, destination, landing coordinates, etc. The machine itself is easy enough to reconstruct, but the real time machine is the remote. The crew at each end, present and past, carries one. It's never far from me, so I'll show it to you later."

"Why me, Walter? I mean, you're tight with Fathers' Andre and Richard. And there's Ronny."

"I need someone young and mature whom I can trust. The people you've mentioned are very dear to me, very special, but two of them are getting on like myself. And Ronny is ... different. Profiled psychologically, he is an adult child. Under stress he could disorganize."

"I don't understand why he hasn't received the marks. He's been hearing and seeing angels all his life. Not to mention his aptitude for languages. These are gifts."

"You all have gifts." A small red vein appeared in Walter's eye. "All of you. Everyone going back. And God did not give those brandings to tell us apart. He doesn't need any help and He certainly doesn't need to showcase his work. They were given to all of you *for* all of you. It's important that you recognize each other—until the millennium. You probably suspected as much. In the first year of the millennium, they will disappear.

"As for Ronny, he's experiencing difficulty accepting his parentage. Learning that his mother is really his aunt, that his aunt is really his mother was traumatic enough. Add to that a father who desecrated his mother and a mother who is a nun and you've got the beginnings of some disturbing emotional problems.

"Children are so remarkably intuitive. As a boy, Ronny experienced the changeling fantasy as most children do at some point. Only in his case it was true. His parents were not his parents. So he decided that if he *earned* their love, they would never abandon him. He would belong. Abandonment is his greatest fear, Joe, a fear augmented by time and truth.

"He feels his aunt and uncle distanced themselves so he could come to know Elizabeth as his mother. And every time Elizabeth resumes her duties as a religious, he feels abandoned all over again. Ronny has to accept. He has to mature. When this happens he will receive the marks. We all have our issues, don't we, Joe? Like Carol Ann who certainly has hers. Dina who is struggling and nearly there from what Alain tells me. Then there's your Maggie who is another story completely."

This was as good a time as any to hit Walter with something that'd been nattering at him. "There's been some negativity regarding your time machine. Carol Ann played devil's advocate a few weeks back and I have to admit, she raised many interesting questions. I'm sure you've heard them. Why does it only go forward in time? What happens if one of us gets lost or trapped there? What if some nearsighted person absentmindedly sets the time log forward? What if anything nasty happens, God forbid, to the machine itself?"

"All questions beginning with 'what if' are fear questions, Joe. Go back a few years. Would God answer my prayer, show me how to build this machine, then take it away in the eleventh hour? What else is troubling you?"

"There have been inconsistencies. The Red Doors for example. People are going through prematurely and getting messed up. Why are they open early since our people won't need them until '95 or '96?"

Walter looked intensely at him. "Many of the group leaders need them now. I think it's time for you to pass through the door yourself, Joe, which you'll be doing many times before you take your people through. Take nothing for granted. Not Rome. Not your awareness. Not your gift. Nothing. I watched you tonight. You're beginning to walk around with one eye shut.

"There are things you're missing. Drop your illusions and during the next few days, really see the people involved. Including myself. *See*, Joe. Be aware. See the ways in which many of us *try* to fail. And this town. Be aware of it, too. All of it, even the nooks and crannies. All the answers are right here in Angelfish Cove. Remember that."

"Something's influencing the group, Walter. Over the years I've felt these intermittent portents dangling over me like a six-ton wrecking ball, but nothing this pervasive. Even Alain's been a naughty boy lately because he isn't sharing stuff. And Maggie ... I get near her and my head wants to explode. She isn't sharing, either. Dina seems to be slipping back into angry mode and Carol Ann is romantically obsessed and drinking. Like Willie all over again, obsession is the cross she's nailed to. And the secrets, my God, the secrets. The dream. The document. Alain. Iris. Angelfish Cove. Now there's Alain's brother, Simon." He stopped talking for a few seconds. No doubt he loved, but did he completely trust? He had to hear himself say the words. "I trust Alain with all my heart. But I know he has information I haven't. You said before that there are things you think I'm missing?"

Walter gave the top of his hand an affectionate slap. "The fact that everything is getting ready to unfold right before your eyes, secret by secret. As I said–pay attention. The child could be within your midst."

"Oh please don't get me *stahted* on the child, Walter," he said, swatting a mosquito that wasn't there. "I mean we all know Alain is the child, don't we? At least that's what I was told."

"But you no longer believe that."

"Not for a long time." The words came out barely audible. He felt a dark cloud forming in his mind. He would let it come and pass straight through him, like the breeze in the poplar. "You're right. I have to hone my instincts, my self-awareness."

"Your instincts are perfect, Joe. Though you're right about the self-awareness. As for the secrets–there are always secrets. But you've been solving them as you've gone along, as the rest of us have. We've all had the same complaint. I've always believed in truth, but I won't push for it. There are things I'm uncomfortable with now as well, apart from my own innate demons. There are evil entities around that seem to suck the air I breathe. What is it you call them? Dark angels? Alain informs me there's one right here in Angelfish Cove, but he's not at liberty to disclose. And I know you're aware of its identity. You see? You may not know everything, but you know more than most."

If Walter were a horse he'd bet him on the nose every time. "I suppose."

"I'm in pretty good health, Joe. However, I did have a mild heart attack two years ago. I gave up the cigars, sugar, caffeine. When I asked God to let me keep the steak and pastrami, I got a picture of little green men dressed in rubber aprons, shoveling out my arteries. So the heart's back in pretty fair shape. Still I feel there are precautions I must take."

"Eat your oats, Walter. We can't finish this race without you."

Walter chuckled. "Sometimes it's tough to differentiate insight from dark angels, isn't it?"

"I'll say."

"Come on. Let's catch a bit more of this night air then head inside, Joe. I want to play show and tell with my remote." Walter's eyes glowed. "And we'll speak of your battle with uncertainty."

16. Oppressis Diabolus

They strolled along the boardwalk talking about Walter's book. Several years back, Walter decided it was not for publication, that like a journal, the book was something of great personal value, meant only for family. Simply written and therefore, easily translatable, its general premise lay in the recognition of truth from untruth. Walter wrote extensively of places where Untruth liked to play and dance, places in the mind and secular world.

He said the prayer asking to restore love and hope to the world in 1967 and wrote the book two years later. Walter told him it began because the escalating 'new age' thinking disturbed him. The rationalizations were so borderline credible that to many they became credible.

"Always the fine line leading to blind alleys," Walter said.

Walter confessed his vulnerability to the disguises of anti-truth, remedied solely from Biblical study. He dedicated his book to his family and had it doubly bound in Corinthian leather. Inspired by the ancient language, he wrote the book in Latin and titled it *Oppressis Diabolus,* which translated, 'Overpowering the Devil'. It grieved him and his family when it went missing after their move back to Boston. Yesterday, Alain told him where the book was and why it could not be returned yet.

"How remarkable that it really has power over the Devil," Walter said as they reached the Inn. "And Maggie painted it in her *Angel Reclining*. Like the red door, she didn't realize what she was painting. Is it true she was totally reclusive for several years?"

He told Walter as much as he could without breaking confidences.

"This is quite a group you have here. And you are all in my Angelfish Cove. Be careful, Joe. Something *is* wrong. I can feel it too, so much that I've decided to cut my trip short. I'll stay over the weekend. Ronny's looking forward to Carol Ann's book fair, but I want to get back to Marianlake and join my crew. Suddenly I'm anxious to bring them home. As we speak, they're scouting locations on the Gaza Strip-Israeli border. Year 5, Joe. Year 5."

When Walter removed the remote from the room safe, his face glowed with pride and pleasure. "Here, take it," Walter said. "Just don't press anything."

"Looks like a TV remote on steroids," he said, transfixed by the buttons, wheels and tiny green and red flashing lights. Recalling the Star Trek bedspread and a simpler life in a long ago bedroom attic, he smiled wistfully at Walter. "What's the solid amber light below 'Lock In' mean?"

"It informs me that the crew is where they should be, that all is well, and the machine is nestled in its bed at home in Marianlake. When active, it flashes bright pink. A minute after the crew arrives in Judea the machine returns to Marianlake where it remains until they're ready for departure. The crew simply sends for it. Should something happen to their remote, I can transport the machine to them using mine. There is no need to have a queer looking, disc-like object hanging around, even miniaturized, in an ancient world." Before he could utter another word, Walter gave him the time-out gesture.

"I'll tell you what every button on this remote means, but first I want to ask you a difficult question. Make yourself comfortable, Joe."

He did as asked, taking a seat on the couch but leaning anxiously forward.

Walter sat down on the coffee table, directly in from of him. "As I said, I have a crew of eight in Judea, Year 5. I've indicated that we can communicate in code through time and space *with* our remotes. I guess you can call them state of the art walkie-talkies. My question, Joe, is *do you believe all of this*?"

Wow. A stunning question. Walter had to go and ask him the million-dollar question he'd been struggling with since Page's opening. He stiffened his back against the couch. "Why do you ask me this, Walter? Or are you just going stall to stall?"

Walter didn't respond.

He rubbed a hand through his hair. "It's so incredible. All of it. I ... sometimes I can't believe I'm a part of it. I've seen so many miracles over the years. Little ones. Big ones."

"Do you believe all of this, Joe?"

Dammit. He felt his right eye going 'off' a little and Walter's eye had become increasingly bloodshot. "I believe it *most* of the time. Other times, especially when I'm around Carol Ann, I believe it's a meaningful hoax, designed to align our paths toward God and enlightenment in some indefinable manner. Back in time? *The* Child? What frightens me is that sometimes the demons are all I do believe in. How can I selectively believe this way after the miracles? The doubts are not all-consuming, Walter, but they're there.

"You spoke to me of self-awareness. Well I'm aware I've had doubts immediately following our return to Angelfish Cove. Alain doesn't know I have them. He's too preoccupied lately. Funny isn't it, like Carol Ann, I feel my doubts will harm this mission in some way. But you asked. Though I don't know why you asked."

"Because I see you vacillating." Walter locked the remote back in the safe then joined him on the sofa. "You should know that I do too at times and I invented the thing. I've been back. Just last month I was in a town called Magdala, strolling along the Galilean shore. There we were, Ronny, myself and two others in my crew—four miles from Nazareth. Imagine it, Joe. *Ancient Palestine!* The bottom of my toe had sand-burned and blistered. Ronny informed me that there is no word for 'Band-Aid' in Aramaic. I knew beforehand we had no business being in Nazareth. We were supposed to be scouting landing sites in Judea, not Galilee. Bethlehem is in Judea and we had logged in for a town called Qumran, which is one town south of Bethlehem.

"At the last minute I ignored my inner voice telling me to mind present business only—and changed the log to Galilee. I had to go to Nazareth. I had to look for expectant mothers and carpenters. I had to *see*.

"And see I did. I saw people there in Nazareth, Joe. Holy people. Evil people. We spoke to no one, but they knew who we were. We left within the hour. Two in my crew returned emotionally fragile, fragments of ancient evil attached to their minds, cancerous shadows. And my toe ..." Walter removed his right loafer and sock, exposing the scarred stump of a second toe. "It immediately became infected, turning blue before my eyes. The doctor couldn't understand how gangrene could set in so quickly. My circulation is fine but my family has a history of diabetes. So he froze it and amputated twenty minutes after the examination.

"I remember lying there thinking about pride. Had I obeyed the internal warning ... oh I don't care about half a toe, but I do care that my men attracted and returned with two negative presence's that likely tailgated us here. Although I was never an Emerson supporter, I can't quite shake something he said, 'everything that God has made has a crack in it.' Evil lurks in cracks and shadows. And faith and love are as vulnerable as always. Remember a little while ago I told you to pay attention to all the nooks and crannies in Angelfish Cove."

It was like riding a carousel and he was on his tenth spin and dizzy as hell. Even a man of Walter Bayard's stature had to see to believe. Now he was paying the price for pride and lack of faith. How did one weigh evil? Some people were pretty good and others exceptionally good. Then you get into your saint category. So how about these 'presence's'? Was there a spiritual barometer out there, an evil *scale*? Redundant question. Like asking if pitch is darker than black.

Again he was glad for the time remaining to whip everyone into shape. During moments like this he found the thought consoling because the five years would fly right on by. Actually, they had four and a half years left and he had to factor in the ways people wasted time. Rationalizations. Comfort zones. Platitudes and clichés. Everybody had 'em and they still got screwed up.

What of the team? Could they make it? The concept of this mission boggled the mind. Already, Carol Ann had begun turning her back on it. So if something were to go wrong ...

Walter must've sensed the dark path he was stumbling along in his thoughts. "Stop it, Joe. Sit back and observe the fear. When an informed person has a negative or allergic reaction to a drug, they have the sense to realize that the drug is the cause. Soon it will be out of their system and they will feel normal again. They are not the drug. We both know what's making us feel this way, don't we? Stay in the light now." Walter put his sock back on then got up to answer a musical knock at the door. He looked back and gave him a reassuring smile.

"Hi there," Ronny said cheerfully, entering the room with his usual unsophisticated vigor. "Came in to grab some gear." Father Richard was with him and everybody got quiet while Ronny changed his Bagel Factory T-shirt, which had coffee stains all over the front. "Hi, Joe. Hope I'm not interrupting."

"I'm only interrupting by association," Father Richard said, sipping Coke.

"Not at all. Sorry we didn't get the chance to talk much at the beach house." Something in Ronny made his stomach quiver.

Alain returned from the front desk shaking a small paper bag. "Extra creamers for your coffee, Walter," he said. "And all wake-up calls are in. I think we should get a couple of those Bagel Factory T-shirts, Joe. What do you think?"

"I'm in," he said, passively. Was this the second or third time Alain mentioned getting those shirts? "Is the party still rocking back at the house?"

"Carol Ann's toast," Ronny said, extracting a pair of boxer shorts covered in musical notes from his suitcase. "I told her I'd help her out at the fair tomorrow. She's gonna need it. She talks a lot about you, Joe."

He had no response for that.

"You two getting caught up on Marianlake business?" Father Richard asked.

"That we are, Richard," Walter said.

Father Richard took the polite exit cue and steered Ronny out the door. Watching Walter put his shoes back on reminded him of the most fascinating part of their conversation–Nazareth in the Year 5. Not that he needed much reminding. "How is it done?" he asked.

"Positive and negative values. And I don't mean in the spiritual or moral sense. Science observes events numerically and thusly assigns positive and negative values. The numerical observation of these events involved experiments with time, and subsequent time travel. There is a scientific motion called 'time reversal invariance' in which events appear in reverse order. We're looking at time reversed with respect to the original motion. If some motion is possible according to known physical laws, then the time-reversed motion is almost always possible."

"Mm-hmm." *Hmm?*

"Einstein recognized that because the speed of light is constant, the measurement of time depends on the observer's motion. Time is frequently described as the fourth dimension. Did you know that? It is difficult to simplify, Joe, but it involves gravity. When light interacts with mass, whatever exists in the immediate area is either attracted or repelled. It can gravitate and accelerate toward or it can regress and decelerate away. Well, we have succeeded in experiments with time regression–non-accelerated *away* motion. And I suspect the human race has been successfully entering the fourth dimension since the turn of the century. Einstein explored gravitational research with Marcel Grossmann around 1912."

Feeling his eyes glazing over, he accepted the limitation of his scientific aptitude, though he remembered hearing something of that time reversal invariance theory before, probably in school. What he wanted now was to power himself beyond the doubts and hearing Walter's stories of their excursions back helped dispel them.

"Anybody else I know, besides yourself and Ronny, who've gone back?"

"A hand-picked, carefully chosen crew," Walter said. "Plus a few historians and researchers, two field archeologists, and four psychologists. They'll be touring around, spending time with all the groups. Beginning very soon."

"Why the psychologists?"

"In theory, the mind can grasp what we have accomplished. In practice, it's another story. Actually being there jolts the mind into a new consciousness— territory unexplored. There's no frame of reference. No safety nets. Again, it has no awareness of the reality. How can it, when it's all so illusory. It's something that has already happened, a historical event. Sometimes, reality is the most difficult thing to reason out. A paradox."

"Like astronauts entering space for the first time. They have to be psychologically prepared."

"Precisely. Here." Walter reached into his pocket and handed Joe a small key on a Marianlake key chain. "This gets you into the control panels beneath the rink, which are larger versions of the remote built into the actual flooring. My original plan. You'll find it under the goalie net beside the Expos sign." Walter snickered and he had to laugh. "It has detectors that identify problems with the machine, things the remote *cannot* do. That was intentional. If anything should happen to me before this mission is over, remember—it must be shut down at the end. As you know, the hockey rink goes back to being a hockey rink. We don't want anyone stumbling upon it years from now and dusting the cobwebs off the technology."

"How do I shut it down?"

"You'll see a circuit board. Just yank the wires. There are so many that no one could ever figure out what was originally attached to what. May take you all of five minutes. Don't lose that key, Joe. A forced entry could do damage. All the circuitry is directly below the rink flooring. If you were to hammer your way in there, the machine itself could blow. That would be messy, dangerous, and difficult to explain."

"You hardly know me, Walter. I don't understand why you're entrusting me with all this." The engrained smile disappeared from Walter's face. For the first time he noted the deep creases in his brow and bloodshot eyes, indelible signs of fatigue.

"Hardly know you?" Walter said. "I would not trust someone with my life's work if I didn't know him, believe me. I know you, Joe. Everybody closely involved with this mission knows Joe Ross. Of course I also know your history ... your mother. Such a tragedy, Joe, I'm sorry."

He patted his pocket. "Never go anywhere without my DEET."

Walter shook his head. "DEET? You've lost me."

"You weren't given details?"

"I know she sustained the fatal injury while working in a stable."

"It was a freak accident when I was nine." He massaged the tightness in his neck. "My mother trained Thoroughbreds and was great at it. We had torrential rainfall in Ocala that spring, so the ranch was a veritable breeding ground for black flies, horseflies, mosquitoes, you name it. We didn't dare open our mouths outside.

"We kept the horses sprayed down and blanketed of course, but it didn't help them much. You'd see clouds of the little bloodsuckers hovering over puddles. I remember bites on the backs and insides of my ears so bad I wanted to scream." He stopped, exhaled deeply.

"Joe, you don't have to—"

"Nope. It's okay. Claxton Farms had a beauty of a Derby contender, a yearling by the name of Fast Forward, regal bloodline on both sides. We all loved him. Nothing scared that horse. He was fearless. A comical, good-natured guy who liked to snatch your hat or your rake, or notebook. I adored him and was so proud when the owner chose my mother to train him.

"One morning Mum noticed a little inflammation in Forward's left hind leg. Nothing serious. He'd popped a little cold splint and Mum was icing him down in his stall. Or trying to ice him. The mosquitoes and horseflies were everywhere, some of the horseflies an inch and a quarter long. Mum cursed at them, batted them away every few seconds. Forward's tail swished, his legs stomping and kicking them off.

"The bugs were driving the horse crazy, so my mother told me to get help. And that's when it happened. I was gone maybe three minutes, tops. When we got back, my mother was lying in a weird position on her side. I remember squatting to see what she was looking at because her eyes were open. Then a second later I realized she was dead.

"I don't believe Forward knew he hit her. Can you imagine the overkill with one kick to the head at fifteen-hundred pounds of pressure per square inch? One split-second kick ended my mother's life."

"Oh, Joe."

"Yeah. They determined she must've lost her balance swatting mosquitos. True enough. My mother knew how to position herself around horses."

"Claxton, you said?"

"Yep. Why?"

"My nephew spent the odd summer in Ocala, stayed with a couple of his Cambridge buddies whose family owned a horse farm."

"No shortage of horse farms in Ocala," he said, still thinking back. "Less than a year later, my dad and I had the accident on my tenth birthday. You know the rest. I went to live with my uncle and his family in Medford."

"Two tragic losses for one so young. What happened to the horse?"

"It was a freak accident. Everyone agreed it wasn't the horse's fault."

"Did you ever get to see him run?"

"Nope. But I followed his career. He didn't win the Derby but he ran in it. The Preakness, too. Even after Mum ... I hated leaving him. And I knew Forward missed her. I could feel it."

"What happened to your dream, Joe?"

It's still here, Walter, buried under a pile of priorities. "Your dream dwarfs mine, Walter. Aw, I completed my equine studies in Rome, and after that, well ... here we are. And believe me I'm here because I want to be."

"But still, your horse farm?"

"Actually I'm looking at some land in Ocala. Flying out in a few weeks."

"Good for you! Never dump the dream."

Funny. He once offered the same advice to Craig Matheson from his hospital bed the day after the accident. Craig also had a theory with the word 'time' in it. But for the life of him, he could never remember the other words in the theory. Couldn't even get it straight at the time.

They wrapped it up shortly after that. He had a bunch more questions, but Walter was definitely ready to stand down for the evening. His complexion had paled and his eyes were extremely bloodshot, and he assured him they'd have more time to talk tomorrow during the book fair. It had been a long day and Walter still had notes to make before retiring. He sensed something wrong, but then it seemed the entire group was sensing the same thing. He shook Walter's hand goodnight and thanked him for everything.

From the doorway he said it again, "I mean it, Walter. Thank-you."

On the way back to the car he reminded himself to ask Walter who his nephew was. Claxton's had bunches of Cambridge guys hanging out during the summers and he was friendly with many. But Craig Matheson, who always called him *Toots,* even in his letters, was the best of the best. Poor Craig.

Who knows—Walter's nephew might have heard him tooting his harmonica around the stables.

Driving along the main drag, he caught sight of his four ladies walking toward Pages and pulled over. He cut the engine and sighed heavily, suddenly feeling depressed as hell at the sight across the street. Maggie and Dina were supporting Carol Ann who was too drunk to walk on her own. A despondent looking Sister Elizabeth trailed behind.

He bolted out of the car and slammed the door loud enough for them to hear. They had to hear. Apart from them, he was the only one on the street. He clamped his jaw and rolled up his sleeves. The women stopped and waited for him, except Carol Ann who was oblivious to his presence.

Maggie and Dina had to brace themselves against the dead weight of her. In all his life he'd never seen a person so drunk. Even Willie. The sight of Carol Ann repulsed him, which brought back the guilt, which made him get down on himself for his lack of compassion, which angered him all over again.

"Didn't anyone see her getting into this condition?" he asked them from halfway across the road.

"She wasn't exactly allowing us to monitor her drinking, Joe," Elizabeth said.

Without assistance from Maggie, Dina gave Carol Ann a hoist. "I'm gettin' sick and tired a this shit."

He and Maggie exchanged looks.

"She doesn't even know you're here," Maggie whispered.

"Let me take her." He reached over and took her in his arms. Carol Ann glanced briefly at him through sleepwalker eyes. "I'll put her to bed. The rest of you can go if you want."

"I want to spend the night with her," Maggie said, tucking in one of Carol Ann's bra straps. "I think she's going to need me in the morning."

"She's not Willie," Elizabeth said to him under her breath. Then she and Dina went on their way.

She passed out the moment he set her down on the bed. Again he wondered if there was anything left, even a spark of the girl he fell in love with. She was so thin. How could he not feel guilty? Her obsession for him was killing her— like Willie. Elizabeth was wrong. Carol Ann *was* turning into Willie and had expressed her fear of making him go through it all again. Damned self-fulfilling prophecies. Maggie was waiting for him to leave so she could undress her. Fine, no problem. Seeing Carol Ann like this had made him nauseous.

"Ronny said he'd take over for her tomorrow," Maggie said, slipping off Carol Ann's shoes. "She briefed him over at your place tonight while she was still lucid. She's been so irresponsible with Pages, Joe. Since day one. It's not like her. What's happening to her?"

He couldn't get into it with her. Carol Ann wouldn't like that. "Stew," he said, staring vacantly at Carol Ann.

"What?"

"Stew. When you put a stew on to boil, the scum rises to the surface. I'll see myself out. Take care of our precious stew, Maggie. G'night."

With the moonlight streaming in downstairs, he took another good look at the Angel Reclining. There was something nattering at him about this painting, something disturbing. Suddenly the lights flicked on and he found himself fencing eyes with Edmon. No small talk. Edmon was out of his league. He had to keep his cool and remember that. Alain was taking care of Edmon. *Don't say or do anything stupid, Joe. No fear.*

"Re-checking the inventory for the morning," Edmon said. "Hope I didn't startle you."

He hated Edmon, hated the idea of him anywhere near Carol Ann. He hated him for making him feel hate. He lowered his voice, "I don't want Carol Ann in that cellar." The thing immediately sent him a gift of that sickening, foul odor, the same odor that made him retch up at Marianlake. He fought hard to keep his stomach contents down.

"And she shouldn't," Edmon said, moving a carton of books to the front door. "I take care of the storeroom. Do all the heavy work. But then you know that. As my father always said, it's so good to have a man around the house."

He got out of there before he killed the thing. Then of course the damned thing couldn't be killed, though he entertained the idea of finding out.

∞∞∞

Ronny showed up at Dina's first thing in the morning with a dozen donuts and three large coffees. It had not occurred to him that the Lodge's famous guest was already receiving five-star treatment. It had not occurred to him that it was seven forty-five and they might still be asleep. But his mother loved those doughy maple donuts and he loved his mother. Nothing bad was ever gonna happen to her again. And the day would come when she would look at him and not be reminded. He wouldn't think about that now. He did his best never to think about that. How his mother came to be his mother, how he was conceived–he never thought about it. Often he would have a nightmare about it, but he would never consciously think about it because it was not to be thought about. Ronny Fergel played this broken record on a daily basis.

"I guess you're on your way over to Page's?" his mother asked.

He washed down the cruller with coffee. "I am. They got a lot of books to push this weekend, Mother. Boxes full. All titles."

"I hope she can sell most of it," Dina said. "Have you looked outside? Awful-looking out there and she's got all those stalls set up."

"Walter wants to head back first thing Sunday morning." He licked the sugar off his fingers. "Joe's giving us a lift into Boston. We're flying back, so you can hang on to the Mustang, Mother, since you'll be staying a few more days."

"Why does Walter want to return so soon? I've hardly talked to him since we got here."

"We have a crew on location scouts." He snuck a glance at Dina. He had to be careful not to say too much in front of her because she had that personality thing. "They're due back sometime Monday, so Walter's anxious for status reports. Oh, I gave Maggie a bunch of Aramaic cassettes that I made but I forgot to get her number. Do you have it handy, Dina? I still have to go over a few things with her in case I don't see her before we leave."

"What's Maggie need with a bunch of Aramaic cassettes?" Dina asked, jotting down the number.

He intentionally stuffed his mouth again. He wasn't supposed to let that slip. "She'll fill you in. I gotta go." Hopefully, Maggie wouldn't mind his passing the buck.

Elizabeth halted him at the door. "You and your book fairs, you big kid," she said, giving him a hug. "Ronny, I'm worried about your being in Pages. I want you to promise me something, alright?"

"I know, Mother. Joe was my wake-up call this morning. He told me to stay out of the *cella*. Can you believe it?"

"Then do as he asked. People have had problems entering that room prematurely. You've heard the stories."

"Won't hurt to stay out of there," Dina shouted from the kitchen.

"Guys." He couldn't believe Joe called. Obviously Walter hadn't filled him in. "Walter. Me. The crew and everybody who's already been back don't have to worry about that door thing. Because we've *been* back. That door is just a head exercise anyway, like it is for students of the Dalai Lama. I know Joe believes the demons are real. We've had numerous debates on this subject. You know that. The demons are of the mind, Mother."

"Then why would Joe tell you not to go down there?"

She could make him so impatient. "Power of suggestion. Our training. Our training in self-awareness. We all know what our demons are and how destructive they are. That room represents the epicenter for the headspace of everyone involved in this project. Geez."

"Do you know what your demons are?" With Dina off in the kitchen banging plates and cutlery around, he pretty much guessed she'd nail him with this question. Again.

"Of course I know, Mother. And I really don't have the time to get into it with you now. I'll stay out of the basement. Okay?" He kissed Elizabeth on the cheek. "Goodbye, Mother."

Ronny disregarded the shudder that passed through him.

∞∞∞

"I think I make your son nervous," Dina said, a sardonic smile on her face. "Think I'll do a little skit with him, Sister. Maybe ask him out. Does he know about us at Marianlake that Halloween?"

"Yes, he knows. Just as he knows about me—and his father, whoever he was. I tell you this so you won't worry about slipping up around him, Dina. I often wonder how he'd handle meeting his father."

"What's to handle, Sister? His father jumped outta the bushes and raped his mother, a novitiate at the time. Ronny might want to redecorate his lower anatomy. Who's this Father Crouse I keep hearing of in connection with you?"

Elizabeth sat back on the couch, stared at the blackening sky over the water. "Father Crouse was my therapist and I adored him for getting me through that nightmare. We still keep in touch some, but seeing him still reminds me of that time. I've learned to accept that I can't let go of some things, that some things I'm taking to the grave."

"I still break into a sweat when I smell lemons or anything mentholated."

"When I look deeply into my son's eyes, especially now that he's older, bigger–I'm reminded of that night, of his father's eyes. It's painful sometimes and I know Ronny can feel it. I live with it, Dina. Don't empower your demons by fighting them. Alain and Joe will help you with that."

"So looking forward to it. I guess you must wonder if he's inherited nasties from daddy."

"That moan. Ronny has the same moan but I would never tell him that. I would never tell him that sometimes I awaken hearing it."

"What made you tell him the truth?"

Elizabeth's smile hardened. "I've been called mother for most of my life, except by my son who called me Aunt Liz. A strong bond had formed between us as aunt and nephew and I wanted more. My sister and brother-in-law haven't completely forgiven me for telling him but they're working on it."

"Any regrets telling him?"

"No, Dina, not a one. Now enough of me and my past. I want to hear about you girls and your present. What happened to Carol Ann last night?"

Dina spiked her fingers through her short curls. "Joe Ross is back in her life—that's what happened."

"You mean she still loves him?"

"Well, whatever it is, she's *still.* I guess she fantasized about them picking up where they left off and it's definitely not happening."

"Even so—but practically drinking yourself into a coma? That's about more than disappointment and unrequited love."

"I know. But here's the scary thing, Sister. It's recent. Carol Ann was never a drinker. Never a pill-popper. This has all been in the last year. It may have been dormant and something woke it up. I don't know but something's going on. It's getting to be like Halloween at Marianlake all over again."

"You're right of course. That entity has disturbed you and Maggie. Naturally it's going after Carol Ann, too. All of us, at some point, at some time."

"Well I might get annoyed with Carol Ann, but I'm there for her. It's like she's getting hit the worst. She had the dyslexia all those years ago. Then the Joe obsession. The drinking. And now that red door thing in her basement. I think she's fought with the most guts, Sister."

Elizabeth smiled and sprung back one of Dina's curls. "I'm inclined to disagree."

"What I don't get is how come all of us missed seeing her get so wasted last night. Where the hell were we? Where did she get all that booze?"

"I know. Maggie and I were wondering the same thing on the phone this morning. Could she have taken something with it? Maggie mentioned sleeping pills."

"No idea. Absolutely none. Next time she could vomit and choke in her sleep. It's all scaring me. Maggie, too."

"I'm happy to see Maggie looking so beautiful."

"Well, if there's a file on all of us somewhere, you must've heard of Maggie's agoraphobia. Two years she didn't leave the house."

"I know. But somehow after talking to her last night, I get the feeling she's been trying to guard Pandora's box for selfless reasons. What do you think?"

"After our visit with her at Dracula's castle, I'm thinking along those lines, too. Then she got the marks and now she's here with all of us. I'm thrilled about that." Dina cleared her throat a couple of times.

"What? What else is there?"

"Maggie is Maggie, Sister. Pandora's paradox. A young, beautiful recluse who keeps her emotions to herself and her private life private. Last Christmas, Carol Ann found her in her bedroom, prostate on the floor."

Elizabeth couldn't help giggling. "Pros*trate* on the floor."

"Whatever."

"Maggie's deeply religious, I can see that."

Dina paused, took a few easy breaths. "Carol Ann thinks Maggie's in love."

"Really? With who? Oh no—not Joe?"

"No, course not. Maggie would never keep that from Carol Ann. She'd risk any relationship to bring the truth forward."

"Who then?"

"No idea. Carol Ann's asked and Maggie shook off the question. Said she doesn't date, so how could she be in love."

"What makes Carol Ann think that in the first place?"

"She says Maggie's symptomatic. Her energy. Captivating smile. Her soft, sexy voice. With all the scary stuff going on with her work, Maggie's still 'out there' somewhere else. I've seen the smile on her face and in her eyes when she thinks no one else's looking."

"But she's smiling, Dina. Not frowning. And when she's ready to talk, she'll talk."

"That's what I said. But you know our Carol Ann Marple."

"So what about you now, Dina? Has the bad press hurt your career?"

"Nah. My life is hash the public eats up. The press knows I've had therapy. They just don't know what for. I prefer they think it's all about the temper, which is partially true." Dina smiled, took a big, healthy stretch of her arms. "Being here with all of you again—I can't tell you what it means to me, how it's helped me.

"It doesn't feel like a virus anymore. That Alain is something else. Wow." Dina's eyes misted a little. "And now it's making me sappy! Look at me. Thank-you, Sister Liz, for all your letters over the years. They kept me sane. I've kept them all and still take them out and read them."

"You're very welcome, my friend."

"Bugged me though, that I couldn't tell anybody about the letters, especially since so many of the postmarks were from Rome. Exciting."

"Bugged me too. Joe caught me mailing a few of them. One time I'm sure he saw your name. But he didn't say anything. He never has."

"I've wondered something about Joe Ross for years."

"What's that?"

"What makes him so, how do I say ... *qualified*? Don't get me wrong, I love the guy, but for lack of a better expression—how does he rate all this?"

"You know about the angel on his tenth birthday?"

"Yeah, yeah Sister, I know. But lots of people have had similar stuff happen. And they didn't get to spend five years in Vatican territory. You've practically lived with him."

"True, and for years I used to wonder, too. All I can tell you now is that Joe doesn't know. And if Joe doesn't know, and nobody wonders more than him, trust me—how can the rest of us know?"

"Bet Alain knows."

"Bet he does."

Dina leaned over and gave Sister Elizabeth a peck on the cheek. "Joe's wonderful. Alain, too. At least there's one good thing I've had to focus on this last while–Alain got that *thing* out of me, and I'm remembering more which means there's fewer of me. Hah! I can't understand why I'm not more frightened. It amazes me 'cause I've been frightened my whole life. I guess I've been worrying a lot about Carol Ann and Joe. Maggie, mostly. Alain says the cross is sometimes a gift. Do you have any idea why Ronny would give Maggie all those Aramaic tapes?"

"None, unless she asked to bone up on the language. Ask her."

Dina went over and stood by the window. Her neck and shoulder muscles had tensed into spongy lumps. "I will definitely ask her. It looks so cold out there this morning. More like November instead of June. Gray streaks across the sky. Black way over there beyond the Cove. Moody weather. Know what Joe would say?"

"What's that?"

"Dark angels are preying."

∞∞∞∞

By noon, Alain showed up with Claude, Tracy and Simon. Simon, who had Joe by the hand, knew exactly what he wanted—Detective Jack Shade in the Case of the Spotted Goose. His parents decided that Jack Shade was really Sam Spade but kept this information to themselves. Simon seemed to prefer hanging out with Joe more than Alain. Joe thought it was odd that a tighter bond hadn't formed, especially since they were brothers who seldom saw each other.

The ambiance between them seemed more friendly than family and they conversed little. Joe kept the boy close at his side. Like Boston's Mattapan after dark, malevolent entities lingered about, only these malevolent entities didn't need to carry heaters. The rest of the Marianlake bunch showed up early in support of Carol Ann who made her appearance shortly before two.

Carol Ann hadn't recovered enough to face any of them and preferred to avoid them as much as possible. Still sick and looking it, she embraced herself in an effort to keep warm while she mingled. She overheard one customer say she looked like a shivering rack of bones. What happened to her last night? How could she abuse herself to this extent?

The sight of Joe and Maggie chatting and munching at the hotdog stand made her regurgitate some of last night's brandy. Oh to go over and apologize, throw herself at the mercy of the court. But she couldn't face them yet and snuck off, leaving the book fair in Edmon and Ronny's capable hands.

While Fathers' Vaux and Andre struck up a conversation with a young tourist couple from Quebec, the crowd thickened on the street. It was such a dismal day. Obviously the townsfolk had nothing better to do, so profits flowed.

By five, Edmon asked Ronny to give him a hand in the storeroom. There was a box containing some bestseller diet book down there and only one copy left in the stall. Edmon made sure Joe had not seen them talking. When Ronny hoofed it toward the basement, Edmon glanced back at Alain and shot him a piercing look. Knowing Alain had been watching from across the street at Corey's, he already had the hardcover in hand. He held up the book and pointed to the title.

Farewell My Lovely.

∞∞∞

Ronny stopped on the bottom stair and checked out the big, cold basement. Obviously, Carol Ann stored the inventory down here in a hundred boxes crammed into four walls of aluminum shelving. The dehumidifier, probably as old as Sanskrit rattled and clicked in the damp, musty room. And there was this other odor, rank, like an unwashed armpit on a crowded summer bus.

The room seemed offensive to the eye as well as the spirit. He was probably creeped out because of all the babble about the red door being down here. Just proved he was right about the demons being of the mind because the dark thoughts were heavier than frozen rope—case in point, like how he was conceived. Or rather—ill-conceived.

All three doors down here were open, one of which lead to the laundry-furnace room. He heard a dripping faucet and the air conditioner click off. It was difficult to tell what the other two were and it didn't really matter anyhow, since he already told Edmon he'd bring up the box of books from the storeroom. He assumed the storeroom was to his immediate left, the room with all the crammed shelves. Ronny looked for traces of red paint on the doorjambs. No traces. Also no traces of the box Edmon asked him to get.

The two remaining rooms were adjacent. As he studied the next from the threshold he scratched his chin and neck, cognizant of his racing heartbeat. Carol Ann had boxes strewn all over the floor so it seemed obvious she'd made a recent attempt to sort through them, particularly the one marked 'Brent'. Seemed the lady wanted all traces of her ex-husband removed from the premises. No darn box of diet books in here, either.

At the entrance to the last room, Carol Ann had a stash of wine on racks. He really didn't give two hoots about wine but Carol Ann sure did. She must've had over a hundred bottles on these racks, probably more than Mr. Corey across the street and he had a bar and restaurant. She'd devoted two rows exclusively to brandy and cognac—Courvoisier and five-star Metaxa. He glanced at the door jamb then read the Greek label on the Metaxa, feeling a swell of pride. He spent five minutes on the label, even though he was able to read it in one. Geez, he should get a move on because Edmon was probably waiting for that box.

Why didn't he grab a bottle of water for the dry throat? He moved closer to the door. At least the stink had stopped. This was a good sign. He checked the doorjamb up close. The inside of this door was a putrid green. He heaved in a breath and gently pulled the door a few inches away from the wall. This was uncool behavior. After all, he *knew* the concept behind this room so he should know better than to get this jumpy.

He looked behind the door. *Oh no. Aw, geez.* There were coats and coats of it. Deep red paint. It looked like blood, dried and caked on. The look of it sickened him and he pushed the door back against the wall. Find the box quick and get the hell outta here. Then he saw it on the floor in the middle of the room just as Edmon had said.

Oh yeah, this was it. Edmon said it was the box with purchase Order No. 214 scrawled on the side in black marker. But where was that other book he wanted? What did he say–old filing cabinet–white cheesecloth lightly thrown over it? Edmon wanted to put it in Carol Ann's antique bookcase. Okay. Get the book, the box, and get out. He rushed into the room like a man collecting his luggage twenty minutes before flight-time.

The cheesecloth fell to the floor when he scooped up the book. It took a few seconds before clicking in, but at least it clicked in. Latin was still his favorite language and Walter had told him about this book years ago. It was the first thing he wrote at length and it was special to him. Holy cow, what an incredible find! Walter's book! No way was this book going into Carol Ann's bookcase. If this book was going anywhere it was going straight to Walter. Carol Ann would understand.

"Carol Ann might, but I won't." Edmon closed the door.

His stomach dropped and he felt a slight stab of pain in his chest. The room smelled bad again. Suddenly it hit him. This man had been down here all along. Following him. Watching him. Oh God. Oh God.

"How did you know I said that? I didn't say that out loud?" Then his voice went childlike, "Did I?"

"Put the box and the book in the hall, Ronny. I'll take them up."

His neck started itching bad and he wanted to claw at it. He had shingles once. This was a heck of a lot worse. Maybe he was allergic to this guy, Edmon. He tried holding his breath in shifts because of the stink.

He summoned the courage to speak with confidence, "I'll be happy to take them up for you but Walter's been looking for this book a long time. You probably don't know but he actually wrote this. So I'd better hang onto it. Anyway, I'm feeling a little under the weather, Edmon. Think I'll head out."

Edmon raised his chin and dramatically sniffed the air. Ronny saw himself in a funeral parlor then, sniffing carnations, sniffing them among rows and rows of empty black caskets. He hated black caskets.

Edmon brought him a chair, bobbed a bony white finger at him.

"Sit."

He shook his head, said he'd stand, thanks. He didn't want to sit down. He needed to keep the feet moving like the Dalai Lama said.

"Sit."

Ronny sat in the chair and watched the room fade away.

17. Behind The Door

Elysium is as far as to
The very nearest Room
If in that Room a Friend await
Felicity or Doom—
What Fortitude the Soul contains
That it can so endure
The accent of a coming Foot—
The opening of a Door—

Emily Dickinson

Ronny stood amidst a sea of caskets with raised lids in an area reeking of old paperbacks and sweaty feet. The corpses were blond with bluish hands gripping sections of taut rope. Most wore slippers, the plush kind, except these had gold question marks embroidered on the toes. He felt compelled to keep walking, to get names. Why the question marks? Why all blond? What did they have to do with him? At the top end of the second row, the corpses began to change, subtly at first.

The caskets in this row had blindfolds pinned to the fold of the interior panels beside photographs of the dead, also blindfolded in the photographs. Trying to steady himself, he leaned against the top frame of a casket and looked ahead, combing this hellhole for an exit. His only escape was through a large opening in the wall about ten feet away. But when he made a run for it, the opening sealed. He heard a scream in his head and found himself at the top of the third row lined with black coffins. He hated black coffins. Oh God, oh God— the blindfolded blond men in this row lay with exposed genitals.

Ronny opened his eyes wide and screamed, for real this time.

Jolted back in the chair and oblivious to solid ground, he saw Edmon sitting across from him, so relaxed and comfortable. The man had kind eyes. So very kind. Was his father in one of those coffins? Which blond guy was he?

"Poor Ronny Fergel," Edmon said in mock remorse. "Only half an identity. I want you to run another errand for me, son. And you will be handsomely rewarded. I'll let you have your book, but first it stays on your person while you take a little trip."

It felt like he was floating on one of those air mattresses. "What trip?"

"To Angelfish Cove," Edmon said. "You love Angelfish Cove. So that won't be a problem, will it?"

"I work for Walter Bayard, and it's his book. I'm leaving now." Ronny made it as far as the door, which his conscious mind remembered as the last action taken in this room.

He felt rather content here on the road. He didn't have to drive. All he had to do was navigate and keep the music happening in the cassette deck. Easy. Holidays were so great. But the bridge a few miles ahead looked high, uncomfortably high. It was one of those multi-tiered jobs, the kind that disappeared into the clouds. He said to his friend,

'You know, we could take the Falcon Road exit instead of the bridge. Be more scenic. It's this next cut-off right here ... '

The friend ignored him and the bridge was fast approaching. Ronny looked up, and up, and up. The car climbed onto the first tier. It was already such a long way down and he was in this crappy, convertible heap. No seat belts on his side. Second tier. More cars with honking horns and raging drivers riding bumpers. He looked up again into a silver maze, hundreds, no, thousands of feet in the air.

'Get us off this bridge,' he hollered at his friend. 'Just get us off, get us off of here!'

The more he hollered the faster the car shot upward until he found himself lying on his back with the car pointed at the heavens. Finally they reached the clouds and the car stopped and slowly, the friend aimed the nose downward. Yes, thank-you, oh thank-you!

His friend looked at him and said, 'Nothing like reinforcing a positive thought, I always say.' He flew out of the car then, falling and dying through miles of steel. At least he could die soon ... except ... there was no bottom.

"Sorry, son," Edmon said. "I flunked the Drivers Ed course." Edmon grinned at his superior, who had been enjoying his creativity. "You need more exercise, lad. Another lap around the Cove."

He wriggled slightly in his chair, like a catatonic braving shock treatments. Was this Hell, he wondered? Why was he here? What did he do?

Edmon wiped the tears from his cheek. "I want you to take Walter Bayard's book back to Marianlake with you, Ronny. And the boss can't know. Do you understand?" When he didn't answer, Edmon looked to his superior, "He understands. I'll give him his instructions and send him on his way."

"Not quite yet," Edmon's superior said. "One last dance with the devil, if you'll pardon the expression. Make it a good one. I did warn Remiel about Iris, didn't I? I warned him twice—Iris goes or somebody important leaves here as damaged goods. He actually challenged me to choose someone better qualified. Remiel doesn't know me as well as Rafe. I take things so literally, so to heart. I'll be on my way now, Edmon. We will see you up at Marianlake."

"Will you be doing any more visiting while you're here?"

The demon's saffron eyes shone with pleasure before taking its leave.

Edmon understood its unspoken answer. "He gets to have all the fun," he said. "And you're not much of a challenge, lad. Your friend, Joe Ross, now there's a challenge. It's hard to rattle his bolts, but you rattle your own. And you thought you could handle this room on your own too, without JR. Or Remiel. You lost your mettle when you learned of your father, lad. Afraid you inherited a few of his genes, are you? Afraid you'll get left behind again?

"Your fears have been our treasure in this mission, Ronny. I'm so fond of Emerson's infamous crack. We thank you. A shame you've misplaced your angels, though. They're a bit like cops, you know, never around when you need one, but I'm getting detoured here when it's you I should be detouring.

"You're going to take a little trip out of here, Ronny, the first of two. A little trip out of here and *back* to here. Hate being left behind, do you? Tell me, which do you find more frightening, abandonment or claustrophobia? We'll find out. In the meantime have a rest now, lad—in the loveliest of ebony coffins, with the lid welded shut. Enjoy ..."

The sun was setting on Angelfish Cove. How he had come to love this place. It was easy to understand why Walter was so anxious to return, why he fashioned it into the timeless place it was. He wandered happily along the boardwalk, stopping outside Corey's Cafe Beanery to smell the lobster cooking in garlic butter. He stepped aside to let a line of cyclists whir by him. Mm-mm that lobster smelled better and better. He would go inside for a bite and say hello to Mr. Corey. Maybe he'd run into some of the gang here.

He gave the inflated bourbon bottle a playful punch. Looked like they were preparing for a party. A party two nights in a row? Wow. He smiled at the waitresses as he made his way to the bar. He hadn't seen bell-bottoms, headbands, and tie-dyed tops since he was a kid. He chose to sit at the bar because it was elevated and he could check out the action.

Mr. Corey was behind the bar talking to some guy in a burgundy suit. If it weren't for the voice, he would never have recognized him. He looked so different. Then everything looked different–the room, the staff, the entire general atmosphere. He began to feel mildly uncomfortable. When Mr. Corey turned around, he gaped at him. John Corey looked twenty-five years younger. He nodded and Mr. Corey nodded politely back. Couldn't be him. Had to be a son or nephew or somebody. Besides, this guy didn't seem to know him. Amazing resemblance, though. Totally amazing.

"Is Mr. Corey senior, about?" he asked.

"Beg your pardon?" the relative said.

"Mr. Corey senior? John Corey?"

"I answer to both," the man said in a friendly manner. "Can I help you? Are you all right?"

"Set him up with the bourbon du jour, John," a familiar voice said from across the bar. "Straight."

Ronny looked across the bar and when he saw Edmon, his stomach flipped over. One look at Edmon brought it all back. The book fair this afternoon. Pages. The Red Door. Suddenly he wanted that bourbon more than he ever wanted a drink in his life. He watched Edmon saunter over toward him. He didn't walk, he sauntered. And he seemed to be taking forever. Ohh, God, forever. Where in forever was he?

Edmon sat at his right, positively beaming. "My advice would be to drink that drink, lad."

He took the advice.

"Good." Edmon gestured for another shot of the same. "Experiencing dark memories?"

"Why did you bring me here?" he asked, knocking back the second bourbon.

"I want to make my requests clear to you, Ronny. What better place to do it? You like it here."

"Yeah, right. Where in time exactly is here? I know about time travel, you know I do. Did you get me here in the machine?"

Edmon sighed. "No, no. So you will be happy to know that our time here is limited. But to be honest, Ronny, that is my intention. I want to bring you back here in Walter's machine. Tomorrow night."

"Am I to understand you're not dumping me here now?"

"Correct."

"What do you want me to do? Did I ask you who the hell you are, I can't remember."

"You know who I am. I dwell in the unholy hall of fame. I, along with my associates am the flipside of the record as I once heard Priest Richard refer to us. We really are that infernal music parents order their children to turn off. I am your sweetest, darkest angel, dear lad. And you are at my service."

"In your dreams, Edmon. I live and work in God's Light."

"And here I am to help you re-affirm your faith. Through me, your faith is strengthened. Yes?"

"What do you want?"

"You will leave for Marianlake tomorrow morning. I want you to take Walter Bayard's book with you. Of course

he cannot know you have it. Tomorrow night you will step into Walter's machine and return it here to me. In 1967. You will conceal the book here in John Corey's attic. Then you can step safely back into your little time machine and go home to your little 1991 world where I suppose you belong. That's it."

"I'm gonna save us a lot of time here by asking what happens if I say no?"

"Your father really was in one of those coffins, Ronny. But that coffin scene sprang out of your own fears. When I fed it back to you, I was just playing. Truth is, your father is very much alive and continues to destroy practically everything he touches. Your mother still lives and works in Brooklyn. As does he. Matter of fact, they inhabit the same neighborhood.

"He knows about you, lad. Unfortunately though, his parole officer caught him stalking your mother and warned him off her. Oh how he would love to be a part of your lives. He lives well, your dad. He has money, and a lawyer second to none. Your mother doesn't know he's around. Yet. The authorities spoke with her superiors who didn't see the need for her to know, to live in fear again. So her superiors are watching him. The authorities are watching him. And he knows they're watching him. But I would not have a problem arranging things for him, Ronny, if you'd like. It's obvious he still finds your mother extremely attractive, and such a challenge."

"What's to keep you from not living up to your end of the bargain?"

"Oh come on, lad. We may have a reputation for being adroit liars, but we never welsh on our promises. Everybody knows that. Don't even think about declining, Ronny. I can read your mind. GOD will take care of your mother and all that. But remember where you are. I can simply leave you

here and find someone else. What will happen to your mission then?"

"Your objective is to destroy this mission."

"That's right. But you have your unshakable faith, God's angels surround you. So what's your faith telling you now? Do you really think God is going to allow me to destroy this mission? Don't you believe I'm going to get my comeuppance? Look on the bright side. I'm affording you a wonderful test of faith here. The greatest tests of faith do not come from God, Ronny. They come from me."

His arms flopped at his side and the lump in his throat actually hurt. There was no way he could fight Edmon from here. No way. No way could he be left alone in this place. In this time. Besides, Edmon said he would only find somebody else to dump here anyway.

"Why do you want the book left here and why return tomorrow night? Why not take care of business now and be done with it?"

"Remiel saw us. Tomorrow night we won't be seen and tomorrow night is when I will update you. This party will still be in full swing. I have to get you home now. You'll have no memory of this until we meet again. When asked, you will say you never were in Pages basement. No one will know. All you need concern yourself with is getting that book to me tomorrow night. Concentrate on the book's destination— Angelfish Cove 1967. Now, before I send you on your way, allow me to give you a few detailed instructions for Marianlake..."

... Ronny took the thick book with the brown leather cover upstairs for Edmon who'd been patiently waiting. It was already dark. Tucking it under his arm, he walked slowly toward the door. The street looked pretty through the Japanese lanterns Carol Ann had strung above the stalls. People weren't minding this horrible weather too much. How nice ... how nice.

"Ronny," Edmon called after him. "Let me give you a bag for that. Here you go. Thanks for all your help today, son. And enjoy the book."

∞∞∞

Alain stood quietly across the street where no one could see him, except Rafe. Huddled alone in the alley by Corey's service entrance he implored Rafe for counsel, but no answer came. Pages Bookstore blurred through his tears.

∞∞∞

Maggie turned up the intensity a notch on her industrial flashlight and re-examined the base of the statue. Aside from two faint scratches made in transit, it looked marvelous as always. It was silly to inspect it in the dark, but they'd just delivered it and she couldn't wait. How wonderful to have it home.

She looked adoringly at the little cottage. With the statue here, the cottage was her real home. Not temporary. Permanent. No more high walls and complex security systems. Freedom. Now if the headaches would ease up she wouldn't have to think about herself at all. She could concentrate fully on this mission, on Carol Ann, and get back to work. The door slammed inside the cottage. Only one person she knew slammed doors this way. Only one person had that endearing clunky walk.

"What're you doing out there in the dark?" Dina shouted from the porch. "Oh, you sent for it! Your Saint Michael. He looks great there, Maggie."

"Have you eaten?" she asked, plodding toward Dina. Every step made her head ache worse. "I made some gazpacho this afternoon."

"I just came by for a visit. Figured if you weren't working we could chat."

She sat beside Dina on the porch swing, her body tensed. "Anything specific you want to chat about?"

"Well yeah, actually. Ronny stopped by this morning on his way to Pages. He mentioned something about giving you a stack of Aramaic cassettes that he made?"

"Mm-hmm. That he did."

"So what gives? We need the basics, right? Don't hide stuff from me, Maggie. I got the feeling Ronny didn't want to tell me something."

She reached over and took Dina's hand. "I'll be staying longer than the rest of you guys."

"What do you mean? How much longer?"

"I paint, Dina. I'll have before me one of the greatest, if not *the* greatest moment. I've been asked to paint the Nativity. And more after that if I want. Which will take me a little longer than twenty-four hours." She searched Dina's eyes.

Dina's chin quivered. "Who all knows about this?"

"Joe, Alain. Ronny, of course. Walter too, I expect."

"Did you intend to keep it a secret?"

"No, Dina. Not a secret. I agreed to do it less than two weeks ago and I needed to keep it to myself for a while. There's no fee for this, but still it's the greatest commission I will ever receive. Imagine it, Dina. The Nativity!"

"How long do you figure it'll take?"

"Three or four weeks. I'm told the Holy Family won't be there much longer than that. I'll have to work fast. But I expect my hands will be guided."

"So ... you're gonna be staying back alone. In ancient Palestine. Communicating to people using what— twentieth century Aramaic for Dummies?"

"I won't exactly be alone, will I?"

"Aw come on, Maggie! You know what I mean. One of us should stay back and be there with you."

"Dina, there'll be groups arriving every twenty-four hours. And they will all know who I am. My status will be logged in every group leader's report for the duration of my stay. Add to that the state-of-the-art communication system Joe and Alain have arranged for me. Don't worry. I'm going to have enough problems dealing with Carol Ann when I tell her. So be happy for me. Imagine. Look what I'll be bringing home."

Dina gave her hand a squeeze. "I am happy for you, Mag. Really. I'm going to be the first one in line waiting to see it the second you get back. It is a thrill pill, isn't it?"

"Yes. But I don't think Carol Ann's going to swallow it."

"Carol Ann doesn't seem to be swallowing any of it these days. It's like she's suddenly turned off everything about this mission. Everything except Joe, that is."

"I know. Her moods are darker. She's suspicious of everyone. Every day I find myself looking for new ways to bring her around. It's like she's hooked on this negative feeling, like she's unconsciously hoping for something to go wrong."

Dina let go of her hand and wiped the sweat from her brow.

"Dina? You okay?"

"What you said about Carol Ann's mood. It seems to be catching. I find I'm more wound up than six musicians before show time. I leave for New York next week to begin rehearsals for my tour."

"I know," Maggie said. "I read it in the *Boston Globe*. I can't believe it's time already. That's quite an entourage you've got there, all those famous musicians joining you. I'm so proud of you."

"The thing is, with so much going on here and this sudden low mood and everything ... I find myself wanting to postpone. I'd really like to stay here in the Cove. I don't want to leave you guys."

"You can't postpone. The last thing you need is another legal jackpot to wrangle out of. You have to go. Besides, you'll be stationary in New York during rehearsals for close to three months, so you can come back here on weekends. It's a forty-minute flight, Ms. Private Jet."

"True, you're right. How you feeling? The headaches?"

She wouldn't worry Dina. Everybody was so easily worried these days. "Migraine. Nothing showed up in my blood tests or x-rays. Probably related to seasonal allergies, that kind of thing. My doctor wrote me prescriptions for antihistamine and Fiorinal." She wouldn't tell Dina or Carol Ann—not even Joe or Alain—that the headaches were getting worse.

∞∞∞

Maggie went inside to answer the phone and she followed, stopping in the kitchen for a bowl of gazpacho. A hit of spicy food would fix her up. Of course Joe and Alain would watch over Maggie. How could they not, and she'd stay on their butts checking on Maggie during stage breaks, if necessary. Poor Carol Ann. She had to stop ragging on her so much. You don't slam people when they're down, especially people you love no matter how nuts they get you.

The soup was making her hot, not horny hot—feverish hot. Dumb of her to eat spicy food during a sweat, but hey, this was good. She couldn't be catching a bug now. No time. Too busy. No bugs, no bugs.

Maggie was holding her long locks on top of her head and said 'mm-hmm' a lot on the phone. Maggie always held her hair up like that when she was thinking hard or questioning something. She gathered Ronny was on the other end of the line because Maggie said the word 'cassettes'.

"That's odd," Maggie said, hanging up.

She set down the bowl and dabbed the sweat from her upper lip. "What's odd?"

"That was Ronny. He called to tell me to copy the cassettes in case one got wrecked or misplaced. Then he says they're leaving first thing in the morning. Joe's taking him and Walter to the airport. Then he says goodbye. Then I say goodbye. Then before he hung up he said, 'See you around Corey's'. When am I going to see him at Corey's? They're leaving. What an odd thing to say."

"I bet he wandered into that room. Bet that's why he sounded weird." She updated Maggie on the morning's conversation.

"Well, if that's the case," Maggie speculated, "Joe and Alain will have to bring him around. I'm sure they've anticipated this happening with one of us."

"Funny how that room's so full of this post-hypnotic stuff."

"I believe that room is filled with much more than that."

Dina finished off the last of the gazpacho and said goodnight. There were calls to make, checks to write, and two contracts to sign. Since the checks and contracts had to be couriered to New York tonight, she figured she'd better get cracking in case this really was a bug. 'At least all my personalities are good businesswomen', she said aloud on the drive back to the lodge. 'We read all of our contracts with a magnifying glass, don't we?'

Although her mood was still low, today had been the first day in weeks she wasn't pissed off about something. She stopped at the front desk on her way in and asked for some hot tea and honey. Those contracts weren't getting read tonight, who was she kidding? She was in rough shape. *Get real, Dina.*

In the early morning hours as her body sweated out the fever, her head was drenched in music from the Lake Oz days. That had to be eight albums and a hundred songs ago. As the tunes played, she watched little Dina and rockstar Dina dance around her bed, with little Dina giggling and rockstar Dina giving orders. Hot. Very hot. Her arms hurt and were hard to lift. She watched while both Dina's stopped and smiled down at her, the sweetest most loving smiles. Smiles to herself from herself. It felt wonderful. *She* felt wonderful. So happy. So loved. Both Dina's closed their eyes and put their cheeks out for a kiss. A young man kissed them. Fair and radiant, he sat down on the bed and kissed her forehead.

"Alain," she whispered, "you look so great. So different."

"You're seeing me through your fever." He traced two fingers across her brow. "What hurts?"

"I don't know. My arms, I think."

Alain took her right arm and cradled it in his own. "Sweet Dina. Thinking and worrying so much about Maggie and Carol Ann."

"Am I getting those marks, Alain? Can you see for me?"

His smile was bittersweet. "I believe so."

"What's wrong?" She wanted to touch his face but her arms were lead.

"We're all in for a rough ride over the next several years. Even Joe. Sing for them, Dina. As often as you can. And never despair. I'm here and God isn't going anywhere. Remember that."

Alain's words didn't stick for long. Later that morning, she awakened with the marks and called everybody to come over quick and see. She felt all goosy woosy when she saw Alain at mid-day and told him most of what he'd said the night before had already slipped away.

"I remember you told me to sing for them as often as I could. But there was something else. It's like a dream now. Hazy."

"It's all still there in your subconscious, Dina." He mimicked her habit of tapping her temple and she cracked up.

"So tell me again."

"I told you to never despair, to remember that I'm here and so is God. Enjoy this day, Dina."

∞∞∞

Joe inhaled the morning air as he drove along the coastal Atlantic to the airport. A day's getaway—hallelujah. After he dropped off Walter and Ronny, he planned to see Regnault's *Automedon With the Horses of Achilles*. The equine masterpiece of Achilles and his two divine horses was currently in storage at Boston's Museum of Fine Arts, but Maggie had made a phone call.

Getting him a private viewing was her way of cheering him up since Suffolk Downs was closed until January '92. Bummer. He would've loved to catch a race but maybe it was best to dodge the old dream, for a while. That Ocala land deal he was going to check out in two weeks had fallen through.

"What are you thinking, Joe?" Walter asked.

He smiled, reminiscent, "My mother's collection of horse ribbons. They're with my grandmother in Medford." He was about to mention the land deal op going bust, but didn't. "Well, I can look forward to seeing equine perfection in Judea 6, that's for sure."

"Only Roman generals and aristocrats ride the cream and their military *trivialis* ride pony breeds. We'll be in cave country, Joe. So, don't look too hard."

These were Ronny's first words in twenty-five miles. They were also his last until they said their goodbyes at the airport. Ronny had a spur stuck in his heel today. Probably down because they'd cut the trip in AFC short. Odd how looking at Ronny now reminded him of Simon and the other night Simon reminded him of Alain.

When Ronny disappeared behind the baggage check he told Walter he'd call tonight, after he did a little consciousness-raising behind the Red Door. He should call Ronny too, although he had no idea what he wanted to say to him. Ronny was sort of a kid, a brilliant kid who made him about as comfortable as sitting on cold porcelain. He had no idea why. It was definitely time for a little lazy two-step in that room.

The curator, a friendly, easy-going guy named George, met him at five after closing and took him down to the storage area.

"Why is the painting in storage?" he asked.

"It was one of the Museum's most popular paintings since it got here in 1890. But like all things popular it went out of style. I intend to rectify that. It's a magnificent painting, but at ten by ten, it does occupy space. I'll be here until ten," he said, nodding at two Brinks guys hauling stuff out of the storage area. "Just stop by my office on your way out and I'll come down and lock up." He pointed out the painting, told him to feel free to look at anything else down here and then left him to peruse.

As it happened, he never got to see Regnault's painting.

"Excuse, please," one of the two Brink's men said. They'd returned with a massive painting and leaned it against the wall where he stood. The elder and beefier of the two was slightly out of breath.

"Need a hand?" he asked. The thing had to be twenty feet high.

"Sure. You can help us unwrap and pull off the cardboard corners. We'll lift 'er up while you yank the paper away."

"Wow," he said, once they had the thing peeled. "What is this?"

"William Blake's *St. Michael the Archangel*," the younger said. "Somethin' isn't it."

He stood back, hands on hip, and looked up and up and up. "Wooo, you said it. A friend of mine would love this." Too bad he didn't grab the camera. He could've snapped it for Maggie.

"Well, we gotta hit the road."

He nodded, still entranced by the painting.

"We'll leave you to it, Joe. Thanks for your help."

"Right. Sure. You're welcome."

He smiled at the sight of the Archangel's foot on the defeated Lucifer's head. Guess there was no getting away from angels, not that he wanted to. Maggie would love to see this. She often spoke of William Blake's work. Interesting. Brinks were so cautious and those guys trusted him alone down here.

The painting seemed as animate as Maggie's statue. He remembered seeing this picture before, though he didn't recall the Archangel without armor. He always had the breastplate, the shield and sword, all of it to its very golden hilt. In fact, naughty Blake had painted him nearly naked. He stared at the painting some more and looked around for a men's room, after which, he'd go see the painting he came to see.

He splashed some water on his face. Might not be such a bad idea to spend the night. He'd passed a Holiday Inn down the road. Sure, why not. A nice dinner, hit the sack early, watch a little TV in bed and check out first thing. It was better to be rested when he closed the Red Door

behind him. He'd go tomorrow night. Tonight, tomorrow
night—no big diff. Anyway, he was tired. He splashed
some more water on his face and mopped it with a paper
towel.

I didn't tell the Brinks guys my name.

Feeling a prickle on his spine, he headed toward the
painting he came to see, passing Blake's towering St.
Michael by a foot or two. He caught a glimpse of the
Regnault and stopped. The prickle had turned to chills and
he swallowed hard. *Oh man, here we go.* He glanced
heavenward then inched back to Blake's St. Michael.

The Archangel now wore full armor of blinding gold.
What the ...? The gold breastplate was the way he
remembered it in photos, same with the shield and gold
sword. No...silver sword now. Wasn't the sword gold a
second ago? Okay, he was clear. He was fine. This here was
a supernatural occurrence because he saw what he saw, so
he could handle this.

Been through this before. Hang in, Joe.

He closed his eyes and slowly re-opened them. Feeling
exposed before Lucifer's wrath, he stared into his eyes, eyes
capable of kindness rather than hatred. Here was a fallen
angel to be pitied. *Christ the Lord.* What was he thinking?
Was he nuts?

He forced his thoughts away from Lucifer's defeat and
focused on Saint Michael's courage, awed by courage born
of unconditional love and adoration. Gaze resting on the
armor, three words came to mind—

Bring them home.

But like words written in smoke, the message burst
forward, blurred and faded away. Bile coated his throat.
For weeks he knew something was wrong and lately the
rest of the group sensed it, too. Alain was disappearing for
hours at a time. Walter was sharing secrets and cloaking

warnings. Ronny's endearing childish ways had ended shortly after his arrival in Angelfish Cove. But it was more than that because ... somewhere a door was closing.

The armor seemed more golden than anything he'd seen in Rome. Its meaning was obvious—he was to prepare for a fight. He had to get home. Something was going on and he wouldn't know what until he got his tail home. It was close to 7 PM when he headed back. Walter and Ronny would be having dinner in their cabin at Marianlake right about now. Either that or Walter was still tinkering with the newest remote.

During the drive he considered everything Walter had said when they talked the other night. More than once, Walter told him to pay attention, to hone his sense of awareness. He would've liked more time with him but he was so eager to get to Marianlake and bring the crew back tomorrow. *Tomorrow?*

Bring them home.

Bats flopping around in his stomach, he hung a hard left into a roadside restaurant. He should call Walter NOW. He dug out his calling card and dialed. After four excruciatingly long rings, Walter picked up.

"Hello?"

"Bring them home, Walter! Tonight."

"Joe? What's wrong?"

He took a deep breath. "No time to explain now. Some kind of high anxiety about your crew. You know what I'm saying or we'd be sipping Buds in the Cove right now. Don't wait until tomorrow morning, Walter. Bring them home tonight. Now." The silence on Walter's end disturbed him. "Walter?"

"Okay, Joe. I'll contact them as soon as we hang up. Are you at home?"

"No, but I'm on my way. I should get there shortly after nine and I'll be heading straight for Pages cellar soon as I hit town. How's Ronny? You know I think he went sightseeing behind that door and he's keepin' it to himself."

"When that thought crossed my mind, I asked him and he denied it. I've got my eye on him."

"Good. I have to call Maggie about something and then I'm heading back. I'll call you again later tonight. Thanks for not asking for an explanation."

"None required, Joe."

He said goodbye and dialed Maggie. He could've waited and stopped by her cabin later, but patience was never his brightest virtue. She had to be home. *Please be home, Maggie.* Maggie would know what he'd seen or hadn't seen in Blake's painting. In Maggie's world, supernatural activity and paint went together like mosquitoes and beer.

It calmed him knowing Walter was sending for the crew tonight and when Maggie answered he managed to inject a little humor into the scenario at the Museum of Fine Arts, especially the part about being paces away from *Automedon With the Horses of Achilles* and not seeing it. Twice.

He reiterated the story, emphasizing the supernatural incident around Blake's painting. Maggie listened quietly, too quietly. He stopped talking after the *bring them home* part. Except for her breathing, he could've been talking to himself.

"Maggie? You with me, hon?"

"Joe, first of all, William Blake did paint Saint Michael, but it was nothing like the one you've described. It's called *The Angel Michael Binding Satan* and he's wrestling with the dragon in it. And it's in the Fogg Museum at Harvard."

"*Hahvid?*"

"Yes ... and Joe?"

"Mm?"

"I know of no twenty-foot high painting. Anywhere. Did you say you helped two Brinks guys unwrap it?"

"Yeah."

"With no staff present?"

"Yeah."

"I think I'll give George a call."

"Don't bother."

"Joe, why on earth not?"

"Because the painting won't be there."

18. The Child

An hour after Walter hung up the phone, the crew stepped off the pod. Of course they looked confused, somewhat harried. How could they not be? Judea in the Year 5 one minute, Canada in Year 1991 the next. Chilled by frayed nerves and jolt in temperature, they hadn't been near the unfinished hockey rink in weeks, and along with their belongings, they reeked. One did not have the luxury of daily bathing in ancient Palestine, unless one was royalty. There were no scented soaps and antiperspirants. Neither was there Imodium and sunscreen.

Squeezing a cordoned section of rope until his palms burned, Ronny watched Walter greet them. He failed to understand why he wasn't standing among them, using his familiar greeting–a firm neck hold, the kind for which chiropractors are renowned. Dave Thomson, Walter's best field archeologist had a love-hate relationship with his athletic greeting but seemed to be missing it today.

Thomson waved vigorously at him from the some-day rink. "Hey language boy, get over here and give us a kiss!"

Ronny tightened his smile and twirled a frayed piece of rope around his finger. He continued to smile and twirl as each man passed and acknowledged his presence, waiting for the neck embrace that didn't happen.

Thomson, last in the queue, would settle for nothing less than the usual gripping fanfare. He dropped his pack and held out his arms. "It's because we stink, isn't it? Hey Mr. Aramaic, one of your tapes melted in Tephon near Mount Gerazim."

"That's what you get for sneaking it back," he said in an unusually reserved tone. "I hope no one saw the cassette player. Did you tell Walter?"

"You're kidding, right? Come on, Ronny, I thought you went to the Cove to relax. Of course I'd be cautious, man. So nobody has to know about the tape. Right? And nobody saw the deckplayer. What's with you? Never mind. Let me take numerous showers and then we'll grab dinner and shoot some darts. I've got amazing stuff to tell you, language-boy. We all have."

"Can't, Thomson. Not tonight."

"And why not?"

"Already have plans. I'll meet you for darts tomorrow night. Gotta go. So, are we on for darts?"

"Sure." Thomson poked his tongue into his cheek. "Don't get you tonight. You always lunge at me for information. Okay, eight tomorrow night at Patsy's and you're popping."

Don't think so, amicus.

∞∞∞∞

Ronny was supposed to join Walter and the crew for a dinner briefing in one hour. As usual he stayed back to record log entries and cross-reference arrivals and departures from the remotes to the panel below the rink floor. This was the only time Walter left the remote in his hands. 'But they're your hands, Ronny', Walter told him the first time he entrusted him with it. 'Safe hands.' Good ol' Walter.

He plodded over to the Gold section and retrieved the book from section six, row six, seat six. What a cornball thing to have done. Three sixes. Really. In a state of absent-mindedness, he set the book down on the pod. Edmon was waiting for him.

"Have you had the chance to read it?" Edmon asked, droning, "Language boyyy?"

His stomach turned. "No. Didn't exactly have the time. Listen, how long is this going to take?"

Edmon smirked at him. "You would ask me that when we have a time machine at our disposal? We're only going back to '67, lad."

He suddenly remembered his nightmare experience behind the Red Door. Huh. Edmon was probably *allowing* him to remember. "Wait, you said you were going to use the machine to get us back. I remember our conversation at the bar now."

"Correct. We need the machine to take the book there. My schooling ended after the course in human transport."

"That's bullshit. I can't take the machine. That would push the time log ahead to the twentieth century. And we can't go back, you know that. We're in 5 AD and we have to stay at 5."

"You failed to pass that information on to me at the bar, Ronny. Perhaps if you had, I would have had time to make alternate travel arrangements. Too late now, though. We really must be on our way within the next few minutes."

"No. I wasn't thinking clearly. I was only thinking of your threat against my mother, not the machine."

"You had the presence of mind to observe that I was trying to sabotage this mission."

"Yes, but with the machine lost ahead in time we'd have no chance, would we."

"That's your faith question."

He took a step backward. "It's not the book at all. The *machine's* the real prize, isn't it?"

"Another tong in my fork, I'll admit."

"Go to Hell! No way. No way!"

"You're not yourself, Ronny. I think I prefer you in moron mode. Set the log to 1967. It's time to go."

The remote shook in his hand as he set the time log forward. There was still a chance. "Okay. Let's go then."

Edmon fanned the air with his hand in a show of disgust. "Ronny. Take Walter's remote and set it as well."

"Why? I know you're not going to leave it behind."

"Set it," Edmon said with brutal detachment.

He did as ordered. Soon as he got back, he would gather the crew together and they would fix this. As a team they could do it. He took his place across from Edmon on the departure pod. "So a deal is a deal, right? You won't leave me there? You'll keep my father away from my mother?"

"A deal is a deal." Edmon extended a veined white hand and he recoiled. "I won't leave you. And your mother is safe from your father. Promise. Now set the clock panel below the floor at zeros so we can carry out our business."

There was only one number to set to zero. The five. Zero zero zero five, it read. He shook uncontrollably as his hand hovered above the green flashing button below the five. Dear God, how were they ever going to fix this? He felt sick and dizzy. The stench coming from the pod nauseated him.

"Set it, you lard-loving moron! Someone's coming." Edmon charged over and smacked his hand away. He changed the five to a zero and dug his nails into Ronny's forearm. The rest was easy enough for Edmon, who slammed the panel shut and shooed his defeated sorry self onto the pod.

Pressing the departure button, Edmon shouted, "*Oppressis Diabolus!*"

Two seconds was the time it took for their surroundings to fade. Hugging Walter's book to his chest, he raised his head when he heard its author shouting his name and running in their direction. *Hope!* He held up his hand plus one thumb to Walter, praying his friend would realize the machine was on its way into the '60s. As their surroundings faded, he dropped his head in his hands.

Edmon was wiping away tears of laughter when they landed behind Walter's favorite poplar. "You held up six fingers. Even if Bayard saw, he'll think you're heading straight into the Year 6. Beautiful. Ah I wish I could take credit for making you do that. Now shrink the disk and put it where you will. We are going to catch the last act of John Corey's party. I can take that book for you now."

He sent Edmon a hateful thought and handed him the book. "Fine. Then you can take over and send me home."

"First I have to show you off to a few friends at Corey's. But I'll save you the trouble and put the book in his attic myself. One of us should certainly stay and enjoy the party."

"I have no intention of staying anywhere here," he said as they started walking. "What friends?"

Edmon didn't answer, but continued to walk silently along the boardwalk while he numbly followed. A group of noisy street kids were playing Kick the Can in the alley by the abandoned glass factory across from Corey's. The sight jolted him. Pages or glass factory. Glass factory or Pages. Was he here a minute ago, an hour ago, or twenty-four years ago? How much of this scene was real?

Edmon was holding the door open for him when one of the kids in the lane hollered victoriously after his win. He stole another look at the glass factory. Curious, last night he could have sworn it *was* Pages. But that was impossible, seeing that Pages did not exist in 1967. Edmon bid him to enter and reluctantly, he went inside.

John Corey was there of course, along with the liquor representative sponsoring this bash. They had 'Needham's

Distillery' signs plastered everywhere on banners, coasters, bottle openers, T-shirts and hats, even the staff aprons. An employee snapped their picture as they sat on the same barstools as last night, curiously available given the size of the crowd. Considering the Needham's glow on all the patrons, the party had been going since late afternoon. Edmon ordered a couple of double bourbons and left him at the bar. Five minutes later he returned–bookless.

"Done," Edmon said, beaming with delight. "Mr. Bayard's book is now tucked away safe and sound in John's attic, out of harm's way."

"Ace the cliché course in Hell school, did you?"

The demon didn't appreciate that remark and it showed.

"What about these friends of yours?" he asked, trying to pump in some courage. The people on either side of them had cleared out. Had Edmon arranged that?

"You can't see them," Edmon said. "But they can see you. That's all I wanted. By the way, when those future San Quentin residents across the street distracted you, I removed the disk from your jacket and returned it to Marianlake. Walter will be happy to have it returned, don't you think? Mind you, I had to set it for 1991. He won't be too pleased about that, though."

Numbed from the bourbon, he held his head low. "The machine was screwed anyway when you made me set it for 1967. So we're going back through the Red Door then."

He searched his jacket pockets for the twin remotes, feeling a modicum of relief when he found them. What good were they now? He put them on the bar and removed his jacket. The lights on one had already stopped flashing. He stared absently at them.

"Junk," he said, aiming one at the garbage bin behind the bar. "As useless as if they were lost." He pitched the first one in, then the second. "Lost remotes. Junk. Waste. Lost."

Edmon gave him a patronizing pat on the back.

"Okay," he said, draining another shot glass, "you win. Let's go."

Edmon shot someone or something in the corner a victory glare. Following Edmon's eyes, he thought he saw a glow in that corner. It was the flashing Needham's sign, that was all. He felt a little like *Dorothy*, only Edmon wasn't exactly *Glinda* and this demonic Glinda was his sole transport home. They would work this out. Him and Walter, Alain and Joe. They would fix this. They had to. He wondered if he would be of any help to them. He wondered to what extent Edmon had messed up his mind.

"Can we go now?" His chest tightened watching Edmon dig out a pile of bills from his wallet.

"I'm afraid you're to stay here, Ronny." Edmon handed him the whole wad. "This cash will feed and board you for a while."

He blinked back a tear. "You promised me you wouldn't leave me here. You promised me you'd keep my mother safe from my father."

"Funny how you thought of yourself first, lad. I'm keeping my promises. Your mother will remain safe. As for the other—I promised not to leave you. I didn't promise not to leave you *here*. So don't worry. I will never leave you, Ronny. Besides this is temporary, no longer than two or three years. You see, without you, Walter's little miracle mission and prayer can never happen. But a word of caution—if you attempt to communicate anything of your plight to the much younger Walter Bayard you will soon meet, I can only be damned for breaking my promise for your mother's safety.

"You'll also have to support yourself which, for a flesh and blood anachronism, will be difficult. You really cannot exist here without me because here you have no identity. So grab on to me, lad. You're drowning and I'm the life buoy."

"Leave me now, then." He felt a death wish coming on and loathed himself for it. "At least leave me this moment for privacy."

"Very well. I can do that for you. See you in a day or two, Ronny. Anything you need here in '67, just mention my name to John Corey. He's your link to me."

"A friend of yours?"

"Nooo. But you have to remember, good people like John Corey are used by the likes of me every day." Edmon produced another twenty from somewhere and tossed it on the bar, smirking at a far corner of the room on his way out.

∞∞∞

"Don't be saddened, Remiel," Rafe said as they watched Ronny drowning his sorrows at the bar.

The two of them stood in the corner with their superior, the Prince of all legions. Though he came to Angelfish Cove to help Maggie, Rafe felt there might be another reason for his presence—another person. The Prince hadn't said much.

"It's difficult not to be sad," Remiel said. "We don't and can't know the outcome. Poor Ronny believes he's been abandoned again. I didn't anticipate this, Rafe. I didn't even see it coming. But you know, don't you, Sir?" He directed this question to their Prince.

"Our lives are governed by more than our thoughts," he said. "Yet our life is as we think. No, Remiel, I cannot know. It is up to them. We do battle for them. We fight for them. That is what we do. My business here is with Margaret, whether she paints in 6 or not."

"Are you saying she may not?" Rafe asked. "Sorry, Sir. You just answered that question."

Anxious to return to Joe, Remiel bid them a good night.

Rafe said to the Prince, "You're here for more than Maggie. Maggie's call is still some time ahead. Is someone dying?"

The Prince of God's legions watched an employee haul the inflated bottle through the door. "Yes," he said.

John Corey wanted a photograph for a keepsake. "Take it, Scotty." He and the liquor rep struck a pose beside the bottle.

Then John slashed his index finger across his throat, a gesture indicating he wanted the stranger in the brown bagel factory T-shirt cut off. He was beginning to attract attention. He'd been mumbling something about a lost remote and looked like a guy ready to jump out of a plane. Only this guy had no parachute.

∞∞∞

"Did Ronny give you any hint at all as to where he was going?" Walter asked Dave Thomson. He didn't know who to contact first–Elizabeth, Joe. Rome.
"Think, Thomson. Anything?"

"I'm sorry, Walter. Nothing. But he was acting weird. Weird for Ronny, that is."

"What do you mean?"

Thomson took a moment to carefully choose his words, which was bringing Walter to the brink of madness.

"He chewed me out for playing one of his Aramaic tapes in Tephon," the field engineer admitted sheepishly. "He knows I've been having a tough time with the language. But he knows I'm cautious. Sir, I've been sneaking the cassettes back for months and Ronny knew that. On one site we researched, he even gave me a lesson. We were miles from any village. How bad is it?"

Walter sunk into the workbench nearest the panel flooring, which he had yet to check. All he saw was a shadow of Ronny holding his hands in front of his face as he and the machine disappeared. Minutes later the machine reappeared–without the remote. Thomson was waiting for an answer.

"It's bad, but I don't know yet how bad. I want you to go back to the others and tell them to carry on with dinner. We'll have our meeting in the morning, eight o'clock. Don't tell them about Ronny until I've had more time to assess the damage. I need to check the panel log and keep my eye on the machine. I'm hoping Ronny will send for it shortly. So if it disappears, that's a good sign. Let the crew think I'm working late tonight."

"Lucky we got home when we did."

Thinking of Joe, he answered, "Yes."

Walter watched until Thomson left the arena, grateful that panic hadn't set in. Yet. His heart had been hammering since Joe's call and he'd been feeling nauseous for the past hour. After checking that the exit was clear, that no one else could sneak up on him, he knelt by the machine's pod and opened the hatch. Perhaps Ronny shoved his remote inside here somewhere.

He glanced peripherally at the time log and observed the first two zeros. So far so good, but something prevented him from giving it a thorough check, perhaps a human instinct for suspending the inevitability of impending pain. If one was given the gift of time to prepare, accept it. In the meantime he took the few extra minutes to search for the remote he knew was not here. He looked down to his right at the time log.

Two zeros. Three zeros. Four zeros. No five, just a fourth zero. He checked and compulsively re-checked. All zeros in the hatch. Feeling light-headed, he brought his knees up to his chest and looked over at the machine. If Ronny left the machine set at AD 5, they still had a chance since the current year was programmed through the remotes only. If the circuit panel under the floor or the machine still showed 5, they'd be fine. It would take him a few days to make the adjustments, but they'd be okay. Now obviously, someone had tampered with the circuit panel, but surely not the time machine's log. If the log showed numbers other than zero-zero-zero-five, they could all be in for heartbreak. Again, he took an extra moment to prepare.

He stood up and looked around–so much work, so many people involved. This was going to be a beautiful rec. centre for the kids. Beautiful. And the reason it got built was because his prayer was heard and about to be answered as he'd imagined. Had this assumption been blasphemous? Suddenly he wondered. Suddenly he was filled with doubt. He and the crew had already returned to the Year 5 where he'd gone against the grain of his conscience. Did it happen there? Did that amputation represent more than the loss of his toe?

The green section of the pod surface was flashing, an indication it was due for miniaturization. As a disk, it would be hidden with a cover of flooring, creating the illusion of invisibility. It was time to notate his personal log. He sat beside the flashing green square and flicked up the top. He stared blindly at the timer. He stared at it for an hour.

It displayed the current year. 1991.

With the twin remotes gone, with the panel under the floor-hatch set at zeros, with the time machine itself set at

1991, he'd have to re-build the spare remote in order to connect the new circuitry and replace the 1991 date on the machine. This brought him to the second and most critical problem—what year was he to substitute with '91? Joe Ross had to find Ronny. Until this was accomplished they could not continue.

∞∞∞

Drenched from the rainstorm by the time he arrived at Pages service entrance, Joe preferred Carol Ann not see him and parked the van a ways down the street. Naturally there was no umbrella in the van. As he turned the key in the lock, he chuckled to himself when he heard the thunder-claps. Was the Door giving him a private welcome? How nice. Walter was right. He should have passed through the Door long before this. He felt ready, though what awaited him was not going to be a pleasant experience and up 'til now he had other priorities. The gang was here and he had to take care of them. He didn't have time for self. But taking care of the self was taking care of the gang. Walter had driven this point home. Thank-you, Walter.

Edmon's *spurine* scent lingered everywhere, that nauseating blend of spew and urine. Ronny must have had quite the time walking around down here. As always, Edmon had left the Door open so no one would see the exterior coats of blood red paint. Why? Since Carol Ann was off limits, who was left to trap? No one in the group would dare come down here ... aside from Ronny.

Joe entered the room with another question—Edmon's whereabouts. He was always around when Alain went in to meditate. And where was Alain? Was he off pursuing Edmon? He wasn't anywhere around when he left for the airport with Walter and Ronny this morning. He might be sightseeing with the Duprielles', but wherever Alain was, his mysterious absences were making him seriously uncomfortable.

He chose to stand. Ignoring the *visitors'* chair in the middle of the room, he paced closely to the walls, guided by three low-volt nightlights. But the light was yellow and therefore ample. He prayed silently, transforming his mind to an uncluttered room. After the removal of fear, he tacked the problems onto an imaginary bulletin board and diligently labeled each. Then he touched them as one would touch a baby's cheek or the wing of a bird.

He untacked the problem marked 'Accident' and quickened his pace around the room. *One Less Bell To Answer*. He could hear the song. But it sounded flat in this cellar room and as he re-lived the accident, he braced himself against the wall, visualizing the solitary running shoe and the Hand. The old directive flashed like a marquee in his mind. *Study in the Spirit and keep the child safe*.

He was coming to loathe that directive. For years he'd heard it, sometimes in his sleep, sometimes in a dream when Alain was a boy and he was afraid to let him out of his sight. If he let him out of his sight, some bad thing could happen to him. And it would be his fault. Keep the child safe. Keep the child safe! The Child! THE CHILD!

He breathed deeply and stepped backward in his mind-room. He tried to replace the 'accident' label with another, but it stuck to his finger. He tried again, continued to try several more times until all ten fingers were stuck with paper, every finger having a different label. There was no use trying to replace the accident with other problems because the accident led to the child, and after the accident, the child lived in every place and in every one. Willie. His grandmother. Angelfish Cove. Marianlake and

Alain. Carol Ann. Rome. The fathers' and the girls. All of the 'mission people' involved in Walter Bayard's miracle.

Tempted to sit in the chair, he knew he had to keep his feet moving. He was here for an answer. Walter wanted him to take an awareness check because he'd been missing something. Something obvious. He'd chosen to take the most painful memory and embrace it, study it, which meant bringing back the fear and embracing that, too. *Okay Joe-Joe, let the problems fly.* He walked slowly around the room, crossing one wrist over the other, gently pushing his hands down on his chest. Within seconds the paper bits wafted to his feet.

"I am in this moment. I am letting the Holy Spirit choose the memory."

He returned to his first night with Willie in Angelfish Cove and floated beyond remorse and shame. He listened to the child's voice,

Joe. Joe? You were supposed to help me, Joe. Help me.

"Who are you?" How many more years would he have to ask this question? *Please, God.* "Show yourself to me again."

The vision reprised.

"Closer. Let me see your eyes. Let me hear your voice."

You have to help me. Please, Joe, help me.

He didn't see the bruises this time, or the blood. He should talk directly to the voice. Why not? "Come closer. Don't be afraid."

The voice and the child's eyes moved closer. *Joe. Joe.*

He saw that these were not Alain's eyes. They were not gray-blue like Alain's, but deep blue. Wistful and blue. Even in childhood, nothing about Alain was ever wistful. Then he had known for some years that Alain was not the child.

"Who are you? Are you Simon, Alain's brother?" There wasn't a trace of French accent in the voice. His stomach fluttered with excitement. He'd seen these eyes somewhere. "Let me hear your people."

The image faded and he listened.

Elizabeth: He's really like a big overgrown kid. Still a child in many ways.

Walter: He's an adult child. Under stress he could disorganize. He has to mature.

Father Vaux: He cried like a baby when Compo died in that lake. He cried for two days.

'You know, Joe, I had an imaginary friend named Joe when I was a kid', Ronny told him ... all those years ago. 'He looked like you. Every time I got beat up, I would call for him to come and help me.'

Dear God. And he thought Ronny wanted to bond. He was practically in his face all the time. Ronny Fergel. "Ronny Fergel is the child!" That damned thing used Simon to distract him. How in hell did he miss that? How?

"You're not the only one with a directive. Want to play Hide and Seek with Walter's book?"

It was the same voice that burst from the intercom and scared Dina into fits. Cold surged from his chest toward his brain. "Where is it?" he asked, drawn to the book's absence on top of the file cabinet. "Who did you use to take it out of here?"

"Lose the child–lose the book. Find the book–find the child."

"Ronny!" He remembered the Blake painting in the museum today. "I saw the armor. It's just beginning, isn't it? The pain and fear. Disillusionment. Where's Ronny?"

The demon groaned with satisfaction.

"Where is he!"

"Joe? Joe, are you down here? What's wrong?"

"Carol Ann, stay out of here!" This time he whispered the question, threatening, "Where is he?" But the demon had gone. It had come only to drop its little bomb.

Carol Ann was calling him from the hall. "Joe, what's going on in there?"

His feet had stopped moving for some minutes now. Oh God, his feet had stopped moving. He told Walter to bring back his crew. He had to call Walter.

He opened the door to find his once beautiful Carol Ann standing there, rail thin, gaunt. She shivered at the sight of him. She had a wine stain on her white satin nightgown, the kind worn by brides. "I'm sorry," he said, unable to ignore Edmon's foul smell this time, to which Carol Ann seemed oblivious. "I shouldn't show up here this late, uninvited. But didn't you hear me shouting to stay away?"

"I heard you shout Ronny's name and I got scared. Walter called me," she said, stroking her throat. "He's looking for you. Something's very wrong, Joe. He said I might find you down here. He wants you to call him immediately."

He grabbed Carol Ann's hand and led her out of the basement.

"Walter would never have sent me down here to look for you, Joe," she said on their way up the stairs, "knowing that room is down here. He didn't sound good at all."

"Have you heard from Alain?" He wanted to hold her in his arms.

"No. Dina was looking for him this afternoon. Nobody's seen him. Can you please tell me what's wrong?"

He touched her cheek and she flushed. "I don't know yet. I'd better call Walter. How 'bout some tea? Got any of that herbal stuff around here?"

He'd rather grow hair in his ears than drink herbal tea, but it took a while to steep and he could get the call in privately. Something horrible must've happened. Where was Alain?

Walter picked up the receiver the instant it rang. "Joe?"

"Hi. I think Ronny is gone, Walter. And your book with him."

Walter's breathing sounded heavy, erratic. "It gets worse, Joe. The time log on the machine has been set forward. To 1991. And both remotes are missing."

"What ... you mean the machine can't go back? Did I understand correctly when you explained the machine?"

"You understood correctly."

"So that's it then. Everything's over. It's over. Carol Ann was right."

"Now wait a minute. Remember I told you I had several more hours of work left on the spare? Remember the spare I didn't think I would ever need?"

Finally he could blow out a sigh of relief but his pulse was still racing. "Of course. Aw thank God, Walter. So you can re-set the time log from the spare back to 5?"

"Yes. But it's a quick fix, Joe. We can backdate *once* only. How do we know Ronny went back to 5? He could be in Judea 6, we don't know. There's more involved here than this fortuitous spare of ours. Ronny's off somewhere with the other remotes. Whatever private mission he's on we have no way of knowing. But we can definitely say he's not in his right mind. Why did he send the machine back with the log set to the present time? Why didn't he return one of the remotes? I have to know where he is, Joe. Before we can continue, we have to bring him back here."

"Walter ... I learned something tonight."

Walter waited.

"I learned that our Ronny Fergel is the child. All these years he's been around and now I learn he is the child I'm supposed to keep safe. Wherever he is, Walter, he's in big trouble. And I'm the one who has to find him. Where do we start looking? I have no idea. Do you?"

"No. But I know you'll find him, Joe. My job is to get you into the apparatus that will take you."

"Maybe he'll send for the machine and return on his own." Yeah, and the moon'll wake him up in the morning.

"I don't think so. You say he took my book. Well we both know where he got it, don't we. Certainly he did not exit that room in the proper frame of mind. Let's not waste time fooling ourselves. You're right. You're the one who has to find him."

"I have to admit I was pretty shaken a few minutes ago, until you reminded me about the spare. I was given a strong premonition in Boston today, which I'll tell you later. I knew your crew had to come home. Somebody's watching out for us. Actually that statement is redundant, isn't it? Of course Somebody's watching out for us. Who would know better than you? Everything will work out, Walter."

"Joe, listen ... I believe that too with all my heart. I do. But it may not work out right away. It may take time. Are you prepared to wait?"

He didn't like the sound of that question, or the hitch in Walter's voice. "Well I know it'll take time. Uh, do you have a guesstimate?"

"A few months maybe. Or longer, Joe."

Was he hearing this right? "A few months?"

"Be prepared," Walter cautioned. "For now, don't say anything to the others, except for Elizabeth. She's his mother. She has the right to know. I don't want to push any panic buttons yet. One of the crewmen knows but I've had a talk with him. And God forbid, we don't want any of the other groups finding out."

"What about Father Andre? And Alain?"

"I'll tell Father Andre tomorrow. Tonight I want to assess the damage so he can give Rome a time frame. They're footing the bill for all this, remember. And Alain ... of course you'll tell Alain, if he doesn't already know."

"How could Alain know?"

"Alain was watching Ronny closely at the book fair. I don't mean that he knows where Ronny is. Certainly he would have called me. I mean he senses something, and you know Alain's senses. Talk to him. And first thing in the morning, after you tell Elizabeth, I need you to help me here at Marianlake. There's no one better to assist me and I need to get started immediately."

"You must be heartsick over Ronny. I'm sorry, Walter."

"Thank-you, Joe. I am. And don't fret about your own group right now. Everyone will be told when I have a remedy to offer them."

"Cushioning the blow, are we?"

Walter laughed weakly. "Something like that."

"Okay then. I'm going to head home. It's after eleven so Alain should be in by now. You should see it here. Thunder. Lightening. It's raining so hard it doesn't look like it's raining at all. Hang in, Walter. I'll be at Marianlake by midafternoon."

He told Carol Ann that Simon was terrified of thunderstorms and had to go. She was not amused, although she bought the story. Sort of. Carol Ann had built-in radar when it came to some things, especially any 'thing' involving him. He couldn't worry about Carol Ann right now. Talking to Walter helped, but the weight of this problem had begun to sink in. By the time he got to the beach house, the 'what if' monster had given him the crazies.

He found Alain sitting on the floor, staring into a roaring fire. How odd to see logs burning in July. But then this was not exactly July weather. "We're in trouble," he said, trying to read Alain's face. He seemed concerned, meditative. "Where are the folks?"

"Spending a few days in Rhode Island. What's happened?"

For several seconds, he couldn't spit out the words. "Ronny Fergel has disappeared in time somewhere. He's taken Walter's book. And he has both remotes with him."

Perfectly calm, Alain asked him, "Where's the machine?"

"At Marianlake. But he's messed with the log. It's set for '91."

Alain turned his attention toward the fire again. "I'm sorry, Joe. I felt something was wrong, I just didn't know what. I guessed it had something to do with Ronny."

He plopped on the couch in front of him. "And for what reason did you not want to share that with me?" Hopefully he wasn't on the verge of saying or asking something he'd regret.

"You had to find your own way to Ronny. I couldn't interfere with that."

Alright, enough of this. "You knew Ronny Fergel was the child, didn't you?"

"Yes."

"How long have you known? Actually let me rephrase my question. How long have you known you *weren't* the child?"

"Always."

He looked up and screamed silently at the ceiling. "You're not gonna tell me, are you? We'll just go on the way we have been, with me knowing you're carrying your little secret, with me accepting, patiently waiting until you can tell me. 1996, right? Allow me to repeat myself—Ronny Fergel is the child, Alain. It's all sinking in. I have to find him.

"Something inside of me knows that no matter how hard Walter tries to rectify this situation, no matter what he does, it's not going to completely work. Walter intimated as much to me. Walter has been trying to wake me up from all sides since he got here. And so have you. What am I missing? How can I feel so close to everything I know is missing and fail to find it? And I don't mean Ronny."

"By doing what Walter told you." Alain sat beside him and put a hand on his shoulder. "By staying in the present with your senses fine-tuned. You'll piece this puzzle together. And I'm here to keep you sane. I can tell you that much. We were brought together by an apparent deception allowed for mysterious reasons. You had to be convinced I was the child, and I had to go along with that for reasons that are a mystery to me as well.

"We were all brought together. You know that is absolute. I don't know what the outcome will be, Joe. That depends on us, on how much we all love and believe in each other. On our hope. We're heading into our darkest time and I don't know how long that time will last. But this I do know—not anywhere in Walter's prayer did he mention despair and heartbreak. This is not what he asked for. This is not what he will receive."

"Keep telling me that over the next while, will you."

"We've been missing each other around here the last couple of days." Alain's smile encouraged him to smile. "Dina's received the marks."

Finally, some good news. "Aw that's so great. So if something like this can be happening now, then this situation isn't a complete horror story. Right?"

Alain nodded. "Love and concern for Carol Ann and Maggie is what did it. Her love for Maggie is pure. As the old Dina would say, 'Mag is my bestest friend in the whole world.' You going to tell Elizabeth in the morning?"

"Yeah." He massaged his fingertips and looked into the fire, pictured bits of ashen paper. "She'll be asleep by now so there's no point telling her tonight. It may be her last good night's sleep for a while. I'll head to the airport from Elizabeth's. Want to come?"

"Best to stay here and keep an eye on things. One day you and I will make the trip back together. You better get some sleep, Joe."

It surprised him being this tired. Wonder of wonders, might sleep actually happen? Perhaps Providence was bracing him for the day and trouble ahead. Yet he slept, nodding off at the start of his prayers. And in his dreams he saw Ronny's frightened face, hands tensed into fists on his mouth.

Drunk, in some cellar-like place, Ronny cried out for God's help.

19. Remembering 1967

The brass greeting shone over the entrance gate. *'Welcome to Marianlake Dominican Monastery'*. It never seemed to change here. The three front steps of the little souvenir shop still sloped in the middle. Black-eyed Susan's and wild daisies lined the roadside for a quarter mile inward. No matter how tired or mentally depleted he got, the smell of Scotch pine mixed with traces of skunk never failed to energize him. Only one person knew he loved the smell of skunk and that person was Willie.

Though Alain had returned on several occasions through the years to deliberate with the Roman unit, a sneak preview of Walter Bayard's time machine and a meeting with all North American group leaders marked occasion's number two and three for him. Both trips were happy occasions. Now here he was again for clearly opposite reasons–in all respects.

It was unusually damp and cold for a July day. In the east pasture the cows appeared jumpy, bobbing and nodding their heads at the darkening sky. Set in a pine clearing, an outdoor classroom of six seminarians scribbled furiously in notebooks. The gardener was de-weeding a bed of impatiens in front of St. Mary's. The lake looked bluer than ever, the grounds impeccably groomed as ever. Everything was as lovely as ever, except for the gloomy sky, the nervous animals ... and the graveyard. Something about the graveyard. On his way to meet Walter at the Sports Centre, he stopped the car to take a closer look.

The graveyard appeared more unkempt and neglected than usual. For years he wondered why it failed to receive the care it deserved. Creeping thistle and dandelions obscured the gravestones and moss sprang between cracks along the pebbly pathway. There wasn't even a muddied old vase with a dead flower set anywhere for these poor souls. It was a disturbing visual. Yet the rest of the grounds were immaculate.

The rain started coming down harder than it had last night in the Cove so he hopped in the car. A mile down the road he caught sight of a woman with a familiar walk, a woman from this time whose walk belonged to another. He felt the warp in his memory, as warped as some of those old 45s Rosa still kept in the Medford attic bedroom.

He hit the brakes and opened the door for her. Not knowing quite what to say he looked questioningly at her while she squeezed the rain from her ponytail. He'd just left Angelfish Cove one and a half hours ago. They could have flown here together.

"Iris, what are you doing here?"

"Alain phoned me last night," she said, snuggling into her jacket. "We're in the throes of a nasty storm, Joe."

He turned off the ignition. "Are you speaking figuratively or literally?"

"Both, I guess."

"Why didn't you come with me?"

"Because I came up last night. Alain told me you were staying back until you could talk to Elizabeth this morning. He felt one of the three of us should be with Walter last night. If you want to call it last night. I got here around two this morning in Dina's plane. Alain asked her if he could borrow it for a little mission business, but didn't tell her why. And your grandmother called here this morning looking for you. I tried to keep it light, but it's as if she feels something."

Once again he noticed that peculiar familiarity about Iris. A shadow. Or an aura. He needed to rewind this conversation and begin again. "What are you doing walking in the rain in those highalized heels? It's almost two miles to the rear property and there are cars at the rectory. You could break something important falling off those things."

"I needed to clear my head. Besides I knew your e.t.a. Figured you would catch up with me somewhere along this road."

He smirked and started the ignition. Always the pat answers. "So we're in the throes of a storm, are we? How's Walter?"

Iris's eyes darkened. "Mentally, he's still the rock, a man of great faith. A great man of faith. Emotionally he's suffering, for obvious reasons. But, physically ... I'm worried, Joe. He's pale and his breathing is labored. He's not a young man anymore and he's walking with a bit of a limp."

Walter would be fine. Walter *would* be fine. Walter *had* to be fine. "Do you think we could lose Walter?"

Iris curled her hand over his on top of the steering wheel. "It could happen. He's accomplished what he set out to."

"But this whole thing evolved from Walter's dream. From Walter's prayer. One man. One man, Iris. My God, it's like the star ducking out of the theater halfway through the premiere. Last night he said this might take longer. A few months he said. Or a year. What if it's longer than that? What if it goes down to the wire? Are we going to make it back? Are we going to go backward so we can move forward? I was so in control behind the Red Door last night. Even with the demon I kept it together. I mean, what have I been learning all these years? It's unraveling now, Iris. I can feel it. This is no anxiety attack.

"Walter told me to be aware of everything. And I'm aware I'm missing signs, all kinds of signs right in front of me." Maybe if he banged his head against the steering wheel he could stop talking. "Spiritual adversaries continue to distract me. They succeeded in using Simon to make me believe he was the child, just long enough to divert my attention from Ronny. To get him out of town. Way out of town. Alain kept warning me. It's all coming at me now. And every time I move to ask Alain why he chooses not to tell me what he knows, my head fills up with this scalding light. I can't know. I can't ask, the light empathizes. I'm not to ask.

"This has been going on for years. Last night when I talked to Walter, I dismissed the feeling as a negative, but now I'm certain ... this minute I'm certain it's going to go on, not for months—for years. Could be to the wire, Iris. Could be. To '96, the absolute wire." He stopped talking suddenly. He'd been ranting. He had turned into a ranting man.

"Drive around to the back of the building, Joe. Walter's in the rink. And don't worry, you can bet we'll get to finish what we started."

∞∞∞

The complex had eight entrances, four tunnels leading into the dome and four to the underground facilities. This is where the smaller rink was going–underground, along with men's and ladies dorms, lockers, showers and offices. The second rink was going in the domed section on ground level and would one day house an NHL-sized rink with seating for a thousand. An Olympic-sized pool was in

the plans as well, though years away from completion.
Naturally, the rinks came first. This was hockey land and
the girls wanted to play, too. He'd heard talk of some
wicked party in the NHL rink. Hopefully, Walter would
provide details.

The rain left mud trails around the Sports Centre
which, to the naked eye, looked extremely unfinished. He
hadn't seen this many workmen on a site since the John
Hancock Tower went up in Boston. The area certainly had
all the appearances of *busy-ness,* but all was not as it
seemed. This he did know. Iris said she didn't mind sitting
in the car while he got rained on.

Leaning against the car door drenched as a diaper
accident, he considered the workmen. To visitors, and
there were many of these, the Centre appeared months
away from completion. But who was it said *the little things
are infinitely the most important?* He took a closer look.
The structure was months *ahead* of completion. The
workmen were laying concrete in the rain and making a
noticeable production with a tilted wheelbarrow—
contents hardened.

Then there were the guys on scaffolds. A little too
much conversation happening there. One fellow was busy
hammering a two by four. Repeatedly hammering. If he
returned an hour from now, the same guy would still be up
there hammering the same two by four. On the dome's
roof a bunch of workers had a dice game going. He sloshed
back into the driver's seat and smirked at Iris.

The same show was pretty much playing on the inside
among builders, electricians and engineers. Given the
budget, the Centre would take another four years to
complete, and the NHL rink an additional two. The locals
weren't squawking since they had the rink in *Nicolet,* a
huge cut above the sub-standard rink they had prior.

Didn't the locals wonder why this project would take so long to complete, even with the limited budget?

As they walked along the foyer on the lower level, he said to Iris, "I'd like to know how Rome stalled all of this until '97. Never mind. I have enough wonder in my head."

The rink entrances were locked so he used one of several keys Walter had given him in Angelfish Cove. Father Andre had a key and of course Ronny had one—wherever he was. "Hey over there," he shouted to Walter, whose only visible body part was an arm and forehead bobbing up from the rink's sub-floor.

The area was in darkness with the exception of the rink, which in no way resembled a rink yet. Walter told them to watch their step, "Stay between the glow-posts! The lights are on the other side."

Walter hadn't miniaturized the time machine and he felt hypnotized by the flashing green light on its log. Major screw-up when the green light flashed. He remembered that from the machine's lexicon and his notes. In a way it was eerier in here than it was last night behind the Red Door. Here lay the proof. This mission was definitely stalled and Ronny Fergel really was lost in time.

"Hey, Walter." The greeting came out as a sigh. "How you holding up?"

Walter struggled out of the small manhole and pointed to the glow-post nearest the panel with the rumpled sleeping bag beside it. "Camped here last night. Thought Ronny might try to send for the machine like you suggested, even though I didn't really believe it. Even if he had, don't know what that would have told me. A few more indicator lights would've flashed from the pod, but that's about it."

"Maybe that would have told you Ronny was alright," Iris said. "Maybe that's really why you camped here. To know that much."

Walter acknowledged her reasoning with an affectionate tug on her ponytail. "Yes," he said. "I suppose that's why. Glad you're here, Joe. How's Elizabeth?"

He tore off several paper towels from the roll Walter handed him and wiped his face. "Dignity, composure, or faith. I'm not sure. You pick."

"I'd pick faith. And faith is never tested during quietude."

"You don't look well. I'm worried about you. Hell, okay I'll admit it–if something happens to you, none of us gets to dance at the ball. Man, I haven't felt this incredibly blind and selfish since Medford. I missed seeing it, Walter. Missed seeing the big picture."

"So did I and Ronny was with me last night. Don't beat yourself up, Joe. Let's go to my office."

"I'll stick around here," Iris said.

They ascended a long sloping stairwell that would one day lead to the mother rink, Walter told him. It was damp going up. He had never seen the surface level. This was the big circle with the four extensions Dina and her private detective were so curious about. Walter led the way with his flashlight and at the top of the stairs was a vast area of unending glow-posts.

"Where does this stairwell lead?"

"Eventually it will be a tunnel ramp leading into the rink foyer. Both rinks will boast NHL-sized ice pads—two hundred feet by eighty-five feet, with fixed seating for a thousand in the big one, as you know. The small rink will seat two hundred in bleachers. Right now and for the next few years, we're using the pool area for offices. Ronny calls it *The Bagel Factory.*"

"For *Ba*yard and Fer*gel*," he guessed, admiring the foyer structure. "What is it I'm smelling? So familiar, what is that?"

"Don't you remember where you are?" Walter was smiling at him.

Joe laughed as the memory of a long ago Halloween filled his nostrils. "Of *coahse*. Pumpkins! We're above Alain's old pumpkin field. I guess the roots are deep and still growing. But it's July. How am I smelling pumpkins in July?"

"Their roots and scent are in the earth. The soil. Eventually the roots will push upward." Walter switched on the lights.

"Wow," he said, noticing the hitch in Walter's stride as he followed him along the foyer. He never got the chance to ask about Walter's leg because he got all distracted over the sign on the office door. Ever the big kid, Ronny had written the sign in a childlike scrawl on a huge scrap of cardboard, THE BAGEL FACTORY. A Ronny Fergel labor of love.

Remembering Ronny's favorite T-shirt, his heart sank. They'd divided the room with office partitions and he counted thirteen desks. He hadn't met all of Walter's team yet and up to now, hadn't thought much about the exhaustive planning it took developing the Judean mission, thus far managing to hide it behind the construction of the Marianlake Sports Centre.

He spotted Ronny's desk beside Walter's on the far side of the some-day pool. An easy guess because it looked like a train wreck and he recognized the oversized white mug Elizabeth had given Ronny last Christmas. It had a black splat on it with the caption *Mr. Messy*. Walter grabbed a set of keys off his desk and they headed back to the foyer.

"Wait till you see this," Walter said, pushing open the large door when they reached the end of the foyer.

He couldn't believe it. It looked like a giant sunburst in gleaming white, the roundest room he had seen since The White House Tour and Oval Office, only twenty times the size. For every five steps forward, he stopped and turned slowly in a circle. He didn't know why exactly, but for some reason he had to stand in the middle, which had an enormous platform. He counted twelve steps up on both sides.

"This is more than a stage," he said, amused by the echo. "Walter, this feels like a dais."

Walter joined him on the stage. "She'll host national hockey championships, curling, live concerts."

He shook his head in wonder. "Live concerts on ice?"

"It'll have a premier ice rink conversion cover. Big party when the last group returns from Judea, Joe."

"Judging by the size of this dais, we'll be hearing a speech or two. So, I'm really going to dance at the ball?"

"You are. And it doesn't matter when we dance, does it? As long as we dance."

"Here we go again," he said. His eye had developed a slight tremor from constant chafing and lack of sleep. "*Tempus caveat*. Why are you giving me subtle warnings of time here? And to which or whose time are you referring– the mission's, the Sports Centre, Ronny's, yours? You didn't call me here because you're afraid you'll crack under the strain, or to help complete a remote control you can probably rewire with your eyes shut. What's up, Walter?"

Walter sat lifelessly on the edge of the dais and patted the spot beside him. "You know what it is, Joe. I need you to locate the year in which Ronny disappeared. For what it's worth, the remote is finished but the process is unchanged. Once you bring him home, we cannot backdate a second time."

"And when I bring him home, what then?"

"You know where my designs and notebooks are, so does Ronny. The problem will eventually get solved."

His stomach rolled, possibly from the pungent scent in the drenched soil. "You never really answered the question about time reversal, what your reason was for constructing the gauge as you did."

"I could have constructed it rearward. I confess to not knowing why. My gut said no, so it was no. Perhaps I was afraid of people playing in the past and altering it. Look at me, I stepped sideways in the past and lost half a toe. No. It had to be for a brief time. Twenty-four hours per group. One year, that simple. You thinking about what Carol Ann said?"

"I am, but as a devil's advocate, not as an infidel. Okay. The year–how in the world do I find the year?"

"I can tell you *where* in the world," Walter said with conviction. "Angelfish Cove. All the answers are there, so follow the clues and let Iris help you lead. She'll keep you from distractions. Spend a few moments alone here, Joe. Remember when you first came to Marianlake. Remember what had happened in the weeks before you came here. When you're done, lock up. My truck's outside, so I'll meet you at the rectory. And on your way back to the airport, I want you and Iris to drop me off at the hospital. We can talk more on the way."

"The hospital? What for?"

Walter removed his shoe and sock. The area around the partial toe amputation had turned purple. He didn't need to spend more thinking time in this room, or at Marianlake. He had carried Marianlake in his heart and head for close to eleven years. Priorities. After seeing

Walter's toe, he and Iris were at his side in emergency within the hour, waiting their turn with a pair of cracked ribs, a cut eye, a handful of bleeding knuckles and a pulled Achilles tendon.

"Do you have any idea where you're going to start?" Walter asked him, as a concerned triage nurse examined his foot.

Joe noticed the bleeding knuckle guy had been staring at him. "I think with John Corey," he said, annoyed when they took in the cut eye. "He was the first local I remember talking to in Angelfish Cove. Willie was with me, or at the bar or something."

Iris looked uncomfortably at the man with the bleeding knuckles.

"Walter," his insides twisted at the sight of Walter's leg. It had swollen and the gangrene appeared to be spreading like vines up a rotting oak. "Your foot looks worse than it did an hour ago. Nurse, I think we need a doctor sooner than later."

"You and your friend can go in now," the triage nurse said. "We have a room ready."

"Remember, Joe," Walter said, having difficulty putting weight on his foot, "all the answers are in Angelfish Cove–from your first day straight through to your last day on this mission. Now you and Iris get going."

He helped Walter into the wheelchair. "Cure that foot, Walter. We have a party to go to. I'll call you in a day or two."

He stared after Walter with a strained smile until the nurse wheeled him out of sight. An ugly question flashed through his mind—since the waiting room was packed to the hilt and triage nurses determined medical priorities, why was Walter first to go in?

The knuckle man shuffled over and extended his healthy hand. "Noticed your wrists. You wanna know something? Running into my own kind practically everywhere doesn't matter anymore." He said this sadly, vacantly.

He shook the man's hand again, pressing his forefinger down on his wrist to verify the marks' authenticity. Affirmative. "These marks are supposed to help keep you out of trouble, not get you into it, man. What happened?"

The young man ignored his question. "It's over. You know how I know it's over? It's over because I don't give a damn who you are or why you're here." Then his voice trailed away as he lumbered off, muttering, "Marks are fadin'. Bye, marks."

In an effort to turn his thinking around, Joe hurried after him and grabbed his arm but the man responded by yanking it away. The enemy had severed this man's connection with the Light. He said nothing more and let him go, sending a positive prayer thought after him.

He took a quick glance at Iris, then the clock above the nurse's station, then back at Iris. "He said the marks were fading, that it's over. Did you hear him? There was nothing I could say."

"No. No there wasn't," Iris said.

"What's happening outside the Cove? People are getting away."

Iris struggled to find an answer. "People have always gotten away. Consider history. Since when is this news? We need to fly back to the Cove, Joe."

"Right. We have to find Ronny. But did you see that guy's eyes? Empty they were. Soulless."

∞∞∞∞

They headed straight to Corey's Café Beanery. Joe considered getting his spleen checked. This lethargy, this exhaustion wasn't in his DNA. 'Course, running around like a new foal in the paddock these last few days didn't help. And the emotional strain. Drain. Strain. Rain. Would the sun ever come out again? It had been raining for days. Now he had that *something about Iris* gnawing at him. He didn't understand this attachment toward her. It wasn't sexual. It was more like asexual attraction if this made sense. He needed sleep, that's what he needed. More sleep. But how could he sleep with Ronny lost in the twilight zone somewhere ... and now Walter ... oh God ... now Walter.

They found John Corey sitting at his office desk, wolfing down a pastrami on rye. It was a little early for dinner, but then John was always up with the dew. Joe liked it back here. The place was so cozy. Mini-kitchen and bar, trundle bed beside a quaint fireplace, one wall plastered from top to bottom in photos. It was cabin-like, resembling Maggie's place, only it had an outdoor patio in back instead of an archangel prince overlooking the Cove. Because of the rain, the worms, which now blanketed Angelfish Cove, and a dead pine on the patio cut in half by lightning, late July business was slow.

"Hey, here's my occasional, part-time and some-time drop-in waitress," John chided Iris, good-naturedly. "Hi, Joe. Would you two like some chowder and a towel?"

"A beer'd be nice," he said. "We dropped in to tell you Walter's in the hospital in Trois-Rivierés. A problem with his foot, he'll explain it. Figured you might want to give him a call." He'd begin with the second reason for his visit, secure in the belief that 'going with the flow' would provide answers. John always suspected something anyway, but regarded Walter's privacy. "And there's something else, John. I was hoping you'd help me take a walk down memory lane. How is your memory these days, by the way?"

"Both socks match, Joe." John handed him a Bud and Iris a V-8. "How can I help?"

"A long time ago I told you about my first visit here in '81, and our chat that night. I remember a picture of this giant liquor bottle. Do you still have that picture?"

"I do somewhere, but geez, that photo goes way back. My guess is it's in the attic in one of my memorabilia boxes. And there's stacks of 'em up there. Wanna tell me?"

He groaned like a sick cow and John had to laugh. "I wouldn't know where to start, John. It's one link in a very long chain of events and no matter which way I tell it, it would violate a confidence."

"Is it true you and Alain work for a Vatican newspaper? This is a small town, my friend."

John Corey's mischievous smile cracked him up. He knew he wasn't getting into that attic without giving him something to chaw on, as John was fond of saying. "Alain and I spent close to five years in Rome, yes. But technically we work as research associates for the V.I.I.D. Vatican Institute of International Development. We gather information and report back."

"Okay, Joe. If you say so. I'll take you up to the attic and show you where the boxes are. That old bottle is still up there, yup, propped in the corner covered in dust, if that's all you want."

"Thanks, but no. I had a dream associated with that bottle. You know how sometimes the subconscious mind represses things. For some reason, an event associated around that bottle is significant, but I don't know how. That's what I have to find out."

"But my liquor rep friend, Frankie Gallagher, gave me that bottle for a party way back in the '60s. Long before your time." John stood up and indicated the way.

"'60s? Guess you don't remember when in the '60s?"

"Matter of fact, I do. It was '67. I remember 'cause that was the year I started slashing all my sevens with that little bar. Frankie's bank returned the check I wrote. Said my seven looked like a one and would he please get me to fix it. Been slashing 'em ever since."

Joe's skin prickled. "Wait a minute. You've told me this before, the thing about the bar through the sevens. The night we first met you told me that. And was that the year you had the party?"

"Yeah, we did. Everybody wanted a picture with that promo bottle. But I'm gonna leave you up there, Joe. I was up there yesterday and it stinks like hell. A rat decomposing or something. I'd sure like to find it before the health inspector does, but I couldn't pinpoint the source. So if you can stand the smell, make yourself at home with those boxes."

"I'll go too and help him, John," Iris offered. "I'm used to rat corpses. Lived near a river once..."

"Good," he said, staring curiously at her again. "The two of us can plow through those boxes in no time."

Halfway up the stairs to the attic he realized this was no decomposing rat. It was Edmon—Edmon Fendi's ever-popular, nauseating calling card. So he had been here recently, but his odor was not as offensive as usual. Though it lingered like a roomful of filthy socks, the scent was old, like it had been aged in this wood and in this atmosphere. *God please help Ronny if Edmon went with him.*

"Aghh," John held the side of his hand under his nose. "You and Iris are on your own, Joe." John showed them where the boxes were and left them.

"Are you going to talk to John about Pages that night in '81?" Iris asked as they began sorting through boxes one and two.

"I don't know yet. My brain is still in a knot over that thing with him and his sevens. Okay. We both know Willie and I weren't really strolling through Pages that night, because Pages wasn't there yet. Another puzzle. Everything else in this town was real—Corey's, the record shop, Marvick's, the boardwalk. It was all real. Except Pages. Why? It's been driving me nuts.

"Pages was the only building anachronistic of its time. And from Pages came the CAP cap I bought for Willie. I figured *c a p* stood for Carol Ann Page the second I met her at Marianlake. She was destined to open a bookstore. Pages. It all fit. But then I knew Dina was destined to sing. I saw Maggie painting. Sister Elizabeth was out for a stroll. All the players, or actors, were out that night.

"But the only person in her proper environment was Carol Ann. I could never figure out why I saw Pages as Pages and not as the old abandoned glass factory. And then what's the significance of the cap?"

Iris chewed on the corner of her lip. "Okay then ... something *inside* Pages. You were supposed to see something inside there that night. That has to be why it was shown to you out of its time, Joe. Has to be."

"I've been over that a hundred times in my head, Iris. What's inside Pages? We know Walter's book is there ... or was there until the other night. We know it was in the storeroom behind the Red Door."

"So you figure you were strolling through the abandoned glass factory? Then you cut your leg in there and all that."

"That's right ... how did you know I cut my leg in there?"

Iris didn't look at him, but continued to file through pictures and papers. "Well, you mentioned it or Alain did."

"I haven't thought of that incident in years until recently. So I never thought to mention it to Alain or anyone."

Iris's gaze challenged his. "Well you must have at some point, Joe. Because how would I know then?"

"Guess you're right," he yielded to her. "Must have."

He didn't have the chance to dwell on the place where Iris was picking up her secret information. John Corey's little seven-slashing story made him remember something else. Some of it was coming together. "Can you see if the blood's draining from my face?"

"You've remembered something?"

"Yeah. A big something. I saw Ronny as a child on the beach that night *and* earlier that evening here in Corey's— well, not actually here, but in a picture I saw here. Then after dinner Willie and I crossed the street to Pages. It happened in a flash before I cut my leg on that piece of broken glass. I was on the upper level where Carol Ann's apartment is now and saw this young guy with his head in his hands. He was blurry or I got dizzy. Something. I didn't get a good look at him. But now I recall seeing a few words on the back of his T-shirt. I only caught one of the words. I remember thinking 'Label' or 'Bagel'."

"The Bagel Factory!"

"Yeah. And you know what else? Maggie painted him in the *Angel Reclining*. I don't have to go across the street to double-check. Did you ever take notice of the man in the painting, standing in front of the record shop?"

Iris thought for a moment. "There's so much in that painting, Joe. Lots of people and things going on."

"It's the rear view of a man, a stocky man. And he's wearing this brownish T-shirt with obscure writing on the back. The only letters I could ever make out on the back of that shirt were *G E L*. So I assumed Maggie was painting the word 'Angel'. But she wasn't painting *Angel* ..."

Iris was all excited. "Bagel!"

"Bagel."

"So that's it then. It's all in the painting. And when you were here in '81, you had a feeling you were in the '60s. The music, the environment–all so you could place Ronny there. He's in 1967, Joe. Go get him."

He exhaled the bad air. "With the new remote finished, Walter has the machine ready to program the year. But until this time-gauge issue is rectified, that machine is still unequipped to move backward in time. I have to be certain he's in '67. If I miscalculate, and it turns out he's in '66, we're all screwed. Again. And there's still missing pieces, Iris.

"Remember when I told you about the accident? I had heard that directive for the first time on my tenth birthday. At the time, those words were very big and very complex for me. Then there was the written message in my prayer book. *Remember your ABC's.* From the complex to the insulting. Years later it hits me. I got an *A* for Angel. I got a *B* for Book. And a *C* for Child. Now I'm all messed up because that *C* can stand for Corey's or Cap. And if that's true, then the *A* and *B* can mean something else, too. And that blasted cap doesn't fit somehow."

"Maybe it's not supposed to fit. Maybe it's just a cap."

He turned his head away to gather his thoughts. "No, if that cap had Carol Ann's initials on it, it meant something."

"Stay on track with the photo, Joe," Iris said, lugging over another box. "You'll figure it all out when you're meant to. We still have eight boxes left."

"At least now we know we're looking for Ronny in one of these pictures. That's all the confirmation I need to go get him."

Two minutes into box number five he found it. Funny how one glance of what was then a stranger in a photograph could bring it all back with such clarity. He remembered sneaking a taste of Willie's screwdriver to see how strong it was. He remembered that overpowering magnetic pull into the future, or destiny as he called it at the time. He remembered the deep, gentle tones of the angel's voice. That was the last night he heard it. He desperately wanted to hear it again now.

The photograph had not yellowed with time. There he was, in the party background, dejected, frightened. Ronny Fergel. A man at the right place in the wrong time. A decade ago. He caught Iris staring at him, something she often did when she thought he was looking the other way.

"Have you got something there?" she asked, revealing traces of embarrassment.

He handed her the picture.

"Here he is! Oh he looks so lost. And look at all those empty shot glasses in front of him."

"I remember something else," he said. "I remember John telling me that Ronny had come in with one of their locals and that he kept mumbling something about a lost remote."

"Joe, you can't go back to Marianlake tonight, not in this downpour."

It was like she could read his mind. Geez. "It's not coming down that hard in Quebec. We've got Dina's plane and Dina's pilot. I gotta get him out of there, Iris. It will take me one minute to set the machine for that night in '67. And the second we get Ronny back, we'll take him to the hospital to see Walter."

"If Dina's pilot gives the OK to fly tonight, I'll hitch a ride back to Marianlake with you." Then she got all solemn on him. "But I can't go with you to get Ronny."

"Then why you heading back to Marianlake?"

"I have other business to get on with there. So now I have to go do my thing."

"What business? What thing?"

"I want to hang out with Walter for a while. And Father Andre wants me to help with some clerical stuff."

It was his turn to stare. After a moment, he said, "I have one question for John Corey before we leave."

Since business was slow, John was tending bar. He approached him fanning the air with the photograph.

"Oh good," John said. "You found it. Did you find what's stinking up there?"

"You were right. Dead rat. I pitched it. Smell will fade in a day or two. John, do you remember anything about the young man in this picture?" He handed John the picture. "I know it was years ago, but———"

"Good Lord. This is Walt's assistant. Young Ronny. But it can't be, must be his father or uncle. I knew I saw his face before, or one just like it. Is this his father?"

He took a pause and then nodded. "Do you remember anything more about him?"

"Sure. He hung around the Cove for a day or two and then disappeared because some guy was looking for him, so said my staff. I remember he was sort of strange. Lost. You know? Not one for conversation. Nothing like *your*

Ronny. There was nothing happy-go-lucky about his dad. Is Ronny looking for him?"

"Yeah." *Bad karma to lie, Joe. Bad karma.* "You said he hung around town for a day or two and then disappeared?"

"Yup. Disappeared and we never saw him again. Wait, Joe. You know who might better help you?"

"Who?"

"Ed. You know, Carol Ann's assistant. Haven't seen him around in a few days, though."

"Edmon? How could he help?"

"Well, old Ed's the one who brought Ronny's dad to Angelfish Cove."

20. The Sacrifice

During the turbulent flight back to Marianlake, Iris ragged on him again for being so hard on himself. He took little credit for discovering that Ronny was in '67 and believed he should have seen this coming. If he had, he could've kept Ronny away from Edmon at Carol Ann's book fair.

The psychological effect of the rain wasn't helping, either. They hadn't seen the sun in days. Dina had been grouchy due to contractual problems with promoters re the new tour. Elizabeth was despondent for obvious reasons. Carol Ann was down to maybe one meal a day. And Maggie's migraines had worsened. Now Iris was taking a powder on some mysterious business.

He was concerned for Iris. Here he was, about to fetch Ronny from the era of seekers and seers and she had bigger concerns, meditating during the entire hour and a quarter flight back to Marianlake. What in blazes outranked Ronny? She was preparing for something—he knew the look. Alain had that same look all summer, what there had been of a summer.

Another nasty thought banging him upside the head was Walter's machine. Last year's demonstrations at Marianlake looked easy enough. A kid could do it. But shouldn't he get a few pointers here? A new pilot doesn't hop in a plane and fly off solo. At least Iris would stick long enough to see him off.

He assumed.

They got back to the rink at nine-thirty. Wasn't he just here before noon today? He shook his fuzzy sleep-deprived head at Iris, making her giggle. "Doesn't matter what time it is," he said, "because I don't even know what day it is. Or the month. Doesn't exactly feel like the end of July, does it?"

"No." She stared down at her empty hands. "You'll be fine, Joe. But I can't stick around. I have to get going."

"Why the smoke? Can't you stick long enough to see me safely into the twilight zone?"

"No. You gonna hug me goodbye?"

There was something about her body, the frame of her back, the scent of her hair. Again, he stared into her eyes that he might read the volume of passion and mystery in them. And again she prevented that, casting her eyes downward. "Why do you always do that?" he barked at her. "Why are you so shy with me? You afraid I'm going to come on to you?"

"No. Of course not," she said awkwardly. "I'm afraid I might come on to you."

Like a jerk he stood there with a tongue full of holes.

"Take a while to get your head in the right frame of mind before you take off, Joe," she said. "And remember– don't lose sight of the big picture. Now I really have to go." She touched the side of his face. "Love you always."

She dashed away like Comet, Cupid, the other one, and Blitzen. How did women not topple over in heels like those? Willie liked high heels. He had the disturbing notion that he would not see Iris again for a long time. He sat in one of the *gold* seats in front of the pod. Iris was right. He had to cast the dark thoughts from his head before he got near Ronny, and that last thought he had when he left Corey's was the darkest ... John said Ronny hung around Angelfish Cove for a few days, then disappeared because some guy was looking for him. A few days. Then disappeared.

∞∞∞

Breath ragged, Iris plodded along the dark ramp to the reception room. The closer she got, the slower she moved. She didn't want to go in there. For a place so enticing, for a place that would one day throw a party to end all parties— if all went well, it held something foreboding now. She stopped outside the door and touched Ronny's sign. Given a choice, she'd turn away. But she could not because of the firm voice that summoned her here.

There were four on the dais, two of whom she did not recognize. The room was stark white, serious white, the hue that meant business for all concerned. Even the white of their skin glowed more radiantly as she drew near. Remiel was here. She smiled at him, and the smile he returned filled her with warmth. Rafe was here. It was he who called her. She straightened her posture.

Oh my, oh my—their Prince was here, the most revered of all the legions, legions that would have been destroyed if not for him! Just his presence transformed her into Love. God had given him such great power, power to lead the entire heavenly host in the battle against dark angels. She trembled. She had seen him once before and he did not speak then. Why was he here?

She recognized the fourth spirit and stopped on the seventh step. This was not so.

"No!"

She moaned, and they all waited for the echo to end.

Remiel walked over and assisted her up the last five steps. "Remember who you are, Iris," he said softly.

"No!" She tried to contain her anger. "You've taken him from Joe, from all of them."

"Iris, walk into my light," Rafe commanded her.

She did as she was told.

"Now speak to him, Iris," Rafe said.

"Walter." She wanted to say his name. Nothing else came to mind.

"Speak to him from your essence," Remiel said, "not from your mind."

"You brought us here, Walter." She felt Rafe calming her. "All of us. And now you're dead. Like me."

Walter seemed to study her. "You would say I'm dead, Iris? You? You who died asking what you could do, you who asked to do it over. Well here you are, doing it over. Living again with no return. As am I."

"But they can't see me here as I was. And what happens to Joe without you? Where will you be now?"

"I'll be with Rafe, learning, studying. After that, how far I go will be determined by how much I learn. As for Joe, in this realm where the Almighty's angels do not have all the answers, how can I? I'm to take you to see Ronny. That's all I know for now."

"Ronny? Now? But Joe's on his way there to get him, if he's not there already."

"His minutes pass differently from ours," Remiel said. "I'll be going as well. We won't be staying long and Walter has to give Ronny a message. You're to remain with Ronny."

Intuiting the answer, she asked her question anyway, wavering, "Will Joe see me there?"

"No," the glorious Prince said. "You are not to see him, as you were not to see Rosa Canites when you were returned here." Without further explanation, he left the dais.

Rafe, who followed him, looked back and said to Remiel, "You have your work cut out for you, Remiel. We all do." He smiled, "Ah, time to get at it."

"*Pax vobis*," Remiel said into their vanishing light.

Iris, remembering her reverence in life for this great Prince, observed that her focus on him had diminished her earthly passion for Joe. Again. The Love he left behind was that pure. Imagine, *Princeps Militiae Caelestis*. The 'Prince of the Heavenly Hosts'. She felt honored and humbled.

"The holy warrior Prince—why was *he* here?" she asked Remiel, still awed.

"To walk me through the veil," Walter answered. "To escort me to the holy table to meet my Creator. I've spent a lifetime longing to behold Him. But I've asked to see to Ronny before my exile here is ended. So I think we'd better be on our way, Iris."

∞∞∞

They walked along the tunneled hallway in Remiel's light, using his light to move back through time. There were certain things Iris preferred to forget, but could not avoid seeing. If not for God's mercy, she'd be with Edmon and his superiors right now.

As they passed through 1981, she relived the hangovers and fixation. She prayed for Carol Ann, asking for the return of her freedom. If Remiel gave her the power, she'd command the demon to stop narrowing Carol Ann's world. With that single prayer, she heard Remiel's voice in her mind. They could not see each other in this place.

"You will have the power of command," Remiel said. "You *are* the wild card, Iris. Remember the night the demon let that slip? And to pray for Carol Ann now, given our situation, is more to your credit than you'll ever realize."

It was beautiful on this misty summer night in 1967. They walked along the boardwalk glancing up at the full moon. Iris felt empowered, strong enough to fight the demon when it showed itself.

She regarded Remiel's exquisite face. "Thanks for the booster shot."

"I think I know where he is." Walter pointed at the abandoned glass factory across the street. Something or someone had scared off three teenagers.

"Odd to look there and not see Pages," she said to Remiel. "What now?"

Remiel turned to Walter.

"He's going to think I've come to take him home." Walter sighed heavily. "He won't even know I'm gone until I tell him. I feel like I'm about to drop a bomb on a city that's already been destroyed."

∞∞∞∞

The place was gray and damp, with centipedes and silverfish darting behind broken pieces of floorboard. It was lonely here, but thankfully, no one bothered him for ID. There was no room service, but Corey's was just across the street. There was no electricity, but he had a camper's lamp and flashlight courtesy of the kids who snuck in to smoke and drink beer. Then there was the mattress, blanket and pillow left behind by kids playing more than Spin the Bottle. Thanks to child's play and raging hormones, he had managed to convert a portion of this hellhole into something of a janitor's corner.

Barely hanging on these last two days, he repeated the same mantras. Someone would come to get him. Walter or Thomson. Maybe even Joe. They would figure it out and find him. They would figure it out and find him. *They'll figure it out and find me.* Yet he almost gagged every time he reached into his pocket to pay for something with Edmon's money. He could be jinxing himself. No. No. Jinx lived in the same house with Superstition. He was God-fearing. The angels were on his side. Oh no, now he sounded like he had pride. He was never proud before. Never say never. Never, never say never. Oh no, too late.

"Hello, Ronny."

It was Walter's voice—Walter's wonderful, brilliant voice. His best friend, the *Bay* in Bagel. *He found me. Thank-you, God. Thank-you, thank-you.* "Walter!" He grabbed Walter by the back of the neck and hugged him. "Have I been waiting for yoooo." Seeing Iris and Remiel widened his smile. "Hi," he said shyly to Remiel. "Great to see you." Iris looked different. As a matter of fact, all three of them looked different.

A wave of anxiety cut through him. Suddenly he felt like the last survivor in the ocean. After treading water for days with the sharks circling, he was about to be rescued, and the wait seemed excruciatingly long. "Okay, Walter, let's do the *Transporter* thing and *energize*. I'd prefer the update in '91."

"Guess there's no place to sit down," Iris said.

He took a choppy breath and gestured toward the mattress and a couple of beat-up chairs. When Walter sat, he noticed his sandals, and his toe ... as perfect as it was the day they left for 5 Tephon.

"They making prosthetics for toes now?" he asked.

"No," Walter said, hesitating. "Not that I'm aware of. Ronny, we have something important to talk about. And we're going to have to do it here."

"There's a problem because I tossed the remotes, isn't there? I don't feel so well. Actually I'm feeling a little sick, Walter. Can't we do this from home?"

"Not yet. We can't get you home yet, but Iris will be staying on with you. I want you to listen quietly while I explain. Seeing you in pain hurts me so much, makes it difficult to begin. You know, I've been through a transition too. And the one I've been through doesn't involve quantum physics or time reversal variance. As you know, others before me have proven that we are unlimited by time and space. But now I find I'm unlimited in a very different way. You can say that I am unlimited by another consciousness. An altered state."

"Please, Walter! My patience is in an altered state. What do you mean 'Iris will be staying on with me'? And what's with the toe? You're telling me you're dead, is that it? No, don't answer me. If I'm losing my mind, Angelfish Cove '67 is the place to do it. What the hell, great music— Groovin —The Young Rascals. *Light My Fire*—The Doors. *Gimme Little Sign*—Brenton Wood! *Release Me*— Englebert Humperdinck!"

Remiel put his hand on his back. "It's always been beautiful, hasn't it, Ronny? And it will continue to be beautiful, as will your role in this mission. Only your role is not what you thought it would be. No one's is. Listen to Walter."

Walter's elastic smile didn't exactly fill him with moonbeams. "Just hours ago, Ronny, I lost my leg and my life. My leg to gangrene and my life from heart failure. The Prince of Light guided me through. Rafe was also with me, but I asked to be here with you now, to talk with you. Otherwise I'd be on my way. Somewhere."

He had to reject this. "No. Your death defeats our entire purpose. No, it makes no sense."

"How does it defeat our purpose?"

"Oh, come on, Walter. It all happened because of your prayer, your work. So you gonna tell me you're not permitted to share the big event with us?"

"How do you know I won't be sharing the big event? Let me tell you something, I'm in the best position to share in it. You're not being honest, Ronny. You're upset because I won't be here to fix everything for you. You're mad at me because you think I'm abandoning you, that you're being abandoned all over again."

Why was Walter treating him this way, now, after everything he'd been through? "That's not fair! Behold my predicament, Walter and excuse me for whining a little. First I'm bounced into a time where I'm three years old by a guy whose name-anagram is 'Demon Fiend'. My ID means squat here so employment is out. Then my best friend shows up and announces he's dead and says he can't get me home yet. So yeah, I'm upset. Yeah, I'm ticked because you won't fix it for me. I mean if you're going to dump me here, Walter, at least dump me here with your credit card."

"Such a victim," Walter said, without emotion.

"Why are you doing this! Of course I feel victimized. Let's turn back the pages to chapter one of Ronny Fergel's life, shall we. I never knew my father, and given the circumstances of my conception, I don't want to. You're the only father I've ever really had. My stepfather or uncle, you see I'm still confused–my stepfather, *slash*uncle was always on the road. My stepmother, *slash*aunt was too conscience-minded to pull off the deception for my biological mother, *slash*aunt, *slash*nun. My life has been the soap writer's dream and it all began because my biological father, *slash*rapist was heavy into power. So you could say I've been playing the victim.

"The only peace I've ever known has come from Remiel and Company. Now everybody's leaving, except for Iris. And even she's stuck between a rock and a hard place. I know. I'm not supposed to know that, but when you grow up with the kind of playmates I did, you know stuff."

He turned his head away to wipe the drip from his nose. He hated making a fool of himself. "Okay, Walter. I've got it together. What's going on?"

Remiel got up and stood with his back to them, so it was a good guess they hadn't much more time together once he saw Remiel's frame elevate.

"I'm here to ask something of you, Ronny. Something huge. And I'm sorry I angered you. Better we surface your anger than the demon, don't you think?"

He loved Walter but this wasn't exactly the time for psychological first aid. "How huge?"

"I'm here to ask you to stay back, that the rest of your friends may move forward. I'm here to ask that you remain here, in this time, to reconstruct the machine's time compass. By now you've guessed that it must toggle backward, otherwise how will we get to the year 6 and subsequently return with our cargo?"

This numbed feeling was probably a good thing. "What do you mean? I thought we were returning to spread the 'good news' all over again. But that's not what you meant by *cargo*. What's the cargo?"

Walter shook his head apologetically.

"Oh come on, Walter! You mean I can't have this information?"

"I couldn't have it either, Ronny, not until a few hours ago. Even Iris is not allowed this information."

"But Iris is d———"

"Iris's circumstances are different." Remiel signaled Walter to hurry along. "You've assisted me from the prototype days. All my diagrams and notes are in your head. I've taught you well. Modify the gauge and then return to your own time."

"But I don't have the materials! The materials are at Marianlake."

"You'll put it on paper, Ronny and complete the process once you get back to Marianlake."

"Excuse me, Walter, but we have a slight problem. How am I supposed to return to Marianlake without the machine?"

"That's Joe's responsibility. It's his job to find you and take you home."

His chest tightened. "Any idea when that's going to be?"

"You'll have an emotional adjustment to make first. Jumping right into the work as you are now would be a waste of time. But I know you. You'll try it anyway. In an effort to get home by next week, you'll try it. Eventually though, you'll take a path similar to the one Joe took in Rome. Joe was in Rome a long time."

He swallowed, tried to swallow. "How long, Walter?"

∞∞∞

While Walter cradled Ronny in his arms after answering his question, Remiel received a gift of prayer. In Angelfish Cove '91, someone close to them had just asked for the right thing. Remiel was offering thanks when Edmon appeared before him. Remiel permitted Iris to perceive the demon's motives—

The demon stared, intensely curious, powerless to know what new information had come to this soldier of Light. It felt weakened, yet stood firm in the knowledge that its mission had been successfully completed. A little more work to do here, then it could move on into the outside world where evil waited for harvest. And now that Walter Bayard's mortality had altered slightly, it was wiser to take the lad home, especially since learning Bayard wanted him to stay. He had tired of these creatures. All they had left was the dream. He had been doing such a good job convincing them of that ...

The demon waited until Remiel opened his eyes and allowed him to pass.

∞∞∞

"Hello, lad," Edmon said to Ronny while moving cautiously around Remiel.

"Oh great." The pulse pounded in his dry throat. "I'm afraid the matinee is sold out. Perhaps you can try the evening performance."

"But I've come to help you exit the stage, lad. You don't want to play here."

"What are you metaphor-bling about now? Ala ... Remiel? Can't you get rid of this thing please, so I can have my time with Walter in peace?"

"It's going to make you an offer," Remiel said. "Better it makes it in our presence."

"Thank-you," Edmon said, his eyes black as sockets. "You want to return home in an amateur attempt to repair Walter's machine, don't you? Well here I am to take you. My route is through the Red Door Interstate. My way you don't need any second-rate time machine, or angels' fair, or ruby slippers. So let's go, lad. Time to leave the Emerald City."

"Yeah? What's leaving Oz gonna cost me?"

"You've already paid it. You helped me disable the machine and re-locate Walter's book into a comfortably inaccessible time. So my mission ends with yours, because I don't believe you have the brain for Walter's work. The other groups are being infected as we speak and hope is dying. Wait until they hear about Mr. Walter here. I couldn't be happier. Lastly, no book is left in your time that threatens power over us."

"I can think of one," Walter said.

Edmon ignored him. "So what's it to be, Ronny? Because once I go, I'm gone for good. Financially, you'll be on your own. Unless you think Remiel's opened a five-figured savings account for you, unless you think he has an identity to give you. Frankly speaking, lad, he's leaving you dick on a paper plate."

"How will I live?" he asked Walter.

"That's my department," Iris said. "Leave that to me."

The demon sneered.

"But I want to know *why* I have to stay back. And for so long. *Why* do I have to do the work from here, in this time, when everything I have is at home?"

"Walter will answer as best he can in the demon's absence," Remiel said. "Make your choice, Ronny."

"He's been through too much, Remiel," Walter said. "He could make the wrong decision. How could we allow that?"

"He has the spiritual tools," Remiel said. "All he has to do is use them."

"This is tiresome." Edmon crossed his arms and tapped his foot. "Decide. Now."

In his heartache he laughed to himself, then laughed out loud over the first ludicrous thought that entered his mind. "I do like '60s music. God help me. Take a hike, Edmon. I can't live in your world, even if your world is my world."

"Your parents are there, lad," it said, making its exit threat, "both of them."

"My mother will be taken care of. Whether she stays with Joe or—goes with Walter."

"Well." The demon seemed happily resigned to this ending. "Best of luck, boy. Sorry to abandon you, but then you must be used to that by now. Goodbye."

"Not so fast," Iris said, stopping it with the resonant command in her voice. "Remove the part of you that lives in Carol Ann. From now on she struggles only with demons of her own making."

"Oh please," it said. "A father wants to be remembered before it moves on. It has a legacy to leave its children. How can you ask me to strip her of her inheritance? Rude."

"Then consider this," Iris continued, fearless, "since I am still treading in middle waters, I am free to dog your every move. In an attempt to undo all that you do, I will follow you everywhere. When I died I stood on the border that overlooks your city. I was there. I know where you come from, how you began, and where you're going. Your superior once called me a wild card. It was right. Now you can appreciate why it didn't want me hanging around.

"Release Carol Ann or I promise you, I will pursue you so aggressively that you won't be left the fraction of time it takes to infect somebody's head. At your every attempt to contaminate, I'll be right there trying to make you fail. And you have to admit, given the law of averages I'll win at least some of the time. So with my soul floating in this temporary oblivion awaiting an answer, don't you think I would do everything in my power to make amends? Don't you think I would do everything in my power to stay out of where you're coming from? Free her."

"Ugh," it said, "an ambitious angel-in-waiting, forever lurking behind me with a tray of milk and cookies. Sorry I can't invite you to join me. Carol Ann isn't worth the trouble. She's released, Iris. I don't want to have to see your face again. Until I see it in Hell."

∞∞∞

Remiel was proud of her and wished he could share what he had learned. *Share the prayer*. But again, this new information was to remain within his circle. This new information was also powerful enough to secure Edmon's permanent departure from Angelfish Cove. This delighted him. Where Walter's prayer ended–this new, selfless prayer began.

∞∞∞

"Okay," Ronny said. Although Edmon was gone, there was this empty place inside, a place he could no longer fill with enthusiasm for the work he and Walter shared. "I get the feeling that you have to go soon, Walter. And Edmon's gone. So tell me why."

Walter clasped his hands. "I feel it was all just handed to them. I wrapped it up in a pretty, tight little bundle and said 'Merry Christmas. Here's a bunch of miracles. Enjoy. There will be hardships, but you're in the world, not in paradise'. Yet everybody seemed to expect paradise. Many abused the bonuses, like the impressions. Again I remind you that these marks are not the Stigmata Christ seldom graces to the deserving few.

"Time and again they were given examples of God's love, but it was never enough to trust the gifts, to relax and enjoy them, to have faith in them. History's mistakes repeat, exponentially each time. I guess you can say that everyone at home is in the desert-wandering stage now. Let them come to know the pain of their loss. Let them be with their pain for a while. This is what I feel, Ronny. Yet I also feel there's more. More reasons. Perhaps something to do with time, or timing. That word is a constant hiccup with us, isn't it?"

"So what you're saying is that you and I are being taken from their lives now so they can appreciate what they've lost? All that clichéd stuff like–not our timing, but God's timing?"

"Ronny, I realize it sounds superficial, but I have other information I'm not permitted to give you. You know that. Not long ago I told Joe that all of us knew different things about this mission, which our gut told us we could not share with the others. He couldn't tell us about Edmon. Years have passed and many of the secrets are out. Many secrets remain. You, Iris, and myself are out of their lives now, yes." Walter checked to make certain that Remiel and Iris were out of ear shot. "All part of the plan, like Remiel knowing you would make the right decision because he wouldn't let you make the wrong one."

He rubbed his eyes. If only he could go to sleep and wake up in 1991. "And we know Remiel has *his* secrets."

"There again—you know more about Remiel because in a way you're connected with him. You know and I don't. So why didn't you tell me, your best friend?"

"Point taken, Walter. You know, I've always had the feeling you thought I had lots of maturing to do. I mean, the way you looked at me sometimes, treated me."

Walter smiled. "You'll mature fast now, believe me."

"So it's going to be some time before I see you again?"

Walter put his hands on Ronny's shoulders. "I think you know how long."

"Yes. That's so long. I'm afraid I'll lose it, Walter. What if I end up as some John Doe in a hospital ward somewhere? I'll be alone. My life and people are not in this place or time."

"You're wrong. You said it yourself. Right now you're three years old and living in a quiet Long Island suburb with your aunt and uncle. And beginning a few minutes ago, you saw your first angel. You can say you're having your batteries recharged. So now you know for certain that all your childhood visitations were genuine. No more doubts. How does that make you feel?"

"Confused, but good."

"Still think you're going to crack up?"

"Guess not. But I still feel so weird, dissociated, like somebody's separated me with a red crayon and ruler. Now

I can understand how Dina must've felt. Scary stuff. Hey, I just thought of something."

"What's that?"

"If that happened to me starting when I was three, then I'm right where I'm supposed to be now. Is that right?"

"Yes," Walter said. "Keep having those good thoughts. They'll be useful during setbacks and self-doubt. Tell me something else? All kidding aside, why did you really decide to stay?"

For once, an easy answer. "I stayed so they can all get back, even if I have to work alone."

Remiel, who had wandered over with Iris, felt the tingling in his wrists that Ronny could not yet feel.

"You won't be alone," Iris said.

His face saddened again. "Joe doesn't know we're all going to miss the mark. Does he, Remiel?"

"He'll know soon enough, and he'll come looking for you tonight—"

"Joe's coming? *Here in '67?* Ronny held his arms out wide. "Walter, you adjusted the spare."

"I did. To regress once. This is where you take over, my friend."

Remiel handed him a room key. "Iris has you registered at The Twin Cedars Lodge as *Tommy Walters*."

He looked wistfully at Walter. "And Iris?"

"Iris will be close by. You'll need to rest tonight, but I suggest you leave tomorrow as soon as you're able. Leave no traces. You know what a bloodhound Joe is. He won't give up until he believes he must give up. If there are no clues, no traces, he'll be forced to quit."

"Will I have the strength to leave in your absence, I wonder. This place is my last link to everything, to everyone at home. I wish I could talk to my mother."

"You'll have the strength," Walter said. "Your mother's hurting now but know she's with good people. They'll look out for her, don't you worry."

"Any idea when Joe will get here?"

"Soon as we say our goodbyes."

"You know, he'll check the inns for anyone who matches my description."

"He won't see you, Ronny. We've got you covered." They all smiled.

"I have to see *him*, though. Please don't talk me out of it. I ... let me find a place where I can hide out and play I Spy or something. One last time ... because it's going to be for a long, long time. Guess I need reminding that the time machine's real before I disappear to work on it. Imagine, I went back with you and I need reminding that it's real. I scouted locations alongside the crew in Tephon 5 and it's all unreal. Still. How do the rest of them feel, have you ever wondered? So I need reminding that Joe's still real, that someday he'll be back ... and I'll be here waiting ... and we can go home and see everybody and party down. I want to see his face, Remiel."

Remiel granted his approval with silence.

"This is the first place in town that he's going to come looking for you," Iris said. "Imagine. We're in the basement of what will be Carol Ann's storeroom many years from now. And we're all familiar with the door to that storeroom. So this is a good spot for you to hide. Joe's so nostalgic. I know. I've known him longer––what I meant to say is, since Joe and nostalgia are often at odds, this is the first place he'll head. But I won't stay. I'll take a swim or something and see you later at the lodge. I ... we already said our goodbyes today, although he didn't know it. I won't see him again for a very long time. And now I'll give you and Walter some privacy."

Iris and Walter exchanged parting words. Then she asked Remiel, "Will I see you as *Remiel* from now on?"

"Yes."

"Because I really miss you-know-who."

Remiel smiled. "When you see Joe again, you'll see *him* again."

Iris blew Walter a kiss and left.

When Walter took his hands and held them, he knew this was it. "I'm scared, Walter. How will Joe find me again?"

"The minute your work is done, head straight back here."

"But how will he know the time?"

"He'll know, Ronny. Concern yourself with your work and I'll never be far away."

His eyes misted. "Yeah, but there'll be no more Bagel Factory. And you'll be near in spirit only. I'll miss you. And I can't believe I'm accepting all of this so calmly." He glanced over at Remiel. "I must be getting another battery recharge. Now I know we won't see each other for ... well ... you told me approximately, but can you tell me *exactly*, Walter?"

"I don't know exactly, my friend. But all that matters is that we will see each other. It'll seem longer for you than for me, but keep life in front of you and laugh once a day. I love you, Ronny. If you keep busy with your work, the time will pass quickly, I promise. Iris will be here and who knows what other surprise visitors you'll have just when you need them. Goodbye for now, son."

Walter held him and kissed him on the cheek. Then suddenly, he was alone.

∞∞∞

After concealing his bedding and camper's lamp, he ditched the donut bag. Joe would take one look at that and know he was around here. Hoping Joe wouldn't hear or *feel* his pounding heart, he wedged himself behind the old furnace and the wall. It was a tight squeeze and he had to hold in his stomach if he wanted to keep his shirt buttons from clinking against the aluminum. Cramming himself behind here seemed foolish and childish, but so what. He had to see Joe's face—here—in this time.

The old furnace was covered in rust fungus and cavities so he'd have his pick of holes to peer through, and Joe wouldn't be able to see in. And he sure wouldn't think to look for him behind a rusted-out old furnace. Besides, Joe would expect him to answer his call. This old aluminum heap hadn't worked in years and yet he felt hot, kind of feverish back here. Hearing a voice might soothe him, even his own voice.

"Scared."

Oh great, he had the shakes now. Maybe he should take a powder while he still could and go find Iris. Hiding was a stupid idea. He didn't have the heart or guts to resist Joe's call. Man, it was getting hot down here. Did he really have the strength to stay back, to not return with Joe to his life? He felt the vibration of footsteps on the floor above. *God please help.*

Through a crack he saw legs coming down the stairs, a body moving closer, what must have been an industrial flashlight because the entire room suddenly exploded in light. Then he saw Joe. His friend, Joe.

"Ronny?" Joe softly called his name.

He stared at him.

"Ronny are you down here, man?"

A tear trickled down his cheeks.

Joe swished away the garbage on the floor with his foot. He looked so tired. He stopped and rubbed his eye. Fixed on the one spot, he looked around the room, then plodded toward the furnace and stared at it, hands on his hips.

He wished he didn't have to breathe. He wished the tears would stop falling because they were stuffing up his nose. Walter was dead. Why was this tragic fact hitting him now? Joe stood inches from him, so close that his shadow enveloped him. Inches and a fractured mass of decayed sheet metal was all that separated them. It seemed that Joe was staring directly into his eyes.

He turned off the flashlight—*what're you doing, Joe?*—and stood quietly in the dark with the moonlight streaming in through cracked windows. Oh no. If Joe was meditating, he'd know he was here. He would find him. This had to be the most nerve-wracking thing ever. He wanted to jump out from behind the furnace and say, 'I'm here, Joe. Let's go home.' Walter would understand. *Walter was gone.*

He didn't feel well. Feverish. Nerves. Extremely feverish. What if everything with Walter a little while ago was all a dream? He had to hang on. He would see Walter again. He would.

He listened to Joe breathing. What was he doing, geez! Another minute of this and he'd pass out, and he couldn't pass out without making a whole bunch of racket. He closed his eyes. For a guy that wanted to give Joe a shout-out so badly, he was sure doing his best to be silent. If staying in this time was the wrong thing, God would've imparted that to him. *Yes, surely.*

He would stay.

He'd stay here in this time and do the work on the machine for all of them ... so they could have that twenty-four hour visit in the Year 6. And the rest of them had to get along without him and Walter for a while, just like

Walter said. They had to be with their pain. *Joy reveals joy, but pain reveals a whole lot more than sorrow—bye, Walter.*

Joe turned the flashlight back on and tapped it on his palm. A minute later he sighed and headed toward the stairs.

Ronny watched his friend leave.

Bye, Joe.

21. The Big Picture

Joe returned to Marianlake at sunrise. A somber Bishop Gianni was at the rink waiting for him. "Don't say anything, Vittorio," he said, depleted. "Give me a silent minute. Please."

"Joe, there's something––"

"Please."

He remained on the pod with his head lowered and his eyes closed. After a moment he looked up at the Bishop. "As you can see, I didn't find Ronny. I hung around––"

"Joe––"

"All night. All night in that twisted twilight zone. And I couldn't find him. Just have to go back tonight, that's all."

He noticed Vittorio's black choir dress cassock, mozzetta and purple biretta. Only bishops wore the purple hat and short shoulder-cape. Almost forgetting Vittorio was a bishop now, he wasn't accustomed to seeing him in formal gear. A jarring adrenaline rush replaced the weariness. Why was his mentor friend waiting for him here at the rink at 6 a.m. dressed in formal liturgical vestments?

He cleared his throat. "Why the ceremonial garb?"

Reaching for his arm, Bishop Gianni told him in Italian that he had sad news.

"My Italian's rusty, Vittorio. Better give it to me in English."

"Joe, the gangrene in Walter's leg, it ... the doctors had to amputate. After that his heart ceased. It could not support the strain of surgery. I'm sorry, Joe. Father Vaux and I have been up all night with his family. They're at the rectory now. Step off the pod, Joe."

"Walter died last night? No, I can't ... I can't uh ..."

"You need rest. Pay your condolences to his family and then rest."

"Yes, um." He stumbled toward Vittorio. "But let me walk back. I need a few minutes ... some time ..."

"*Sì.*" Vittorio lapsed into Italian again, asking him if he wanted company.

He shook his head. "Who all knows? Does everybody know?"

"The fathers and Alain know. Father Andre is making announcements through proper channels. By tomorrow, everyone involved worldwide will know."

"Is Iris at the rectory helping him?"

"Iris? No. Iris is not here."

"Was she at the hospital last night? Maybe she's still there."

"Joe, I haven't seen Iris around here for days."

He walked along the road, shaking, ducking his chin inside his collar. It had finally stopped raining. The ground in the little cemetery was thick with mud, but the storm had washed the pathway clean and flattened the weeds. He read parts of the headstones as he passed. French priests, mostly. A few sisters from the Order. The elements had completely obscured the writing on one cluster of headstones. Drawn to the middle stone because of the small statue of Saint Michael on top, he kicked away the weeds in front.

He took no notice of the first few letters he uncovered in the name. He was not in the right frame of mind to read nor think, nor plan. Walter was dead—that was a fact. Ronny was lost somewhere in 1967. Another fact. Since last night he'd felt Ronny in that broken-down building.

Fact number three. He'd probably missed him by an hour, tops.

It was time to pay his respects to Walter's family. He turned and shuffled off toward the rectory. If this had been any other day in his life, any other day, he would have seen this headstone. He would have seen it and been greatly disturbed by it.

Alain Girard Duprielle
Naître: Août 24 1970
Mort: Août 25 1970

∞∞∞

By New Year's Eve 1991, Edmon had not returned to Angelfish Cove, not even for the three expensive suits he left behind. His landlady packed up his belongings and asked Carol Ann to store them. She said she'd take a pass on that. If Edmon hadn't returned for them by now, Edmon wasn't returning at all. Like a late night train whistle, memories of Edmon Fendi sometimes haunted her. Joe likened the memories to phantom pains after an amputation.

Ronny and Iris were missing and everyone had this silent pact not to mention it tonight. But then no one had mentioned it for days. The day of Walter's funeral, she started a journal. There was much to catch up on and in spite of their loss and sadness, she felt optimistic. She had gained back ten pounds and felt a little like her old self. She always believed that the 'mission' and the 'machine' were too far-fetched, yet this last month, while her friends distanced themselves from the dream, she had come to believe in it. This dream mission was now a *plausible* thing.

Carol Ann pondered the word as she watched Joe fill the ice buckets, and watched his grandmother watching him. This is what everybody had been doing these past months–watching each other watch each other and saying little. At midnight, they all stood around like wilted heads of lettuce listening to Joe mouth a bunch of words in which he held no trust.

"Well, two things collapsed in '91–the Soviet Union and our mission. Here's to '92. To conquered fear and restored hope."

That was her first glimpse of the tiny crack in Joe's armor. Of course he was human, no matter the gift. But she wasn't jealous of his relationships with Maggie or Alain anymore. As he talked, she looked into those soulful, brown eyes and remembered the first time she prayed for the return of his happiness, whether it included her or not. That was when Ronny disappeared and Joe went looking for him. It was also the end of her obsession with him. How freeing it was, she wrote in her journal, to love Joe and not obsess about Joe.

Through the spring and fall he stopped in Pages every day to read the paper. He'd spend no more than an hour with the paper whether or not he finished reading. After folding and stacking it neatly on the table, he'd go down to the basement and close the Red Door behind him. Twenty minutes later he'd come up and shake his head at her. On the way out he'd always remind her to call if anything needed fixing. Sometimes they'd grab a bite across the street at Corey's, but mostly he'd walk back to the beach house. Though the thirteen-kilometer daily walk kept him fit, he no longer rode, went to the races, or hunted down property in Ocala. 'Go to Ocala', she told him. 'Go look at properties. Here's an idea—go riding'.

He'd just twist his face at her and say, "Meh."

Now that the mission was off, nothing interested him anymore, including her. All he thought about, to her knowledge, was finding Ronny Fergel. At least once a week he'd say to Alain, Maggie or herself,

"The answer's right in front of me. Right here in Angelfish Cove. I know it."

∞∞∞

Christmas of '92 was too depressing for him. He was reminded of old acquaintances 'unforgotten', like Ronny and Iris. And the hockey rink in Marianlake's Rec. Centre was having its grand opening the first weekend in January. Originally, Rome had planned to stall the opening to '97 on the pretext of lack of funds due to the withdrawal of a major investor. They had it all beautifully and believably worked out–the 'stalling sting', the 12-month mission, the disassembly of the time machine. Then in '97, miraculously, the investor would come through, construction would resume, and the rink would open within months.

Joe attended a few of the games but found it difficult to concentrate. His eyes would dehydrate from glaring at the camouflaged time machine. Why was he worrying this much? The panel was undetectable and safely insulated. He still had the disc and Walter's remote set from the last trip in '91. Then there was the half-finished remote. Technically, he could travel forward in time without adjustment to the rink panel. But of course, the coordinates were unchangeable, so they needed to arrive and depart from the rink. And one thought of another attempt at time reversal without Ronny equaled one night of insomnia. So far he calculated the loss of a year's sleep.

Two days prior to Christmas, the day they decorated the rink for the big opening, a gang of young vandals broke in and spray-painted graffiti on the ice. In seasonal red and green, they wrote *Finally The Puck Gets Going Snoozebags*. Then they painted a Happy New Year hat over the double o's in snoozebags. Father Vaux said it was rather creative. Missing the humor, Joe suggested there was no need to wait on dismantling Walter's machine. But he didn't mean that, not really, and waited patiently for someone to talk him out of it. Alain managed to do that over the telephone. "You're too hard on yourself, Joe," he told him. "You're literally dis-Spirited. 'Total trust', remember? Get it back."

Elizabeth stopped returning to Angelfish Cove on weekends in January of '93. She'd accepted a transfer post with the Carmelite Order in Las Cruces, New Mexico, teaching grade twelve Art and History. Although she believed Ronny was fine wherever he was and would show up unexpectedly one day with coffee and a bag of donuts, everyone could see she wanted distance. So they threw her a goodbye party and off she went. With Joe's dark night of the soul as obvious as an eclipsing moon, he said to Elizabeth, "I've run clean out of pretensions."

∞∞∞

It was 104° at Aggie Memorial Stadium in Las Cruces during Dina's July tour-stop. Safely tucked away offstage, surrounded by press and private security staff, Elizabeth watched the first dozen rows of the audience get hosed down. She saw many temperature changes that night, especially Dina's, whenever someone made reference to the marks on her wrists. Once again the marks had attracted attention. With stories re-circulating, it was clear their quiet time in limbo was at an end.

Those marks never were adequately explained and the press began hounding her. Why were so many people with the marks getting into trouble? A brawl in a tucked away bar in a quiet, Spanish villa. A scene outside a church in Detroit. A skydiving accident that looked suspiciously like a suicide attempt in Newfoundland. All bore identical markings. What fascinated the press most were their similar statements during questioning.

The marks used to be more prominent, many said, but had almost faded now. *Why are the marks fading*, asked one anchor on a major city news station? *What do they mean? What the hell were they in the first place*? Carol Ann took out the journal and made a point of recording this in great detail, as she did most things. The journal was already an inch thick.

It was obvious that Dina Amodeo was no longer sought. She was hunted. In mid '94, caught in a mob scene with fans on the European leg of the tour, she sustained two broken ribs and a fractured wrist. A press photographer captured her fixing to deck a guy who got hold of her sleeve and wouldn't let go. But something held Dina back.

'I just have to remember that night,' she wrote Elizabeth, 'when all of us were together again and we first heard of the mission. It keeps me from losing it. It can't all have been for nothing. Can it? You guys keep me sane.'

∞∞∞

Maggie sent the Saint Michael statue out for re-facing in the early spring of '95. The Cove winters had been hard on it—and her. Frequent migraines forced her to shut out the sun she so loved and keep the blinds drawn. But she always managed to paint, even for fifteen minutes on the worst days.

Determined to keep the mission dream alive, she didn't tell them she still listened to Ronny's Aramaic lessons. She was fluent now, especially since she spent so much time lying in bed. Energized by instances of recurring portrait images in her head and visions of ancient canvases— messages came through, came *back*. She longed to share this with the others but a powerful force within urged silence, secrecy.

This was *their* secret, a secret between herself and a loving source of light. She'd often have visions of a cloudburst shifting into emerald plumes with thousands of eyes. Other times she'd see armor and a shield with undecipherable writing. Token glances were all she got.

By October of '95, Maggie left her cherished cabin to be nearer to her physician in Suffolk County, New York, and temporarily returned to the old mansion. Angelfish Cove was her home now and once she got this headache business straightened away she'd head back. Diagnosed with severe migraine headaches, the attacks came without warning and sometimes lasted for days, making the most potent forms of medication impossible to avoid. Maggie rarely complained.

Still she managed to paint and after an attack she wondered how she could paint this well, considering she was a zombie most of the time. Her doctor said it was a miracle she could get out of bed at all during these attacks, let alone paint. But 1996 was fast approaching and she had begun worrying about Carol Ann and Joe. Actually, she'd been worrying about all of them from Rome to Angelfish Cove to Marianlake and now—New Mexico.

She wanted them to join her in New York for New Year's Eve since staving off depression was always easier to do in a group. This December thirty-first would have been their departure date for Judea 6. Ronny Fergel had been missing for five years.

The New Year's Eve party was not going to happen for Maggie. This latest spell was the worst yet. Carol Ann arrived early Christmas Eve and seldom left her side. She set down a pot of taheebo tea on her night table.

"I'm staying," she said in that voice of hers, the one she used when no one could talk her out of anything. "I'm going to stay and ring in '96 with you."

"You know, they can all still come," Maggie said in a whisper, holding a cool facecloth over her eyes. "Because I'm sick is no reason--"

"Maggie, you need absolute quiet. No noise. Even this house isn't big enough to drown out party noises. Besides, you don't want everybody walking around on crushed eggs, do you?"

"No. But everybody sounds so lost. And I don't buy Joe's act. He's been putting on a brave front for too long. I don't care how many times he's danced with the demons and come out of it. He seems to have forgotten what he's learned and Alain's away so much."

Carol Ann slid back in the chair by Maggie's bed. "He hasn't forgotten. It's just that his thinking has become emotional. He told me that as more time passes, he becomes increasingly unaware. And the more he focuses on regaining his sense of awareness, the more it eludes him. He grasps and it eludes. And what's so frustrating is that he knows this principle. He knows the answer is not to grasp."

"I have sketches for everyone," Maggie said, happy that Carol Ann seemed to have learned the principle herself. She removed the facecloth and made strong eye contact. "Lately I've been too weak to paint because my hand keeps slipping. So I've been sketching. Remember that sketch I did up at Marianlake all those years ago?"

"The one with the door and those grotesque bat creatures?"

"Yeah. Remember how I couldn't remember sketching it?"

"You're not going to tell me you're sketching those things again, are you?"

"No. But in my latest state of oblivion, I did sketch one and this sketch is very unusual. I've sent the original to Joe as a Christmas present but had a couple of copies made. They're tucked in back of my sketchpad on the lounge over there. This sketch could be what it takes to brighten everybody's spirits, Carol Ann."

"What's it of?" Carol Ann yanked out the pad buried under Maggie's bathrobe and handed it to her.

"It's of Ronny."

∞∞∞

On New Year's Eve, Joe and Father Richard sat in the front row of the Marianlake rink while Pancake played high in the stands, scratching his back and yipping at the echo of his bark. Father Richard let Pancake mosey while they sat expectantly with Maggie's sketch unfolded across their laps.

Joe checked his watch for the fourth time in twenty minutes. It was 11:40 PM. "Gettin' there," he said to Richard, who didn't look overly pleased to be here. "Come on, Richard, what's with the gloomified face? You don't want me to be disappointed if this doesn't go down, is that it?"

"Just don't shoot all your pucks in the wrong net, Joe."

He had to laugh. "Have to dust the cobwebs off the hope." He tapped the circled date in Maggie's sketch. "And this, Richard—*this* gives me the most hope I've had since Ronny and Iris disappeared."

Maggie had sketched a thinner Ronny with wrists heavily-bandaged, in a workshop environment, desk covered in pieces of scrap metal, crumbs and a donut bag. In the midst of this mess was his *Garfield* mug and half-eaten donut hanging off the rim. Maggie didn't know about this habit because he'd asked her. He could've matched laps around the track with a yearling when he first saw what Ronny was working on—a duplicate of Walter's remote.

Father Richard smiled. "At least twice a week Ronny grabbed the donut instead of the handle. Walter was always buying paper towels for Ronny, who'd grab a handful, sop up puddles of coffee and carry on, oblivious."

Behind Ronny was a window framed in holly and tinsel with a view of a distant bridge. The sun hung high over the bridge, so it looked to be midday. Two items stood out like a pair of red bulbs on a string of blue lights—the lime-greenish light on the remote in Ronny's hand and the large calendar by the window, flipped to December 1971. A spiral of circles enclosed the 31st with the word 'MID' underlined below.

If Maggie's work was as prophetic as ever, then Ronny might try to get a message through at midnight. What better place to relay the message than the panel below the rink floor? Definitely a long shot worth checking. After all these years, wherever Ronny was hangin' his hat, he still *believed.* His work on Walter's remote was the proof in the Christmas pudding. Minutes before midnight while remembering that long ago promise from the angel, his stomach fluttered at the prospect of two miracles-in-waiting—a message from Ronny and the angel's voice in '96. He folded up the sketch and put it back in the tube.

"Come on, Father. Let's get closer."

Yipping and tail wagging, Pancake joined them at the retaining board behind the goal cage.

"I could never fathom," Father Richard said, "why there's been no inquiry into the disappearance of Iris Valez. It was like she never existed."

"There was always something about Iris," he said under his breath, fingers curled into the net. *Come on, Ronny.*

He and Father Richard checked their watches at the same moment. "11:58," Richard said. And at 12:02 he said, somewhat dejectedly, "Happy New Year, Joe."

He couldn't take his eyes off the ice. "You too, Richard. Happy New Year. *Come on, Ronny.*"

"Yes. Come on Ronny."

Pancake yipped once.

Maggie's work had always played a mysterious part in the game plan. For many this was a difficult night and she'd passed around the hope pot to everybody. If all had gone according to plan, they'd be on the pod now. Ronny would be roll-calling the checklist, including items *not* to take, things like paper and pens, watches, roll-on deodorant and pocket calculators, jewelry with fancy clips. Boxer shorts and prescription bottles. And of course, obvious things like eye and sunglasses, and lastly–the cross and crucifix.

At 12:03 a spark of green flickered under the ice. He took in a gulp of air and nursed it. "Richard? Did you see that?"

A strong band of green flashed below the surface.

"Yes, Joe, I see it!"

It grew stronger and brighter and he cheered it on. "Ronny, you little dammer, man! You're still with us. Come on home!"

The green light flashed until 12:10, Ronny's way, no doubt, of reinforcing his message to whoever was here watching. "Yes! We're back in business."

"Happy New Year, Joe," Father Richard said again, and then again, giving him a hug. "Happy New Year."

"To you too, Father," he laughed. "Joy in '96."

'Ease up on yourself, Joe. Always, there's a bigger picture. Front and back.'

He closed his eyes. Father Richard did not hear the amazing voice he'd been waiting sixteen years to hear again. That night driving out of the Cove with Willie, it had told him Carol Ann's name and reminded him to study in the Spirit. Then it said he wouldn't hear his voice again until 1996. This was the voice of his angel. Renewed hope for their *big picture* filled him with peace ... peace as fleeting as Ronny's icy band of green.

∞∞∞∞

Their renewed hope in the mission brightened the long New England winter. Dina felt it as far away as Bali where she had been hiding since her last tour. After receiving Elizabeth's letter in January, she wrote a ballad called '3 Minutes'. The three minutes referred to Ronny's 12:03 message. 'His watch always did run three minutes slow', Elizabeth wrote in that letter. 'Joe said it's another clue. My son's coming home!'

But as the months passed, no new sketches came from Maggie and before they knew it, New Year's Eve had come round again. Throughout January of 1997, Joe spent an hour a day behind the Red Door trying to reconnect with his angel's voice. Nothing. And although Edmon never returned to the Cove, he seemed to have left his seed in each of them.

Alain assured him that Light would obliterate all dark angels of the mind. No seed would propagate. All these years of mis-timing and waiting were, of course, for a reason. Reminded that he was hanging on too tight, Alain's attempt to talk him into a vacation went for naught until Alain and Carol Ann ganged up on him. He felt like he was abandoning them and absolutely refused to go until Carol Ann got blunt.

"Listen, Joe—we actually *require* your absence. We need you to go get spiritually juiced somewhere so you can return with fresh eyes and find Ronny." He still refused, but the next day when he went down to meditate behind the Red Door, Carol Ann had it padlocked. "My house, my door, my lock," she said. "Have a nice trip."

He decided to bone-up with Vittorio in Rome and had his hand on the phone when Tim Pink called and invited him to Mardi Gras in New Orleans. He could lose himself there, the way he did at Patsy's Bar back in the fall of '81. On his way to the airport he told Alain, "I've had shadows dangling carrots under my nose for twenty-seven years. Now if one of these carrots stick, no play on words intended, you call me. I am so sick and tired of living in and waiting for *the future*. And I don't even know when that happened. At first I thought it was when Ronny disappeared. Now I'm thinking it was before that. From day one in Rome, we were taught to live in the present. Who knows, maybe I'll find the present in New Orleans."

"Look softly," Alain said. "Remember, you found Ronny once. You'll find him again."

He said nothing, save, "Keep the home fires burning ... *Remiel.*"

Although Mardi Gras was a slice of crazy, he had himself a good time with Tim and his family. He loved New Orleans, even polished up the old blues harp and jammed with a few bands on Bourbon Street. In April after deciding to stay a while longer and not wanting to wear out his welcome at Tim's, he rented a little shotgun house in the French Quarter and said 'Where yat' a lot.

It bothered him when Carol Ann refused his May invitation to spend a vacation week or two with him in New Orleans. 'Pages is too busy right now', she had said. It was bothering him when he rented a car and drove eight and a half hours to Ocala to look at two horse farms for sale. Though the dream had a bit of rust on it, he still had the dream.

So he rode, hung around Ocala for a week, groomed a few horses, even paid a visit on Claxton Farms, all the time avoiding the barn. He didn't need to go in there, didn't need the nightmare memory. Just that he'd heard the sons were considering listing the farm since Claxton Senior's death. But neither the sons nor anyone else from the old days were around, so he sat in the car for an hour, staring at the outside of the tumbledown barn, listening to phantom whinnies and tasting the dust and chaff in the air. He thought about the day his mother died, wondered whatever happened to Fast Forward. Mum had the Kentucky Derby and Breeder's Cup fantasy for Forward, but it was like the horse fell off the planet. Figuring today wasn't the day to get the zip back into the dream, he left. Besides, the bugs were biting.

He called Carol Ann his last night in Ocala and drove back to New Orleans the next day. Maybe it was time to go home *home*—back to Angelfish Cove. Back to that little strawberry blonde who'd become charmingly unavailable. He still had no clue where to find Ronny but he no longer felt the weight of the problem. Alain and Carol Ann were right. The vacation was a good thing. Once he got home he'd be clearer.

His second last night in the French Quarter he strolled into the *Cajun Cabin Restaurant* around midnight for jambalaya and clams. While the band fiddled and tuned for the next set, he made himself comfortable at a small table near the stage. The waitress promptly appeared and he had to admit, waitresses always promptly appearing in front of him was another thing to be grateful for.

But this waitress didn't have strawberry blonde hair or a cluster of freckles on her nose or ask questions from out of left field like, 'Is there a feeling you're trying to ignore? Maggie says the number 2 pencil is the most popular—so why is it number two?' Or continually peppering their conversation with facts like dogs having elbows or one-third of the population can't snap their fingers. Her questions made everyone else's sound boring.

"Can I get you a menu?"

By the time the waitress returned with his order, he'd tuned into one of the musicians, an elderly man with eyes like pools of wisdom and fingers that mesmerized guitar strings. He asked her his name.

"Albert Lomax," she said, eyeing his shoulders.

"Please send him whatever he's drinking and ask if he'd be kind enough to stop at my table after the set."

Twenty minutes later, Albert Lomax stopped by and thanked him for the drink. After inviting him to sit, they shared an odd first moment. Quiet. Albert Lomax stared at his wrists, while he stared at Albert's cap. He spoke first.

"Your bass wails, Mr. Lomax. Thanks for joining me."

"Pleasure, son. And it's Albert." The musician bobbed his finger at his wrist. "You know, I know what the real SC stands for. Seen a few of them around over the years. Saavve theeee Children." Albert had drawled this out almost lovingly.

"What if I tell you it stands for 'Second Christmas'?"

Albert gently shook his head. "For the others, maybe. When you get old, you learn to pay attention to the words that come outta your mouth, the words–and more–the thought that beats the words there. And I ain't even psychic. Or if I am, we all are."

"You're aware," he said, distracted by Albert's words, and his cap.

"Aware? That's the buzzword now, is it? Could explain it."

"How does *SC* make you aware in connection with me?"

"Simple. Cause it was the thought I got. And I keep my thoughts simple. So don't ask me to make them complicated. You understandin' me?"

Joe laughed. "I hear you. Can I ask you about your cap, Albert? I have one just like it and I thought mine was an original."

Tilting its brim at him, it was Albert's turn to laugh. "An original! You sure do hail from the far north, polar boy. *C A P* stands for *Civic Air Patrol*. Got its base set up two States over. CAP headquarters is at Maxwell Air Force Base in Alabama. These hats are all over the South." Noticing his drugged-like expression, Albert asked, "You look like an alligator bitten in the butt. What's wrong, son?"

"I thought that cap meant something else. In a way, it's been part of a puzzle I've been trying to solve for many years. That cap hasn't exactly kept my life uncomplicated."

"See my bass guitar on that stage up there?"

"Yeah."

"I've played that bass in the company of thousands of musicians. Most of them I never laid eyes on before. But one thing I do know—when I jam with strangers, until I flow into their rhythm, all I got is my own chord. So I stick with it, mixing their licks with mine. Then soon we make sweet music, Joe. Real sweet music."

"I'm not sure I follow."

"I'm sayin' you gotta stick with what's familiar. Until you jive with the man, you stick to your own pattern. And you ain't gonna find that pattern until you remove all the confusing bullshit. That's when you find your chord. You understandin' my words?"

"I'm feeling ya, Albert."

"I don't know about this puzzle of yours, Joe. But if my cap isn't what you thought it was, then it's probably not part of your puzzle at all."

Joe remembered Iris's words to him that day in Corey's attic, *"Maybe it's just a cap."* Then it really hit him, the last thing Iris told him before she said goodbye. *Don't lose sight of the big picture. The front and the back.* And his angel's words, *Always, there's a bigger picture. Front and back.* "I think I found my pattern," he told Albert, "which was in the picture all along. Literally."

He bought a cassette of Albert's songs and for the first time in years, listened to music in the rental car over the three-day drive to the Cove. *Thanks, Albert.*

∞∞∞

Pages had closed by the time he got into Angelfish Cove. He didn't know what to go for first–the Angel Reclining or Carol Ann. Of course mission business had to come first, but then a few moments shared with Carol Ann after all these months was the polite thing to do, and she was expecting him. Mission business. He smiled at the thought as he rapped on the door. How many years had it been since thinking about mission business was not torture? Carol Ann opened the door and that gorgeous, wide smile of hers stabbed at his heart. What was different?

"Six!" he said to her first thing, and then laughed.

"What?"

He entered past her and closed the door. "Six. It all feels right again after six years."

"It's on again, isn't it, Joe? I can feel it. And Maggie's never stopped feeling it."

He looked at her all over and she blushed. He didn't mean to do that. It just happened. After a few more enjoyably awkward seconds, he hugged her and kissed her cheek. Holding her in his arms felt as warm and smooth as the Mystic River in July. "Glad I'm home," he said over her shoulder.

"Are you really *really* home?"

"We all are, Carol Ann. And *all* includes Ronny."

"Ronny? You know where he is? Tell me! Tell me what you wouldn't say on the phone."

It didn't take him long to recap the Albert Lomax story, especially with the painting in his peripheral view. Carol Ann had moved it from the top of the stairs into the bookstore. He couldn't wait to get into it and somehow she sensed this.

"I have a couple of distributors to call on the West Coast," she said, "and it's near the end of their working day there. So I'll leave you with the painting for a bit, okay?"

He nodded, remembering the first time he saw those freckles on the bridge of her nose. She had a new hair-do, bangs, and a short page-boy combed behind her ears. She was looking pretty adorable.

"If I put the puzzle together tonight, we'll go back to the beach house and crack open a bottle of wine. And we'll tell Alain. Is he in town?"

"I'm not sure, Joe. I haven't seen much of him." She smiled and left him with the *Angel Reclining*.

He leaned against the wall, crossed his arms and studied the painting. Wow. It still packed a mystical charge, still connected past with present like magnetic poles. Every significant event had occurred in the past. All the puzzle pieces were in the past. Or were they? Though he felt grounded here and now in 1997, he could visualize John Corey slashing that seven for the first time like he was there *with* John.

Sometimes you have to go backward to move forward. That first night in town with Willie popped into his mind.

Pages was the only place anachronistic of its time. When they left Pages, he felt so drawn to the painting it was difficult to leave. Even then. So all along it was the painting he was meant to see in Pages that night. Had he studied it then, he would have anticipated the answers when Maggie painted it for real years later. With a little help from John Corey, the *Angel Reclining* located Ronny the first time. Now it was about to locate him again.

Warmed by the Spirit in and around him, he spotted a beam of light across the street and flung open the door. Yards away, two small orbs of light dissolved into nothingness, leaving a twinkle in their wake. Whatever they were, they were still watching him, and this time the presences were positive. Heart fluttering, he returned to the painting.

He observed the little blonde-haired girl in daisy dungarees catching a triad of rays with her magnifying glass—one on the barn some distance behind her, one on a silver toy subway car or a train club car, and the last on Marvick's storefront. 98 Main Street. Maggie painted the numbers in rainbow colors, psychedelic-like. 98 Main Street. He stepped in closer. The even numbers were on Carol Ann's side of the street ... on this side.

He plucked one of Carol Ann's business cards from the gold candy dish by the register. Pages address was 52 Main. No way on earth could Marvick's number be 98. The numbers didn't even reach 98 on this street. He couldn't get across the road fast enough.

The number was still rainbow-colored, all right. Old Len Marvick hadn't changed that. But the real number on Marvick's was 57. It had always been 57. *My God.* He let out a spirited whoop, so spirited that Mr. Marvick and several other tenants flicked on the apartment lights above the stores. He waved at them and padded back to Pages, which seemed like the longest walk he'd ever taken.

He had lost Ronny back in 1967. And for every New Year that followed, he'd secretly toasted Ronny in the current year. Ronny Fergel was twenty-four years behind ... in '73—making '73 *his* '97. This was the year he was going to bring Ronny home! *Oh Maggie, our Maggie. You're the angel.* He wanted to yell up to Carol Ann and tell her to get down here. But he had to figure out when. What month? What date? There were six months remaining in this year. Now that the brain was clear, he knew the answer was two minutes away.

It didn't take him the two minutes. More like thirty seconds. Maggie had painted Marvick's having a firework draw, with a large box of fireworks in the window and a sign on top.

Contest Draw - Noon July 4th.

How many times had he walked by this painting over the years and seen this box? A couple hundred, maybe? What an amazingly perfect day to bring Ronny home– Independence Day. July fourth. But this was '97 and Maggie had painted '98 over Marvick's. Pieca cake now to figure out. This was their true mission departure date. In the first minutes of the New Year 1998, Ronny Fergel could finally roll call that itemized list. He knew one other thing, too—if he could convince Father Andre to verify the dates on the ever-mysterious Roman document, those dates will have miraculously altered. 1991 would now read 1998. He was sure of it! So all bets were on again. And in less than three weeks he could bring *the child* safely home.

∞∞∞

From an orb of light across the street, Remiel said to his superior, "Joe has so much joy ahead, many wonderful surprises. But they will have their price. Will he be seeing you, Sir?"

The Archangel Prince smiled. "Yes, twice more in this exile. And Remiel?"

"Yes, Sir?"

"The *price* most often becomes their greatest consolation. Is Margaret ready?"

"Almost."

"And when are you going to reveal your identity to Joe?"

"At the Jubilee, Sir."

"And Iris?"

"Also at the Jubilee."

The Prince of Light left then, leaving Remiel to his Jubilee thoughts.

22. Silver Sword

July 4th

It was 3 PM in the Cove. 3 PM, *1973*. Some of the kids were lighting sparklers and setting off cherry bombs on the boardwalk. He and Carol Ann strolled along Main Street, grinning at bell-bottom jeans and Afro hair-dos. Carol Ann said that bell-bottoms were worn by sailors because they fit easily over boots and could be used as flotation devices.

The air smelled of wet wood, musk oil and patchouli. From the corner of his eye, he checked to see how Carol Ann was adjusting. He could tell she loved it in spite of the tension in her shoulders, understandable since it was she who had to fetch Walter's book from John Corey's attic. Not the most pleasant of tasks. But they each had their directives and finally they could carry them out.

The old glass factory looked pretty much the same as the day she and Brent began renovations for the *surreal* estate business. Her pet name for it. Somehow she always knew that neither the biz nor Brent would last very long. She smiled at Joe. They hadn't made out since they met in 1981. Now they were in 1973, which was eight years before they met. What was *surreal* now?

"I wonder how much Ronny's changed," he said, reading the sign in Marvick's window.

Congrats to our contest winners Sanford and Tisha Blewett. Don't blow yourselfs up tonight. Happy 4th of July. Len and Tammy Marvick.

He worried that negative forces had messed with Ronny here in the '70s. And what about the late '60s? He considered the Monterey Pop Festival back in '67 and the Harvard Prof they called Big Daddy. Timothy Leary. Now what was his mantra? *Turn on. Tune in. Drop out.* Yep, those could do it, especially if Edmon was hanging out with him. Ugh, the thought.

"--I would think he's matured in un-Ronny ways," Carol Ann said. "What he's been through would do that."

"But some things never change, I hope. I'm thinking about Maggie's sketch of him with his mug and donut. Wanna bet we find him in Corey's?"

"Oh boy, my nerves could stand a complete overhaul. If I took Valium, I'd take Valium. How 'bout you?"

He put his arm around her waist as they walked. "I just want to get him safely home. I didn't exactly keep him safe all these years, did I?"

"You did everything you could. Seriously. Wasn't it all meant to be this way? Slowly, we've all been finding our way home. That yellow journal of mine's an inch and a half thick now. What if John Corey's hanging around?"

"I doubt he will be or we would've looked familiar to him years later. This may be the weekend he's away for the holiday. I'm nervous too, Carol Ann."

They chose an umbrella table in the middle of Corey's patio. This way they could scan the action from both ends of Main Street. They would wait as long as it took because he felt certain that Ronny would drop by at some point. He always loved his food and Corey's had the best in town. Ronny Fergel could not have changed that much. Once they found him, Carol Ann would sneak off into the attic, do her thing, then they would bring Ronny home to Marianlake. The whole gang was waiting, except Alain. Father Andre had closed the Rec. Centre for the weekend on some ridiculously believable pretext. And Alain–his elusive Alain–was off somewhere on mission business. There was much to do.

They tried to pass the time making small talk but that didn't work too well. Given the anomalous circumstance, it was difficult just trying to stay in the present moment. He knew Ronny was finally coming home, that in the deepest part of him were answers to a life's worth of questions. During meditation behind the Door last night, some dark, burning horror had been unchained. Though the release click of the lock distressed him, he felt certain this horror would soon be crushed. But ohh ... his poor, sad earth. A silver sword lay on the ground beside the chain, the only two discernible things in the vision.

Joe inhaled the pungent scent of hay and rancid oranges—overpowering, seeping down his throat, and then *poof*—gone. He coughed, straightened his back and glanced around the patio.

"What is it, Joe?" Carol Ann asked. "Now I've really got the jitters, what is it?"

He didn't answer. He didn't answer her because he was preoccupied with the man entering the patio. The man, fair, heavyset and bearded, sat down at the table directly beside them. He was carrying, of all things, an old *Civic Air Patrol* bag. Seeing the CAP letters widened his smile.

He continued to stare and smile. The man ordered an iced coffee and asked for the specials. His eyes misted when the man's eyes wandered past the waitress and landed at his and Carol Ann's table. The man stood all the way up. Slowly, he stood up. The man looked at Carol Ann, then back at him, and he laughed out loud when Ronny tipped over the chair in his excitement. They rushed at each other and firmly embraced. They stood there, continuing the embrace and saying nothing. Everyone on the patio stopped talking.

"Joe!" Ronny nearly knocked him over with his weight. "Oh, Joe! Man I can't believe it's finally you!"

"And finally me you too!" he said and several people laughed. "Six long years, bud. Welcome home!" Needing to look deeply into Ronny's eyes, he released him, thanking God for finding him, and asking God to let him bring him all the way home. *Doesn't matter what happens to me. Just let me get him home safe*. This was not the first time he had said this prayer. "Are you all right?" Ronny's wrists were deeply scarred, more so than his own.

"Yeah, Joe," Ronny said, dabbing the corner of his eye. "I'm very all right. Now who do we have over here?"

"I hope you recognize me without my hangover," Carol Ann said, giving him a hug.

"You've been hangoverless since the time I disappeared." Ronny seemed to enjoy her mystified expression. "You okay, Carol Ann? I know you're here with Joe because of Walter's book."

The threesome sat quietly down.

"I'm jittery," Carol Ann said, displaying her shaky hands, "but I'll be okay. I know I will."

"We have so much to talk about," Joe said. "Which end of the pool do I jump in?"

"How's my mother?"

"She's good, Ronny. She's waiting for you at Marianlake. Everybody is—except Alain can't be there. But as soon as Carol Ann gets the book, we're out of here. My God ... so many questions."

Ronny reached over to the other table for the *CAP* bag. "Don't worry, Joe," he said, comically twitching his eyebrows. "It's in the bag."

"Really? You fixed the gauge?"

Ronny drummed the table with two fingers. "Just drop me off at the Bagel Factory so I can play."

"How much playing time, maestro?"

"We still leaving New Year's Eve?" After he said yes, Ronny asked, "As soon as the clock ticks '98?" When he answered yes again, Ronny said, "More than enough time. I should have all the kinks out by early fall."

"Wonderful. Just don't kink yourself into the twilight zone again."

"I plan not to do that."

"So the gauge now toggles *backward* in time?" He had to hear Ronny say it.

"Yes, Joe. That it does."

"How did you know I began straightening my head out just after you disappeared?" Carol Ann asked.

When Ronny hesitated, he thought again about personal directives. Whatever would he do for secrets when this was all over?

"Iris was here with me all this time, Carol Ann. She prayed for you when she decided to stay behind with me. That was the night Walter died. I also got the marks that night. So considering the state I was in, I knew her prayer for you was answered."

"How did Iris get here?" he asked, half expecting an answer. "She was with me during that time and I took Walter's machine."

Ronny tightened his face. "Sorry, Joe. Iris travels however she travels. Best let her fill you in."

"Okey dokey. And Iris is where?"

"She left me a note yesterday saying she was on mission business and I'd see her in a few days. You know Iris–mysterious as ever."

"I miss her," Carol Ann said. "I was so messed up when she left. So paranoid. I had it in my head that she betrayed me. I still feel bad about that."

"You'll have a chance to get hassle-free with her on New Year's Eve."

He laughed. "'Hassle free'? Is that '60s vernacular?" Ronny laughed, too. "I won't even ask about current events in the '90s yet. Don't think I'm ready, especially since my headspace is still in the '70s. And in a few months we'll be in Judea 6. Man. Get me home, Joe."

He asked Carol Ann if she was ready to go do her thing. She said yes and he put his hand on her cheek. "You said it yourself–you know you're going to be okay. I agree. I'm sure Ronny agrees, so it's unanimous. But don't yag all over that pretty summer outfit."

"Is that your way of telling me there's going to be evil up there?"

"I promise you, Carol Ann, it's being restrained. It can't touch you, not up there. Besides, I've done enough throwing up over the years for all of us. And in the nicest places, too."

"I'll put in a word to Michael the Archangel," Ronny said. "Satan's conquistador, remember?"

"Vaguely," Carol Ann said. "I remember the scales and the armor. And his glistening gold sword."

"Silver."

Joe leaned forward. "What?"

Ronny searched his eyes. "Silver sword."

"Well ..." Carol Ann stood and took a deep breath. "I think I'm ready to sneak up to John's attic and get this over with. Wow, it must be a hundred degrees on this patio."

Taking her straw purse, which was more of a fancy shopping bag, she strapped it over her shoulder and gave them a brave salute. "Don't go anywhere without me." Then she walked off toward the stairs to John Corey's attic.

"You know, no one would object to your reading Walter's book before you return it to his family," he said, trying to forget the million questions he wanted to ask that Ronny probably wouldn't or couldn't answer. "Who knows? I have the feeling they might even allow you to make several hundred copies." He used to kid Ronny about his boyish, gleeful expressions, but not today. So much for trying to stuff the Q's. "Let me share another feeling with you, now that you're home—I suspect that the departure dates on Father Andre's covert document have mysteriously morphed from '91 to '98. Now my question is—do you think, that after all these years, he would finally let me see it?"

Ronny took a swig of his iced coffee. "Don't know. Father Gianni was also one of the big three, and your pal. But I guess you've tried him already."

"Yeah. Although Vittorio's a bishop now, Father Andre is his senior. He will always respect his wishes."

"Joe, what is it with you and this document?"

"Not knowing the A to Z of it has always grated on me."

"Well you know what's in it. A bunch of headliner names involved in this mission gig. And the dream that the three of them shared. When was the last time you asked Father Andre for a look-see?"

"Shortly after you disappeared. He promised me I could see it when the mission was over. At that time I believed everything was over."

"It's not over yet. You may have to wait a little longer. What is it you think you'll find in it? I mean, the altered date thing is recent, so obviously you're looking for something else. Was there a name on it you wanted to check?"

"Yeah," he said. This was a day to celebrate. But Ronny guessed correctly. There was a name on it that he wanted to check.

∞∞∞

With the attic door closed behind her, Carol Ann leaned against it. First get to that window. She needed to open that tiny window over there. Lord, it was stifling. Actually, she could see the book from here but felt too sick, dizzy and hot to go for it. She had to breathe first. Yes, breathing was a good idea. The window.

The thought of Iris praying for her got her legs going. Thankfully, John stored his old hockey skates up here and she used a blade to pound the rusted window lock. She asked God to bless Iris for all her trouble. Finally the lock gave and she raised the small window, but the attic was still hotter than ghost peppers and her hands and wrists were killing her. *For cryin out loud, Carol Ann, get the book. Just get the book.*

She lunged for the book and pressed it to her chest. Walter Bayard's book. Maybe it wouldn't be too easy making a run for it. The fever had the con now and in this condition she could take a flyer down the stairs. So much for an inconspicuous exit. She got herself back to the window and breathed deeply. There were maybe five or six steps to the door.

Through blurred vision she checked her wrists. The air was heavy, but oh, what a lovely, *floaty* feeling. Such light and peace.

"Lord, so many are going. Thousands. Take care of them. Take care of my Maggie."

'From Love, the gift multiplies, Carol Ann. Now go.'

One. Two. Three. Ohh God! She felt Maggie here somewhere. Four! "My Maggie—five!"

Carol Ann didn't recall those last five steps. As long as she lived, she never would. And the message of Love had already left her.

Joe and Ronny were waiting on the other side of the attic door. Joe gave the book to Ronny and put his arm around her waist. He looked at her wrists. "Better to wait a bit. You should enjoy this."

"We don't have to wait," she whispered. "I am enjoying this. And I'll be enjoying this wherever we go."

"My my," Ronny said, wiping the dust off the book with his sleeve. "I'm remembering how I made this scene. Can you walk okay, Carol Ann?"

"Yes. I don't think we need to be here any longer. I think we're wanted at home now."

"So let's go home," Joe said.

"*Ciao, settanta's!*" Ronny took a bow. "Hey, what about my income tax? Did anybody file tax returns for me? They're gonna nail me for six years of tax returns––"

∞∞∞

They were all at the Marianlake rink, waiting. Elizabeth. Dina. Maggie. Fathers Andre and Richard. Bishop Gianni, the Duprielles and Ronny's entire crew. Even Rosa. She had made it her business in recent years to learn what had been going on. In the past, Joe had discussed her with his superiors and since he had no problem, they had no problem. Joe trusted her. That's all they needed to know. And Rosa so loved the Cove and these people. Being near them made her feel close to Willie and feeling close to Willie meant that Willie had to be around here somewhere.

Father Richard had the rink decorated with multi-colored balloons and *Welcome Home, Ronny* banners. He had five made, one for each corner and one taped straight across the rink. For an extra chuckle, he had a table set with six boxes of assorted donuts and one of those gallon-sized coffee machines. He even had a tape of Ronny's favorite '60s picks amped up from all the speakers. Ronny always did love that '60s stuff. Little did he know he'd end up there. Be careful what you wish for, Father Richard cautioned. At first he thought Ronny might be sick of this music until he reminded himself of the man's work progress in that era. Obviously something quite positive had come from the late '60s and early '70s.

Elizabeth cried when he came into view. While everyone else clapped and hooted, Elizabeth cried. Ronny headed straight for her arms and she welcomed him home in Latin, his favorite language, at least it used to be. He kissed her and responded in Aramaic.

"Just to keep you on your toes, Mother."

She hugged him again, observing the remarkable change in him. He could still be the big kid, but he was more confident, matured. The fear had left him and there seemed to be no hidden burdens in her slightly-slimmer, bearded son. Motherhood was astonishing. She got all this from his demeanor, his voice and his caress.

Keeping mission matters light, they had a happy reunion. At sundown Claude set off the fireworks display. How grand it was to enjoy their own Independence Day back at old headquarters on Canadian soil. Joe suggested Ronny continue swilling the java. A midnight display was waiting for him in Angelfish Cove.

"I had the plane, *our* plane re-named for you guys," Dina said. "In honor of Walter and his partner here, it is now *Plane Bagels.*"

Ronny kissed her cheek and asked her to sing a ballad, which made everyone misty all over again. At nine-thirty, Andre, Richard, and the Duprielles said goodnight to them at the plane, telling Ronny they would see him back here for work in a few days and they had the Bagel Factory all shined and polished for him.

"Well don't worry, I'll fix that pretty quick," Ronny kidded.

The rest of them boarded *Plane Bagels* and partied through the hour and a quarter flight back to Angelfish Cove. When Alain greeted them at the beach house shortly after eleven, they were feeling no pain, Carol Ann excluded. She was still high on her own experience and preferred to keep it to herself for a while, except from Alain who noticed straight away. She was the last to receive the marks and considered the others around the world sharing the phenomenon at the same moment. Later when no one was looking, she snuck away to the little Chapel of Saint Joseph down the road from Maggie's to say a private 'thank-You.'

∞∞∞∞

"How thrilled you must be," Rosa said to Sister Elizabeth as they watched fireworks brush the sky with color, "to have your son back so happy and healthy. This old noggin' of mine can hardly comprehend all of it."

Elizabeth removed the snapshot from her jacket pocket. "Ronny just gave this to me. It's of him and Iris. Taken last week right in this town in another time. Imagine! I don't know if you know Iris. She's been a wonderful friend to my son."

Rosa slipped on her bifocals. "I've talked to her on the phone a few times over the years," she said, holding the photo up to the light. Then her eyes brightened and she grabbed onto Elizabeth to brace herself. "This girl. Her eyes. I'm frightened ... frightened!"

Joe saw her reaction from across the room. "R! What is it?"

"The picture," Elizabeth said, "something in it has upset her."

Rosa didn't want to let it go.

"Come on, R, let me see the picture. Let me see what's upsetting you."

Rosa collected herself somewhat and handed it to him. "I'm fine, Joe. Just that something about her reminds me of Willie. Suddenly, these days, everything reminds me of Willie."

"But why would that frighten you?" Elizabeth asked.

"I don't know now. The feeling went as quickly as it came. It's gone. Don't worry, Joe, I'm fine."

Odd. He always thought there was something about Iris, as well. But Iris was nothing like Willie. No, nothing like Willie. They had the same warm-colored skin and rich brown eyes. That was all. Except for the heels. Good old Iris and her 'highalized' heels.

"Rosa okay?" Ronny strolled over after Elizabeth took R in the kitchen for tea. "Sorry my picture of Iris upset her."

"She'll be fine." Ronny looked flushed or sheepish, probably the beers.

"Joe?" Ronny tugged him by the T-shirt tail into the hall. "Got something to tell you. And now'd be a good time since I'm inebriated partially."

"Oh no, not the gauge. Don't say it's the gauge."

Ronny chuckled. "The gauge is good. The bottom line is–I'm gonna go with my crew. Walter would want that and so do I. I should be with the crew. So there's an extra spot to fill, if your grandmother wants to fill it."

"That's good of you, Ronny. Thanks man, but Father Richard already offered and she just can't grasp the language. He even suggested she go mute, but she doesn't want to screw it up for the rest of us. That's her primary concern." He looked over at Alain who seemed involved in a heavy conversation with Maggie. They'd been at it for an hour. What could they be talking about? "Alain already mentioned you might want to go with your crew. That'll make them happy. But thanks, anyway."

"Thank-you, Joe," Ronny said tenderly. "Thank you. I can't say that enough. And here comes Bishop Gianni. This might be the perfect time to mention you know what. Maybe he'll talk to Father Andre for you." Then Ronny took a powder so they could speak privately.

"I heard the last of that," Vittorio said, eyeing him curiously. "Why don't you just spell it?"

"That's *spill* it," he ribbed.

"Correcting my English colloquialisms is no way to batter me up, Joe." His smile widened. "What's on your mind?"

"I want to see the document."

Vittorio coughed on purpose. "Joe, we've been through this so often. Father Andre won't let you have it until the *Jubilee*."

"Jubilee? What's ... what's ...?"

"Our party, you know, our big New Year's Eve 1999 bash."

"Oh. I didn't know they named it. Will you at least verify one small thing on that document for me?"

"And that would be?"

"The departure date. I want to know if '91 mysteriously evolved into '98."

"I've already checked in Rome. They have. That is, all three of them have. My copy, Paul's, and Andre's. And that's all I can give you of the document. But I will give you another gift."

"What's that?"

"Remember Walter's original story, the one where God asked his angel to find a place?"

"Oh of course."

"The dates on that have also changed. It's time, Joe."

"What do you mean *it's time?*"

Vittorio rolled his eyes, "What do you think it means? *Bethlehem Anno Sei*. What else?"

Everybody was so into Italian and Latin these days. And the word 'time' had a different ring to it. Then there was the vision of the silver sword. Somehow the two seemed connected.

∞∞∞

Joe didn't have to be back here at Marianlake this morning. For once, the problem was not his problem. Ronny was home now. Technically, his role in this mission had already been accomplished. Not so. They were a team. That was not about to change. He would make himself available for whatever they needed, whenever they needed it. Besides, he still felt partially responsible for Ronny's safety.

It was such a kick hanging out in *The Bagel Factory* with the team. Ronny was sure on a natural high, sprinting around the Sports Centre all morning like a puppy in a field of tennis balls. His first remark regarding their corner of these unusual office headquarters was that it was 'too neat'.

"The only thing allowed to be neat in here should be Walter's desk," Ronny said, winking. "So I'm going to, *ahem*, straighten things out for you. So to speak."

Dave Thomson, *Bagel's* top Field Archaeologist, chose to keep his desk behind the stage, as far away from Ronny's as possible. He adored Ronny, they all did, but one by one they wheeled their chairs and desks away from the organized chaos around Ronny's work station. They kept Walter's desk as he left it, as a memorial and Walter's desk flanked Ronny's. And now that the 'child' was finally home at Marianlake, seriously at work, his desk was as he left it, aptly described by crew mates with words like heap, clutter, grunge and spillage.

"I'm sorry to lay this on all of you my first day back," Ronny said, shaking off the chill from the rink tour, "but we have a serious problem here."

"Not the gauge," he said. Carol Ann told him an office chair with wheels travels eight miles a year.

Ronny laughed. His obsession with that gauge amused Ronny to no end. "No." Ronny looked at Fathers' Andre and Richard, Thomson and two more of his crew. Bishop Gianni was on his way back to Rome. "We gotta shut down the rink."

"For how long?" Father Andre asked, stone-faced.

Ronny set down his oversized mug. "I'd say until about January 2nd, 1999."

Everybody was too stunned to say anything.

Before they all started talking at once, Ronny continued, "Look, surely all of you realize how the altered dates change everything. Originally, the rink wasn't to open until we were through, until the last group came home. And you know the rest of the story. The problem is this—not only do I have to install the new gauge below the rink floor, I have to test it and test it. And retest it. We have to jaunt back and forth. Thomson's crew has to return with a fresh batch of materials for Maggie.

"She has paints and canvases to prepare. And of course we have to scout more locations. Then, beginning after midnight next January first, we're going to have groups moving in and out every night—for one year. Do we really want twenty or thirty hockey teams playing around all this?"

"Can't we somehow arrange all arrivals and departures for after midnight?" Richard asked.

"Too risky," he said. Carol Ann said he should ask the crew about mosquitos and black flies. She knew he despised getting bitten. But this was hardly the time to ask. "I don't want to be an alarmist, but we must consider mis-timing, illness. I recall Walter once telling me about two cases of serious sunstroke."

"That's right," Ronny said. "We're all familiar with plans gone awry, then factor in the human condition. We're up against too much to add hassles with time. No other way to do this. Sorry. We have to shut down the rink. But for what reason? What are we going to tell the people?"

"For a year and a half–it's going to have to be serious," Andre said. "And it's July. Hockey season's just begun and we have a full roster for months. What about the rest of the facilities? The basketball court, the gym, the pro shop?"

"They can all stay open. Thomson, any ideas?"

"The cooling system and de-humidifier comes to mind. We have six miles of piping directly below the rink, with pipes four to five inches apart. If one of the pipes malfunctions, it rejects the entire cooling system."

"Yeah, but we don't want any accidents. I want a player or coach to notice something is wrong. That way they bring the problem to us, from the outside. Suppose we begin quickly but subtly. You mentioned the de-humidifier."

"Right. It keeps the retaining windows from fogging up. So let's fog 'em up. It'll take two hours. Those retaining boards and windows are four feet high. The walls will be covered in moisture even sooner. Twenty minutes."

"That's good," he said. Maybe he could spray some DEET in an antique bottle or something. "Everybody gets told the rink has to close for a day or so in order to repair the de-humidifier. And in the interim, the staff notices the ice is softening."

"Done." Ronny pushed up his sleeves like the problem was already solved. "Now, one final nut to crack ... It doesn't take a year and a half to fix a cooling system."

He interrupted their brainstorming with an idea. If they agreed he would have the satisfaction of knowing his presence was somewhat contributive. "How 'bout a phony lawsuit? That would table things."

The team agreed.

∞∞∞

"Oh, Alain," Maggie said from behind the Red Door. This room continued to unnerve her, even in Edmon's absence, however temporary that was. "I can handle it all, except the thought of pain without medication. What am I going to do there without the occasional shot of Fiorinal? That's the demon I live with now–the thought of my future in a past with no medication."

"It's this room," Alain reminded her. "You express the same thought every time you enter this room. Are you aware that's the first thing you always say?"

"Do I?" She became thoughtful. "This room does hold up the mirror, doesn't it. Are you aware that your voice always sounds different here? Deeper, more melodic, not even a trace of a French accent. Allow me to tell you something? How you process or comment on my observation is up to you."

"I don't know, Maggie."

"Please?" She knew his silence meant yes. Alain always answered yes that way. She continued cautiously. Perhaps she was out of line here, but this room had an odd effect on her. "I see you in my sketches sometimes. I never told anyone. And your voice, the one you use here, I hear it in my dreams. You always seem to be talking to someone else. There's this cloudburst. Then I see a shield, a silver sword, and a couple of times I've seen heavy chains. I've had this dream five or six times. The shield frightens me. There's an inscription on it I can't make out. And it ends with my hearing your voice talking to the man with the shield."

"What am I saying?"

"You say, 'Will you be unlocking the chain for them soon, my prince?'"

"Why didn't you tell me this before?"

"In a way, even though it's frightening, it's the most beautiful dream I've ever had. I wanted to keep it for myself. You know how I like to do that."

"So why now?"

"I finished a sketch the other night–my first night back at home in the cabin. Angelfish Cove is our real home, that's how all of us think of it, you know. Yes of course you know. Anyway, this sketch, it was of a grave. It was a gravestone, Alain. And it had *your* name on it. And below it was your birth date–August 24th to August 25th. A baby's headstone. A baby who lived one day." She waited for him to respond, but he said nothing. Nothing. She hated doing this, but she had to know. *Poor baby. You are incredibly beautiful. I wish I didn't love you so. Ohh, I love you so––*

"Stop it! You can't have these thoughts about me. They're not real." Then he realized what she was up to. "Our beautiful, Maggie. So smart. Why did you do that?"

"Because tricking you is the only way I can get you to reveal more of yourself. And I can do that in this room. Handy, huh? I'm sorry, Alain, but I see you. I really *see* you and I can't pretend otherwise. In a few months my entire life will change. I need who you truly are to be with me."

"Let's not talk here. We'll go across to Corey's—"

"Oh no you don't. I'm not stepping out of this room."

"Maggie, I can't reveal more of myself without revealing *all* of myself. And that is what you're asking of me."

"Can't is not in your vocabulary. I know that for a fact."

"No more games." He was right firm with her now, a side of him she hadn't seen. "It's true. I do have another identity. But the details of that identity are to be shared first with Joe. Even you with your gift, you can't know. Maggie, you will have a guide, I promise. You won't be alone there. And this guide is so magnificent that he makes the soul dance. Next to him I'm a speck of dust. That's all I can tell you."

"You won't tell me who Remiel is?"

"No."

"And the man with the shield in my dream, do you know who he is?"

Alain remained silent.

"So you won't tell me who he is or the meaning behind your question to him?"

"No."

"And the grave with your name on it?"

"It exists, Maggie. That's all I can tell you. Remember, my first loyalty is to Joe. Please respect that. Thank-you for not showing him that sketch."

"No need to thank me. Many of my sketches are like a diary to me. It's just that I'm so anxious. We all are, more now that we're so close to departure."

"I know."

"And my guide who'll make my soul dance ... can you tell me who *he* is?"

"That's his job. Now do you think we can get back to business?"

"Boy, I can certainly appreciate Joe's frustration. Do you know that your skin doesn't have a pore in it? You should do something about that. People will notice."

Alain laughed. "You want to poke me full of holes?"

"I know. I'm stalling. Alain, once I prepare those canvases, maybe then the reality of Judea 6 will sink in. It hasn't yet. I wish to God you'd answer my questions."

"They'll get answered. Tell you a secret. The reality hasn't completely sunk in for the thousands of others, either. And it won't, not even when they step off that pod into the year six. Reality will happen when they stand beneath that star, when they see that Face. Then in subsequent months, the memories will fade. And that's the way it's supposed to be. For everyone."

"Except me."

"Yes, Maggie. Except you."

23. Judea 6

Carol Ann placed Joe's present front and center under the tree. Unlike the 'good old days' when she spent half a day getting ready before seeing him, she was scrambling now thanks to a party of last-minute shoppers in Pages, for which she had no complaints. Sales were just as welcome at the end of the workday, thank you very much and Merry Christmas. She had a little bounce in her step as she set the table, thinking about her gift to him. It sure took long enough putting it together. Joe always dropped in on Christmas Eve, but tonight was different. Tonight felt like a date. She wouldn't get her hopes up.

He liked to toot his harmonica outside the door. Tonight he knocked. She took a deep breath, let it out and opened the door to a large box that she assumed had a head behind it.

"Hey," she said, sliding Christmas bags off his arm, "is that you back there?"

Joe set down the box and kissed her cheek. "Hey back. The box is actually for the bookstore but you get to open it up here. The place looks great and you look greater."

Her stomach fluttered. "All these for little old me?" she asked, watching him put the presents under the tree.

"Plus a little something for Maggie and Dina when you see them tomorrow. If you wouldn't mind toting them on the plane?" He flashed that adorable tightened smile. Yeah, right. Like she could say no to him.

She poured them a glass of Châteauneuf-du-Pape and they settled on the sofa mooning at the tree. As always, Joe waited for her to speak first, which she'd never had a problem with.

"Did you know that artificial Christmas trees have outsold real ones every year since 1991?"

"Is that right?" he said, chuckling.

"This amuses you?"

"Your factoids amuse me."

"Staggeringly useless information, mostly."

"Staggeringly amusing, I'd say." He started to move closer then changed his mind. "So? We leave a week tonight. How do you feel?"

"I have concerns."

He scratched his beard, which he couldn't get used to, but the men had to go bearded. These were the rules. "Your outfit itches."

"That and ... Maggie's migraines. She won't be able to inject the Fiorinal."

This time he moved closer. He smelled like orange and lavender. "We haven't told Maggie yet, but one of Thomson's guys has engineered an ancient-looking hypodermic made from bevels and reeds. This way if she's caught injecting, she can wing an explanation."

"Reeds? Like reeds-from-river-beds reeds?"

He smiled and she swallowed. "How will she measure the dose?"

"I understand it's simple. They're showing Maggie the minute she gets back, so stop worrying."

"I'm surprised they're allowing the Fiorinal, but relieved."

"They have no choice. Her migraines are worsening. Besides, Fiorinal doesn't have a scent, unless it goes bad, then it smells like vinegar. Trivia for *you*."

"She has another check-up before we leave next week."

Joe reached over and caressed her hand. "We'll bring her back at the first sign of trouble, Carol Ann."

Joe didn't know Maggie as well as he thought. She'd die before leaving that Nativity unfinished. "Would you light the candles while I get dinner?"

"At your command," he said.

"So how come Alain gets to go beardless?" she asked from the kitchen.

"Alain doesn't look a day over twenty."

"Notice how his voice is sometimes deeper than other times?" She put two bowls of linguini with clams on the table and gestured for him to sit. "He's more serious than he used to be, too. Preoccupied."

Joe stared distantly at the linguini twirled around his fork. "I get the feeling Alain will stick around for one more year, tops."

No surprise there because Alain wasn't around much now. Time for a change of subject. She hated making him sad. "A company in Taiwan makes dinnerware out of wheat, so you can eat your plate." That got him smiling. He seemed so nervous tonight, but then they were all nervous about the trip. "Did Dina mention her unique problem to you?"

"You mean her singing the syllabic groups? Well that's okay. If she wants to sing to everybody in that cave, I'm sure Dina'll pull it off."

"She's worried about the Aramaic. I am, too."

"Women do scarcely more than nod and smile in public. Even the site crew hasn't had to speak much. Will you stop worrying?"

"I will if you will."

Joe raised his brows at her. "Stalemate."

She leaned forward and said *we are following the star. Good morning,* in Aramaic.

Joe leaned forward and said in Aramaic, *in the Child, we are one. You are a beauty.*

She felt her neck and cheeks grow hot. "We'll be fine there."

Over dinner they talked about supplies the crew brought back for Maggie, materials to prepare the canvases, including paints and brushes. What puzzled her was why Maggie needed to prepare a third canvas. She understood she would paint the Nativity plus one more of the Holy Family later on. But three paintings would keep her in Judea too long, unless she was finishing it back here.

Joe wasn't on foraging and excavation detail so she wouldn't bring it up. She'd see Maggie tomorrow anyway and Joe had enough on his mind trying to keep the rest of them from worrying. Aside from reassuring them emotionally and spiritually, his job was pretty much done. But Maggie's was just beginning.

"Maggie's using her middle name in Judea—*Joanna.* Fortunately it's an ancient name so she won't need to explain it."

"*Ann's* obviously special to your parents."

"To Dad. My grandmother's name was Leanne." She set down the Apple Crostata with caramel sauce. "Maggie's been spending a fair bit of time at Marianlake the last couple of months. Have you noticed?"

Joe took a bite and swooned. "I imagine she's preparing canvases and checking supplies. Your sister has the lead role in this play."

"How much time can it take to prepare two canvases? Actually, three." She couldn't help herself. She had to mention it.

"Okay, Inspector, what's on your mind?"

She poured their coffee. "She's been reading up a lot on ancient Galilee." She had his full attention now. "I've asked Maggie if she's moving forward in time and I got a 'tsk-tsk' and 'Oh Carol Ann, really.'"

Joe leaned back in his chair and got all reflective.

"What are you thinking?"

"Maybe the rules don't apply to Maggie."

"What!"

He waved it off and went back to dessert. "It makes perfect sense that she'd want a third canvas handy. And nobody but nobody's venturing out of Judea. Walter lost half a toe when he took the crew to Galilee. Nope. Besides, Ronny would never let her break the rules and she wouldn't lie to you. You asked and she answered."

Ronny might not but Dave Thomson would. He adored Maggie. She swallowed a forkful and widened her eyes. "I asked and she evaded."

After Joe shrugged it off, her stomach rolled mulling over the next question, debating whether to ask what Ronny and Dave Thomson wouldn't answer. She had to know. Or maybe she had to know if Joe trusted her with information. No, she wouldn't ask. "Joe, since we're on the subject ... Ronny's been back and forth with his crew mapping locations, mapping *the* location ..." She stirred her coffee with her finger. What did she think she was doing stirring her coffee with her finger?

Joe reached for her hand, soggy finger and all, and walked her over to the nativity she'd set up in a bookshelf by the tree. "This is what you're asking me, right?"

She nodded, hoping he'd lie and tell her he didn't know if he did know. She'd rather that than his telling her he did know but couldn't tell her.

Joe's eyes softened. "They found the cave last week. They've seen *Him*, Carol Ann. Alain told me Ronny and the crew returned with lightened minds."

"Enlightened?"

"Lightened."

"I guess I'm to keep this between us?" she asked, stumbling out the words.

Joe glanced at her lips, then at her. "Yes."

They stood quietly in front of the crib for a couple of minutes and then she asked him to open his gift.

"Mine first," he said. She followed him to the tree and sat on the floor beside him. "Open the big box first." He slid the box out for her and stood it upright. When she finally got inside the thing, which wasn't easy because he'd used duct tape, she yanked out four acrylic shelves.

She furrowed her brow. "Um, thank-you."

"The rest of it's at the beach house," he said with enough enthusiasm for the both of them. "The sides and the base. Now your display will look like it's floating."

"What I always wanted."

He reached into his pocket, took out a small velvet box and handed it to her. "I know you won't like this as much as transparent shelves, but ... well ... we can always swap it for a desk to match the shelves."

Wow. He'd given her diamond and emerald palm leaf earrings. "Oh my God, Joe! Oh, Joe." Yippity-do, this was *no* friendship gift. She kissed him, then shyly pulled away and held the box next to her ears for him.

"You like them?"

"Are you kidding, I love them. Oh, Joe." She had to stop saying that.

"Put them on."

She got so excited after putting them on and getting several more compliments from Joe that he had to hint at the whereabouts of his gift. "Your gift! Yes, of course! Your gift." She reached under the tree and passed him a medium-sized box wrapped in gold paper that she took great pains with. It embarrassed her to give it to him now. How could it stand up to diamonds and emeralds? As he slid a fingernail under a piece of tape, she stroked one of the earrings. "Oh, Joe." Gawd, she said it again.

"Nice paper," he said, taking his time with it. "Wrapped like this, I'd be happy with the box and ribbon."

"Great, now you tell me." Maybe this was a dumb idea. Maybe she should've got him something practical.

While Joe unrolled the gift from the bubble wrap, she swallowed a lump in her throat. This really was a dumb idea, but he looked pleased. Very pleased. Okay, so far so good. "This looks ancient," he said, holding the small spherical flask against the tree lights. "Absolutely ancient." In that sexy, playful way she loved, he narrowed his eyes at her. "Carol Ann?"

"It's an *aryballos*," she said, relieved. On his feet now, he held it under the bronze table lamp by the sofa. "The ancient's used them for perfume or oil. The cork is ancient, too."

"How ancient?"

"Are you asking me where your gift came from?"

"Sort of."

He hadn't asked what the liquid was inside it yet. Oh boy. "Okay I confess, I've been bugging Ronny since you got him home—I described what I wanted and asked him to bring it back."

"Bring it back *from*?" He sat on his heels in front of her.

She stuck her tongue in her cheek and he laughed. "Judea 5."

"What! You got Ronny to break the rules?"

"Yeah well, you'd just rescued him and I kinda used that."

"It's fabulous. I can't believe you talked him into it. An *ary* ... what?"

"Aryballos." He was all smiles. This was so great. So far.

Joe shook it gently. "What's in it?"

She took a deep breath. "Pyrethrum oil."

"Say what?"

"Pyrethrum oil. One of the oldest pesticides known to man. It's made from the seed coating of pyrethrum daisies." The ear to ear grin dropped off his face. He was now expressionless, somewhat in a stupor. Maybe she should keep talking. "It's said that the plant proliferated along caravan routes of the ancient world ..." Oh God, what was he thinking? "It's toxic to bees, wasps, lice, and your personal favorite—mosquitos." He gingerly set the flask on the bubble wrap and stared at her, eyes shining. "I ... I can't take a lot of credit for this gift, Joe. I got the idea, did the research, but it was Ronny who found it for me. After I pestered the hell out of him. Um ..."

He knelt close to her and cupped his hands on her face. The tree lights twinkled in his eyes.

"Um ... I'm guessing you like it."

He licked his lips and pulled her up into the kneeling position against him. He put his arms around her waist and drew her in tight.

"*Oh, Joe ...*"

Her heart hammered as he kissed her, his kiss demanding as she yielded to him. He tasted like caramel. She ran her hands through his hair as he pressed in on her back. He kissed her neck and traced his lips around her ear.

"*I love you,*" he whispered, and she could've died happy right then and there.

She melted into him and returned his kisses. "*Right where we left off at Marianlake,*" she whispered back. His body slackened when she said that and he loosened his hold. *Oh no, what did I say?* She kissed him and he returned the kiss with less fervor.

Joe shifted his legs and cradled her in his arms. "I've loved you since Marianlake," he said, running the back of his finger up and down her cheek. "That never stopped. You have no idea how many times I thought about this little cluster of freckles right here." He kissed her nose. *Don't spoil the moment, Joe, please.* "I'm sorry I had to stay away from you, that I took so many years from you."

She tilted her head to kiss the top of his hand. "You had no choice. And I was so selfish and pushy. It took years before I considered what you'd sacrificed for this mission."

"We've all made sacrifices. A million times I wanted to ask Maggie if you were dating, if you had met anyone special. Then I lost my nerve because I didn't want to know." He looked like a little boy asking permission to take a cookie. "Have you? Are you seeing anyone?"

"No, Joe. I guess I'm breaking all the rules saying this, but you have my heart. I've dated but ... I'm all yours."

"What rules?"

He could be so adorably naive. "Girl stuff. Why did you pull away from me a few minutes ago?"

"A week from this minute we'll be on holy ground. I want to do it right with us, the old-fashioned way. How do you feel about that?"

She threw her arms around him. "I'm just happy we're going to be doing it at all."

Joe looked cautiously at her. "There's something you should know." He sat up and held her hands. "Women who've loved me have ... died. I know it's superstition which goes against everything I believe, but there are fears I haven't been able to shake, Carol Ann."

"I know that, Joe. None of us will die from good health, right? Their deaths were not your fault. Our time is up when it's up. Some of us will get hit by a bus. Some of us will get a horrible disease. Some of us will be murdered or martyred. And some of us will die peacefully in our sleep. Their deaths were never your fault."

"Consciously, I believe that, too."

"What are you telling me, Joe?"

"I don't want to make you nuts looking over your shoulder. You need to live your life."

"What kind of life do I have without you?"

"I'm also concerned about losing my zapper."

"Your what?"

"My zapper, my gift. I used to feel Maggie's headaches, Dina's anger, your longing. I can't synch in anymore. God took away the empathic gift. Why? The last thing on this earth I want to do is push you away ... but I'm afraid I might."

∞∞∞

Plane Bagels touched down on an icy patch of private airstrip in Trois-Riviérés at noon on the 31st. He considered telling them it was all over now, but wasn't trusting his humor today. All Alain's fault. With the twenty-five below wind at their backs, they walked slowly, trailing the women. The last time they were here together, Alain was ten years old and neither of them had looked back. Then, he'd had the feeling they'd have years together. Now, he felt the opposite. As the others hurried ahead toward Father Richard's van, he tugged Alain's coat-sleeve.

"It's nearly over, isn't it, bud?" When Alain didn't answer, he let the sadness pass through him. And it took its sweet time.

"Spot any dark angels around here?" Alain asked, smiling.

"No. They're all waiting for us in Judea."

"There will be sentinels everywhere, Joe. You don't have to worry. *'May you have a good journey, and God be with you in your way, and his angel accompany you'.*"

"Extremely close company, I'll bet. Your voice is changing, bud."

"Pitter, patter, Joe."

Noticing a bunch of hugs going around outside the van, he rushed over, knowing he was about to greet an old friend. "Iris! Well well. '70s, eh. What did the flower children think of those heels?" He hugged her. And again that queer familiar feeling returned. She hadn't changed at all. How could that be?

"Well, they tried to get me into sandals," she laughed, kissing him on the cheek. "And that's when I said, 'Okay. I'm outta here.'"

Joe lifted up her earmuff. "We've all missed you. Welcome home."

"Yes." Carol Ann tapped her affectionately on the hand. "Welcome home."

∞∞∞

Two minutes to midnight, Ronny returned with a very dirty, very peaceful crew. Exhausted but eager to embrace the world, they were anxious to return to their lives and go to work, gently or as dynamos, whatever it took. Good news was good news and they'd happily spread it in their individual ways. Ronny hugged his mother and the site crew smiled and touched the arms of Joe's group as they passed. It had been arranged that all returning groups remain quiet in the presence of departing groups. The reasons were obvious.

Ronny padded over. "Go drink it all in, Joe. It's ambrosia." He turned his attention to the group, "Now let me check your lists and baggage for no-nos, boys and girls. We want to get you on your way."

It took Ronny fifteen minutes to clear them. He cleared Father Richard and Bishop Gianni first. Father Andre, who had a little high blood pressure problem, had to have it checked. Ronny grinned at him. Andre would never blow this. This past year, his self-care had been exemplary.

Next came Elizabeth, Dina, Carol Ann and a weary-looking Maggie. Although Dina wrote her Aramaic notes on plain, beige paper, Ronny said no way and confiscated them. He smiled sympathetically at Maggie. Noticing her swollen, bloodshot eyes and labored breathing, Ronny told her it was okay to delay departure an hour or so. Maggie thanked him and refused. She was the one who had to go, no matter what. Even if she was dying, she had to go, though she would never complain. Not Maggie. The headaches had gotten bad, so an hour more or less wouldn't make a difference.

Ronny cleared Alain and Iris with a nod. The others didn't seem to notice but this intrigued him. He would've checked the heels on Iris's sandals, but hey, Ronny knew his job. He stood behind them. As their team leader, he waited until the nine were physically and emotionally comfortable. Watching Maggie sneak a little rub on the temple filled him with melancholy. *God, feel free to zap Maggie's migraine over to me.*

"You all right?" Ronny asked after checking his list.

"Let's say I'm all ready. Ready for all my answers. Happy New Year, Ronny."

"Happy New Year, Joe. Happy New Year, everyone!"

∞∞∞∞

Ronny's team coordinated the disk to land in the deepest hollow of the cave, an area with high crevices well lit by torch-lights set in clay pots. The psychologist had instructed them to remain still for several minutes. They had to ease into the atmosphere by first acknowledging emotional reactions, after which followed prayer for the recognition of evil and the ability to stand firm in the face of it, a meditation they had practiced behind the Red Door. Subsequently, it would take an hour to attach the truth of this to the 'reality of this.'

The star would set them on their way. For this moment they had prepared, as here in these hills lived the Highest Good. Yet in the shadows, evil awaited its prey, aching to destroy, angered that these eight mortals were trained to combat *its* most powerful weapon–fear. Too, the one holding the silver sword protected these mortals. When informed of his presence, even the monarchs of opposing forces went rigid with dread.

The night was cold, hovering around zero. Joe walked a few feet from their cave and gazed at the surrounding hills. Torch-lit caves dotted the mountainous countryside. How did the sky hold all these stars? And the auroral activity— arcs, rays, and coronas of red and deep blue. He had once seen the Northern Lights in Yellowknife, dwarfed by this divine vision, rare phenomena in Judea. More divine was the star ... His star. So bright. So awesome—a word he would use twice more in his lifetime.

Joe glanced at the others, off standing alone, looking up, faces serious, and eyes unblinking. Twenty minutes off the disk and no one had spoken. He bathed his spirit in the atmosphere and delighted in the sounds of this ancient night ... the bleat of lambs echoing from distant hills. A shepherd's whistle. A dog's bark. Crickets. The smell of campfire smoke. He continued listening, watching the star in awe. Maggie wandered over to him and broke the silence.

"Did we do the right thing, Joe?"

The tone in her question disturbed him. It had begun, the doubt, the fear, and to Maggie of all people. With the others busy setting up camp, they could speak privately. "Do you mean coming here by way of modern science and technology? Do you think we crashed the party?"

Maggie tucked her hands in her cloak sleeves. "In a way. Could be we're not supposed to be here. I mean, think of how difficult it was getting here, all the obstacles. Could be we forced this, Joe."

Maggie's eyes were still red and she was pale, weakened. He took her wrist and held it upward. "And these marks ... did we force these, too? Are they the result of Walter's invention? On a few thousand people? Take a minute for yourself and concentrate on the star, Maggie. It occurs to me that you are the most vulnerable here."

She looked up as she spoke. "I am scared, Joe. It's like my life-light is expiring. But back in the Cove when my mood was optimistic, I saw another light, a light brighter than my life."

The mention of the light strengthened Maggie. She looked up at the star again, and he saw it flicker, as though talking to her. "See that, Maggie? Draw from it."

"The anxiety is leaving me. Oh, thank God. And the shield in my vision has brightened. The vision has followed me here. I can actually see it separate from my dreams."

That was odd phrasing for Maggie. She wasn't normally so esoteric. "The shield? What do you mean, *shield*?"

"I've had this recurring dream about a sword, a shield, and a chain ..."

Why did she hesitate and stop? Was she holding something back? He had to know more about the sword and shield. "Fascinating. I've had the same dream minus the shield. What's the shield look like, Maggie? What's on it?"

"It's bronze and worn. Ancient. And there are words on it, but I can't make them out."

He laughed. "More acronymics? Acronymic puzzles have been my life. Oh the joy."

"I'm into joy," Alain said, pulling up the hood on Maggie's cloak. "I couldn't help overhearing the acronymic part. Permit me to join in the fun?"

"Watcha got?" Thoughts of the silver sword had him straining to remember. A shield in his studies. Latin writing. *Leave it alone. Don't force it.*

"An acronymic question." Alain said this loud enough for Father Andre to hear. "I happened to catch a sample of our Jubilee invitations." He smiled mischievously at Father Andre.

Warming themselves by the fire, the others listened.

"You did, did you?" Father Andre teased, "A provoking little puzzle."

"Acronomycs *and* alliteration," he said. He wanted to contribute to their play, but more than anything he wanted to remember the shield.

"Regarding our marks," Alain said, "on the inside of the invitation at the bottom, we are being asked, 'What does SC mean to you? The right answer will shower you with blessings.'"

"I thought SC meant Second Christmas," Dina said.

"Who's asking, Alain?" Elizabeth's voice echoed in the hills. She lowered it, "Who wants to know?"

"Good question," Carol Ann said.

"Actually, it's from me," Vittorio admitted, sheepishly. "I posed the question."

"You're toast now, Vittorio," Richard joined in.

∞∞∞

Iris edged closer to the fire and warmed her hands. They weren't all the way into this time and place yet, but most certainly would be within the hour. Over the next range a liar approached—an adversary with the power to contaminate the ocean with one drop of mercury.

∞∞∞

For the first time he observed Iris's startling resemblance to Willie. Was it this light? This night? "Tell us, Vittorio," he said, grateful he'd learned to discipline his thoughts. "If it's not Walter's *Second Christmas*, what is it?"

"Sorry, Joe," the bishop apologized and stood for a stretch. "No answer will pass these lips until one year from tonight. And don't drive yourselves crazy, people. Or you'll have SC's coming out of your ears."

"Hm. SC," Maggie said.

"How 'bout process of elimination?" Carol Ann offered. "We know what it isn't. We know it isn't *Second Coming*. Too obvious. We all know that's inevitable."

"Uh-oh." He slipped an arm around Carol Ann's shoulder. "Don't get her going."

"Hey, safe in Christ!"

"Safety of God's children."

"Sign of the Cross."

"Sign of the Covenant. Soviet consecration?"

"Salvation or condemnation?"

Bishop Gianni flagged his long arms at them, "I told you. Don't do this or you'll drive yourselves *pazzo.*"

And so it continued for twenty minutes until they withdrew into silence. Their informality disturbed him.

How could they be so casual over something God had carved into their flesh, and seeing the Christ Child? SC was the reason they were here. The psychologist did say it would take time for the reality to sink in. Right, no argument.

"Is someone coming?" Richard asked in a cautious whisper. "Look way over there in that cluster of caverns to the left. A light moving closer. Do you see?"

At once, he and his group of nine awakened to the present moment.

Waves of anxiety cut through him as he examined the approaching man. He had a dog with him. The man plodded, supporting himself with a tall curved stick. Something about him seemed familiar and as crooked as a farrier's knife. Then he recognized him ... and waited for the others to recognize him. They didn't. *How could this be? Those eyes.* Even with the body concealed by the winter mantle and hood, how could they forget those pseudo-soulful eyes? Lord above, how to resist telling them, shouting at them! But the team had to reach their own conclusions while all he could do was guide. Guiding might be tricky considering he once entertained the idea of killing him–just to see if he could die.

Though their exchanges were in Aramaic, communications transmitted back in English. They'd received this illusion from a most powerful presence, a presence oblivious to them and the approaching stranger, except him, Alain and Iris. Why Iris? He couldn't take time to wonder about that now because the preternatural fireworks had begun.

Wake up guys, wake up.

The temperature plummeted and the wind intensified, forcing them to scurry for more wood and fan the fire. Before introductions, the stranger pointed toward a wood stack, partially hidden by an enclosure of rock. The wood stack was not there before, he realized, trying not to fuel his anxiety with malice. He looked up at the star and silently pleaded for help. As before with Maggie, it flickered back.

"Greetings," Elizabeth said, reaching down to stroke the dog, a lifeless-looking thing. "Sit with us and warm yourself."

"Do you gather to view the child?" the man asked them, glancing sideways at Maggie.

"Yes," he answered. How clever of him to alter his voice and appearance. Why were their eyes continuing to deceive them? Here of all places, why could they not recognize Edmon Fendi?

"My name is Joanna," Maggie said, extending her hand. "Yours?"

"My name is Chemosh," Edmon said.

Not even Carol Ann placed him. And Maggie? Maggie painted those eyes. This was insane. What was happening here? Why was he back? "Are you here to see the Child?"

"I have already been. They are saying this is Elah's son. A beautiful child, no question. They are saying that star above is *his* star."

"And after seeing Him, what do you say?" Andre asked.

"I am saddened," Chemosh said. "The world is foolishly apt to believe untruth. I have journeyed one day and a half from Hebron, knowing all the while that this child the land speaks of is already born. He is now six in years and lives with his family in Alexandria. Their region is unknown. He was born as the prophets foretold ... in the Year One. Truly I say, I have come seeking the identity of these pretenders. By discrediting them, it is my wish that Elah will look upon me with favor."

"I did not realize Scripture foretold His birth year," he said, already sensing doubt among his teammates, patently among one cleric. "And—" Eliminating their doubt was his responsibility, "—it is my understanding that the Family did not stay in Alexandria nearly so long as six years. I believe this child is *The* Child."

He wanted to disclose Chemosh's identity, just blurt it out. But they would never accept what they could not see. And he had to accept the *reason* they could not see, whatever it was. How did Ronny do it? Edmon had taken him all the way to Hell's gate and dumped him. Only one way Ronny kept his sanity–he had help. Amazing generals, these dark angels. They had years to study the enemies' weakness before attacking their most vulnerable area, which in this instance was here and now ... Judea in the Year Six. And in their hearts where faith lived.

Did they force the Hand of God by coming here? No. Ronny and his group returned unscathed. Who had helped Ronny? Who was the unseen dominant force here? It wasn't Iris. It wasn't Alain, not this time. And what they lacked in awareness, he was receiving empathically. Around this campfire he felt a surge of negative emotions, as though surrounded by nine Red Doors.

He sat on a limestone slab, rigid as a hex bolt, helpless to prevent Edmon from playing his ace.

"The chosen people of Elah are saddened," Chemosh said, feigning doom and gloom. "Many have seen these impostors who carry the mark of Satan. All disciples carry the seal of the condemned. They are Satan's cognomen, Satan's children. Sinners. Corrupters. Heed this warning– their mark infects the land. I have seen them near the impostor child, heard them say he is the Messias. Remember, the rightful Messias is already born. Stay clear of these false disciples. I must take my leave. I am on my way to visit friends in Gaza. May the true Elah of Israel bless you all."

Everyone stood except himself, Iris and Alain. Edmon's dog trailed slumberously behind.

He studied their faces and eyes, eyes that narrowed at the sight of their wrists. He waded carefully into his words, "Well. If he's on his way to Gaza he's heading in the wrong direction. Gaza's below us on the Mediterranean strip and he's heading toward the Jordan River. Misguided chap, isn't he." He found their silence alarming. "Hey, come on. *Seal of the condemned, Satan's cognomen, Satan's children? Sinners. Corrupters. Stay clear?* A bit overdone, don't you think? Vittorio wasn't kidding when he said we'd have SC's coming out of our ears. But 'positive' SC's. Remember always–positive over negative."

"Like your old '80s logo," Carol Ann said, voice dry with melancholy.

"Exactly. Now is the time to remember everything you've learned. You must stay in the light here. Draw on your years of experience in battle. Look up at that star. Is *it* false?"

"Suddenly it does not look as large, Joe," Vittorio said. "I have had I suspect, too many years of politics and education. Old doctrine. Old doctrine slightly altered. Old doctrine doctored. My mind is clouded with facts. I was prepared to accept the Year Three, Joe. But *Six*? Year Six does not coincide with Herod's death in 4 BC. Herod the Great was King of Judea from 37 to 4."

"Our dream, Vittorio," Andre reminded him, "You, Paul, and myself. Remember it now."

"I believe in the dream, Andre. And I will always remember. But did it prophesy this mission? Did we fight for something not meant to be?"

"Oh, God," Maggie said, "I thought that, too."

"Maggie, it was by your hand that we found Ronny," Alain spoke for the first time, much to his relief. "Do you think Elizabeth prayed for him to be left behind in that limbo Angelfish Cove? Did Ronny return with his mind poisoned? No. He returned a man, filled with the light of true faith and the knowledge that Walter's death had meaning.

"There's so much you forget—how we all prayed for and supported one another through the dark years. And Iris. Iris stayed with Ronny for six years. Does a sacrifice of that magnitude come from darkness? We are here because we are meant to be here. This trip's been booked a long time. And we are to take something precious away with us."

"The years I spent with Ronny," Iris said, speaking mostly to Elizabeth, "he worked with total faith, total trust. He knew he'd get back, knew he had lessons to learn. And he knew he'd eventually return with the goods. He always believed in Walter Bayard's prayer. So must we."

With those words their fire fanned itself and instantly warmed them. Warmed further by recurring thoughts of the silver sword and chain, and now the shield, he stared across the fire at Maggie. She looked so ill, her face drawn and pinched. Yet there was an aura of clear light around her, an aura no one else had. One other thing was clear. Whoever carried the silver sword carried it mostly for Maggie. She had told him she felt her life-light expiring. He could not easily dismiss her words.

"So do you think that Chemosh guy was a distracter, a non-believer?" Dina asked no one in particular?"

"Are you kidding," Richard said. "He had more SC's than *Campbell's Soup*. I believe Chemosh was a demon in human form. A demon who, along with his disciples, has not had the identity of our Savior revealed to him. The Adversary will not know for certain who He is for another thirty-three years. Even as I speak this they are not permitted to hear. Incidentally, Chemosh is a fallen angel in Milton's *Paradise Lost*. Oh and another thing—Satan does not translate as *Satan* in Aramaic."

Kudos to Father Richard. Now what would happen next? Vittorio's mood was still gray. Could he lose one of them? Vittorio was a bishop. So what. Anyone, regardless of spiritual credentials was corruptible. History proved it. Anti-popes permeated the fourteenth century. Even after living with Christ, Judas went sour. The Apostles doubted. Yes, he could lose one of them. Days before the accident, he overheard Aunt Pam remind his father that 'many are called, but few are chosen'. That night, his prayers consisted of two words, repeated until he fell asleep—*Pick us. Pick us. Pick us.* It was time to seek out their protector. There would be no souls lost on his watch.

Although he managed Edmon on his own, caution had to be taken with his superiors, making it vital that he free himself and the others from all malicious distractions. To receive individual gifts required a clear head. A clear head would insure his return home with at least one answer to his four remaining questions. The contents of the dream document, Alain's secret, Maggie's next work, apart from the Nativity, and lastly, the meaning of the recurring sounds and smells from his dream–a sword being thrust into a scabbard, the unchaining of some horrific thing and the rancid smell of hay and burnt oranges.

As for the true meaning of SC, he already knew. These past moments the answer had been revealed to his mind.

∞∞∞

They went on their way before sunrise, carrying spears and swords. Apart from the harsh terrain and weather, there was the threat of lions and wild boar. And bandits. Solitary travelers generally teamed up with large caravans, often as many as three hundred people. Ancient Palestine was a dangerous place, in all respects.

As they walked through the hills enjoying the distant view of the Dead Sea, they encountered many caravans. It had taken only forty minutes to walk to the Child's cave. Now it seemed it would take hours to get inside. There were people everywhere. Some had set up camp outside the mouth of the cave. Clearly, judging by the anxious-looking faces, everyone wondered when their turn would come, if it would come. Then the oddest thing happened.

Alain removed Maggie's paints and canvases from his pack, occasionally glancing at one of them to pass on a comforting smile. Handing over to Maggie as much as she could carry, he took the remainder of her gear and hoisted it onto his shoulders. Then he gestured for her to follow and they made their way through the crowd as easily as ripples through water. The eight of them watched with amusement as people moved to one side as they passed, as though expected, as though called. A few moments later, he sent Andre and Vittorio through. Again, the crowd moved aside.

Elizabeth and Dina went through next, then Richard and Iris. After these last two disappeared inside the mouth of the cave, Carol Ann turned to him.

"This is it, Joe," she said, her breath ragged with expectation. "Even though I know the enormity of this moment, I want to say that if you exit that cave feeling differently about us, I will understand. By tonight none of us are going to be the same again anyway. I love you. No matter how you decide to spend your future, I now know that you'll always love me, too. Because it's not what we want, is it? It's what God wants. I finally learned that. And at last I'm finally receptive to that. I feel peace inside, Joe."

He leaned over and kissed her tenderly. "Funny thing about love, even in its spaces it doesn't go anywhere. I've loved you since that first night in Patsy's Bar. I used to think we lost what little we had. Now I think we have it all. I wanted to wait until we got here so we'd have a nugget of gold to take home from this time. Alain implied that what we see inside might become dreamlike after a while–but not outside, not here. I love you, Carol Ann." He took her hand and kissed it. "Thank you for your love and endless patience." He sighed dramatically and she laughed. "I hope you still want to marry me as much as I want to marry you. Please be my wife, Carol Ann." He laughed in kind when she let out a little squeal. "Most men would take that as a firm yes."

"Yes, I do," she said, eyes cloudy. "I mean I will. Yeees! I'm yours, Joe. I've always been yours."

Then they went inside.

There had to be fifty people in the cave. Despite the numbers it was like a quiet lake at dusk. A misty morning nod to a smiling passerby. How many were holy guardians and sentinels? They all stood quietly, heads slightly bowed. He felt this intoxication of the spirit. They were all truly here. From this angle, his view being obstructed by flickering torchlights and a small group in front, he squeezed Carol Ann's hand and edged his way through. He did not think to look for the others. They were safe here, safer than they had ever been.

He spotted Maggie attempting to set up her easel and canvas several feet to his right. He followed her eyes, watching where they stopped. It was still impossible to see anything from this point. Carol Ann released his hand, whispering that this was Christmas in the truest sense and she wanted him to open this present alone.

"Time for your private moment," she said, then moved off in Dina's direction.

Edging in closer, he noticed that many faces here seemed familiar. It was thrilling and frightening to see resemblances to his parents and Walter. Even Willie. Ah sweet, deceptive torch light. It had to be the Child's Spirit doing this to him. So beautiful. So incredibly beautiful. *Thank-you.*

Like the marks, his recollection of these precious steps to the front would soon fade. They were meant to choose or yield, not have their choices thrust upon them. They were here to take home love and hope, not distract themselves with sentiment or raise themselves above men. Feeling a strong hand on his forearm, he looked up into the eyes of a tall slightly built man. Joe's soul spoke to him, *this is His foster father.*

"I am Joseph," he said. "My family welcomes you and your friends. Come and meet our Son."

He followed the Child's Foster-father to the front. Joseph. Saint Joseph himself placed his hand on his arm and escorted him to the holy crèche, a fact his mortal mind could not completely fathom.

The Infant's Mother was the beauty he'd imagined, except smaller, younger, a womanly mother who resembled a girl. Yet she was a Woman, a Queen. Their eyes locked. Did She know him? Her eyes were soft indigo blue and her hair lustrous, the color of sandalwood.

At last he was looking at the Child.

He knelt at the foot of the small feedbox by the Savior's bed. Poor beautiful Savior Child. Such humble beginnings—an animal trough filled with one large bale of hay. Wrapped in fine cloth strips from his chin to his toes, He couldn't move his little body. He couldn't kick out his legs nor wriggle his fingers. He had no blankets, nothing to keep out the dampness, no medicine to stave off infection. Would they mind if he placed his coat over Him? What could be wrong in warming Him, making Him more comfortable?

He is comfortable and warm, a Voice spoke to his soul. *Does the breath of the animals not warm him? Remember who cares for Him.*

He removed the piece of straw brushing against His brow and put it in his cloak. *Thank-you. I did not come here to ask for anything or even to ask something for another. I simply wanted to say thank-you and I want to hear, really hear.*

Contemplating SC, he looked at Jesus and wept internally. He heard the thrust of a sword into a scabbard, signifying victory. He heard the release click of a lock and the Voice—

Enjoy this moment and receive. Speak to Him.

"It really is You. I love You." He said it loud enough that everyone heard.

The Child stared at him through honey-colored eyes while the Man-God spoke to his soul. *'Unless the grain of wheat falling into the ground die, itself remaineth alone. But if it die it bringeth forth much fruit'. Speak to Me.*

It seemed it was just the two of them when his thoughts spoke.

You are so awesome. The rest of mankind entered the world to live. But You–You are the only One who entered it to die. Maggie's dying, isn't she? You don't have to answer, Lord. Somehow I know. And she has to leave something with us, with the world. A message in her work? We'll know when You're ready to tell us, Lord.

Ask Me.

He gazed into the Child's eyes. *Please don't let anything disturb our relationship with You. Our salvation is everything. Walter wanted to return hope and love to the world. SC, my Lord. 'Study in the Spirit and keep the child safe'. The child is me. The child is all Your children. 'The salvation of God's children. SC'. I love You, Jesus. Please save souls.*

Forgive me, I am impatient to know my purpose in this mission. Please tell me what remains to be done for Maggie. And for You. Always for You.

The Child spoke to his soul, *You will receive your answer tonight before you leave Judea. In your vision, follow the one who carries the shield. As God's champion, I have commissioned him to help you. Regard his actions. Heed his words. Obey him.*

The Queen of Heaven stepped in and bundled Jesus up in her arms. Watching her tap her finger on his tiny chin, Joe nearly died of love.

The last thing inside the cave he remembered was Dina's voice. She knelt beside Him and sang a song she'd written, lyrics flowing in Aramaic, the tongue for which she had no aptitude. The beauty of the melody brought them to their knees and as Dina sang, he felt the Spirit of total trust entering his soul.

24. Who Is Like God?

They took their leave from the adorable Child an hour before sunset. He'd wanted more time and envied Maggie for being allowed to stay. The astonishingly beautiful face of His Mother was still with him. He trailed behind his friends, contemplating the vision before him. *Before you leave Judea.* Since they were here until midnight, it would happen sometime during the next six hours. It was all incredibly over the top as Dina was so fond of saying, and though he was curious to know what his friends remembered, he kept his nose out of their business. Privacy was a thing highly regarded amongst them.

He sensed someone following him.

At first glimpse of their campsite, he called Alain back. "Will you keep an eye on them? I'd like to be alone for a while. I'll be over there on that incline if you need me." He pointed toward a gentle slope overlooking the Dead Sea. "The sun's setting. Be a nice place to watch it from."

"You go ahead. I'll take care of the kids."

Joe looked dreamily at his best friend. "You've seen Him before, haven't you, Alain?"

Alain didn't answer. So of course that meant yes.

"If Edmon shows up, come get me."

Alain smiled, remembering, "You know, a long time ago I told Edmon I'd see him around the campfire. Then last night he showed up around the campfire. Don't worry about Edmon and enjoy some time alone." He walked off taking long strides toward the others.

Joe stretched out his legs on the incline, waiting until they were all out of earshot. He said quietly, "Okay, you got me alone."

∞∞∞

Certain the presence following him to be of God, he felt dizzy with fear. As the presence neared closer to his soul, its power intensified. What God was sending him now was one with the power to take him to the front lines of reality. He assumed he'd remain on Earth during the vision but maybe he was wrong. What if his point of view was about to significantly change? He'd never known fear like this.

The sun in his mind's eye spun on its axis. Yielding to the weariness, he used this meditative state to wait out the solar vision and in a flash, found himself in a place of vast dimension, surrounded by a high, jeweled wall. Several feet ahead stood the first of four bridges of skyscraper proportions at the fringe of a wall, over which he saw a partial view of a golden city, a city of Daylight. *The New Jerusalem*. The city appeared guarded by flaming tongues of light, thousands of them. One left its center post, approaching the distant end of the bridge.

It began moving slowly toward him.

At the foot of the bridge to his right was a gold shield, erect and ostensibly supported by one of these *tongues*. On the ground at his left were gold gladiator-type sandals, holding a presence because the leather strapping around the foot to the ankle seemed animate. Another tongue flickered approximately seven feet above the sandals.

The approaching flame was a few feet away now. Nearly blinded by it, he turned his head and saw a shepherd's crook imbedded in the road leading to the bridge, under which a lane veered to the right and downward into a void. He stole a peripheral glance at the flame, which was beginning to grow, taking the shape of a man. Only this was no man. Once again, his spirit filled with warm cleansing waters.

Above its shoulders, extending to its sides as far as his eyes would take him, were specters of pale green and white wings. Its head was pure light and it hurt his eyes to look at it, most particularly his right eye. The eye burned and he clamped it shut. In a heartbeat he would sacrifice the eye, both eyes, to savor this vision. Tongues of fire sparkled and danced in the presence of this magnificent creature, a creature so glorious and terrifying that he thought he would die unless he turned away. He could not turn away.

The creature flooded him with its consciousness.

It moved close enough to touch. As the blinding light and wing apparition faded, it extended an exquisite, powerfully formed hand over his right brow and healed his eye. The voice in his mind instructed him to say a prayer of thanksgiving for the Nativity vision granted to them. Having done this, Joe saw before him a great angel of remarkable beauty.

He had seen a whisper of the glorious angel in Maggie's first mural. Short locks of satiny, golden hair framed his sculpted face. Downy, apple blossom skin and wisteria-blue eyes that gently admonished. Glistening seven-foot iron-muscled frame. A scabbard hung from his waistband containing a silver sword and he held a shield bearing the inscription *Quis Ut Deus*. Familiar with the inscription, for it meant *Who Is Like God,* Joe recognized him. This was Satan's conqueror, God's Grand Marshal and Champion. Still, he had to hear the first and greatest of saints identify himself.

His voice trembled, "Who are you?"

"I am Prince of the Church of Jesus Christ, chief commander of the heavenly hosts, guardian to Israel and souls of humanity. I am Michael. The Archangel."

He forbade Joe to kneel in his presence. "In this place, one kneels solely for the King and Queen." Michael directed him to follow, instructing him to remain silent from this point onward. When they began walking, his heart leapt at the notion of crossing the bridge, but sank as quickly when the Archangel Prince lead him away to their right ... and downward into the void.

Depression beat down on him as they walked, thickening with the descent. Thoughts became infected with memories, filling him with guilt and despair. Thoughts of Willie and that night on the beach in September of 1981. Suddenly he felt ill and wanted desperately to leave here. The holy Prince set aside his shield and from a place in the depths drew a massive chain of considerable length. On one end was a bladed, iron manacle, an opened manacle. Michael picked it up and stretched the collar between the blades, holding it open in front of him.

Joe had come to understand his dream. He did not need words to explain what and who was shackled on this chain. But when did this happen? And when was it released? But he dared not ask. If it were for him to know, he would be told.

The majestic archangel flung the collar to the ground and removed his sword from the scabbard. With indescribable swiftness of hand he made two revolutions in the air before pausing briefly with the sword pointed upward, followed by two perfect revolutions back, returning the sword to the scabbard. Though he couldn't be certain and was too awed to ask, the gesture seemed to signify victory. He rocked his footing into place and dabbed the corner of his eye. Michael's love for God and Queen were unconditional. They journeyed back to the bridge in silence.

At the foot of the bridge, Michael spoke, "Margaret's paintings will bring blessings and myriad conversions to all who look upon them. Once her paintings are brought home, the examination process will begin directly. Exhaustive carbon dating and botanical tests will circumvent all scientific explanations. Results will confirm the work to be truly of God, as the elements combine both modern and ancient matter. This mystery will draw millions to her opening exhibit at The State Hermitage Museum in Saint Petersburg, Russia. In this place, the seeds will best take root.

"Wait until the night of your celebration to speak of this vision. Wait until the key is removed from beneath the desk. Though God desires the success of this mission, He continues to give his children free will. Speaking of it too soon could alter the course of events. Now listen carefully, Joseph.

"Did you hear the silence, the deceiving tranquility in this dark place? It was the wail of the serpent you heard not. Lucifer was temporarily released in 1864 and took with him a 'fiend'. Although it is alarmingly inconspicuous, the brief period of peace on Earth is over. Since the serpent is freed, its disciples' rage has swollen.

"As custodians of Margaret's work, you, together with your companions, joined by their companions will return many of God's flock. Be reminded that during this period, taking naught for granted because their power is unequaled to mine, fallen angels continue to soldier on. Worldly man is easy prey for the Prince of the Earth. Oh my son, remain aware and on guard.

"When this term of chaos is over, I will shackle the devil for the last time, after which, the Queen will crush its serpent's head. This signals that the end soon follows. I anticipate your thought. We do not know how long God will permit it to attempt the ruin of souls. But you can see now the critical state of affairs. Amidst plagues and wars, the world continues to enjoy peace in comparison with the coming times. Man is denied witness to the serpent's snares. Remember the great power God bestowed upon me, Joseph, and pray to me evermore for protection."

At his point of entry at the four bridges, Saint Michael said, "With regards to Margaret, you are correct. Be courageous in your grief as I am soon taking her. I will see her directly to God. I delight in personally safeguarding her soul, as she has been devoted to me these past twenty-five years. And since you are dear to my client, I may present you with another favor, if the favor has merit.

"Again, the same question remains uppermost in your mind. Neither can I speculate for you. God does not tell His angels the length of the end times and it is not your duty to make people listen. This mission's yield and your love will accomplish that. It may be years or centuries before our Queen crushes the serpent. The answer rests with the choices of mankind. As it frequently has, prayer can soften the Father's heart. Now you may present a petition, then we must both return to our duties."

He wanted to ask why he'd been so favored but this was not the time to lobby for himself. With that ridiculous notion aside, it took two seconds to search his soul for the petition.

"I ask that the success of this mission result in the good of all concerned."

A trace of warmth lightened the eyes of the Archangel Prince. "*Fiat,*" he said.

Let it be done.

Joe was kneeling when he came to, The Dead Sea reflecting moon and auroral activity–crimson red and electric blue arcs and coronas. His body ached and his wrist throbbed. The discomfort was a joy to bear since it brought with it a flashback of the entire vision, unlike the Nativity, parts of which were obviously banned from memory. He would write it all–every sight, emotion and word. Then he could read it over each day for the rest of his life. There would be no day like this again, not while he was alive. He almost envied Maggie. Maggie...

With all his heart he ached to return to the Child's cave. No. There certainly would not be a day like this again. How would he fare? What if, for the rest of his life, every day was ordinary? No more miracles. He'd had his fifteen minutes of spiritual fame. No more guest passes, Joe. Saint Michael said he would get another favor if *considered necessary.* So, God help him, now he had to go out there and live like everybody else. Yet no day had to be ordinary. It was so easy to fall into despair, even now in the wake of a vision, in the afterglow of a life of visions. Saint Michael warned him to remain on guard–to be aware. Dark angels preyed.

Even here.

A few minutes past eight he found his friends writing in their journals. He delighted in their writing tools—paper scrolls fashioned by Maggie and Ronny's team, feathered quills, and a thick black substance that resembled ink. They each acknowledged him with a smile and a few words then carried on. All agreed the tongue was unjust in its description of the experience. But the words flowed on paper with nothing lost, or rather, nothing they were permitted to recall.

Carol Ann and Father Richard were first to finish and began preparing their supper–herbs with oil and bread. They had packed a dozen wineskins–ten with water, two with red wine. At nine-fifteen they sat down together. Joe longed to share his vision but had been asked to wait one year. He would honor that. However long it took, he would obey. Just that it was frustrating leaving out details concerning Maggie. She was so close to his heart and her work had been their visual core.

What did he mean, *if the favor is considered necessary*? If only Maggie knew. Then again, if Maggie knew her escort from this life into the next was her inspiration–the Archangel Prince himself, her hands would start shaking for sure. And yet she'd been given a taste of what would soon come. She had sensed her declining 'life-light', had seen the shield, without the revelatory inscription and felt renewed. He would miss her. He would miss her terribly.

A few minutes before midnight, with their few belongings packed and on the disk, they said their goodbyes to Maggie. Dina told her she would be right there waiting at Marianlake for her on her return, sometime in the spring, Maggie speculated. Carol Ann stepped aside to give him a private goodbye with her.

He ached inside. He might never see his friend again and had to keep it to himself. What did Saint Michael mean by 'soon'? Next year, next month? "You are the heart in this mission, Maggie. I know you'll create your best work. I wish I could stay and watch."

Maggie reached for his hand. "I wish you could, too." Then, as if she knew... "What a glorious ride we've been on in this Divine carnival. Roller coasters and merry-go-rounds. Target shooting. Now I'm leaving the park, Joe. Remember what Emily Dickinson said, 'Elysium is as far as to the very nearest Room'. Well, I intend to paint it. The

New Jerusalem. And once that's done–I intend to see it, Joe."

He hugged her. "If anyone can keep us anchored in the light, Maggie, you can. Bye." He stepped back to give the sisters' space and saw the pale aura around her. Seemed she had one foot in Elysium already.

Carol Ann looked uncomfortable with all this high drama. "I love you," she said. "And I'm so proud to be your sister. Paint masterpieces and make sure you send me messages via group leaders. Promise?"

"Promise. Maybe I'll message you in a painting or on ancient scrolls, who knows." Maggie's eyes were etched with sorrow. "I love you, too. You know, you and Joe should get married." She glanced at him and winked. "Now there's a message *I'd* like to get."

Carol Ann's face beamed, "Actually I was getting to that. Joe proposed right here in Judea 6. You'd already gone in and ... well, fall wedding, you my maid of honor. Say yes right away. The centuries are flying."

Maggie hugged her tight. "I'm so happy," she said.

The sisters' goodbye hug left him breathless. Time froze that moment.

At 12:15 a.m. on January 2nd, *Meat and Potatoes* Group Two returned to Marianlake. Ronny and Dave Thomson welcomed them home. By 12:30, Maggie Page was greeting Group Three ... five miles south of Jerusalem in a town called Bethlehem Ephrata. Year Six.

∞∞∞

"Hey, Inspector!" Joe called down to her, "The Nativity's home, so pack a bag."

The painting came home to Marianlake the first week in April. Alain had found a place for Maggie to stay in Beth Bassi, a few kilometers southwest of the holy cave. She worked fast, sending sketches to Marianlake with groups shuttling back and forth. Dave Thomson stayed close, replenishing supplies and visiting, using every excuse he could to spend time with her.

Joe and Carol Ann decided to make a long weekend of it and drove the five and a half hours to Marianlake to see the painting. They found Fathers' Andre and Richard in the rectory office glued to the painting when they arrived, reflective and captivated. With one look at *The Nativity*, he understood why.

Sitting on the edge of a straw bed, the Mother held the Child. Joseph sat by her side. Such a simple picture. A family portrait which millions would eventually see, via the Internet. Would a part of them know they were looking at the real Family? How would they feel and to what degree would they feel it?

For a moment, these Faces came back to him. He had described their faces in his notes but the memory never returned clear and intact, until now. That walk through the cave entrance up to the front was like a dream and this ... *this* was reliving it! If only he could return to the holy cave and see Him again. He'd saved the straw of pale gold hay that had brushed against the Baby's brow, took it out every night at bedtime and inhaled its sweet fragrance.

"They're going to be testing these paintings for a hundred years," he said, dreamily. "Maggie blended ancient materials with present-day. They'll never be able to explain it."

Carol Ann was already sitting in front of the painting, lost in it. "That's what will draw them from all over the globe. They'll *never* be able to explain it." During dinner, she toyed with the food on her plate. "I wish Maggie were here to celebrate the painting's homecoming. She doesn't seem to want to come home anymore, does she? All I get from her are notes and blurbs. She never mentions a word about the time she's spending with the Holy Family."

"Has she titled the new one?" Father Andre asked. "We haven't received any sketches yet."

"She hasn't mentioned a title, Father. But she did write that she has preliminary sketches and hopes to have the new painting finished by August."

"She still getting migraines?"

"No mention of her state of health, either. My sister— the woman of few words." Carol Ann slid out of her chair and walked over to the painting, which was having dinner with them. "I wonder why she didn't use her own canvas."

"What?" he and Fathers' Andre and Richard said in stereo.

Carol Ann giggled at their gaping mouths. "This isn't her canvas. Is this observation important?"

"Are you sure, hon?" Father Andre helped him pull the painting and easel away from the wall.

"I never thought to mention it, but it's a quirk of Maggie's to put a small checkmark after her name on notes, letters—and finished canvases. Bottom right. See? No checkmark. She fixes her corners with sets of wood blocks. These corners are fixed with single, angled wood strips. And you could bet if this had a frame, it'd be lined with sponge or cloth so as not to scratch the painting. She's fussier than hair in a heat wave when it comes to canvases and frames."

"So she's chosen to use a period canvas," he said, fascinated.

"It would seem so."

Three days later, Father Andre phoned to tell her Maggie had sent home a blank canvas.

"That means there's still two out there," she told him over a beer at Corey's. "If she's going to use period canvases, why didn't she send home all three?"

"Maybe she wanted to mix them up."

"She's there to paint two pictures. She's done one. She has one left to paint. She's sent one home. So what's the extra canvas for?"

"Mistakes? Fire?"

She shook her head. "Maggie paints over mistakes or scrapes off the paint. And I don't think fire concerns her."

"Not sure where you're going with this, Inspector."

"Me neither. But still—I wonder what my sister's up to."

∞∞∞

The few times Maggie hitched a ride back to Marianlake with one of the groups, she never stayed long. And for some reason, even after Father Richard's coaxing, refused to call Carol Ann. Instead she called her parents and gave them messages for Carol Ann.

"It's because she knows I've got questions," Carol Ann said in June. "Well she has to talk to me sooner or later because she's my maid of honor. I'm getting worried, Joe."

The first week in July, he and Carol Ann were denied permission to visit Maggie in Judea. "'She's concerned about distractions and she says she's behind schedule', was the reason Father Andre gave."

"A load of crap," Carol Ann said. "She told the folks everything's going *wonderfully.*"

"Let's sneak back to Marianlake," he said. "Maybe we'll catch her there."

They missed her by three hours.

"Dave took her to the hospital yesterday." Father Richard said. During a walk to his old cabin he said Maggie was showing signs of wear and Dave insisted she go to the hospital. "They injected her with Fiorinol and her color returned by the time they got back. Just a bad bout of migraine. Something else is concerning me. Maggie asked to complete the painting in Judea. Not come home at all until she's done. She said this jutting back and forth in time in one and two-minute increments are wreaking havoc with her metabolism."

"I hope Father Andre said no," Carol Ann said.

"He did. He said no."

"What's the problem then, Father?" he asked.

"She didn't present a case. Didn't turn a hair."

"Oh, God," Carol Ann said, stopping dead on the road. "Asking for permission was just a courtesy. She's not coming back, I know her. She'll stay put until she's done."

He put his arm around her. "Better call Dina and have her stand in as maid of honor. Just in case."

With *The Nativity* in Rome, safely sheltered from the world until the exhibit, Ronny personally presented Carol Ann a note from Maggie the second week in July. She'd given it to Dave Thomson during a visit to replenish supplies,

Please don't be mad at me. I've taken the coward's way and decided to <u>not </u>have to deal with my very determined, inquisitive sister while I'm in the home stretch! I'm feeling fine—no migraines, just a little headachy. So stop worrying. You know what my staying means, Carol Ann...I can't be your maid of honor. It wouldn't be fair to you to get me piecemeal during this time. Dina would love to proxy for me. Love to the folks, Joe and Dina. I love you and miss you. Maggie xox √

The checkmarked letter was a mix of relief and disappointment. She was happy Maggie was okay and had expected her to pass the maid-of-honor-baton to Dina. But she had to stick her nose into the arrival and departures at Marianlake thus learning that the last two groups hadn't seen Maggie painting in the holy cave or at the group site. In fact no one had seen her except Dave Thomson. But Dave wasn't too accessible these days. Ronny explained again and again that Dave was busy. If he wasn't off with the crew in 6 raising shekel and denarii for group leaders, he was seeing to Maggie's needs.

The last week in July, Carol Ann received a call from a Dr. Briard at the hospital in Trois-Rivierés, Quebec. She was at Corey's having a late breakfast with Joe when her pager went off the moment Alain walked in.

As always, Alain's timing was perfect. Joe laughed to himself. All these years, every time Alain needed privacy, a phone or a doorbell would ring. In this instance it was a pager. Most people agreed it was a coincidence. He knew better.

Carol Ann gave him a kiss, waving to Alain on her way out. He grabbed a cup from the table beside him and poured Alain a coffee. "What's up?"

"I just got off the phone with Dr. John Goldberg in Trois-Rivierés. Name sound familiar?"

He leaned forward. "Yeah, vaguely."

"He's going out with a group next spring."

"What business did you have with him?"

Alain waited until the waitress cleared Carol Ann's setting. "John Goldberg is Head Coroner at Trois-Rivierés Memorial, Joe. Our people need protection. If anything were to happen, John has the power to keep the wrong people from discovering certain facts."

"Like the explanation of scar tissue that isn't scar tissue above a main artery?"

Alain didn't answer.

"Like ancient pollen and fiber particles on a body?"

Nothing.

"Like time of death?"

A nod.

"I don't think I'm enjoying this conversation."

"Did you know that Maggie showed up at Trois-Rivierés Memorial for a shot of Fiorinol a couple of weeks ago?"

"Sure. Dave took her."

"Did Dave mention she almost didn't get the shot?"

He bounced a fist on his mouth. "We didn't get to speak to Dave. Why?"

"Doctor Briard insisted on having her records faxed. At first, they faxed over the wrong records. A Mr. Michel Paget's records, who had had x-rays taken the same day as Maggie. Shortly afterward they told Maggie she was suffering from acute migraines, which she already knew. So they administered the shot and sent her on her way.

"But Mr. Paget was told he had a small growth, by all indications a cancerous growth in the oculomotor nerve. Probably there for some time. It's also difficult to spot, ironic since it's this nerve that enervates eyeball muscles. After more tests, they found they could not do an exploratory until they reduced his blood pressure. He's been closely monitored in hospital for two weeks. They did the exploratory yesterday."

He knew where this was going and already felt queasy. "And?"

"And nothing. No tumor. Joe, the call that Carol Ann went to return ... I suspect it's concerning this matter."

"They mixed up their records, didn't they."

Alain put his hand on Joe's forearm.

He was not going to panic. He would be calm. "Okay. So we grab her and get her home, like now."

"You know that's not the way it's supposed to go. Joe, it gets worse."

"Say it."

"I just learned Maggie's been missing for a couple of days. Since this is typical of Maggie when she's finishing a painting and since her family can't do anything, Rome made the call to wait, to give her more time. But she's changed lodgings and left no forwarding address. Maggie is considerate of others, so she must have big reasons to keep her location secret. Dave is there now with most of the crew."

"Oh God." He could think of two things—what the Archangel Prince had said about Maggie. And Carol Ann. What would he say to Carol Ann? Alain wasn't finished. "What?"

"Some are concerned Maggie may have moved forward in time, Joe."

∞∞∞

"She has cancer!" Carol Ann had been spinning in circles, throwing random items in a suitcase. "And now she's missing! Lord help us. Do you know the first three hours are the most crucial? If a person isn't located after three hours...I can't think about it. And she's lost somewhere in ancient Palestine!" She slumped on the edge of the bed and put her head in her hands. "She has cancer behind her eye, Joe."

It killed him that he knew what he knew and couldn't tell her. Saint Michael said he was soon taking her, but he didn't think it would be this soon. He hoped she had two or three more years, maybe until the Judean paintings were on exhibit and she'd had time to witness the miraculous effects of the work. But that wasn't going to happen, as Alain said—it wasn't the way it's supposed to go. If Maggie's time had come and if they did find her, they'd find her dead. What could he say to comfort Carol Ann? What could he do? Nothing. He could do nothing except hold her and continue lying to her.

This time they flew. Dina offered *Plane Bagels* but couldn't get it to them until tomorrow night. Carol Ann refused to wait. They left Angelfish Cove at 7 a.m. to catch the 9:30 a.m. flight from Boston to Trois-Rivierés. At 11:55 a.m. they shot past the Marianlake gates in their rented Chev Astro. The grounds were bustling, probably time-travelers because they all had that tranquil expression. They found Fathers' Andre and Richard in the rectory dining room. Ronny and Dave were with them and all four looked glum.

"Any news?" Carol Ann asked going from hug to hug.

Ronny looked worn out and Dave was flustered. "Dave and I returned from Joffa an hour ago," Ronny said, holding out a chair for her which she didn't accept.

"What's this place—*Joffa?* I don't recall any Joffa around Bethlehem."

"Let's all sit," Father Andre said. "We know Maggie's ill. Alain called. I'm so sorry, Carol Ann."

"Yeah, well ... thank-you, Father." She sat and Joe sat beside her and took her hand.

"Where's Joffa, Father," he asked Father Andre.

"Three kilometers southwest of Nazareth."

"Wait a minute." Carol Ann about squeezed the blood from his hand. "Nazareth's in Galilee. Right?"

"Right." Father Richard took in a deep breath. "Maggie is in—"

"I'm responsible for this. Only me," Dave Thomson said. "Carol Ann. Joe. Long story short, at Maggie's request, I snuck her ten years ahead in time to Galilee. She insisted on finishing the painting there and asked for my help. I found her a reputable innkeeper family to stay with.

Hushai and his wife, Hannah. Ronny and I were with them this morning and Maggie hasn't been home since I last saw her two days ago."

"God."

"What else did they say?" How fast could they suit him up? He'd taken his Judean gear back to the Cove and packed it away. Why didn't he think to bring it? *Damn.*

"We checked her room," Ronny said, "and there are supplies all over the place, but no canvas and no painting. My guess is Hushai's holding out on us. Hannah seemed rattled, but we couldn't get anything out of them."

"I can try," he said to Carol Ann.

"Oh no, Joe, please. We're not supposed to be there. None of us. We were supposed to stay in Judea and only Judea. Look what happened to Walter. And now Maggie. Don't go. I don't want you to go."

"Baby, we can't not look for her, you know that. And I'll have Ronny and Dave as my wing-men."

Carol Ann shook her head, adamant. "I love my sister. But ten years ahead—I believe that time in Jesus' life is forbidden, Joe. I think God meant the Family to have privacy during those years."

"Maggie is sick," Dave said, "so we need to bring her home."

"I don't need you to remind me my sister's sick, Dave! Thank-you very much for dropping her in the forbidden zone, by the way."

"I'm so sorry. She's just ... it's hard to say no to her."

"I know," Carol Ann's voice broke. "Believe me, I know. But now my fiancé wants to go traipsing after her. I can't lose him, too. Joe—do you think Maggie is ... do you think she's really sick somewhere?"

This was a new kind of hell. "I think we have to face that possibility, yes. Still, we need to bring her home, Carol Ann."

"If the other groups get wind of this they'll want to travel ahead," Father Andre said. "Carol Ann's right. That place and time are forbidden."

∞∞∞∞

With Ronny tucked away on the edge of Hushai's property and Dave behind at the helm, Joe found himself back in this ancient land without having had the time to psychologically prepare. In recent years his empathic gift was proportionate to his faith. But if he could tap into a kernel of emotion or find something Ronny and Dave overlooked, it might help them locate Maggie. They discussed his spending the night at the inn but Carol Ann wanted him back in 1998 as soon as possible.

He stepped out of his sandals and curled his toes in the red soil. One could cross a border into another country and feel a slight difference in ambience. But this wasn't about ambience. This was about a phenomenon that rocked the soul, the spirit, and for the untrained–the potential to waffle the brain.

The area smelled of rich pasture, meadows and sweet grass. The ground-level inn, made of red clay and stone, had a well-maintained but vacant appearance. Aside from nesting birds in hillsides turned pink and white from oak and rockrose trees, life was curiously quiet here. He waited several minutes before the innkeeper answered his knock. Judging from the anxious expression on the innkeeper's face, he immediately sensed something amiss.

They didn't seem to want him to venture beyond the inside of the door, so he put on his best smile and introduced himself as *Josef.* The innkeepers, Hushai and Hannah, told him they were taken with Joanna, that it was her habit to paint for days in her room. She dined once a day and preferred to bring back her meals from the cooking room. He had a number of questions for Hushai and hoped his Aramaic was equal to them.

"My intended is Joanna's sister and she is worried because Joanna is not well." He must've got through to them because they strained to hear. "We have medicine for her and ..." *Oh crap.*

"Did you bring medicine?" Hushai asked and he should've seen this coming.

"No. My friends have the medicine with them. I was hoping I could look at her room."

"Your friends looked at her room," Hushai said and his wife nudged him. "Yes, you may look at her room."

"*Taudi*," he said and followed them through a narrow hallway to the far side of the house. Maggie's room, situated apart from the other guest rooms, was her preference, no doubt.

There wasn't much to the room—a straw mattress and spread in the corner plus a wooden bench and large window with a table under the ledge where Maggie organized her paint and supplies. A nightdress, blouse, skirt and paint-splattered apron hung from iron spikes hammered in the stone wall. He was familiar with the ancient-looking paintbox the team fashioned for her. Apart from the canvases, nothing seemed to be missing. Wherever she was, she hadn't taken much in the way of supplies, not that he could detect.

"Did she keep her painting in here, Hushai?"

"Yes. Where else she keep?"

Strike one. "Of course. Did you see Joanna when she left?"

"No, not see." Hannah's eyes shifted away and looked down when they met his.

"Has she had visitors here apart from me and the men you met this morning?"

Hannah moved to speak but her husband beat her to it. "We see once but not get good view."

"One person? Two persons? Man or woman?"

"One person who walked like a man. Couldn't tell age. Hard rain that day. Everyone covered up."

He looked at Hannah who was still focusing on her toes. *Well Sherlock, this is going great.* He smiled weakly at them and ran his hands over Maggie's paintbox. From the only uncluttered area on the table, he picked up a tiny bundle rolled in blue cloth and folded at the sides.

"I give," Hannah said, her face softening.

He smiled. "You give to Joanna?" He removed the cloth and observed the small wooden carving of a dove. He held it up to Hannah. "Beautiful."

"No not bird. Give cloth to wrap bird."

Maggie had wrapped it carefully, almost reverently and kept it apart from her tools and supplies. "May I take this with me?"

"Not ours to give," Hushai said, eyeing the dove proprietorially. And that answer told him what he needed to know. Hushai and his wife truly cared for Maggie, and they respected her privacy and belongings. He made a show of wrapping the dove the way she had and put it back as he found it.

"Thank-you very much. *Taudi.* May I return to await Joanna? Would this be agreeable?"

They nodded in unison and made moves to show him out.

He could've been more inquisitive but didn't want to scare them off. Why should they trust him anyway? On the other hand, Maggie was gone and so was the painting. Even if they had stashed it somewhere around the inn he couldn't very well go pulling their house apart. But Maggie was okay, he sensed that. Or maybe he needed to sense it for all of them.

Two men, sweaty and soiled from the day's work, turned off the road toward the inn. He greeted them, "Laborious day?" he said, hoping the word 'laborious' translated as such.

"The body needs fluid today," one said.

"Do you work here in Joffa?"

The second man pointed up the road, indicating a place beyond Joffa. "Sepphoris," he said. "The city is good for work."

"What is the distance to Sepphoris?"

He was confident the man answered something in the neighborhood of seven miles.

"Are there smaller villages along this road?"

The second man wiped the sweat from his neck with the fold of his tunic. "Yes, friend. The next village is close to three miles southwest."

"What village, sir?"

"Small village of Nazareth. Little to see."

He bid them a good day and stared up the road, blood humming through his veins.

∞∞∞

Maggie stared down the road. She couldn't do that walk to the inn today. Not today, not in this heat. She leaned back in Yosef's favorite outdoor chair and slid her hands back and forth on the arms. This had to be the closest place to Heaven, the perfect place to live and to die. She couldn't thank them enough for storing her canvas in their home. Apart from three favorite brushes and the neutral and flesh-colored paints, everything else belonged to Yosef, and it pleased him that she made use of them. He didn't want her carting her canvas and supplies in this heat, either, and the last few nights the family insisted she stay over.

This was the best part of the day. Eashoa had finished his chores and was bringing her pomegranate juice. Then he would bring out her canvas and set up her easel. He loved to do things for her. And she loved Eashoa, loved him with all her heart. He set down the juice and placed his palm on her forehead. A flicker of sorrow passed through his almond eyes.

"No pain today?"

"No pain today," she said.

He had this wonderful habit of thinking before he spoke which always made her smile. "Soon you will finish your painting, Joanna. Then you will go *home.*"

He always emphasized the word home. "Yes, my Eashoa. Thank you to you and your mother for being perfect subjects."

He laughed. "Back to Father's work soon. But joy comes from his work and yours also. Joanna, I will finish your painting for you. If you wish." He regarded her in his special way.

Her heart skipped a beat. "Finish it?"

He bowed his head. "You have completed the face and hands. Only part of the chair and a foot to finish. I do well with chairs."

This was the thrill of her life. "That you do." She got dizzy with excitement. Eashoa made her drink a little juice. "I would love for you to finish my painting."

"Then it is done. After I will bring it to Hushai ben Issachar and your people will have it."

Her thoughts froze for the moment. "You can bring it to me at the inn, dear Eashoa. Then I will bring it to my people at home."

"You may go *home* sooner," he said, reaching into his tunic. "I made this for you." He gave her the tiny carving.

"A lamb!" She kissed the little lamb. "Oh, thank-you."

Eashoa was thinking again. "Joanna, while the painting must go with your people, the dove and lamb must remain with mine. Prepare a letter in your words and Hushai will write it in Aramaic. Then copy the letter in your hand. This is your will, Joanna."

Was he really only eleven? Of course not. "Oh? My sister cannot have them?"

"No. The Father desires that only the paintings link our worlds. But the dove and lamb will remain in your heart, in this world and the next." Then Eashoa grinned mischievously. "Yet paintings hold many links ... is this not so?"

Maggie looked tenderly at Eashoa's beautiful mother who approached with the cutting tool. She smiled and wiggled the tool at her son. "Eashoa, bring Joanna's painting. It is time to sit for her."

∞∞∞

Joe planned to wait one day before returning to Hushai's inn until he phoned Alain who advised him to wait a week. "If you can stand the wait," he added. Carol Ann agreed and suggested they go home to the Cove. Maybe Maggie would show up before he returned to Galilee.

"If she's not well she might come home on her own to get checked out," Carol Ann said during the drive back. "Then we can sit her down and discuss the next step."

She looked to him to say something comforting. Instead he nodded at the wheel and the I-91 ahead. He didn't really take notice of the long, scenic I-91 at St. Johnsbury, Vermont because he had another road in mind. A scenic road in an ancient land.

They rolled into town at 8 PM and stopped at Corey's before unloading the car. Though he wasn't hungry, Carol Ann insisted he eat.

"I know you're worried as much as I am," she said. "All you eat is fruit when you're worried." How well she knew him.

The only available seats were at the bar and they'd ordered a couple of beers when Alain walked in from the patio. "I have a table and a surprise waiting," he said, all smiles. "Follow me."

John Corey was working the bar and winked at them.

Carol Ann spotted her first and ran ahead to give Iris a hug. Suddenly his appetite spiked. Geez, it was good to see her, and Carol Ann sure could use the moral support. So could he.

"Hey look who's here!" Carol Ann said and he kissed Iris' cheek.

"There she is," he said and laughed. "All five-feet-two plus four-inch heels of her."

"I wear them just for you now," Iris said.

They had a nice reunion. Iris had flown in from Rome but was group-hopping across Europe with the psychologists these past months. She'd written often and called once a month, but now he sensed she was home because she'd heard Maggie was sick and missing. He'd wait for one of the girls to mention it and got busy draining his second Budweiser. Iris was first to drop the shoe.

"The group leaders have been told Maggie's having a bad bout of migraine. That's all. That's all they need to know."

"Father Andre fill you in?" Carol Ann asked.

"Vittorio," Alain said. "He called to ask if there are any clues about Maggie."

Iris looked questioningly at Carol Ann and himself. He shook his head and ordered another Bud.

"I'm praying Maggie will come home on her own, especially if she's not feeling well," Carol Ann said, then suggested he order something to eat.

She won't be coming home, baby. I'm so sorry.

"Right, Joe?"

He tapped the freckle patch on her nose. "Right. How long you in town, Iris?"

"I can hang around awhile," she said. "You're returning to Marianlake in a week, right? Alain told me."

"Right. A week." He slugged down some more beer. "Why, you wanna hitch a ride back?"

"No." She clicked her heels under the table. "I think I'll stay put and do girly-girl stuff with Carol Ann."

If you say so, Iris.

Without Iris in the Cove, Carol Ann would have insisted on returning to Marianlake with him. However, he did have instructions to call her the moment he stepped back on present-day soil. Funny how Iris always showed up at the best times—and the worst times. The girls dropped him at the airport and after he kissed Carol Ann goodbye, Iris shot him a brief knowing look that made his stomach lurch.

∞∞∞

Since the groups always came and went at midnight, he and Ronny slipped around them unnoticed late mornings or early afternoons. In the interim, Father Richard made certain the rink stayed locked. Ronny had to fend off an overly-excited traveler in the vestibule who tried to get him to share 'just one' Judean experience. It took a while but they settled him down and convinced him to focus with a bit of prayer and meditation.

"I can use a bit of centering myself," he told Ronny while they changed clothes.

"I've logged a hundred and five trips over the years," Ronny said. "And once in a while I still come back emotionally fried."

Fifteen minutes later they surfaced in Galilee behind a small grove of prickly juniper. After Ronny sent the disk back to Marianlake, they took a quiet moment before heading toward the inn. He glanced at Ronny who was standing with his hands on his hips staring at the sky. The poor guy had already served his time, so to speak, and he didn't dare set himself to worrying about his little Inspector. He looked heavenward, same as Ronny. It was time to bring Maggie home.

"You haven't said much since you got to Marianlake today," Ronny said as they hot-footed it along a grassy slope on Hushai's property. "Wedding jitters?"

"Maggie jitters. She planned this you know." He dodged a mosquito and slipped on a pile of cow dung. "Gah!"

"You okay?"

"Yeah. Carol Ann told me at Christmas that Maggie was reading up on Galilee. It slid right over me. How could I let it slide right over me?"

"Pleasantly distracted would be my guess. Geez it's quiet down there. In this heat, what're they doing inside? It's not like they have AC."

Ronny called out for Hushai as they strode along the path.

"Maybe they're all at the mall." *Oh Lord, help us.* Joe knocked at the door and again waited several minutes before Hannah answered. She looked relieved and unnerved at the sight of them.

"Come come," she said, agitated. "I'll get my husband. Hushai! Hushai!"

Hushai's feet slapped hurriedly from the back of the house and upon seeing them, raised his arms. "Ah, you have come for Joanna."

"Is Joanna home?" he asked, dizzy with emotion.

"We are so remorseful, Josef. So remorseful."

"Hushai, where is Joanna?" Ronny asked.

Hannah started to cry.

Not ready, St. Michael. Not ready.

"Joanna returned ill to us two days ago," Hushai said, gesturing for them to sit. "Pain here." He pressed in on his temples. "And later, fever. Joanna is now at peace with Elah."

A hoarse guttural sound emerged from Ronny's throat.

"Tell us, please." The Archangel's words weighed heavy on him, *I am soon taking her.*

Hushai put his arm around his wife's waist as she fought for control to speak. "Joanna returned pale and beautiful. I did not see who was with her. She entered alone holding carved lamb mystery friend gave her. It made Joanna happy and she tell my husband she leave painting outside." Hannah sniffed and dabbed at her nose. "My husband went to bring in painting and painting stand and set it in her room. She did not want to eat and asked Hushai to write letter."

"A letter?"

Hushai nodded and shrugged. "She asked me to write in Aramaic what she tell me to write. Then she copy Aramaic in her own hand. She ill so letter took three hours and more for her to copy."

"Where's the letter?" Ronny asked, a shade away from an accusatory tone.

"With Joanna. With the dove and little lamb. When we bring, we show you, Josef."

"Did Mag...Joanna say why she wanted this letter?" he asked.

"She say important her friends understand some things must remain behind."

"Not her painting?" Ronny nearly jumped all over the innkeeper, but Hushai shook his head and clarified.

"No. Joanna would never leave painting behind. After she finish copying letter she go to room to rest."

"Later I go to see her health," Hanna said. "She look often at dove and little lamb and say she would take food now. So I bring bread and legume soup and Joanna ate little. Then I stay until she sleep and I close her door."

Hannah started weeping again so Hushai spoke for her. "In morning, my wife go to tend Joanna and find her reclined on bed holding little lamb and dove. She was beautiful like an Egyptian queen, forever sleeping. We do not know what happened to Joanna. We do not know who she was with during these last days."

I think I know.

"We are so remorseful. We cooled and wrapped her in herb and salt compresses. And last evening, certain that family would not come to claim Joanna, we moved her."

"Where did you move her?" He glanced at Ronny whose eyes were darting around the room, searching.

"Come," he said. "She is in our family resting place."

While they trailed the innkeepers along a narrow pathway to a small cave, a fifteen-minute walk behind the inn, they explained that they needed to collect Joanna's things. In the past the crew returned to her with everything from wildflowers, dead bugs, horse hair and soil. What else did Maggie leave behind? There were no other caves around here. No sheds, except a barn and a coop for chickens and doves. What was missing in the picture this time?

He felt Ronny's heart pounding harder than his own. This was an inopportune moment for the return of his empathic gift. So say him. What God had in mind was clearly none of his business. When Ronny stopped Hushai and Hannah to talk outside the cave, he used the moment to take in a deep breath and send home a blessing to Carol Ann and her parents.

"It will not take long to prepare Joanna and transport her home," Ronny said. "Is the painting in the house?"

Hushai nodded. "Yes, we love." He set aside three planks covering the mouth of the cave and entered. "I will light lamps. There is room for two inside."

"Is this your family resting place?" he asked Hannah.

She pointed to a plot of land east of the cave. "We prepare here and bury there. We are not wealthy enough for a family crypt. We would have buried Joanna with us in our earth."

"Thank-you," he said, swallowing hard.

"There is light inside so you may enter." Hushai came out and gave him Maggie's letter, which he promptly passed to Ronny. An explanation to the innkeepers that he couldn't read Aramaic may have prompted questions. Better to stay silent. "We give you privacy," he said, and walked off with Hannah, talking low.

"Do you want to go in alone, Joe?"

"That's considerate, Ronny. Yeah, think so."

"I'll read Maggie's letter and when you come out I'll go in and pay my respects. I think we should take her back to the juniper grove and leave from there. We can't risk being seen and I don't have the coordinates for this area."

Unable to think about that yet, he went inside.

There was such serenity in her beautiful face. He wondered how it was possible that she was dead and not sleeping. They had laid her on a type of white porous cloth on a board raised by boulders at each end.

"Oh, Maggie." He set the dove and lamb on her heart and held her hand.

Her body showed no trace of decomposition and her skin seemed oddly moist, especially her hands. The innkeepers had placed the dove and lamb in her hands and dressed her in an ankle-length tunic with a pale blue sash at the waist. The sash was damp and oily where her hands had been. He took the lamb from her other hand and it too had a mysterious oily fluid seeping from Maggie's fingertips onto the sash. Perhaps the oil was a Jewish custom.

He raised her hand to his cheek, and upon doing so, the tomb filled with a heavenly perfume of roses. The oil, still oozing from her fingertips smelled of roses.

Dark with sadness, he stroked the top of Maggie's head. "It's like God sent you roses to welcome you home, then showered a path of petals from your deathbed to His throne."

"And an angelic cortege," Ronny said, entering. "Joe, I had to come in ... that scent ..."

"I know. Hushai must've rubbed her down with it. A custom, I would think."

After thirty minutes of silence, Ronny asked him to step outside. "This letter, Joe—it reads as a will."

He shook off the drifting feeling and squinted at the letter he couldn't read. God, it was hot. "Anything that will disturb the family?"

"I don't think so. She says she wants to change her place of burial to Marianlake. That aside, she wants everything in her original will to stay the same." Ronny gestured to the small cave entrance with his chin. "Except for the wood carvings, which she's leaving to the innkeepers. That's all. What's the big deal about a couple of wood carvings?"

Maybe he knew. "Maybe asking to be buried at Marianlake is the bigger deal."

"Either way it doesn't matter. We have to get Maggie home. We'd better find that painting."

25. Forbidden Fruit

Since the innkeepers seemed to have disappeared again, they let themselves in, walked down the hall to Maggie's room and knocked in case the room had a new occupant. No answer, still no people—and no painting in the room. Time to locate Hushai and handle this as delicately as possible. The couple did not call the authorities to take Maggie. Instead they scented her with oil and would have buried her in their family plot. Why? For a lodger? This was a magnanimous gesture towards one they barely knew.

They found the couple sitting outside, the deepening hue of shame cast in their expressions.

"Where is the painting, Hushai?" Ronny asked.

When Hushai hesitated, Hannah became clearly agitated, provoking her husband to speak.

"Hushai ben Issachar, Hannah bat Reuben," Joe said, "Joanna's paintings are all her family has of her now."

The innkeeper made a placatory gesture, "We are so remorseful. Please forgive. The painting was with us during your previous visit. Joanna, she had finished and store in our home."

"Why did you keep us from it?" he asked.

"Our loyalty is with Joanna. If you are truly her people, why did she hide? We choose to wait until Joanna returns and instructs us what to do. When I saw your faces when we impart tragic news, we know you are true to her. Now we be true in return. Come."

The couple took them to their bedroom. Upon entering, his breath caught by what he saw—a room filled with people, sitting, standing, leaning, all silent and staring reverently at the painting. Clearly, the inn wasn't devoid of guests at all. They remained silent when he and Ronny approached the paintings.

"My God," he said, forgetting to speak in Aramaic. Maggie's work was magnificent. "My God." Maggie called it *Arma Dei*, Latin for *Armor of God*. It made his heart flutter.

The painting was a pictorial roadmap, only these roads were not of Earth. Maggie said she wanted to paint the New Jerusalem and that she did. In the upper segment she'd painted a circular city exploding with light, surrounded by a high jeweled wall.

At the top, bottom, left and right, four bridges led to the city or out of it depending on the viewer's interpretation. The bottom bridge was almost twice as long as the others. At the end of each bridge a road circled to meet the other three, so if one were to walk around, they could get to *Paradise* by taking the circular road onto any one of the bridges. The road glowed with thousands of small, dazzling orbs.

In front of the bridge at bottom center was a gold shepherd's crook. At bottom right an angel bore a golden shield and to the left another angel wearing gold sandals. He had been here! In his vision he'd stood in this place! And so had Maggie. She wasn't in that small cave at all, not really. She was in the *City* she'd painted, in the place he stood less than five months ago.

She'd signed 'M. Page'. How strange this signature must have looked to the Joffa innkeepers. Taking in more detail, he shook his head with delight. The golden color appeared to be the metal itself. Pure gold. Floating over the void at each midsection of the four bridges were more angels, all with golden flakes woven into their clothing. Topping the painting was a cross by the end of the bridge, an anchor at the left midsection and what appeared to be a heart-shaped pool at the right midsection. Again, the shepherd's crook was at the bottom.

Given the measure of detail in the painting, he would have to stand here all day to take it in, like the winged face on the bottom middle bridge outside Paradise—an effigy of a deceased soul or the soul in flight, perhaps? With tongues of fire everywhere, a permeating darkness rose from the void below. The tongues, it seemed, represented sentinels.

He could scarcely breathe. Somewhere in this painting was a hidden message.

Ronny's eyes were still searching, but no longer at the painting. "Where is the other canvas, Hannah?"

Of course! When Hannah looked to her husband, he pulled the painting away from the wall. Everyone started whispering. "This is not a period canvas," he said to Ronny. "This is Mag...*Joanna's.*"

"Hannah?" Ronny asked her again. She was still looking to her husband. "Joanna has another canvas that she brought with her."

"Yes, we know of it," Hannah said, cheeks burning. "Joanna finished *Arma Dei* long while ago and took empty canvas off our property. We do not know where."

Hushai sighed. "My wife speaks the truth. She must have been storing new painting with subject of painting. In beginning she returned to inn with paint on clothing. Later she did not return for days. I have informed you of this."

Ronny moved abruptly to one side. "Did you not question her? A woman travelling the road alone in this land cannot be safe. You let her go off alone?"

"She insisted Elah is with her." Hushai flapped his hands as he spoke. "What we have done? Joanna not our daughter."

Everyone in the room began whispering again.

"You have both been kind and generous," he said. "And we are grateful. We will take Joanna home now and her painting. Do you have boards and rope, Hushai? I will return them."

"Yes, but you may have."

He cleared his throat. "I must find Joanna's last painting. I will return another day. Her work is truly important."

"Yes," Hannah said, gazing adoringly at the painting. "We know Joanna's work is important. Her family must have. The world must have."

The world must have. Hannah bat Reuben had no idea how prophetic her words were.

∞∞∞

He resisted the violent temptation to speak of the Saint Michael vision and helped Carol Ann through her grief as best he could. Knowing he could abate her pain was a new torture for him, especially since their collective worlds revolved around Maggie's legacy. Iris had hung around and was a great help to Carol Ann. Thank God for Iris.

"Why, Joe?" Carol Ann asked him at the viewing. She knelt by Maggie's casket and stroked the side of her face. "Maggie should be here to enjoy the impact of those paintings. You know, I'm seriously considering suing that hospital. Maggie could have had that operation if they hadn't mixed up those records. I can't bring myself to tell my parents the coroner's results. They're standing over there, a few feet away ..."

During the funeral Mass after Dina finished singing the *Pange Lingua,* Carol Ann whispered to him, "I've decided. I'm going to sue."

Joe said nothing. He put his arm around her and kept her close.

The one available plot of ground in Marianlake's small cemetery straddled the fence, facing the road to the rear property. The Pages hated it but respected Maggie's request. As they squished into the area, Dave Thomson drifted by, mumbling under his breath, "*This could have been prevented.*" Had Dave directed the comment at him? No way to be sure except to ask him, but already he'd walked off, obviously preferring to stand alone. Poor Dave. He'd never seen him so low.

Amidst the smothering heat, hotter than it had been in Joffa, he smelled roses at the gravesite. Carol Ann clung to him on one side, Dina on the other. Bishop Gianni, Sister Elizabeth and Tim Pink stood across from him, with Dave withering away in the distance. Did any of them notice the floral scent rising from the ground? He looked at Ronny and Alain, then at Iris who was staring back at him. Good ol' Iris drove his Syclone here from the Cove while he and Carol Ann flew to Brooklyn to deliver the heartbreaking news to her parents. Iris smiled weakly at him.

"Do you smell the roses?" he whispered to Carol Ann. She looked at him strangely through swollen eyes and shook her head. He looked to Dina who had overheard. She too shook her head. Ronny was on the other side of the casket. He'd have to ask him later.

Unable to focus at the wake, he was uncapping his third beer when Elizabeth strolled over with Ronny.

"I'm glad the wedding's still on for October. Maggie would like that," she said, eyes lingering on the bottle.

"That's why we didn't postpone," he said. "Did either of you smell the roses at the gravesite?"

"There were bouquets of roses on the casket, Joe," Ronny said. "Can I talk to you privately for a second?" Ronny led him out the back entrance of the rectory to the parking lot. He stole a swig of his beer and handed it back to him. "You haven't been yourself since we left for Joffa, Joe. This can't be all about Maggie."

"I have to go back there. I have to find that painting." *No. It was more than that.*

"Well we will. Alain's flying back to Rome with Vittorio in a couple of days. Why don't you grab Carol Ann and join them for a week or so. Get your sea legs first."

He held the cold bottle against his forehead. "How soon can I go back?"

Ronny raised his chin and scratched it. "What you gonna do when this gig shuts down in four months? Horse farm still a go?"

He couldn't think about that now. Or Maggie or Carol Ann. Not even the wedding. "How soon?"

"Give it another couple of weeks, Joe. Carol Ann will need you at home. I take it you haven't mentioned a return to Hushai's? Or the third canvas?"

The beer sloshed in his gut like water in a janitor's bucket. "I couldn't. She's had enough to deal with. I want you to do me a favor, Ron-man."

Ronny glared at him skeptically. "If I can."

"I want to go alone."

"*Non futurum,* man. Not going to happen!" He threw up his hands. "Nobody goes past-hopping alone."

"I did. When I went looking for you."

Ronny narrowed his eyes at him. "I wasn't there to stop you."

He looked at Ronny in earnest. "You owe me, don't you think?"

"Joe? What is this? Don't put me on the spot, man. We just lost Maggie. We're not losing the groom, too. Why would you want to go alone?"

He handed Ronny his beer and scrubbed his face with his hands. "I've had it good all these years. You've all suffered and I've had it good."

"Like with your parents? Norma? Willie? You've suffered, Joe. I don't get where this is going."

"That happened before the mission. I've had it good since, running this little show from my comfortable little corner."

"Uh, okay, so what're you saying, you wanna go to Galilee to suffer it up?"

"Of course not. It's like I'm running to catch up, that I'm missing something. You've all faced your demons and returned the better for it. Me, I'm still checking the life raft for holes. It's all been too easy for me, Ronny."

"You've been there for all of us. Sacrificed your studies and that horse farm."

"I'm not talking about my little disappointments and setbacks. There's something I'm missing, dammit. And I believe I'll find it there."

"But why go alone, Joe? Can you explain that much?"

"It's a test."

"A what? A test?"

"Yeah. A test."

"I'll consider it. But you'd better tell Carol Ann."

Doctor Goldberg omitted and *altered* certain details in his coroner's report while Alain persuaded the undertaker to keep the markings on Maggie's wrists confidential. Of course Carol Ann didn't sue. Settling Maggie's affairs consumed enough time and the press attention was exhausting. Dina Amodeo canceled three nights of her concert tour for Maggie's funeral and that made headlines. Lives touched other lives in many ways.

A week later he drank beer and paced in the Pages living room while Maggie's lawyer read the will. She bequeathed her art collection and Long Island mansion to Carol Ann on the proviso that it be used as a combination art school and student gallery. All monies were equally divided among Carol Ann and her parents with generous sums donated to Marianlake's Building and Maintenance Fund, the Church of Rome and Elizabeth and Ronny's retirement. Her sketchbooks went to him, the little jewelry she owned to Dina, and the Saint Michael statue to Holy Name of Mary Church at Marianlake. The Angelfish Cove cabin went to Dina and she established an additional fund in trust, appointing him and Carol Ann CEO's of the school and Dave Thomson, Managing Director.

The guilt for leaving Carol Ann in the midst of grief and wedding plans to return to Joffa was driving him to the brink of madness. Plus he had to wait four more months before he could tell them of the Judean vision with Saint Michael. One didn't go breaking confidences made with the Commander of God's legions, no matter how tempting. He tried to get answers behind the Red Door five minutes after they got home from the reading of the will. But the Door had been useless since their return from Judea 6. The Doors had systemically closed for the groups who'd been back and remained open for the groups in line to go—four months' worth as Ronny pointed out. Four more months … and then what?

He phoned Ronny again to pester him for a decision and Ronny said he'd give him eight hours. One full day alone in Galilee. If he hadn't returned by 6 PM, the team would storm-troop him twenty miles in both directions on that Joffa road. There was a condition, though—he had to tell Carol Ann.

She was helping Judith with a new display when he snuck up on her, mid-afternoon. He'd had a couple of beers but Carol Ann wouldn't be able to tell. Beers helped settle the restlessness and two or three never showed on him.

"You've been drinking," she said, taking a break with him on the patio.

"How did you know?" She gave him one of those looks that said *I love you but you can be so lame.* What a woman. "I know, I know. I don't even like drinking all that much."

"True, you don't. I've been waiting for you to talk to me. Is it wedding jitters? We can put it off, Joe—"

"I'd marry you tomorrow if you wanted."

"Then what?"

He 'fessed up about that last hour with Hushai and Hannah, telling her he didn't believe the blank canvas was so blank. But he could do without the repeat conversation he'd had with Ronny at Maggie's wake. "So you were right last Christmas when you thought Maggie was up to something."

"Okay. So drop the other shoe."

"I intend to bring you that missing canvas. A wedding present."

She leaned over and kissed him. "No surprise there. I'm glad Ronny's including you. I think you're as knowledgeable as anyone else on his team. When do you go?"

Oh crap. "Five days. Saturday. So I'll leave Friday morning." Weekends were busiest at Pages and Judith couldn't work this weekend. She had a wedding in Brimfield and Iris left two days ago. Carol Ann had no one to mind the store, which is why he picked it.

"Nuts. Too bad I can't make the drive in with you, but Judith has a family wedding."

"Oh right. That's too bad."

"Joe? Why didn't you tell me sooner about the canvas?"

"You had a lot more on your mind and I thought you'd freak at the idea of my going back again. You did the last time."

"I'm getting used to it and Ronny's been a gazillion times with the team. But what's got you all beer-buggery? You've been weird for a while. I thought it was the wedding."

How could he explain what he didn't know? Maybe Ronny had hit on part of it. "In four months I pull Walter's time machine apart. After these last twenty years, Carol Ann, raising Thoroughbreds is looking pretty dull. I think I'm already going through withdrawal. During the years Ronny was missing, I could've got the farm going then. So what stopped me?" Lord help him, he was turning into such a whiner. And a deceiver of fiancé's and good friends. "I'm sorry. You've just lost your sister and I'm droning on about myself."

"Well Joe, we'll be perfect when we're in Heaven."

He hardly slept for the next four nights. On Friday morning he stopped off at Carol Ann's to kiss her goodbye and dish up a little more deception. Too tired to slap himself conscious, he barely remembered packing his bag, though he did remember to throw a bunch of CD's in the car to keep alert. Music in the car still annoyed him to no end, but it was an eight-hour drive to Marianlake. He should've flown.

"I packed you some fruit wedges and a few Cokes," she said. She'd just tossed a Jabba the Hutt-sized cooler bag in the front seat and was now searching his eyes like she was looking for a light at the end of a dark corridor, "and I put in a jar of that peach jam for Father Richard. Did you know Coca-Cola was originally green?"

This time it was a strain to smile. "Carol Ann?"

"Yeeeees?"

"Ronny's agreed to let me spend eight hours on my own in Joffa. Only because I begged. I need time alone there and I can't explain why, not even to myself."

"I know, Joe."

"What? Again? How did you know?"

"I sensed you were off your wick a bit. And knowing you'd never give up until you found it, I called Ronny a few nights ago and made him promise to drag you forcibly back if it looked like you guys couldn't locate the canvas. That's when he let it slip you were looking for it on your own. He assumed you'd told me, Joe."

"I'm sorry."

"For the record, I wasn't going to let you drive away without telling you I knew."

"Because?"

"Because I want you guilt-free in Joffa, and in the proper frame of mind."

"I love you and every single freckle on that adorable nose."

"Phone me the second you get back. I'll answer quick. Women always answer quick because they think somebody's calling to tell them they've won something."

"I will." He kissed her nose, her ear, her mouth. Then he kissed her mouth again. And for the next fifty miles he got jittery knowing how haphazardly he tossed everything into his duffel. It bugged him so much that he stopped to search. The first item he searched for was Carol Ann's insect repellent, heaving a sigh of relief when he found it. He'd never forget to pack the bug repellent no matter how exhausted he was. *Thank-you, God.*

Still, when he got to Marianlake around 7 PM, he got there antsy, and he got there thinking about Walter Bayard's partially amputated toe, which he'd been thinking about for the last three hundred-plus miles.

∞∞∞

He slathered himself with the repellent and joined Ronny, Dave and Father Richard for a hearty but broody breakfast. Father Andre joined them mid-breakfast, albeit somewhat disapprovingly, and inquired after his physical and emotional needs.

"I'm fine in all respects, Father," he lied. "I have water, cheese and almonds and a bit of fruit."

"Keep Proverbs 19:21 in mind, Joe. 'There are many thoughts in the heart of a man. But the will of the Lord shall stand firm'."

"Okay."

"Okay, Joe," Ronny said when he stepped on the pod. "Hushai's water clock is inaccurate, but most farmers and merchants have sun dials. So if you can't figure it out—ask. Six-O-one, Joe. Then we're comin' for ya. Don't wander down that road any farther than six miles."

"Right."

"That painting isn't worth getting yourself into a jackpot over."

"Right."

Ronny got him in a neck clinch. "Safe trip. See ya at six."

Dave Thomson looked on from a distance, mouth downturned and eyes cold.

∞∞∞

This time Hushai answered the door after a few seconds with Hannah on his heels.

"Josef!" Hushai whisked him in the door. "It has come! Joanna's painting has come and painting have mount around edge."

"When? How?" Was this rock in his stomach disappointment? Maybe he was using the search for the painting as an excuse to go looking. *No maybe's about it, Joe.*

"Last evening. Always you arrive pre-destined."

He stood there like his ankles were tangled in swamp sludge.

"What is wrong? Come see Joanna's portrait."

Maggie had done another portrait? "Portrait?" Hannah had him by the arm, gently tugging him to their room.

"Joanna reminded me of my son many times when he was a boy," she said. "A memory for mothers. And for fathers to laugh and walk away."

"Look," Hushai said, beaming at the painting like his own child had created it. "A boy bring to us last night at dinner. I ask if this is him in painting. He say yes."

Joe sat on his heels, admiring the painting's simplicity and humor. "Boy?" he said, dreamily. Someone had framed this painting for Maggie.

"Yes. He say he paint bottom part of chair. *Here.*"

Hushai indicated the section of chair on which the boy patiently sat while his mother cut his hair with two fine blades joined at the handles. Shaded by an olive tree she sheared dark curls that settled like satiny brown ribbons on the white and grey-striped cloth wrapped around him. Folded hands peeked out of the cloth at his waist. Pale tan eyes like moist clay widened in interest below a sympathetic slightly-raised brow.

With a hint of blue in her downward gaze and a trace of amusement in her expression, his mother's concentrated loving hand trimmed the hair above his ear. She wore two veils secured by a headband and a modest indigo *chiton* or long ankle-length tunic, gathered at the waist by a tasseled cord. A grey shawl of the same length draped her shoulders.

Joe's fingers tingled as he ran them along the part of the chair painted by the boy—the boy, he recognized, was the boy in the long white nightshirt in the *Angel Reclining*. Maggie sure had friends in high places. He blinked his eyes shut for a moment. *Are you here with me now, Maggie? I can't go straight home, you know that, right? Say one for me, Maggie.*

"The language we do not understand," Hannah said, referring to the title. "What its meaning, Josef?"

Maggie titled this one in English. "*Obedient Son*," he said, feeling the same rush he had the day he met Carol Ann, which meant he had a lame smile on his face. Hushai and Hannah smiled along with him. "Do you know this boy?"

Hushai squatted beside him. "No. He ride on mule with mounted painting. Joanna allow him to paint part of chair and foot, he say. *Eashoa* is his name. He did not say where he lives, but home must be near. Boy riding mule alone? Father would not allow if son had to travel far."

"*Eashoa,*" he echoed. Ronny would know the etymology of the name. "Did you tell him about Joanna?"

"I told him Joanna go away and he seemed to understand. He did not ask for explanation. He did ask of dove and lamb and Hannah say Joanna give to us as gift. This pleased Eashoa."

"Did you see which way he went on the road?"

"He went north," Hushai said. "You go to look for Eashoa?"

"Yes. I will pick up the painting late this afternoon on my way home. Is this agreeable, Hushai?"

"Of course, Josef. But the day is hot. And you do not have proper cover for head. Hannah, bring Josef a *tallit*. You return tallit to me when you pick up painting. Stay in shade side of road."

Inhaling the smell of copper, olive oil and smoked fish, he'd walked all of one mile north on the parched stony road when his sandal strap split open a blister. He'd smeared sunscreen on the tops of his feet, but either sweated it off or deactivated it with repellent. A fly the size of a humming bird escorted him across the road to the blessed shade of an olive tree. The 'humming bird' dive-bombed him. Did they have attack flies in this time? He sank under the tree, batting it away. It returned and circled his head twice until it lighted upon a dung pile. Unease shifted from his stomach to his thoughts. The fly dwarfed the biggest horseflies he'd seen in any barn anywhere any time. Mercifully, there were no mosquitoes and if there were, Carol Ann's Christmas gift was an arm's length away in his shoulder sack.

"*Eashoa*," he said, feeling inside the sack for his water. "*Where are you?*" He took a hard swallow. "Walter lost half a toe here. Not going to happen to me, right God?"

People walking to and fro on the road started noticing him. Why? Didn't they take siestas in this time? A family slogged by, trailed by a panting dog and a packed mule. He nodded. They nodded back and whispered amongst themselves. *Thanks for stopping. Nice chatting.* He had to get up. Had to get to Nazareth. Had to find the Family. Two more miles up this road. Tops. Maybe he'd walked farther than he thought because he had no sense of time here. *Oops. Sorry, Ronny. You might have to liberate me from this road I'm not supposed to be on, man.* He might've thought to offer Hushai a few denarii to rent his mule for the afternoon. Too late.

Dizzy from the hot air rolling over him, he continued onward, sounds clamoring in his ears—cowbells and the bleat of lambs, the clopping of horse's hooves and nauseating aromas like sweat and manure mixed with olives roasting in the sun. Ahead, voices rose. Aramaic piecemeal translated as *fasten. Tie. Hoops.*

Fragmented words evolved into sentences as he neared a small somber-looking home built from lava rock. He took for granted the exchanges with Hushai and Hannah, never offering up a thank-You for the Aramaic he'd come to learn through the years. He grasped most of the conversation between a man and boy lunching outside—

"Nahir, eat small last meal and large first meal. Yes? Else you will grow fat like your Uncle Itzak."

"Uncle Itzak says he is bloat, Father."

"No. Your mother was bloat before you came. Uncle Itzak is fat."

He took a deep breath and approached them. They had to have a well around here somewhere. Never in his life had he consumed as much water as he had today. He'd minimize the words. A good decision considering he wasn't nearly as fluent as Ronny.

"*Shlamak,*" he said. *Oh little drinking well, come out, come out wherever you are.*

"*Shlamak,*" the man said, snatching the boy's bread from his hands. The boy pointed at his sandals and the man he assumed was the boy's father, spoke. "Your feet are fire. Your skin is not accustomed to this land. You are a stranger here?"

"Yes." He shook his blistered foot and the boy giggled.

"Rest, stranger. And my son will cool your burning traveler's feet with sour wine. Nahir, go."

"*Taudi*," he said, and moved aside a large hoop propped against a sycamore trunk. He peeled off his sandals and reclined against it. Something buzzed by his ear. *Oh no.*

"I am Tuvia," the man said, "and that is my son, Nahir."

"Josef." He couldn't ask or answer questions that would draw attention to Eashoa or his family. So a lie was probably best, if such a thing was ever best. "I am staying with Hushai ben Issachar and looking for work in Nazareth and Sepphoris." Two lies, actually. The boy set down a large bowl filled with, no doubt about it, vinegar.

Tuvia asked the type of work he sought, how long he'd been in the area, where he came from. He was up to lie number twelve now, and the buzzing around his head increased with every lie. What would he tell the Holy Family if he did find them—that he was a friend of Joanna's? That would work. But what else? What else could he say that wasn't a bold-faced lie? He could say he came to re-visit their Son, that he was at the cave of His birth. Ah, finally! Some truth, *Josef.*

"The traveler looks stricken with heat, Father," Nahir said, daubing something globby on his blistered foot. "He must continue to walk when the sun is higher."

Did the boy say traveler or *intruder*? Another bloodsucker landed on his arm and he smacked it with such force his hand left an imprint. The mosquito bit him though, and the bite had to be a quarter of an inch wide. Father and son glared at him like he was one fig short of a fruit basket as he trashed his sack looking for the repellent. He could've sworn the boy said *intruder*.

"Come inside and sleep for an hour," Tuvia said, helping him up. "The stone is cool and damp."

"Thank-you." *Forgive me, Lord. I'm not following the playbook.* "Thank-you for your hospitality. For an hour then."

Nahir's mother took over at the door, barely turning a hair as she escorted him, a stranger, to a darkened room that resembled a pantry. She brought him a blanket and a roll for his head, saying something about being cool as she smiled her way out the door. He laughed out loud at the being cool part and managed to get a grip when she re-entered the room and set down a water jug. He lay on the straw mat and was drifting off when he heard his least favorite sound. *Buzzz. Buzzz.* He pulled the blanket over his ears. *I'm intruding here.*

What was he doing? He had a painting to return home. He had responsibilities—to the team, Carol Ann. To the world. Walter didn't selfishly deny his team the same opportunities. He groaned and rolled on his side. Who was he kidding? Of course they knew he was here to find Jesus. Why else would he choose to go tripping down the road in this basalt furnace? What rights of entitlement did he have? *Absolutely not a one, Joe. You have no right to be here.*

Buzzz. Buzzz.

He hadn't considered Ronny having to round up the boys and come searching for him. Why was it sinking into his seared brain now that getting Maggie's last painting home was the reason they were all here?

"God forgive me."

He'd take the hour to rest and then get his tail home. At the end of Tuvia's path, he would turn left, as much as he ached to turn right. But could he make that turn with Jesus living just down the road? Making that left turn would take all the strength he had. What if he couldn't do it?

'*What you gonna do when this gig shuts down in four months?*' Ronny had asked. Fair question.

"What did I do to get here, Lord? Why have You rained miracles on me all these years?" He rolled onto his back and opened his eyes. This was the million-denarii question.

Though he managed to get himself in the alpha state and rest, he couldn't sleep, not with that infernal buzzing in the room and Nahir playing outside. He felt bites come up behind his ear and another on his ankle. Startled by a thud against the rock wall between him and the outdoors, he raised the cloth covering above the quasi-window and smiled at Nahir.

"*Sh'lam*," he said. The boy had a playmate with him, chasing a hoop in the distance.

"Nahir! Leave the traveler alone," his father shouted. "He is resting."

He stuck his head out the window to assure the boy's father. "It is fine. I am gathering my belongings."

"I am sorry," Nahir said, eyes rounded and soft.

"It is fine, Nahir." He reached out and patted his cheek, remembering Alain when he was that age. About five minutes ago. "My feet are cooled and the blister has hardened. Thank-you."

"Nahir, leave him alone!"

"My father calls me away," and off he dashed around the corner of the small house.

He folded up the blanket and poured the rest of the water from the jug into his wineskin. *Pitter patter, let's get atter.* Time to hit the heat ... and head back to Hushai's. Still weak and somewhat dizzy he thanked Tuvia and his wife for their hospitality. Nahir was off playing somewhere.

"I will return to Hushai," he said.

"This is wise decision," Tuvia said. "Animals say there will be breeze and rain tomorrow. You return then to look for work."

His stomach tightened. He could never return and in four months he'd make sure no one else could, either. "Goodbye and thank-you again." *God bless Tuvia and his family.*

He stalled at the end of the path hoping Divine Providence would give him a shove toward the right. It was around two or three in the afternoon and the heat wasn't as suffocating. But no shove came. No instruction, no inkling, no voice.

"Flash the left turn signal, Joe." He'd grown accustomed to talking to himself here. It felt good to drop English words in this ancient land, like they could float onward and remain long after he'd left. Invisible floating words were the only change he could make, the only part of himself he could leave, and to Galileans the words would be incoherent babble. He prayed the words floated *rightward* and turned left.

Ten minutes into his walk he ruminated over the leavings in his life—Ocala after his father's death, Medford after Willie's death, Carol Ann and Marianlake for Rome, Rome for Angelfish Cove and now this ancient world in exchange for a new life with no more miracles. But none of those leavings meant as much or hurt as much as the untraveled road at his back. He shuffled his feet as he walked, desperate for answers, realizing he'd been desperate for answers since the day his father died.

"I desperately want to turn around, God. But if it takes leaving You to get closer to You, I'm leaving You."

"Nahir! Nahir!" a young voice shouted behind him. "Watch! The man, the man!" He heard a whirring sound and turned halfway around and *thwack!* Next thing he knew he was flat on his back staring at a bunch of fuzzy-looking clouds.

"Josef! I am sorry again!" Nahir was kneeling over him. He heard the sound of running feet as he got himself into a sitting position. "Please forgive again!"

He shook it off and laughed at poor Nahir who was finally coming into focus. "I am fine, Nahir. All is forgiven. What hit me?"

"His hoop," a second young voice said, helping him up. "Nahir meets many people knocking them down with his hoop."

"This is my friend, Eashoa ben Yosef," Nahir said.

Joe's heart stirred and leapt at the sight of Eashoa, the boy in the *Angel Reclining* and *Obedient Son!* "Hello, um ... *Shlamak.*"

Eashoa offered his hand in greeting.

Say nothing. Ask nothing. Just send Him love, Joe.

"*Shlamak,*" Eashoa said.

"You are returning to Hushai now?" Nahir asked.

He nodded, swallowed, tried to swallow. Eashoa's hair and eyes shimmered under the sun and there wasn't a bead of sweat on him. *Thank-You, God.*

Eashoa held his wineskin to Joe's lips. "Recently I have been to Hushai ben Issachar's," he said without further explanation. "Drink, please."

"I had better turn back," Nahir said. "My father is not pleased with me today. *Shalom.*"

He said farewell to Nahir and returned the wineskin to Eashoa with a trembling hand. "*Shalom.*"

Eashoa traded the wineskin for his sack and slid it on his shoulder. Eashoa's fingers brushed against his on the strap. "*Shalom*, Josef. Elah will bring you peace at the end of your journey."

Hushai had wrapped the painting in cloth and fastened a rope-tie so he could carry it effortlessly. He insisted the couple accept the rest of his denarii. He certainly had no more use for it and Hushai and Hannah deserved much more than he had to offer.

"You were kind and devoted friends to Joanna. The rose oil you anointed her with scented the air—from the ground on her day of burial."

Eyes moistening, Hannah shrugged at him and Hushai frowned. "We did not use scented oil on Joanna," Hushai said. "We use herbs and salt."

"I see." God must've sent her roses to welcome her home. *Oh Maggie.*

After bidding the innkeepers farewell for the last time, Joe coasted over the hill to the prickly juniper grove and found Ronny and Dave already waiting.

Dazed and numb with joy, his fingers tingled as he raised the painting in greeting.

∞∞∞

Ronny explained that although Yeshua is the most widely used transliteration of Jesus' name, *Eashoa* is the most accurate. Jesus from the house of Joseph becomes *Eashoa ben Yosef.* "You should've been with me to meet Him," he said to Ronny, stroking the bite welt on his arm. "I'm such a selfish snake."

"If I was with you," Ronny said, "we would've grabbed *Obedient Son* and hightailed it back. You never would have met him. But hey, you brought Maggie's last painting home, so lighten up."

A week later on the phone with Ronny, he mentioned that the mosquito bites hadn't healed. "I'm hoping I can keep them. They're kind of like *holy* bites."

Ronny took a big gulp of whatever he was drinking. "It's odd, you know."

"What is?"

There are flies everywhere in Israel, but not many mosquitos. They must've packed their little mosquito bags and tracked you down, man."

∞∞∞

With their wedding arrangements sorted out by the end of September, the bride spent her time compiling the first draft of Maggie's work, which included many of the horrific 'Red Door' sketches from the early days. Dina introduced a new spiritually-themed CD. *Variety's* cover page headline read, **Dina Amodeo, From Rock's Gladiator Goddess to God's Ladyjock.** Elizabeth assembled a traveling band of teachers. Using the acronym SEAN, they christened their organization *Spiritual Educators for American Natives.*

The three Fathers', having written a paper on the turn of events since Vatican II Council, became politically active. Vittorio's status as Bishop opened doors to the private sector, an area strictly reserved for ecclesiastical hierarchy. The paper began making waves. Old friends sadly became new adversaries. Old adversaries became new friends. Iris spent most of her time in Rome as acting secretary on this project.

After averaging six hours a day on the phone with Carol Ann's parents, Rome and the director of the State Hermitage, Joe was in the final throes of setting exhibit dates for Maggie's Judean work plus the *Angel Reclining.* Today he was having problems putting the director off any longer. In fact, lately there had been several annoying details gone awry.

The director was anxious to get on with it and Joe wanted to stall him until Rome safely insured the *Obedient Son.* But as the rightful owners, the Page family merited time with the painting before sending it off. They kept it for three weeks in Brooklyn until Carol Ann's parents decided they could part with it—and so the delay.

Joe preferred to wait for the *Obedient Son* since these three paintings were the providential design of their entire mission. Also, he had a slight personality conflict with Heidi, Maggie's agent, so Alain acted as liaison. Joe did not care for Heidi's controlling, busybody ways and she did not care for his secretiveness. The St. Petersburg exhibit was the Crown Jewels of the art world and he was grateful to Alain for handling Heidi. Alain—his best friend, his right hand, his best man. Once the mission was over, would Alain stick long enough to Godfather their first child? He felt a big negative coming on.

∞∞∞∞

It would have thrilled Maggie to see them marry, especially during a torrential rainfall which she believed was good luck. But she would always add, 'Though I don't believe in luck. I'm just partial to torrential rainfalls.' So, marry they did–on Saturday October 31, 1998, seventeen years to the day after that horrifying Halloween at Marianlake. They didn't plan on this date. Joe told people the date *evolved*. He and Carol Ann were transforming a terrifying memory into a joyous one.

The groom spoke rapidly and swayed to the background music as he fastened the buttons on his shirt. "Well it only took us seventeen years but we're here!" he said to Alain.

It was like the guests were told to BYOP—bring your own puddle to Angelfish Cove's St. Joseph's Parish. While Ronny and Dave passed out paper towels inside the front entrance, the bride slipped in the side entrance under a beach umbrella. Yes, rain, thunder and lightning were a good thing, a great thing–leprechaun lucky, not that he believed in luck, either.

"Little did Carol Ann know it would take us this long, thank God. She would've had smoke under her *Nike's*." He said this to the best man who was checking the bottom of his shoes for prankster commentary. "Did they have *Nike's* in '81, bud?"

Alain laughed and held up the back of the groom's shoes by the heels. '*Help Me*', someone had boldly painted in white. Though it was an old gag it always got laughs–but not this time. Alain went at them in the kitchen with a bottle of *Fantastic*, a scouring pad and coffee grounds.

Joe sat shoeless in the rectory passing the time with the residing pastor and fathers' Andre and Richard. Richard was performing the rite with Andre as the con-celebrant. They had considered having the wedding and reception at Marianlake, but the Massachusetts area was more accessible for the guests. And of course their hearts preferred Angelfish Cove. Although they met at Marianlake, the warm and timeless Angelfish Cove had been home to them.

By 3 PM, amidst peals of thunder and ringing chapel bells, he beamed at her from the altar. Dina sang *The Look Of Love* from the choir loft while the bride glided a little too swiftly down the aisle causing her dad to fall out of step. The guests giggled as Dina clumped down the stairs from the loft after her song and rushed to take her place at Carol Ann's side. When Father Richard pronounced them husband and wife, Joe said to his bride, "Thank-you for trusting in us enough to wait. I love you, Carol Ann Ross."

∞∞∞

Since Dina left Gerrybarry and Plane Bagels at their disposal for one month as a wedding gift, they decided to spend their first night in the old Marianlake cabin before heading on to Italy. The Fathers' were obviously in on it since they filled the cabin with yellow roses and set a chilled bottle of Dom Perignon, fireside. It was twelve forty-five in the morning when they took all this in, senses reeling from seventeen years of memories.

"Bless all their ever-lovin' hearts," Carol Ann's voice choked as she read the card. "It's perfect."

"Speaking of hearts, I lost mine to you in this cabin," Joe said. "I cried after we said goodbye that last morning. Right over there." He pointed to the lumpy wing-backed chair by the couch. He walked over to Carol Ann and put his hands on her face. "But you cried for many years afterwards. Let me make all that up to you. Starting now."

He carried her upstairs and when they undressed and lay on the bed, it was yesterday. He looked down at those five wonderful freckles on her nose. They hadn't changed. Nor had the adoring expression in her eyes.

"Joe," she said, "My heart still pounds when you walk into a room. You don't have to do anything. All you have to do is stand there."

∞∞∞

They honeymooned in Italy and took the rest of fall and most of winter getting the school's paperwork in order, hiring instructors and mapping out the criterion for student acceptance. But it sure passed the time while they anxiously waited for the big night at Marianlake. In all their years together they were the busiest they'd ever been, so busy that by the third week in December they barely noticed their fading marks.

Though happy, Joe felt a disquieting distraction as once again, some important detail eluded him. He even felt occasional shades of Edmon. Yet nothing seemed to bother the rest of the team and an atmosphere of total trust filled their spirits. So he thought it best not to mention his unease to anyone, except Carol Ann. He too trusted, but after all these years he'd become warily wise.

"Missing raisins again," he said to her. "I might ask you to put your inspector's cap back on."

He missed discussing his deepest feelings with Alain. Then Alain, who was busier than any of them these days, had vacated the beach house for Marianlake in preparation for New Year's Eve. So with Alain moved out, he and Carol Ann agreed it was best to move Rosa in, especially now that she felt poorly. They could keep an eye on her in the Cove and while they preferred the loft above Pages because he did not want the *Willie memories*–Rosa did, saying Willie seemed nearest to her at the beach house.

"But Willie always seems near when you're near, *mi querido,*" Rosa said.

Rosa finally listed the Medford house and moved to the beach house three days before New Year's. Though he still hadn't found the time to source his unease, at least on the big night he could tell them, glory hallelujah, of his vision and for a change enjoyed the pleasant distraction over the 'nagging' one.

∞∞∞

By New Year's Eve afternoon with the grounds packed and the mother rink in the throes of set-up, the atmosphere tingled with excitement. He'd stayed up most of the previous evening in prayer and meditation and felt tired and hungry, hungry because he'd been fasting since the twenty-sixth. He wanted his spirit fine-tuned, just in case Saint Michael favored him with another vision. Tonight was the night. After midnight he could tell them about the Judean vision. Already, the last of many blips on the screen, another year was over. But his stomach quivered all the time now and sometimes the hair stood up on his arms. For no apparent reason he had the feeling of being watched.

He'd caught Alain in flashes these past two days. Either he was down on the lower level at the Rec. Centre tending the early arrivals, or he was in the office writing, reading, or talking on the phone. Late morning, he made a point of catching up with Alain in the rectory kitchen. The girls went to town for hair appointments and Tim hitched a ride with them to do some sightseeing. He'd hoped to share this quiet time for a catch-up with Alain, but Alain obviously had his hands full.

"Sorry, Joe, I won't see you until after opening ceremonies. But we'll have a long talk tonight. Be prepared—you'll be getting some answers."

He flashed his best friend a tight, false smile. Suddenly he seemed farther away than the Rec. Centre's lower level. Alain had the similar aura Maggie had when they said their goodbyes in Judea. What was that last part of Emily Dickinson's poem? It came flooding into his brain—

What Fortitude the Soul contains
That it can so endure
The accent of a coming Foot–
The opening of a Door

Since it was the only unengaged area on the grounds, he headed toward the little cemetery. Seeing Alain just now reminded him of something he said Christmas Eve—that apart from Maggie, no one had been buried there in the last sixty years, save one. The Order preferred to be buried with families or with founding houses in Quebec City and France, so there hadn't been any requests to expand. When he asked Alain who the *one* was buried there, Alain clammed up on him. This piqued his interest as Alain likely knew it would.

After a visit with Maggie, he approached three isolated headstones near the fence. The last time he was in this end of the cemetery was that horrible, tragic day. Walter had died. Ronny had disappeared. The mission had stalled. It marked the beginning of a test of faith that would last for many years. His prayers had been so empty, his mind cluttered with details, but Alain was the match that kept his faith ignited. He had been his guardian angel.

This section of the little cemetery seemed freshly tidied–*seemed*. Could this be so? He stopped in front of the unknown child's headstone, the one with the tiny sculpture of Saint Michael on top. This had to be the headstone Alain spoke of. During his last visit, brine and soil obscured the name. He wanted to share the Judean vision with Alain before anyone else, and wasn't sure why. Carol Ann should be first to know. He felt something like a warm hand on his back and spun around. No one was there.

The brine covered most of the stone facing, except the first four letters in the name– *A l a i*. For a moment his surroundings blurred and his body tilted right. It felt like a mild earth tremor. Though it seemed everything was vibrating, only he was vibrating. It reminded him of the first night he saw Ronny in Pages. Or rather—the vision of Ronny.

Cloaked in dreamy gauze, he cleared away the brine and read that a child by the name of Alain Girard Duprielle, born August 24, 1970, died a day later on August 25th. He gazed upward and took a breath before re-reading the name to make certain there was no mistake, that it was not a namesake relative or something. It was not. He and Alain shared the same birth-date. He and Alain shared a lifetime in the Spirit. His mind filled with dark shadows. Who was this poor child who lived one day? Who was Alain?

Again he felt the warm hand on his back and prayed for the dead child, asking Michael for revelation.

Then he went looking for Alain.

26. Remiel

Joe had to flash his ID three times to access the main foyer in the Marianlake Sports Center. There were people everywhere, smiling people, hauling boxes or unfolding chairs or pushing carts. The burly guy in the lumberjack parka hanging pictures must have been hanging for days because he'd reached the end of available wall space. Joe stopped to chat, hoping Mr. Burly would know where Alain was.

"Hi there. What are all these pictures? They look great."

The guy set his nail gun on the second rung of the ladder. "Mission folk. Faces and places through the years."

"Take it they're just for the party?"

"Yep. Party favors for the guests. They'll get to pick 'em right off the wall."

He squinted at him, "Any from Judea 6?"

The young man laughed and reached for his Coke. "Don't we wish. Nope. Everybody respected the rules. You're Joe Ross, aren`t ya?"

"I am. Have we met?"

"No," he said, all smiles. "But everybody knows you and Alain. Ronny Fergel, Dina Amodeo. It's an honor, man. Thanks to you guys, the rest of us got to make the trip."

No thanks to him since he couldn't begin to fill the shoes of the others. Others like Craig Matheson. Walter Bayard. And Maggie, of course. *Still don't know why I'm here.* "On behalf of the others, you're welcome. Name?"

"Josh Levy."

"Good to meet ya, Josh. Would you know where I can find Alain?"

"Sure. I think he's down on the lower level."

"In the small rink?"

"Or the offices. All the tunnel doors are locked, though."

"I have a set of keys. How long since you've seen him?"

"Couple hours." He put down the Coke and grabbed a picture from the box at the top of the ladder. "Watch your step on the ramp, Joe."

What could Alain be doing alone down here in the dark for two hours? Unless he wasn't alone. He plodded down the ramp to the baby rink, mulling. *Oh still mystery of mysteries why I'm in this group. Why I'm in such illustrious company. Why that angel upstairs waited so long to marry me.* The new key slid easily into the lock to the lower level foyer. After flipping the light switch, he rolled his neck and shoulders a couple of times. He hadn't exactly planned what he'd say to Alain. *Oh by the way, is that a secret relative buried in the cemetery? Oh really? No worries, bud. What's one more secret kept from best friends, right?* The area seemed devoid of souls but he called out for him anyway.

No answer.

Maybe he was inside the rink. Maybe tonight's group was returning early and Alain had to be here to get them. But that was Ronny's job. Hands on hips, he stomped a foot on the concrete.

"Alain!"

After another excruciating long silent moment he unlocked the door to the rink and entered.

"Alain?"

The air was unusually muggy and it stank. Someone had been here. Or maybe it was ancient Palestine he smelled, a musty, sour scent that lingered around the time machine. He rattled the key ring and slumped on the bleacher nearest the pod. Tonight was the night. Yep. He'd yank Walter's work of art apart and by tomorrow at this time—sayonara time machine. All over. Really bye-bye this time. A dull, empty ache gnawed at his soul.

'Walter, thanks for the great ride, man.'

A high-pitched undecipherable whisper struck his senses like a current slammed against a riverbank. The hairs spiked on the back of his neck. "What the...?"

"*We will stalk you now. The way is clear.*"

Joe stared catatonically at the rink. For the first time in twenty years, he felt completely alone.

∞∞∞

Minus Alain and Iris, Joe's *Meat and Potatoes* group swept through the foyer door promptly at 7 PM. Guests' had designated colors on their invitations and sections so eight hundred and seventy-seven people could arrive and depart as effortlessly as possible. Marianlake organizers originally intended to host all thirty-seven hundred travelers, but the number made it unworkable. A party that huge would've attracted more press attention than they were getting now, which was considerable.

Once the Page family agreed to show the paintings at three more parties before the St. Petersburg launch at the end of January, Marianlake heaved a sigh of relief. They couldn't accommodate that many, nor could the small town inns and hotels in the area. Quebec City was an hour and a quarter's drive away, Montreal an hour and a half. With the party on New Year's Eve, guests would need to reserve before invitations went out.

The invitations enclosed a map indicating the two Centre entrances and parking, accessed by a separate road. Marianlake couldn't have a constant stream of cars cutting through their property on party night nor any other night thereafter. In all respects it was still a monastery. Outside the monastery gate, sentries re-directed guests to the access road and deterred crashers. Without an invite and ID, the Pope couldn't get on the grounds, Father Richard said, adding that the sparrow had to pass inspection tonight.

The first news crew arrived in Trois-Rivierés yesterday afternoon, skulking around Marianlake's perimeter and local hotels, trying to glean information about the big New Year's party at the monastery on the edge of town. One reporter tried to land an interview with Marianlake's bone-weary head pastor, but Andre managed to fend them off. The press's sizeable base camp in Trois-Rivieres would be issued a statement tomorrow evening.

Though the press managed to dig up vague party descriptions like *Jubilee* and *New Year pre-Centennial and pre-millennium preparation celebrations*, no one in town knew anything in-depth, which intensified curiosity, especially the letters *SC*. Over the years, the letters adorned T-shirts, sweats and hats and other novelty items. Most of the world had seen these letters on wrists, or squiggles that resembled them.

Press majority felt the story had grown cold, mysteriously cold. People seemed indifferent. A double paradox because their indifference concealed the undiscovered link between the party and Maggie Page. The art world and Maggie Page fans anxiously awaited her posthumous exhibit at the State Hermitage Museum. And as for *SC,* where there was once a pull toward the meaning of these letters, which would explain all the hats and T-shirts, etc., there was now an apathetic acceptance of them.

∞∞∞

As usual, Ronny chose to arrive with his crew but headed straight to the small rink to await the last group returning home.

"Apart from Bishop Gianni, I don't know any of the speakers on this program." Dina said, running a quarter-inch fingernail down the list. "So it looks like we're sitting through speeches before we can get nosy."

"I've heard most of them and they're impassioned speakers," Elizabeth said.

Carol Ann was anxious to hear about the testing of Maggie's work. "There'll be a lot of buzz about Maggie and Walter. Thomson believes the work will stagger the art world and so do I." Making theatrical gestures with her long arms, she spoke as if to a crowd, "Here come the big boys and gals––National Endowment for the Arts, American Horticultural Society, The P-l-a-n-e-t-a-r-y Society, Geographic Society, American Bible Society. Mensa."

"I think you're pushing it with Mensa," Father Richard said. "How about the *Union of Concerned Scientists?*" and they all tittered.

Still feeling this afternoon's sting on his nerves, Joe whispered to Father Andre, "I saw a certain headstone in the cemetery today. Enlighten me, Father?"

"I will tell you anything you want to know–*after* you speak with Alain."

"And the elusive document? Rumor has it I'm finally going to see it tonight."

"So I'm informed, Joe. Big unveiling tonight."

A gold carpet runner extended the length of the upper foyer with chairs lining the walls, and the vast number of photos hung by Josh Levy drew them in like kids to a kite festival. Signs posted at opposite ends of both walls read, *Photos compliments of Marianlake. Help yourselves.*

Hundreds huddled around their group shots. They pointed. They laughed. They remembered. And they plucked them off the walls.

Father Richard spotted their first group shot of Elizabeth's going-away party when she accepted the New Mexican post. Joe found several of the Bagel Factory crew, including Walter in the early days. Quebec, Boston, New York—and the uncomplexified years with Alain and Vittorio in Rome.

He tapped his bride on the shoulder. "This shot here," he said. The picture showed him scowling at a bowl of stewed calamari set before him. Alain looked a gleeful twelve while Vittorio prompted him to sample the squid. "Vittorio kept saying, *mangiare. Eat up*. We were in a restaurant with a seating capacity of four and a half and I had promised I'd try it. I was remembering you and me and our first meal in Patsy's. The whole night, all I thought about was you. Couldn't get you out of my mind no how."

A big stereophonic 'awwww' echoed forward and Carol Ann cracked up. Dina and Tim were right behind him.

"You're so tweet," Dina said, an elbow on Tim's shoulder. "Aw, isn't Joe tweet, Tim?"

"Exceptionally tweet," Tim said. "And such a twell guy."

Savory smells of roast beef wafted from the banquet hall buffet set to feed them from six to eight, then again with a lighter, late-night buffet from ten to eleven-thirty. A licensed LLBO bar was in place for wine and beer, served by Judean 6 travelers who'd volunteered their time.

Joe chose to fast with juice, which he did one day a week, though for this occasion he'd fasted on fruit and vegetable juices for five days. Probably why he was so receptive to *the voice* this afternoon. He didn't want to mention it to Carol Ann until after the party, but Alain was going to hear about it. If he could ever find him.

They ate and reminisced over the photos until eight-twenty, ten minutes before commencement ceremonies began. They were happy cherishing these moments and Carol Ann's dreamy smile moved him whenever she sensed Maggie's presence, as they all did in their own way. What didn't move him was faking the party mood for their sakes. That *thing* at the rink had rattled him more than he realized. And his best bud was still on the MIA list.

The elegant red-carpeted dais, front and center in the converted rink, had five Florentine high-back chairs to the right of a stand-up microphone, with Maggie's paintings placed on easels at opposite ends, magnified on two video screens. A giant Crucifix hung above the stage. When they hit the lights, ribbons of colored strobes filled the room and the approximate eight hundred guests gasped in wonder. Someone tapped the mic to test it and the crowd fell silent.

He glanced around for Alain and Iris. No sign of them.

"I've got to wander," he whispered to Carol Ann. "I can't just sit here."

"You're going to go looking for Alain, aren't you? What if he takes his seat and you're gone?"

Vittorio walked onto the dais below, followed by four clerical dignitaries of multi-denominational faiths. Vittorio adjusted the mic to his height and asked them to stand in prayer. He stood and told Carol Ann this was a good time to slip out.

"I don't think Alain is going to show for the speeches, but maybe I'll run into him below. Oh well, time to go pull the plug on a miracle."

"You okay? Don't try fooling me now. I'm on to the Mr. Pollyanna act."

How did he deserve this angel? "The thought of dismantling the time machine's making me a tad wistful. But it shouldn't take long, Inspector, so keep your dancing shoes on."

"Alright but be careful down there. Remember what Mark Twain said, 'Name the greatest of all inventors. Accident.'"

"Last group just left the deck, Joe," Ronny said, folding down the creaky seat behind them. "They're a little gamey but they're home." Ronny handed him the disk. "Don't forget to toss this in. So? Any time you're ready to rock and roll."

He tugged Carol Ann in close. "All due respect to Mr. Twain, the chocolate chip cookie was invented by accident." Then he kissed that adorable freckled nose and slipped out.

∞∞∞

Ronny had left all lower level lights on for him. After calling for Alain a couple of times he approached the light coming from an office transom at the end of the foyer, but found the door locked and turned back. His gait felt stiff and halfway to the baby rink his knee cramped on him. What was it? Was he out of practice eliminating fear? What happened to lessons learned in Rome and behind the Red Door? Most likely he'd forgotten how to out-muscle fear, was therefore rusty, and a sitting duck should the demons choose to turn him into a toy for eternity.

Inside the rink, he steadied his breathing. The master plan was to dismantle the machine after the last group came home. *Shut her down, Joe. Forget this afternoon and get moving. Don't get distracted. Big party happening upstairs.*

He sat beside the pod and fanned the air, half-expecting that thing to return with another threat. It would take a day to ice the rink floor and another day to dust the cobwebs off the place. By next week the kids would be in here aspiring to Olympic heights. Next week the rink would return to being a rink.

Taking the crowbar from the workbench he pried off the two floorboards covering the machine's access panel. It was mind-boggling that the last group had returned from Jerusalem less than an hour ago with the sharp scent of ancient Judea still in their gear. This was going to be tough, given the memories and even the hassles. He unlocked and raised the access panel. Time to start yanking wires.

Sitting in a scattered multi-colored heap of wire fragments, something blew on his ear. He sat upright and stiffened, finding nothing but cold emptiness. Distracted by jitters, he didn't look twice for the missing time gauge. He had entertained the idea of keeping it for a souvenir, an idea not all-consuming right now.

Something was in here with him.

Even with the burning crawl on the back of his neck, he forced himself to hang back. He wanted to do this right. Loose ends had to be double-checked. He took a nail, scratched the miniaturized disk and tossed it into the sub-floor compound. The Ice guys would never guess this was anything other than an old fuse box, nothing more than a bunch of junk in a hole. He could get the hell out of here now.

A foul breath blew on his ear, garbled whispers echoing like tuning forks against his eardrums. He ran down the hall to the office with the light on and banged on the door.

"Hey come on, I know someone's in there! Open up!" The whispers became intelligible and sickeningly blasphemous. "Open the door!" He took in a breath and said to the voices, "I thought our business was done."

Greeted by that phlegmy, high-pitched voice ingrained in his memory, he listened with numbed horror, "Our business with you is never done," Evil said. "Show me how well you pray with your right hand cut off. Like sympathetic pain following amputation, you *will* feel the hand you cannot see."

He closed his eyes and leaned back against the door. "What do you mean? What amputation?"

"Your right arm," it droned. "Alain. How well will you fare against me without Alain? Let me show you."

It impaled his mind with more blasphemies, making him cough from nausea and fear. Faith. God, where was his faith! "I believe in both angels of darkness and Light. But my allegiance has always been with Light and so has my trust." He leaned into the door for support, affirming his belief, belief carved on his heart from years of chasing God. The voices stopped and he sensed a gentle softness in the air. He opened his eyes and gaped in stunned silence.

"Joe? Joe, are you alright?"

"Well well," he said, forcing down a drop of saliva, "Iris. Iris ... Iris."

"Joe, you look like you've been wrestling with the devil himself."

"Close enough, my friend. What are you doing down here?"

"Looking for you. I knew we could speak privately down here. Let's go into this office."

"Locked," he said, trying to gulp fresh air into his lungs. He laughed weakly when Iris simply turned the knob and opened the door. "Ah, what is it about Iris? Know where Alain is?"

She hesitated. "He asked me to spend a little time with you first. He'll be catching up with us later."

He slanted a brow. "Watcha got for me, Iris?"

"Oh just a certain document written and notarized by three priests in 1970."

"Okay ... happen to have it on you, do you?"

She removed a taped key from somewhere under a shabby aluminum desk and unlocked a drawer.

Wait until the key is removed from beneath the desk, Saint Michael said.

His heart hadn't stopped racing from that last episode yet, now it felt like it was a beat away from a chest massage at Trois-Rivierés emerge. He sucked in his lower lip as she took out two stapled documents from a large brown envelope stamped *confidential* and motioned him into the desk chair.

"The original's in Italian. The other's been translated for you. Remiel figured your Italian might be a little rusty."

"So it's *Remiel* now, is it?"

Iris smiled, almost apologetically, "Tonight it is, Joe."

Gently, he ran his fingertips over the document cover sheets like they were a rare hybrid rose. "Can I keep one of these?"

"Sorry. The original goes back to Rome. The copy gets shredded. I'll come back and lock up when you're done. An hour long enough?"

He gave her a noncommittal shrug. "I have been waiting twenty years to read this. Have you ever worried that your body couldn't handle the healthiest plate of food? You think 'I don't know if my body can digest this. It may reject food this healthy'."

"You won't reject it." She said it like it was a promise. "See you in an hour." Then she left him alone.

Remiel was right. His Italian was rusty so he jumped straight into the translation. Then he'd read the original. Then he'd probably read them both again ... and again—

Written as directed by: <u>A Messenger of God to three of</u> <u>His ministers</u>

Date: <u>August 24, 1970</u>.

Signatures and Name: <u>Andre Georges</u>, <u>Vittorio Gianni</u>, <u>Paul Crouse</u>.

Location of 'idem est sómnium': <u>Old Gardens between</u> <u>the Art Gallery and Academy of Sciences in Vatican City</u>.

Copies received by: <u>the Holy Father, three Cardinals</u> <u>{names}, two Secretaries {names}</u>

Joe was well acquainted with Walter Bayard and his prayer, his work, and his personal directive. This was the content in the first couple of pages, a profile on Walter, followed by a second profile on him. He had to read about the accident all over again. His loss. His vision by the roadside that tragic day. His angel. It was still painful to read and he wanted to skim over this part too, until his eyes reached the paragraph where the messenger first appeared to the priests' in their identical dream—*idem est sómnium,* the night of the accident. The messenger spoke of the prayers he said in the nights before and after his birthday on August 25 1970, prayers long forgotten. He continued reading—

... the boy Joseph has sent up many simple prayers for his friend, prayers that have so touched the heart of God that He has chosen to link Joseph Ross with Walter Bayard. Joseph was so deeply concerned with the welfare of his friend, Craig Matheson, that he deferred his personal sorrow over the loss of his father. If young Joseph had not convinced Craig Matheson to persevere with his hypotheses on *Time Reversal Invariance,* Walter Bayard would not have completed his nephew's work and the time machine would not have—

"Craig was Walter's nephew?" His mouth flew open. "Craig Matheson?"

—existed. In his humility, Joseph believed his was a selfish prayer, a game. Again God's heart was touched. Therefore I, Remiel, am commissioned by God to impart miraculous phenomena from God and His angels to Joseph Ross.

From this point onward, the words seemed to fly off the page, words like—Down's syndrome, terminate pregnancy, angel child, consecrated ground. Struggling to remain calm, he read on, knowing life would never be the same once he'd finished. Referring to himself as a 'messenger of God' and speaking in the third person, Remiel continued in the final subheading—

'Duprielle, Claude and Tracy: In February of 1970 in the first week of her second trimester, Tracy Duprielle awaited test results at Mills Center Hospital in Maskinongé, Quebec. Ultrasound markers showed the presence of several fetal anomalies, and additional tests confirmed that the child would be born with severe Down syndrome. Mills Center specialists urged the parents to terminate the pregnancy. Horrified, the Duprielles decided to terminate Mills Center and its physicians, informing them that their son, Alain Girard, would be welcomed into this world in six months.

'On the eve of August 24, 1970, Tracy Duprielle went into labor at Saint Michael's Hospital in Cap-du-Madeleine, Quebec. The night before the birth, Claude Duprielle was told in a dream that yes, their son would be born with Down syndrome and cyanotic heart disease. He would live one day. However, after twenty-four hours, a messenger of God would take the child's soul, then return in the child's body. No one but the parents would know of their loss. To staff at Saint Michael's Hospital, this was a healing miracle. The baby would leave the hospital one week later, perfectly normal. To the Duprielles', this was much more than a healing miracle. Twenty-four hours after the birth of their son, God's Light entered the child while he lay in his mother's arms. There were four others in the room. Only the Duprielles' saw God's Light. It was my privilege to escort Alain Girard to *Paradiso* then return in his place to effectuate Walter Bayard's petition and guide Joseph Ross, his aide.'

'In his dream, Claude was instructed to bury their son as if there were a body, for in fact, 'he has departed'. They were further instructed to bury a casket in consecrated ground at Marianlake Dominican Monastery in Trois-Rivierés and confide in the monastery's rector. Claude was shown Andre Georges face. In closing, the messenger informed Claude that God was moved by their faith and their decision to keep the child. In ten years' time they would be rewarded with another son. All of this was done in answer to another man's prayer–to return Love and Mercy to the world. To accomplish this, the Lord would arrange a 'mission'. In the years henceforward, thousands would be as 'seeds' for a great harvest.'

These were the last words, and again the three priests testified by giving sworn oaths to the Bishop of Rome and Pope Paul VI. So here it was and it certainly exceeded anything he'd imagined–his and Walter Bayard's prayers, Craig Matheson, the disclosure of Alain's true identity, of which he was still reeling. And seeds for a great harvest. What harvest?

How God? How am to process this information? I was given years to prepare for Judea. I've had less than a day to prepare for this. It seems my best friend belongs to You and soon he will be returning to You.

So what was he going to say to Alain when he saw him? 'It's been swell, see ya?'

After the fourth read through the document, twice English, twice Italian, he began pacing the office, picking up objects at random, setting them down, waiting for the voice to return. Although foreseen, how could he possibly prepare for a moment like this? Alain Girard Duprielle was ... he'd been living with ... he wasn't even Alain Girard Duprielle, not really. He was a heavenly spirit ... *Dear God, help me. Let my words to him come out right.*

When Iris returned at ten-thirty, an impatient edge had crept into his voice, "Iris, where's Alain? I have to talk to him."

"I'll be taking you to him in a bit."

He noticed she avoided eye contact. He studied her as she took the documents from him and locked them back in the drawer.

"How are you digesting your food?" she asked.

"Fine I think, but I'm a little light-headed-from the fasting. I uh ... very light-headed. Where did you go?"

"Up to the party. I told Carol Ann you were reading the document and that you'd be a while yet. Then I said goodbye to Ronny."

"Goodbye? Why goodbye?"

"Mission's over. Time to move on."

"Listen ... Iris–"

"Really Joe, everybody's moving on, right? Maggie's paintings are almost ready to show so there's nothing left for me to do but read reviews."

"Fine, Iris, whatever. But I think I'd really like to see Alain now."

"Joe?"

"What!"

"Until we receive permission to call him Alain, we address him as Remiel."

"Perm ... Iris, he's my best friend. And I have never called him 'Remiel'".

"You will when you see him."

He was getting a trifle scared, not dark angel scared, God-fearing scared. He felt this way when he drifted into the Saint Michael vision. Wasn't he ever going to see Alain again? Wasn't Alain a part of Remiel? He missed him and wanted to see him. Would God allow that? Would Remiel? He was starting to sweat. Remiel wasn't human and he was having difficulty processing this major detail.

"Tell me something, Iris. I assume you've read the document. Is that right?"

"Yes."

"However did you manage it? Andre and Vittorio made me wait twenty years."

She hesitated again. "Remiel will explain that."

"I surrender," he said, throwing up his arms. "Take me to your leader."

He followed her back through the rink, out the players' exit and down four small steps into another dimly lit room toward *another* door. It was obviously some type of sub-level hideaway, the only one of its kind it seemed because it looked like it had been dug out. He wasn't sure how much more walking he could do. His legs felt weak and the smell from the freshly dried concrete had begun to nauseate him. And oh gee what a surprise—Iris seemed to know.

"You'll feel better soon, Joe," she said, opening what he hoped would be the last in this labyrinth of doors.

The room was spectacular. Again its base was white, this time with a peachy glow. Even the light from the three-tiered crystal chandelier was soothing pink and the carpeting dense and plush. An enormous, triangular glass desk with sculptured gold legs stood on the far side of the room with pale blue and crème-striped satin easy chairs at opposite ends. A royal would consider a candidate for an ambassadorship at this desk. Like it was beckoning, he headed straight for the super-comfy-looking sofa. Delighted by a sudden trance-like feeling, he sat his formerly nervous behind on the supple white leather. No darkness permitted here. Uh-uh. The room looked like it had been sprayed with a rainbow.

"This is the mellowest, comfiest sovereign's nest I've ever seen," he said to Iris. "This is no office."

"No," she said. "Remiel wanted something nice for you tonight. But it is formal, Joe." She said it like it was a warning or something. "Remember you're not in vision yet, so please remember who Remiel is at all times. I'm not permitted to join you until he calls for me."

Now he was nervous all over again. "But I will be seeing Alain? Right?"

"I can't answer. I honestly don't know how much of Alain he will show you. I know it's hard but try to relax because he'll be here soon. It'll be fine, Joe." Then she left him alone.

With his thoughts focused on *who* was about to enter this room he decided it might be a good idea if he could manage to keep from passing out. This particular *who* wasn't his best friend, not really. He was no longer mortal. The child Alain was a day old when his soul was taken. So any minute he was going to sit down and converse with what—an angel? This was a fact. How does one converse with an angel? Would they have tea? A beer? Prozac?

He kept thinking about the grave this afternoon. It was a baby's grave and in a way it was also Alain's grave—his Alain. In recent years he would sometimes look at Alain and see hints of Remiel. He knew it now, could admit it to himself. There was no French. There was no accent. There was less camaraderie. When he said 'I do', it was Remiel who passed him the ring. At the reception supper, it was Alain who made the speech. In Judea, Remiel carried Maggie's bag into the holy cave. In Judea, Alain left him by the Dead Sea before he went into vision.

How should he digest these changes in Alain? The deepest part of him was aware, but it was aware in this secret place, a place sometimes secretive even from himself. When Alain was a boy, maybe since that day he stood in the cabin with Compo by his side and a single drop of blood sparkling on his forehead like a blinding ruby, he knew he was no ordinary child. Even the age was all off–he was ten and sometimes seemed five. He was ten and sometimes seemed twenty. Nothing ever seemed the way it *should have* seemed. And it all began, really began the day they drove off this property. Now they were back on this property with an ending and a goodbye-in-waiting.

The clocked shrilled ten times. He hadn't noticed the wall clock, or that he'd been pacing the room in a slightly altered state of consciousness. Quiet footsteps approached on the other side of these walls. He stopped and stared at the door, waiting for the knob to turn, but it didn't turn right away. The footsteps stopped at the other side of the door and he held his breath. He felt them staring at each other through the block of wood that separated them. Suddenly he could hardly stand it. He wanted to call out to him to enter, but whose name would he call? Was Remiel a name he ever used? Watching the doorknob turn, he shivered like a dog left out in the cold. Then *he* stepped into the room ... and during these seconds, Joe forgot who he was and where he was...

"... Remiel," he said, dazed by the transformation.

He was taller, luminous. Like Saint Michael's, his eyes gently admonished, but they were filled with love. He had never seen the eyes of love stare at him with such force–

and from an almost exquisitely expressionless face. Remiel's thick blond hair was combed back, off his forehead. He was wearing ganymedes and a white ankle-length tunic, cinched at the waist by braided rope. He bore a slight resemblance to Alain.

"Would you like to sit, Joe?"

He went over to the glass desk instead of the couch because this was formal and he had to remember that, not that he was in any danger of forgetting. Remiel gently touched his back when he went around him, touched him in the same way he'd been touched this afternoon in the graveyard. Was it Remiel? Was he with him in the graveyard? Why was he here tonight? He wanted to ask and couldn't. Why couldn't he ask all the things he wanted? What was happening to his voice? From Remiel's reflection in the glass, particles of a substance like crystal snow radiated and fell around him. The silence continued until he got up the nerve to look into Remiel's eyes. They had shared hundreds of expressions over the years. This one was new. Remiel broke the silence.

"You read the document, Joe. How do you feel?"

"Uh ... Craig Matheson ... blown away."

"You put love for a friend first and here we all are. It's all right, Joe. Take a deep breath."

"I can't describe how I feel. I don't know where to begin asking."

"Talk to me then. Just talk."

"In the graveyard this afternoon, I saw the headstone and felt a presence. An hour later I felt and *heard* another presence–dark. For twenty years I've been familiar with both. But not like today. Today I tasted the end and feel like the graduate clutching the diploma. I earned it, I have it, so now I go out and do my level best with it because I'm on my own. And the professor's retiring, am I right?"

The first sign he'd seen of Alain was in Remiel's non-answer answer. No answer always meant yes, but he really didn't have to ask. He knew, even before today, he knew, but there was one thing he insisted on knowing. Like right now. "Were you the angel at the roadside?"

No answer.

"In Angelfish Cove and on the beach?"

"As the child-boy, you thought I was your directive. But really–you were mine. I've been with you since the eve of your tenth birthday."

"Ah. A fabrication. I didn't think seraphs could do that."

"In what way did I fabricate?"

"Many years ago we had a chat on the dock. You told me about the TV inside your head and the other man. You said you saw me on the beach with Willie."

"It was Ronny speaking to you at that moment. And I was there with you both, along with two of my friends. And regarding the information that I had and kept from you, remember God gives us charge over you. I had to guide, lead, and instruct, but I could not give you all the answers. And *Jesus* was the other Man Ronny saw in his head. As a Child and as a Man, He kept Ronny company in his early years. Given the painful circumstances of his background, God took particular care of him."

"And Iris? She disappeared when he did."

"Iris volunteered to go with Ronny. It was a sacrifice made for a friend, and the strength to make it came from a prayer."

"What is it about Iris? She keeps surfacing like a new penny, and she had the privilege of reading the document before me. Somehow, she *is* a wild card. How is that?"

Remiel looked deeply at him, making him feel that trance-like state again. No, not now! He didn't want to go into vision now. Not yet. "You're slipping me an angel-dust mickey, aren't you? Why won't you answer?"

"I will, Joe. But there are realities I need you to deal with on a spiritual level. You're still having difficulty processing the document, difficulty adjusting to me. Trust me. Let me slip you that 'mickey of angel-dust' as you put it. Because after we're done here, I'm escorting you into vision. And your friend Iris is coming with us, so leave your questions about her for later. Do you remember the little white prayer book and the note I wrote in it?"

"It said 'Remember your ABC's, Joe.'"

"Right. Remember the boy who adored word puzzles? That never changed, did it? God's blending of His humor with your sense of play. Eventually *SC* came along. Then in Judea, you received an answer—for to God, nothing is more important–nothing—"

"The salvation of His children."

"Yes. All of God's children are part of the whole. We are connected. You know that Walter's selfless prayer started it, connected us. Selfless prayer is about selfless love, something your Willie learned at the end. No matter how distracted we are, God listens."

"So in an attempt to pray, when we're really obsessing about unpaid bills, God is still paying attention."

Remiel nodded.

He thought about their distractions and struggles with time over the years. "Judea 6. Never said a word to the others, but it's always bothered me what Vittorio said about historians confirming Herod's death in 4 BC. The only consoling thought I had is that Year 6 was perhaps an illusion and a test of faith. Was that all it was–a consoling thought?"

"Yes. We were never there in 6, but the demon used that number as an assault against all of you. The princes of the earth always fail when surrounded by faith. That one number you all believed was the cause of so much grief truly united you. We were there close to the Year 3 in your years. I know the exact moment Christ was born, but it is difficult to give you a secular calendar date. Astronomers verify the approximate time by the position of that great star which we know to be under two thousand years past."

Recalling the night he stood under that star, he sighed peacefully. "Close to 3 is answer enough. And relating to another matter pertaining to time, what of Saint Michael's chaining the dragon? The thousand years of peace––"

"Joe, this has not been about the end of the world and the Second Coming. You know that. The world knows that is an eventuality. Anyone can read the myriad signs. Again, this has been about—"

"I know–the harvest—gathering souls, the salvation of God's children."

"Seeing was never enough to fully believe in the miracles, was it, Joe? Without faith, the effects of miracles eventually fade."

"But faith is a gift. Not everyone is given this gift."

"One needs only to ask. Persistent prayer shows God one's true colors. Like the Angelfish."

"The Angelfish?"

"Yes. Ever wonder why Walter named a place after a fish that is not indigenous to North America? The Angelfish are the most colorful of all fish and this varying coloration warns off intruders. Its colors are even more brilliant in the face of danger. So remember that faith is miraculous of itself. Without it, you could not have stood up against Edmon."

"An associate of his paid me a visit in the rink this afternoon and again tonight. It said it would always stalk me. Referring to you as my right hand, it asked how well I would fare with my right hand cut off. It knows you're leaving. It was telling me I'll be alone, an open target."

"A time will come when you will not hear the demons' voices as you've known them. An open target? Alone? I told you I had two friends with me at the roadside. Michael was there to escort your father safely home. And your guardian was there as your guardian is here now, beside you. Only I can see him and you can't. Never worry about being alone." He pursed his lips and Remiel laughed for the first time. "What do you want, Joe? An introduction? You've seen him. You've heard him. He's the light in your peripheral vision. He's the *voice* of your conscience. You've heard his voice when you've been half-awake and half-asleep. The word he often speaks is 'no'."

"And his name?"

"Like everyone else, you will be given his name when your life in this exile is over. Next?"

Big question to ask, but Remiel had given him back his nerve. "Were you at the Creation?"

"Do you remember exiting your mother's womb? I have faint recall of a testing, the trial, but that's all I remember. These things you want to know are too complex for mortals and even angels to comprehend. The higher Orders understand more because they revolve around God's throne. We could talk of explosions, bursts of supernatural color, the Creator's Hands. But that's all I can tell you. You will not understand the Creation until you quit your body and step through the veil. Not even I, as Remiel, could come remotely close to helping you understand."

"What about the trial you mentioned, and the Fall? Do you remember?"

Remiel appeared to wait for something before answering. "The Lucifer Uprising. Of course I remember.

The battle was titanic with millions of us in a quasi-paradise. I remember vibrant colors and how the ground thundered when Lucifer denied God. We all heard Lucifer's answer, bold and belligerent, 'I will not bow to Them!' The ground thundered more when he repeated it. Then he stretched out his arms, bidding his soldiers to come to him. And they did. One third of God's legions.

"Another voice was heard then, echoing from the depths to the Throne, 'Quis ut Deus! Who is like unto God?' 'No one,' millions shouted. You know the voice, Joe. It was Michael."

Remiel was actually there. Imagine. His brain couldn't grasp the enormity of it. "Here you are now with me. Then there you were—in some place before time was even Time–listening to these voices, hearing that proclamation, never to be rescinded. *Be gone.* You were actually there to witness Lucifer's transformation."

"I didn't see him fall. I was in combat. But I did see the appalling ugliness. And there was stench and darkness until it was over. At the end, the Creator called Michael forward and made him His champion, His grand Marshal, and Prince of all His legions. It was an unparalleled moment. We stood watching in awe, millions of us, while God glorified Michael, saying, 'Tell men to ask of you whatever they wish. Tell them your power with Me is very great'."

"Did you see God?"

"I saw Him as Light. I heard His voice, felt His Spirit entering me. Although we had proven ourselves, we stood on the threshold of Paradise and Throne. But as the newly appointed Prince of His legions, Michael saw Him. Since that time, I have neared closer to the Throne where I am permitted to speak with the higher Orders. Soon I will be spiritually prepared–able–to see all Three Persons in the Holy Triumvirate."

Remiel would say nothing more on the subject, though with that last statement he seemed flooded with joy. "You were a soldier then. And still are. What about you as a child? Were you a child? Or were you Remiel straight from the Creation, soon to be Alain?"

"I was the child Remiel, without recollection of who I was on the roadside or who I was at the Fall and certainly not at the Creation. Remember, we are only slightly superior to man. We too are God's free-willed creatures. I had already made my choice, therefore I belonged to God and as His instrument, He could do with me as He pleased. And He was pleased to send me to the Duprielles in answer to Walter's prayer—and yours." Remiel paused and searched his eyes.

"The child in the *Angel Reclining, The Nativity* and *Obedient Son*, you know who He truly is now. I realize you've had much to digest this evening, but have you given any more thought to that?"

"Apart from the stunning realization of it all—no."

"I watched Maggie's face when she saw Him in the cave. Radiant. And when she realized she had already painted Him, she fell to her knees. Can you imagine what that moment must have been like for her? The recognition! Only Michael knows when and why God sent her the vision of His Son. Many years ago when you and I were in Turin viewing the Shroud, a God-loving man stood beside me. I recall telling you what he said when he first laid eyes on it."

"I remember. He said, 'Isn't it just like God to leave us a photograph'."

"Yes, and there was no doubt in the man. He was right. Isn't it just like God to leave us a photograph. One has to wonder what else He's left us out there."

He wondered that, too. Every day. "The last series of tests made them crazy," he said, thinking about all the detractors they'd have to face down the line. "The pollen samples date the season and approximate year the work was finalized, so does the canvas and some of the paint. But what of our current period materials, which are mixed in with the ancient materials? How are we going to prove that these materials, which were used the way they were, can possibly *be* what they are?"

Remiel's eyes twinkled. "You're not going to prove it. The experts will prove it. And the beauty of it is, they will want years in which to prove it. And they should take years. Since the '80s, testing is so much more sophisticated than mere carbon dating, such as botanical testing. And while preliminary test results are surfacing, you can imagine what else will be taking place–the rumors about Maggie, all the rumors of a secret mission to the past involving thousands of people. The marks. All the rumors once so annoying will now be purpose-fully timed. And they will remain rumors because you and your companions will never be able to confirm them, nor will you be able to refute them.

"Recall what Michael told you about the circumvention of scientific explanations. Remember he said the results will confirm the work to be truly of God, as the elements combine modern and ancient matter. Again, the tests will take years. For a change, time is your friend, Joe."

"Yes, quite happy about that. I remember how I let it bully me."

"Time and tests will put the fiat on this mission. In the meantime, one glance at those paintings brings—"

"Graces?"

"Graces, blessings, elevation of souls, and conversions, though some will hold and some will not. But the seeds will be there for harvest, remember?"

"I remember. When Carol Ann and I first met, I told her that seminary means bed of seeds. And a seminary is also a hermitage ... and ... well here we are. The *Hermitage Museum* in St. Petersburg, Russia."

Remiel smiled. "Marianlake was your bed of seeds. You're feeling better now, Joe?"

His not so glowing display of cowardice at the rink today curbed his enthusiasm. Nice way to demonstrate his faith after being Mr. Spiritually Privileged for twenty years. If Alain were here ... well, no matter ... now he had to sit across from Remiel with no ball cap to pull down over his nose. *Alain, I miss you, bud.*

Remiel stood and held out his arm to him. "Clothe yourself in God's armor during spiritual combat and remember that demons are omnipresent entities, intrusive as tripwire. In gratitude for your years of service and sacrifice, Michael has honored you with a favor. He believes your choice will have merit. This mission is almost over."

"Almost?"

There was a knock at the door and Iris entered the room. She looked compassionately at him as though she was reading his mind. He hoped Remiel remembered that he had questions for her, too.

"It's time to go, Joe," Remiel said.

27. The Hand You Cannot See

Remiel's tunic was a blur of white, blended with speeding ribbons of color. Familiar places of the heart on Earth regressed and dissolved, places like Marianlake's chapel, Main Street in Angelfish Cove, Carol Ann in their bed, the sky, the sun, and himself–on the sofa in the room with the glass desk. Murmurs came to the fore, faint at first until a male baritone instructed Remiel to 'bring them to the bridge of charity'. Iris' breathing was soft and uneven beside his weightless self.

Feeling a gentle fanning against his skin, like a baby's breath on a whisker, he awakened at the foot of the longest of four bridges. He had stood in this place with Saint Michael, had recognized it in Maggie's painting. Actually, this *was* Maggie's painting. Was he about to walk around inside the *Arma Dei*? He smiled at Iris, whose eyes seemed different. Something. Something was very different about Iris.

Radiantly clad in his armor, St. Michael approached, attended by a legion of exploding paths of light. The Prince of Light acknowledged him with a nod and turned to Iris.

"You have demonstrated remorse through sacrifice for self and friends," he said, placing his hand on her head. "Eternal peace will soon be yours."

Leading his army of soldiers, Saint Michael descended into the void below. What did he mean about eternal peace? Why was Iris here, anyway!

While Remiel conversed with two soldiers, he decided to come right out and ask her but caught her on tippy toes, distracted by the jeweled wall across the bridge and whatever was on the inside of it. Keen on getting a closer look, Iris stepped fearlessly onto the Bridge of Charity beside an Angel holding a shield.

"No," the Angel scolded. "Step back."

"I'm sorry," she apologized to Remiel. "I wanted to see those flashes of color inside the gate. Hear that enchanting music."

"You will as we get closer. Walk behind us while I spend time with Joe. Soon he will understand where he is and who you are. Then you'll be on your way."

They began to walk to the right along the circular road, stopping at a floating angel holding a gold shield. Joe looked back at Iris who was still preoccupied with the mysterious activity behind the jeweled gate. The angel bowed his head in acknowledgement. Iris had trailed behind and stopped at the foot of a bridge. She had become too much of a distraction, even here. What was Iris so rapt about? Remiel walked back and spoke with her. He couldn't hear what was being said, but Iris covered her smiling mouth with her hands. Her cheeks shone and her eyes glistened.

Unable to stand the suspense any longer, he treaded over. But Remiel cut him off halfway.

"Iris is going to remain here for a while," he said. "You can say your goodbyes to her at the Bridge of Charity when we're through."

Remiel mesmerized him, but ... *Alain? Yoo hoo—Alain? Would be nice to see you, bud.*

"Crossing these bridges usually takes a lifetime," Remiel said, taking peripheral glances at him as they walked.

"Many never make it onto the bridges. Many fall off the circular road into the void below."

He'd be happy forever circling this road marveling at the sights. So how much more wonderful was the City behind the gate? What was Heaven really like? He knew what it took to get there, but what was it really like? He hadn't realized he posed the question aloud. Or maybe he hadn't.

"The mortal mind has no concept of how beautiful Paradise is, how perfect. Perfect peace, Joe. The perfect happiness for which man was created. So now you know the unabridged meaning of Maggie's *Arma Dei*."

Arma Dei–God's Armor. He knew the Latin translation straight away. What Maggie had painted were the words in Ephesians 6 about the armor of God. Actually he had lived the passage during times of unwavering faith, but had no awareness of it. It used to be that Alain was always around to help him resist sentiment and embrace awareness. But Alain wasn't around anymore. He just wasn't around.

Remiel had emphasized the word 'unabridged' using it drolly. This was something Alain would do. Sensing the tour was about over, he decided to ask Remiel if he could say goodbye to Alain. *If you don't ask, you never know.*

"Joe?"

He looked up at Remiel, so beautiful, a divine creation, and Alain was buried somewhere inside.

"Joe?"

"Yes?"

"The horses for the track, Joe."

His skin tingled. "That's the track for the horses." He noted that sweet, gentle teasing, the lighthearted loving expression that always showed in those gray-blue eyes when he was on the verge of discovery. The lips pursed tight into a smile. The forehead hidden by a blond fringe of silky bangs slightly parted to one side. Right leg out in front, hip leaning to the left. And ... ! ... the sudden whoosh of air from ballooned cheeks!

"Alain?"

"Always been here. Never left."

"*Ahh*," he said, beaming. "Have I missed *you*!"

Alain snatched his harmonica from his jacket and gave it a toot. "Thought I'd come back for the finale."

Joe embraced him. "Welcome back, bud." And considering that he had no idea what was going to happen next–he didn't know what to say next. This was after all, their finale.

"Almost twenty years," he said. "So this is it, right? This is what you've been preparing me for."

"This is it. Except for one or two muddy creeks to cross." Alain waved the harmonica at him. "I need to get serious, Joe."

"That's clear. Look where we are."

"And where you've been. What you've been through together. What you've all become. What a lovable cast of players. Ronny played the assumed child, cameos by the archangel Raphael as Rafe. The divine painting cameos– the archangel Michael in Maggie's first angel mural, Jesus as the Child in the *Angel Reclining*, *The Nativity* and *Obedient Son*. And the holy Family, the real Family. And then there's Iris."

Finally. The Iris puzzle. "Iris?"

"Shall I call her over?"

"Please do."

She was already halfway across the Bridge of Love, walking toward them. She had this little loose-boned gait that seemed hauntingly familiar. Amazing how the click of a loved one's footsteps could touch a heart in profound ways. Loved one? Suddenly he wondered why he was always gaping at Iris's heels.

The eyes were rounder and the cheekbones more prominent. The hair was different, too—ponytail gone, it fell in thick black layers to her shoulders. She stopped a few feet away and those loving, penitent eyes filled with tears and the tiniest choppy whimper rose from her throat. He walked up to her and wiped away a dangling teardrop from her chin. This was not Iris.

Recalling how the cherry Jell-O shook on the spoon the first time he saw her sweet face, he saw that this was Willie's face.

"Yes, it's me," she said, "God has given me this chance to ask for your forgiveness, since He gave me his and so much more. Please, Joe, I'm so sorry. I died asking God to let me fix it, to let me make it up to Him. And to you."

"Willie. Willie, there is nothing to make up! It's your forgiveness I need. I was the one who pushed you to the edge."

"No. My un-love did that. My obsession for you is what pushed me to the edge. My selfishness, my attempts to manipulate God's will. I saw the face of the demon as I was dying in the tub that night, Joe. If not for God's mercy, I'd be in Hell right now. And Hell *is* real. I've seen it. But God let me live long enough to express genuine remorse. Three seconds of heartfelt repentance and He saved my soul. Then I asked to help you—from the other side of the veil. From here."

"Joe?" Alain said, "would you recall for a moment that awful night when Ronny disappeared?"

"If you insist. One of my worst days."

"I know. I was there that night. So were Walter and Willie. Ronny was held up in what was then the old glass factory. So there we were that terrible night with Ronny frightened, Willie still in pain over the past she shared with you, and myself, receiving from your guardian the second selfless prayer from you. You were in your cabin. You went down on your knees and asked God to do only His will. Then you added that if it were His will, you would give your life to bring Ronny safely home.

"Well my friend, that prayer of yours secured Edmon's permanent departure from Angelfish Cove. Twelve prayers were said over all, including yours. You already know of the first three–Walter, Willie and the Duprielle's. Walter asked that love be brought abundantly back into the world and Willie asked to make it up to Him, to fix it. Then when she saw Carol Ann suffering the same way she had, she prayed that she get over her obsession for you. And tonight after reading the document, you learned that the Duprielles willingly gave their son to God, who sent me in their child's place, and gave them another son."

Alain continued, "Our three ministers have prayed daily for the success of this mission. Paul Crouse too, has prayed fervently, although for Elizabeth's sake, he chose to be active in another group. Elizabeth now, has offered her suffering to God every day since Ronny's birth, that it may help someone in a similar situation. For years, her secret letters to Dina gave Dina strength and courage. Now we come to Dina. She asked to forget herself for the sake of Carol Ann and Maggie. She wanted her two best friends cared for more than she wanted fame or wealth. Not once did she ask for either of those things.

"Ronny's courage was most pleasing to God. When he was trapped in the late '60s, he prayed, 'I'll stay here and work alone. Just let them all get back to the Year Six.' God sent Willie to keep him company." Alain smiled, "Ronny had many companions there. Then there's your Carol Ann. When she saw you despairing after the ostensible failure of the mission, she prayed, 'I will give Joe up, if You will keep Joe from giving up.' She never would have had the strength to let you go if Willie had not prayed for her. They all intertwine beautifully, don't they?"

His eyes misted. "Yes. And Maggie?"

"Ah, there's our angel. Our Maggie. Her entire life was a sacrifice. She was in love with God and there wasn't enough she could do for Him. When she realized how sick she was, she asked that her body be used as a magnet in order to repel evil from all of you. That's why she isolated in that house. She could have asked to be cured, Joe. Long before, because He was so taken with her, God sent Michael himself to protect her. She first sensed Michael's presence after painting the wall mural that Christmas. In later years, she saw his eyes every time she closed her own— right there, always protecting her, battling her demons, and bathing her soul in warmth."

"The demons Maggie saw in her sketches were the demons I lived with," Willie said. "You know who kept constant company with me? Edmon."

"As Iris," Alain said, "Willie was the wild card. If all of you failed then of course Willie would fail in her attempt to make it up to you and God. This was Edmon's mission. By her failure, he would win her soul and sabotage the mission. That's why he pursued Ronny so aggressively. Ronny was Walter's right arm."

"He didn't seem to have an effect on Walter or Maggie."

"As you learned tonight, Maggie was a client of Saint Michael's, who was also close to Walter since his earthly exile was almost over. The demons, even Lucifer, are terrified of Michael and our Queen. Stay close to them and one has nothing to fear."

"Edmon used to bring me vodka on a tray with burnt roses," Willie said, her face paling from the memory. "He would force me to watch Carol Ann's self-abuse, that familiar all-consuming pain. We even had the same player in our little black passion play–you. I lived through it twice. And worst of all, I watched you live through it twice. Then ... when Edmon took Ronny and you began despairing ... Satan himself made my acquaintance."

"Oh, Willie."

"No, please don't. Don't feel sorry for me. I saw clearly what prayer accomplishes. God is Mercy itself, Joe. He forgives the worst sin from a contrite heart. I came to learn that if I wanted a better future I had to break patterns of the past. Sometimes you have to move backward to move forward."

"Your death put the fight in me, Willie. What happens to you now?"

She looked to Alain for the answer.

"Willie goes through the Gate now," Alain said. "She has repeatedly proven herself. Her purgatory is over. You may watch her as far as the Gate, Joe."

"Then this means she's ...?"

"I'll give you both a few moments to say goodbye. Then I have to get you back."

He walked Willie to the foot of the bridge and for a moment they stared deeply at each other. "If I wasn't in vision I know I'd be begging to go with you now," he said.

"You have things to do yet. And you and Carol Ann can start a family."

His eyes misted again. "Probably be a girl. I've always been––"

"Ambushed by women, I know."

"You know, you and Alain are my best friends?"

"And now you feel like you're losing both of us?"

He just got her back. Too soon to say goodbye again.

Willie gave him a playful jab in the arm. "Well I heard through the *Grapevine* that a certain special somebody's step-cousin will be permitted to say the odd 'hello' on special occasions. So when you're half-asleep or half-awake—pay attention!"

Nine Angels approached from across the bridge and he realized they were for Willie. She was finally going home and she looked radiantly happy. There was only one thing more to say before he could let her go.

"I love you, Willie."

"I love you too, Joe."

And as quickly as she had returned to him, she was gone.

Alain joined him and they watched the holy cortege escort Willie through the Gate and disappear into Heaven's arms.

"I couldn't accept that Willie's death wasn't my fault. Fooled myself into thinking I had. Through all the miracles, I still blamed myself. Couldn't let it go."

"God brings some along slowly, and so you have your awareness, Joe. Now I must show you one last thing."

They crossed the Bridge of Love and Alain gestured for him to sit by a small rippling brook. Alain extended his arm over the water and fanned it back and forth.

"Hula lessons?" he joked. Hey he could do that now, here. This was his best friend.

"A lesson of sorts," Alain said. "Just setting the scene. You know me."

"Setting the scene for what?"

"Look in the water, Joe."

As usual he obeyed, noticing the baby brook had stopped gurgling. What was this? Swirling colors now? "Alain, can't you just *tell* me?"

"What? And deprive you of the movie? Watch."

The scene took form and the backs of two people came into view—a male and female. The woman had long hair. *Wait a minute.* Red hair. And they were in an outdoorsy type room surrounded by paint paraphernalia.

"Maggie!"

"Maggie."

"Who's that with her?"

"Patience, Joe."

Maggie removed a cloth cover from a painting set on an easel. It was the *Obedient Son.* She said something to the man who moved the painting and easel to the other side of the room, away from the window. The man looked at her as if to say *is this all right here?* He ... he .... "It's Dave. Dave Thomson." He frowned at Alain. "Dave's not ... dead?"

"Dave is as fine as can be under the circumstances. No, this scene took place shortly before she died. Dave helped Maggie in any way he could. He loved her, Joe."

"No secret there. Speaking of secrets, he knew all along about that third canvas."

"Pride, even in love, often shuts friends out."

"Well, we all know that's true. Dave is proud and tight with his feelings. Even at Maggie's funeral. Why are you showing me this? Is Maggie okay? She's with Willie, right?"

"Maggie is perfectly happy in Paradise. I'm showing you this because of the paintings. God will uplift the soul with a glance at them."

"I already know that."

Alain pointed to the scene. "Watch a little more."

Maggie and Dave crouched on the floor in front of the painting. She ran her hands lovingly along the bottom of the frame, smiling that beautiful, reverent smile while Dave eyeballed her like she was Helen of Troy, Athena,

Scheherazade and a strawberry soufflé. Then Maggie leaned forward and kissed the frame and the scene faded away.

He felt Alain's hand on his back. "I'm afraid it's time to say our goodbyes, Joe."

"Whoa, hold on now! Nobody's saying goodbye until you tell me what that was all about."

"Maggie's work, of course. With particular focus on her last four paintings. *The Angel Reclining* was your first introduction to her work. It's always been your roadmap, hasn't it? It helped you identify Walter's book, locate Ronny and identify Jesus as the Child. It's a key that will always open doors for you. It's important to remember that.

"*The Nativity* was the first painting in the Judean work. Ancient and modern ingredients. The Family. The Child. The world's recognition. The St. Petersburg exhibit.

"*Arma Dei.* God's Armor. As you know, we've been walking around in it—the Ephesians 6:11 passage. *In all things taking the shield of faith* ... use the shield against the demon, Joe.

"*Obedient Son.* The painting you felt compelled to find and fetch alone. The painting to which you're most drawn. The painting of Jesus in a time forbidden to us. No doubt it's Maggie's favorite and will become the most celebrated work of the series—for many reasons. She kissed the frame, didn't she? We'd better head back."

His heart thrummed. Too soon for goodbyes. Too soon. "If I weep like a war widow, just know it's because we've been through a war and I'm already missing you. What's my life going to be like without you in it? Alain, I can't begin to tell you what you mean to me."

"Remember the day we met and roamed the pumpkin field? I knew then that the best years of my existence would be with you. We'll see each other again, Joe. Not in the same way, but I'll always be there for you."

Joe stopped on the bridge and weighed his words. "So? Where to next?"

"Haven't been informed as yet."

"Would you tell me if you knew? Never mind, don't answer. I just said it to Willie, so how can I not say it to you? I love you. You know, your expression reminds me of the day we left Marianlake the first time."

"That moment was five minutes ago for me. And it's been the best five minutes in a long, long life. But for you, time runs on a different lock."

"A different *lock?*"

"Did I say lock? Meant to say clock. I left you a belated Christmas gift, by the way. In the office where you had your meeting with ..." He grinned and cleared his throat, "*Remiel.* There's some rough track on the backstretch, Joe. Remember to check your tack. Still like solving puzzles?"

"Sure. I'll start with your last few sentences," he answered, snickering.

"Happy to hear it. Now don't forget this." Alain returned his harmonica. "Spiritually combatant equipment, this. Never stop talking to me, and I'll see you in *five minutes*, my friend."

He wept some as they embraced. He'd prepared as best he could, but tears had their own timing as Carol Ann liked to say. As the colors swirled around him like concentric circles in a pond, he heard Alain's loving voice—

"Joe. The demon was right about one thing. You will feel the hand you cannot see. But it will be my hand. Keep your shield up. I love you, too."

He found himself back in the office seated at the glass desk, where for an hour he replayed the vision in his mind.

At the end of the hour he remembered he had a gift waiting, though he wasn't sure it was the gift to which Alain referred. Fine. He loved puzzle-play and the biggest puzzles were finally solved. Or were they? He took a stretch and sighed, then spotted it nestled on the sofa cushion—the cubical device no bigger than a ring-box, set on an opened page of his little white prayer book, set on the message Alain wrote the day of the accident.

Remember your ABC's, Joe.

Unwrapped with no note, the gift said it all. He laughed and placed it lovingly on his hand and made a gentle fist over it. Recalling the day he kidded Ronny about the patriotic colors, he spun the four numbered wheels. A mini red, white and blue dot separated each wheel and he teased Ronny mercilessly the day he installed it.

'Red, white and blue dots?' he had said. 'Such patriotism moves me.'

It was the time gauge.

∞∞∞

He discovered his wife in the Bagel Factory, squatting in front of the *Obedient Son* like a property inspector searching for defects. Why was the painting not on the dais in the party room? Tim, Dina and Ronny were slumped in desk chairs a few feet away. Mourning their fading marks, they were, reminiscing about what SC meant over the years. Recently he'd spent time in the Land of Miracle Withdrawal himself, so their wistfulness seeped into his very pores.

"I just heard a good one," he said by way of hello. "*Spiritually combatant.* What are yas doing in here?" He helped Carol Ann up and gave her a hug. "Wow," he said, raising his eyes at her. "Big night. Big answers. Big vision."

"You okay?"

He took out the harp and tooted. "Lots to tell you."

"Thomson had to leave," Dina said. "His dad's had a small stroke. He said to wish *Mr. Solo* a Happy New Year."

Dave hadn't been too pleased with him since he insisted on taking that last jaunt to Galilee alone. Too bad about his dad. Dave would've enjoyed hearing about the vision in the brook and he would've enjoyed telling him. It also would've been nice to hear Dave's explanation as to why he kept *Obedient Son* a secret.

"Iris and Alain said goodbye earlier." Carol Ann's eyes moistened and her focus returned to the painting.

"And the fathers' and Mother are at the party where we should be," Ronny said. "So? Walter's machine's pared down, I trust?"

He shivered at them. "Gave me the willies in there. Like I was followed. Okay, before I continue, I must know what the *Obedient Son* is doing here?"

Tim stood and gestured him over to the painting. "The work was fastened to this portable wall at three points using mirror plates and screws. But one plate popped out somehow. Father Andre decided it was best to park it here."

"All the paintings bed down here for the night, anyway," Carol Ann said, hand on hip, eyes still scrutinizing the work. "Climate control. No big sources of heat."

"What's wrong, Inspector?"

"She's been glued to that painting all night," Dina said.

Carol Ann crossed her arms at the shoulders. "Don't know. Just something familiar about it that's driving me crazy. I can't place it so let's forget it. Joe, tell us everything."

He set the time gauge and prayer book in the center of Dave Thomson's ridiculously neat desk and about broke his tongue recounting the St. Michael vision, the

Document, his meeting with Remiel in and out of vision, *Willie*, seeing Maggie and his goodbye to Alain. Carol Ann made him tell the Maggie part twice, listening calmly as they all did, the way he'd listened to Alain speak in peculiar racing metaphors.

He began to feel mildly uncomfortable. Alain's last words sounded weirder and weirder as he replayed and processed them in his head. *Rough track on the backstretch,* he'd said.

The group could've been talking about two-way toothpaste or slurp guards just then, because he didn't hear a word. Because Carol Ann's distraction seemed clearly justified. Of the three Judean works, *Obedient Son* cast the largest mystical net. He'd felt it since the first day at Hannah and Hushai's. Works of art, beauty, grace and he should start taking one baby aspirin daily, just in case. He could use another hit of angel dust, too, and not the PCP kind.

"Joe?" Carol Ann gave his bicep a squeeze. "Concerns?"

He stumbled back a step and laughed. "Temperamental zapper."

"So what else is new?" Ronny said, plucking a strand of hair off Dina's shoulder. "You worried about the paintings?"

"'R what?" Tim said.

"All is well, all is well." He ran a hand along the bottom of the painting. *Maggie had kissed the frame.* "A thing of grace. Of ..." He touched the frame and smiled, loving the tiny ghost prickles that shot up his arms and the feeling of spring in his heart when he caressed Jesus' brush strokes on the bottom of the chair. Stabbing waves of anxiety shot through him.

"Joe?"

"*Not this time,*" he said to no one in particular. Again, he caressed the brush strokes.

"'R what, Joe?"

"A ballet in my heart, a song in my head whenever I touch the frame."

"Don't follow, hon."

His gut hardened. Could be he was emotionally off, seeing Willie again and saying goodbye to his best friend. His *zapper* needed a charge, that's all. Right. So why did Alain show him that last vision? Alain never did anything without purpose. Even his meaning had meaning—sometimes a double meaning behind everything Alain said and did. If only he could segue in from a comfortable place.

He grabbed a desk chair and wheeled it over to them, but couldn't sit. "You're all thinking I've smoked something."

Three of them nodded in agreement.

"Maggie said she would try and send a message back in a painting. Remember? Maybe Carol Ann's right. Maybe we're missing something." He waded in a little deeper. "I've got my toolbox here, you know."

"Joe!" Carol Ann was somewhere near aghast. "Rome would kill us! So would my parents, who haven't forgotten the lemon geranium and oats, by the way. That painting is much more than a painting."

"That much-more painting is on a plane out of here in three days."

She hesitated for only a second before her lips curled upward. "Okay then, I'm with you, hon. Don't worry, I'll stand in front of you when they start shooting." She challenged the others with a stare that made his heart flip-flop.

"You want to take it out of the frame?" Dina asked. "Tonight?"

All heads turned back to him.

"What say we do it in the morning after Mass?"

"Do you think you can separate the painting from the frame without damaging it?" Ronny asked.

"I do." That was the easy part. The hard part would be if he was wrong. What, if not the painting, something else was calling him? Was he again prey without his right hand?

"So what do we do with whatever we find?" Dina again.

"We put it back. Then we attend the St. Petersburg opening and watch the ripples in the pond."

After pondering a few seconds they agreed, then headed back to the party to ring in the New Year. But like Carol Ann, he couldn't tear himself from the painting. *She kissed the frame, didn't she?*

"*Davay,* Joe," Ronny said, already practicing his Russian. "Come on."

In the morning, he and Carol Ann hung out with a group of stayovers after Mass. Of the eight hundred and seventy-seven time travelers who attended last night's shindig, eighty stayed over at the seminary and were just now getting ready to leave. The call came through on his cell in mid-flight on the stairwell while assisting in a luggage run. He flew down the last four steps to the next level and picked up.

"Front desk. Bellhop."

"Joe. Did you take the *Obedient Son* back to your cabin last night?"

"No." It was Ronny and he sounded wired.

"I'm in the BF office and it's not here. Not at the rectory, either. I'm fairly alarmed here."

Joe nodded to the traveler who'd returned for his suitcase and waved goodbye, then leaned against the wall, stomach rolling. "Uh ... maybe the security people packed it? Popped plate and all."

"Checked with them already. Discreetly. Lord help us, Joe. I think someone's walked with it, and we have a hundred cars pulling out and no way to stop them. You better get up here, *statim*."

"Meet me at the cabin. Does Father Andre know?"

"Just you. I'll see you in five." Ronny hung up.

Fathers' Andre and Richard were last to arrive at the cabin. Ronny tried reaching Dave at his folks' in Pontiac, Michigan, but no one was home. Sister Elizabeth had tucked herself into a couch corner beside Rosa and had hardly moved. Vittorio kept taking deep breaths. Dina clung to Ronny, gazing expectantly at him. Eyes to the floor, Tim paced behind the couch. And Carol Ann stood frozen by the window, staring out at the lake, hand covering her mouth.

As Marianlake's patriarch, Father Andre was responsible for the paintings. In spite of the disturbing turn of events, he remained calm. After Ronny finished recounting his search, Joe added his two cents about the plan to separate the painting from the frame in hopes of finding a message from Maggie. Father Andre's eyes hardened momentarily before he spoke.

"We'd better get the security people in here and call the police. Most likely the painting is in the trunk of one of the cars now leaving the premises."

When Father Richard moved toward the phone, he cut him off. "Don't think that's necessary, Father. He hadn't called Richard *Father* in a decade and this got everybody's attention.

"Joe, we have to move. The police can set road blocks, maybe."

"What do you mean 'you don't think it's necessary'?" Father Andre asked.

Oh man, how to explain? No way to explain so he might as well risk sounding nuts. Wouldn't be the first time around this group. "As you know, the *Angel Reclining* has always acted as a roadmap for me. A key. Give me a few hours with it and I'll figure it out."

Finally, Carol Ann took a step away from the window and turned to him. He gave her a reassuring look and told those who still hadn't heard, about his vision and goodbye to Alain. After emphasizing Alain's final cryptic remarks, of which they'd also experienced numerable times over the years, Father Andre consented.

"And when you do locate the painting, Joe, take Ronny and Tim with you. I insist. No going alone this time."

Sorry, Father. Sorry, Carol Ann. "I promise I will not go alone, Father."

Rosa made the sign of the Cross.

They left him in the Bagel Factory to meditate on the *Angel Reclining.* He eased it off the portable wall and carried it to the opposite end of the office that would one day house an Olympic-sized pool. Isolating himself on the floor in a corner, he set the painting against the wall and sat facing it in the lotus position. When the answer hit him at exactly 3 PM, two and a half hours later, he wanted to ram his fist into something. But first he had to stuff his emotions in his back pocket, get off this property, and somehow manage to hide his anger from Carol Ann. He could do that. Pieca cake. No worries, Joe, no worries. Carol Ann'd never guess the extent of his fear, or his anger.

Heart pounding and hands shaking, he called Patsy's Bar.

"Patsy. Happy New Year, man."

"Same to you, Joe. Still on for darts later?"

"That's why I'm calling. Something's come up and I need your help. Need to catch a flight out of Montreal, asap. And I doubt the buses are running today. Can you get me there?"

"Sure. Giving Marianlake the slip, are we?"

"Yeah. Carol Ann, too."

"Uh-oh. When did you want to leave?"

"Right away, if possible. Got an overnight bag I can borrow?"

"Uh, sure."

"Your cousin, Jake, still leave his gear lying around?"

"Uh, yeah—"

"Okay good. Here's what I need you to do ..."

"Why are you so angry?" the Inspector asked.

"I'm not angry."

"You are so. That vein in your neck always pops when you're mad. It's positively purple now."

"Guess I'm needing a walk to reboot the zapper."

"So you don't know yet—where the painting is?"

He hated lying to her, hated the deception. Even more, he hated that he was so good at it. He pulled her into his arms and kissed her neck, ears, lips. Geez he didn't want to stop. But he had some hatred to attend to. "I'll get it back for us. I'm going to take that walk, clear my head. The twenty-below wind-suck out there oughta do it."

She studied him a minute and stuck out her bottom lip. "Give me your wallet."

He reached for his wallet. "And why am I doing this?"

"Because I don't trust you not to take a powder."

He handed her the wallet then held up his arms. "Look, no luggage up my sleeves."

"Right. Now your cell."

He passed the cell, grinning—God she was smart. "Can I take a powder now, Mrs. Ross?"

She bowed to him. "You may, Mr. Ross. But while you're powdering, remember what Abe Lincoln said about falsifiers, "'No man has a good enough memory to be a successful liar'."

"Yeah, but the man practiced law without a degree." He caressed the side of her face with the back of his hand and slipped out, as coolly as possible.

Figuring the little Inspector was watching from the window, he kept a standard pace trudging through the snow along the road until he knew he was out of sight, and then booted it to the front gates. He was wrong about the temperature. It had to be closer to thirty below, but hey, it was a lot hotter where he was going. Patsy was already waiting outside the gate in his '66 Grand Prix, about as inconspicuous as an ocean liner in a shopping mall.

"Rented a car for you," Patsy said as they barreled down the road. "And I managed five hundred in US lolly."

"Aw that's great, Patsy, thanks." Anticipating Carol Ann's move, he'd stashed his MasterCard and driver's license in his pocket, but left the cash in the wallet. Hopefully she wouldn't notice the card and license missing straightaway and sic Ronny and Tim on him. "You are a jewel of a guy, you know that? I really appreciate this. And the use of your cell."

"I tossed the charger in the overnight bag in case you need it. And I threw in a couple changes of underwear, which Jake won't miss because he rarely changes his underwear. Also a pair of shorts, socks, T-shirt and sunscreen. Plus toothbrush, paste and a girl razor. Sorry, man, that's all I had around."

"That'll work just as well, bud." He wouldn't need DEET. Not in January in Florida. Patsy skidded into a half rolling donut and his gut rolled along with it. He clenched his jaw.

"You look like you could box a few rounds, Joe. Sure you don't want reinforcements?"

Enough people had died on his watch. *No more.* "Thanks to you I'm good to rock, Pats. What time's the flight?"

∞∞∞

"GOOD AFTERNOON LADIES AND GENTLEMEN, THIS IS YOUR CAPTAIN SPEAKING. WELCOME ABOARD UA FLIGHT 207. FLIGHT DURATION IS TWO HOURS AND FIFTY-ONE MINUTES AND WE WILL ARRIVE IN GAINESVILLE AT 8:16 PM. WE ARE CURRENTLY LEVEL AT THIRTY-THREE THOUSAND FEET, WHICH WILL BE OUR CRUISING ALTITUDE TODAY.

SHOULD WE ENCOUNTER SOME UNEXPECTED TURBULENCE, PLEASE FASTEN YOUR SEAT BELT SNUGLY ABOUT YOU. IN THE MEANTIME, SIT BACK, RELAX, AND ENJOY THE FLIGHT. IF THERE IS ANYTHING THAT ANYONE OF US CAN DO TO MAKE YOUR FLIGHT A MORE PLEASANT ONE, PLEASE LET US KNOW. ONCE AGAIN, WELCOME ABOARD."

He passed on dinner, passed on a drink, passed on a snack. He didn't tell Carol Ann where he was going when he called from the airport, which ticked her off even more. She didn't holler or threaten, but he'd hurt her. She was scared for him, worried because he sometimes took inappropriate risks when angry. 'Are you angry because the painting's stolen, or is it something more?'

He couldn't answer. And there was no way to soothe her, except to tell her he was safe and would take every precaution to remain that way. He told her he loved her and hung up remembering how he never got around to telling her he knew Maggie was dying. What if she found out he knew first and kept it from her? This could destroy her trust—maybe jeopardize their marriage.

"Are you sure I can't get you anything?" the stewardess asked.

"No appetite, thanks." The plane smelled like a hospital corridor. "What's the weather doing in Florida?"

"Beautiful, you're lucky."

"Why is that?"

"They've just come off a four-day hard rain, which is unusual during the dry season. So is the temperature. Seventy-four degrees!"

As far as he was concerned, hard rain followed by warm temperatures meant one thing in Florida—mosquitoes. Clouds of them.

He consoled himself with thoughts of locating the *Obedient Son*. After nibbling on a fruit plate, he started to feel better. For about a minute. Could be the *Angel Reclining* was pointing him in the wrong direction. What if the painting was on the other side of the world? What if it was damaged, or worse, forever lost?

When he disembarked at 8:21 PM, his state of mind was so messed up he had to call Patsy for the name of the car rental and hotel. Finding *Mavis Cheap and Friendly Car Rental* was no easy feat, either. After a wrong turn and a lineup in the men's room, it took him forty-five minutes to backtrack, only to be saddled with an ancient Mazda Miata convertible. If he did find *Obedient Son,* he'd have to ride with his gear in order to fit the painting securely in the trunk.

"Don't you have anything larger?" he asked the rental agent. "I'll have to fold my legs like origami to fit into a Miata."

The agent pursed her lips in an exaggerated pout and handed him the keys. "Sorry. Maybe if you take your boots off..."

He yanked off his boots in the *Stay Inn*, the kind of motel where one got nervous about finding nasties on the sheets and mildew in the coffee maker. Patsy, clearly a loyal friend and a man with a heart as big as Finian's rainbow, was not one to research hotels prior to booking. No matter. Getting to Ocala by first light was his primary concern. If necessary, he'd sleep in a tent inside a moldy sleeping bag.

We will stalk you now. The way is clear, the demon had said. To think it was only yesterday. After pondering yesterday some more, he prayed himself into a restless sleep.

At 5:30 a.m. he asked the front desk if a call came in during the night regarding his query. No, they said. The desk still hadn't received word from EquiState Horse Properties. So he left yet another message on the realty's voicemail telling them he was on his way to survey the farm. *My name is Joe Ross. I am not an intruder. If you see me walking around the property, hold your fire.*

It was a forty-five-minute drive to Claxton Farms, an area he remembered well from boyhood and last year's visit. But last year he hadn't driven at dawn grinding his teeth, heart racing. He pulled over on the 441 S and shone the flashlight he borrowed from the desk on the road sign. *W. Silver Springs Blvd and 3rd Avenue.* Right. Onward and upward.

He arrived before sunrise and Claxton Farms rose to greet him with the scattering wind and the scritch of tree branches against the barn windows. Part of him wanted to charge into the barn to begin the search, but he couldn't risk a slip in the dark and damage to the painting. The sun would be up in twenty minutes. Time enough to pray, recharge his spiritual batteries, punch a hole through the curtain and say 'good morning, I need you', to Alain.

The scent of oily exhaust and men's cologne wafted under his nose then evaporated like jet spray. And with the rising sun came a cloud of mosquitoes, a shadowy fist hovering over the rundown barn's cupola and corroded weathervane. Why didn't he wait for the stores to open to buy some DEET? Why did he have to come alone? Geez, would he ever learn. Something unholy stroked the back of his neck, dark like a spurned lover's kiss.

He hustled out of the car and, braving the buzz and whine assaulting his ears, leapt over rainwater ponds and puddles covered in mosquito pupae. Car grease and cologne again. Trailing the scent behind the barn, he came upon a '95 Ford LTD with mud-caked tires, hood and windshield coated with bird guano. The paperwork on the dash caught his eye.

"Well, whaddya know," he said, unsettled by the discovery, "Mavis Cheap and Friendly." Whoever rented the LTD, rented it from the same company, possibly from the same airport.

Breath bursting in and out, he entered the barn into forks of morning light and dire memories thickened by time. It was his fault. *My fault Mum died.*

"Hello! Anybody need help in here?"

The stink of musty cologne drifted toward him as he edged his way to the old stall, Fast Forward's stall. His eyes moistened with the flood of rising emotion. The mother he loved had received one fatal kick from the horse he loved—in the stall just yards away.

Someone sniffled, rustling the hay in the area of Forward's stall. Probably the guy with the LTD. Did the Miata have a med kit? He hadn't checked.

He booted it toward the stall, "It's okay! Help's here! I have a cell, so ..." His heart slammed against his ribs at the sight—

"Hello, Joe."

"My God, what is this?" Dave Thomson sat cushioned against the back of the stall beside Fast Forward's, legs outstretched, eyes red-rimmed and cloudy. "Dave?"

Dave pressed the side of his nose and snuffled. "Wouldn't have a tissue, would ya?"

"I ... are you all right?"

Dave looked at him incredulously. "Am I all right? Let's see, Maggie's been in the ground for about six months now. Sure, Joe. I'm in clover all over."

"What's this about, Dave?"

"Retribution, I suppose. But you can make it up to me. *Mr. Solo-man.*"

Dave's stinging tone and expression of malice gave Joe the chills. He took a quick glance around and in the rafters.

"Lose something?"

"You have the painting with you, don't you?"

Dave ignored the question and took a lazy stretch. A daddy longlegs crawled up the leg of his jeans and he watched it dispassionately. "*Angel Reclining* get you here?" Dave didn't wait for an answer and flicked the spider in his direction. "Figured it would."

"Okay, Thomson. Enough games. Let's get you and the painting out of here. We'll talk later."

"I say we talk here and now—"

A familiar voice boomed from out of the shadows. Thomson, suddenly animated, jumped up as Edmon Fendi lead an anxious old horse into Fast Forward's stall. The horse pinned its ears and lunged when he closed the gate.

"This horse needs to learn some stall etiquette," Edmon said.

The horse's hindquarters grazed what had to be the painting, propped against the stall under a filthy blanket. "What have you done to Dave?"

Edmon passed Thomson a handful of tissues that seemed to come out of nowhere. "Poor David has a cold. He spent the night here waiting for you, Ross."

He had to get Dave out of here and the painting out of that stall. Devising a strategy would be tricky since the sight of Edmon Fendi repulsed him beyond belief. "Why are we here?" He stole a glance at Dave who looked like he was off somewhere, floating on a dark cloud. And the air had shifted from cologne and car grease to the sickening stench of burnt hair and urine. He knew the urine odor came from Edmon, but the burnt hair was omnipresent and intensifying.

"Pay attention, David," Edmon said, thrusting out his chest. "Suppose you tell your friend why we're here, son."

Dave sat on the tack box in front of the stall and wiped his nose. "I want you to restore the time machine. I want to go back and ask Eashoa to cure Maggie. And if he won't, I'll bring her home for treatment. Against her will, if necessary."

My God, how Edmon must've messed with Dave's head. No argument could sway Dave, he could see that. Maggie was in the ground. Dave was at her funeral. It would be a sacrilege to go back in time now, but he could never convince him of that and in any case he wasn't about to try.

"You were there New Year's Eve. You knew the plan. Why didn't you grab me then, before I yanked the wires?"

"And you would've said what? 'Oh of course, Dave. Anything to help out a bud.' Sure, Joe."

Something was off here. Edmon could've piloted this scenario at the rink the other night, allowing Dave to take the machine by force. Why not? He was desperate enough.

He clenched his fists and glared at Edmon. "You wanted me here, trapped with the *Obedient Son* to discredit me. No one knows Dave took it. I get caught looking like a thief and along with me, my family gets disgraced. I can imagine the repercussions. The exhibit gets cancelled. Bad press. Doubt in Maggie—and her work. But you'll fail, Edmon. Stop to consider how I got here."

Edmon glared at him, eyes mocking and confident. "Oh we know all about the A.R. being your map and compass. But we're renowned for charting a course or two ourselves, Ross."

He held his breath in intervals. The burnt hair now smelled like what—cigar smoke and ... *oranges*? "Good for you. You can't touch me, so what do you want—me and Dave to duke it out for the painting? Not going to happen."

Edmon's tongue flicked his bottom lip, and with each flick of the tongue it lengthened, becoming snake-like and furred. He smiled, head bobbing on his shoulders like a doll, eyes like white moons rolling back into the sockets.

Dave got off the tack box and dry-heaved. "He wants the painting, Joe. Do what he says."

"Oh that's not all he wants."

Edmon nodded at the horse in Forward's stall and the animal stomped and kicked his hind leg, missing the painting by inches.

"You won't get that painting, Edmon. You've been flashing the same badge for years now. Your superiors' out on the big command, are they? And here you still are.

You'll fail again. You couldn't stop Walter from continuing his nephew's work, nor did you succeed at destroying Willie's faith, or driving Dina insane. Or keeping Maggie a prisoner in her mansion."

"Enough!"

"You failed with Carol Ann and Ronny." Joe felt dizzy from the stench, his vision blurred by the rising sulfur. And the horse had become increasingly agitated. "No doubt you were promoted a rank or two when you took off with Ronny. I can't imagine the stripes it cost you when I brought him back."

"I've been amply rewarded for my loyalty, Ross."

"Right. But if you lose again today, you go from low rank to no rank. You'll be lucky to boil water in hell's kitchen if you return to your superiors' empty-handed. Again."

His core saturated in malice, Edmon sneered at him. "No house can stand divided against itself, Ross. Didn't the little holies teach you that?"

"A house requires a foundation to stand."

"Joe!" Dave hollered, then broke into a coughing fit. "Are you crazy! Quit fencing with him. Now I've agreed the painting stays here until you get me back with Maggie."

"Then what, Dave? Edmon turns the painting over to us and everyone's in *clover all over*?"

The color rose in Dave's face. "I don't care about the painting. You'll still have the other paintings."

"Right. And I'm ruined. Why should I take you back? What's in it for me?"

"I've told the lad the theft won't be traced to you if you get him back to Maggie."

"Uh huh, and have you told the lad what's in it for you?"

Patience waning, Edmon's hatred burned into him. "In all fairness to David, he wasn't too concerned with my needs."

"Care to enlighten him now?"

"I aim to please. David, fetch me the painting from the stall, son."

"Don't do it, Dave. That horse is unsettled."

Dave wiped his nose on his hand and opened the stall door, brushing away Joe's hand in an attempt to stop him. The horse pinned its ears and paced back while Dave inched inside.

"Dave. Go slow. No sudden moves."

Dave edged his back along the wall in baby steps. When he reached the horse's flank, it delivered a solid kick, busting a hole clean through the board.

Amused, Edmon retrieved a small twig from his pocket. *Dear God, no!* Edmon threw his head back and laughed and the horse reared around, butting Dave with its head.

"Get out of there, Dave. Slow and easy."

"Don't forget that precious painting, son."

Dave skirted the horse's flank and slipped into the rear corner of the stall. After that—mayhem. Edmon tossed the twig to the ground and stepped on it. The twig cracked and the horse went berserk, kicking and rearing, eyes wild, ears pinned. Dave managed to slide the painting a few inches but the animal knocked it out of his hands and Dave landed on his back.

"Dave!" One thing came to mind. One thing—he reached for his harmonica and gave it a toot.

Something happened.

The horse's ears pivoted and it bobbed its head at Joe. Joe tooted the harmonica again and the animal moved forward. Then *they* came, a cloud of them. Massing and swirling. Harmonica falling on the ground. Dark fist

descending—whipping the animal into a frenzy. A cloud
of mosquitoes biting. One dive-bombed his ear, buzzing
and spinning inside it.

"*Arghhhh*!" The mosquitoes swarmed him, biting his
eyelids, swooping into his mouth and nostrils while
Edmon cackled with joy. Stomping in the stall. A thump.

"Dave!" *Bite me, you bastards! Go ahead! Feast!*

Flailing them with both arms, he felt around the
ground with his foot for the harmonica, reaching it before
Edmon kicked it away.

Again he tooted and the horse quieted. He played
softly. Dave was in there shaking it off, on his feet now.
Good. Oh, good. "Dave. Slide the painting into the next
stall and come out. Nice and slow."

The mosquitoes dispersed. Was it real? Had it
happened? Then he saw the horse for the first time—saw
the irregular star and white snip on the horse's nose. The
brown spot on the front pastern. Chills prickling his body,
he played an old tune while Dave staggered out of the stall
and yanked the gate shut.

Nickering softly, the horse brought his head closer and
nuzzled him. He put the harmonica in his pocket and
patted an old friend.

"Oh, Forward," he said, voice cracking. "My Fast
Forward. How are you, boy? You didn't know what you
did, did you? My poor boy. All you knew is that I went
away."

"So touched, well done," Edmon said dispassionately,
smile fake as canned laughter.

Dave retrieved the painting from the next stall and
when he handed it to Edmon, Edmon backed away a step.
Interesting. Very interesting.

"It's clear you're ruddig the show, Joe," Dave said, mid
wheeze. He leaned the *Obedient Son* against the tack box in

front of the stall adjacent to Fast Forward's. "Thig is, I'll call upon the forces of Hell if I have to, to get Maggie back."

"Careful, Dave. You gotta know what you're saying." He would not get the chance to explain further. With the dispersal of the mosquito cloud, came the sequel to this nightmare.

28. Secrets Dense with Splendor

A second entity moved forward.

He'd felt it all along—the intermittent scent of cigar smoke and—*oranges*. The look of terror in Edmon's eyes spoke volumes.

A smoky, eerie mist filled the barn, from which he heard the whispering of voices, many voices coalescing. He heard Edmon's name, and Dave's name. He heard the order, "SEND HIM OUT!" The barn door slammed behind Dave's voice, fist banging and foot kicking in an attempt at re-entry. Then the room stilled except for Fast Forward's edgy, over-breathing. Numbed in front of Forward's stall, cold gushed through Joe's veins.

The sound of voices was distinct—Edmon's monotonous drawl subdued by this new voice, sepulchral and superior. Chilling. He felt the demon commander assess him from the mist, a proud and powerful entity, bloated with self-importance.

"This man is correct in his appraisal, *Inferiori*," it said. "You stand on broken ground."

"This has been a complex case, Lord Praefectus. One angel of the true realm against several of Michael's plunderers. May I say I have performed well on my own?"

"You have never been on your own, Inferiori. Are you suggesting your lords have failed you?"

Edmon seemed to have lost his voice.

And what have I lost? My mind?

"Leave me with this man."

"Lord, shall I remain outside with the man, David?"

"No. Have him sleep in the vehicle and take your leave, Inferiori. We will discuss your ineptitude at a later date."

Edmon couldn't bolt fast enough. But now what? He had to remember he wasn't alone, had to reinforce the thought. Legs weakened, he leaned against the stall and Fast Forward nuzzled his shoulder. The demon moved closer in the darkness, close enough for a kiss, nearly choking him with its rancid scent. Was it petting the horse?

"This horse has great love for you," the demon lord said, voice low and emotionless. "Will you leave it to despair again? It has suffered much cruelty."

"No ... I ... will bring him home." *Cruelty? He's suffered?* "You said Dave is *sleeping* in the vehicle?"

"Your friend is fine. For the moment."

"Why not reveal yourself?"

He sensed the demon's annoyance. "Rome's failure to teach patience? The horse has been maltreated. The whip. Failing to meet expectations. Bad handlers. Then with un-performance ..."

I'm so sorry, Forward. Forgive me, boy. Please forgive me. He reached out to stroke the horse and his hand tapped an icy patch of skin. Cringing, he recoiled in the darkness. "Identify yourself and tell me what you want of me."

The foundation shook and Fast Forward neighed and stomped his feet. "That should be clear, Ross. I want the painting destroyed. I want you destroyed. But first we'll take inventory ... your mother—she died in this stall." The sound of long fingernails clacked on the gate. "My condolences."

Joe scratched at the bites on his arms. *Think! He had to think!*

"A shame the horse was not sprayed sooner. Then you were only a child. Your mother should not have made you responsible for the horse."

But he had a role in her death, to be sure. *My fault.* "I should've sprayed him soon as I was told."

"'*Get the citronella and spray, Joe. Start with Forward. I want him rubbed from ears to hocks'.*"

Mum's voice! Mum's voice in the darkness! "No. That can't be my mother."

"It is your mother. Two hours later she was dead. You're right. Perhaps you should have sprayed the horse soon as you were told. Tell me now, why didn't Joe Ross save Maggie Page?"

"Maggie's fate was never in my hands."

Two more voices tormented him from the darkness, his own and Carol Ann's, "'*We'll bring her back at the first sign of trouble, Carol Ann.*'"

"'*Joe? Do you think Maggie is...do you think she's really sick somewhere?*'"

"She had a tumor and I had a confidence to keep. How could I—"

"You deceived your fiancé. Didn't it occur to you to save her sister? Maggie was in Nazareth, two miles down the road. Even your sleeping friend had the idea to return and petition for a cure. Not once did you think of saving her. Remiel told you she was sick and you settled. Just down the road you were. Two miles down the road. Your fiancée, now your wife however temporary, has begun to wonder."

"That's a lie! Carol Ann would tell me. She's always spoken her mind. Show yourself! I have a right to see my accuser!"

"Very well," it jeered, and the mist dissolved.

The demon revealed itself in pale streaks of morning light—tall and androgynous with shoulder-length black hair, tipped with grey. It wore a black, floor-length tunic, tightly fitted and single breasted with a moldy green trim. Pinned below its left shoulder was a gold pentagram brooch slashed with a lightning bolt. In Edmon's world, the brooch undoubtedly signified a rank of great distinction. This was the demon in Maggie's sketchbooks.

The demon lord regarded him with mocking eyes. Eyes with black sclera. Eyes the color of coagulated blood. How could a thing look both horrifying and beautiful? Its stare penetrated him, flaunting centuries of amassed wisdom and power. And malevolence. Icy fingers of fear stroked Joe's spine and neck. His scalp tightened.

"Like what you see, Ross?" It gazed sensually at him, focusing on his groin.

Aroused suddenly, he filled his mind with the memory of Eashoa's eyes shimmering in the sun. *Elah will bring you peace at the end of your journey.*

He heard a slap and Fast Forward's blood-curdling groan. The horse's knees buckled and he went down in the stall. "Forward!" Joe rushed the gate, but the demon stretched out his arm and sent him flying into a rusted wheel barrow.

"You could've saved her, Ross! You let Maggie die!"

"No!" He rolled over on his side and propped himself up on semi-paralyzed hands swollen with bites.

"Your mother would still be alive. Your father, as well—consumed with grief he failed to maintain the car. You ignored Willie. You knew she was in love with you and you did nothing."

"No! I talked to her, I tried—"

"In the eleventh hour, you tried. What did The Bard say? 'I will about it; better three hours too soon than a minute too late. Fie, fie, fie! cuckold! cuckold! cuckold!'"

No, no, Willie was fine. Willie was at peace, happy. He'd just seen Willie! "Willie is at peace!"

The demon sent him spiraling against the gate on Forward's stall. The horse groaned with fright and lit into the wall with an explosive kick. Another kick like that could shatter the canon bone.

Breathless, he pulled himself up. "Let the animal be!"

"Are you *petitioning* for a favor, Ross?" Its eyes softened with interest.

"Of a sort. Call it a trade-off." He had a favor coming from St. Michael. But he'd die before using it on himself. 'Keep your shield up,' Alain had said. Ephesians 6—the shield. He signaled the demon to wait before throttling him again and treaded cautiously to the painting. He picked it up and asked, "Will you spare Dave Thomson and myself if I destroy this?"

The demon eyed him suspiciously. "What do you intend to do, put a fist through it? And you'd make a bargain with me, you'd trust me? Well, I'm disinclined to trust you, Joe Ross."

"Then it's a stalemate, isn't it? If you want it destroyed, you'll have to be the destructor."

The red sclera shone in the demon's eyes. "Now you know the destruction of the painting is your sole privilege. Though I would have preferred credit for the idea. Very well, proceed."

"And after I destroy the painting?"

It tilted its head and smiled. "We'll negotiate to our mutual satisfaction."

Joe gulped down the knot in his throat and inhaled deeply. *She kissed the frame, didn't she?* Gripping the

Obedient Son single-handed, he took aim with his fist, blocking the demon's view. The demon didn't care for the obstructed view and closed in on him. By his side now. Good.

He whimpered and squeezed his eyes shut. "*Ahhh!*" *Oh God, make this work*. He cradled the painting against his chest.

"Get on with it!" It moved within inches of him. "NOW!"

Joe repositioned the painting at eye level and again took aim with his fist. In one move he unclenched his fist, seized the right side of the painting—*she kissed the frame, didn't she*—and slammed the side of the painting into the demon's collar bone. Its eyes rolled back and flames shot up at its feet from a widening, fiery chasm. Moans, weeping and screams of the demons cried from the bowels of the earth. Assaulted by waves of nausea, Joe braced his hands against the wall and vomited from the smell of hydrogen sulfide, road kill, and more odors too foul for this world.

"Master!" the demon cried, arms splayed at its side, fingers like plunging arrows. "Master! Receive me well and I will avenge thee beyond the Day of Judgment!" Smoldering corpses and a sea of clawing hands sprung from the depths and yanked at the hem of its tunic. The demon implored, begged, "I will avenge thee!" A funnel cloud of ash and bleeding eyes encompassed it, drew it inside the vortex and sucked it into a fiery catacomb.

Joe buried his face in the crook of his arm and coughed away the fading stench. When he opened his eyes, the chasm had sealed, and the floorboards returned to normal. *Hah, normal!* About as normal as playing with your thumbs. He smiled hard at the obscured netherworld.

"Were you *petitioning* for a favor, barbecue bait? Sorry, not going to happen."

Sunlight streamed into the blissfully silent barn onto Fast Forward, now up and nickering softly in the stall. The stench cleared, replaced by the dewy scent of pasture and sweet-smelling hay. It was like the nightmare hadn't happened, like Hell never laid a foul finger on this place. Dazed and confused, though physically unscathed, Dave Thomson lumbered toward him.

"Joe? Joe, you all right?"

He nodded and reached for the painting with throbbing, swollen hands.

The painting was intact. Not a mark. Not a scratch.

Now what to do—about Fast Forward, about Dave. And about the mystery element in the *Obedient Son*. What in the painting had spiritual muscle powerful enough to toss that demon commander out on its barbecued booty?

Joe didn't have much time to find out. First thing tomorrow, the Judean work plus the *Angel Reclining* was on a jet to private party stops in Dar es Salaam and Sydney, followed by the big world reveal—the Page *Arma Dei* Exhibit in St. Petersburg, Russia.

∞∞∞

Dave was in no shape to travel. By morning his cold had worsened and Joe couldn't risk flying him back to Marianlake. Even the icicles in Quebec were wearing mitts and gloves. Carol Ann was on the frosty side herself and how could he blame her? He started out giving her the *Reader's Digest Condensed* version on the phone, but true to form, she extracted the entire story from him, scene by scene, horror by horror. Of course he omitted the demon's accusations. Not meant for the phone. And of course he omitted how badly he'd been bitten, that the doctor sent him back to the motel with a shopping bag full of antihistamines, topical anti-itch lotion and an EpiPen in case of emergency.

"So you've arranged to courier the painting here first class?"

"Mm-hmm."

"And you're staying on with Dave another day or two?"

"I can't leave him, hon."

"And I'm guessing you don't want me going there?"

Of course he wanted her. But he looked like the inflatable fish guy and she was freaked out enough. "Of course I want you here." God, how he meant every word. "But I need you there. Something's hidden in that painting, Carol Ann. I know it and so do you. Find out what, 'K? You'll only have a few hours with it before it's on that jet. The gang still there?"

"Yes."

"Get them to help, and take more pictures."

"I will. I don't mind asking my friends for help." Ouch. He deserved that. "What about your horse friend? Will it take long to locate the owner, do you think?"

Bless her sweet, animal-loving heart. "It shouldn't, no."

"Well, offer whatever it takes to get him home. Oakcrest may not take a thirty-one-year-old horse. But Garrow's will. I'd stable him there."

"I love you."

"I love you too, but I'm still ticked you took off like that, Joe."

"I know. I'm sorry."

"We're going to have to talk about that."

And the demon's accusations. They'd have to talk about that, too. "Okay."

"What do we do about Dave?"

"That's Father Andre's call."

"Poor Dave."

∞∞∞

In the land of bygone Russian aristocracy, of empresses and tsars, artists and dreamers, is the mystical city of St. Petersburg, home to the State Hermitage Museum. Founded by Empress Catherine the Great, the museum houses the world's largest collection of paintings. Works of da Vinci, Raphael, Rembrandt, Van Dyck, and many more occupy six historic buildings strung along the Palace Embankment like pearls glistening in the snow. Historians say Catherine never got a hot cup of tea. Since the Winter Palace is a block long with the kitchen and suites at opposite ends, it wouldn't be a leap to say she never got a hot meal, either.

Awed by the ethereal shimmer of snow on the palatial city, Joe halted his morning power walk with Vittorio along the Embankment to marvel at the wintry, fairy tale setting. What lifestyles nobility must've led back in the day. Vittorio, noticing he'd stopped to take in the view, walked back and joined him at the balustrade overlooking the Palace Square. Vittorio had flown in two days ago with him and Carol Ann, and the team, minus Father Andre, was due in three hours.

Dear Vittorio. Standing in for Alain, perhaps? He felt blessed to have such amazing friends. They were coming for the opening of Maggie's exhibit tomorrow, sure. But mostly they were coming to celebrate Carol Ann's birthday. His in-laws wouldn't be blowing out any candles, however. Mrs. Page's rheumatoid arthritis was not conducive to Russian winters. Or U.S. winters. The Pages wintered at their Bajan condo and did not set foot out of Barbados until late March. And Father Andre had to stand down because Marianlake needed him. He preferred to come in the summer, he said. 'For those glorious White

Nights'. He said. But Joe suspected he wanted to hang back to cut Dave Thomson some slack.

Father Andre and Marianlake's acting psychologist, Father Paul Crouse agreed to spring Dave from his temporary home at Marianlake. He had two weeks in St. Petersburg to make amends and reap the fruits of this twenty-year mission. Dave's liberty was conditional, though. He had to convalesce at Marianlake until Fathers' Andre and Paul decided he was fit to return to his life.

Since Maggie appointed Dave Thomson Managing Director of her art school, they mutually agreed he had to be right with her memory if he was going to spend the rest of his life surrounded by it. If Dave didn't meet the terms of the conditional offer, well ... Father Andre would report the theft and the position of school director and acceptance of the occasional archaeological assignment would be moot since he'd probably be in jail—or *the Jug,* as Ronny referred to it. Asked by Ronny and Carol Ann if he thought Father Andre would make good on his threat, Dave replied, "How can I know? He never gave me the option to decline."

Team Bagels had returned to their lives. Dina purchased forty acres of land seven miles north of Angelfish Cove and was working with the architect on her future home and studio. Ronny was off on an archaeological dig in Palestine next month to act as translator extraordinaire. Currently, Dina was the main attraction in his life.

Joe and Tim had grown tighter since his visit to New Orleans. Tim had resumed his life, too. Wife, two little ones, and a wicked land surveying business. 'From suits to boots', Tim always said.

Sister Elizabeth helped the absent Dave launch the school, assembling student lists, starting with SEAN.

Though busy teaching plus a variety of other priestly duties, Father Richard said he wouldn't miss the *Arma Dei* kick-off for all the chocolate in Belgium.

"Did I tell you I misplaced my harmonica?" he said to Vittorio. Carol Ann was in a meeting back at the Hermitage and had kicked him out since he'd practically set up camp by the paintings.

"Oh, Joe. You've had that since childhood, yes?"

He commenced walking, slow-footed, less animate. "I had it in the barn, that's how I calmed Fast Forward. So many years I've had it. Didn't notice it missing until I got to the walk-in clinic with Dave. After I got him settled at his hotel, I DEETed myself up and went back to the barn. Scoured every inch."

"It must have been difficult for you to return."

"I wanted to check on Forward and was waiting for calls about him, anyway. But the harp wasn't there. Only a bunch of nightmare memories."

"I'm sorry, Joe. But the horse is fine?"

"Oh," he laughed, "in the pink seeing me again. Hearty appetite. Rolling around in the paddock at Garrow's. Funny how Edmon got away with walking him off like that. But Edmon had, shall we say, certain *abilities*." Coward that he was, he still hadn't told Carol Ann about the demon's accusations. "Vittorio, all these years, no human on the team has seen a demonic entity. Why me?"

"What do you mean? Edmon Fendi, Joe. Everyone saw Edmon."

"Edmon looked normal, well, normal as Caligula's great grandfather could look. That demon commander looked like nothing I'd ever seen. Really, why me?"

"It was forced to appear after Edmon failed. As always, the devil wanted the mission sabotaged. Discrediting you and your family would certainly discredit Maggie. But you've already surmised this. It used Dave as bait to trap you, and the horse to emotionally destabilize you."

He couldn't help smiling at Vittorio's choice of words. "Edmon wanted to use Forward as a weapon to destroy the painting and somehow get me caught in the act. That's when I reached for the harmonica. You know, since we got here I keep hearing *Run-Around* by Blues Traveler everywhere I go. My favorite on the harp."

"The song is glued in your head?"

"No. Actually *playing*. Radio. Lobby. Gift shop. Elevator. I guess it's just becoming popular here, maybe." A bleak, wintry feeling tugged at his heart. "Are you okay, Vittorio? I mean, minus the miracles and with everything behind us?"

"We can always count on change, Joe. This thought comforts me. I'm coming along fine, my friend. You, I suspect, not so?"

"Dave had a point."

"When he said we yield better results as a team?"

"Yeah. He didn't appreciate my doing things unassisted. Which I don't understand myself. A person is the way a person is. Some things we can change. Some things we're takin' to the grave."

"'Serenity to accept the things we can't change and the courage to change what we can'. You were alone during the most tragic circumstances of your life. Perhaps you didn't want to risk a friend's life in a potentially dangerous situation."

He smiled reverently at Vittorio. "I hope Carol Ann will forgive me for putting her in the number two slot. We're celebrating her birthday tonight and all I can think about is solving the mystery vibe in the *Obedient Son*."

"Don't wait too long to discuss your other worries with her, Joe. The demon always mixes lies with the truth.

Sparing Maggie's life or taking it was up to God. Carol Ann will understand this."

"Will she? I know Dave doesn't."

∞∞∞

"I think I froze my *zadnitsa* off," Ronny said, doing a one-two step around his suite in the Hotel Astoria.

Joe got the largest, most luxurious suite for Ronny because, somehow, everyone always ended up in his room for the nightcap, the talk, the plan or the party. The suite had a massive sitting room with a fireplace and two large couches facing each other, a bedroom with a king bed and a second fireplace, and convertible kitchen/boardroom. The doorman accepted Ronny's tip and laughed at whatever Ronny said before he shook his hand and left.

"So," Ronny said, crossing broad arms over an expansive chest. "Here we are, most of us. Together again like Ripley and his Believe It or Nots."

He wanted to give the big guy a hug but slapped him on the back instead. "You're looking fit. How much weight have you dropped?"

"About forty. Dina's my donut monitor."

"I sensed a little something on New Year's. Or is it more than a little something?"

"Think we're heading in that direction, yeah. Life is a down duvet, Joe. All it needs is a good shake and back she bounces."

Father Richard walked in, followed by Dina, Dave, Tim and Vittorio. Sister Elizabeth was in their suite helping Carol Ann organize her not so surprising surprise birthday party.

"We're all on this floor together! This is happening," Dina said. "I hope Carol Ann likes what I got her."

"Carol Ann always likes your gifts." Actually, that was stretching it. Dina's gifts were either opulent or bang-on. It was a fifty-fifty thing.

Dina frowned, said, "This one's different. On the tame side, so we'll see."

They all started chatting merrily, happy at being together for another Plane Bagels Fest as Tim referred to it. The Fathers' stood by the window with Tim, pointing at palaces while Dina helped Ronny unpack. Dave Thomson strolled over to him.

"I'm glad I could be here, Joe. You have no idea. Well ... maybe you do."

"And I'm glad it all worked out. How much longer is your exile at Marianlake?"

"Until I've grieved well, Father Andre says. Living by Maggie's grave, by the time machine's grave—difficult to stuff the grief. I still blame myself for not bringing her back, Joe. I blame you, too. And Alain. But Father Crouse is qualified to help me work it out and he's doing that. Thanks for everything. Thanks for getting me sprung to be here for Maggie's opening."

"You're welcome. You were right, you know, about me being Mr. One-man Team. Always trying to calm the waters before inviting my friends into the boat. I saw the waves it created in our friendship and as usual, ignored them for personal priorities."

"Well, you can't fight fire with fire. You actually need water," Dave deadpanned. "So? This is about more than tomorrow's opening and Carol Ann's birthday, isn't it."

For an instant, he averted his eyes to the others, who'd grown quiet in an attempt to catch the drift of their conversation. "It's the *Obedient Son*. You of all people remember how I felt compelled to go to Galilee and find it.

Well, déjà vu, my friend. I feel like I'm about to have a love affair and you're all here to keep me from straying."

"It's the mystery you're infatuated with. So let's solve the mystery."

They dined in a private section of the hotel restaurant and he made Carol Ann's birthday a priority. Though he couldn't divert his mind for an instant from the *Obedient Son,* he had become rather adept at portraying the merry host. He loved these people and was touched they'd come, and he owed them. So if they were as obsessed with the painting mystery, they didn't show it, God love them. But he felt the rising tide in them, the quick pulses and the rush. In Elizabeth and Tim, he noticed controlled movements. In Dave, he felt tight muscles and inner tremors.

Ronny whispered something to Dave, who nodded.

"I'm fine," Dave said.

"Okay, Joe. We're all here. So tell Team Bagels all about it or Carol Ann's not getting her presents." This from Ronny.

"Uh-oh. Tell you about what?"

"How you found the painting. Give, son, give."

"Better tell them, Joe. I want my presents."

He raised his eyebrows at Dave. "You didn't tell them on the plane?"

"I thought I'd let you do that," Dave said, casting his eyes downward. Obviously the poor guy still felt raw. "And I had a head full of cold when you told me."

Hard to forget. Difficult to remember. "It was easy. But it took me almost two hours to relax into the painting. Remember the little blonde girl with the magnifying glass?"

"The little girl copping rays? Sure." Ronny reached for another roll and Dina snapped it away. "Cutesy."

"One of the rays polarizes a section of barn far in the background."

"I don't remember a barn," Dina said.

"Well it's there, greener than St. Paddy's beer, with a cupola and a golden horse weathervane."

"Sure," Father Richard said. "I remember the weathervane."

They instantly recalled the weathervane, except Dina, who seemed somewhat distracted tonight, more so than the rest of them. "Well ... Claxton Farms had a green barn. And a golden horse weathervane exactly like the one Maggie painted. Though it wasn't looking so golden last time I saw it. Anyway, that's when I knew."

"Did you sense anything about me?" Dave asked, expression slack in his dull eyes. Carol Ann gave his shoulder a squeeze.

"I didn't, Dave. I knew you were annoyed with me when I went on the hunt in Galilee without you and Ronny. Aside from that, no. I'm sorry, guys. I've always had this manic fear of getting another person I love killed."

"We all understand this, Joe," Vittorio said.

"Bless your little pea-pickin' heart," Tim said. "Don't matter Joe-Joe. No apologies."

"Hey come on, everybody." Carol Ann rubbed her hands together. "Let's do presents. Yes. Presents, please."

"Anybody bring *me* anything?" he asked.

"*You* get horseshoes," Elizabeth said.

He snuck a sideways glance at the ghost town that used to be Dave Thomson. No more wisecracking, happy-go-lucky straight man. He felt Dave's longing. It was like he had a date with Maggie at that opening tomorrow. And the waiting was torture.

Carol Ann got a cashmere travel wrap from Tim, mink ear muffs from Father Richard, flannel-lined jeans from

Sister Elizabeth, a Russian/English dictionary wrapped in long johns from Ronny, ice grips and thermal socks from Father Gianni, and a collapsible duffel bag from Dave.

"What did Joe get you?" Dina asked.

With a wicked hint of a smile, Carol Ann began stashing her gifts in the duffel. "*The Tale of Benjamin Bunny* by Beatrix Potter."

"'R what?" Tim said.

"It's a first edition. Signed." She slipped her arm around his. "And on the card he wrote 'this card entitles the bearer one guarantee that her husband purchase his horse farm in the Boston area'." They all whooped and clinked glasses. "Joe already has three properties lined up when we get home. Soon, Fast Forward'll have a forever home with the Rosses."

Ronny nudged Dina.

"I know," she whispered not too silently. She wrinkled her nose and handed Carol Ann the tiny silver-wrapped gift box. "It spoke to me. Actually it hollered at me. But it's not exactly designed to keep you warm."

"It'll warm my heart, I'm sure. Besides, I love all your gifts." He had himself an inner smile at that one. His adorable Carol Ann. The tactician.

He didn't pay much attention to the wooden locket until Dina fastened the clasp for Carol Ann. While they cooed over the workmanship and the smoothness of the wood, he leaned closer to her throat like a drooling vampire. Damn if his heart wouldn't stop pounding, because for the moment, the Russian winter had taken a powder. Birds chirped. Canals rushed. Easy breezes smelled of lilacs and sweet grass.

He ran his fingers across the locket and inhaled. "Beautiful."

"What, Joe?"

He inhaled again, sighed. "I've seen this before. The elliptical shape. The soft lines and the flush of the wood. Where'd you get this, Dina?"

Dina moved her chair as close to the table as it could get. "A little jewelry shop in Toronto. Actually, I'm glad you love it, Carol Ann, because I'd picked out something else first. An amazing brooch shaped like an open book with multi-colored stones."

Carol Ann stifled a wince. "This is perfect, Dina. Elegant."

"What made you choose the locket?" he asked, nose to Carol Ann's larynx.

"Told ya. It's like the thing shouted at me. I bought both the brooch and the locket. And you know what? I haven't looked at the brooch since."

"What's inside?" Father Richard asked.

"Nah, Father. That's up to Carol Ann. I thought about putting something inside—but nah."

"Any idea where you've seen it?" Dave asked him.

He rubbed the back of his neck and told himself to take a breath and slowly release, release, *release!* "No idea."

They managed to get off topic for several minutes but he couldn't stop eyeing the thing. Couldn't stop fidgeting. Waiting to ease into what he wanted to say, intended to say, was about as comfortable as wet socks. *Let's go up to Ronny's suite, spread the Obedient Son pictures over the boardroom table and glue ourselves there until we find something.* But it was Carol Ann's birthday celebration. So, 'nuff said, forget it. Bulldoze the emotions and be a good little host. This was one of the world's most fascinating cities and he owed them a good time.

It took them all of twenty minutes to change into winter gear and meet in the lobby. Their excitement still flowed through him like surging waters, more forceful than any place they'd been in the world, with the exception of Judea 6. Perhaps it was the end of their adventures this time—the final *period—finito*. It could be years or never before they got together again. But Maggie's one-year Hermitage exhibit felt auspicious of more than closure.

The front desk recommended a cozy little subterranean jazz club in the Nefsky Prospekt area called *The Blue Fox*. Tim and Dave sat at the bar and ordered drinks while he pushed a couple of tables together. Vittorio and Richard were still standing outside blowing into gloved hands and staring across the canal at the Winter Palace, sparkling on the water like a horizon of stars.

"How popular are you in Russia?" Elizabeth asked Dina, checking out the crowd to make certain no one had recognized her.

Dina undid her parka and slung it over the back of her chair. "Nobody's gonna recognize me in this getup, don't worry. I used to hate my chameleon looks. Not anymore."

The club was atmospherish and dark, with an unpretentious piano in the corner and an unpretentious piano player playing. Tim and Dave returned slogging two trays loaded with creative-looking concoctions plus *imbir'-el'*/ginger-ale for Elizabeth and coffees to thaw Vittorio and Richard. Zapper's got juice tonight, he thought, picking up on more controlled movements and distracted delight—especially the birthday girl.

"Hey, birthday girl," he said, sipping on a chocolate something or other with a whole jalapeno in it. "*S Dnem Rozhdeniya*, baby. Sip sip." His happy birthday sounded more like Sin-yum-rush-deen-ya. Somewhat off the mark, but it didn't completely suck. He glanced proudly at Ronny but Ronny was in Dina-land.

Carol Ann took a sip and cough-laughed. "Wow! So much for getting to the Hermitage first thing in the morning."

They all put down their drinks at once. It was like watching glass dominoes.

"Well, I intend to be there first thing," Dave said.

"I'll nap in the aft," Ronny said.

"Soon as the doors open."

"Won't stay on the porch when I can run with the big dogs."

"Up with the sun. *Subito.*"

"Right."

"Check."

He was enjoying this. Could it be the painting had summoned them as well? He'd stuffed a few photos of the *Obedient Son* in his parka lining. Just because Dave had heavy things on the brain these days didn't mean he'd forget his penlight. The thing was like an extra appendage. He extracted the three photos, waved them at his friends and lined them up on the table.

Elizabeth wiped away drink rings and Dave produced the penlight. They huddled in closer.

"*Dove cercare,*" Vittorio said, frowning. "Where to look? Where to look?"

The pianist stepped up the beat.

"You told us Maggie kissed the frame," Ronny said. "Something in the frame, maybe?"

The pianist switched on some background noise equivalent to a piano fortissimo in his ear. Could it be *Run-Around*? Again? And on the piano? Geez, he missed his harp. "What!"

"The Frame! Maybe something in the frame!" Tim shouted, shining Dave's penlight on a photo.

He covered his ears. "I'm leaning in that direction." Not one of them heard what he said.

Carol Ann stood up. "Oh for Pete's sake! We have two weeks to club hop. Let's take this party back to Ronny's suite."

They may not have heard her, but they caught her drift in a hurry. So he tossed a few thousand rubles on the table and within the half hour, they were up in Ronny's suite. Joe fetched the rest of Carol Ann's photos and spread them on the boardroom table.

"Okay," the birthday gal said, "everybody grab a picture."

Holding a photo in front of him, Father Richard thought out loud, "We know there's nothing hidden in the canvas or paint material. We know, praise God, that Jesus himself painted part of the chair. So what else do we know?"

"We know we're concentrating on the frame," Tim said. "Joe is curious about why Maggie framed this one. Must say, my Yankee doodles, I am too."

"*Si*. Myself as well." Vittorio tapped a corner of one photo. "But, Maggie stayed with the carpenter of all carpenters. Correct? Why *not* frame it?"

Carol Ann had three photos lined up in front of her and looked to be in another world. "Good question," he said. "Why not frame it? But one of the last things Maggie said when we parted in Judea 6 was that she might send a message back in a painting. Inspector? What's got your attention there?"

Carol Ann rested her chin on her palms. "The four corners. Do we have a magnifying glass?"

"I'll call the desk," Ronny said.

"You think you see something in the corners?"

Entering into a discussion of the four carved frame corners, they got to talking about the 'shadows' scanned and authenticated by Lloyd's. The team agreed with the experts—the crossed wood pieces accounted for the shadowing. They'd admired the beauty and simplicity of the workmanship and aside from the cloth pieces used to keep the wood from scratching the canvas—the vote was unanimous. Maggie hid nothing underneath the frame.

Joe vehemently disagreed. "Maybe not *under* the frame. Vittorio, you've seen the reports from Lloyd's. What exactly did the reports say about those shadows?" All heads turned toward Bishop Vittorio Gianni.

Vittorio raised his shoulders. "Again, they're indicative of where the wood overlaps the corners. Dowels are used in this frame. Not nails. Yes? So. Those shadows are wood and dowels. Nothing more."

Following a knock on the door, Ronny returned with the magnifying glass, passed it to Carol Ann, said, "Joe, we're with ya. Firm as turtles crossing the freeway. But where haven't we looked?"

"The x-rays show nothing but shadows, which the experts have confirmed are nothing more than shadows," Dave reminded them.

Dina took a thinking girl's stretch and peeked over Carol Ann's shoulder. "Funny. The frame corners remind me of Carol Ann's locket. Don't you think, guys?"

"What?" He flew to Carol Ann's side of the table. "That's it. Oh my God, that's it!"

"A bit more, Joe," Father Richard said.

"Dina's right. That's where I've seen the locket before. Astute observation, Dina. The corners are near reproductions of the locket."

They all gathered around Carol Ann, who, holding the magnifying glass over one of the frame corners, still hadn't said a word.

"Amazing," Elizabeth said. "The fine lines carved in the frame are different, however."

Carol Ann picked up another photo and held the magnifying glass over a different corner.

"True," he agreed. "There's just a squiggle on the locket. On the frame corners, it looks like the number eight."

"I noticed that before," Ronny said. "It's not a symbol of any kind. At least not that I'm familiar with. Dave?"

"Not a symbol. Not an icon."

The fathers' agreed with Dave and Ronny.

Carol Ann chose another photo and hunched over it.

"Notice the grooves around the elliptical shape," Tim said. "Interesting."

Carol Ann glanced peripherally at Tim, smiled faintly, and returned to the photo.

"Okay, Inspector. Lay it on us."

"Pen and paper, please," she said, grinning.

"Come on, Carol Ann." Dina started snapping her fingers. "Chop chop."

Carol Ann drew a large elliptical shape on a piece of paper. "Observe."

From the upper middle of the elongated circle she drew a curved line that completed in the bottom left hand corner. Returning to the top, from the upper right she drew another line that crossed the first line in the center and completed at the bottom right hand corner.

"Okay, dear," Father Richard said, "We've got the lopsided figure eight again. You've lost me."

"Look again, Father. Everybody? See anything apart from the figure eight?"

The realization seemed to strike them all at once.

He hugged his brilliant, adorable, wise wonderful wife and laughed. "Of *coahse! SC!*"

"*SC*," they repeated, not exactly getting it, still looking confused.

"Joe," Vittorio said in a cloudy tone. "I don't want to be a wet blanket pooper, but *SC* had many meanings throughout the mission years, often meaning something different to each of us."

"My point," he said, belated Christmas bells tinkling his heartstrings.

"So what do you think it means now, Joe-Joe?" Tim asked.

"Sugar pie honey bunch, would you remove your locket, please?"

Carol Ann removed the locket and handed it to him.

'Time runs on a different lock. Did I say lock'? Joe flipped open the locket, looked at each of them and waited.

"Got it!" Elizabeth said, eyes the size of gear wheels. "*SC. Secret Compartment!*"

"Bingo," he said.

∞∞∞

Carol Ann had private numbers for the administrator, director and three of the two hundred curators employed by the State Hermitage Museum. For the next eleven and a half months, she, her adoring husband, and her folks had only to call to request private viewings. Names had to be cleared of course, and arrangements made in advance. Private viewings were available prior to the 10:30 a.m. opening or after closing at 6:00. So when Carol Ann learned the team would be here for the opening, she arranged a private viewing for 8:30 a.m. the day of.

Along with rye toast, coffee and black tea, staff had the paintings spaciously set on easels in a roomy office on the third floor of the Winter Palace. Security had no intention of leaving until Carol Ann charmingly persuaded them off the premises.

"Well, here we are again," Ronny said. "Joe, this is your show."

His heart was pounding so hard it hurt. "It's the *team's* show." He smiled at Dave and squatted by the *Obedient Son*. "Okay. Let's think corners. No doubt we all stayed awake last night pondering. Tim, you said you found the grooves interesting."

"Yeah." Tim squatted beside him. "Your secret compartment is obviously behind one of the elliptical shapes. But which corner, which one? Look—they all have grooves."

"Or—the corner shapes *are* the secret compartments," Dave said.

"May I deek in?" Carol Ann asked, her inspector's nose at the ready. "The corners appear recessed. Anybody else see that?"

"If that is so," Vittorio said, moving closer, "those corner buttons might turn."

"Give one a twist, Joe," Dina said. "Just go for it."

"If we're wrong, it could break off." Richard grinned like a harvest pumpkin, "but I don't think we're wrong. Joe?"

What an intoxicating moment, waiting for the hidden wonder behind one or all of these 'buttons'. He looked up at his lovely wife, whose sister was the foundation of this mission. His lovely wife who lost her sister and sacrificed big time for the mission and him. As they all did. "Carol Ann? Pick a corner and twist."

"Oh, Joe, I—"

"Come on, girl."

"Go ahead, dear. Gently."

"Before the White Nights, Carol Ann."

Carol Ann pressed her lips together. "Okay. Here goes."

She sat on the floor, inhaled deeply and twisted the elliptical button on the bottom left, counter-clockwise. And just like a screw, it turned. Gently, slowly, she turned it until the ornament detached, falling in the palm of her hand.

"Now," she said, breath raggedy, "this thing has to open somehow."

"It's so delicate and lovely," Elizabeth said.

Carol Ann handed it to him. "Joe, I don't know how this opens."

He was dying to give it a try, but passed it to his friend. "Ron-man? Open it, bud."

Ronny swallowed hard, turned over the ornament and held it up to the light.

Tim looked at his watch. "Ronny, we have about twenty minutes, man."

Ronny applied gentle pressure with his thumb and forefinger and the ornament twisted open.

"My God."

"Ohh, Joe."

"Oh my Lord!"

"*Capello de Cristo!*"

'Did I say *lock?*'

The team gathered around Ronny and stared in awe and silence at the wondrous relic in front of them all along. In retrospect, Maggie couldn't have been clearer. Secured inside the ornament was a braided lock of hair.

Vittorio reached over, gently removed the lock of hair from the ornament and placed it in Dave's hand.

"Joe," Dave's voice caught in his throat, "Maggie was with *Him*. And he knew she was sick. He must've had his reasons for leaving her that way." Dave opened his cupped hand and grazed his lips along the divine treasure. In that moment, Dave Thomson got his life back.

"What about the other three corners?" Dina asked, voice hoarse.

As it happened, they didn't have time to find out. They had just set the lock of hair back in the ornament and twisted it into place when staff and security entered the room. It was ten minutes to show time, ten minutes to the big reveal. Emotional and silent, he thought about beginnings—a tiny, clerkless record shop, a field of pumpkins, a girl discovering her voice in a rowboat, a certain strawberry blonde. And a little boy dressed in a Yoda costume.

You here, Alain? Maggie?

He glanced at his wrists, no hint of scarring. Sadly smooth. The mission was over.

∞∞∞

Much to Joe's consternation, organizers placed the exhibit in a far corner on the third floor of the Winter Palace. But he had no worries, not with Saint Michael's personal guarantee that millions would come. The exhibit's curator believed it would catch on *slowly*, and he told her she might want to rethink keeping it on the third floor, lest she planned for a gridlock on the Jordan Staircase.

The curator contended, "There will be no congestion issues because there will be no congestion, not in the opening weeks." Right. He believed that like he believed in glass hammers.

"Thing is," he told this nice woman who, if anything, found him amusing, "once the rowboat is full, you only have so many options."

So on day one of the exhibit he sat back smug as smirks watching staff manage the traffic jam on the staircase. On the average day, sixty-eight hundred people visited the Winter Palace. The first day the count approached ten thousand and by the end of day two, the numbers had grown exponentially. Next night, the Director intervened and ordered the paintings moved to the first floor, adding gold-braided rope stanchions for queuing. On day three, Carol Ann passed the curator the salt and pepper to complement her breakfast of crow.

The initial tests proved inconclusive but Lloyd's of London chose to insure the works based on Maggie's impressive credentials and celebrity. This did not mean the testing was done. The testing would never be done. He was glad about that. Carol Ann and her folks were always happy to authorize more testing. Why not? Test results brought further publicity and publicity circulated worldwide. The seeds had taken root.

Yet, numerous details needed explaining—like two-thousand-year-old pollen samples mixed with synthetic fiber. Like the oil paints used in the *Angel Reclining* that identically matched the Judean work. How could they explain that the same artist painted the work over a span of two thousand years?

Well, they couldn't explain it, but people hoped. They believed in miracles. They believed in the mystical nature of the work. And that was the catalyst that brought them in from all parts of the globe. How did Maggie Page do it? These *wrist people* had found a way to jaunt back and forth in time, how else? Possible but improbable was the general consensus.

Then came the question of the *child's* identity. The child's dress—the white tunic and towel on his shoulder in the *Angel Reclining* and *Obedient Son* was identical—identical and painted using two-thousand-year-old materials. Though the boy was profiled in the *Angel*

Reclining, he had the same coloring, size and hair as the boy in the *Obedient Son*. So it had to be *the* Child. And if it was truly Him, then that was truly his Mother, then that was truly his Foster-father. Then *yes!* The artist really did travel back in time!

∞∞∞∞

"Joe? *The Rembrandt Room*, Joe. We've been here three weeks and you still haven't checked it out." It mystified Carol Ann how unenthusiastic he was about beholding masterpieces. This was their last night in St. Petersburg, they were flying out in five hours and he still hadn't seen the works. "*The Return of the Prodigal Son, Descent from the Cross*. Rembrandt, Joe. You've heard of Rembrandt? You can't miss this. You just cannot miss this!"

Here they were, finishing their coffee in the Hermitage Café, inside one of the world's greatest museums, if not *the* greatest and they'd been ragging on him for only wanting to hang out at the *Arma Dei* Exhibit. Didn't they get it? Rembrandt they could look at on the Internet or in a coffee table book or on a postcard, for crying out loud. But this was Maggie's exhibit. The big kahuna. The pot of gold at the end of the rainbow. The last period at the end of the last sentence. Getting here was what the last twenty years was all about. Anyway, he and Carol Ann were returning next summer during the White Nights, so he could ogle the masterpieces then. *Come on, guys, you held a lock of His hair in your hands!*

"Dina has us cleared for 10 PM, Joe. At least come see *The Return of the Prodigal Son* with me. It's on this floor, practically around the corner." Ronny flashed Carol Ann a grin that said *good luck with that* and waved bye-bye to the both of them.

"I'll check it out before we leave," he said. "I want to hang with the art students for a bit. Don't you want to spend these last hours with your sister's paintings?"

"Not entirely, Joe, no. And my sister would not want me to miss the works she aspired to and dreamt of seeing." Hand on hip, she waited for his response.

"Okedoke." He folded his arms across his chest. "Enjoy."

Carol Ann sighed, crinkled that cute freckled nose and walked off.

After chugging the rest of his coffee, he headed back to the exhibit, passing marble columns and ceilings depicting the gods of Olympus. The art students from I. E. Repin piled in at the end of the day once the crowds thinned. Admission was free for them and mostly they didn't have to queue up between five and six. This was his best time, too. He got to chat up the critics and those adoring fans *stirred to the core*—another SC he told himself, for lack of telling Carol Ann and company, off drooling in Rembrandt Land by now.

Yet tonight, he didn't feel much like talking. Tonight he wanted to listen. What did the work mean to them? What moved them? Were there spiritual sensations? Standing with his back to two art students, he cozied up to Maggie's sketches, pretending to read the commentary. Ah what a lovely night for eavesdropping.

The more demonstrative of the students, a tiny bird of a girl, dark-haired and animate with her hands, feet, and even her eyebrows, clapped her hands in awe. Joe took a few steps to the right and stole a peripheral glance. All aflutter, she fished a notebook out of her knapsack then cradled it against her chest. Forgetting the pen, she shook her head and sighed adoringly at the *Obedient Son*. Were her eyes misting? It was difficult to tell at this angle.

The student, whose name was Zoya, brought a friend, a seemingly troubled, fidgety young woman. "We must hurry, Zoy. The weather. The snow. It's getting heavy. We must be on our way."

Zoya refused to budge until the friend took a good look, a deep look at the paintings. "Don't look *at* them. Look *in* them. Look in them with your heart."

The friend scowled, moving from painting to painting. But something in each painting slowed her. When she got to the *Arma Dei,* she stopped and leaned in. Zoya asked what she thought.

"My mind has gone from worry about snow accumulating beneath my tires to marveling at snow falling from above. It makes me want to ask questions. It disturbs me and it sets me at peace."

Zoya nodded, knowingly. "There are many stories about the artist. About the obstacles she overcame to paint them. There are stories of angels. No, Anna, *real* angels! And thousands of people baring identical lettering on their wrists—all to do with these paintings. Imagine!"

"Oh yes, Zoy, I have heard this. A virus, nothing more. And not letters, this is propaganda. Bumps and flourishes on wrists do not letters make. You have been reading too many newspapers."

She would have none of it, for she was one of hundreds he'd seen these past three weeks with the same captivated expression, undoubtedly experiencing like emotions, the same stirrings of the heart and soul. "Look at *Obedient Son.* The patient way he sits for his mother as she cuts his hair. Every night I come and see something different in my walk through the paintings."

"I have never thought of myself as spiritual," Anna said, "but after looking at these I can, for the first time, understand the inclination."

Rembrandt, eat your heart out.

"You favor the modern one, I can tell." Zoya nodded at the *Angel Reclining.* "Am I right?"

"Yes, so right. The color and the light—from the little girl's magnifying glass. Light is central in the picture. Central in all the artist's work. Page lived in the light, I think."

Hmm. He'd never thought of Maggie's use of light and shade in relation to her life. He was a puzzle-man, first, last and always. The mystery pulled him in. Only the mystery. These girls looked at the painting with their hearts.

Zoya glanced past him at Maggie's sketches. "She knew darkness, too. She extracted the purpose of evil to create these, Anna. Think of it! Just to discover the purpose! Ohh, how she must have made the devil weep!"

"There's much talk of a connection between the soul and the paintings," Anna said. "Do you believe the talk?"

"I feel something divine was behind these works, yes."

"I can't yet."

"You don't have to, Anna, don't worry. The soul knows real beauty even when we don't know what we're looking at."

The closing bell dinged throughout the Palace and people began filtering out. When the students headed off with promises to return again tomorrow, he toddled up to the *Angel Reclining.* This time he didn't need to go searching for clues. For once he could look at the painting with his heart, the painting that had figured so prominently in the curve of time around them. Maggie wove strands of their lives in her work—like the lock of hair in the *Obedient Son.*

The little girl with the magnifying glass made him grin again. Would he and Carol Ann have a girl someday? The toy train or subway car gleamed below the sunlit rays.

Would they have a girl who liked to play with trains? Aha, she'd be an engineer. He squinted at the train. What was this now? Hmm ... heart fluttering, he stepped closer. Could it be? Oh yes, of course! All these years he thought it was a subway car or train reflected by the glass.

It was neither and he bit down on a smile. The tiny train was in fact a harmonica, silvery-blue and shiny in the sun's eye. This meant Alain was with him in the Claxton barn, because only Alain would stick that tune in his head. Perhaps someday, the harmonica would find its way back to him.

'*Spiritually combatant equipment, this.*'

As for the remaining three corners of the *Obedient Son* ... he wanted to wait. Like his friends, he wanted to 'savor'. The exhibit's next stop was the Guggenheim, followed by the Art Gallery of Ontario, and after that he hadn't a clue. Maybe they'd get together in two years' time and give the ornament on the top right a twist. And what of Saint Michael's favor? The archangel prince trusted him to use it wisely. How he hoped. For now, it was fun to speculate, to ponder. For now—there was only now.

He blew the little girl with the magnifying glass a kiss and hurried off to The Rembrandt Room.

THE END

Dear one, thank you for reading. A favorable review is the best gift any writer can get. Not only does it increase sales, it tells a writer that we're not wasting our time, that we should continue, that our work has actually touched someone—a lovely stranger who is no longer a stranger. Now we've generated a little karma DNA out there and we owe that to you and your kind review.

God bless,

Liz

And—please page over for info on a couple of FREE novels, one of which is a companion to *Dark Angels Prey*. Enjoy!

Acknowledgements

For my mother, Anne, Shirley Traynor, for editing and reading this doorstopper more times than you had to. For Karen Lukas, George Robins, Anne Pickett, Linda Warner, Sondra Elliott, John Mlynarsky, Father John Brennan, and for my brother, Ron, who convinced me a whole bunch of years ago that 'there is no such thing as the self-made man'.

I would like to express my gratitude to those who saw me through this book, all who provided support, talked things over, read, wrote, offered comments and assisted in the editing, proofreading and design.

DEDICATION

This book is dedicated to S.M.A. and Shirley Traynor, best friend and sister soul mate who called me late at work one night and said, "You have to publish this. You just *have* to." Well, here it is, Shirl. Thank you.

Other titles by Elizabeth Genovese:

The Astral Shore

He has the fame ... She has the power

Troubled model, Laurel Ariss wants rock star Mark Grant out of the astral and into her life. With the help of a cautioning parapsychologist, she succeeds. But it takes more than beauty, brains and a magical connection to hang on to a rock star--it takes *power*.

Because now that she has him, she'll do whatever it takes to keep him ...

THE ASTRAL SHORE — a standalone tale of supernatural suspense.

Frankie G's Miracle

A supernatural novella
FREE at elizabethgenovese.com
In all formats!

Only Two Men Hear the Music...

In the 'summer of love' 1967, hippie buses painted with psychedelic graffiti head west while liquor rep, Frankie Gallagher buries his wife in Boston. Guilt-ridden, sick and boozing too much, Frankie settles in the mysterious town of Angelfish Cove, believing life has little to offer.

Until he witnesses a miracle.

But when a sadistic teenager exposes his secret shame and the glow from Frankie's miracle fades with the threat of scandal and prison, he opts for a supernatural solution—and faces the fight of his life.

Website: elizabethgenovese.com

email: Liz@elizabethgenovese.com

Twitter: https://twitter.com/lizgenovese

About the Author

In the mid-eighties, nervous novice writer, Elizabeth Genovese attended a taping of Toronto's *Front Page Challenge* where a friend introduced her to Canadian icon, Pierre Berton. When Mr. Berton said he was interested in reading her novel, Elizabeth said she 'just happened' to have a manuscript in the trunk of her car. "Up front I'll tell you, if I don't like it I'll say so," he warned, "I will not embarrass myself by submitting a bad manuscript." Two weeks later at 7:00 a.m., the phone rang: "Elizabeth! Pierre Berton here. I think you've got yourself a book." Following a previous publication, a title change and several re-writes, that book became *The Astral Shore*.

Elizabeth's books combine supernatural suspense, mystery, and time travel with recurring themes of obsession and idol worship. *Dark Angels Prey* is a supernatural tale of suspense and adventure. The book's companion, *Frankie G's Miracle*, highlights the life of a character briefly portrayed in *Dark Angels Prey*. Though the novella introduces DAP's main characters, they can be read and enjoyed as standalone books. *Frankie G's Miracle* is free on *elizabethgenovese.com*.

www.ingramcontent.com/pod-product-compliance
Lightning Source LLC
Chambersburg PA
CBHW030327030726
47495CB00013BB/1264